Praise for Shadows of the Apt

'The insectile-humans premise is inventive, shaping the world in all sorts of ways' *SFX*

'Epic fantasy at its best. Gripping, original and multi-layered storytelling from a writer bursting with lots of fascinating ideas' *WalkerofWorlds.com*

'Superb world-building, great characters and extreme inventiveness' *FantasyBookCritic* blog

'Adrian is continuing to go from strength to strength. Magic' *FalcataTimes* blog

'Reminiscent of much that's gone before from the likes of Gemmel, Erikson, Sanderson and Cook but with its own unique and clever touch, this is another terrific outing from Mr Tchaikovsky' *Sci-Fi-London.com*

'I cannot even begin to explain how much I enjoy the Shadows of the Apt books. Their level of originality and their sheer epic-ness makes for some of the best fantasy entertainment out there' *LECBookReviews* blog

'Tchaikovsky's series is a pretty great one – he has taken some classic fantasy elements and added a unique (as far as I'm aware) twist . . . Tchaikovsky has created a world that blends epic fantasy and technology' *CivilianReader* blog

'A novel brimming with imagination and execution . . . The Shadows of the Apt series is quite distinct, mainly due to the insect-kinden and Tchaikovsky's fertile imagination'

***SciFiNow.co.uk***

'Tchaikovsky manages to blend these insect characteristics with human traits convincingly, giving a fresh slant to the inhabitants of his classic tale' ***SFReader.com***

'I want more and there's nothing I can do but sit it out and wait' ***GraemesFantasyBookReview*** blog

# The Scarab Path

Adrian Tchaikovsky was born in Woodhall Spa, Lincolnshire, before heading off to Reading to study psychology and zoology. For reasons unclear even to himself he subsequently ended up in law and has worked as a legal executive in both Reading and Leeds, where he now lives. Married, he is a keen live role-player and occasional amateur actor, has trained in stage-fighting, and keeps no exotic or dangerous pets of any kind, possibly excepting his son.

Catch up with Adrian at www.shadowsoftheapt.com for further information about both himself and the insect-kinden, together with bonus material including short stories and artwork.

This is the fifth novel in the Shadows of the Apt series following *Empire in Black and Gold, Dragonfly Falling, Blood of the Mantis* and *Salute the Dark*.

BY ADRIAN TCHAIKOVSKY

*Shadows of the Apt*

Empire in Black and Gold
Dragonfly Falling
Blood of the Mantis
Salute the Dark
The Scarab Path
The Sea Watch
Heirs of the Blade
The Air War
War Master's Gate
Seal of the Worm

Guns of the Dawn

SHADOWS OF THE APT

BOOK FIVE

# The Scarab Path

ADRIAN
TCHAIKOVSKY

TOR

First published 2010 by Tor

This edition published 2012 by Tor
an imprint of Pan Macmillan
20 New Wharf Road, London N1 9RR
Associated companies throughout the world
www.panmacmillan.com

ISBN 978-1-4472-2111-1



A CIP catalogue record for this book is available from
the British Library.

Map artwork by Hemesh Alles
Typeset by JCS Publishing Services, www.jcs-publishing.co.uk

*To Val Patchett,*
*who taught me much of the writer's art*

# Acknowledgements

Again, I couldn't have done it without Simon Kavanagh, constant fount of cautions and advice, Peter Lavery of the masterful pencil and wine glass in equal measures, Julie Crisp and Chloe Healy and everyone else at Tor, and Jon Sullivan for his sterling work on the covers. I should also thank Lou Anders of Pyr for all his help and support across the water. Furthermore, anyone who turns up at signings, conventions, or posts on www.shadowsoftheapt.com, is also entitled to no small measure of thanks.

For the better edification of the reader, there is a complete cast list at the back of the book, as well as a complete cast list for the series on the website.

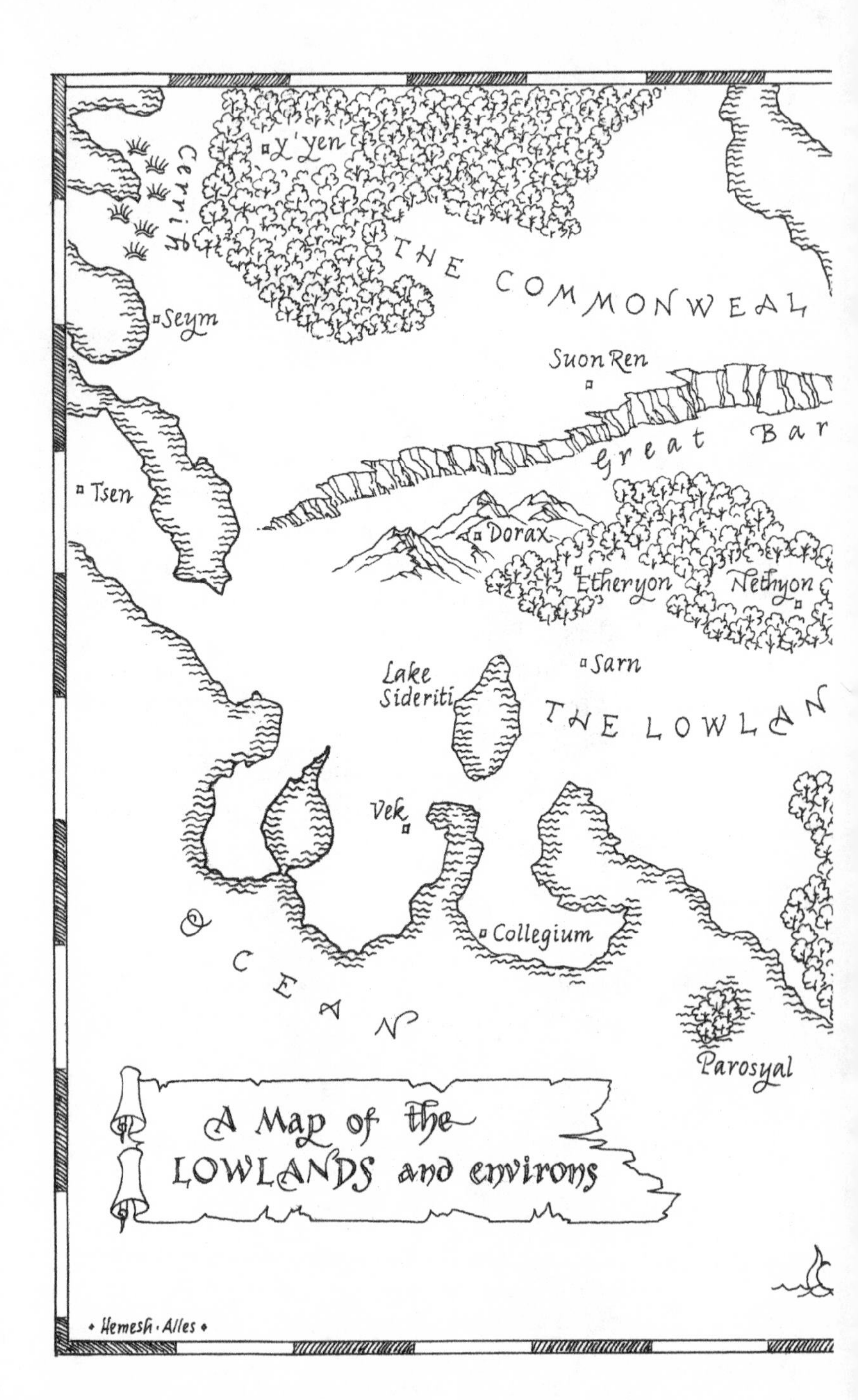
Y'yen
Cerrig
THE COMMONWEAL
Seym
Suon Ren
Great Bar
Tsen
Dorax
Etheryon
Nethyon
Lake Sideriti
Sarn
THE LOWLAN
Vek
Collegium
OCEAN
Parosyal
A Map of the LOWLANDS and environs
Hemesh · Alles

Lake Limnia
Jerez
Shon Fhor
Luscoa
Sa
WASP EMPIRE
Maynes
rier
Ridge
Szar
Myna
Darakyon Forest
Tharn
Helleron
Asta
DS
Akta
Merro
Tark
Egel
Thord
Felyal
Seldis
Iak
Dryclaw Desert
Everis
silk road
Araketka
Kes
Toek
SPIDERLANDS
Siennis
Mavralis

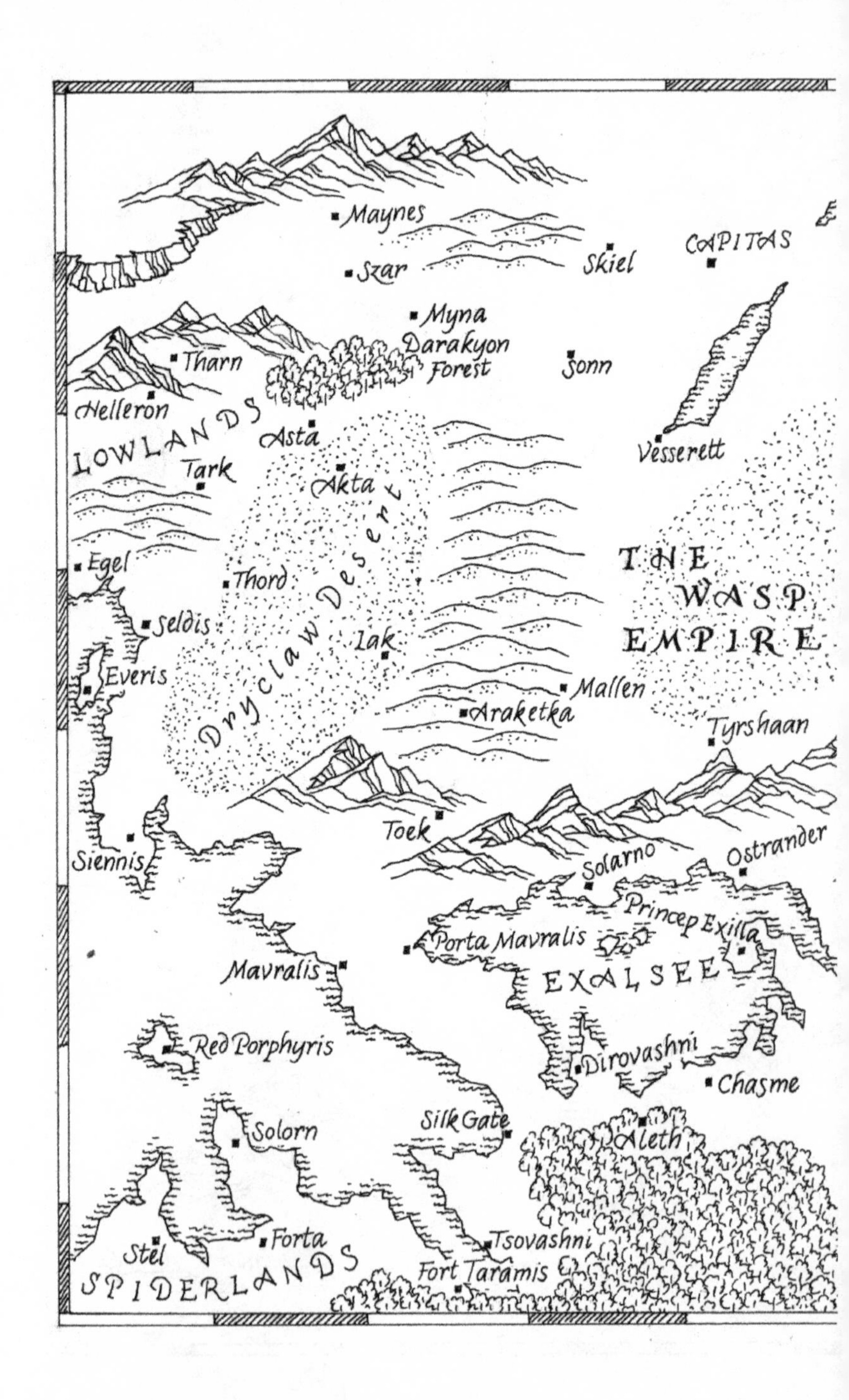
Maynes
Szar
Skiel
CAPITAS
Myna
Darakyon
Forest
Tharn
Sonn
Helleron
LOWLANDS
Asta
Vesserett
Tark
Akta
Egel
Thord
Drycland Desert
THE
WASP
EMPIRE
Seldis
Iak
Everis
Mallen
Araketka
Tyrshaan
Toek
Siennis
Solarno
Ostrander
Princep Exilla
Porta Mavralis
Mavralis
EXALSEE
Red Porphyris
Dirovashni
Chasme
Silk Gate
Aleth
Solorn
Forta
Stel
Tsovashni
Fort Taramis
SPIDERLANDS

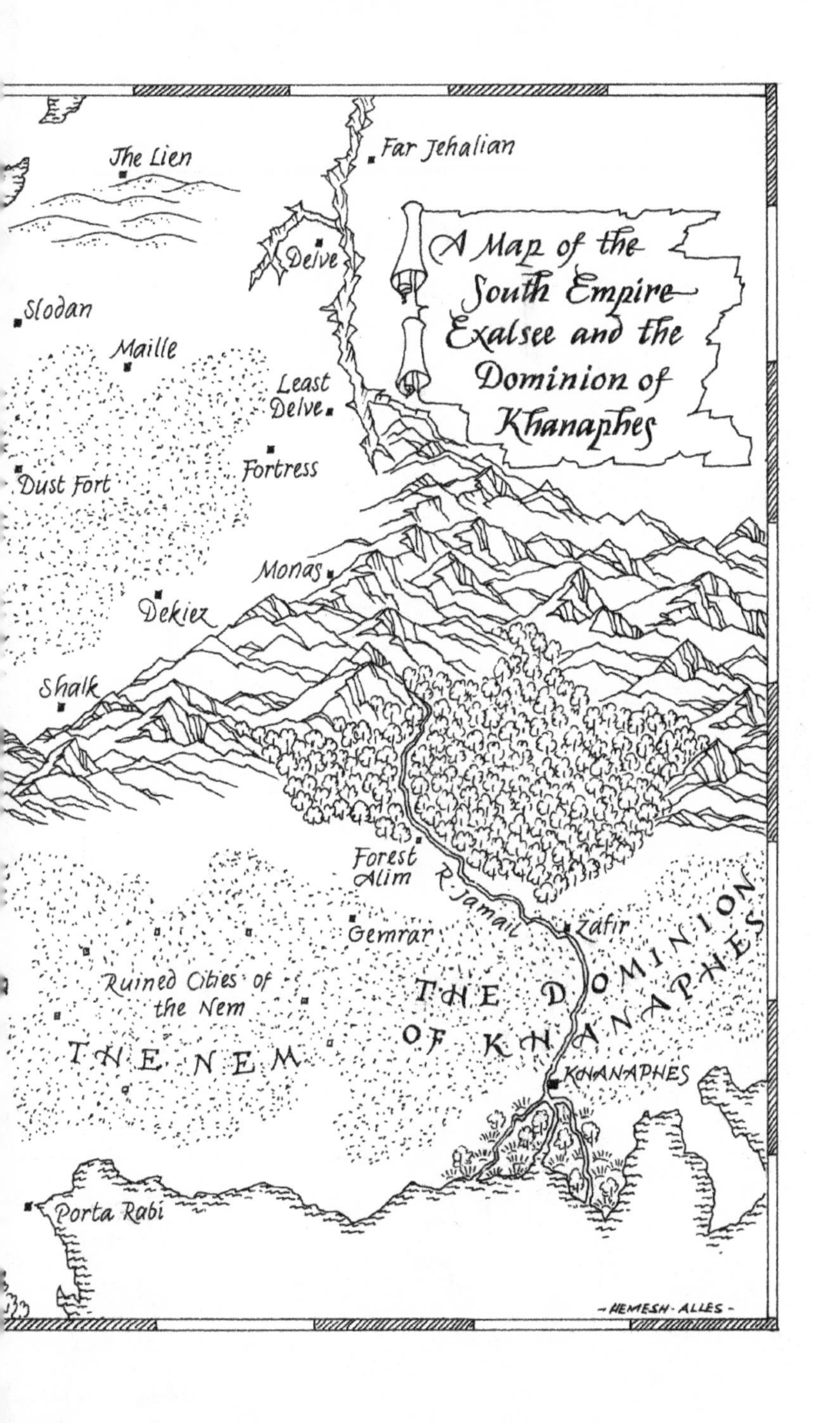
A Map of the South Empire Exalsee and the Dominion of Khanaphes
The Lien
Far Jehalian
Delve
Slodan
Maille
Least Delve
Fortress
Dust Fort
Monas
Dekiez
Shalk
Forest Alim
R. Jamail
Zafir
Gemrar
Ruined Cities of the Nem
THE NEM
THE DOMINION OF KHANAPHES
KHANAPHES
Porta Rabi
- HEMESH - ALLES -

# Summary

*The war that the Wasp Empire brought against all the cities of the Lowlands has ended in a stalemate and an uneasy truce.*

*The Mantis-kinden weaponsmaster Tisamon, in his dying moments, destroyed the Shadow Box that held all the darkness of the Forest Darakyon and the twisted history of his race. In the same clash, the Emperor himself died, as did the Mosquito-kinden Uctebri, who had sought to use the Box to make the Emperor's sister, Seda, an immortal puppet-queen. Now Seda has become Empress of a people never ruled by a woman before, and while she tries to hold onto power, the rest of the world is safe from Imperial ambition.*

*At Seda's side is Thalric, once an officer in the Rekef, the Imperial secret service, and then a fugitive on the run from his own people. His war record is one of dubious deeds done for both sides, but he provides Seda with a male figurehead while she rebuilds her Empire.*

*In Collegium, Stenwold Maker works on preparing his city for a return of hostilities that he sees as inevitable. Reminders of the toll that the war took are all around him, though. As well as Tisamon himself, it is the loss of the Moth-kinden, Achaeos, that cuts most deeply. Dying of his injuries during a ritual that invoked the power of the Darakyon, Achaeos left behind two women whose lives are shattered by his death. One is Stenwold's niece Cheerwell, Achaeos's lover. The other is Tisamon's daughter, Tynisa, who gave him the wound that eventually killed him.*

*Part One*

# The Road to Khanaphes

# One

He was Kadro, Master Kadro of the Great College of the city of Collegium, which was half a world away and no help to him now. A little Fly-kinden man, long hair going grey and face unshaven, waiting for the pitchest dark before beginning his work. *Oh, I have striven all my life against the way my race is seen.* The perception of Fly-kinden as thieves, as rogues, as a feckless, rootless underclass in any city you cared to name. He had thought that he was beyond that, Master Kadro the antiquarian and historian, who had stood before a class of twenty avid scholars and propounded his learning. He had stood on a box, certainly, so as to be seen over the lectern, but he had stood there nonetheless.

And here he was, skulking like a villain as the evening drew on and the city below him grew quiet and still. The farmers would have come in from their fields by now. They would be lighting the beacons along the great wall. They would eventually be going to sleep. Those sentries that remained would be blind to the night hanging beyond their small fires. Kadro, who could see in the dark as the locals could not, would then strike. It was a poor way for a guest to treat his hosts, but he was beginning to believe that his hosts had not been entirely honest with him.

*We sighted the walls of Khanaphes today. After the wastelands it was a view to take the breath away. Golden stone raised higher than the walls of Collegium or of any Ant city-state – and with statues piled on that – architecturally bewildering but, given the people that live here, I suppose it's not surprising. Huge buildings and broad avenues; every major building constructed vastly out of scale. For a man of my stature it was daunting – even for the locals it must make them feel like midgets. Beyond the walls, the strip of green that is the river's attendant foliage runs north, a single channel of life in the desert.*

*Everyone apparently pleased to see us – especially pleased to see Petri – much polite interest in Collegium but a little standoffish, as though news of a city inhabited by their close kin was something they heard every other day. Evening of the first day, and we seem to have been absorbed – found a place and now genteelly ignored, as the life of Khanaphes moves around us like a sedate and well-oiled machine.'*

Kadro reread it with a shake of his head. *How little I knew, then.* Crouching high above the plaza, with its great hollowed pyramid, he watched the torches of a patrol pass indolently by. He had not been noticed, either in absence or by presence. His heart was hammering. This sneaking around was not his trade. The deftness of the Fly-kinden, his birthright, had mouldered for a good long while before being given an airing now. He was lucky his wings still worked. *How they would scoff at me, back home.* Collegium born and bred, and living amongst the cumbrous, grounded Beetle-kinden all his life, he had almost forgotten that he was more than a pedestrian himself.

*Now!* he told himself, but still he did not go, locking into place instead, clutching flat against the stone like a badly rendered piece of sculpture. They were mad keen on their carvings here in Khanaphes. It was obviously the main outlet for all their stunted creativity, he decided. They could never leave a stone surface blank when they could chisel intricate little stories and histories into it. Histories that revealed nothing. Stories that hinted at everything. This whole city was just a maddening riddle created specifically to drive an aging Fly-kinden academic insane. And here was the culmination of his insanity.

It was totally dark now. There was a patchy spread of cloud above, too, which had recommended tonight to him: a rare occurence out here on the fringes of this nameless desert. Nameless in the eyes of Collegium, anyway. In a lifetime of poring over the oldest of maps, Kadro had seldom come across the city of Khanaphes. The name existed only in those ancient, unintelligible scrawls that the Moth-kinden left behind, after the revolution had forced them out. The maps of Beetle merchant venturers barely admitted to its existence, barely gave it credence or fixed location, as though some conspiracy of cartographers existed to deny that a city called Khanaphes had ever taken physical shape. *East, somewhere east*, the stories ran: a city founded by the Beetle-kinden, and whose name, to those few academics who cared, was inseparable from legend and Inapt fancy.

And here he was, looking over this city, this great river Jamail with its acres of marshy delta and the desert that the locals called the Nem – all nothing but names to the academics of Collegium, until now.

It was the war, he knew, that had opened up so much more of the wider world to the Lowlands. Suddenly there had been a lot of new faces seen in the city, in the College even: Imperial diplomats and their slaves of many kinden, Solarnese Fly-kinden or the sandy-skinned near-Beetles they bred there, Spiderlands Aristoi, and even the occasional brooding Commonwealer. The world was bigger than it had ever been, and yet Kadro had found new territory still. The ever-talking Solarnese had eventually got around to comparing maps, and there, lying at the edge of their world, had been the winding blue line of a river with a jewel at its mouth: Khanaphes.

He shifted on his high perch, digging fingers into the reliefs to keep his balance. *They build high here, yet they never look up*. Rents in the cloud passed bands of silver moonlight over the Scriptora, the big, brooding mausoleum that served Khanaphes as the seat of its administration. The ember glow of a rush-light was visible in one high window as some clerk continued working all hours for the implacable bureaucracy he served. Below the window rose great columns that supported the building's facade, carved from huge slabs of stone to resemble scaly cycads. This was such a serious city, where nobody hurried and everyone was busy, and it was all just an act. He was sure of that by now. It was all to take one's attention off the fact that there was something missing from the public face of Khanaphes. The city was intrinsically hollow.

> *This city of contradictions. To find an outpost of what should be civilization all these miles east of Solarno, untouched by the Wasp Empire, untouched by the squabbles of the Exalsee or the machinations of the Spiders . . . and yet to find it untouched, also, by time.*
>
> *Khanaphes has welcomed me, and yet excluded me. Petri does not feel it, but she was always a dull tool. There is a darkness at the heart of this city, and it calls for me.*

Last night's entry. He should have left this journal with Petri, just in case.

The heart of Khanaphes yawned for him, here overlooking this grand plaza. They liked their space, here. After they had won a victory against the Many of Nem, they had paraded their chariots all around this square, their soldiers and their banners, before immortalizing their own triumph on further expanses of stone. But who had they been parading for? Not for the ministers, who had stood with heads bowed throughout; not for the common people of the city, who had been away at their daily tasks. It had been for the *others*.

There *were* others. Kadro was convinced of that now. They were spoken of so often that their name became meaningless, and therefore they were never truly spoken of at all, as if held so close to the face that they could not be focused on. *Here* was the heart, though. If Khanaphes was holding a secret, then it was here in the tombs.

In the centre of the plaza stood the pyramid. It was a squat thing, rising just thirty feet in giant steps, and was sliced off broadly at the top, to provide a summit ringed with huge statues. From his high vantage, a vantage that the structure's earth-bound builders could never have enjoyed, Kadro could see that within the ring of statues' silent vigil there was a pit, descending into a darkness that his eyes had yet to pierce. It was the great unspoken *what* at the centre of Khanaphes, and tonight he intended to plumb it.

A bell rang deep within the city, maybe a late ship warning the docks of its approach. The sound took up all of the night, low and deep as wells, for the bells of Khanaphir ships were as hugely out of scale as the rest of the city. Aside from the faint scratchings of crickets and cicadas from the riverbanks, there was no other sound in the darkness.

Petri would already be looking for him. By tomorrow she would be asking questions of their hosts, in her well-meaning and perplexed manner. She would bumble about and make a mild nuisance of herself, and yet be utterly, patently oblivious to what was going on. That was good. It meant that, if something bad happened to him, if he was caught, then they would not suspect her of any complicity. He hoped that was the case, anyway. He had no guarantees.

With a flicker and flare of his wings he coasted gently down to stand between two of the statues. The Khanaphir really loved their statues, and these were huge and strange. It had been the expression on their white stone faces that had drawn him here in the first place. *They know something.* They were older than the rest, and bigger than most, and better made, and *different.* There was no man or woman in Khanaphes who could lay claim to those beautiful, arrogant and soulless smiles.

He now crouched between the pyramid summit's edge and the pit. The same rush-light ember still glinted in a high-up window of the Scriptora, that diligent clerk hard at work. Or perhaps it was a spy, tracking Kadro in the darkness? The Fly-kinden huddled closer, trusting to the bulk of the statues to conceal him. *They would have come for me, by now, if they knew*. He had no choice but to believe it. They had a word here: *reverence*. It was not the word that the Collegium scholars thought they knew: here it carried tomes of unspoken fears. It was stamped on all the minds and faces of Khanaphes.

He peered down cautiously, into the black. The shaft fell into a gloom that even his eyes wrestled with. *The Royal Tombs of Khanaphes*, he told himself, and Kadro of Collegium will be the first outlander to enter there in a thousand years. The thought brought a rush of excitement that dispelled the fear. He had always been a man to dig in strange places. Back in Collegium he had been a bit of a maverick, dashing all over the Lowlands to look at unusual rocks or talk to wizened mystics. There had always been method in his research, though, as he negotiated with grim Moth-kinden or bandied words with shrewd Spiders. There had always been a trail to follow and, although he could not have known at the start, that trail led here.

All around him the statues kept silent guard, and he even summoned courage enough to grin at them. If the Khanaphir had wanted to keep him out, they should have posted a living watch here. The white faces stared impassively out into the night over the sleeping city.

Kadro hunched cautiously at the top of the steps, staring downwards. Fly-kinden had no fear of darkness or confining walls. They were small and nimble, and left to their own devices they built complex warrens of narrow tunnels, impossible for larger folk to navigate. There was a cold breath coming from that hole below him, though: chill and slightly damp, and he wondered whether the tombs connected to the river.

No matter. He had not dared this much only to fall victim

to his own imagination. He shifted the strap of his satchel and took a deep breath. *Into history,* he spurred himself.

He glanced across the pit and saw one of the statues staring at him, its blind white eyes open at last, and now darker than the night sky behind. Something moved close by, and he gave out a hoarse shout and called up his wings to take flight, but by then it was already too late.

# Two

It was all over before they arrived, the charred wood and ash gone cold, and just the smoke still drifting into a cloudless sky. The sail-mill, the warehouse, the miller's home, everything had been systematically razed. By the time word was rushed to Collegium by the neighbouring hamlet, it would already have been too late to stop it.

Stenwold stared at the ruins, his hands hooked in the belt of his artificer's leathers. The miller and his family and staff would all be dead. This was the third attack to occur hereabouts and the pattern was dismaying in its precision. Around him the guardsmen from Collegium were fanning outwards from the automotive, some with their shields held high and others with snapbows at the ready.

'You think we did this.'

He looked around to see one of the Vekken ambassadors staring at him. The Ant-kinden's expression was one of barely controlled dislike. The man's hand rested on his sword-hilt as though he was waiting for a reason to slice Stenwold open. Stenwold was wearing a breastplate over his leathers and he was glad of it.

'I don't think anything as yet,' he replied patiently. A lot of effort had been involved in there even *being* a Vekken here to talk to, and most of it was his work.

'Yet you have brought me here for a reason,' the man said. He was smaller than Stenwold, shorter, stockily athletic where the Beetle was broad. He would be stronger than Stenwold too. His skin was dark, not the tan of the Sarnesh or the deep brown of Stenwold's own people, but a slightly shiny obsidian black.

'You insisted on coming with us,' Stenwold reminded him, 'so we brought you.' He bit back anything else. 'Touchy' was an understatement, with the Vekken. Stenwold's men were moving cautiously further out. There was still enough cover left, in fallen masonry and half-standing walls, to conceal some bandits or . . .

*No bandit work, this.* But who, then? Collegium had its enemies, more than ever before, but there was currently supposed to be a general peace. Someone clearly had not been informed.

He heard a scrape and scuff as the automotive disgorged its last passenger. His niece hesitated in the hatchway, looking unwell. She shook her head at him as he made a move towards her.

'Just give me a moment,' she said, as she eyed the wreck of the mill bleakly. 'This is bad, isn't it?'

'Quite bad, yes.' Seeing the officer of his guardsmen backing towards him, he said, 'Che, would you look after our Vekken *friend* here while I see to something.' He had not meant to put so much of a stress on the word, but it had come out that way.

Che dropped to the ground and staggered, before catching her balance. The journey had been hard on her. The Vekken was staring at her, but if her discomfort meant anything to him, it was lost in a generic expression of distaste for all things Collegiate.

'Do you think . . .?' His look did not encourage discussion but she pressed on. 'Do you think someone could be causing trouble between our cities?' In the absence of a reply, she added, 'We are west of Collegium here, and Vek is the closest port.'

'As I said, you believe this is our work,' the Vekken said flatly.

'Che, get back in the automotive,' Stenwold said suddenly. 'You too . . .' He looked at the Vekken and obviously could not put a name to him. The Vekken squared off against him, wanting to see whatever was being hidden from him.

'Now!' Stenwold shouted, and then everything went to pieces. Without a sound, there were men popping up from all sides, their crossbows already clacking and thrumming. Every shadowy corner of the mill's wreck that could afford a hiding place was disgorging attackers. One of Stenwold's soldiers was down in that instant, another reeling back with a bolt through the leg. All around was the sound of missiles blunting themselves against shields, or rattling off the automotive's armoured hull.

'Pull in!' the officer shouted. 'Protect the War Master!'

'Uncle Sten!' Che cried. She was already halfway back inside the automotive, an arm reaching out for him, when she noticed the Vekken ambassador was sprawled on his back. A moment later he was lurching to his feet, but he had a bolt embedded up to its metal fletchings in his shoulder. His sword was out, offhanded, but he did nothing but stand there in plain view. She rushed over to him, got her hand on his shoulder.

He cut viciously at her. If not for his wound, he might have lopped her arm off at the elbow. She retreated, seeing him loom over her with blade raised, at that moment prepared to kill her without another thought. She was an enemy of his race and had dared to touch him. He must really have been what passed for a Vekken diplomat, however, because he let something stay his hand.

'Get inside the automotive!' she urged him. 'Please!'

'I am in no danger,' he replied, and she thought she had misheard him at first, barely catching the words over the shouting. Stenwold collided backwards into the automotive's side with a curse, as a soldier thrust him back, one-handed.

There was a bolt lodged through the man's left arm, and with his other hand he pressed his snapbow into Che's grip.

'Take it and use it. Come on, Master Maker!'

'Wait!' Stenwold crouched lower. 'Wait – look at them!'

The attackers had mostly stopped shooting now, and instead were forming up a line of shields, preparing to rush in and finish the job. Meanwhile the automotive's driver was pointedly letting the steam engine whine and rumble, as if trying to get the idea of escape across. Che looked down at the snapbow, glinting fully loaded in her hands.

*If only I could.* But it was a deadweight, useless to her. She dropped it into the automotive's waiting hold.

'Look at them!' Stenwold was shouting, pointing for the benefit of the Vekken envoy, and Cheerwell suddenly realized what he meant. The line of attackers, who were moving in even as the Collegium guard tightened around the automotive, were all Ant-kinden. Specifically, they were Ant-kinden of Vek.

'They are a detachment from Tactician Akalia's force,' the Vekken – *their* Vekken – explained. 'They are merely obeying their last order, which was to harass Collegium in any way possible.'

'But they shot you!'

'My people are skilled soldiers.' The Vekken sounded insulted. 'I had no time to announce my presence to them before they commenced their ambush.'

Stenwold was shouting now. 'Then tell them you're here, you fool!'

'They are already aware,' said the Vekken, as another volley of crossbow bolts drove the Collegium men further back towards the vehicle. 'They have advised me to leave before they begin their shield-charge.'

Stenwold reached for him in frustration, but then thought better of it. 'Tell them that the war is over. You're an ambassador – Vek is sending ambassadors to Collegium, for Waste's sake!'

'I do not have authority to countermand a Tactician's order.'

At that moment Stenwold was physically shoved further into the shelter of the automotive's hatch by the injured soldier. 'Tell them!' he roared desperately. 'Don't you think that if your King was here he would order them to stop?'

The idea of second-guessing the Monarch of Vek was obviously beyond consideration for this particular Vekken. He just stood there, staring at Stenwold with patent loathing. The guardsmen had now raised a cordon of shields around him and Cheerwell, with snapbowmen ducking down behind it to reload, then up again to shoot. Che noticed that there were a good few Vekken dead as well, as the bolts tore through their shields and armour both.

'Well?' Stenwold demanded. 'Can't you admit to logic, just this once?'

'Your men are the only ones still shooting,' the Vekken observed.

Stenwold forced his way out of the automotive again. 'Put up your bows!' he called. 'Hold!'

The Collegium soldiers waited tensely, the snapbowmen with their weapons still levelled above the shields of their fellows. The Vekken force mirrored them, big shields steady, crossbows loaded and aimed. There was a long, fraught pause while Stenwold caught his breath.

'We cannot go on like this,' he declared at last. The Vekken ambassador eyed him as though he was mad.

'Put up your bows,' he said again without anger, sounding only tired.

The officer repeated the order with obvious reluctance and the barrels of the snapbows lifted.

'What is going on?' Stenwold asked.

'As I have said, these men were given their last orders before Tactician Akalia's force was defeated.' That defeat was obviously a bitter memory for the Vekken.

'And now?'

'They will seek further instructions, on the off chance that their orders will now be changed.'

'*Off chance?*' Stenwold exploded.

The Vekken's expression suggested that attacking Collegium agriculture was an eminently appropriate thing for bands of Vekken soldiers to be doing.

'And are there any more of these soldiers?'

There was a pause while the Vekken remained silent, obviously communing mind-to-mind with his kinsmen. 'Yes,' he replied at last. As Stenwold drew breath to speak he said, 'I have suggested, as an officer of Vek, that this band recommend they too seek new orders. I have no absolute authority, however, and they may disagree with my assessment.'

*And you secretly hope they will.* Stenwold felt an urge to strangle the man. He cautioned himself: *Diplomacy, remember.* He had tried so hard, so very hard, to make things work. He had started with this premise: *they are people, just as we are,* but he should have known better. Since then he'd had plenty of cause to remember that Ant-kinden were not remotely like the sort of people he understood.

The Vekken were now attending to their wounded. 'Do you want me to provide them with doctors?' Stenwold asked, seeing the opportunity for a peace offering.

'They require no Collegiate doctor,' the Vekken ambassador snapped, without hesitation.

'At least let us attend to *your* wound then . . .'

The look he received was poisonous. 'My own people will tend to me in due course. For now, should we not be returning, as you have solved your mystery?'

Stenwold took ten minutes' respite from diplomacy, as the automotive began to rumble its way back to Collegium, to think every vile thought he could about both the city of Vek and its bloody-minded inhabitants. After that satisfaction he leant forward to address the envoy again.

'Do you at least see now, though, why your presence in

our city is so necessary? Misunderstandings occur so very easily, between our people. Surely you must understand that there is no need for this violence, not any more?'

There was no hint of understanding in the Vekken's face, in fact no expression of any kind. Stenwold sighed again.

'You are here in Collegium for a purpose.' *A purpose other than spying on us, surely*, he added to himself.

'Master Maker,' the Vekken replied, 'we are here for now, but how long do you think your plan will work? We are here because you have spoken so many words that some within our city have become curious. We know that your people hate us. We know that support for you in your ruling body wanes. Matters will soon resume their natural course. What do you hope to accomplish?'

It was a surprisingly long speech, for one of his kind. Stenwold sat back and reflected. The Vekken initiative had been his idea, true, and almost a single-handed effort. He had traded a lot of the prestige he had accumulated during the war for this chance at a lasting peace.

*And he's right, the bastard. He sees it very clear. It wouldn't take much of a shift of opinion in the Assembly to have us rattling our spears again.*

The Vekken was looking at him without expression, except for a tiny wince of pain each time the automotive jolted. The studied loathing still evident in his eyes presaged the future.

# Three

'Khanaphes,' said Master Jodry Drillen and, although it was twelve years since the man had been a teacher at the College, Stenwold still heard in his head the squeak of chalk on slate.

'Khanaphes, indeed,' he murmured. The two of them had appropriated one of the smaller conference rooms at the Amphiophos. Nearby, the Assembly, the great elected mob that governed and failed to govern Collegium in equal measures, had only recently finished sitting.

'Something must be done.' Master Drillen was a great, fat Beetle-kinden man a few years Stenwold's senior. He had exchanged academia for politics years ago and never looked back, his influence and waist expanding in tandem as though by some demonstrable formula of statesmanship. At the moment he wore a little greying goatee beard in the Spider style, which Stenwold thought looked ridiculous but was apparently all the fashion.

Stenwold shrugged. 'The city of Khanaphes is a living, breathing city, rather than something consigned to the histories of the Inapt. That's no great surprise, is it? After all, the Moths left us with only the scraps from their table, academically speaking. No wonder, five centuries on, we're still rediscovering things that they have known all along. As for what you can mean with your "Something must be done" then it's simply one more field of study for the

College geographers, unless you're now proposing going to war to wipe it off the map. It has been only recently added by the cartographers. The paint is probably still wet.' It was now two tendays after the incident at the mill, and Stenwold was feeling, at least, a bit more rested. Any good humour these days seemed to be fleeting, so he made any use of it he could.

'Sophist.' Drillen gave him a grin that was surprisingly boyish. 'You *know* why this is important.'

'Do I?'

'It's all the fault of the Solarnese, of course, all those squabbling little provincials huddled around the Exalsee – why are you laughing now?'

'Those "squabbling little provincials" have been teaching our artificers things we wouldn't have worked out for another ten years,' Stenwold said mildly. 'But do go on. You were blaming them for something.'

One of Drillen's servants arrived just then, having finally tracked down the right vintage in the Assembly's cellars, and the two statesmen took a moment to sip it appreciatively. 'The Solarnese,' said Drillen eventually, 'with their stupid names with all those extra vowels . . . what was that ambassador they sent? Oh yes, he wrote it as Caidhreigh, but then when you introduced him it turned out he was called Cathray. Anyway, everyone seems agreed now that they're some kind of stable halfbreed stock, Ant-kinden and Beetle-kinden combined. You can see it in their faces, and most especially you can see it in their Art, after we finally convinced them to talk about it. They're like those other fellows you were always banging on about.'

'Myna,' Stenwold agreed.

'Exactly. But they're obviously no relation because of their skin colour, and so the ethnologists started asking "Where did they come from?"'

'Nobody cared when it was just Myna,' Stenwold said.

'Two reasons, old soldier.' Drillen enumerated them on

his chubby fingers. 'One: public attitudes were different back then. Two: Myna's within spitting distance of an Ant city-state – and not so very far from Helleron. No mysteries there, then. There are no Beetle-kinden around the Exalsee, and yet the ethnologists are adamant in their conclusions, so whence the Solarnese? Well, of course, we ask them that question, when politeness permits, and they show us their maps, and tell us their earliest word-of-mouth records say their ancestors came from Khanaphes. The Beetle-kinden city of Khanaphes, no less, just as some of our ancient-history fellows have been banging on about for ages. So now every scholar in that field is publishing his flights of utter fancy, saying that we came from there, that they came from here, all manner of lunacy. It makes you wish the Moths had been just a little more forthcoming with their menials, before the revolution. If there's one thing a man of the College hates it's feeling ignorant.'

'You are still a scholar at heart then?' Stenwold said. 'That amazes me. I happen to agree with you, but I'm surprised that a man of importance like yourself can still find time to concern himself with such abstruse academic matters.'

'There is more at stake here than scholarship,' Drillen said fiercely. 'You must be aware that people are looking at the world in a different way now, after the war. For me, I'd just as soon everyone went back to not really caring what lay east of Tark and north of Helleron, despite all the trouble that attitude has caused us, but it's too late now. Go into any taverna in the city and you'll hear scribes and guardsmen and manual labourers all talking about places like Maynes and the Commonweal and bloody Solarno, as though they were planning on going there tomorrow.' Drillen was becoming quite excited now. Stenwold sipped his wine and watched him with interest.

'And the romances!' the fat man continued. 'Have you any idea how many talentless clerks are writing "true" romances boasting of their supposed travels in distant lands? And still the printing houses can't get them to the booksellers fast enough to satisfy public demand. Everyone wants to read about foreigners, and I'll wager that not one of those people writing about them has so much as stepped outside Collegium's walls. It's all lies, but people are gobbling it whole. Foreign is fashionable. People are falling over themselves to be more misinformed than their neighbours about distant lands. And then there's Master Broiler.'

Stenwold pressed his lips together, locking away his automatic reaction to the very name. The fact that Broiler had always been his vocal political opponent was something Stenwold could live with: such free debate was after all the cornerstone of Collegium governance. However, he had his own suspicions about precisely who had bought the man's loyalties.

'What is Broiler doing now?'

'Courting public support, as usual, by pandering to the latest fashion.' Drillen reached into his robes and came out with a smudgily printed volume whose title proudly proclaimed *Master Helmess Broiler, His Atlas of the Known World and His Account of His Travels Therein.*

'The shameless fraud,' growled Stenwold, the historian in him genuinely shocked.

'Quite,' Drillen agreed. 'He's taken every damn map he could copy from the library, put them all together in no particular order, even the ones that are obviously made-up or wrong, and called it "The World". And he's written about his incredible adventures, this man who would get lost just walking from his house to the marketplace. I swear that Helleron appears in three different places in his so-called "Known World", and on at least one of the maps he's got the sea and the land the wrong way round. And you know what?'

'People are reading it?' Stenwold said.

'People are lapping it up,' lamented Drillen. 'They think Broiler's the best thing since the revolution. Stenwold, it's time for Lots soon enough, meaning all change at the Assembly. We have to do something before then.'

'We?'

'I have to do something,' Drillen corrected, 'and, unless you want to see Broiler as the new Speaker, so do you.'

'Where do I come into this, then?' Stenwold asked, thinking again about the Vekken and his final words. *I am fighting for our future and my footing is being eroded like sand shifted by the sea.*

'The people like you, Stenwold.'

'But the Assembly loathes the sight of me,' Stenwold pointed out. 'I remind them of how they were wrong.' It was a point of pride with him.

'Yes, but the people like you. Everyone out on the street there remembers how *you* won the war. They fought alongside you. They watched you go out and send the Wasp army packing. *People* – I'm talking about that majority without political aspirations – respect you. That's one reason why I'm going to be seen shaking hands with you in as many places as possible.'

'Why should I prostitute myself like that?'

Drillen's grin resurfaced. 'Because I make sure that you get what you want. I was almost the only person backing your Vekken initiative, when you put it forward, but I wrestled enough support to push it through. You're not as detached as you pretend, old soldier. You don't give a fig for power, but there are things you want done, and for that you need people like me. Which is convenient, because people like me need people like you in order to defeat people like Helmess Broiler.'

Stenwold scowled, but he had no argument to hand that could refute the other man's logic.

'I need to trump Broiler's atlas if I'm to get enough lots cast in my direction to secure the Speaker's podium,' Drillen explained. 'Now, I could just match him, map for map, but I have no guarantee that my fraudulent cartography would be any better than his, so I rather thought I might produce something genuinely scholarly, just for the fun of it.'

'That is not the thing the political future of the city will hang on,' Stenwold told him.

'Believe me, stranger things have been known. Our cousins, our kinsmen, our estranged family of Khanaphes . . . I have planted a few seeds of rumour already. People are already beginning to talk about it. I will raise some pertinent questions at the Assembly, and you . . .'

'What?' Stenwold said finally. 'What do you want from me?'

'Your seal of approval. I happen to know a little more about Khanaphes than most. You remember Kadro the antiquarian?'

'Vaguely, yes. I haven't seen him around recently.'

'I'm not surprised, as he's been in Khanaphes for several months. He'd followed the Solarnese trail long before anyone was looking in that direction. I know because he's been writing to me for money, and I've been sending it. That makes him my man.'

'And what has your man found out?'

'My man has been keeping his cards close to his little Fly chest.' Drillen grimaced. 'Which is why there will be an expedition sent to help him out. The first official Collegiate expedition to Khanaphes. Our ambassadors will extend the hand of friendship to our estranged brothers. Master Kadro will receive his due, but I need results.'

Stenwold nodded patiently, letting the quietness spin out until he was finally forced to ask. 'So where do I come into all of this?'

'Aren't you roused by the sheer academic challenge of it all?' Drillen asked, still grinning like a fool.

'As it happens I am, but where do I come in?'

'You propose the expedition, which I then agree to sponsor and fund.'

'Do I now?'

'Because if I tried it myself, then Broiler would be all over me, and I'd be fighting tooth and nail every step of the way to stop him making it *his* expedition and *his* triumph. You, though . . . Broiler hates and loathes every inch of you there ever was, but more than that, he doesn't have the guts to take you on. If it's your expedition, he'll mutter and complain, but he won't dare stick his neck out, and you know why.'

Stenwold cocked a surprised eyebrow at Drillen, seeing that his own suspicions about Broiler's loyalties were obviously not unique. He shrugged philosophically, waiting for the catch.

'*Please*, Stenwold,' Drillen said, in a pleading tone that surprised both of them. After an awkward pause the fat man continued, 'I'm a devious bastard whose only aim is my own betterment, I freely admit it, but I'm also on your side. A coup involving Khanaphes could be enough to swing the voting next Lots. We need each other.'

Stenwold sighed. 'This sort of politics has always been exactly the sort of thing I've tried to avoid. So you want me to go to Khanaphes?'

'No, no, I need you here to continue shaking hands with me in public. I just want you to drum up a few scholars to go there in your name, with my money. So people will like me more and Broiler less. And also the academic knowledge of the College will be expanded by another few feet of shelf space. That's a secondary consideration for me, but I do still care about it.'

'I know,' said Stenwold tiredly. 'That's the only reason why I've been listening to you for this long.' Inside he was fighting his own battle. There was a lot of him saying that once he started making these deals he was on a slope – and his kinden were notoriously clumsy. That the future of Collegium might depend on closet conspiracies like this one made him feel sick about the whole business. Drillen was right, though: Stenwold needed support in the Assembly, and he must pay for any services rendered.

And he was intrigued. Despite himself and despite everything he was intrigued. A Beetle-kinden city located beyond Solarno. *What might we learn there?* And on the back of that, another thought – the possible solution to another personal problem.

'I'll do it,' he said. 'I'll regret it, but I'll do it.'

'That's my old soldier!' Drillen clapped him on the shoulder with a meaty hand, and poured out another two goblets of wine.

Stenwold took his and drank thoughtfully, turning implications over in his mind. 'I suppose you'll want everything to look spontaneous,' he mused.

'Oh, of course,' Drillen agreed heartily. 'The serendipitous meeting of two great minds.'

'Best if it looks that way,' Stenwold muttered darkly. 'I'm not thinking about Broiler now, but about the Imperial ambassador.'

Drillen blinked at him blankly.

Stenwold looked unhappy as he continued. 'Think about it: Stenwold, implacable enemy of the Empire, entering into secret negotiations that will send agents to a city that is not so very far from the Empire's southern border.'

'The war's over.'

'The war isn't currently active. Both the Empire and I understand the distinction.'

Drillen shrugged. 'Whatever you want. You're in charge. It's your expedition.'

She was still in mourning, but mourning was difficult for her.

In Collegium the official colour of mourning was grey. True, it was not customary any more for widows and grieving family to parade around the city in drab vestments for tendays, or even just days, but for funerals at least, grey was the order of the day.

For Cheerwell Maker, though, grey was *his* colour,

therefore a life colour, the colour of her happiness, in the same way that black and gold had become colours of death. She could not make grey the colour of her mourning because that would be a negation of his life.

In the end she had tracked down a Moth-kinden, a pallid trader from Dorax, and not left him alone until he had explained the customs of his people. For the Moths, the concept of colour seldom entered their lives, since they lived in a midnight world where they could see perfectly without need for sunlight or spectrum. For death, though, they made an exception. For shed blood, they took on the hue of blood. She learned how Mantids did the same, dressing their honoured dead in scarlet, and then entrusting them to the red, red flames. The Moths, who had been the Mantis-kinden's masters since time immemorial, had become infected by such superstitions.

And red was the colour of the Mynan resistance, their emblem of red arrows on a black background proclaiming their impossible triumph over the Empire. And Myna had been where he had died, for her, though he had been so many miles away.

So Che wore red, and thus caused public comment. She wore a tunic of deep wine colours edged with black, or else black arrowed with resistance scarlet. Even though she also wore a Moth cape of grey sometimes, nobody realized that she was mourning.

When she had gone to Tharn, after the war, they would not let her in nor tell her what rites had been performed over the body of poor Achaeos. They would barely spare two words for her. With the Empire beaten back, the old hatreds had resurfaced. She was Beetle-kinden, therefore a despoiler and an enemy. Her previous history as a Moth seer's lover had been erased and, in the end, the Moths had forced her, at bow-point, back on to the airship. Only the intervention of Jons Allanbridge, the aviator, had prevented her being shot dead there and then.

She had tried to tell them of the mark, of the affliction she had been left with in his wake, but they had not wanted to know. Instead they had told her to leave promptly or they would throw her off the mountainside.

Mourning was so hard for Che. Her own people had not understood her choice of lover, and now they did not understand her grief. She was surrounded by her own folk, yet feeling more alone each day that passed.

Yet not alone enough. Sitting here on her bed, with the bright light of day blazing in through the window, she felt a sudden presence beside her. It always happened the same way: the movement did not manifest as such, at first, neither flicker nor shadow, but just as a concrete awareness of *there being something there*.

If she moved her head to look, it would be gone. If she stayed very still, though, and emptied her mind the way he had taught her, and waited . . . then sometimes there would be a greyness at the edge of her vision, a tremor in the air, a *something*.

Mourning was difficult for her because she knew that he was still there. He had been a magician, after all, which she now finally believed only after his death. He had been a magician, truly, and now he had become something else. She had been far away when he died, having left him to the failed mercies of his own people. Now, posthumously, he was close to her, and she could not bear it.

She stood up, feeling the non-presence recede away instantly, knowing that it was still there somewhere, beyond her notice. At the same time she heard the front door, the hurried feet of Stenwold's servant running to greet his master. She drifted out on to the landing in time to see her uncle down below, divesting himself of his cloak. He complained so often of being old and tired, and yet seemed to her to be possessed of boundless reserves of energy. He complained of being mired in politics and intrigue, yet he fed on it with a starving man's appetite.

He still wore his sword, one of the few Assemblers who did. Stenwold was still at war, they would joke, but their laughter had a nervous quality.

She drew back into her room, knowing he would come to speak with her soon enough. He did not understand, could not fathom, what she was going through, but he did his best, so she could not complain. He was perpetually a busy man.

Downstairs, Stenwold stopped himself from turning his head as he heard the landing creak. Either she was still there or she had retreated and he did not know whether her absence or her presence was more disturbing: this ghostly, red-clad apparition that his niece had become.

*I need help.* But there was nobody to help him. The war had stripped him of both allies and friends. Above the fireplace, he had finally had framed and hung the old picture that Nero had done of Stenwold and the others when they had just been setting out. Dead faces now, only Stenwold Maker living on out of all of them.

*How is it that I am still here, after all of this?* He had a sudden sense, almost like vertigo, of all the people he had sent out to die or get hurt: Salma, Totho, Tynisa, Achaeos, Sperra, Scuto, Tisamon, Nero – even the madwoman Felise Mienn. There was no justice in a world that preserved Stenwold Maker after all that loss.

But it was worse when he considered the survivors. The Assembly was crawling now with men boasting of their exploits in the war, but Stenwold could not remember seeing *any* of them defending the walls at the time.

He glanced up, at last, to find no scarlet watcher above. The war had left so many casualties, with so many different wounds that he was powerless to cure.

'Lady Arianna sent word that she would be expecting you at her residence, sir,' his servant informed him. The thought stirred an ember of a smile, but he was so tired that it could be no more than that.

He began the slow clump up the staircase.

There were books all over Cheerwell's room, open, bookmarked or stacked, lying on the bed and at her desk. They looked old and valuable, and he knew she was trading on her family name to extract favours from the librarians. On the other hand, it was not as though the topics she was researching were required reading for College scholars. Most of these tomes had not been opened before during her lifetime, perhaps not even in Stenwold's. The sight of them reinforced his disquiet, reminded him of the scale of the plight they faced.

'How was the Assembly?' she asked him. She sat demurely on her bed but there was a brittle aura about her, as of some fragile thing delicately balanced.

'Tedious as usual.' He racked his mind for something amusing he could recount to her, was forced to accept that nothing amusing had occurred. 'I did my normal job of making friends, so I'm surprised they're not burning my effigy in the square before the Amphiophos.'

He saw her smirk at the quip, a reaction more than the words warranted. 'You have no idea,' Cheerwell told him. 'You should get her . . . get Arianna to go to the play with you.' She stumbled a little over the woman's name, but only a little. She was at least trying.

'Play?' he asked blankly.

'Haven't you heard? At the Rover on Sheldon Street?' Her smile was genuine, though a sadness shone through it. 'They call it *The Shell Crack'd* or something like that. It's about goings on in this city when the siege was under way. It's all people leaping into each other's beds and arguing.'

'There's a play about the war and it's a *farce*?' said Stenwold, quite thrown off course from what he was originally going to say.

'Yes, but you're in it too. You're the serious bit in the fourth act, like they always include,' Che told him. 'When you went out to confront the Wasp army and got them to surrender and go away—'

'It wasn't like that—'

'Tell that to the playwrights. Tell that to the audience. You're a hero, Uncle Sten.' Her shoulders shook briefly with mirth, for a moment like the Che he knew from before it all. Then another layer of solemnity enveloped her and she said, 'Your man from Paroxinal came back today.'

'Oh?' and he was serious at that news, too.

'He said he'd report fully to you, for what it was worth, but nothing.'

'He found nothing, or they'd tell him nothing?'

'Nothing either way. Nothing at all. He found no trace of her.'

For a moment they just looked at one another, chained together by an equal guilt, until Stenwold bared his teeth in annoyance and looked away.

'Damn the girl!' he said. 'Why—?'

'You know why,' Che interrupted him flatly.

'Oh, I know what sparked it, but why go off—?'

'You know why,' she repeated firmly, and he had no answer to that, because he did know.

Feeling weary to his bones he pulled the desk chair out and reversed it, sitting so he could rest his arms on the carved back. He heard it creak at the unaccustomed strain. *I'll be as fat as Drillen, one of these days.* 'Che, I've had a thought about . . . something for you.'

She sat very still, waiting warily. It was not the first time he had tried to find things for her to do. She knew he meant well, but he did not understand that her current problems could not simply be left behind.

'Che . . . you did some good diplomatic work during the war.'

That took her by surprise. 'When?'

'In Myna, for example.'

'Sten, they nearly killed me there as a traitor.'

He smiled slightly at that. 'Same here . . . and with death, it's all about the "nearly". The way I hear it, you finally got their rebellion inspired to the point where they could throw off the Empire.'

'It wasn't like that,' hearing in her voice an echo of his own words.

'Tell that to my agents. Tell that to the Mynans. Che . . .' Staring at his hands as he always did when he sought inspiration. 'You need something to do . . .' One hand rose, quickly, to cut off her objection. 'I *know*, I know it won't stitch the wound, and it won't make everything better, just to be doing something, but you need time to heal, and at the moment it's just you and the wound, and nothing else. I have a job I need doing, and you need something to do – and you're good at it.' When she just stared at him he continued, 'I need an ambassador. An official ambassador representing Collegium, bearing the seal of the Assembly and everything.'

For a moment she continued to stare, then she laughed at him incredulously. 'You can't be serious.'

'Why not? You've already proven your worth: in Myna, in Solarno, in Sarn. This isn't just Uncle Sten finding jobs for his family. You've shown you're more than equal to the task, and—'

'And it would give me something to do,' she finished sourly. 'And where, pray?' A thought struck her. 'The Commonweal?'

'Not the Commonweal,' he said. 'We're being . . . very careful there. They're a strange lot, up north. They don't really seem to understand yet why ambassadors are necessary. We may even have to buy into their "kin-obligate" business, not that we really understand it.' He waved his hand impatiently. 'No, it's a place called Khanaphes.'

She stared at him, which he interpreted, incorrectly, as ignorance.

'The Solarnese know a path to reach it. It's east of the

Exalsee, a long way off any Collegiate trade route.' He left the appropriate pause before revealing, 'A Beetle-kinden city, Che.'

Since her return from Tharn she had been deep in the old tomes of the Moth-kinden. She had been immersing herself in the world that the revolution had shattered, in an attempt to find some cure for her own affliction. In the very oldest of the books and scrolls remaining to the College, amid the most impenetrable shreds of ancient history, there had been a city of that name. It was a relic of the forgotten world that the Beetles had shrugged off in order to become what they were now.

'Think about it, please.' Stenwold took her silence for reluctance. He wanted to tell her that it was a golden opportunity, that she should look to her own future, capitalize on the respect she had won in the war. He wanted to tell her, in short, that no mourning could be for ever. He knew better than to say it. 'Just think about it. You are a student of the College after all, and the possibilities for scholarship alone are—'

'I'll think about it,' she said, a little harshly, and he nodded, standing up to go. 'Another thing,' she began, her voice sounding strained. 'You . . .' She paused, gathered her courage together. 'Please tell the new man about the doors again. He forgets.'

Stenwold stared at her, a welter of different emotions momentarily at war across his broad face.

'It's not just me . . . it's . . . I'm thinking about Arianna as well.' Che's voice shook under the sheer humiliation of having to say it.

'Of course I will,' he said. 'Of course. I'll have a word with him when I go back downstairs.'

The expedition was approved by the Assembly, despite anything that Broiler and his supporters could say against it. The Town vote, comprising the merchants and magnates, scoffed at the expense, but the Gown vote of the College masters was mostly for it, and Drillen's promise to secure funding without troubling either College or Assembly coffers sealed the matter neatly. There was no suggestion that the proposal had been stage-managed from the start.

The very night of the Assembly meeting, however, found a clerk working late. Drillen was a rigorous employer who demanded results from the least of his underlings, so candlelight in the late evenings was nothing unusual. This clerk, a young man who had hoped to make more of himself, and had lived beyond his means, was just finishing his last missive. The letters seemed nonsense, strings of meaningless babble, but an informed eye would have deciphered them as:

*Urgent. Codeword: 'Yellowjacket'. You told me to keep an eye on all dealings of Stenwold Maker, so this should interest you: the expedition being launched to Canafes (sp?) is not as it seems. JD and SM met twice beforehand re: this matter. Unusual secrecy. Believe JD and SM have their own purposes aside from those stated. Thought you would appreciate knowing.*

He folded the note over, and went over to his rack of couriers. Drillen used these various insects as missive-carriers across the city. They rattled and buzzed in their tubes, each tube with its label to show what place the creature was imprinted on. The clerk, whose responsibility these carrier-creatures were, selected one carefully: a fat, furry-bodied moth. It bumbled out of its tube and crouched on his desk, cleaning its antennae irritably as he secured the message to its abdomen. He had no idea where it went, or to whom, save that it would not be the man who had originally recruited him into this double-dealing. He only knew that the insect would be returned safe, along with a purse of money, to his house. This told him two things: that his shadowy benefactors were wealthy, and that they knew where he lived.

The insect whirred angrily off into the night, swooping low over the streetlamps but impelled by an inescapable instinct to return home. Before morning the Rekef operatives in Collegium, placed there with exquisite care after the close of the war, had something new to think about, and other, grander, messengers were soon winging their way east.

# Four

She was dreaming, and she knew she was dreaming. The problem was that it was *his* dream. Worse still, she knew that the things that she was witnessing through his eyes were real.

Her mind was full of chanting voices, overlapping and blurring together. She heard no distinct words, just the ebb and flow of the sounds interfering with each other until it was like a great tide, rolling in towards her endlessly.

And she saw robed shapes . . .

She saw robed shapes. They were atop a mountain, and the air around them was bending and fragmenting under the strain of what they were doing. She could not tell which one of them was Achaeos. Because it was also *her* dream she rushed from one to another, to find him. She never could. Their pale, grey Moth faces, their blank white eyes, were all transfigured, so that each face looked the same. The ritual had gripped them with an identical hand. She shouted at them and tried to shake them. She warned them that he would die, if they kept tearing at the world like this. Because it was his dream, and she had not been present, they ignored her.

She knew that she was running out of time. It was not *his* time, not the time remaining until the barbed peak of the ritual, when the power they invoked would come thundering down through the city of Tharn, and his fragile body would be unable to take the strain. Instead it was the time until the *other* arrived.

It had always been there beside them, although she had been blind to it for so long. From the very first moment their minds had touched, he venturing among the ghost-infested trees, she imprisoned in the hold of a Wasp heliopter, it had been with them. Now she felt it rising from beneath them, through the warrened rock of the mountain, through the very weave of the world. It was surging upwards at a fierce, relentless pace, but it was still a good distance off because it was pursuing from five hundred years ago.

She thought of flying over the Exalsee and seeing the lake monster rushing for the surface, the great pale body of it forming from the depths.

The chanting grew even less and less coherent as the voices of the Moth-kinden fell into the echo of that older, greater ritual. Around them the rock of the mountain itself began to crack. Thorny vines thrust themselves violently into the air, then arced round to penetrate the stone once more, to pierce the flesh of the ritualists, yet they did not seem to notice. Transformations were being wreaked on them. Che would run faster and faster from one to another, trying to find Achaeos before the things of the Darakyon did. There were shadows all around now, the shadows of great twisted trees, of Mantis-kinden writhing, bristling with barbs, gleaming with chitin. The shadows were closing in, encompassing the ritual. The robed figures were being consumed.

She felt it again, as she had felt it in life. She felt the sudden silence, that utter silence as though she had been struck deaf. It was a silence so profound it left an echo in the mind. It was the moment when the wrenching strain of the ritual, the fierce attention of the Darakyon, had become too much for him, the moment when his wound had ripped open and he had died.

Had died, and yet not left her.

Behind the Tharen mountain top and the shadow-trees of the Darakyon lay the streets of Myna, the ziggurat of the governor's palace, her own dream evolving in the shadow of his. She saw a tiny figure break from the barricades, and then charge towards the soldiers clustered around the broken palace gates. She saw, as she had not seen at the time, the great clawed tide of the Darakyon hurtling forward, spewing uncontrollably out of that lone running figure, thrashing about her like a headless, dying thing. The last dregs of the Darakyon, now poisoning the minds of the soldiers ahead of her, making her into a vessel of terror.

She woke to find the shutters still dark, no piercing slants of sunlight. She, who had once slept late by choice, now woke regularly in darkness and saw every dawn arrive, tugged awake by shreds of a nocturnal life that had not been hers.

He was with her.

There, in the darkness that was no darkness to her, she could see him as a grey smear hanging in the air, formless and faceless. It moved and changed shape, and she received the impression of a dreadful urgency. He was trying to tell her something, desperately trying to make her aware of something, and yet he could not form words or even pictures for her.

'Help me to understand you,' she told him. 'Achaeos, please. I can't . . . I'm not strong enough to make you real. Just tell me what I have to do.'

He grew more agitated, and she thought of him trapped between life and death, a knot in the weave, shouting and screaming at her to help him. But she could not. None of the books she had trawled from the Collegium library had helped her. She was too dull a scholar, their old language too intricate, too occult.

He was fading now. It was only just after she woke each day that she could see him clearly. He would always be there, though, a half-sensed presence hovering over her shoulder.

Mourning was difficult, for Achaeos's death had left her with an indelible legacy. The sorrow of losing him still had its hooks into her, but the horror of having him still – in this horrible, half-formed way – was worse.

By the logic of her people, she was simply deranged. If she had gone to see a Beetle-kinden doctor, he would have told her that she was suffering from these hallucinations as a way of dealing with her loss. Alas, she could no longer subscribe to the logic of her people. The books she had pillaged from the library were written in the crabbed hands of Moth-kinden or the elegant loops of Spiders. The one thing she had learned from them was that, by *their* logic, she was not mad. There were precedents for her situation, though she was not sure that this was any reassurance. Being haunted was surely worse than mere madness. Especially being haunted in a city where nobody, not even her open-minded uncle, believed in ghosts.

During the ritual atop Tharn, Achaeos had called out to her, and she had lent him as much strength as she could, and possibly contributed thereby to his death. Her mind and his had been touching when the mouldering evil of the Darakyon had stirred itself to answer his call for power. When he had died, therefore, something of him had stayed with her. The logic – since all insanities have their own internal logic – was faultless. The books were silent on remedy, however.

And there was more than that: she was not whole, any more, after the war.

She stretched herself and shook her head. The ghost of Achaeos was gone: still there in the back of her mind but no longer apparent to her eyes. As she dressed, she saw the first pearl-grey of dawn glimmer through her shutters. She approached the door carefully, as though it might suddenly become a monster, a jailer. It was ajar, though, and she went out on to the landing.

Stenwold's door stood open, which meant he had not come back last night. She smiled at that. She knew that she was a burden on him that he could not shift, so it was good that he still had Arianna.

Che and Arianna had not got on well, not at all, and the real problem had been Stenwold himself, who simply did not know how to deal with them both at the same time: on the one hand his young niece, his daughter in all but name; on the other his lover, scarcely older than her, with whom he was a different man entirely. The confusion it threw him into had obviously amused Arianna at first, but then it had become inconvenient and, in her smooth Spider-kinden way, she had secured a first-floor residence across town. Stenwold was abruptly released from the pressure of having to be two men at the same time, while Che and Arianna did their best not to meet. Life was easier that way.

Che pulled her grey cloak on over her mourning reds, taking only a moment to look in the mirror. With the hood raised high her reflection always surprised her: her skin appearing too dark, her eyes disfigured by iris and pupil rather than blank white. Seeing any face framed in grey cloth, she expected to see his face and not her own.

'Achaeos,' she said softly. He must be able to hear her, from his vantage point at the back of her mind. 'Help me.' Sometimes she saw him flicker in the background of mirrors, but not now. She lifted the bar on the front door. There was no lock, only the simplest latch.

Collegium was a city of the day, but good business came the way of early risers. By the time she ventured out, the sky was already flecked by Fly-kinden messengers, and a big dirigible was making its way in slowly from the north towards the airfield, bearing goods and news from Sarn, no doubt. There was currently a law about running automotives through the city streets before a civilized hour of the morning, but handcarts and animal carts were already rattling across the cobbles, and she could hear the slow shunting of the trains almost all the way across the city, in the still dawn air.

Stenwold lived in a good part of town, not far from the College, and the short walk took her through what was now called War Harvest Square, because of the mummery that was enacted here every tenday. Collegium looked after its own. Collegium was wealthy enough, despite the costs of the recent war, to do that. She spotted the queues ahead of her, and knew it must be the day when the War Harvest was doled out.

It could have been worse. Collegium medicine was some of the best in the world, and modern weapons were efficient enough to kill more often than they maimed. There were enough, though, who had fallen between the extremes of kill and cure, and every tenday they made their arduous way here. These veterans, the men and women of Collegium who had fought for their city against the Empire or the Vekken, or else gone out to fight for the Sarnesh, and whose injuries meant they now had no trade left to them. Men and women missing legs, missing arms, missing eyes, they came and queued here every tenday, and the Assembly ensured that they were given enough to live on. There had been a bitter dispute over it at the time but, in the flush of peace, the Assemblers of Collegium were not going to turn their soldiers out to beg or starve. It had made Che proud of her kinden, and the veterans who gathered here for the handout had been left a little pride, a little self-respect. Passers-by saluted them, cheered them, and acknowledged their sacrifice, while the two tavernas nearby did a good trade from citizens buying them drinks.

The problem came with those whose wounds were less visible. She knew there were many: those who had not been able to bear the blood and destruction, the loss of loved ones; those who had retreated into themselves; those who could not hear a shout or a loud noise without being flung back into the fighting. Victims of the war without a mark on them, they were not provided for. Instead the doctors prodded them, frowned at them, and shrugged their shoulders.

She herself had not gone to see a doctor. They would not understand.

It had come upon her as she went by airship to Tharn, to try to visit Achaeos's ashes. Before then the shock of his death, the whirl of events at the end of the war, had kept her off balance. It had only been on that return journey that she had realized.

She remembered the waves of nausea first, losing her balance at the slight sway of the wind. She had crouched on the deck, feeling her stomach churn in sudden spasms. The movement of the vessel beneath her had seemed as unnatural as water on fire.

*This is what he felt*, she had reflected at the time, remembering how Achaeos had always been so uncomfortable with modern transport. She had assumed that was just because he was new to it, then.

She remembered staggering towards the stern, clinging to the rail, where the concerned expression of Jons Allanbridge had wavered through her view, a meaningless image. She had stared at the engine, the blur of the propeller, and felt a chasm gape beneath her. It was *wrong* – worse, it was meaningless. She had stared at all that pointless metal, its inexorable convolutions, its parts and pipes and moving things, and she had felt as though she was falling.

The white elegance of the College was straight ahead of her now. The library's great gates were still closed and barred, this early, so she went to the side door and knocked and knocked, until a peevish voice responded from within, announcing, 'It's not locked.'

Che drew a deep breath and knocked again. 'It's not locked!' called out the librarian, thoroughly irritated now. 'Either come in or go away.'

She stared at the handle, feeling tears prickle at the corners of her eyes. Her memory told her that this was simple but her body had no path for it, her mind no connection. She rattled with the metal ring, but the door would not move.

She could not understand the process. It made no sense to her. In her final moments, while touching Achaeos's mind as a channel for the Darakyon, something fundamental had been ripped out of her.

At last someone came to the door and yanked it open. The librarian was a stern old woman, her face devoid of sympathy. 'What do you want?' she demanded.

'I want to come in,' Che replied in a tiny voice, fighting the urge to weep in frustration.

It would have been worse if there had never been Tynisa. Che had grown up with her as though they were sisters: Stenwold's clumsy niece and Tisamon's halfbreed bastard – although neither had known Tynisa's heritage at the time: Tynisa, who was graceful and beautiful and accomplished in every field save one. So it was that Stenwold had made alterations to his house, and given his servant special instructions about the doors and the locks. That servant had died in the Imperial siege, though, and the new man was taking a while to learn. It was not surprising, for the instructions were baffling to him and Che could hardly blame the man for forgetting. At least Stenwold was used to the idea; he could pretend he understood.

Walking through the streets of Collegium, she was nevertheless a cripple. She looked up at the slowly manoeuvring airship and felt that it should fall on her. It was too great; it could not stay up. The sounds of the trains, which had lulled her to sleep ever since she first came to Collegium, were now like the cries of strange and frightening beasts.

Yet she had spent years learning mechanics, basic artificing, forces and levers, power and pressure. Now it was as if she had spent all that time learning how to walk through walls or turn lead into gold. She could clearly remember being able to do it once, but not how. The logic had deserted her and she had become like *him*. She had lost her birthright, the basic tools that made the modern world comprehensible. She had become Inapt, unable to use – to even comprehend – all the machines and the mechanisms that her people loved so much. She was crippled in her mind and nobody would ever understand. There was a division between the races of her world: those who could, those who could not. Che had fallen on the wrong side of it and she could not get back.

It was worse now because of Tynisa. Of all the people in the world, Che could have spoken to Tynisa about it. Tynisa would have understood, would have helped her. Tynisa was gone, though, to Stenwold's fury. Che had not understood, at first, why Stenwold had reacted so angrily.

*I drove her away.*

And it was true. Not anything Che had done but the simple fact of her. In the end Tynisa had not been able to look at the sight of mourning Che without recalling whose blade had lanced Achaeos, whose hand had inflicted the wound that eventually killed him. Che did not blame her. Of course, Che did not blame her, but that did not matter. Tynisa had lived through the violent death of her father and come home to find herself a murderess. She had stayed as long as she could bear it, growing less and less at home in this city she had dwelt in all her life, unable to talk to Che, grieving a dead father, nursing a killer's conscience for all that Che tried to reach out to her. At the last she had fled Collegium. She had gone, and not one of Stenwold's agents could discover where.

Stenwold's rage, Che finally understood, had been over the undoing of twenty years of civilized education, over all the care and time he had spent in making Tynisa the product of Collegium's morality. In the end she had shown herself her true father's daughter. She had gone off, Stenwold felt sure, to lose herself in fighting and blood – chasing her own death just as Tisamon always had done.

*Hooray*, Che thought. *Hooray for those of us who won the war.*

*

The vast stacks of the library normally absorbed her. The Beetle-kinden claimed this to be the single greatest collection of the written word anywhere in the world. The Moths scoffed at them for this boast but nobody had performed a count. There were texts and scrolls here that dated back to before the revolution, to a period when the city bore a different name. They kept them in cellars whose dim lighting offered no impediment to Che. She had been searching for months, now, trying to find a cure to her affliction, a way of helping Achaeos's wretched shade.

All of a sudden she found she could not face it, not today. The thought of poring over more ancient scrolls that she could barely understand, of another day's fruitless delving into an incompletely rendered past, was more than she could bear. She searched her mind for the reason for this change, and found there Stenwold's offer of the previous night. At the time she had not cared, but something had lodged there, waiting for the morning light.

'Khanaphes,' she said slowly to herself, and it was as if the word created a distant echo in her mind. Ancient histories, old Moth texts: the city name would barely be found in any writings that post-dated the revolution, but if the diligent student dug deep into the writings of the old, Inapt powers, that name glowed like a jewel, ancient even to those antique scribes.

She needed to talk, but who could she talk to about Khanaphes?

Two dozen bemused students had turned up for the aviation lecture: Beetle-kinden, Ant and Fly youths, all wanting to be pilot-artificers – *aviators* as the new word went. They were without a teacher. So far all they had were some scribbled notes left on the chalkboard, instructing them to fold flying machines out of paper. This was now what Che discovered.

She knew where to look, as the avionics students did not, yet, though it took her a fight with her courage to cross town to the new airfield and enter the hangar. The shapes there, the winged things arranged in their untidy horseshoe pattern, looked only predatory. The air was filled with the sounds of metal and cursing artificers. It was a sharp reminder of her former self that she could have done without. She had encountered this and beaten it before. Had she wanted she could have shut herself away and never had to deal further with her affliction, but that was not her way: she was still Beetle-kinden, and Beetles endured. They were tough, both within and without.

'Taki!' she shouted, whereupon the little Fly-kinden pilot looked up, delighted.

'That,' she said, 'is the first time in five days that someone's addressed me properly, instead of "Miss Schola". I should never have told them my full name, honestly.'

She was looking well. Taki had also been crippled by the war, but in her case the damage had been made good by artifice. Her beloved *Esca Volenti* had been destroyed over Solarno, but here she was fine-tuning the *Esca Magni*. It was the perfect fusion of Solarnese know-how, Collegiate industry and Taki's prodigious skills as a pilot. She claimed it as the most agile flying machine in the known world. The boast had been put to the test and so far never proved false.

'It's good to see you again.' Che eyed the opened innards of the machine, fought down a brief stab of queasiness. 'Something wrong here?'

'Not wrong, just could be made better. One of your fellows at the College came up with an idea about air exchange, so I reckon I can get another few per cent efficiency out of the rewinding gears.' She grinned in the face of Che's polite expression, because she didn't know what was behind it. 'I want to try a non-stopper to Capitas.'

'Capitas in the Empire?' It was a stupid question, Che knew, but it leapt out before she could stop it.

‘Where else? They’re keen on their fliers up that ways. I’ve had an invitation.’ She shrugged. ‘If not there, then there’s an exhibition in Helleron in a month’s time, and I won’t miss that.’

The *Esca Magni* was sleek, hunched up from nose to cockpit, then with a long sweep of tail. The two wings, silk stretched over a frame of wood and wire, were currently folded back along her length. Beneath the nose emerged the compact fist of a pair of rotating piercers, another Solarnese innovation in the world of aviation. Taki, just three foot tall in her sandals, sat on its hull like an empress, mistress of all she surveyed.

‘What?’ Taki asked her. ‘I know that look. What’s up?’

‘Taki . . . have you ever heard of a place called Khanaphes?’

The Fly gave her a surprised look. ‘Well, of course, but how did that come up?’

‘It’s just that . . . people have been mentioning it.’

Taki shrugged. ‘Well, why not? Big old place down the east coast from the Exalsee. All a bit, you know, backward thataways.’

‘Backward?’

‘Not really keeping pace with progress, you know.’ Taki made a vague gesture. ‘We get food from them, trading through Ostrander. Now, Ostrander’s a strange place, and you never saw it when you were over . . .’ She saw something in Che’s expression. ‘But Khanaphes? What’s to say? Let’s get a drink and then you can ask your questions.’

The Fly had never actually been there, was the first thing Che learned. Taki’s life had always been fiercely centred on the airborne elite of the Exalsee.

‘They don’t have flying machines in Khanaphes?’ Che probed.

Taki made a condescending noise. ‘They don’t have *machines* of any kind in Khanaphes, from what I hear. Like I said, backward.' She looked amused, her eyes flicking across the clientele of the taverna as though she included them loosely in the same definition.

That took a moment to sink in. 'But they're . . . I thought they were supposed to be Beetle-kinden.'

'Oh, yes, yes they are. Not anything like your lot, though. I remember how Scobraan went there once, for a bet . . .' Her voice twitched for a moment, another colleague dead in the war. 'He said they'd never seen anything like his flier – didn't know what to make of it. Didn't want to know, either. And he couldn't get it refuelled, of course, had to get it shipped back to Porta Rabi by boat.'

'But that doesn't . . .' Something odd moved inside Che. 'And have they been settled there long?'

'Oh, you might say that. Long enough to have founded Solarno.'

'Seriously?'

'Oh now, this is long, long ago – and I'm remembering back to my school days for this, too. They used to own halfway around the Exalsee, way back before anyone can remember. But that was long before the Spiders and my own people came over – a thousand years before, something crazy like that. Then I suppose they just . . . got left behind. The way I hear it, they haven't changed much since those days. They still own a fair bit of territory up and down the river where they are.'

Che digested these words, thinking: *the past.* It made no sense: she *knew* Beetle-kinden even if she could not quite claim to be one of them any more. It made no sense. *Something doesn't add up.* It gave her a strange sense of excitement. *Khanaphes – what might I learn there?*

It struck her then, and she actually jumped up, knocking back her chair. Taki was in the air in an instant, wings a-blur and a knife in her hand. A few of the other taverna patrons had gone for their weapons too. The war was not so very long ago.

She sat down, made herself give an apologetic wave around the room. Taki stood on her chair back for a moment, wings flicking for balance, before consenting to sit down.

A city of Beetle-kinden without machines?

A city of *Inapt* Beetle-kinden?

'Yes,' she said, thinking of Stenwold's offer. 'Oh, yes I will.'

Stenwold was enjoying an after-lunch bowl of wine in the College refectory when someone came brushing past behind him, murmuring, 'The Vekken are after you.'

His stomach sank and he looked back. 'Which ones?'

His informant, a natural history master, shrugged. 'Who can tell? They all look the same.'

This was Stenwold's chance to make himself scarce, but he did not seize it. 'They're *my* problem,' he replied, whereupon his benefactor shrugged and made a quick exit. Stenwold braced himself mentally for another taxing encounter. His Vekken initiative which, in their mutual derision of it, had at last provided Collegium and Vek with something in common. Yet nobody understood how important it was. He was trying to do what Collegium should have done in the first place, instead of relying solely on the strength of its walls and assuming the Vekken had been defeated a generation ago. Stenwold was trying to make sure that there would be no third Vekken war. He was trying to build bridges. The result of his months of careful diplomacy was that the Vekken had at last sent four men who claimed to be ambassadors, and were more probably spies.

Two of them located him soon enough after the tip-off, and came marching up to stand before his table.

He couldn't even tell which two of the team they were. Ant-kinden all looked like siblings, and the Vekken seemed to have sent four ambassadors who were absolutely identical. They stared at him now as though they had just found out he had sent assassins to kill their families.

'Masters . . .?' He made a motion at the table, offering chairs. They stared at the seats as though they were venomous, then turned the same expressions on him. His Vekken initiative had been worth it, if just for this. He had always known the dislike of his own people for the city of Vek, inspired by two repelled attempts at conquest, but he had not guessed at the reciprocal loathing felt by the Vekken because of Collegium's successful resistance. They hated the Beetle-kinden and, because they could not see how mere Beetles could resist the might of an Ant city-state, they feared them also. Stenwold was working as best he could to disarm that enmity but there was a lifetime of ingrained distrust to overcome.

'We are aware of your plans,' one of them said, and then paused as if waiting for him to admit everything.

He looked at them blankly. 'I have many plans,' he said at last. 'Which ones do you mean?'

'You are gathering allies,' said the same one, speaking with the flat courage of a man who expects his hosts to have him killed. 'You are sending to another Beetle city to secure them.'

That gave Stenwold pause, but he was good at handling surprises and just drained his wine bowl while he pondered, *Now that's interesting. If* they *think that, then who else does?*

'Your silence indicates admission,' said the same ambassador. They had an identical expression of dislike etched onto their mirror-image faces, but no more than that. As with all Ant-kinden, the real feelings were expressed inside their heads, secret among their own kind.

'You're talking about the Khanaphes expedition?'

'So,' the Vekken said, all their fears confirmed.

'What of it? It's simply an academic expedition to study a city of our cousins . . .' He was about to ask them if they would not be similarly interested, in his position, but they would never be in a similar position, because any other Ant city was automatically their enemy.

‘So you say,’ said the Vekken. ‘But we see more.’

‘Please sit down,’ he suggested, but they would not. They continued standing there with their hands near their sword-hilts, waiting for the worst. He had a sudden dizzying thought of what it must be like for these envoys, surrounded by those they *knew* to be their avowed enemies, while deprived of the comforting voices of their own kin that they had lived with all their lives: just the four of them cut off and alone in an alien sea.

‘What do you want?’ he asked them patiently.

‘Warmaster Stenwold Maker is sending an expedition,’ declared one of the Vekken crisply. ‘He tells us it is peaceful and that no harm is meant. He will not deny a Vekken presence, therefore.’

They waited for his furious objections as he stared at them, mind spinning. They saw a military purpose in everything, and that purpose forever turned against Vek.

At the thought, it was all he could do not to laugh, but that would not have been diplomatic.

‘If you want to go, I shall make the arrangements,’ he agreed.

They betrayed nothing in their faces, but he knew he had caught them out. They did not know whether to rejoice at defeating him, or curse at themselves being defeated.

He only wondered what they would make of Khanaphes.

# Five

*Greetings and salutations of the Great College to my good friend Master Kadro.*

*It has occurred to me that you may think we do not allow sufficient importance to your far-flung mission.*

*Similarly, communicating as we do by such inadequate means, your discoveries to date – as opposed to your renewed requests for funding – have not been communicated to us here so well as I am sure you would prefer.*

*As the first College Master to study such a fascinating people as the Khanaphir, I can tell you we are all agog to learn what you have discovered, and to assist in furthering your studies.*

*So it is that no less a man than War Master Stenwold Maker, whose decisive role in the recent war cannot have escaped your attention, has proposed that we send some further members of the College to assist you in your labours.*

*Rejoice, then! For an ambassador of Collegium, none other than War Master Maker's own niece, shall be travelling to assist you, be the distance never so far. She shall take with her certain other academics who have expressed an interest – as who would not? – in the vital work you are doing. They shall of course bring equipment and funds to assist you, and they will be keen to hear from you regarding your theories and evidence.*

*I do hope you can arrange for them, with the Khanaphir authorities whoever they might be, appropriate lodging and similar conveniences.*

*Your most dutiful friend and sponsor*
*Master Jodry Drillen,*
*of the Assembly of that most enlightened city of Collegium.*

Petri Coggen read the letter again and felt like weeping.

She sat at the little sloping lectern which the Khanaphir had given her for a desk, and put her head in her hands. They were so *obtuse*, those old men at the College. Worse, they had a gift for bad timing. Beside Drillen's letter was one of her own, completed last night and ready for sending. It read:

*Good Master Drillen,*

*Forgive me for writing to you directly but I am the bearer of terrible news. Master Kadro is gone. He disappeared only two days ago. There is no trace of him. The Ministers say nothing, but I am sure they* <u>*know*</u>*.*

*Something terrible is happening here. There is a secret in Khanaphes and Kadro was close to it. They have done something to him. I am sure he is dead.*

*Please tell me what to do. I do not want to stay here longer, but I fear what might happen if I try to leave.*

*Yours*
*Petri Coggen, assistant to Master Kadro.*

She wanted to cry. She wanted to laugh. Instead she took her own letter and folded it, then put it inside her tunic. Perhaps, somehow, it would arrive in time to do some good. Assuming it arrived at all.

She buckled on her belt, carrying her purse and her dagger. It was the only weapon she owned but she would not know what to do with it if she was forced to use it on another living thing. Petri Coggen had never been much more than an aide and secretary to Master Kadro, who had been the great academic and explorer, dragging her out here so that she could scribe his exploits. But now she was alone, and the city of Khanaphes had become a brooding and hostile place. She was merely a Beetle-kinden woman edging towards her middle years, short and stout and prone to getting out of breath. She was certainly not the woman to avenge Kadro's death, but she felt she must at least try to investigate his disappearance.

She had shared a third-storey room with Kadro, a little box with two windows squeezed under the flat roof of a warehouse. Kadro had chosen it because the landlord was a merchant, and therefore used to dealing with foreigners; also because the place was cheap and lay close to the little stew of villainy that cluttered this side of the river beyond Khanaphes's great Estuarine Gate. This was a busy market by day, a tent city by night, and the tents often grand and elaborate, for there was a great deal of money changing hands at any given moment, and people in Khanaphes – legitimate dealers or otherwise – liked to show that they were doing well. It was a place that, in other circumstances, she would never have dreamt of visiting on her own, but nowhere else in Khanaphes might she find some kind of answer to her questions.

She made good time. A few hurried glances detected no followers, but the streets were teeming this close to the docks. There were always ships coming to the river quays, and then a swarm of dockhands, fishermen, merchants and rogues to pester them. Despite the time she had spent here, the heat still raised a sweat on to her skin, and the bustle of bald heads, the murmur of quiet voices, remained densely impenetrable. *These are my kinden but not my people and I cannot understand them.*

In the shadow of the Estuarine Gate, she paused. The gate itself was out of sight, supposedly deep in the waters of the river, under any ship's draught passing between those gargantuan carved pillars. Again she looked round and saw no soldiers of the Ministers come to apprehend her, no skulking cloaked figure with eyes fixed on her.

*And a poor spy it would be that I would notice!* She did not know what to do next. Her training at the College, all that history and architecture and philosophy, had been no preparation for this crisis.

She slipped past the gate by the narrow footpath, wall on one side, the choppy brown waters on the other. She did not look up, past that monumental pillar, to see the great stone likeness that was set into its southern side. Those inhumanly beautiful, blandly smiling features were constantly in her dreams. She had begun to fear them, for all they were a thousand years dead.

The maze of tents and awnings that awaited her was known to the locals as the Marsh Alcaia. She had come here twice before, both times with Kadro. Each time he had been cautious. Khanaphes was a well-run city, law-abiding and peaceful, but there was a froth of uncertainty where the external world met its walls, here before the Estuarine Gate. Other foreigners were not always so respectful of Khanaphes's laws. The golden Royal Guard sometimes swept through here with lance and sword, arresting and confiscating and slaying those that resisted, burning the tents. Khanaphes needed its trade, though, and so long as it did, the scum of the Marsh Alcaia would always re-establish itself before the Estuarine Gate, just outside of the city proper.

Entering the Marsh Alcaia was like stepping underwater, as the faded orange and yellow cloth closed over her and muted the sunlight. She was abruptly in a different world, stuffy, gloomy, reeking of spices and sweat. As she stood, a silhouette against the bright day beyond, the denizens of the Alcaia jostled past her. They did not look at her, each preoccupied with his own business. Every one of them was armed, a hand always close to the hilt of a broad-bladed dagger, a short sword with a leaf-shaped blade, a hatchet. Some bore as weapons simply the extrusions of bone that the Art had raised from their hands.

She finally conquered her fears and pushed inwards. Kadro had walked here without fear, or at least he had shown none. She tried to emulate him, even though she was big and clumsy and kept getting in the way. Porters with sacks of flour and sweet spices jostled and cursed her. A be-ringed merchant's retinue pushed her aside against the counter of a jeweller so that she upset his scales in a tiny clatter of brass. Her apologies fell into the abyss: they all maintained the Khanaphir reserve. Whether they were the local Beetle-kinden or the sinewy Marsh folk, or one of a dozen breeds of foreigner or halfbreed, they looked at her as though she was not wanted there. *As though I do not belong.* She did not belong. She had no wish to belong. It was just that she had nowhere within this city to turn. Khanaphes was the problem. If a solution existed, it must be somewhere here.

She regained her balance. The offended jeweller was a Khanaphir Beetle, shaven-headed as they all were. With that narrow-eyed, unreadable look they all adopted when looking at her, he finished restacking his weights and measures. She tried to remember what route Kadro had taken through this maze of shifting streets, hoping it was still good. Her memory was not up to it, though: the Marsh Alcaia was a world without reference. Each day the faces here might be different, and if there was a code in the colours of the awnings that might have directed her where she needed to go, she had no way of reading it. Recognizing such patterns had been Kadro's strong point.

'Excuse me,' she said to the jeweller, the effort almost having her in tears again. 'I need to speak to the Fisher. Do you know her?' The title was all she knew. Most of the darker denizens of the Alcaia had left their real names behind a long time ago.

The jeweller stared at her with the Khanaphir stare reserved for foreigners. It was not hostile, in fact very polite, but suggested that she was speaking some kind of infantile nonsense that the man could not possibly be expected to understand. It humoured her without admitting any comprehension.

Petri bit her lip. Reaching for her purse, she took out a pair of coins – Helleron-minted Standards and a long way from home – and put them on his counter. With a deft motion he slipped them on to his scales. Weight and purity of metal was everything here. Her money from home was disastrously devalued and she knew that in exchange he would give her a fraction of the value that unadulterated gold of that same weight would have brought her.

'Please?' she asked. The jeweller still said nothing but, as if by magic, a small child appeared at his elbow. He muttered a few words and the girl ducked under the counter and ran off into the Alcaia. A nod of the jeweller's head then suggested that she follow.

Where the girl led her was nowhere near where she had gone before, but headed deeper into the Alcaia than she had ever been. The thought came to her, within three turns, that she was being led into some kind of trap. By then she could only follow, because she was lost already. She was out of breath from keeping up with the girl's skipping figure, with dodging all the other bustling people doing their secretive deals beneath this all-embracing cloth sky.

The girl had stopped, ahead of her. Petri put a hand on her dagger-hilt, feeling it so unfamiliar in her grip. There was a tent ahead, which surely could hold a dozen people inside, all ready to lay hands on her. 'This . . . this is it?' she asked. The girl looked back at her, as blandly unreadable as any local. She still had hair, cut ragged to just above her shoulders. The ubiquitous head-shaving was an adult affectation.

Deprived of an answer, Petri took a deep, harsh breath. She could wait out here as long as she wanted, but all she would accomplish would be to make herself look indecisive and lost. She had to move forward, so she pushed into the tent.

The Fisher lay there, attended by a quartet of young Khanaphir men serving her wine and grapes. She was spread out on a heap of cushions, wearing Spiderland silks that must cost a fortune to import here, and adorned with gold all over: armlets, anklets, rings, pendants, even a band of it across her forehead. She was compensating in some way, Petri suspected, for the Fisher was a halfbreed of mixed Khanaphir and Marsh people stock. Her skin was an oily greenish colour and, somewhere between the solid Beetle build and the slight grace of the estuary folk, she had turned out shapeless and baggy. Her eyes were yellow and unblinking as they regarded Petri. A servant handed her a long-stemmed lit pipe made from smoke-coloured glass, and she accepted it, wordlessly.

*How did Kadro do this?*

'I . . . er . . . I wish to do business,' Petri began, trying to keep her voice steady. Responding to a small tilt of the Fisher's head, abruptly one of the servants appeared by Petri's arm, offering her a shallow bowl of wine. Gratefully Petri took it and subsided on to the cushions. It was hot and airless in here, and the bittersweet pipe smoke made her head swim.

'Please . . .' she said, before she could stop herself.

The Fisher continued to regard her silently, waiting. Petri summoned all her reserves of strength.

'I wish you to find someone for me.' *How would Kadro have put this?* 'I know that, of all the knowledgeable people in the Marsh Alcaia, you are renowned as being the one who can locate anyone or anything.' Compliments were important in Khanaphes, she knew.

A slight nod revealed the Fisher's acceptance of Petri's clumsy offering. 'A friend of Kadro of Collegium is always my friend too, of course,' she replied. 'But a curious woman would wonder at the purpose of such a hunt. Perhaps some fool who has insulted you, and is therefore deserving of death? You should know that there is another who would be keenly interested in such dealings.'

Petri's mouth twitched. 'It is no such matter,' she stammered, 'only that a friend of mine has been . . . too long out of touch, so that I am now concerned for him.'

'Your sense of duty does you credit,' the Fisher told her,

with a shallow smile. 'The path to my tent is not the worst that you might have chosen. Who is this ailing friend?'

Petri drained her wine for courage. The local stuff was strong, and she waited for a moment of dizziness to pass her. 'Ma . . . Kadro. I need you to find Kadro.' Never *Master* Kadro, not here. Here, the word had other meanings.

The Fisher's slight smile did not flicker, and its very fixed immobility told Petri that something was wrong. The halfbreed woman took a long puff of her pipe, then handed it back to one of her servants.

'Fisher?' Petri pressed, knowing that things had gone awry, but unable to see precisely how or why.

In a single movement the Fisher stood up, her face still devoid of expression. 'Alas, what you ask is impossible,' she declared. Her servants had moved closer to her, as though expecting attack. Petri stood up as well, mouth working silently, searching for words.

'But . . .' she got out finally. 'I have money!' It was unspeakably rude, by local standards, but the Fisher did not visibly react to it. Instead she simply retreated further and further. What had seemed a wall of cloth parted for her, and then she had vanished beyond it, her servants following silently. Petri was left in sole possession of the tent, deep within the Marsh Alcaia.

Her heart was beginning to pound. She had the sense of something chasing her. The Fisher had known something, had known enough not to want anything to do with this. Petri was fast running out of places to turn.

There was someone, though: there was the very person the Fisher had alluded to. The Khanaphir loved middlemen. Even in the business of seeking another's death there was someone to go to, who would then find someone else to wield the knife. Petri had never met the current holder of the office, but she knew the name from a casual mention by Kadro.

When she asked for the name of Harbir, people drew

back from her, turned away, refused to speak. She persisted, and suspected that carrying the name before her made her proof against the petty robbers and killers that haunted the interior of the Alcaia. Somebody who had business with Harbir the Arranger, however they might seem, was not prey for smaller fish.

But it was Harbir who found *her*. After she had spent a half-hour wandering at random through the coloured maze of the Alcaia, and regularly dropping his name, a cowled Khanaphir woman approached her, tugged once at her sleeve, and then retreated deeper into the gloom. Petri followed meekly, again because she had nowhere else to go.

Harbir's tent was bigger than the Fisher's, and inside it hanging drapes cordoned off the man himself. Petri found herself in a surprisingly large space, empty save for overlapping rugs on the floor. Two men stood by the door, bare-chested Khanaphir Beetles with axes in their belts, whose stare did not admit to her presence or existence.

'You have bandied my name a hundred times beneath the roof of the Alcaia,' came a voice from the tent's hidden reaches. It was a male voice, but Petri could tell no more than that. Even if this was the Arranger's tent, it could have just been another servant speaking.

'I . . . give you my apologies if I have caused any difficulties.' She stumbled over the words, which was poor, knowing the Khanaphir valued eloquence.

'There are many who come to me seeking a final arrangement,' the man responded, with the unhurried measure of someone fond of his own voice. 'The wealthy speak to me of their rivals, the bitter regarding those who have wronged them, the desperate concerning those who have more than they. Honoured Foreigner, have you been in our lands so long that you would be prepared to take part in our pastimes?'

'No . . .' The word came out as a squeak, so she calmed herself and started again. 'I only wish to know, great Harbir, whether a friend of mine has been arranged . . . has had an arrangement made about him.'

She hoped she had remembered properly what little Kadro had said of the traditions here. Amongst some assassins, she was sure, such a direct question would transgress etiquette – perhaps fatally.

'You have not come empty-handed, expecting to bear away such a weighty answer?' the voice enquired, upon which she finally relaxed a little. She reached into her purse and came out with a fistful of currency: Helleron Standards, the local lozenges of metal stamped with weight and hallmark, even a few bulky and debased Imperial coins.

There was a slight sound that might have been a snigger. 'And who is it that is so fortunate as to have you solicitous after their health?'

'Kadro . . . Kadro of Collegium, the Fly-kinden,' she replied. The words dropped heavily into the tent and left a silence.

'Please . . .' she said again, before biting off the words. The locals never said 'please'. Their indefatigable politeness danced around the word.

'Go,' said the voice.

'Please tell me!' she managed, suddenly very aware of the two axemen by the tent-flap.

'His name has not been passed to me,' said the unseen voice. 'Now go.'

The axemen had subtly shifted their stance, and Petri was suddenly very afraid. She tripped on the rugs, stumbled, and was out of the tent before she realized it, into the stifling alleyways of the Marsh Alcaia.

She looked around her, having no idea what path might lead her out of this warren of fabric. She had known she was intruding too far, but somehow had envisaged, after a successful quest, that the way out would open before her. But her quest was not successful, and no clear exit was to be seen. The one thing she could not ask the locals was *How do I get out of here?*

Petri started walking. She tried to make her gait seem determined, as of someone who frequented the Marsh Alcaia every day. But she was a foreigner, dressed like a foreigner, wearing a head of hair like a foreigner. She no longer had any names of power to awe the locals. She passed through avenue after cloth-roofed avenue, each lined only with the openings of tents. People stopped to watch her pass, and eyes from within the shadows picked out her movements. She was aware of this scrutiny but did not stop, just kept walking to who-knows-where.

A man fell into step alongside her. He was a Khanaphir Beetle, short, shaven-headed, wearing a simple robe. She glanced at him out of the corner of her eye and found he was not looking at her.

'Pardon this no doubt unwarranted observation but you look like one who is seeking the direction to where she should be,' he said, smiling out at the canvas sky.

'E-excuse me?' she stammered. She felt hope steal up on her, now, although she had no reason for it.

'I know where you need to be, and I can assist you, Honoured Foreigner,' said her companion. She stopped and turned to look at him directly.

'Please help me,' she said.

'Why, of course.' He smiled broadly. 'What you wish, of course, is to be in company with myself and my fellows. Who would not?'

She looked behind her and spotted the gathering of rogues that were his fellows. There were a full dozen of them, Khanaphir and silver-skinned Marsh folk, halfbreeds, and even a Spider-kinden woman from somewhere far, far off.

'No, please,' she whispered. 'I don't want to go with you. I just want to get out of this place.'

'Who would not want to leave here?' the Beetle agreed,

still smiling at her. 'And what better companions to leave with than such stout fellows as we? We have a fine ship, too, which lacks only one of your elegance to complete her company. Surely you will be our guest.'

She understood then: *slavers*. The rogues were meanwhile drawing closer to her in a kind of casual saunter. Any one of them looked as though he could outrun her and they had broad-bladed daggers, short-hafted axes, sported spurs of bone.

'Please, I . . . I am a scholar of Collegium. I will soon be missed.'

'Then surely your friends will reimburse us for our hospitality,' replied the smiling Khanaphir. There was a dagger in his hand, its blade as bright as a mirror even here under cover of the tents.

She opened her mouth to protest again but he grabbed her tunic, twisting it at the collar and drawing her up on to her toes. His smile stayed robustly unchanged. Another of his men was abruptly close enough to take hold of her other arm.

'Please—!' she cried, just as a spear plunged so far into his chest that its leaf-shaped head emerged complete and red-glossed through his back. His eyes popped wide open but the smile, horribly, stayed quite intact as he dropped. Petri fell back and sat down heavily, staring.

They had found her at last. She saw their gold-rimmed shields inlaid with turquoise, their raised spears and drawn bows, the gilded and alabaster armour of the Royal Guard of Khanaphes.

The slavers made no attempt at fighting. At the sight of the Royal Guard, they took to their heels. Petri saw the three guardsmen holding bows calmly aim and loose, and heard the solid sounds behind her of arrows finding their mark. The lead guardsman was now approaching her, one hand held out to draw her to her feet. She saw it was their captain, Amnon, who had always terrified her. He was over six foot

– very tall for a Beetle – but he seemed at least a foot taller still. He seemed larger than life, packed with energy and strength, bulging with muscles, with hands that could have crushed rocks: so fiercely alive and strong that she felt his presence as if he were a fire. She cringed away as he reached out, but he put her back on her feet one-handed, the other grasping a second spear behind his glorious oval shield.

'Honoured Foreigner Petri Coggen,' he said, grinning at her with white teeth, 'how fortunate that we found you.'

She could only nod. This was the First Soldier of Khanaphes, the Captain of the Royal Guard. He was everything she had been trying to escape from, to warn Collegium about. He was part of what had taken Master Kadro, she felt sure of it.

'Come, we will take you to your new rooms,' Amnon informed her, putting an arm about her shoulders. He made her feel like a mere child, like a Fly-kinden. He had come accompanied by only five men, but twice the number of slavers would not have dared face him, for he could have walked into the Marsh Alcaia on his own. Amnon was a legend here, and his position in the city was well earned.

At last his words got through to her. 'New rooms?' she asked timorously.

'Of course.' He drew a folded paper from inside his broad belt. It was the same letter from Collegium that she had left on the desk back in her lodgings. 'Your people are sending friends, so we must ensure that our hospitality is not wanting. We will prepare a proper welcome for them.' His smile was guileless, yet as savage as the sun.

# Six

'I have travelled in more luxury, in my time,' said Mannerly Gorget. 'When they said we would be travelling on the *White Cloud,* I allowed myself to get excited. I hadn't realized they meant as freight.'

'You exaggerate,' Praeda told him. 'Also, the padding you bring to the ship should be luxury enough.' She had made herself comfortable, or at least as comfortable as possible, against a bulkhead. It was not actually the cargo hold they were in, but three compartments alongside it that had probably been originally intended for crew. By unspoken agreement, Che and Praeda had taken the bow, the men had taken the stern, and the middle compartment was where they habitually sat and complained about the arrangement.

Since the war, Solarno and Collegium had not been strangers. A two-way trickle of scholars and artificers had begun, all keen to learn or to profit from the shortcomings of the one city or the other. The sheer distance, and the intervening cities of the Spiderlands, sufficiently complicated the journey to still make most forms of trade uneconomical. There was a certain market, however, that had grown up very recently between them, and that was aptly represented by the *White Cloud.* Just as Spider Aristoi had been using Solarno as a holiday retreat for centuries, so the idea had grown up amongst the richest of the Collegium magnates. Solarno, that beautiful lakeside city, with its civilized comforts and entertainments, had become *the* place to go for a certain class of the very wealthy. Deep in the Beetle mind there had always been a sense of grievance with the world. Beetle-kinden felt themselves looked down upon. They came from old slave stock. They were unsubtle in their dealings. Compared with the elegant grace of the Spider-kinden, they felt like club-footed children. It was a thorn in the minds of all of them, especially those rich enough to discover that there were things that money could not buy. Solarno, lying outside the Spiderlands proper, had given them a place to go and flaunt their affluence. They would promenade alongside the glittering Exalsee, throng its tavernas, watch its excitable locals and pretend that, by doing what the Spider-kinden nobility did, they had become their equals. What the Spiders thought of it all was unknown, but Solarno was raking in money hand over fist. The *White Cloud* did not lack passengers for the return trip, either. The Spider-kinden who lived in Solarno were sheltering from the Dance, and it provided a backwater allowing them to play their games in safety. The introduction of Collegium into their lives, a whole city crammed with the naive and the adoring, had enlivened their social scene considerably.

Captain Parrols of the *White Cloud* was possessed of unusual acumen, himself a Helleren Beetle of dubious provenance. He had almost ruined himself to fit out this little airship with as much tawdry opulence as possible, but he had since made it all back and more, even with only a single round trip every month. The sort of people who took the air in Solarno could not afford to be seen looking cheap. Parrols had been less enchanted with the idea of carrying a grab-bag of academics on his ship, but he owed Drillen and so had grudgingly acquiesced. Their current station within the bowels of the vessel was testimony to the stalemate reached between Drillen's influence and Parrols's parsimony.

The Khanaphir Expedition of the Great College consisted of either three, four or six people, depending on your point of view. The fourth person was Cheerwell, and she found herself with an uneasy and ill-defined role. Although a scholar of the College, she was not present here as an academic. The other three had credentials, while she was merely a student with a colourful recent history. She had been given the over-large title of Collegiate Ambassador to Khanaphes, even though Stenwold could not furnish her with much idea of what such a grand personage might do. Khanaphes itself sounded a confusing and contradictory place, so she would have to think on her feet and try not to upset people. On a more mundane level, although she was not the expedition's leader and had none of the academic prestige, she seemed to have inherited most of the practical responsibility. When they reached Solarno, it would be her job to find locals prepared to take them further. She was positively looking forward to it, if only for the fact that being crammed here into the underside of an airship with three bickering academics was making her ill. She could barely eat, she slept badly, she constantly fended off Mannerly Gorget's half-heartedly lecherous advances. She worried all the time about what they might find in Khanaphes.

The academic contingent of the expedition was a triad of conflicting personalities who were either genuinely enthused by the project or indebted in some way to Jodry Drillen. Che was not sure which criterion applied to whom. Their leader was a staid old man called Berjek Gripshod. He had been better known to her simply as Master Gripshod since before Che started her studies, but she understood there to have been a first name attached to him at some point. He was a College Master who cared nothing for politics, therefore Stenwold had chosen him as a historian who would not twist the revelations of Khanaphes to fit his own pet theories. Drillen, for his part, had chosen him as a man whose academic and political reputations remained unsmudged:

someone that people would listen to on his return. Those were his good points, at least. He was in his mid-fifties, hair grey and thinning, dignity etched over his face in deep lines. He had a desert-dry humour and no interest in conversing with people outside his own discipline. College students said the best way of attracting his attention was to have been dead for three hundred years.

In contrast was Mannerly Gorget, who was younger, broader, livelier and lewder. He eschewed College robes for brightly coloured Spider silks that strained over his stomach. Manny was a rising star in the Natural History department, Che understood, as well as being a better cartographer than Helmess Broiler. This was only the case when he could be bothered, however. He came from a rich family, and so work and discomfort were both unfamiliar to him. He had made a corner of their common room his own, where, at cards and dice, he fleeced – and was fleeced by – off-duty members of Parrols's crew. He seemed happy about everything until halfway through the journey, when he exhausted his private stock of wine. That had since triggered his more or less constant complaints about their travel arrangements. He dressed his moans up as badinage, but it was clear that he felt hard done by that Drillen's largesse had not extended to housing them in the upper berths.

Praeda Rakespear was a scholar of architecture and artifice. She did not drink wine, or gamble. Her first action, once the *White Cloud* was under way, was to definitively rebuff Manny Gorget and make it clear that she found him repulsive. The airship itself she found interesting, and she spent a tenday sketching the workings of its engine. She had a fine precise hand that would have been much admired, had she not made it clear that she valued nobody's admiration or praise. She was somewhere near thirty, impeccably neat and attractive save that her face might as well have been carved in dark stone. The ship's crew, as well as Manny, had begun to call her the Cold One. She cared not at all. She was abrupt with everyone, not from hostility but because she lived her life without any luxuries, including manners. Che's attempts at friendship had not been rebuffed, just retreated from. Praeda had not lived a happy life, Che gathered. Collegiate scholars had a phrase, 'the armour of the mind', and Praeda wore it night and day.

Before halfway Che had decided that of the three of them, Manny Gorget was the only decent company. At some level she was even glad that her roiling stomach kept her out of everyone's path for much of the time.

Then there were the other two: the Vekken. Stenwold had explained to Che why they were there, with apologies. 'They should likely keep out of your way,' he had advised – and they had. They stayed together, shoulder to shoulder, and said nothing. They wore real armour all the time, their swords always close to hand. They were ever waiting for treachery: Che could read it in their stance quite clearly. The concept of mounting an academic expedition to a far city, even one with a political undertone, made no sense to them. They had come aboard without names, and Che had eventually had to force her presence on them. 'I need to know what to call you,' she had said. They had stared. 'I might have to introduce you,' she had said. They had still stared. 'I was told you were ambassadors,' she had told them, now at her wits' end. They had reluctantly given her names: Accius and Malius. They looked almost twins, but she gathered that Accius was the one who spoke infrequently, Malius the one who spoke not at all.

They spent a lot of time up on deck and stared down both the crew and Captain Parrols when asked to go below. Cheerwell saw them most often at the stern, and guessed they were looking towards their vanished home and wondering if they would ever see it again. Looking at them, and their fearful hostility towards everything around them, she decided that her uncle's plan for conciliation with these people was doomed.

Captain Parrols was beckoning her over. He was a grizzled, unshaven man of near Stenwold's age, dressed in garish finery. Rumour placed him as being a sea pirate, not so very long ago.

'Look,' he told her, gesturing grandly over the port bow. His paying customers were present too, and they oohed and aahed at the sight. Cheerwell, at least, had seen it before: Solarno, the city of white stone set before the silver expanse of the Exalsee. The sun was lowering in the west into a bank of clouds, and a shoal of rain was scudding across the surface of the lake like a living thing. Parrols was giving a rambling and mostly inaccurate account of the city's history, but she ignored him and leant on the rail. Out here, with the wind in her hair and the cool fresh air all around, she found it almost bearable. The impulse to just spread her wings, to coast all the way to Solarno under her own Art, was very strong. She knew she was not flier enough for it, alas.

Even at this distance, she could pick out places that she knew. She saw the tangled street market of the Venodor and the mansions of the Spider-kinden families where she had once guested. She wondered which party now controlled the Corta, the city's intrigue-ridden council. It all seemed so long ago that she and Nero had been Stenwold's agents there.

*So long ago, and so many gone.*

They parted company with the *White Cloud* without much sorrow. Che engaged some locals to carry the surprising amount of luggage that three academics had been able to accumulate and found her way by memory to a Fly-run taverna where she installed them all in separate rooms. Manny Gorget was already talking about finding a bath and a whore, in no particular order. Praeda Rakespear and old Gripshod were talking in low voices about the merits of Solarnese building. In the morning it would be time for Che to find them a suitable road to Khanaphes.

★

'Well, if it's just a matter of the getting there,' replied the bearded Fly-kinden, 'then no problem. Tell you the truth, you don't even need me. Just find yourself a caravan, find a ship. It's not like people don't ever go there.'

Che nodded. 'It's more than that.' They were sitting on cushions around a very low table in something called Frido Caravanserai, which she understood was the place to go to find trading parties heading east. As well as the bearded man there was a Solarnese woman who looked as if she had been told something displeasing just before Che sat down, and was unable to forget it. Their quartet was rounded off by a lean, scarred Dragonfly-kinden who said not a word. In that restricted company Che and the Fly were making most of the conversation.

'Tell me about Khanaphes,' she said.

'Ah, well.' The Fly took out a clay pipe and filled it carefully with nimble fingers. 'They're strange over there.'

'They're my people, I hear. My kinden?'

He snickered, at that. 'They look like it, sure. They ain't, though. They're a law to themselves, the Khanaphir. Very secretive.'

'Will we have trouble getting into the city?'

'I don't mean secrets like that. No, they got secrets all over, absolutely everywhere, but because they're secrets, you can't see them. You just know that they're hiding stuff from you – and you never get to see their leaders. There's just this big pile of clerks running everything. And you have to be real careful what you trade with them.'

'What do *you* trade in?'

The Fly looked to the Solarnese woman, who scowled at him. 'In Khanaphes you buy food,' she said. 'Also gems and precious metalwork. They're good at that. You sell raw gold and iron, unworked metals of any kind. You sell cloth, Spider silks especially. Timber too.'

'That doesn't sound that odd to me.'

The woman made a despairing noise. 'My dear, you see them working in the fields with draught-animals and ploughs, or else they potter about on their river with oar-galleys. They are, in a word, *primitive*. Now, I knew a fellow who imported the parts for an automotive, set it up outside the walls to demonstrate it. He was going to start his own revolution. But nobody would deal with him. Nobody would even talk to him. They all got busy elsewhere, like nobody could find the time. He went back the next year with a hold full of the best timber you could find – and nobody would buy. It bankrupted him. The same thing happened to a woman I knew who tried to fly out there and trade from her airship. They wouldn't have it. They're not just barbarians, they're *wilful* barbarians.'

Che felt an odd feeling of excitement rise within her. Inapt Beetle-kinden? People who would understand her curse, perhaps even be able to help her? She looked to the Fly-kinden.

'All true,' he confirmed. ''Course, it doesn't mean squat to me. I'm just the caravan master and trading's what other people do. I just put them where they can do it. Which brings me to you.' He smiled at her brightly. 'Now, you're looking for a caravan master, and I just happen to be one, and currently free of hire. What are you carting?'

'Just passengers and their effects,' Che said. 'Six of us. And we'll retain you to stay on with us in Khanaphes just long enough for us to learn the ropes.'

The Fly rubbed at his chin. 'Don't know if there's enough time in the world for that. Don't think outsiders ever do work out what Khanaphes is all about.'

Che smiled to herself and thought, *Try me*.

They were not the only party making business arrangements in the Frido Caravanserai. Two Spider-kinden drank and laughed amongst their Solarnese retinues, while their fingers flicked and spun loops of silk in a silent language. Across the room, three tattooed Dragonflies were making a secretive deal with a pair of armoured men who caught Che's attention. Their tabards were dark grey, and the device on them seemed scarcely a different colour, and yet some trick of the cloth made it stand out plain: a heavy armoured gauntlet held open. An open hand meant peace, of course, except in the Empire it meant threat.

'Who are they?' she asked.

The Fly turned to see where she was pointing and made a dismissive grunt. 'Can't seem to go anywhere without seeing them these days. All over the Exalsee, they are. Iron Glove Cartel. New boys out of Chasme, but they fix up some good stuff.'

'What do they make?'

'Weapons,' said their quiet Dragonfly unexpectedly. 'Armour. Things of war.' He lapsed into silence again.

Che regarded the two Iron Glove men, who wore armour of studded leather all over, even visored helms. They made her feel uncomfortable at some deep level, and for no obvious reason. With a little shiver she turned back to the Fly-kinden.

They haggled over money a little. She knew in the end that he had got her to agree to more than his services were worth, but it was Drillen's money and she had no emotional attachment to it. Anyway, she reckoned that she could probably keep tapping the Fly for information by riding on the guilt of his good fortune.

'I'm Cheerwell Maker of Collegium, by the way,' she informed him. 'What do I call you?'

He leant across the table to clasp her hand with his much smaller one. 'You may call me te Rallo Alla-Maani, Bella Cheerwell,' he said proudly.

'That's your name,' she acknowledged, 'but what do I really call you?' She saw the surprise in his face, at a foreigner knowing this much. The Solarnese woman snorted.

'He's just Trallo,' she said. 'Nothing more than Trallo. And you'd better watch him, Bella. He's a rogue.'

Trallo's easy smile neither confirmed nor denied it.

When Che returned to their lodgings that night, she found Praeda out on the balcony, a silent figure against the raucous background noise of Mannerly Gorget and at least two Solarnese strumpets. The Collegiate woman could almost have been one of the Vekken, and engaged in their silent communion. They had not sufficient funds for a view of the lake, and so Praeda was staring blankly at the buildings just across the street. Che would have gone straight to her own bed and tried for some sleep, save that there was something uncharacteristic about the way Praeda was standing there.

'What are you doing out here, Miss Rakespear?' she asked, joining the woman in the open air. Fly-kinden buzzed overhead, either messengers or just late in going home.

'Not stabbing Manny,' Praeda said flatly, keeping her face turned away from Che.

'He didn't—?'

'He decided to subject me to another broadside of his affection,' Praeda snapped. 'And I do mean broadside.'

'Drunk, I suppose . . .' said Che and then caught herself. 'Meaning no reflection on you, save that he always seems to be.'

Praeda's shoulders shook, just briefly, hunching forward about her feelings. Che suddenly felt horribly awkward.

'I know what they say,' the other woman said. 'Don't think I haven't heard. I'd hoped to get away from . . . that kind of talk, save that wretched Gorget has brought it with him. Che . . .' But she killed the thought, the reaching hand snatched away. 'I apologize, Miss Maker. I will soon be myself again.'

'Cheerwell, please. In fact, I'd prefer Che,' Che told her. 'And can I—?'

'Praeda, please,' Praeda confirmed. 'Thank you.' She turned, valiantly, and Che could see the redness round her eyes. 'It's been a long journey and I'm tired,' she said with dignity, at which Che could only nod.

*

'It's a three-stage business, the road to Khanaphes,' Trallo explained. Despite the warnings about him, he had been working hard for his money in making arrangements. 'We may as well fly to Ostrander. There's a regular run of airships making the jaunt there. From Ostrander we'll fall in with a larger caravan, hiring pack animals and porters. There's always a pool of villains there waiting for work. We go overland to Porta Rabi, almost the longest part of the journey.' He had taken Che to a Fly-kinden chocolate house overlooking the water, and ostentatiously insisted on paying for everything. She was not sure whether this was business as usual for a Solarnese caravan master or whether he was trying to impress her.

'Why not fly straight to this Porta Rabi?' she asked.

Trallo laughed unkindly. 'You're a foreigner, so perhaps you don't know about our neighbours in Princep Exilla.'

'The Dragonflies – you mean air pirates?'

'Any airship near Princep is fair game. So we go overland, and in company, since it's not the safest of roads. From Porta Rabi we find a ship heading for Khanaphes: there'll be one every few tendays.' He shook his head. He had met Master Gripshod and the rest earlier that day and not seemed much impressed. 'They don't like questions in Khanaphes, Bella Cheerwell, so I hope you know what you're doing.'

'So do I.' Here in Solarno, such a long way from home, all of Stenwold's plans and Drillen's ambitions seemed weak and hazy.

'Tell your boffins that we'll take ship in three days,' Trallo continued. He had not met the Vekken yet, which was probably for the best.

'They'll be ready. They're keen to investigate new ground. Solarno has been the talk of Collegium for months.' She hoped that was true for all of them, since Manny had shown a particular liking for the seamier side of this city.

Trallo stood up with a flick of his wings, then changed his

mind and sat down again, abruptly waving to a servant for another bowl of chocolate.

'I don't know this place you come from,' he said. 'So I asked around – what's this College place like, I ask them. Nice, they tell me. Busy, hard-working. A bit fond of the pomp and gravitas. They don't tell me about the politics.' His voice had lowered.

'Politics?' Che felt something uncomfortable stir inside her.

'People here are taking an interest. Nobody's been so crass as to offer me money yet, but I'm almost waiting for it. You're being watched, and it's not just cos you're new in town. Anything particular I should know, is there?'

She shook her head slowly. 'I don't think that can be from back home. It's too far, surely. Who . . .?' She stared at him for a long time. 'Tell me, does the Wasp Empire keep any . . . people in Solarno?'

'Oh there's an embassy, an ambassador,' he replied lightly, but he was looking straight into her eyes and nodding. 'I don't mind, but it may cost extra, and it's only right I should know.'

She shook her head. 'It must just be because of the war. They probably still keep tabs on every Lowlander in Solarno.' He was looking doubtful, though, and she hardly believed it herself.

'Change the arrangements at the last minute,' she suggested. 'Make it two days, not three. I'll pay for any inconvenience. If someone's interested, let's surprise them.'

Trallo nodded, already making the changes in his head. 'Wise,' he muttered. 'Very wise.'

Across the mirror of the Exalsee, the glitter and dance of an aerial duel was takng place. Che leant on the rail, fascinated. She could just make out the combatants. The match was something peculiar to this region, uniquely uneven: a dragonfly-rider from Princep Exilla was flying against a mechanical orthopter. The insect was vastly nimbler in the air, hovering and darting in circles about the machine. Its rider had only a bow and throwing spears. Barring the luckiest shot, he would merely waste his arrows. If the orthopter's rotating piercers found their prey then it would be over in a moment but the machine, sleek and deadly as it was, seemed to lumber through the air. Eventually it would run short of fuel and the pilot would have to break off from the contest. The Dragonfly would count that as a win.

Trallo joined her, stretching theatrically. Their current transport was a more utilitarian beast than Captain Parrols's piece of luxury. The *Fighting Craidhen* ran passengers and light cargo in short, quick hops around the Exalsee. Aside from the impressive engines, which stank of a mineral oil that made Che feel queasy, there was no spare weight or needless decoration in the airship's design.

'Here.' Trallo handed her a spyglass. She took it, abruptly glum, and even looked into it. She saw only blurs and smudges wheeling and dancing at the lens's far end. It made her think of Trallo's little people.

'Your kinden . . .' It was an awkward thing to ask. 'Some of you are Inapt, yes?' She already knew it was so. She had even seen Fly seers in Tharn.

'Hardly,' Trallo said, nevertheless. 'What use would they be?'

*In Solarno things are different.* Still, she stared at him until he shrugged.

'Oh a few,' he admitted. 'A few are born each generation. Less and less, I'd guess. They have a blasted hard time of it, I'd guess.'

'Quite.' She handed back the spyglass to him.

The *Fighting Craidhen* flew on through the night, and the academics were given nothing but some blankets thrown over the bare boards of the hold on which to sleep. Che made it plain she had no time for their complaints. She had not explained to them why they had left Solarno so precipitately. When Praeda questioned the wisdom of hiring Trallo, she had likewise not been drawn into debate. To her astonishment, her fiat on such matters was grudgingly accepted. *They all think I know what I'm doing!* She could have laughed. *I'm making it up as I go along.* She knew that Stenwold would have done better.

Trallo came to shake her by the shoulder, a very little after dawn. She twitched awake suddenly, reaching instinctively across the hard floor for a slight man who was not there. For a moment she felt disoriented. Surely Achaeos had been kneeling beside her only now. Where was she, and where had he gone?

The avalanche of a year's history brought her back, trading happy fantasy for hard fact. 'Oh,' she said. 'Oh, yes. What is it?'

The Fly-kinden tugged his beard, which she recognized by now as a sign of good humour. Leaving the academics to bicker, and the Vekken to their stony silence, she had been spending most of her time with the caravan master. His cheerful talk reminded her of Taki. There was an open flamboyance to these Solarnese Fly-kinden that their Lowlands brethren lacked.

'You should see this from the air,' he said. 'We're coming up on the place now.'

Blearily she stumbled up on deck. Dawn had done little to shift the night's gloom, but she could see that beneath them the water was giving way to solid ground. Trallo had reached the bow rail with a flicker of his wings, while she trod heavily after him.

'What am I looking for?' she asked him. After a pause, she changed that to, 'What am I looking at?'

It was a mountain, only it was too narrow, altogether too smooth. She could see the cluster of buildings at its base: a walled enclosure of huts and houses built in its shadow. It cut into the sky like a knife blade, looming bigger and bigger as the *Craidhen* neared it.

Che shook her head. 'I give up,' she said. 'What?'

Trallo was grinning. 'There's a fellow I once met who went deep into the Forest Aleth – that's all the green stuff south of the Exalsee. He went real deep, said that these things were all over there, just rising up from the canopy, big as you like, with some kind of albino Ant-kinden just building them up from the ground. Anyway, that's one of them. Been abandoned for a long time by whoever did make it, but it's like a castle. There's rooms and passages and all sorts inside, and even more underground. A tribe of the Alethi live there now, won't let much anyone in. I hear they're only using a tiny portion of it, though.'

More light struck the vast dagger of earth and stone, turning it the colour of honey. It was a hundred feet high, perhaps more, for the scale of the buildings in its shadow was hard to guess. Che had a strange feeling in her stomach at the sight which, after some hesitation, she identified as excitement.

Ostrander was but the door to greater mysteries. *We are leaving behind the things that we know.*

# Seven

They ran into trouble at Ostrander. It caught them unawares, having come so far without.

Trallo had found them lodgings in one of the shacks within Ostrander's wooden walls, and was now busy making arrangements for the trek onwards to Porta Rabi. The Vekken ambassadors would not venture out, because Ostrander was a hostile Ant city-state as far as they were concerned, even though the Ants of the Exalsee seemed to behave differently to their Lowlander cousins. (*But doesn't everything, here?* was Che's thought on that.) Che herself shadowed Trallo, because he was always good company and because his companionship was teaching her something of his trade. The academics she left to their own devices, which would also prove to be a learning experience.

Trallo had spent the day haggling with a succession of merchants over pack animals and automotives, and had concluded his dealings with each by angrily springing up and declaring that he would never do business with such a villain ever again. They would then meet the next day and renegotiate. It was a way of trading that exactly suited both the hot-blooded Solarnese and the proud Dragonflies of Princep Exilla, and the trading crowd in Ostrander was made up of both. There were a few Spider-kinden as well, and a miscellany of renegades and halfbreeds from Chasme. The actual locals took no part in Ostrander's role as a caravan stop, save by tolerating the rabble of newcomers' buildings in the shadow of their artificial mountain.

Che spotted the natives around, although fewer than she had expected. They were Ant-kinden of an unhealthy shade, greenish-white and anaemic-looking. The vast majority of them did not venture beyond the caverns of their pirated home, and they only came out to tax those who sought shelter in their shadow. They carried spears and crossbows and wore a mismatch of armour, from clattering vests of chitin shards to Solarnese plated leathers and full chainmail. Che already knew that most of the Ant-kinden of the Exalsee lived nomadic lives in the Forest Aleth and were reckoned a primitive lot, by the Solarnese at least. The Ostranden, however, had broken from that lifestyle, settled down in their inherited fortress and acquired civilized vices. In fact they were starting to become a mirror of the fiercely territorial Lowlander city-states that Che knew all too well.

With evening coming on, Che and Trallo found themselves sitting discussing alliances with a Spider-kinden woman and a Solarnese man. Travellers did not set off singly down the road to Porta Rabi, for the desert fringe held too many dangers to be travelled alone. The Solarnese was a rug-trader, the Spider was a slaver, and Trallo had brought them together and, as a reward for the introduction, earned a place in their company. Che had the vague impression they would be paying him for the privilege as well but, as they only made veiled allusions to money, she could not be sure.

Manny burst in just as they were concluding their business, thundering through the door and almost falling at Che's feet. The Solarnese and the Spider had drawn blades on the instant, and Che found her own shortsword in her hand by some instinct she had not known she still owned. The fat man was running with sweat, his fine clothes ripped down the back.

'Hammer and tongs!' Che swore at him. 'What's wrong with you?'

Manny shook his head so hard that his jowls quivered. 'Not me,' he got out, 'the others . . . Soldiers come to the lodgings . . . trying to arrest everyone—'

Trallo was out of the door at once, wings a blur. Che ran after him, trying to resheathe her sword as she went. The wretched Mannerly Gorget was left to recover his breath.

They found a dozen greenish Ant-kinden standing some distance from the lodgings as they arrived. Che saw that they had apprehended Praeda already, holding the Beetle woman tightly between two of them. A dark bruise was emerging on the scholar's face. Armed with crossbows and bows, the Ant-kinden were keeping a respectful watch on the lodging-house, and Che noticed movement in one of the ramshackle building's upper windows.

'What's this?' Trallo demanded, touching down ahead of her. 'What's this? Open arrest on the streets of Ostrander?' He pitched his voice loudly enough to carry to all the traders and travellers and caravaneers loitering nearby, all the other foreigners. The Ostranden Ants remained packed close together and Che could see that the incident had already attracted more notice than they were happy with.

*It must be the Vekken*, she decided, with a sinking heart. Had they not been able to resist antagonizing enemy Ant-kinden?

'You claim responsibility for these?' demanded one of the Ostranden, a woman. 'They have transgressed against us.'

'What? What have they done?' Che asked. She spotted a pitch-dark face at the upper window, and guessed that the Vekken had crossbows ready up there, and better ones than the locals.

The Ostranden woman stared coldly at Che. 'We demand our rights for trespass,' she insisted.

Che saw Trallo visibly relax. 'Oh, money,' he said, almost dismissively. 'We'll talk *money*. We'll come to an arrangement.

Let's go do it now, before nightfall. There's no need for all this.' He glanced along the street, leading Che's gaze in the same direction. She saw another score of Ants approaching, called by their comrades' silent summons.

The Ostranden turned away, along with her soldiers, then turned back sharply. 'Tell *them,*' she said, jabbing her spear towards the lodging-house, 'they must leave. If they are still here at tomorrow sunset, we will burn them out, if we must.'

Che stormed off towards the house, determined to set some limits on ambassadorial freedoms. Behind them she heard Trallo begin to negotiate for the return of Praeda.

A crossbow bolt flowered suddenly in the dirt five feet ahead of her. She stopped dead, glaring up at the windows. She saw one of the Vekken there, knowing it would not be the shooter, who would now be out of sight and reloading. *I cannot let these madmen have free run of the world*, she decided. *We must observe reason.* She took a deep breath and marched towards the door. There was no second bolt.

She stormed upstairs, and they were waiting for her, standing almost shoulder to shoulder. One kept an eye on the street outside, the other faced her, expressionless.

'What have you done now?' she demanded. They said nothing. She waited a count of five for their answer, and then pressed on. 'There is an entire mountain full of Ant-kinden just over there, so what do you hope to gain?' She was fighting to keep her tone reasonable, though not entirely succeeding.

The Vekken stared at her for a moment longer. 'We defend ourselves,' said one, who must therefore be Accius. 'They bring the war to us and we defend ourselves.'

'By doing what?' she asked him. 'Trespassing, they said. Where did you go? Were you spying on them?'

There was a dry cough from a corner of the room. She now noticed Berjek Gripshod there, looking somewhat the worse for wear. His robes were dusty and there was a graze across his forehead. She had been so intent on the Vekken that she had missed him entirely.

'My apologies, Madam Maker, but the trespass was mine – mine and Miss Rakespear's.'

Che stared at him and the old man gave her a weak smile. 'We went to look at their home, that extraordinary construction. It would seem we were paying too much interest. One forgets how Ant-kinden can be.'

Che heard footsteps on the stairs and a bedraggled Praeda Rakespear stepped into the room. She had obviously heard the end of Berjek's statement, because she was nodding agreement.

'Suddenly they were looking at us in an unfriendly manner,' she said, always given to understatement. 'We decided to withdraw. They followed. Then they caught me when I stumbled.'

'I'm afraid for our Vekken friends here it was something of a confirmation of all their fears,' said Berjek. He was shaking slightly, but she thought she discerned a dry amusement now that the immediate crisis was past. 'They broke out the crossbows and starting sending out warning shots at the locals. If you and the Fly had not arrived when you did, then matters might have become considerably worse.'

There was no particular gratitude in his voice but Che realized that it was thanks nevertheless. She waved it away, mumbling something about it being due to Manny Gorget's finding her. Underneath, the two scholars were still reeling from having been under such unaccustomed threat so recently. Che felt the Vekken still staring at her. She supposed she should be thankful that they had not shot any of the Ostranden dead. All of a sudden she felt very tired.

'Well, it could have been worse,' she declared.

Berjek exchanged a sidelong glance with Praeda. 'It may even have been worthwhile,' he suggested, choosing his words carefully. 'What expense we have unwittingly incurred, I shall cover from my own funds. Madam Rakespear and I observed some remarkable things in the short space of time we were allowed. It has quite whetted our appetites for Khanaphes.'

That night, for once, Che absented herself from Trallo's company, leaving him to play dice with Manny and a pair of Solarnese he seemed to be looking to hire. Instead she sought out Berjek and Praeda, as they sat together in a corner of the lodging house's common room. The old man nodded when he saw her approach.

'I thought so. Still some scholar there beneath the ambassador.'

'What did you see?' she asked them.

They exchanged looks. 'The building . . . or perhaps artifact . . . is entirely artificial,' Praeda explained. 'It is made of stones and earth cemented together. I have never seen anything like it before, and so it is impossible to say how old it is, but . . .' She gestured to Berjek.

'There are carvings,' the old man continued for her. 'Around the base – to a height of perhaps twenty feet. Continuous carvings, made of many small, discrete images. They have eroded so far that it is impossible to make out the detail, but the style . . . I have seen some of the papers that Master Kadro sent back to Collegium, though I had to pry them out of Jodry Drillen's hands. The style of carving is Khanaphir, no mistake: Kadro had made rubbings and sketches. The tradition that was responsible for etching this monument, long before these Ostranden took up residence, is alive and well in Khanaphes to this day.'

In her dream she was below ground, walking beside a subterranean river in a darkness that was no darkness to her. The walls she passed were heavily carved, the details obscured by moss and damp. Ahead, where watercourses met and crossed, there was a plinth and a statue rising from the murk. The statue was long ruined. Only its broken base, showing the lowermost folds of a robe, still spoke of whatever dignitary or hero had been immortalized here. It was all so old that, in her dream, she wondered, *Is this Khanaphes?*

When she awoke she realized that her dreamscape was no more than the sewers beneath Myna: the ones they had rushed her through after rescuing her from Thalric's cells and torture chambers. For a moment she laughed at herself, but then she thought again: *old.* The Mynan sewers, seeming impossibly large, had been carved for another city – were the only relic of a time when the Apt folk of Myna had been mere slaves. There were also buildings in Collegium – parts of the Amphiophos and the College – that dated back to before the revolution. They had been put up by Beetle hands, but not for Beetle masters.

*We know so little.* For the Beetle-kinden, history proper began five centuries before, when they had thrown off their chains and driven out their masters. Of what had gone before that she had never really thought, until she had met Achaeos. The world appeared different to him, for he stood on the other side of that historic line. To him, the history of the world stretched back and back, full of ancient wars and pacts and rituals, but had been stripped bare in the last few centuries by the voracious jaws of progress.

*And I am standing on his side of that line now.* Achaeos knew of entire kinden that his people had once fought, traded with, defeated and cast into the darkness, that were mere myths to the Beetle-kinden, or less than myths. The scholars of Collegium were only now rediscovering the deep roots of the world they lived in, and their tragedy was that they would never understand what they uncovered. Their Aptitude, and therefore the limits of their world-view, would always stand in the way.

*There was magic in the world, once.* And her fellow Collegiates would never believe it.

*

On the road to Porta Rabi, only the slaves travelled first class. The Solarnese rug merchant had not been able to conclude his business in time, and so the Collegium delegation were obliged to set out beside the Spider-kinden slaver and her merchandise. She rode beneath a parasol in a howdah atop a burly, plodding beetle, while her stock in trade sat in a covered wagon drawn behind her. They had shade, they had water, and they were always fed first. The guards rode on footboards alongside the trailer, exposed to the sun and dust. Only after a day into the journey did Che realize that these guards were also slaves.

'Why don't they escape?' she asked. 'Why not free the others and escape?'

Trallo gave her the look he reserved for mad foreigners. 'Why should they? They've got it good: get fed, even get money. Only thing they ain't got is freedom, and that's an overvalued commodity.'

He had secured them a rattling automotive in which to make the trip, together with a pair of Solarnese to serve as driver and guard. The machine was broad-wheeled, all wooden save for the steam engine and its casing. Most of its open rear was loaded with coal and waterskins to quench the automotive's constant hunger and thirst. The academics and the Vekken were crammed into whatever space remained. A smaller beetle scurried behind them, so loaded with their luggage that only bags and legs could be seen of it. They kept pace easily with the slaver and her bulky animal, giving them plenty of time to reflect on the flesh trade.

The guards were Solarnese, as were most of the slaves within the wagon. All were debtors, petty criminals or the plain unlucky. Their patient, uncomplaining presence made Che feel wretched. It was not just that slavery was outlawed in Collegium: it was that she herself had been where they were now. True, slaves of the Wasps were treated worse, for the Wasp slave corps cared little for the physical condition of its stock and more for head count, but slavery was slavery.

Che was watching a crime taking place here, and she knew she should make some protest, but there was nothing she could do. She seemed to be the only one who cared. Praeda and Berjek studiously ignored the whole slave party, and Mannerly Gorget had a speculative look in his eye. He leant over the side of the automotive thoughtfully but, when Che challenged him on it, he shrugged his rounded shoulders.

'They do things differently here,' he said. 'I mean, yes, I *know* it's wrong. Morally wrong and economically unsound. I've been to all the same lectures as you. Only we of Collegium are rather the exceptions, because most of the world is quite happy about it. And you haven't had the trouble with servants that I've had. Sometimes I do wonder whether the Spiders have the right idea.'

Che clambered forward to where one of the Solarnese stood beside the simple levers that controlled the machine. She was a lean, scarred woman with her hair cut very short. Her counterpart, a solidly built man, stood behind, ready with the next waterskin when it was needed. They both carried slender, curved Solarnese swords, and the driver also had a winch-crossbow slung across her back. She gave Che a wary nod when the Beetle girl reached her. The heat from the engine only added to the heat of the day.

'This is a desolate place,' Che said, trying anything for conversation.

The woman shrugged lopsidedly. 'This is the edge of the Nem,' she replied, one hand taking in a landscape that was merely scrub-covered hills and dust-filled air as far east as the eye could see. 'This is friendly. Go east and you'll know what harsh means.' There must have been a sudden change in the tone of the engine that Che had not detected, for the woman now turned from her levers and rattled a hopper of coal down into the furnace, shouting at her colleague for more water. *I should help*, Che thought, and then recalled, *I can't.* She had lost all sense of how things worked. She would only get it wrong, yet not be able to see why.

★

The road between Ostrander and Porta Rabi was like a string of three pearls, each pearl a water stop. The first was a great stinking steam-powered pump with a caravanserai enclosed by a palisade wall. The second was an oasis, where the land fell down almost sheer towards a sheen of dark water, fringed with an absurd riot of ferns and horsetails. Trallo's party were not the first to take advantage of it. As they drew near, with evening visible already in the sky to the east, they spied two pitched tents, one gleaming white and the other painted in jagged patterns. Trallo hopped aloft and flew ahead, his arms out to indicate peace, to see who they would be spending the night with. By the time the slaver's entourage had coaxed her huge beast to the water's edge, there was a welcome ready, of sorts. Che saw two handfuls of hard-looking men and women with weapons to hand, but lowered. They were waiting to see if this was a trick, if they would have to fight. It was an insight into Trallo's world, for all his smiles and banter. The caravan life was clearly an uncertain one.

There were a good eight Dragonfly-kinden there, reminding them how close they were to Princep Exilla, with its piracy and violence. They had long-hafted swords and recurved bows, and they wore loose clothes with cuirasses of leather and painted wood on top. Their faces were tattooed into scowls.

Beside them was a smaller knot of armoured men. They wore dark metal, with helms that hid their faces, and their shimmering tabards showed a dark hand prominent on a dark field. *Iron Glove Cartel,* Che remembered. There were only three of them, but their facelessness, their stillness, gave them a greater air of menace than the posturing Dragonflies. Che found her attention coming back to them over and over, as though their very presence was a secret she could not read.

The Spider slaver was helped down from her mount,

giving both groups an impartial nod. Trallo flitted over to instruct his two hirelings where to pitch camp.

'Once we're all set up,' he said, 'we'll pitch torch-posts around everyone, get us a fence. We're about as far from home as you can get on this road, so I don't think anybody minds cosying up.'

'What are they here for?' Che asked him. The Dragonflies and the Iron Glove men had gone into one of the tents, leaving a single painted warrior standing watch outside.

'Not that they exactly told me,' the Fly said, 'but it's the weapons trade. I hear the Monarch of Princep doesn't like the Gloves and won't deal with them. They make the best kit, though, so all the little chiefs are falling over themselves to set up deals like this. No need to say, we've none of us seen any of this.'

*Wake up!*

Che did. She started awake in the tent, shocked out of a deep sleep to utter wakefulness by the urgent command. Her eyes were already penetrating the dark without her summoning the Art. She sat up.

The others lay crammed around her. Praeda Rakespear was a sloping, blanket-covered form to one side, and the Solarnese teamster was curled up on the other, knees drawn up almost to her chin.

*Wake up!*

'I—' She stopped the words, realizing the voice was inside her, not in her ears. She formed the name in her mind, as tentatively as touching a wound. *Achaeos?*

*Get up! Now!* The voice inside her was harsh, impatient. She stumbled to her feet, shaking off her blankets like a landslide, colliding with the tent pole. Her hand found her scabbarded sword by instinct.

The voice was urgent. *Now!*

*I'm going mad.* She slung her grey cloak over her nightshirt and blundered from the tent, hearing the Solarnese woman cursing sleepily behind her.

Outside, the world was immense. The sky reached cloudless, star-studded, from every horizon. For a moment she could only stare. *Is this what he wanted to show me?* She had not guessed at it, how vast the sky was, out at the desert's edge. It was well worth seeing.

Then: *Hammer and tongs but it's cold!*

'Bella?'

She jumped. The Solarnese, Trallo's hired man, stood nearby, frowning at her. The two of them stood in the middle of their triangle of tents, and beyond was the big marquee of the Spider slaver and the pitches of the Dragonflies and the Iron Glove. She stared about at it all, trying to read a secret that the scene did not possess.

There was a shimmer and a shadow in the air. The Solarnese man clearly could not see it. It was there nonetheless.

'Achaeos . . .?' she said, and she reached out, and who cared what anybody thought. 'Please . . .'

*Draw your blade!* the voice snapped, and the weapon was in her hands in the same instant. There was a startled shout from the Solarnese, a whisper of steel as his own curved sword leapt out. The shout further drew attention. A Dragonfly woman Che had not even noticed had abruptly stood up, drawing back her bow. One of the Spider's slave-guards appeared, running round the edge of her tent with a crossbow at the ready.

Everyone was staring at her.

'. . .' Her voice was dry. There were words inside her, but she was fighting to keep them down.

*Say it.*

'There's . . .' *I don't know this. I can't say this.* 'There's about to be an attack.'

They continued to stare at her. She saw that Trallo had put his head out of the tent he shared with Manny and

Berjek, and that one of the Vekken was also looking out from their compact little billet.

'There's going to be an attack,' she said helplessly. 'An attack. Going to be an attack.'

'Woman . . .?' Trallo said hoarsely. The Dragonfly woman let loose a shout, and abruptly their tent started moving as her kinsfolk began to rouse themselves. Everyone else was still staring at Che, but the Dragonflies were moving. *They're Inapt. They're Inapt and so they . . .*

*No. They can see better in the dark.*

She turned, using her Art to penetrate the night, seeing the dust they were throwing, no matter how carefully they approached.

'There!' she shouted, a real shout now, born of true knowledge. 'There! There! There!'

The camp seemed to explode with life. It seemed that Che was now the only still point in it, the hub of a spinning wheel. The two Vekken were kneeling before their tent, each buckling the mail hauberk of the other with absolute concentration. There were half-dressed Dragonflies spilling from their painted tent with spears and bows. The Spider-kinden woman stepped fully out, wearing a nightdress of silk and with a rapier in her hand. She snapped out single words, and her guards were hurrying past her. *To safeguard her slaves,* Che realized. Her slaves were the most valuable thing at the oasis.

The first of the Iron Glove men was out now, half-armoured, helmed. There was a slender weapon in his hands that Che barely registered at the time.

The raiders arrived, breaking into a run as they neared the camp. There was something monstrous in front, a shape that Che's eyes could not piece together, rushing across the ground in a sudden scuttle, with something high above it. Behind it were men, huge men. She saw their blades first, great bludgeoning swords and massive axes that they held in hands jutting with claws. They wore patches of dark armour: hide and metal. Their skins were white.

*Scorpion-kinden.* For a moment she could only think of old Hokiak in Myna, but these were the wild version, the real thing, Scorpion raiders from the desert.

There was a rattle of crossbows as the Spider's guards loosed their shots. Che saw at least one of the attackers go down, then the tide was on them. The vanguard thing was revealed as a scorpion longer than a man, its sting poised like a fencer's blade.

Trallo knelt beside her, loosing a bolt from one small crossbow, then taking up a second. 'Someone load for me!' he snapped, and to Che's surprise it was old Berjek who took the slack weapon and wound the string back.

The huge scorpion lunged forward, and the Spider's guards scattered out of its way. Arrows seemed to spring off its carapace as the Dragonflies loosed, but it just shook itself once and lunged forward again. This time it caught a man in its claws. Che heard bones snap and then the sting darted in delicately, and stopped his heart.

A huge man loomed in front of her, drawing back his axe for a swing. The weapon was as long as she was tall and she stalled, sword loose in her hand, unable to strike. A crossbow bolt flowered in the giant's side, slowed by his armour, and he turned on Trallo instead, bringing the axe down. The Fly-kinden abandoned his bow and darted up and away, the axe-head following him with surprising deftness. Che lunged.

She had not meant to. Her blade skidded and then dug in and she looked up into that furious white face, with its monstrous, tusked underbite. Another shortsword raked shallowly across the man's ribs and he roared, turning with axe raised high. As it went up, the second Vekken rammed his own blade into the Scorpion's armpit all the way to the hilt with effortless strength, and then the two of them were moving on, wordless in their teamwork.

The great scorpion had torn a gash in the Spider's tent, and her guards had taken up spears to keep it back.

Abruptly there was a series of harsh snapping sounds and the monster recoiled, claws raised high in threat. Che turned to see the three Iron Glove men calmly reloading, slipping finger-length bolts into the chambers of their snapbows.

*Snapbows?*

There was no time to wonder. Another Scorpion-kinden thundered past, another giant. They were *all* at least seven feet tall for sure. She stumbled back, seeing the huge man take a sweep with his greatsword, catching one of the Dragonflies and almost cutting the woman in half. The Scorpion roared in defiance, and then his head snapped back, the fletchings of an arrow jutting from between his eyes.

Abruptly there was nothing to fight, and Che was wandering amid a trampled camp with her sword in her hands. The Scorpions and their monster had fallen back into the desert. She spotted them regrouping, assuming themselves unseen, two hills away.

A lot of people were looking at her, with expressions she lacked the strength to analyse. She sat down heavily, feeling drained.

*Achaeos?* She said it in her head, but there was nothing but the echo of her own thoughts. *Achaeos, thank you, but can you not give me more? Thank you for saving us all, but . . . But I love you and it is hard for me, with you dead and so close.*

She found that she was crying, the tears streaking down her cheeks. Without warning the cold struck her, making her shiver uncontrollably. The sword fell from her hand. The two Vekken ambassadors were nearby, watching her doubtfully. She did not care. It was all too much. Her sobs escaped whether she tried to stifle them or not.

Trallo draped a blanket round her. It was hours from dawn but nobody would be getting any more sleep. There were five bodies to bury, and as many dead Scorpions to move from near the water. She heard the Fly give a businesslike sigh, steeling himself to his task.

There was no answer within her. Achaeos – or his ghost or her madness – had done his work and left without a word. *Oh, you have grown cold, since you died.* She felt like screaming for him to either stay and let her know he still loved her, or leave her for ever – and who cared if the Scorpions killed her? It was hard, it was so hard.

# Eight

She was a prisoner in her own lodgings.

There were no guards. She was not bound. The door was not locked. Still, Petri Coggen felt her confinement as keenly as if the manacle was around her wrist. She had felt a sense of doom weighing on her since they had brought her back from the Marsh Alcaia.

They had given her servants, for the Khanaphir had been solicitous of her comfort to the point of patronizing her. The foreign lady must have everything. The servants cleaned her rooms and brought her food, and would have dressed and bathed her if she had let them. They ignored her when she told them to leave her alone. Shaven-headed Beetle men and women with fixed faces, they glided in and out of her life like tidy ghosts.

They made no attempt to stop her going out into the city. She had tried to escape their attention, to get her letter out, but the servants had followed at a respectful distance. She had tried running, but when she had stopped, wheezing for breath, they had been there still, or others like them, standing patiently by. There was no reproach in their faces, only polite concern for the stranger. She had run until heat and exhaustion had brought her to her knees, but they had been waiting there wherever she had run to, with slight smiles at her odd behaviour.

As her last resort, she had gone to the docks. Khanaphes

traded all down the coast and across the sea, so there were always ships.

The first she had approached was a solid Khanaphir trawler. She had climbed halfway up the gangplank, already reaching for her money, before she saw the expression on the captain's face. He *knew* her. He had been told about her. Standing there at the rail, eyeing her with the polite disinterest of his city, he informed her, without needing words, that there was no way she was leaving the city on his ship.

So she had then looked for foreign ships. Surely the sinister influence of the Ministers could not be absolute. There would be ships out of distant ports, and at this point she would take a berth for anywhere. Even the dubious hospitality of the Spiderlands would be preferable.

She found a Spider-kinden trader, all elegant swept lines. She looked around for the captain, and saw her in conversation with a mild-looking Khanafir man. The Spider glanced at Petri and gave a faint shake of her head. Petri stumbled away, ran back down the quays. She did not care who stopped to watch the crazed foreigner make an exhibition of herself.

There was a broad-beamed cargo-hauler at the very end of the quays. Its crew was a mongrel mixture, halfbreeds, Mantis-kinden, lean and sallow Grasshoppers. They looked as disreputable as anyone Petri had ever seen. She rushed up to them, noticing their hands drift instinctively for hilts and hafts.

'Please, I need passage out,' she gasped. 'I have money.' She felt as though she was throwing herself from the jaws of one monster into the pincers of another.

One of the Grasshopper-kinden shouldered his way forward and crouched at the top of the gangplank, elbows crooked over his bony knees. 'Come up,' he said. He had a scar, jagged and twisted, down the side of his long face. In other circumstances she would have been terrified of him.

She made it up the gangplank, the villainous crew watching, narrow-eyed.

'You haven't been in Khanaphes long,' the Grasshopper captain observed.

'Long enough. Months now.'

He laughed quietly, shook his head. 'The blink of an eye. You have the city's interest, little helpless one. We have heard. There is no shipman who does not know.'

She felt a shudder go through her. 'Please . . . I must leave.'

'Anyone who took you away from here, while you bear that mark, would never trade here again, or ever be welcome. They carve their memories in stone here. They *never* forget. I could pass my ship on three times, and neither she nor I could put in safely at this port again, nor my sons, nor theirs.'

With a wrenching despair she realized that the incongruous tone of this vicious-looking creature was only sympathy.

'They will kill me,' she whispered. 'Please . . .'

'They might,' he said. His shrug indicated that the incidence of death punctuated his life as regularly as meals and sleeping. 'Or they might *vanish* you. Or they might lose interest and let you go. But we cannot help you. You do not have the money to compensate us for what we would lose.'

She left his ship, with feet dragging. Her concerned retinue was already waiting.

At Porta Rabi, it felt like the edge of the world.

The desert petered out into a scrub of sawgrass and thorns, and then the land fell away completely in a tangle of vines. Stunted strees clung grimly to the cliff edge, leaning at mad angles over the rocks far below. The cliffs were relieved only the once, where the land slanted steeply down to a beach of broken stone. It was there the intrepid Solarnese had built Porta Rabi. They had used the pale grey stone of the cliffs, but the buildings were the same odd burlesque of Spider styles, all pointed arches, tapering columns, grillwork screens, but all looking slightly wrong. They had made a Solarno in miniature, a little stepped crescent of buildings gathered about two long piers that went far enough into the sea to allow big ships enough draught to moor there. Above, where the cliffs took over, there was a reaching scaffold of wooden floors and scaffolding, rooms and buildings suspended before the rockface, all of it looking open-plan and half-built. Che identified this as Dragonfly-kinden work. There was a sizeable presence of them here from Princep Exilla and, putting aside their normal rivalries, the two kinden worked together to keep the port open in this inhospitable corner of the world. Even so, Trallo warned them, the streets were not safe after nightfall. The merchants who ran Porta Rabi retired early to their well-guarded compounds, and everywhere else became lawless after dark.

They came in close to midday, but the cool air off the sea worked against the pounding sun. The port was seething: a dozen ships moored at the piers. Most had sails furled about their rigging-webbed masts, but one possessed the stout funnels of a steamer, and another was constructed of copper metal and had neither sails nor a visible engine. The largest of the ships had triple rows of holes along each side, and Trallo explained that if the wind dropped it had slaves to row it. Che recalled the human commodity she had recently travelled alongside, and hoped they were bound for a better future than that.

While the others settled in a taverna under the watchful eyes of the two Solarnese, Che followed Trallo to the dockside to see about arranging passage. Standing there, with the grey sea stretching, windlashed, to the far horizon, she felt dizzy at the thought of how far she had come.

'What sea is this?' she asked, touching Trallo's shoulder. She was past the edge of all her maps. Was this the same sea that washed Collegium's wharves? 'Where does it go?'

He smiled up at her. 'This is the Sunroad Sea, and they say it goes all the way to where the sun comes from, if you could but sail that far.' He added, 'We'll have passage on that ship,' and pointed out a sleek Spiderlands felucca, two-masted and painted gold and blue. 'She's the *Lord Janis* out of Portoriens – that's the furthest east in the world that the Spider-kinden claim, the very eastern limit of their satrapies. And you know what?' He was grinning widely now. She shook her head slowly to show she did not know, and he finished it gleefully. 'You know what? That's *west* of here.'

Che felt weak at the knowledge. The Lowlanders tended to assume that the Spidlerlands just extended as far as they needed to go. She was standing at the shore of a whole new ocean, being jostled by sailors and traders of a dozen kinden out of who-knew-what distant ports. This was not Collegium's wilful ignorance of the Empire's ambitions, or the self-spun mystery of the Spiderlands, or the deliberate isolation of the Commonweal. This was *far*. She found herself searching the crowd suddenly for a familiar style of dress, a brooch or a sword-hilt whose style she recognized. There were Solarnese there, in their flowing white, but no more. She was the only representative of the Lowlands, at the docks of Porta Rabi. She was all the world she knew.

Trallo put a hand to her elbow. 'Steady now,' he said kindly. 'It was the same for me, when my dad brought me here the first time. Around the Exalsee we mostly look west and south to the Spiderlands where our ladies and lords come from. It was a shock for me, too.'

The captain of the *Lord Janis* was now coming towards them, and Trallo nodded respectfully to her. 'Here,' he said sidelong to Che, 'you know why Spider-kinden always name their cities and their ships after men, don't you?'

Che mustered a small smile. 'Why?'

''Cos they're both ruled by women,' Trallo answered, and then he bowed before the Spider-kinden captain as she arrived.

★

She dreamt she was on board ship. She *was* on board ship, of course, rocking in her cramped bunk, above Praeda, as the *Lord Janis* steered wide of the cliffs and reefs of the Stone Coast. As she dreamt now, though, she left the cabin and clambered aloft. The crew was gone and the sky above was starless. The skeleton of the rigging was without sail. Only one man stood on deck, stood at the rail and stared out to sea, grey-robed and narrow-shouldered. The ship itself was dead still, the waves all about frozen into jagged teeth.

'Achaeos,' she said, and in the dream it was. He turned to her, and she saw his white eyes, his grey skin, and she ran forward.

She stopped close to him, but not close enough to touch. She remembered that harsh, commanding voice, its angry, distant tones.

'What is it?' she asked. 'Please, Achaeos, tell me what I have to do.' There was a scowl building on his face, piece by piece. The sight made her cower away from him.

He had always been a gentle man who seldom raised his voice. He had never struck her. In her dream she thought he would strike her, on the deck of the stilled ship.

'What is this?' he demanded. 'In dreams? Must you dredge my memory up in dreams? Is this what I have become, just a knife for you to prick yourself with?'

'I don't understand,' she said, but a wind had struck up along with his reproach, tugging now at the empty rigging. She had to shout it again. 'I can't put you down! You won't let me!'

He shook his head. When he spoke again, his voice was the wind, just as the voice of the haunted forest Darakyon had been the myriad sounds of the leaves. *You put yourself on the rack of my memory. You turn the wheel yourself.*

'That's not true!' she shouted at him. 'It's not fair. I want you alive, but I can't have you alive, and nor will you be dead! What can I do? Do you want me to follow you?'

Standing there beneath that featureless sky, she wondered if she might already have done. *Is this death, this petrified sea?*

The wind died abruptly, leaving nothing but the two of them staring at each other. 'I am dead and gone, Che,' he said, and it was once more the voice of the man who had loved her, against all the dictates of history and his own people. 'Do not raise me up like this to injure yourself. I am gone. Just let me go.'

He made to turn away and she rushed at him, determined to hold him in her arms. For a moment she had the cloth of his robe in her hands, but then he was gone, and the rail was gone too, and she was falling with a shriek towards the razor-sharp claws of the frozen ocean . . .

Waking, suddenly, for once she remembered exactly where she was. She slipped from the bunk, felt herself swaying in time with the ship's pitch and yaw. Praeda muttered something and turned over, looking pale with her face sheened in sweat. All the Collegium academics had turned out to be poor sailors, and the Vekken were keeping to their cabin so obstinately that the same was probably true of them. The sea along this craggy coast did not rest easy, but Che had found herself proof against it. She dressed in her tunic and cloak, and pattered barefoot out into the walkway running between cabins. Around her the wood of the ship creaked and shifted, and she found it an oddly comforting sound, a created thing behaving in the way it had been intended.

Up above, it was cold but the change was refreshing to her. There was a handful of sailors still at their duties, Spider-kinden all and mostly men. If not for the dream, she might just have watched them work. They did everything with such conscious elegance, as though they had stayed out here not to work the ship but to perform for Cheerwell Maker. It was not the killing grace of the Mantis-kinden, but something more showy, and which they took more joy in.

She scanned the rails, finding nothing, no smear nor

smudge of him. The sails billowed and the waves rolled the ship up on to their backs, and then sloughed it down the other side. The sky above boasted stars and a slice of the moon, save to port where the cliffs ate out a deeper darkness, unrelieved by anything.

She took a deep breath of the sea air, feeling the deck shift beneath her feet, her toes flexing automatically for balance. Below, the others would still be sleeping fitfully, groaning, or staggering off to be ill. Che, who had suffered the airships and the automotive, had at last found a vessel she was comfortable with.

*But of course.* The *Lord Janis* was built by the Inapt, crewed by the Inapt, and it therefore carried her along with it smoothly, while it dragged the others by force. She smiled at that, despite all her worries. Of all the rest, only Trallo had been weathering this rough sea well, and she guessed that it was sheer experience, in his case. He had made such trips so often that the sea held no more terrors for him.

The ship changed its tack noticeably, slanting away from the cliffs. Ahead, along the dark and starless line of the land, Che could see a red spark high enough to challenge the moon.

'What is it?' she demanded of the nearest sailor. He looked at her mockingly at first, but swallowed some flippant answer and said, 'The Light of Suphat.'

'The what?'

'A great fire atop a tower, that warns us where the rocks are.'

'A lighthouse,' she realized.

He shrugged. 'Stay above decks, lady, you shall see two more along the cliffs, named Amnet and Dekkir. When we have passed Dekkir, which shall be near dawn, we shall be within reach of the harbour of Khanaphes.'

After the ship had passed the Light of Dekkir, and after dawn had come, sluggish, to the Sunroad Sea, the land had changed, the cliffs falling smoothly away until the *Lord Janis* made its smooth progress across a shoreline of sand. The beach ran inland as far as the eye could see, and Che realized it was the desert, the true desert.

'How can it be so dry, right next to the sea?' she asked. There were odd defiant clumps of gorse and thornbushes, and a big ridge-shelled beetle was carefully collecting the dew that had condensed across its carapace. Other than that, life seemed to have abandoned the place.

'Dry means no rain, that's all,' Manny Gorget pointed out. He was leaning heavily on the rail, still looking green despite the easier going. 'Find me a map and I'll show you where the rain stops. It's all in the wind and the landscape. Salt water's no substitute.' When he could be persuaded to talk on his subject, he was quite competent.

Che turned to Trallo, who had been making some arrangements with the captain. 'Have you been there? The desert?'

'Just the once.' His smile was thin-lipped. 'Not nice. And you have to pick a time when the Scorpion-kinden aren't on the warpath.'

'But how can they live out there? How can anything survive?'

'Bella Cheerwell, you have to look cursed hard to find a place where *nobody* lives. People find a way, always. Now, Sieur Gorget, would you go roust your fellows? We're going to be coming up on the city soon and, frankly, if you visit Khanaphes, you should see it from the seaward side.'

'What happens when we arrive?' Che asked him, as Manny lurched off unsteadily against the ship's swell.

'I find out how welcome we are, to start with,' Trallo said. 'They're odd fish, these Khanaphir. They're quiet as you like, hard-working, polite, and if they don't like you, you might as well turn around and go away, because you'll never change it no matter what. So I'll take a sounding, as the sailors say, and find out how best to stay on their good side.'

‘I’m glad we’ve got you along,’ she told him.

‘The labourer is worth his hire,’ he said. ‘I’ll see about letting word trickle to the Ministers, about you being an ambassador. Until they come to you, you mustn’t try to push in on them.’

‘I’ve no intention of it. All I really need to do is make sure Master Gripshod and the others get to study the place, and they can probably do that just by standing and looking.’

‘Hmm, two things,’ Trallo said. ‘First, don’t poke and pry until I give the all-clear. They are a very private people, the Khanaphir. Second, don’t call him that.’

‘What?’

‘*Master* Gripshod – or *Master* anything. Local customs, local rules. They keep the word “Master” for other purposes, and it’s got nothing to do with people like us.’

He was quite serious. She waited for him to elaborate, and he shrugged.

‘I’m not saying that I understand it. I’ve been to Khanaphes a score of times and I still don’t understand the place. But, take my word for it, find some other way to make introductions.’

She was below when the *Lord Janis* began to tack, but she felt the change in the timbers, and ran up on deck to see.

The desert had turned green. While her back was turned the land had been colonized by a vast expanse of reeds and spidery-rooted trees and huge arthrophytes twice as high as a man, all sprouting from a maze of little water channels. The *Lord Janis* was taking in sail, slowing down, and Che saw that it was angling for a broad watercourse that cut through the marsh ahead, a river in its own right.

The others were assembled on deck by now: the three academics standing forward of the mast, the two Vekken sullenly behind it. Che went to join Berjek Gripshod, watching the riot of vegetation pass by on the port side.

‘The Jamail delta,’ Trallo clarified for them. ‘Goes on for

miles. Once a year they dredge the main channel clear of silt, but it still moves around a bit. It all does. They say nobody but the natives can find their way in there from day to day.'

The channel itself was wide enough for five ships like the *Janis* to have sailed in abreast. It was a truce with nature, for beyond those carefully maintained borders the greenery ran mad. There were flies and dragonflies near man-size quartering the air over the water, and she saw something huge and brown and slimy-looking surface to peer at the ship with goggling eyes.

'This river is life, basically,' Trallo was saying. 'This river is Khanaphes and all the other towns north of it. This is the line of green through the desert that everyone here needs to survive.'

Something caught Che's eye, something too rigid and angular to be natural. Between the ferns and the articulated trunks of horsetails, she saw huts – a rabble of little straw-roofed hovels lifted out of the water on stilts. She caught a glimpse of people, and then a boat gliding through the shallow channels, half-obscured by the green. A moment later it cut out on to the river behind the *Lord Janis*, a long, low boat with a high bow and stern, constructed only from reeds and rope. A woman with silvery-grey skin was effortlessly poling it near the bank. Almost unsurprised, now, Che recognized her as a Mantis-kinden. She looked anxiously at the Spider sailors, but none of them paid the native the slightest attention.

*They do things differently here.*

'And there we go,' said Trallo.

Che followed his gaze and caught her breath. The academics, too, were abruptly at the rail, staring.

'Khanaphes, the majestic, the mysterious,' said the showman, Trallo, as though he was charging admission.

Ahead of them, the river was flanked by squared pillars of stone four storeys high, vast at the base and barely tapering as they reached up to support the sky. The stone of the pillars was a dusty tan, while the statues set into their faces gleamed white. They stood almost the entire height of the pillars, carved seamlessly from marble, a man and a woman, barely clad and walking forward. The sculptor had lavished infinite care on their colossal proportions, the man's body heavy and broad-waisted, the woman's rounded breasts and hips, the flowing cascade of long hair down both sets of shoulders. Their faces viewed the marsh and the sea with cold beatitude. These were the countenances of a man and woman who ruled everything they saw as far as the wave-stirred horizon and beyond. Before that commanding, all-encompassing gaze the academics momentarily quailed. Che felt a shiver go through her, witnessing such perfection in stone. Those were beautiful faces, but they were appalling in their utter lack of empathy. It was no failing of the sculptor, though: the hands that had shaped them had carved and chipped to instil them with just such a coldness.

They were certainly not Beetle-kinden. No trick of style could ever have transformed them out of something so mundane. Che had never seen anyone or anything that even approached them.

'The Estuarine Gate,' Trallo announced, but she barely heard him. The blind stone gaze seemed to follow the matchwood thing that was the *Lord Janis* as it passed through the gulf between them and they saw Khanaphes proper.

It was a city built of stones – more so than any other place Che had seen. Houses raised of tan masonry clustered thickly about both sides of the river, and beyond the single-cell dwellings of the poor loomed the edifices of the wealthy. Avenues flanked by pillars led off toward statue-adorned squares where great squatting palaces faced one another, rising higher and higher, each surrounded by a miniature city of smaller structures, and the gaps between them filled with meaner dwellings and workshops.

'Well, rack me,' Berjek Gripshod exclaimed softly. 'Now look at that.'

The *Janis* pulled in skilfully at a dock near the gate, and the crew tied up. With the gangplank down, Che led the way on to the wharves of Khanaphes. Even the pier they were moored to was of stone. *How many pairs of hands, how many years, to make all this?* And yet so little of it looked recent. Time had laid its rounding hand on each surface and angle.

'Look,' said Berjek, and he sounded as though he was going to weep. Even the buildings nearest to them, mere stone huts, were intricately carved. Some simply had borders of angular, stylized images etched on to them, others bore whole panels of complex, intricate, indecipherable work. Looking around, Che could not see a single surface of stonework, even the pier beneath her sandals, that had not somehow been illustrated.

'We should have brought more people,' Berjek said hoarsely. This was hopeless. It would take an army of scholars all their lives to record this. The city was its own library.

Trallo was meanwhile organizing the luggage, his two Solarnese hauling it down on to the quayside. Che stepped aside from the academics, and the brooding Vekken, and stared into the crowd. The docks were a continuous bustle, a dozen ships unloading, the same number again preparing to cast off. There were men and women of many different kinden there, together with a swarm of the ubiquitous bald-headed Beetles. Her eyes had grown used, not so long since, to being wary of crowds. Helleron, Solarno, Myna: the war had given her instincts that had become stubborn guests.

As she looked, so she found. The face leapt out at her, a moment's eye contact across the crowded docks, but that was not a face she was ever likely to forget. Not five minutes after stepping from the ship, and her world was reverting to its old faithless ways once again.

*Thalric.*

*Part Two*

# The Black and Gold Path

# Nine

The grand army of General Vargen had arrayed itself before the city of Tyrshaan, black-and-yellow armour crossed with a sash of blue, the old badge of the Kings of Tyrshaan that had not been seen during this last generation. General Vargen, whose rank was self-given, and who was elsewhere known as just another one of the traitor-governors, had decided to risk a field battle, not trusting his forces to endure a siege. It was not necessarily a poor choice, for Thalric had seen the siege train that the Imperial forces had brought with them. Tyrshaan's walls were neither high nor strong.

Vargen's men made a fierce spectacle at this distance, but Thalric had heard the scouts and the spies report. There was a core of Wasp-kinden, mostly the garrisons of Tyrshaan and neighbouring Shalk, that would fight to the death. Dying in battle was preferable to dying in the fighting pit or at a public execution, especially given how inventive the new Empress had become. The bulk of Vargen's force were Auxillians, though, who had less to gain from victory, less to lose from defeat. Those solid blocks of armoured Tyrshaani Bee-kinden would see no reason to throw themselves on to the pikes of the enemy on behalf of their usurper lord. They now made dark squares against the tawny ground before the city walls: halberdiers, crossbowmen and masses of the interlocking hexagonal shields that the Tyrshaani favoured. The Bees were no match for the trained and keen soldiers of the Empire, either singly or en masse. Their only battle virtue was an implacability of spirit that Thalric suspected they would not be deploying today.

Vargen had placed a quartet of solid-looking automotives in the vanguard of his force, but Tyrshaan had always been a backwater, and their boxy, six-legged design was now twenty years old. By contrast, the punitive force had brought orthopters, snapbows and mobile artillery.

'I make it five of theirs to four of ours,' said a lieutenant next to him, peering through a spyglass. 'Not counting the Flies.'

'Well, who would?' sniffed Colonel Pravoc, the Imperial commander. 'So we outnumber them four to five. Good.' He gave Thalric one of his sickly smiles. Pravoc was a lean man who looked as though he lived primarily off ambition and a joy in the downfall of others. He had been chosen for this role because he was an able battlefield commander, and because having a mere colonel sent to oppose him would throw the self-made General Vargen into a rage. Altogether, Pravoc was a man of few words and fewer compliments.

'I trust it all meets with your approval,' he said, a flick of his fingers encompassing the might of the Imperial army that was falling into place around them.

'I'm not here to approve,' Thalric told him.

Pravoc's answering look said, *And why are you here?* but he was too much concerned with his own future to say it. The presence here of the Imperial Regent had inspired rather than shaken him. 'They'll be marching for us soon, according to our spies.'

Thalric shrugged. 'I'll leave you to your command, Colonel.'

He went to look over the black and gold of Pravoc's divisions: the usual array of light airborne waiting behind shieldwalls of the medium infantry which were supplemented, now, with snapbowmen. Those slender new weapons were about to make a sorry mess of the Bee-kinden armour, Thalric decided. It was just as well the Empire had suffered its crisis before the weapons had spread to the provinces.

General Vargen was not unique, of course. There had been a full score of provincial governors, mostly in the East- and South-Empire, who had decided to strike out on their own. A few had banded together to make little realms – Empirelets? – Emporia? – of their own, but most had been stubbornly solitary. It had been the succession that had provoked it, and Thalric was surprised it had not turned out worse. Emperor Alvdan the Second had died with no legitimate children, nor even a living bastard, having been so ruthless in dealing with potential threats to his power that he had put into danger everything that his father and grandfather had built. The rescuing hand, when it arrived, had been that of his sister, now Empress Seda the First. That had not sat well with many, because in the Empire men held power and women served. It was a tradition that went back to when they had all been squabbling tribes stealing each other's wives. There had never been a woman soldier or merchant or chieftain, and certainly there had never been a woman as ruler.

Seda had done her groundwork, though, and her allies were formidable. In the end, the central Empire including Capitas, Sonn and the neighbouring cities had bowed the knee to her. The West-Empire was lost for the moment to rebellion among the slave-races, and with it any dreams of conquering the lush expanses of the Lowlands. That could wait, however. Men like Vargen could not.

Vargen, like all his peers, had not believed that Seda's rule would hold. He had staked his future on her grip failing, on more and more turning against her. She was, after all, only a woman.

Thalric chuckled bitterly over that attitude. He, of all men, knew Seda, and how she had grown up with a knife at her throat every minute of every day and night, the only surviving relative of the paranoid Emperor Alvdan. It had taught her a certain outlook: Seda had become a woman of iron and Thalric would not want to cross her. If he had his time again, he would make sure he had nothing to do with her. The offer she made him had seemed too good to be true. Only now, when he was too close and had learned too much, did he understand how it was exactly that. How many men envied him: Imperial Regent, most important man in the Empire, and even sharer of the Empress's bed? It meant nothing, however. It meant that he was a mere figurehead, a man for the Empress to parade in front of those who expected to see a man close to the seat of power. He had no power, only an awful knowledge. He knew Seda now, when it was too late.

He was here to oversee the extinction of the traitor Vargen and the return of another piece of the Empire into the proper hands. He was here, as a sign of the Empress's favour, to inspire Pravoc and the rest, and to remind them that they were fighting for the true Imperial bloodline.

The thought made him twitch.

He was also here because, lately, he had seized any opportunity to be out of the presence of the Empress herself. He was a man in his middle years, a veteran of the battlefield in his youth, a veteran of the games of the Rekef for two decades and more. His skin bore the burns and scars of his history like medals. He had survived where others had fallen. He had killed with his blade and his sting and his bare hands, started and quelled rebellions, tortured women and slain children, hunted and been hunted. He had done all of this and Seda was still just a slip of a girl, barely of age, yet he feared her like nothing else. His skin crawled at the thought of her.

He heard a horn sound, way out on the plain, as Vargen's host began its slow advance. He saw the dust start to rise from hundreds of feet, as compact formations of Bee-kinden started to trudge forward. To left and right, Vargen's

Wasps moved out in loose order, ready to take to the air, and behind and around them was a great mass of Fly-kinden from Shalk, Vargen's other conquest. They were not reckoned a dependable asset on a battlefield, Fly-kinden, but these wore striped leather cuirasses and carried bows. Thalric suspected that Vargen was depending on them to pin down the Imperial airborne until the crossbows of the Bee-kinden could be brought to bear.

That prompted a smile: Vargen's tactics were sound, his politics less so. Thalric had already seen the little figure of the Shalken ambassador skulking into Pravoc's tent, confirming that the Flies always knew where their best interests lay. At a certain point in the battle they would vanish like last night's bad dream, leaving Vargen exposed on both flanks. Thalric had no doubt of their commitment, just as he had no doubt that their abrupt disappearance would come only when the battle turned against Vargen. Fly-kinden had an impeccable sense of survival, and the skill was in knowing how to use it to one's own advantage.

He next heard the orthopters starting up their engines. Pravoc had only a dozen of them, but they were all new-built Spearflights, which were swiftly becoming the workhorses of the Imperial air force after their achievements over Solarno.

*And didn't we lose Solarno? And since when did we ever have an 'air force'?* But progress was the watchword, now. Battles against men like Vargen were small change in the pocket of history. Every strategist within the Empire knew that one day they would be turning towards the Lowlands again, looking for a more worthy adversary. The battle of Solarno had at least taught them that mechanized air power was a solid part of their future.

The fliers lifted off in an almost simultaneous leap, their pilots casting them low over their own troops, and then reaching for height as they turned to approach the enemy. There went a new breed of Wasp soldier: the warrior-artificer who lived at speeds Thalric could barely imagine.

The flying machines now banked over the insurrectionist army, and a little cloud of the more optimistic enemy airborne rose to try and confront them. Thalric barely heard the first explosive as it landed, saw only the plume of dust and smoke arise over the army's right flank. The steady, slogging Bee-kinden advance faltered there as a hole was punched into one of their tightly packed squads. The battle had started.

At a signal from Pravoc, the loyalist shields began their cautious advance. It was a slow pace, almost an amble. They were more than happy to let the Tyrshaani do all the walking. Thunder spoke from behind Thalric, a single cough that rattled the ground, and another great geyser of dust flowered from thirty yards in front of the enemy advance. The mechanized leadshotters were finding the range in a leisurely manner.

Thalric turned back to his tent. The Imperial camp was close behind the Wasp lines but, unless Pravoc's reputation was merely hot air, the battle should only move further off towards the doomed city once the Tyrshaani got into snapbow range. It was not that Thalric had no stomach for watching an Imperial victory, although perhaps that thought did not fill him with the same joy it once had. It was just that the inevitable grinding of Pravoc's workmanlike battle tactics was unlikely to provide enthralling entertainment. Outside, the leadshotters thumped again, two or three of them in unison, so that the wine jar and bowl rattled on the table. Thalric stared over at his armour, set out for him by some diligent menial. He was supposed to have someone around to dress him in it, as a mark of his rank. The thought made him irritable: as a soldier, he could shrug his way into a banded cuirass without flunkeys.

He had no need for armour at all, of course, but there would be men of the Empire fighting and dying, so it seemed wrong to eschew it. Being without it with a battle nearby made him feel naked.

He put on his special undercoat first. This was long force of habit, although the copperweave shirt was not the torn and battered piece that had saved him in Myna, in Helleron and Collegium. The stuff was murderously expensive, but rank had some privileges, after all. The undershirt did not rely on the copperweave alone, either. There was an extra layer beneath it, for occasions when mere metal would not suffice. Over the copperweave, that was so fine and fluid that it would be almost undetectable, he pulled on his arming jacket and his cuirass, shrugging it out until the plates hung straight.

*Now at least I look like a soldier.*

He felt better for that, since Seda's court was full of men who did their best to look anything but. Thalric hated them all, both individually and collectively.

He turned for the tent flap and saw the assassins.

They were so clearly such that, in other circumstances, it would have been funny. He had caught them in the act of creeping in, two Wasp-kinden men in uniform with drawn blades and narrowed eyes, wearing expressions of horrified guilt. It must have seemed to them that he had been somehow expecting them, that he had carefully armoured himself in preparation for them, then waited patiently until they entered the tent.

His sword was still attached to his civilian belt lying on the ground. With a convulsive movement he ripped it from its scabbard, slashing a wide arc across the rear of the tent. If this had been a simple soldier's tent, that would have been it: the freedom of the sky open to him in an instant. He was no longer a simple soldier, though, and this tent was made out of carpets and needed three men to carry. His blade barely cut into it as the two assassins rushed towards him.

One loosed a sting bolt from his open hand as they charged in, but the other assassin was so eager that he nearly caught it in the back. The shot went wild and Thalric tried to bring his sword back into line to parry the quicker man's incoming thrust. He twisted aside as he did so, but the man's blade went home anyway, digging in at his side where the regulation armour plates did not cover him. The sword dug in hard, but skittered off the copperweave mesh underneath. *That trick isn't going to save my life for ever*, Thalric considered. *Someone's going to stab me in the face eventually.* Meanwhile he was putting an elbow into the man's ear and thrusting his palm forward at the second killer, almost in the same moment. They loosed together, crackling bolts of energy lighting up the tent's dim interior. Thalric felt the heat as he ducked, letting the stingshot sear past his face. His own shot punched the man across the shoulder before it scorched its way into the tent fabric, which promptly started to smoulder. Now he had a chance to look he saw that, behind him, it was actually on fire.

*Who in the wastes made this tent? It's a deathtrap!*

Abruptly none of them much wanted to be inside it, and yet the two assassins were giving him no leeway. The swordsman had recovered from the blow enough to try and stab again but, this close, Thalric was able to trip him and then stamp on him hard before barrelling for the tent entrance. The second man got in his way and they tumbled over each other through the tent flap. Thalric punched him in the face by instinct, then called up his sting before finding that his sword had already run the man through, slipping between the plates of his mail.

Feeling light-headed, Thalric got to his feet, the sword-hilt greasy in his fingers. He heard the other man approaching from inside the tent and turned to catch him, hearing distantly a sharp 'snap' but not recognizing it for what it was.

Something slammed him hard in the gut and he went over, mind turning utterly blank. There was quite a lot of pain, and he felt a warm wetness of blood. Breathing was difficult, as though a strong man had kicked him under the ribcage. It was all he could do to stay conscious, keep his eyes open. He heard footsteps running closer.

The second assassin emerged from the tent, looking singed and angry. He glanced past Thalric at the newcomer.

'Took your time,' he said – and Thalric shot him under the chin, cutting him off without even a scream, the killer's face vanishing in a sudden inferno. Thalric rolled over, feeling a brutal stab of agony in his side. The third man went stumbling away from him, his face slack with shock, feeding another bolt into his snapbow.

Thalric extended an arm towards him, but the pain made his head swim and he missed his chance. As the snapbowman finished his fumbled reloading and raised the weapon, Thalric gritted his teeth and hurled himself away on to his good side.

His impact with the ground and the impact of the bolt came at the same time. The metal bolt ripped across his left arm, opening a shallow line across his biceps. He gritted his teeth, clinging to consciousness, and loosed his sting over and over. The first three shots went wild, but the man was idiotically trying to reload again rather than watching his enemy or using the weapon his Art had given him. Thalric's fourth shot burned him across the leg and he dropped to one knee, spilling bolts across the ground.

Thalric hissed in pain and then shot him in the chest. Under other circumstances he might have wanted the man alive, but just now he simply was not up to the bother. Feeling the drain on his body's resources he put another two searing bolts into the corpse just to be sure.

He sat down abruptly, hearing the tent crackle merrily behind him. The bruised ribs from the thwarted sword were nothing, and the gash on his arm would mend well enough. With shaking hands he reached for the first snapbow bolt, lodged in his stomach. He kept his eyes closed, because he could not bring himself to explore the wound any other way than by tentative probing.

The little bolt had punched a jagged hole in his cuirass. Carefully – oh so carefully – he unbuckled it, whimpering as that jogged the bolt. He then slid a hand under it, blindly feeling.

His copperweave had fared no better, but the bolt was jutting proud of it, however much it might feel that it was buried in his guts. The delicate mesh had parted like string before the snapbow missile. They had always told him those weapons were good, but he had never expected to be on the receiving end of one so soon.

The bolt had cut into him, but shallowly. His third layer of armour had stopped it going further: Spiderlands silk. The early tests by the inventor had confirmed its efficacy. Like an arrow or crossbow bolt, the snapbow's missile spun, which made it accurate, but also meant that it snarled hopelessly in silk. Thalric had three layers of folded silk pressed beneath the copperweave and, after penetrating two layers of metal, this mere cloth had slowed the bolt to nothing.

It hurt him as badly as it had being stabbed, that one time outside Vek. He could not have felt much worse if the bolt had simply run him through. He wasn't going to die, though, and in a little while he would be ready to stand up and walk around. And then he would want some answers.

Out on the field, the battle ground towards its predetermined ending. The double line of snapbows that Pravoc fielded ripped into the heavy Tyrshaani infantry, butchering them in their uncomprehending hundreds. Predictably, as the scales tipped, the Fly-kinden rose up in a great cloud and simply vanished away, fleeing for either the city or the wilderness, depending on their faith in the victors. A few were bold enough to put a final arrow of farewell into some Tyrshaani officer or other that they had reserved particular contempt for. Meanwhile the orthopters had started preliminary bombing runs against the Tyrshaan gatehouse, on the assumption that the city would require a little extra persuasion to open up.

⋆

Colonel Pravoc's entry into the governor's palace in Tyrshaan went unopposed. By that time the controlling elements of the Wasp garrison had been almost completely obliterated, and to the Tyrshaani themselves it meant nothing which slavemasters held their leash. The surviving Bee-kinden soldiers surrendered in good order, laying down their weapons and sitting down outside the walls of their own city, while tearing off the blue sashes that had never been more than empty symbols – Vargen's illusion of autonomy. Wasps being what they were, there were a few incidents of revenge killing, just as there was some looting once the Imperial forces got inside. It was all within the tolerated bounds of military discipline, and Pravoc's orders were for the city to be left intact and simply returned to the Imperial fold.

In the governor's own war room he found Vargen, already doubled in stiff rigour over the table, scattered markers and tiles oddly mirroring the fate of Vargen's own crushed army. The man's face was purple and twisted, his tongue protruding and his eyes wide.

There was a pair of Fly-kinden waiting there for Pravoc, one in the drab of a servant, the other dressed in Imperial black and gold, and not a blue sash in sight. Pravoc raised his eyebrows at them, seeking explanations.

'When it became clear that his cause was lost,' said the better-dressed of the Flies, 'Governor Vargen took poison. Tragic.'

Pravoc, seeing the outraged and horrified expression on the dead man's face, wondered if Vargen had known that was what he was doing, when he had taken the wine. He noted the Fly's careful use of the word 'governor' rather than 'general'.

'Who are you?' he demanded.

'My name is te Pelli. I am a factor of the Consortium out of Shalk,' the Fly replied, his face displaying nothing more than polite deference. 'I wanted to be the first to assure you that we of Shalk were only yoked to Vargen's schemes through threat of force.'

Pravoc sniffed. He had no illusions about how little a threat would have been necessary, nonetheless it suited him well enough if the Fly-kinden were happy to do his job for him. The faster he could report an unequivocal victory, the higher he would rise in the eyes of his masters.

Thalric found him there later, after the ex-governor's body had been removed, along with the poisoned wine.

'What happened to you?' Pravoc asked, and then added, 'Regent,' a moment later. 'Get caught up in the fighting? Unwise.'

'It came looking for me.' Thalric studied the man's narrow face and found it devoid of anything meaningful. 'Some assassins tried to kill me.' As he said it, he found the words sounding petty in his own ears. Had he still been Major Thalric of the Rekef it would have been a reasonable thing to say. It would have been the preface to organizing a plan of action, a counterplot, a piece of espionage. Thalric the Regent was not free to pursue such courses, and so it came out sounding like a whine for attention, a demand that something be done.

Pravoc's change of expression, however slight, conveyed the same opinion. 'Makes sense. Vargen was against the Empress and you're her man here. Makes sense that he might try to remove you.' He left a measured pause. 'But you came through all right, I see, Regent.'

With his ribs pulsing in pain, his arm bound up, Thalric felt unexpectedly lost for options. The Rekef man he once was would have accepted none of it. With the threat of the entire secret service behind him, he would have ensured that colonels, even generals, would gabble out anything they knew, rather than offer cool insolence. The Regent, though . . . he felt, as Regent, that he should have more respect from this brusque soldier, and at the same time the thought made him sick of himself. Respect for what? Earned how?

'I survived,' he said, turning to go. As he reached the doorway he stopped. 'I was surprised there were none of your men at hand, Colonel. When the attack occurred the camp all around me seemed quite deserted.' He turned, but surprised no admission of guilt, no new expression at all, on Pravoc's face.

'I was fighting a battle,' Pravoc said firmly. 'If you'd asked me for bodyguards, I'd have found them. Complain to the Empress if you want.'

Thalric's smile in response was thin. He appreciated this man's confidence in his own abilities, in his refusal to bow to such an empty thing as the Regent of the Empire, but also he did not trust Pravoc at all. For a Rekef man, trust came hard and often never.

'The Empress shall know that you have done your work here adequately,' Thalric declared blandly. 'What else is relevant?'

He made sure that his gait revealed nothing of the stabbing pains in his side, where the snapbow bolt had been within three layers of silk of killing him. Someone out there knew now that he had fought off three men and was still alive to complain of it.

*Let them worry*, he thought.

# Ten

Thalric had decided against returning home with the army. Even an Imperial army with a mechanized baggage train moved at a snail's pace. Besides, he was expected to return with it, and at this juncture he did not feel like doing anything that was too obviously expected. The fewer opportunities he gave his hidden enemies, the better.

So he commandeered an automotive. What was the point of being Regent of the Empire unless you could do that? *He* knew it to be an empty honour, but that was not general knowledge. His two-man crew of driver and engineer/artillerist were more than happy to break away from the plodding convoy and make best speed along the dusty roads leading north to Sonn. What Colonel Pravoc thought of it, Thalric did not attempt to find out.

Sonn was one of the earliest conquests of Alvdan the First, one of the linchpins of the Empire. It had been conquered by force but the Beetle-kinden residents had soon seen the benefits of Imperial rule, and the place was now the heart of the Consortium of the Honest, the mercantile arm of the Imperial administration. The Beetle-kinden traders, slavers, shippers and bankers had soon made themselves an indispensable part of the Empire, and their kinden had proven the very best of second-class citizens.

Changes were happening in Sonn, and changes for the better, as far as the locals were concerned. Thalric had heard how the city was being expanded, with factories and foundries being thrown up as fast as was humanly possible. The loss of Szar, as a manufacturing base, had been a blow to the military and industrial capability of the Empire, but the Beetles of Sonn were quite willing to make themselves more essential. Even forewarned, the bustle of the place surprised Thalric. There were acres of scaffolding and part-completed buildings lining the road. The Beetles had planned to expand their city by almost as much again, and this addition would all be factories. In a year's time, Thalric guessed, you would barely be able to see the sky for all the smoke generated. It would be like a new Helleron, he thought.

When he disembarked, he realized why. The place was seething with artificers already installing the factory machines, the boilers and steam-powered toolbenches and assembly lines. Many were local people but many more were not. Thalric had travelled enough to recognize Helleren men and women. They had come here in their droves, wearing their scuffed leather and canvas, to sell their expertise to an Empire that only last year had claimed conquest of their native city. Helleron was now proudly neutral again, and no hard feelings, so tramp artificers were flooding in to help the Empire rebuild its losses and to take Imperial coin in exchange for the uncertainties of working for such a belligerent employer. The Helleren were good at what they did, better than any of their Imperial counterparts. They swallowed their pride and doubled their fees, and there were so many of them in Sonn that there was talk of building a railroad.

Thalric had heard that the late General Malkan of the Seventh Army had conquered Helleron single-handed merely with a threat. When the Empire turned its attention west again, he reckoned that the reconquest could probably be effected by letter.

He abandoned his automotive at Sonn, leaving the crew

to enjoy some leave in the city until Pravoc's army caught up. As of a month before, there was a rail-line from Sonn to Capitas. It was ridiculous of course. The new peace with the Lowlands was making the Empire strong enough that the next war, when it came, would be over in tendays.

By train he travelled to Capitas wearing anonymous Imperial armour, just a soldier engaged on official business. This anonymity served a purpose, but he was surprised to find what a weight it lifted from him. For such an empty honour, the title of Regent was a heavy thing to bear.

The weight of it came back to him once the outskirts of Capitas began passing by on either side. The rail depot was located in view of the great ziggurat of the Imperial palace. The sight of it made his stomach twitch.

*Someone tried to have me killed.*

Just seeing the palace, and what it represented, he could barely think about the assassination. *There are worse things in life than being killed.*

They had put up a gilded statue of Alvdan the Second before the gates of the palace. It was interesting, in Thalric's opinion, how the glitter of the gold distracted from the fundamentally mediocre workmanship. He passed it quickly, because the really clever statue was inside. The grand entrance hall of the Imperial palace had once been darker, all guards and armour and the iron fist of power. The Empress had since ordered two more windows to be sunk through the stone, so it was now as bright and airy as a garden when the sun came from the right quarter. At its heart the first thing every visitor, general, dignitary or ambassador saw was the statue.

The likeness of Seda was stylized but unmistakable. The sculptor genius had eloquently portrayed her determination, her youth, her femininity. It showed her with a spear held proudly in one hand, a shield in the other, representing the hope of the Empire. Her image was at the centre, but kneeling, and around and behind her stood her people.

They stood tall, protecting her without overshadowing her, and they were cast in the same heroic manner – blocky, larger than life, projecting loyalty and fervour. There was a soldier in the armour of the Light Airborne, an artificer with his toolstrip, a Consortium factor with his scales and quill. The fourth figure was still being chiselled out of the stone, and Thalric wondered who he would be. A Rekef agent? An aviator? He would stand with the same pride and passion as the others, one hand raised, palm outwards, at the world in defiance and a threat of power. The whole piece was a work of art and even Thalric, cynical as he had become, felt his heart swell with pride when he saw it. Pride at being Wasp-kinden, the superior race.

In this statue, he could look on the face of Seda and not quail. Now he braced himself for the real thing.

The style at the Imperial court was currently for robes, or for tunics with long sleeves that hung uselessly behind the arms like limp wings. Thalric, however, dressed like a military man of high station, in white tunic and a cloak edged with black and gold. It was a kind of desperate defiance, his private little rebellion that he knew would be overlooked.

Alvdan had kept his throne room empty, that was another thing. He had held his councils and conferences, but afterwards the great room had lain empty save for dusting servants. Seda kept a proper court, however. It was part of the strategy she had devised.

By that strategy, she had made them love her. That was her own genius, of which the sculpture was just part. The Wasp-kinden were ruled by men, had been led by men always. On her accession, even with the support of many of their leaders, Seda had been hard pressed to prevent anarchy. If she had merely relied on her own right to autocratic power, issued orders and demanded obedience, she would quickly have fallen. They would have torn her apart in the streets.

She had made them love her. She had assumed the traditional role of a Wasp woman, meek and subservient and weak, and made something of it. She did not demand servitude from her men, she begged their protection. She made them see her as vulnerable, as the last faint hope of the honoured Imperial bloodline that only they could save. She wooed them with her needs, her inabilities. She was the Bride of the Empire, and each one of them, in his way, was her guardian and partner. She made each man believe that by serving her he was personally saving the Empire. In flaunting her weakness, in inviting their support, she got them to do anything she wanted, and made them love her in the bargain.

They fell over each other to display to her their loyalty, their strength. She juggled them like an expert and they never ever realized. Thalric, from his privileged vantage point, had seen it all. He might have found it amusing had he not known.

As he walked in, heads turned. They were all here, three score of them and more: military officers, Consortium factors, scions of wealthy families. Each day they came to the palace and huddled and talked and schemed against one another, and waited. They waited Her Imperial Majesty's pleasure. They waited for her to make her appearance, so that they could prove themselves to her.

There were some there, especially towards the far end of the room with its seven thrones, who were not Wasp-kinden. There had already been a few when Thalric had gone off on campaign but there were more now. They were some of Seda's more select advisers. His heart sank further on seeing them, and that was not because these lesser races now had the ear of the Empress: it was what they represented.

'My Lord Regent,' said a clipped voice.

Thalric turned to see a broad-shouldered Wasp of about his own years, a man with a soldier's physique. He was wearing his fashionable garments with neither panache nor awkwardness. They hung off him as if draped on a mannequin.

‘General Brugan,’ Thalric acknowledged. ‘I trust you are well?’

‘When the Empire is well, I am well,’ Brugan confirmed. As the Lord General of the Rekef he was the most powerful man in the Empire, and one that even Thalric had a wary respect for. It was no secret that his support had turned the balance of power in favour of Seda, nor a secret that he had murdered his chief rival over the late Emperor’s dead body. He was ruthless and intelligent and ambitious, therefore a model Imperial general.

‘The Empress has been missing you,’ he said blandly. Brugan was not one to be misled by Seda’s public face. He surely must know as well as Thalric the true woman behind it. ‘Also, when your official duties permit, I have some news of an old friend. I’d appreciate your views.’

‘As you wish, General,’ Thalric said. Brugan was one of the few people he was both careful and also happy to oblige. The man was good at his job and good for the Empire.

Thalric passed on towards the top end of the hall, towards the clustering robes. He noticed a nod in his direction from the absurdly tall, hunchbacked figure of Gjegevey, but Thalric ignored the grey-skinned, long-faced creature. The old slave was a favourite of the Empress’s now, one of her inner council, and it was people such as he who were the problem. Beyond Gjegevey stood a Grasshopper-kinden, in a robe of pale lemon, whom he did not recognize, but saw as another slave risen above his station. Beyond that . . .

‘You,’ he began, before deciding whether he should. ‘Moth-kinden.’

The grey-clad shape turned, and Thalric was surprised to see a Wasp face looking out from within the cowl.

‘Alas no, although the mistake is understandable.’ The man was short and balding, but a Wasp nonetheless.

Thalric stared at him. ‘Who are you?’

‘You are the Regent Thalric,’ the man replied. ‘I recognize you from the portrait in Her Majesty’s chambers. My name is Tegrec. I am the Tharen ambassador, for my crimes.'

It took Thalric a moment to connect name and place. The result was displeasing to him. 'Weren't you a traitor?' he asked, his voice loud enough for a few people to look round.

Tegrec only smiled his implacable smile. 'Weren't you, O Regent?' he asked, so that nobody else heard. Thalric looked on him without love, seeing behind him two other grey-robed figures, real Moth-kinden this time.

'What's brought you – and *them* – here?' Thalric asked bluntly.

'Times change, O Regent,' Tegrec said mildly. 'I am here for Tharn, and the Moth-kinden thereof. The war is now over between my birthplace and my adopted kinden.'

'Is that so?'

The ambassador's face was all sly knowledge. 'It is true that the Moths managed to drive out the occupying Imperial force, but only at great cost. Current conditions now suggest that a more open relationship with the Empire will be beneficial to us all. The Empress herself has expressed a personal interest.'

'Of course she has.' Thalric's tone was bleak.

'Her Majesty has pronounced herself especially pleased with our gifts.' Tegrec made a grand gesture towards the head of the hall like a magician and, like magic indeed, the doors opened at that exact moment and the Empress made her entrance.

She had an honour guard, he noticed. Thalric felt weak. It had been a concern of hers, before he left, that she ought to have an honour guard, but how could she have trusted one? There were too many throughout the Empire who wanted to see a man on the throne. It seemed the problem had been solved, and he now understood Tegrec's gift. The Moths of Tharn had been clever.

There were only six of them but he doubted she would need more. Tall and slender, wearing armour of delicately crafted mail and leather that had been enamelled in black and gold. Each bore a narrow sword at the hip, a clawed gauntlet on his hand.

'How . . .?' he began, but was unable to say more.

'How can she be sure of them?' Tegrec asked, standing close enough that Thalric wanted to strike him. 'Why, they are sworn to her protection, dedicated wholly into her service by command of the Skryres of Tharn. I think you know how seriously the Mantis-kinden take their honour.'

They took their place and stood there, still as statues around her throne, their faces hidden in the shadow of their helms. In their midst the Empress Seda looked young and demure, dressed in the minimum of finery. Her own natural beauty was all the adornment she needed. She smiled warmly at Thalric and held out a hand. He made himself walk forward and take it, stepping within the Mantis circle to seat himself beside her. Her touch felt shockingly warm.

It was like sitting next to something venomous: a scorpion with sting raised. He sat there very still, tried to ignore the brooding presence of the Mantis-kinden who had been sold into her service.

'You will be joining me in my quarters later, of course?' she said.

'Of course, Your Imperial Majesty,' he replied, with a broad, despairing smile.

The next day he lay recuperating in her chambers, pale and feverish. The day after that, he made himself scarce from any public engagements, retreating to the palace storerooms to seek out Osgan.

Theirs was an unlikely association and it had come about through Thalric's desperation. Had he still been his own man he would have spared the wretched Osgan not a word, would as like as not have despised him.

This was not the first time his eyes had been opened to the sort of man he was. When he had been on the run from the Rekef, he had viewed his life from the outside and the world, he knew, held more pleasant sights. *I was a model Imperial citizen,* he reminded himself. Filtered through his experience, the thought was a painful one.

'You look like I feel,' Osgan remarked and it was broadly true. Mid-morning and Osgan was still unshaven, eyes red-rimmed in a sagging grey face. Once a solidly built Wasp, he was now fast becoming simply heavy. There was already an open bottle on a crate beside him. The Rekef man behind Thalric's eyes looked at him and recognized a liability.

Images from the night before last still recurred to him as he sat down opposite. He and Osgan avoided each other's eyes, both of them men who had seen too much.

Osgan shook a pair of dice out of a leather bag, a handful of small coins from another. 'Might as well make use of the time,' he grunted. He was an appalling gambler, but Thalric made sure he did not lose too much. Only a year ago Osgan had been a rising star in the Consortium of the Honest: supply officer for the Ninth Army, stationed in Capitas, with his hands immersed in the stream of Imperial funds, even holding the favour of the Emperor, but now . . .

He held his current position among the steward's staff because Thalric made it so. If not for that he would have been a debt-slave by now, meat for the fighting pits, conscripted into the Auxillians. It had all fallen down for Osgan, on the day the Emperor died.

It had fallen down for Thalric: same day, different reasons. Thalric who had been a traitor, just as Tegrec had named him, who had killed a Rekef general, who had been brought to Capitas in chains. Thalric who had been saved from a bad fate for, he was discovering, a worse one. Thalric who found the Empress's court at Capitas that bit stranger each time he was dragged back to it. Thalric, who had grown used, in his career as a traitor, to having people around to talk to.

The Rekef man he had once been could not have cared less. That Rekef man had underlings and superiors and enemies. The traitor he became had stood alongside such as the redoubtable Stenwold Maker, the Mantis butcher Tisamon, the enigmatic Achaeos. *They saw more of me than my own people were ever allowed to.* It had seemed right, then, but he had not thought he would ever be coming back.

*But I grew used to having someone to talk to.* Well, now he had Osgan. He could say what he liked to Osgan. Nobody listened to a shaky supply officer who was drunk most of the time. Nobody cared about this man, except Thalric.

*And who cares for me?* The image of Seda's face came straight to mind. She must feel *something* to draw him back and back again, but he had no word for that emotion. She had summoned him to her chamber, where he had been bathed and readied by the slaves, dressed in Spider silks and then taken to her bed. He knew there were many who would give everything to swap places with him. He would give anything to oblige.

'So what's new, chief?' Osgan asked, making a cavalier throw of the dice that spilled them off the crate entirely. The bottle was near empty, and Thalric took it up and drained it until it was. The bitter soldier's beer Osgan had purloined tasted of honesty.

'Someone's trying to kill me,' Thalric said.

Osgan made a grotesque mime of surprise. 'News? Since when's that news?' He retrieved the dice. 'Give me a quill and a week, I'll draw you a list of them that want you dead. Lowlanders, Comm'wealers, even your own friends and neighbours. So what?'

'They had a solid try at it outside Tyrshaan.' Thalric frowned. 'Wasp assassins, so not Commonwealers. And the Lowlanders who know me wouldn't send assassins. Not since the Mantis died.' Osgan flinched at that. Thalric grimaced. 'Someone inside the Empire wants me dead,' he finished.

'Everyone wants you dead,' Osgan muttered. 'Everyone but me. And why not? If they hate Herself, then they hate you too. If they like Herself, then they hate you. Some of them probably just hate you anyway.'

Thalric nodded glumly, conceding the point. His position had endeared him to few. 'I would shed this role if I could.'

Osgan was sober enough to grimace at that. 'I know, I know,' he said, almost whispering, 'but don't *say* it. I don't want to hear it in case they come after me with their hooks to find out what I heard.' He fumbled out another bottle, drew the cork with his teeth.

When Thalric had entered her chambers two nights ago she had been waiting for him, wearing a dress of white silk that hung from one shoulder and followed to her body's every line. There was that happy glow to her that he had learned to recognize, just as he recognized the taste on her lips.

She had offered him a goblet.

Thalric grabbed the bottle from Osgan and took a great swallow, because that taste had suddenly recurred to him.

'I have to get out of here,' he said desperately.

Osgan shrugged. 'Door's right there, chief.'

'You know what I mean.'

'I know, but it's like the army, chief. You don't get out till it's had its full use of you.'

Thalric had looked into the red, red liquid in the jewelled goblet, and he had drunk deep of it, because she would accept nothing else. The taste of salt and rust had coated his throat. She had kissed him, drawn him towards the great bed.

*How long can I survive?* A lucky man could retire from the army, but there would be no quitting this post. *She took me as a prisoner and a traitor. She saw just enough in me to be worth keeping. Now she devours me at her leisure.*

She would ask for him again tonight. She always left him a day and a night to recover. He wondered what arrangements she made when he was absent.

The most terrible thing about it was that he thought she

did feel something for him, some attraction, even some affection. She was cold, though, and everything new she learned from her select advisers was making her more distant still. She was *different.* Everything about her appearance suggested simply a young Wasp woman who was little more than a girl. Her beauty almost broke his heart, but only because he knew that under the skin some part of her had been stripped away.

This last time, he had not looked into the antechamber where the detritus of her preparations would still be on display. He did not wish, when sipping from the red cup, to know what vintage she had provided him with.

*She will be the death of me.* It was no more than the truth.

General Brugan let him stew for a tenday before calling him in. Thalric spent the meantime in standing dutifully beside the Empress with a tight-lipped smile, or in hearing the words of those who courted his own favour. He spent his time in sloping off to talk with Osgan down in the cellars, and dulling the edges of his life with drink. He spent it in Seda's chambers, stepping into her embrace, meeting her red lips as her slender body entwined with his.

Sometimes, as she arched atop him at the very climax of their coupling, he saw something in her eyes: a girl whose childhood had been lived in the shadow of death, and who had seized her only chance to live. The image was despairing, and it called to him for help. He wondered if she saw some similar plea for rescue in his.

He had lived his previous life hoping that a Rekef general would never call for him, but when Brugan's messenger came, it was only a relief.

The office was lined with racks full of scrolls and shelves of books and next to it was housed a coterie of clerks who sifted every word that came into the Empire, searching for the least drachm of significance. It had belonged to Brugan's rival and predecessor, yet he had changed nothing, and

Thalric wondered whether this was to celebrate Brugan's victory, or remind him that nobody lasts for ever.

'Ah, Lord Regent,' he said without expression. There was a Wasp-kinden woman sitting in the corner, ready to record whatever was said.

'General,' Thalric was aware of the absurdity, 'you can call me Major, if you want, sir. I think I still own the rank.'

Brugan shrugged. There was no warmth towards Thalric in his expression, but it was not the job of a Rekef general to like people. 'I suppose I am calling on you for information, as I would with any agent,' he said carefully, with a curt gesture for Thalric to sit. 'I am aware you had a many-coloured career in the war.'

Thalric took the one seat before the desk, wondering how many others must have sweated and trembled here. However, he did not rise to the barb.

Brugan's lips twitched slightly. 'That may be of use,' he continued drily, 'now that you are a good son of the Empire once again. You were in a position to see things that sounder agents had no chance for.' His eyes said *traitor,* but Thalric met them without flinching. For a long time they stared at each other, with neither breaking from the other's gaze.

'Do you consider that you're immortal, Regent?' Brugan asked at last.

'I am sure that if you thought it in the Empire's interest, you'd make an end of me,' replied Thalric. The thought rose in him, *If you must, then do it sooner rather than later*, and he swallowed it down.

'Apparently someone tried to have you killed,' Brugan went on. 'Outside Tyrshaan, I am informed. The Regent may do as he likes, but perhaps Major Thalric should have made his report before now?'

Thalric looked down, at last. 'You are correct, of course, sir.'

'Well, it is now known to us and we will determine who is responsible,' said Brugan dismissively, as if now bored with the subject. 'Stenwold Maker, you met him, I believe?'

'I did. Several times.' This change of direction threw Thalric temporarily. 'What of him?'

'My agents there say that Collegium believes in peace, but what does Stenwold Maker believe in?'

'He believes that the peace is transitory,' Thalric replied. 'May I speak frankly?'

'Do.'

'He would make a good Wasp. Indeed he would make a good Rekef agent. Perceptive, loyal and selfless, he lives for his people and he sees threats to them very clearly. He foresaw the invasion of the Lowlands an entire decade early and spent all that time laying plans and training agents.'

'You admire him.'

'He has many admirable qualities. It is unfortunate he is our enemy.' The brief time he himself had been Stenwold's agent-captive, and the work he had done for Stenwold's cause, flickered briefly in Thalric's memory.

'He's sending agents out again,' Brugan growled. 'South of the Empire now. To places we will be looking to, once the South-Empire is fully ours. It would make sense for the Lowlands to make our Imperial ambitions there difficult, and they already have allies around the Exalsee.'

Thalric nodded. 'It's a good move for him. I can understand him making it.'

'We are far from ready yet for another conflict with the Lowlands,' Brugan said. 'Is he likely to force war upon us?'

'No.'

'So certain?'

'Stenwold will not start a war, not fought by his own people. He may, however, start a war with others' blood, as he did at Solarno.'

Brugan nodded. 'You are well informed.'

'Old habits die hard, sir.' Some emotion had stirred in Thalric's chest. 'Sir, you'll be sending out agents to keep an eye on Maker and his people?'

Brugan studied him with narrowed eyes but remained silent.

'Send me,' Thalric said. *Please, send me. Send me away from here. Give me my life back.*

'Why?'

'Why not? I am Rekef, still – Regent or not. I was good at my job. I know Stenwold Maker better than any agent you have. Give me a small team, embassy credentials perhaps. Who would be better?'

Brugan stared at him for a long moment, his heavy face expressionless. Rekef thoughts would be scuttling through his head.

'An Imperial embassy to Khanaphes,' he spat out finally. 'Ever heard of it?'

'I could soon learn,' Thalric replied.

# Eleven

'The roads are good all the way to Tyrshaan,' said Captain Marger. 'With the insurrection there quelled we should make good time.'

Thalric nodded, eyeing the automotive that Brugan had found for him. It would not be a comfortable journey but he was used to that. The hold, hastily fitted out for passengers, consisted of a metal and wood box slung between the huge-spoked rear wheels, while the driver and his mate would be sitting up front amid the dust. It was a conveyance meant for couriers, travelling fast and without luxury.

'How does it manage off the roads?' Thalric asked.

Marger raised his eyebrows. 'Well enough, if we had to.' Long-faced and sandy-haired, he was about five years Thalric's junior and slight of build for a Wasp. He looked wholly inoffensive, which was the best way for a Rekef man to look. Brugan had chosen an embassy as the ostensible reason for a Wasp team descending on Khanaphes. Thalric would provide the public face, and act as special adviser on the Lowlanders, while Marger would conduct the Rekef Outlander operation proper. It was a delicate balance of power.

'We'll go to Shalk,' Thalric decided. 'Not Tyrshaan.' *Let's make it difficult, just in case.*

Instead of protesting, Marger digested this proclamation. 'If you want. It shouldn't affect our timing much. With the mining trade the roads are probably better.' His team was loading the automotive now: two more Wasps and a Beetle-kinden strapping crates and rolled-up canvas to the vehicle's sides, before returning to the row of storage sheds for more. 'I'd ask why, though.'

'Why not? Shalk's as good,' Thalric told him, 'besides, I've seen Tyrshaan recently. I'd rather see somewhere else.' *Let them think of me as the Regent, not the Rekef Major.* He had other good reasons for wanting to go to Shalk, but those were not for sharing.

Marger shrugged, which he did a lot of. 'It's your call,' he said, and went off to help his men. Thalric leant back against one of the rear wheels, feeling the machine rock and jolt as they continued loading it. Marger was opaque: it was impossible to know yet whether he would cause problems. The captain's subordinates gave few clues, either. The Beetle-kinden was an artificer, a paunchy, grey-haired veteran put in just to reassure the locals. The other two Wasps looked like men more comfortable in armour. They showed Thalric a careful deference but otherwise said nothing.

Thalric was making maps in his mind: envisioning the Fly-kinden warren of Shalk, the quarry mines there, the descent to Forest Alim and the river Jamail. It was all book-learnt stuff, for his travels had never taken him much through the South-Empire and not at all beyond its borders.

*I will be happier once the war starts up again, to give me an excuse to return to the Commonweal or the Lowlands, to places I know.* Save that would mean crossing swords with Stenwold Maker once more. *We cannot afford to let each other live. The next time I will have to remove him, or he me.* The thought brought with it an unwelcome stab of conscience, for Stenwold could have had Thalric killed several times already. Instead he had stayed his hand. *Though for his own advantage!* Still, it did not sit well that Thalric's too often pawned loyalty must await that final twist of the knife.

*The Lowlanders have come close to ruining me for a proper*

*agent's work.* His outer shell of Good Imperial Servant had taken too many knocks and shakes while in their company.

Marger stepped away from the automotive, a soldier's tension abruptly in his manner. Someone came running unevenly around the storage sheds towards them, and Thalric saw one of Marger's people put down the big crate he was carrying and crouch beside it with hand ready to sting.

'Hold!' Thalric called out, and he went to intercept the newcomer before any damage could be done. 'Osgan,' he exclaimed. 'What are you doing here?'

Osgan had dredged up his old uniform from somewhere: a Consortium factor's greatcoat, quartered in the army colours. There was a shortsword at his belt, the baldric crossing the strap of his satchel. He had even shaved, although he had made a ragged job of it, and his eyes were red-rimmed but his gaze steady.

'I'm coming with you,' he panted, short of breath.

'You aren't,' Thalric snapped. 'What's got into you?' With a firm hand on Osgan's shoulder, he led the man a short distance from the automotive, meanwhile signalling for Marger to carry on.

Osgan looked at him miserably. 'You've found your escape, now. You're going, yes? Going far.'

Thalric nodded and scowled, his last words with the Empress recurring to him. As she had made a public farewell, before the whole court, she had reached up to kiss him and murmured, '*You shall return to me. You shall always return.*'

'Let me come with you,' Osgan said. 'Please, Thalric. I'm dying here.'

'You're more likely to die on the road. This is Rekef business, Osgan. Stay here and keep to your cellars.'.

'Each time you find some way of getting out of this place, it gets worse for me,' Osgan complained, almost in a whisper. 'They hate me. They hate me because of you – and because of me. They know I've broken. You'll come back and find me gone, and nobody will even remember my name.'

'You're exaggerating.' Osgan was probably not exaggerating but Thalric couldn't agree to it.

'And what of you, anyway?' Osgan asked. 'You think you'll go back to your old ways, your old trade? You think they'll let you? Them?' Even his jabbing gesture towards the automotive looked crippled, his fingers crooked. 'They won't let you back in, Thalric. They won't forget who you are. What you were.'

Thalric glanced around, despite himself, seeing Marger watching him. The man bore his placid, accepting expression that Thalric had not yet been able to scratch. There had been no sense of complicity between them, no admission that they even lived in the same world. Thalric had wanted to protest, *I am a major in the Rekef,* but now he realized that he did not even know Marger's true Rekef rank. The 'captain' was army-issue, meaning less than nothing on a covert run like this.

'If you can't keep up with us, I'm not sure I can save you,' he warned. His Imperial conditioning raged at him: *What is this? Mercy? Compassion?* A strong man did not bow to such emotions. He had no duty to save Osgan from the results of his own dissipation. Better for the Empire that the man just vanished away, making room for someone who would be better at his job.

*I am tainted.* Thalric had seen too much, done too much. He had been born a true Wasp, but now he'd become some kind of halfbreed of the mind.

He turned back to the waiting automotive. 'Captain Marger,' he announced, 'one more for the journey.'

Marger hesitated over that, taking in the sight of Osgan. 'I wouldn't advise it,' he said. 'We'll be short of space and supplies.'

'Comfort is never a soldier's companion, and there are enough way stations to supply us.' Thalric felt as though he and Marger were facing up to each other in duel, looking for the other's weak points. 'This is Lieutenant Osgan and he's on my staff.'

Still, Marger was unhappy with the idea. 'This is a Rekef operation and he's no agent.'

'We already know our paths will be diverging, once we reach the city,' Thalric said reasonably. 'It will make more sense for me to have Osgan there with me than to have to call on you for assistance.' He held Marger's gaze, waiting to see if the man would stand firm, or fall back.

The final answer was a shrug, the man's easy acceptance reasserting itself. There had been a gleam in there, of Rekef steel, but this was not a battlefield Marger would choose to fight on.

'Your call,' he said again, then, 'We're just about loaded. Are you and your . . . staff ready to move out?'

Many Wasps wondered why Fly-kinden, who had the sky as their plaything, chose to live so much of their time underground. On the surface Shalk appeared merely a collection of little huts and mounds almost lost amid the sweep of the surrounding hills, and only anchored by the bulk of an Imperial garrison's barracks. Thalric knew that most of the town lay beneath, in a complex of narrow tunnels and broad chambers that were impossible to navigate unless one was both tiny and airborne. Military tacticians had often speculated on the difficulties of forcing an Imperial presence on the Fly-kinden, in the unlikely event that they decided to resist one. It would certainly be possible, but drastic measures would be called for and Thalric, having heard of the gas-weapon disastrously employed at Szar, thought it a good thing that the Shalken and their ilk were proving so compliant. Nobody would profit from a rebellion here.

Of course the Fly town itself was only half of it. Beyond the hills the land suddenly stopped and dropped, so the anatomy of the earth he stood on was exposed in stratified layers where the ground had simply fallen away as a result of some ancient cataclysm. It had since become the Empire's largest quarry and mining complex, with several thousand slaves working there day in and day out. If the insurrection had allowed these toiling wretches any reprieve, that was well and truly over now.

After they had docked their automotive at the garrison's stables, Thalric took Marger aside.

'Find me transport to Forest Alim from Shalk End,' he requested. 'We'll take the river from there to Khanaphes.'

'Shalk End?' Marger said. That meant the Shalk below them, the quarry and its slaves. It was certainly possible to shortcut to the plain below by descending the face of the mine workings, but not usual. 'Is there something I should know?'

*If you were meant to know, you'd already have been told*, Thalric thought, still with assassins in mind. 'I like a bit of variety, Captain,' he said. 'Besides, wouldn't you like to see the Empire's largest quarry in operation?'

Marger shrugged, predictably. 'I'll go lean on the foreman,' he replied.

Thalric nodded. 'Osgan, go find the Consortium and get enough supplies for a tenday for the six of us.'

The man started on hearing his name and seemed to wrestle with the words before agreeing.

'Good,' Thalric nodded. 'The rest of you, wait by the machine until we're ready.' He smiled at the Beetle and two Wasps and they regarded him cautiously. They had none of them decided precisely what he was, and he wondered what they might have already heard.

*Which leaves me at liberty in Shalk*. But he would have to be quick. No doubt Marger would be prompt enough in doing his job.

The garrison at Shalk was unusual at the best of times, but even more unsettled now since the insurrection. Its purpose had always been to safeguard the mines and the quarry, rather than to intimidate a naturally obsequious populace. The current military personnel were all new, the traitorous old guard having been rooted out or fled, or else died on the field before Tyrshaan. The staff, though, the underlings who kept everything running, were the same old faces. For most such garrisons they dragged Auxillians from halfway across the Empire, putting them among foreigners to limit any chance of betrayal.

The Shalken themselves were an exception, however. Where most other kinden were unwilling partners, slaves of the Empire with their families and home cities held hostage for their good behaviour, Flies and Beetle-kinden had proved willing subjects of the crown since the Empire's early days. The halls of the Shalken garrison were busy with diminutive forms – in the air and on the ground – of cleaners, messengers, scribes and servants. They went about their duties deftly, with the eternal pragmatism of their kind.

Thalric sought out the records office, where messages came in either for filing or passing on. The Fly-kinden had long made Shalk the South-Empire's great message hub, which had been difficult while the traitor governors divided up the South between them. Now everything was returning to business as usual, and the same faces were to be found at the same desks. All except one.

It had been a lucky piece of research, but Thalric liked to keep in touch with his old friends.

He spotted the man quickly, just another Fly-kinden sorting papers in a pool of sunlight under a window. Thalric made his way behind the man's desk, appearing to peruse a rack of scrolls thoughtfully, and in a low voice murmured, 'A strange place to find a lieutenant of the Rekef, one might think.'

The Fly did not pause in his work, did not even twitch. 'If one thought that, one might wonder whether it was common knowledge,' he said, as if speaking to the ledger he was marking.

'Not yet,' Thalric replied, and he heard the smallest sigh.

'Some of us fall despite our best endeavours, some of us rise despite our tribulations,' the Fly observed. 'For instance, I saw your name included on an execution list, shortly before I decided to retire.'

'You don't ever retire from the Rekef, te Berro.'

'No, they retire you instead.' Thalric heard the misery in te Berro's voice. 'Might one ask how it is that a dead man is now Regent of the Empire? I've followed your career with interest.'

*Of course you have.* For te Berro was a Rekef man, and that training did not sit idle. Even here, in hiding, he had clearly put himself in a position to gather information, even if he was doing so only for himself. It reminded Thalric of his own behaviour in occupied Tharn, when he had been acting as Stenwold's agent. Old habits like that didn't die.

'You must have jumped ship from Reiner's people, if you got to see that list,' Thalric noted.

'Oh, I was on the good ship Maxin a while previously. But then a high-up operation went sour and I judged it a good time to vanish. And now it appears I didn't vanish well enough.'

'With all the changes at the capital, they haven't even started cleaning house properly,' Thalric reassured him. 'Still, it's only a matter of time. I hear Solarno is nice, this time of year. Perhaps you're due for a holiday, assuming they don't hear about you shortly.'

Another sigh. 'What do you want, Thalric?'

'Information. There was an attempt on my life in Tyrshaan. What was the follow up?'

'They strung up three of Governor Vargen's men within days. Case closed.'

Thalric stifled a chuckle. 'And after that?'

'There's a very definite kind of . . . silence from that direction.'

Thalric nodded, satisfied. It meant that General Brugan

had matters properly in hand. After public executions that would reassure the real wrongdoers, the Rekef would start their own covert investigation. It was a way of doing things he had used himself often enough.

'Anything else?' he asked, as if still talking to the racking. 'Don't hold out on me, now.'

'Everything's still upside down here in the South-Empire,' te Berro complained. 'Reliable news is hard to come by. They're still purging Tyrshaan.'

'Who hates me that much, te Berro?'

The Fly made an amused noise. 'Grief, man, who doesn't? They hate the Empress? They hate you. They worked for General Reiner? They hate you. They're just loyal Imperial citizens who remember too much about the war . . .'

'I get the message.' Thalric gritted his teeth, hearing again the truth that Osgan had already given him. *I am now a foreigner in my own country.*

'Well, we make good messengers.' The Fly appeared at Thalric's elbow and started filing scrolls with care. 'Not that I've got anything against reunions, but you're a dangerous man to be around. What happens now?'

The image came to Thalric of a rooftop garden in Myna, of te Berro saving his life with a well-placed arrow. 'I go south and I advise you to get yourself outside the Empire's borders while they change the guard. Maybe, when the next big war looms, they'll look to their old agents, especially those who have been making a life for themselves meanwhile in Solarno or the Lowlands. Until then, I'd keep my head well down, if I were you.'

Still not looking at him, te Berro nodded. 'A holiday on the Exalsee?' he mused. 'I think I've earned it.'

They were winched down the face of the Shalk quarry among descending bundles of mining supplies and a barrel of firepowder charges. The Empire's slaves crawled across the scaffolded rock-face, cutting and measuring, hacking and breaking. There was a scattering of Fly-kinden artificers there for the technical work but the rest were imported labour – Flies were physically and temperamentally unsuited to such hard toil. Instead, Shalk had inherited hundreds of the Empire's most robust. There were Ant-kinden and Beetles, prisoners from Szar and Myna, and everywhere the vast, lumbering shapes of the Mole Crickets. Almost half the adult population of Least Delve had been herded here after the Empire had taken the place twenty years ago. They were not a numerous people but their skill with stone was such that they were ruthlessly put under the whip wherever they were found. Back home at the Delve, their families – especially the children who lacked the Art to simply slip away into the earth – were closely held as strict surety for their parents' continued industry.

The air was so thick with dust that Thalric's party was forced to breathe through cloth. They observed the quarry's vertiginous workings through goggles that had to be cleaned and cleaned again to stop them silting over, and the air was painfully dry. Work in mines and quarries was the Empire's rod for its worst offenders, the final destination of those whose luck had entirely expired. Here, sharing the forced labour of the Mole Crickets, were the deserters, the prisoners of war, the traitors whose physical strength would now serve the Empire they had betrayed until it gave out on them and they died.

Thalric, surveying all this as their lift jerked and shuddered its way downwards, thought, *I, too, could have been here, so easily.* Certainly there were enough other Wasp-kinden toiling at the cliff face.

At the foot of the descent there was the pit, where the quarry had been extended further into the earth. The entire cliff face above was riddled with blast-holes and mineshafts. There had been a web of gold here once, long since exhausted, but now they had found rich seams of iron. Overlooking the quarry itself stood a squat, brooding ziggurat that housed more of the Shalk garrison, with the workers' pitiful huts corralled all around it.

Marger had been conscientious in his arrangements. There was a Slave Corps expedition setting out that was already waiting for them before the garrison. They would travel along the line of the ridge, stopping at each spring and waterhole to trade with the desert Scorpions, until they reached the river and the green edge of Forest Alim. There the slavers and Thalric's expedition would part company.

Thalric found surprisingly little curiosity in himself about his destination or his journey, even about the Lowlanders he was heading off to spy on. *All that matters is that I'm moving further away.* He felt the Empress as a constant pressure in the back of his mind, but he was now putting the miles between them, and there must come a point where her presence would fade.

*You will come back to me*, she had said. He shuddered, successfully hiding it in the rocking motion as the crude lift touched down. Marger and his people unloaded their supplies, and Thalric automatically shouldered a crate himself, without even thinking of his elevated position. When he realized, halfway across the quarry-pit and into the shadow of the garrison, he smiled to himself. *O Regent, see how I escape you.*

# Twelve

The river Jamail was the child of the slanting sheets of rain that fell daily against the Morgen Range, the clouds emptying themselves over the dense forest and denying the arid Nem water and life. From a hundred channels deep inside the forest, coalescing from a forest floor that in the wettest seasons was actually submerged, arose the snaking Jamail that began its long, looping progress south, out of the woodland, cutting its course through the dry lands and bringing fragile abundance to those who claimed its banks. From Alim, the logging town up against the forest's petering edge, all the way downriver to the marsh delta, extended the Dominion of Khanaphes, as it had done since time immemorial.

Thalric had expected something rough from Alim. Researches had told him that, as the furthest-flung outpost of Khanaphir territory, it served as nothing more than a port for forest timber. He had expected only a collection of wooden huts and a pier, and was therefore surprised.

Forest Alim was dominated by what he first assumed was a fortress, but then revised as a fortified palace. It was ancient, partly overgrown by the forest's resurgence, looming over the waters from the river's far side. Beyond the wall, as the slavers approached, he caught occasional glimpses of colonnades and ornamented rooftops. A stone pier jutted into the young river, dominated by a great, broad barge half loaded with timber, while half a dozen smaller vessels huddled in its lee.

The slavers were not interested in this place: it was simply the point where they would turn around and head back to Shalk. As Thalric's band approached carefully, he noticed a little patchwork of fields on the near side of the river, divided and subdivided by irrigation dykes excavated outward from the river itself. The men and women working in the fields were solid, bald-headed Beetle-kinden and paid them no notice whatsoever. In the face of their stoic labouring, which seemed to admit nothing of time or progress, Thalric felt his mission, the entire Empire, being subtly dismissed. *You are not important to us*, they were saying. *We shall work here and you shall pass, and we shall continue on.*

Outside the walled palace, which Thalric guessed would house the garrison and administration from distant Khanaphes, Forest Alim consisted of a cluster of warehouses and a sawmill. Even these buildings were stone-walled, however, converted to their present purpose from whatever ancient rites they had been built for. Thalric had taken a quick look into the sawmill, where he watched men slicing trees into planks by hand, working with huge two-man saws, or with foot-powered circular blades. By Imperial standards it was laughable, but they worked fast and with no sign of tiring.

Marger, and the two Wasps in his team, had gone to enquire about securing passage downriver, and Thalric was left hoping that he would find something faster than that ponderous barge. Aside from a scattering of fishing boats, the only vessel of any stature was a narrow, open craft, piled with cushions at one end to seat a privileged passenger, and equipped with eight oars and a single mast. It had been left unattended, as though the simple status of its owner was sufficient to see off any unwanted attention. Thalric was even considering whether it might be worth making off with, if nothing else presented itself.

'You know, for a logging town, they don't seem to fell many trees,' observed the Beetle-kinden Rekef man, who had been staring into the forest for some time. Their seat near the quay gave them a good view of the darkness between the tree trunks.

Thalric glanced at him curiously and the prompt died on his lips as he saw it – so obvious that it had escaped notice. 'No stumps,' he concurred. 'No cut trees at all. Not the sound of an axe, nothing beyond the sawmill.'

The Beetle nodded. His name was Corolly Vastern and he was old enough to have been a veteran before the Twelve-year War. He was strong, though, with his kind's long-reaching endurance. His face settled into a slight smile, calculated from long practice to dispel any Wasp ire towards an inferior race. 'I've been watching for a while, and all the wood comes from deeper in. These Beetles've got it worked out so they don't even need to cut their own.'

There was a steady trickle of outsiders heading into Alim. They were not Khanaphir but men and women with skin the rich colour of teak. Some kind of long-limbed, loping Ant-kinden, they appeared bearing wood. Chains of them bore whole trees aloft out of the forest, from who knew what distance, or floated them down the river towards the sawmill. Thalric saw Khanaphir scribes carefully noting the arrival of each group on their scrolls. No money changed hands and he wondered if these forest Ants were slaves of Khanaphes in some way. It occurred to him belatedly – and it oddly disturbed him – that he had no idea at all what precise kinden these forest-dwellers were. They were at the borders of the Empire, but the forest of the Alim was an utter unknown. Imperial expansion had been so rapid that their own scouts had barely been able to keep track of it.

Osgan, lying back, began to snore softly, though for once it was not due to drink – or not entirely. Thalric had been keeping an eye on him, and the man had barely taken a sip at his hip-flask. It was the unaccustomed pace that had worn him out.

'Major Thalric . . .' Corolly began, in a subtly different tone.

'I know,' Thalric interrupted. 'The Khanaphir sitting over there, he's been watching us for almost twenty minutes now. Maybe it's just that the locals are curious.'

'Don't know about that,' Corolly muttered. 'In fact, that's the one thing they aren't. Six men of the Empire turn up on their doorstep, and nobody even turns a head to look. Except him.'

'Well, then,' said Thalric, 'let's force the matter, shall we? I'll go and ask some directions of a local.'

'Directions?' the Beetle said, a tilt of his head indicating that the only meaningful directions here were up the river or down.

'Something similar.' Thalric stood up, casting his eyes over the quay again. They were loading the barge with more planks, teams of Khanaphir labourers sweating and hauling as they sang a low, rhythmic tune with words he could not follow. He sauntered over towards the watcher, expecting the man to suddenly find urgent business elsewhere. Instead he stood his ground, so Thalric had a chance to examine him properly. He was not young, although these Khanaphir were difficult to age, what with their bald scalps and dark, sun-creased faces. He wore a white robe that fell from one shoulder, leaving half of his chest bare. Thalric noted a respectable quantity of gold: rings, amulets, pendants, even gold tassels on his robes. At Thalric's approach, he only nodded politely.

'Excuse me,' Thalric said. 'I don't suppose you know who owns that boat over there?'

The man smiled at him as if he had been handed a compliment. 'Of course I do, Honoured Foreigner, for it is mine.'

Caught off balance, Thalric blinked. 'Then you are . . .'

'O stranger, I have been waiting here for you to ask me to carry you to Khanaphes. If your need is so great, there was no need to be reticent.'

'How did you know?' Thalric asked, through gritted teeth. His agent's senses were abruptly alert, feeling great wheels moving invisibly around him. The spy in him was compromised, his mission open knowledge. *Escape. Fall back.* Except there was no falling back here, because the mission had not even started.

The old man's smile remained the same faintly puzzled piece of politeness as before, as if Thalric's tension had passed him by unremarked. 'Where else would a party of foreigners of such distinction wish to go?' he asked. Trying to read the man's face was exactly like trying to read a good spy, a spy who might or might not be working on the right side.

'My name is Akneth, and I am a gatherer of taxes for the Masters of Khanaphes. If you would do me the honour, O Foreigner, of voyaging upon my ship, then I will be ready to cast off in the morning.' The old man had been sitting on a mooring post, and now pushed himself to his feet with a grunt suggesting some effort. Hearing it, Thalric added another ten years to his estimated age. 'I would be glad of the company,' Akneth continued, then made a short bow, one hand pressed briefly to his stomach. Thalric managed a nod in return but, in the face of that patiently avuncular smile, all of his instincts were clamouring for him to draw his sword.

'Well,' he said, as he rejoined Corolly, 'we have secured our passage downriver.'

'So what is he?'

'Oh, he's a spy,' replied Thalric. 'Probably not a professional, but he's a government man who's keen to know what the armed outlanders are doing here.'

'Lucky for us he came along just now,' said the Beetle, but with a noticeable stress on the first word.

'Tax gatherers must be passing up and down this river

all the time,' observed Thalric, a little hollowly. 'It's just coincidence.'

*Of course, it's just coincidence.* He made himself sit down calmly beside the drowsing Osgan, as if he couldn't care less. Inside, his instincts were shouting at him: *He knew. He already knew. He was waiting.*

They kept him in darkness.

It had now been three tendays since they caught him, that was his best guess. Denied the sun, the moon and stars, awareness of time slipped away from him. He tried counting meals, but they fed him unreliably. He slept only fitfully, always startled to wakefulness every time the guards tramped overhead.

They had brought him to Capitas in chains, shoulder to shoulder with a gang of slaves. He, who had enslaved hundreds of wretches while he was in the Corps, now tasted the irony in blood and sweat. They had even displayed him in Armour Square, for the good people of Capitas to jeer at his deformities. Then they had cast him down here.

His name was Hrathen. It was about the only thing they had not taken from him, and they had left it because it was of no earthly use. A Wasp name, from his mother.

The bolts rattled overhead. These were the deep cells situated directly beneath the Imperial garrison. You had to be distinctly *bad* to end up here, but being Rekef and biting the hand that fed you was a good enough qualification. They had made sure his guards knew he had once been Rekef, as well as Slave Corps. It was rare that the ordinary army soldiers got to take out their fear and hatred on a real live Rekef, so Hrathen was stiff with the bruises.

He did not miss the light, the air, the freedom, so much as he missed the game. When he had been what he had once been, standing between his mother's people and his father's, he had been unique. He had been a servant beyond the reach of his master. He had been part of the game, and he missed the thrill of it more than he ever missed the sun.

He had already turned his head away before the searing beam of light lanced from the opened hatch above. He flexed his arms, his hands, against the leather bindings that had been his constant companions since they threw him down here. He possessed killing hands, so they would take no chances. Still, he constantly flexed and strained, working against the tension of his bonds to keep himself strong. He had been taught to believe in opportunity. His father's people were strong believers in such.

He heard a whir of wings as two guards dropped down beside him.

'This him?' one asked. 'Ugly bastard, isn't he?'

'Just get the harness on him. Hey, halfbreed, you're going places.'

Hrathen squinted at the pair. After all the pitch dark even the glow of lanternlight from above seemed glaring, but he had the eyes for it: eyes bred for the fierce desert. He met the gaze of the first guard, and saw him take a step back without wanting to.

'Oi, enough!' The second man shoved a fist into his back and Hrathen grunted. He was tough all over, though: leathery skin and solid bones that had taken worse.

They put a strap around him, under the armpits, and two men above began hauling him up with much complaining. Once they had him up top, which meant a corridor buried deep beneath the cellars of the garrison, they stepped back from him.

'Big bastard, isn't he?' the first guard remarked, noticing how Hrathen topped them all by a head. The prisoner rolled his shoulders, eyes still half closed against the light. Now he was up and on his feet they kept their distance, firmly bound as he was. The sight of their uncertainty brought back some of his much-abused pride. *Let them come close, I'll put my teeth in them.* He obligingly bared his tusks at them, that motley snaggle of jutting fangs that had worn scars into his lips.

'Just move him out. He's not our problem any more,' urged one of the guards. A spear-butt jabbed at his back and he stepped briskly forward, almost leading the way. He made his stride, his demeanour, offer no admission of captivity. *You cannot cage what I am.*

They led him up two levels until he could see sunlight and sky through a window. Further still they led him upwards. Servants stopped and stared when they saw him, richly dressed courtiers shied away from him. He leered lasciviously at every woman he saw. After all, if he was going to be executed, he had nothing more to lose. The guards kept him moving, embarrassed at the attention.

He had lost track of where they were now. Suddenly the corridors became nearly empty, with only guards and more guards to mark his passing. Hrathen began to reconsider his immediate fate. Any execution would occur publicly, or they might decide to torture him instead – though he had not imagined he knew anything worth ripping out of him by such methods.

*Perhaps some scholar wants to anatomize me.* He was not such a fool as to think that he could withstand torture for ever, or even for very long. The Rekef were very good at it, and possessed all the latest machinery to help them. Over the years, Hrathen had learned a few tricks to stave off pain, but they had their limits. He would give his tormentors a run for their money but, as with most hunts, the end was predetermined.

They hauled him into a side office that he thought maybe he should recognize. A moment later it caught up with him: it was a spymaster's den, the desk and papers and scrolls and carefully ordered documents. The guards jabbed him in the back of the knee until he knelt on the floor, and then they retreated to the edges of the room. He kept his head lowered, but from the corner of his eye he kept watching. *If only my mother had given me better wings.*

'Well now,' he heard a voice, 'what kind of monster have we here? My sources were sparing in the details, when I thought they exaggerated.' Boots passed within Hrathen's range of vision, and then a man sat himself at the desk. He was a strong-framed Wasp-kinden, his hair just starting to turn grey and his eyes the colour of water and steel. He studied Hrathen with fascination: after all, halfbreeds of Scorpion and Wasp were not that common. Hrathen had inherited his Scorpion father's bulk, his tusks, his small, yellow eyes and waxy skin. Otherwise, he had features like a Wasp, disfigured by the snaggle of teeth and the narrow eyes. His captivity had endowed his heavy jaw with a tangle of beard, and his scalp sprouted patchy tufts of hair that he was itching to have cropped. His hands were his finest feature, but they had bound them palm-to-palm to smother his sting, and then tied together the thumb and forefinger claws as well.

'Do you know why you were arrested, Hrathen?' his inquisitor asked.

Hrathen looked straight back at him. 'Well, if you don't,' he said, 'can I go now?'

A slight smile quirked the man's mouth, then one of the guards kicked Hrathen in the side hard enough to send him sprawling, cracking his head against the stone flags.

The man behind the desk sighed. 'You were once a Rekef agent, as well as a captain in the Slave Corps. That's a heady rank for a halfbreed, but the slavers are a law unto themselves. You were given responsibilities by the Rekef, which you did not take seriously. Instead you indulged yourself. It is believed that you let yourself . . . go native.'

Hrathen struggled back into a kneeling position, saying nothing.

'It happens, of course. Officers who must work closely with the Auxillians, especially the more savage types, have to make adjustments. Men who are assigned to the Hornetkinden, or the Scorpions, say, must develop within themselves a commensurate savagery, just to ensure the willing respect of their men. That is well known, but when such men begin to act against Imperial interests, in favouring the lesser race, then we step in. Particularly if such men are also Rekef.'

Hrathen tried to shrug. 'What do you want?' he demanded.

'What do *you* want?' the man asked him. 'To go back to your desert and vanish? Or would you serve us once more, if the Rekef found a use for you?'

All through the dark hours, Hrathen had been clinging to one thought: *They have not killed me yet.* Behind that lay another thought, seemingly the only explanation: *I am of use to them.* He was not a man endowed with so many talents that he could not immediately see why. In all the Empire there could not be many individuals who knew the Scorpion-kinden as well as he did.

'Terms?' he enquired.

'Do you believe that I can harm you?' the man asked. 'Do you realize that I have at my disposal all that man has ever discovered of pain and persuasion?'

'I believe it of the Rekef,' Hrathen agreed, staring the man in the eyes.

The half-smile had reappeared. 'I *am* the Rekef,' the Wasp announced softly, holding Hrathen's gaze as he said it. The conviction evident in his eyes was absolute. 'I am Lord General Brugan of the Rekef and there is nowhere you could go that would prove far enough to escape my personal wrath. As you fear the Rekef, then so fear me.'

Hrathen felt a cold shiver run through him despite himself. The words had been uttered quietly, understated, for Brugan was a man who did not need to shout. Still, there was more in that shiver than just fear. *A* general *of the Rekef? And* the *General, if I hear right. What does he want with* me*?* Because underneath it all, despite the tainted blood and the sliding loyalties, Hrathen was still Rekef. He was Rekef through and through because it was the best game in the world – invitation only.

'Tell me about the Scorpion-kinden,' Brugan instructed.

Hrathen grinned despite himself, displaying a nightmare of bristling teeth.

'So you're a tax gatherer?' Thalric began.

'I have that honour,' the old man replied. Akneth was reclining on his cushions beneath a tautly fastened awning that screened out the sun. His six guests now occupied the somewhat cramped section of deck between himself and the labouring oarsmen.

'You don't seem to be interested in collecting any taxes,' Thalric suggested, exchanging a glance with Marger. They were both of a mind that this much-needed offer of transport was all too convenient.

'One collects the taxes during the journey upriver,' Akneth explained. 'If one then collected them downriver also, I daresay there would be complaints.' It was impossible to tell from his expression whether this was a joke.

*A subtle people, these Khanaphir*, Thalric thought. *It's more like talking to a Spider-kinden than a Beetle*. He felt as if Akneth was speaking two languages at once, and that Thalric could only understand one of them.

'Surely anyone who wished could just watch out for your ship on the return journey and rob it,' Marger put in. Aside from the eight oarsmen, and a young girl who had served them grapes and wine, the old tax-collector travelled alone.

Akneth put on a shocked expression. 'But who would dare defy the Masters of Khanaphes?' he asked. 'To raise a hand against me is to raise a hand against them, too.'

*He means it*, Thalric decided. It would have been the work of a moment for them to kill Akneth and his people, and seize the boat. They were trained Wasp soldiers, even Osgan – a flurry of sting-shot and it would be over.

Akneth met his gaze with that ever-present smile, mock puzzlement, polite curiosity, utter self-assurance.

The banks of the Jamail were lined with fields irrigated from the river. They were dotted with villages, and each village, amongst its reed huts that looked flimsy enough to blow away in the wind, boasted at least one structure of stone. It seemed to Thalric that these were the markers to show where original villages had stood centuries before, and around them other buildings had come and gone, but the village itself had lived on.

They had passed the town of Zafir the day before, with its twin walled fortresses situated on either side of the river, joined by a spanning arch that rose high above their ship's mast. The higher reaches of the twin forts had been decorated with statues, although Thalric had not been able to discern, from midstream, what they might represent. He had leant in to Corolly, who had been staring up at the bridge with his mouth half open.

'Could we make the likes of that?' he asked.

'We could bridge this river,' the Beetle artificer replied defensively. It was not the same thing and he knew it.

'What do you want to know?' Hrathen asked.

'Think of me as a wide-eyed scholar eager for knowledge,' General Brugan said. 'Indulge me.'

*So you can see how fondly I still hold them,* Hrathen decided. *Well, scholar, a lecture you shall have.*

'We divide the Scorpion-kinden we have met so far into two,' he began, 'the Aktaian Scorpions who live in the Dryclaw desert, south of the West-Empire, and the Nemian who live in the Nem south of the East-Empire.'

Brugan nodded, showing neither interest nor boredom.

'The Scorpions of the Dryclaw have dealt with civilized nations for a long time. They have preyed on the eastern edge of the Lowlands and the Silk Road, and they have traded with and been employed by the Spiderlands since time immemorial. They have also worked with our Slave Corps for two generations.'

'In which capacity you yourself were introduced to them,' Brugan noted.

'Indeed.' A pause. Brugan nodded his head for him to continue. 'Well,' Hrathen went on slowly, 'their way of life revolves around others now, whether it is through their raiding or their slaving. Between the Empire and the Spiders, they work for the highest bidder and take whatever they can.'

'Including Imperial supplies,' Brugan remarked. 'Tell me, Captain Hrathen, did you fall from the path of duty by action or inaction? Not that the difference is material.'

Hrathen scowled before he could stop himself. 'You . . . do not understand what it is like, to live amongst them.'

'So tell me.'

'Strength,' Hrathen explained. 'Power is all they value – the power of the arm's reach. If I had cried foul when they took the supplies and killed the men, they would have turned on me. To run with them, you must live as they do, believe as they do.' Brugan was now staring at him as though he was something in a menagerie, but he pressed on. 'But if you can run faster than they, kill more swiftly, carry more spoils, care less, dare more, then they will welcome you in and make you theirs, without care for either kinden or blood. Any man may be free, amongst the Scorpion-kinden, if he is a greater monster than they are.' He paused.

Brugan's smile showed delicate distaste. 'Are you such a monster?' he asked softly.

*Well, what does he expect me to say?* 'Look at me, sir,' Hrathen said. 'I am the Empire's monster, but I am a monster.'

'Tell me about the *other* Scorpions,' Brugan prompted.

'They are . . . not so used to civilized nations,' replied Hrathen. 'The tribes of the Nem call themselves "the Many" and, unlike the Dryclaw Scorpions, they are unified, most of the time, under a single warlord – whoever is the strongest of the strong, both in mind and body. They are not so nomadic as the Aktaian, either. The Nem had cities once, before it dried up. There are ruins in the mid-desert, beyond the fringes, and the Many dwell in some of them, wherever the wells still give water. They even raise some crops there – or at least their slaves do. There are cities in the deep desert, too, but even the Many do not dwell there. The reasons for that are . . . confused. The desert of the Nem has never been mapped. The Imperial scouts never penetrated it. It is said to contain . . . unusual threats.'

'Would you venture amongst the Nem, if I asked you?' Brugan said.

'Yes.'

'Would you hold the Empire in your heart, even so? Look at me as you answer.'

Hrathen met his eyes, but the answer was long in coming. 'I am Empire,' he replied. 'I am Rekef. I shall do what is needed to fulfil your tasks, but I must do it in my own way. It may be that this seems to harm the Empire, but I know the Scorpion-kinden, of whatever tribe, and I know how to deal with them. General, will you trust my judgement?'

'Why else would I propose to send you?'

'Then give me men and supplies, and perhaps, as my second, an officer you are not overly attached to. With that I shall go to the Nem and accomplish whatever you wish.'

Brugan smiled widely then, his teeth very white. 'I shall give you soldiers, and artificers. I shall give you siege engines and better weapons than the Many of Nem will ever have held. I shall give you all of this, Hrathen, and for one purpose only.' Abruptly he was on his feet and walking round the desk. There was a knife in his hand.

Hrathen knelt very still. The knife flicked once, twice, and the bindings about Hrathen's hands and arms were severed and he hissed in pain as his long-constrained joints were shocked into motion.

'I shall send you now into the desert to destroy a city: to have your precious Scorpions shatter its walls and slay its people and feast in their halls. I give the Many of Nem the city of Khanaphes to play with. I buy them with that coin. Do you understand me?'

He was still smiling, and Hrathen matched his grin despite the pain, his fangs bristling in delight.

'General,' he said, 'I do.'

*Part Three*

# The Sacred City

# Thirteen

Accius of Vek made sure that he was one of the first to reach the quayside. It would not do for the city-state of Vek to be thought fearful of these foreign lands. Inside, he *was* fearful: no Vekken had ever travelled so far, unless perhaps some luckless slave sold to the Spiderlands. He had no clear idea of precisely where he was. They were off all Vek's maps.

At the rail of the ship stood his brother Malius, watching over him. Only the contact of that one other mind gave him strength. Around him was a seething, babbling bustle, the unscripted chaos of this Beetle-kinden city. Numberless hordes of the locals, bald and indistinguishable, were heading in all directions, jostling and pushing, carrying loads and setting them down, meeting and talking. The air was full of it. Accius was amazed that anybody could hear anybody, that all those thronging words did not choke the whole dockside with their din.

*I wish we were in Vek,* he thought.

*I know,* came Malius's answering thought. *I too, but we have our orders.*

Accius stood by the gangplank, a hand on his sword-hilt, feeling the weight of the chainmail beneath his tunic. It was not precisely concealed, for the sleeves and the hem of it extended beyond his civilian garment. The latter was his concession to being polite, and beyond that he would not go. He was a soldier. *Yet they have made me an ambassador.* It was an empty title, but the Beetles of Collegium were mad and an ambassador was what they wanted. Somewhere in Vek was Collegium's own ambassador, being treated civilly, enjoying the tranquil, industrious quiet of a properly ordered city-state. Accius envied him.

The Beetle woman in charge was talking to her Fly-kinden servant now, as locals hauled down all the baggage that Beetles seemingly needed to travel with. Accius had added such an excess to the long list of things he did not understand. They were so slow, so clumsy; they loaded themselves with such unnecessary clutter, physically and mentally. Yet their journey across so many miles had been so deftly handled, with barely a hitch. They took everything in their stride, where an Ant would call a halt and regroup.

*They have many dangerous qualities, our enemies.*

*True*, came Malius's instant response. *Most especially their way of making friends.*

The Collegiates were seeking allies here, it was plain, even though Collegium already had so many. It was crystal-clear in the minds of Accius and Malius that there would come an attack on Vek sooner or later. Vek and Collegium were enemies and, inevitably, enemies fought. All the confusing words of Stenwold Maker and his kind could not change the way the world worked.

*Can we stand against them, with the Sarnesh, with their other allies?* The future was a sword hanging over the city of Vek. When Accius thought of his city, he felt his heart twist at its beauty, its order, its solitary vulnerability. *Vek must be saved.* To save Vek they must dispense with its enemies, and to dispense with its enemies they must strike. All military theory taught that the attacker, by choosing the time and place of assault, gained key advantages. Vek must be saved, so Collegium must be defeated. The theory was sound.

*But the theory,* came Malius's dry whisper, *does not take account of this.* His mind-touch took in the writhing chaos that was the docks of Khanaphes. It was only his company that steadied Accius, that allowed him to stand here surrounded by these hordes of chattering *others* without drawing his sword.

The other Collegiates were disembarking now. There was the thin old man, the fat man, and the reserved woman who seemed the most clever and potentially dangerous. In her quiet, focused way there was a touch of the Ant about her, Accius decided. The other two seemed mere fools, but it was so difficult to read these people. Their faces and their voices were loud, but their minds silent. They were deceitful, hiding a hundred contradictory thoughts behind their constantly jabbering exteriors. *Real people are honest and truthful.* To go like this, amongst foreigners, was the ultimate sacrifice for an Ant-kinden to make.

*And we are proud to make it*, he and Malius chorused exactly together. It made Accius smile inwardly.

*Brother, there are soldiers*, came the brief warning, and his sword was drawn by instinct. He saw the Maker woman, the expedition leader, turn towards him, stepping back. Her hand was also to her sword-hilt, although she did not seem to have realized it. Accius ignored her, knowing that Malius was watching out for treachery. Instead he stared at the bewildering crowd. *How many? How close?*

*A score. They are on you now.* Even as the warning reached him, he saw the soldiers pushing through the crowd. They had big shields like tapering ovals that were covered with a shiny brown carapace, and edged with gold. They wore armour, hauberks of gilded scales, greaves and tall helms. They had spears in their hands, and swords with leaf-shaped blades at their belts. Everything was chased and trimmed with precious metals, and they had elaborate gorgets about their necks embellished with turquoise and red stones, and more gold. They were an escort, Accius saw, for the old Beetle man in their midst.

*The locals are kept in good order here*, Malius noted, almost approving. Everyone had given the soldiers a wide berth. Work had stopped, everywhere labourers putting down their loads and waiting. The Maker woman glanced at her compatriots, had a quick word with the Fly-kinden teamster.

'Put your sword away,' she told Accius. 'What do you think you're doing?'

He regarded her. *Your time will come,* he silently admonished. *Do not think you can command the Vekken.* He felt Malius agree with him, but the words rang hollow even in his own mind. This was a show of force: the Khanaphir had arrived with weapons, with soldiers. One met a show of force with a show of force, or one retreated. These Beetles did not understand that.

'It's only an honour guard, a ceremonial display,' the Maker girl hissed. 'Look at them.'

*Their spears are real, as are their swords. The gold trimming does not mean that their armour is not functional, you stupid woman.* But he simply did not understand. A lot of people were staring at him now. Somehow, despite the fact that their minds were all so obstinately separated, some idea had travelled between them all, excluding his brother and himself. He sheathed his sword, though his training resisted fiercely. As he had so many times before, he wanted to shout at them, to rage at them. They would not hear, though, because they could not. He had spent whole evenings cursing the Maker woman and the others, as loud as he could, with Malius competing with him for the most apposite phrase. It was wasted – more, it was misconceived. She had got them here without any apparent difficulty, and he could not understand how she had managed it.

The aged Khanaphir was stepping forward. He wore a white robe that fell from one shoulder to mid-shin, reminding Accius uncomfortably of the Assemblers of Collegium. He was barefoot, but he wore a considerable amount of jewellery. Like the other locals he was bald, although he wore a thin gold band about his forehead, the ends of it spiralling together above his brow. To Accius's eyes he differed from all the rest only because he was clearly so old, his face lined and wrinkled.

'I give you greetings, ambassadors sent from our distant kinfolk,' he began. His voice was very quiet and yet clear. Everyone, locals and foreigners alike, had fallen completely silent. The sounds of the city beyond were now a distant tide surging behind him. 'The city of Khanaphes is seldom graced with such an honour as to meet more of our long-lost family. My name is Ethmet and I am privileged to be the First Minister of this city. On behalf of my Masters, I extend the full welcome of Khanaphes to you and all your people.'

The Maker woman stepped forward and said some words in response, the usual patter of meaningless pleasantries that Accius had heard before. They said so much that was unnecessary, these Beetles, or so much that defied interpretation to a poor Ant-kinden of Vek.

Ethmet, the First Minister, was making some offer of accommodation, which had apparently been accepted. Local porters were coming forward to take up the Beetles' baggage. Accius felt Malius, on board ship still, reach down to shoulder their own compact belongings. No doubt these local Beetles would understand privacy as little as their Collegiate cousins.

*Who are his Masters?* Accius wondered.

He felt Malius shrug. *More Beetles. No doubt we will meet them in time, instead of this functionary.*

*And then what? What does the King expect of us, here?*

*We only observe,* Malius replied, but he sounded uncertain. *The Collegiates have some purpose in coming here, and it can be no purpose friendly to Vek. Perhaps they seek military supplies or aid.* He looked about the crowded dockside, noticing there was a distinctly primitive feel to it. *Perhaps they seek expendable soldiers to send against us. They could plan to offset our superior troops with sheer numbers.*

It was Accius's turn to shrug. Everyone was now moving on. Malius brought up the rear, keeping watch over him as he forced himself to wade into the rushing torrent of people, seeking to keep pace with the Maker woman.

He reached out, felt Malius's presence. *I would go mad. How can they live like this?* The business of the docks was picking up again all around them, so many flapping mouths, so much wasted noise. *Have we made a mistake in coming here? Is this merely a diversion? Perhaps our comrades in Collegium have been killed by now. There may already be a war.*

Malius had no answer for him. Surrounded by his enemies, it was all Accius could do not to draw his blade again.

Everything was going well. Everything was falling apart.

*The Empire is here in Khanaphes.* Che recited the words to herself in a tone of urgency. That, she insisted, explained the shock she felt still resonating through her. *Thalric is in Khanaphes.* She did not know what to make of it. When last they had met, over a year ago now, he had been the big man in the Empire, consort of their new ruler. What would such a prominent figure be doing here?

*Concentrate on the Empire,* she urged herself. *Hypothesis one: the Empire is here because we are. Hypothesis two: the Empire has an independent reason for being interested in Khanaphes. Which leads us on to hypothesis three: We are here because the Empire is here, and Uncle Sten didn't trust me with the information. So when was I going to find out?*

She knew now that she had to seek out their people in Khanaphes as soon as possible. In light of this new discovery, it made sense that they must be Stenwold's agents as well. She had heard not a whisper that Stenwold had been plying his trade this far out, but then a lifetime in the intelligencing business had made him highly secretive, even with his own niece.

*Too cursed secret, Uncle Sten.*

But there was nothing she could do about it now. She pushed forward a little to walk alongside Ethmet, very conscious both of the Khanaphir honour guard around them, and the twitchy Vekken following just behind her.

'Excuse me, First Minister.'

'What may I provide you with, O Beautiful Foreigner?' he asked, with an elegant gesture of his spreading hands, from his stomach outwards. The mode of address put her off balance, for all that it was an obvious formality.

'Well . . . I was wondering, there are some scholars from Collegium in the city already. I was hoping to meet with them soon, just to catch up with their news.'

'Why, this has already been anticipated,' Ethmet replied, with a small smile. 'You shall see as much, when we reach your dwelling.' His manner should probably have reminded her of the magnates of Collegium, but he lacked their vigorous pomp and vanity. There was a quiet, self-contained authority to him, an assurance that put her more in mind of Spider-kinden Aristoi or the seers of the Moths. Here was a man who was absolutely sure of his place in the world.

She fell back until she was close enough to Berjek Gripshod and the others to converse with them. 'Well?' she said.

'Speechless,' Gripshod admitted. 'I mean, look at the place – so much stone and so large. How long did it take to piece all this together?' He shook his head. 'We were right to come here. I've never seen anything like it.'

'But *we* build in stone,' Che pointed out.

'Not like this,' he insisted. 'New buildings in Collegium are constructed of brick, or perhaps wood and plaster, at least above the first storey. It's only the grand old structures, the College and the Amphiophos, that are entirely of dressed stone. And that's only because they date from before the revolution. Our erstwhile masters preferred stone – and so, clearly, do the Khanaphir. And look – every piece is carved. Every piece.'

With all the rest on her mind, after seeing *Thalric* here in Khanaphes, she had not noticed it. Now the facades of the riverside warehouses and residences came into focus as rank upon rank of elaborate inscriptions. These carvings were hand-sized, square-ish, abstract, and everywhere, arranged in rows as high as a man could reach, on every surface of stone she could see. On some buildings, which looked older, they reached even higher, ascending all the way to the flat roofs. The myriad pictures swam before her eyes, marching for ever and for ever along every stone in an innumerable sequence.

'I've seen similar, and not just on the big mound-fort at Ostrander,' Berjek continued. 'I believe they tell stories, even histories, in pictorial sequence, but they're so stylized as to defy comprehension. So much to study here! Give me another twenty years!' He shook his head sadly. 'Give me a Moth-kinden's lifespan and I'd unravel it.'

Che felt suddenly dizzy, stumbling so that Berjek had to grab her elbow to keep her upright. For a moment she had seemed to perceive something more in the carvings. It was as though she had seen the message behind them, not just a series of drawings but as though words had been scribed there – jumbled words, nonsense words. She felt the world lurch for a moment, on the edge of some revelation that would still not come.

'Steady there,' Berjek murmured. 'The heat, I know. We all feel it.'

She shook her head, frightened at the sudden shift in perspective. The carvings were just carvings. She did not look at them, again, but focused ahead or glanced downwards. Yet still she was aware of them, pressing on every side.

'Look at the bridge,' Praeda Rakespear murmured suddenly. Khanaphes rose on both sides of the river, and a solitary bridge spanned the flow to link the divided city. It was a single soaring span resting on three pillars, and all faithfully inscribed with large and comprehensible representations of hunting and farming surrounded by the endless little pictograms continuing their never-ending procession.

'Architecturally remarkable,' Praeda declared, and Che knew her well enough to see how impressed she was beyond that cool exterior.

'Socially remarkable,' Berjek countered. 'Look how low it sits. Then consider the docks behind us and think about it.'

Che understood instantly. 'A ship couldn't pass beyond the bridge – not without taking down its mast at least.'

'And so they have total control of the river, simple as that,' Berjek agreed. 'There must be riverside docks on the other side. Anything coming in, anything going out, of any size – it must stop at Khanaphes.'

The city had grown strangely, its original plan still visible but blurred by time. They observed many great buildings, statues, columned arcades, palaces and gardens, and in between them were the smaller homes of the artisans and labourers of the city, huddled close together and yet always in sight of beauty. At first Che approved. How much better was this than the squalid stews of Helleron! Then she began to wonder if it had been intended that way at all. It seemed to her now – she could almost envisage it in her mind – that there had once been empty space between those grand edifices, and the people had taken over that space and made it their own, built houses and workshops where once the great lords had strolled. It was as though the architects had lost interest in their original design, abandoning it to those who would actually live there.

The mere sight of the gold-trimmed guards served to clear them a path ahead. The locals stepped aside into side streets, into doorways, and watched in silence. Che expected the fear that armed guards seemed to generate everywhere, even in Collegium, but there was none of it here, only a quiet respect.

'I am afraid we have received no emissaries from your people previously.' Ethmet clasped his hands apologetically. 'So we have had to borrow an embassy building for your use. I hope that we will have caused no offence through our choice.'

'Ah . . . I'm not sure I understand you. We weren't expecting you to have, what . . . *built* something for us . . .' Che replied uncertainly.

'Ah, no indeed, but we have played host to foreign potentates before, though none for some time . . . not until recently.' The guards stopped suddenly, and Che nearly crashed into the one in front of her. Ethmet had stopped simultaneously with them, of course, and his expression generously overlooked her clumsiness. 'We are now at the Place of Honoured Foreigners. Pray do me the honour of following, and I shall show you what we have managed to set aside for you.'

He stepped into a smaller side street overlooked on one side by three-storey facades marked out with small doors and smaller windows, and on the other by a looming blank wall whose expanse was pierced only by an arch. Ethmet stepped through this entrance, and Che and her company could only follow.

She bent to whisper to Trallo, 'Do you know what's going on now? Is this their usual welcome?'

The Fly's lips were pressed together and he shook his head.

They stepped out again into a world of sunlight and wonder and the sound of running water. Che's breath caught in her throat at the sight of it.

The Place of Honoured Foreigners was a broad open square, lined on three sides by great buildings, veritable palaces. There was a continuous band of rushes fringing the open space, interrupted only where little bridges crossed them to reach the steps of each palace, and where two archways gave access to the wider city beyond. In the centre was a pool, a marble-floored rectangle floored with an intricate mosaic that promised meaning and delivered nothing, just like the ubiquitous pictograms. Che could not stop herself from running over to stare into it. The water was clear as glass, no more than twelve inches deep. Tiny fish and water insects sculled across it, wholly oblivious to their audience. Benches of carved stone lined the pool's two long sides, and the quarters of the square around it were set with four crescents of green, tall grass and ferns.

Che shook her head. 'It's beautiful,' she said, forgetting diplomacy and just divulging what was in her mind.

'We are pleased that you find it so,' Ethmet said mildly. The academics were meanwhile staring about themselves like people in a dream. Only the two Vekken remained aloof, doubtless waiting for some trap to be sprung. Even the removal of the guards had not improved their mood.

'The larger arch, in the far wall, leads into the Place of Government and the Scriptora, where I and my fellow servants of our Masters dwell. Once you have had a chance to acclimatize yourselves, perhaps you would consent to visit us there. We would hold a banquet in your honour, if you would agree. For now, we have set aside this house to be your residence, while you are among us.' One of Ethmet's hands indicated a column-fronted building adjacent to the arch through which they had entered.

Che turned to look at it and she could not help giving a cry of dismay. As she recoiled back, only Berjek's quick grab for her arm stopped her toppling into the pool.

Each of the palaces – the embassies she supposed – had statues standing before it, flanking the door, but she had not registered that they were not statues of locals. They were not even like the cold, beautiful watchers flanking the Estuarine Gate. These were faces she recognized, or some of them.

The stone visages that met her gaze were those of cowled Moth-kinden. In that first glance, the male of the pair had seemed close enough to Achaeos to nearly stop her heart.

A lot of people were talking to her, but she could not focus on what they were saying. For a moment the air about the statue blurred, and she feared that his ghost would emerge from it to chastise her. The impression was soon gone, though, the blur due only to the heat. She felt stifled by the sheer number of people trying to find out what was wrong with her, and she virtually elbowed her way past Berjek and Manny and Trallo, until faced by the old man Ethmet.

She had finally elicited a genuine expression out of him, and it was surprised concern. Nobody had laid this trap deliberately, it had all been mere chance. Predictably, the Vekken had drawn their swords, but she did not feel she had the strength to reason with them again.

'It was . . . it was nothing,' she got out.

'We have displeased you,' Ethmet said mournfully. 'You must forgive us our ignorance of your ways.'

'No, no, please,' she said, and she looked the statue directly in its cold face.

*Can I live with this, even for a tenday? What should I say, if I cannot? How could I explain?*

*I must live with it. The alternatives are too humiliating.*

'Please . . .' she said. 'Please, it is just . . . the journey was long and I am tired, very tired.' The Vekken resheathed their blades sullenly, obviously resenting their inability to use them.

'Of course,' said Ethmet. He made a quick signal and the porters began moving the expedition's baggage inside. Che heard a startled cry from within, but she was already gazing around at the other embassies, the other statues that adorned them. She saw Spider-kinden, clearly recognizable by their features, although the garments were strange. She saw long-faced, hunchbacked people she could not name, and beside them were lanky Grasshoppers. There were even two that might have been Dragonflies.

'How long . . . how old . . .?' she murmured to herself. The carvings that circled the pillars and scaled the walls writhed under her gaze, and now seemed on the threshold of forming actual words, to reveal terrible secrets of time and antiquity.

She heard the sound of running feet behind her, and the all-too-familiar leather whisper of the Vekken drawing their swords again. A Beetle-woman burst out of the Moth-flanked embassy, knocking over a porter in her urgency. Che stared at her, wondering *What is wrong with her*? and seeing a moment later that it was the hair, of course. She had hair, which meant she was no native. When the woman cried out, 'Please, wait. Listen to me!' she had a Collegium accent.

Everyone had gone quiet, waiting for what she would say but, after a sidelong look at old Ethmet, she said nothing. The pause grew awkward.

'I'm sorry,' Che addressed her, 'who are you?'

'I'm . . . Petri Coggen. I'm Kadro's assistant,' the woman got out. She looked as though she had not changed her clothes or combed her hair for a tenday. Her eyes were wide and flinching. Che shared a frown with Berjek, then knelt beside her.

'What is it?' she asked. 'What's the matter?'

Petri's eyes kept being drawn to Ethmet, despite all her efforts to stop them. Che recognized a physical struggle within her, to control some outburst.

'I have to tell you things. Please—'

'Where's Master Kadro?'

'Ssh!' Petri's eyes went wider still. 'Not that – never that!'

Trallo had said as much when he briefed Che in Solarno. 'Where is . . . Sieur Kadro, then?' It seemed disrespectful to give a Master of the College nothing more than his name, and so Che compromised on the Solarnese title.

'Disappeared. Gone.' The words were barely a murmur on Petri's lips. 'This place . . .' Again her eyes were dragged over Che's shoulder towards Ethmet, whose expression suggested polite puzzlement at the ways of foreigners.

'Perhaps we had all better go inside,' said Che loudly, part worried about this woman's state of mind, part embarrassed at making a spectacle in front of their hosts. The porters had completed their job and Che saw a row of Khanaphir men and women lined up in the entrance hall, obviously the staff waiting to greet them. Glancing back she saw that the two Vekken still had their swords drawn, standing shoulder to shoulder, tilted away from each other.

'Please forgive us . . . First Minister.' In between turning to him and remembering his proper title she had caught, for a brief instant, a strange expression on Ethmet's face. It was the look of a man listening to a voice only he could hear. *Are these people mindlinked too, like Ants?* But this was something else, and she realized what it reminded her of. As she stepped over the little bridge, she put a hand on the Moth statue's shoulder, remembering how the magicians of the old races could speak to one another, distance no object. Achaeos had told her so many times.

The races who had graced this square in times past were all Inapt. The lords of the Days of Lore would have sent their emissaries here, before the revolution had put paid to their world. Those days, those far-off days, were engraved here in the very stone, enshrined in the reeds and the water, in the very faces of the locals. She felt her own loss, her deficiency, very keenly, but it was different here. Here, amongst the Khanaphir, it was surely no deficiency. Instead, it put her closer to them. *Have I found a home here? Will they have words for what I have become?*

# Fourteen

'They're setting up right opposite from us,' Vollen observed. 'That's convenient.'

'For them and us,' Thalric mused. With Marger and Corolly off making arrangements with their hosts, Thalric had been left with the two other Wasps in Marger's team, a pair by the names of Vollen and Gram. Vollen was taller, thinner, and Thalric reckoned his role was the specialist sneak, perhaps even an assassin, whereas Gram, even out of uniform, looked every bit the professional soldier.

'I count four Beetles: two men, two women. There's a Fly-kinden there, too, and a couple of Ants,' Vollen went on.

'Ants? What city?'

Vollen shrugged. 'You should look yourself. You're the Lowlander expert, sir.'

*I suppose I have no choice but to go to the window then.* Thalric went over, displaced Vollen from his post, and looked down. He experienced an odd sense of trepidation as though he might fall. Everyday sounds reached him – cicadas out in the greenery, the clatter as Osgan organized their supplies and gave orders to the servants below – but it all seemed to come from very far away. He felt very detached, looking only at the knot of people assembled across the Place of Foreigners.

She was there, of course. *Cheerwell Maker, I didn't think I'd see you again this soon, perhaps ever.* She was wearing

Mynan colours, which made no objective sense, but made sense to him. He would always associate her with that city.

*Did I pay my debts, through what I did in Myna?* He felt emotionally split, his mind running on different rails at the same time. Part of him was thinking of old Stenwold Maker, how he had sent his niece out into danger yet again. Did it mean that this mission of theirs was so important to the Lowlands that he had risked his own flesh and blood to guide it? He never would keep her safe; it was an odd blind spot to Stenwold. Ever since Thalric had known him he had been doing his best to get his family killed. On the other hand, perhaps Che had put herself forward, and if she had done so then all of Stenwold's careful attention would not have been able to stop her. *Yes, that would be just like her.*

He caught the thought, the slight smile, and killed it. Enough of that.

Underneath such personal considerations ran the professional: how to proceed now against the Lowlanders. Their hosts were playing games in this place, it was clear. The Empire and the Lowlands could spy on each other here without even going outside the door, while the Khanaphir could keep an eye on them both. 'Do you think we can infiltrate a spy amongst their servants?' he asked.

'I don't know the local character well enough,' Vollen replied. 'They seem poor, subservient. We should be able to corrupt one.'

*Or perhaps they would simply expand their game, double our agent back on us, feed us false information.* Thalric was a man used to finding his way around in strange cities, amongst strange people, but Khanaphes had yet to open up for him. *There are important things that are kept hidden here. I can almost smell them.*

'What city, sir?' Vollen asked him abruptly. Thalric blinked, losing the point of the question and then remembering. *The Ant-kinden?* He frowned when he looked to the two identical men standing a little apart from the rest.

‘Vekken,’ he declared, and ransacked his memory for news of Vek following the abortive siege of Collegium that he had been so instrumental in prompting. Had there not been some word of Vekken ambassadors in that city, since? He thought maybe there had, but why were they *here*?

Because whatever Che Maker was searching for in this place, it was important. Whether it was seeking an alliance or information or ancient buried treasure, the Vekken were obviously interested, perhaps even willing partners. That seemed next to impossible, considering the way they regarded Collegium, but if anyone could solder together that breach, then it would be Stenwold.

The Lowlanders were going in now. If their embassy was anything like the Empire’s, they would find an embarrassment of riches and service to get used to, giving the Empire a day’s clear start in keeping an eye on them. Thalric watched closely as Che herself went in, the others filing dutifully after her. *She’s definitely in charge, good for her.* Only when she had gone from sight did he permit himself the liberty of the third line of thought that had been brewing. It was a notion that had sparked when he had seen her at the docks, having gone there to see who the Lowlands had sent. Having seen, he should have backed into the crowd: Gram had been plucking at his sleeve, but he had stood his ground, watching. *Unprofessional, for a man of your experience.* The answer to that question was there in plain sight, but he had avoided it, up until now.

*You wanted her to know that you were here.*

He tried to make some capital out of this action, for the Empire. Surely he could wrestle it around to benefit his mission. He felt Vollen watching him, and knew that he was not above reproach, here. *Brugan probably told them to keep me on a careful leash.*

‘I recognized their leader,’ he said lightly. ‘An old acquaintance.’

‘Sir.’ Vollen’s tone remained carefully neutral.

Thalric turned away from the window, putting himself out of sight of the building opposite. 'It gives us another option, in working out what they're after.'

Vollen nodded, waiting for enlightenment.

'I'll make contact,' Thalric declared, sounding very relaxed, almost flippant. 'Since they know the Empire's in the city, I'll think up some story and make contact. For old times' sake, you know.' *What have you been told about me?* he wondered, looking directly into Vollen's face. *What have you been warned about?*

Vollen appeared all business though. 'That would make sense,' he agreed. 'We can hardly keep avoiding each other, being lodged so close. We might as well have some formal contact, and it sounds as though this is why the General sent you along with us.' Thalric saw no hint of suspicion, nothing but a Rekef man mulling over a problem.

*Is it quite so easy? Are my treasons forgotten?* But that was the curse of running agents and spies, of course. Consider those men and women who spent their lives under false pretences, and how was their spymaster – how was *anyone* – to know their true nature? How, eventually, was even the spy himself to know where his loyalties lay? Pretend hard enough and it builds a shell of reality, as difficult to scrub off as barnacles from a boat. *I remember learning that the hard way from my agents in Collegium.* He felt a stab of regret at that, and shame at his own failure. They had been good Imperial agents until he had told them that Collegium must be destroyed, and it was then they had discovered that they were really citizens of Collegium, ready to fight him to protect their city. No one could have known that, until he had put them to the test.

*And now I am put to the test, am I? Who would I betray, given the chance?* Then a pang of self-pity: *Is there anyone I would not?*

'What do you make of this city, Vollen?'

The other man shook his head. 'Speaking frankly, sir, it's

an armpit. You saw those fields on our way down the river. My people are farmers, back home. I know how it's done. We didn't spot a single automotive on the way in, nothing but a few watermills. They do everything by hand or by beast labour here. The guards don't even have a crossbow between them. If the Empire wanted this place, we could walk in tomorrow.'

'Just a primitive little backwater, then?'

'Exactly.' Vollen's expression precisely indicated a Rekef man who wanted to be elsewhere: this assignment was not, his face said, the stuff a career was made of. Thalric realized, with a stab of guilt, that the man was talking to him as one Rekef to another, without any of the reserve that had marked their journey so far. Vollen must have caught himself at the same time because he added, 'Sorry, sir, if I've been too blunt.'

'Be as blunt as you like,' Thalric told him. 'If it helps, I agree with you.' Only he didn't agree, merely *wanted* to. It was clear to him, he who had made a career out of finding his feet in foreign cities, that there were parts of Khanaphes still being kept hidden from him. There were too many inconsistencies all around him. *If only, though* . . . because, if Khanaphes was just some misbegotten hole of peasants and primitives, then it could not in any way be important. And if it was not important, then it could not really matter what he did here, since nothing was at stake. *After all, my purpose – my true purpose – in coming here was to escape the Empress, if only for a little while.*

There was a crash of breaking pottery below, and he took it as his cue. 'I'll see how Osgan is managing.'

Vollen's expression showed just what he thought of Osgan, but he nodded.

*I was a traitor for such a short time*, he thought as he descended the stairs. *Why do I miss it so much?* Prisoner and fugitive, beaten, hunted. *Such times*, he thought drily, but there was a nub of truth there. His life as Regent was no garden, after all, and it had not even honesty to recommend it. It had been different when he had been a traitor.

What was Che to him? He realized that she was the closest thing to an old comrade he had.

He wondered if Cheerwell Maker would want to talk over old times.

'So tell me what happened here,' Che said.

Petri Coggen stared at her, wide-eyed, then her gaze slid over towards the servants who were carefully setting down Che's meagre baggage. The other academics crowded about them as well, so that Che felt a sudden surge of claustrophobia.

'Out, everyone out,' she said. 'Let me talk to Miss Coggen alone. You all go . . . pick your rooms or something.'

Mannerly Gorget was first out the door, his future comfort very much in mind, and the rest began to follow him.

Berjek went last, frowning. 'Are you sure . . .?' he enquired. 'If there's something amiss here we all should know it.'

'Master Gripshod . . .' Che began, and saw the servants visibly flinch. She gritted her teeth. 'Berjek, please,' she continued, 'I don't think an extra pair of hands is going to help, here.' With a tilt of her head she tried to indicate Petri Coggen, who now sat on the bed, looking dishevelled, shaking and red-eyed, hugging her knees.

Berjek pursed his lips in irritation, but nodded and made his exit. Che waited for the servants to go too, but they continued patiently unpacking.

'Sorry, could you leave us alone for a moment.' She had to say it twice before they registered that she was actually talking to them. Their expressions were those of frozen surprise, as though a chair had just spoken to them. *Servants, or slaves?* Che wondered. She remembered her brief sight of the Spiderlands, on the way to Solarno. There had been slaves everywhere, yet they had been invisible, for that was the custom: it was considered bad manners even to look at them. 'I'm sorry,' she addressed the servants again. There were three of them – two young women and a middle-aged man, all as bald as the rest of the locals – wearing simple white tunics that hung off one shoulder.

'Where I come from, we are not used to such hospitality,' Che explained carefully. 'Please would you leave us for a little while.'

Blank-faced, they filed from the room, and Che closed the door after them. From recent experience she thought instantly, *Have I locked myself in now*? But there was no catch on the door, only a loop of cord and a hook. The sight of such Inapt measures was absurdly thrilling to her. *This is it. I've found it. There can be no mistake.*

'They're still listening,' Petri Coggen said in a whisper.

Che opened the door again, quickly, but no eavesdropping servants were revealed. The nearest one, dusting a display of pottery down the hall, could have heard them only if they shouted.

'No one's listening.'

'They're *always* listening,' Petri insisted.

Che closed the door and took a deep breath. 'How long since you slept, if I might ask?'

'Four days. I . . . If I sleep, they might . . .' The woman shuddered. 'I don't want to sleep.'

'Where's Master – where's Kadro?' *I need to break myself of that habit as quickly as possible.*

'He's disappeared!' Petri almost wailed, surely loud enough for any servants outside to hear whether they wanted to or not. 'He was investigating the city . . . he had found something, their great secret. He told me as much, and then, and then . . . gone. Just vanished.'

'What was this secret?'

'He didn't tell me *that*, just that he was so close – that he knew where to go.'

Che took a chair and sat down across from her. 'What sort of investigations was he making? Where did he go?'

'He went everywhere – at night, mostly. You know how Fly-kinden can see in the dark. He would copy down inscriptions from the oldest buildings. He went into the desert once, too, to see some ruins out there. Or he would go out beyond the gates to the Marsh Alcaia – the black market. He was always asking questions, piecing things together.'

Che put a hand up to stop her. 'It sounds . . . forgive me for saying this, but it sounds as though Kadro was fond of dangerous places.'

'He knew what he was doing!' Petri snapped back, then put a hand over her mouth, horrified. 'I'm sorry, I'm sorry,' she said after a moment.

'But did you tell our hosts that he was missing?' Che pressed her. 'Did they look for him?'

'They *know*!' Petri insisted. 'They did it. They took him, because he found out something. They made him vanish.'

*But can you prove it?* Looking at this shaking woman, Che knew the answer already. In this state, Petri Coggen was of no use to anyone.

'You think I'm mad, don't you?' Petri visibly sagged. 'You don't believe me.'

Che studied her and saw haggard exhaustion, hysteria, but not madness. 'Something has clearly happened to Kadro, so I will need to meet the local leaders. I'll ask them about him and see how they react. How would I get an audience with the Masters of Khanaphes – or will they send for me?'

Petri laughed out loud, a wretched and unexpected sound. 'You can't,' she said bitterly. 'You can't. And if they send for you . . .' She laughed again from pure despair. 'Kadro wanted to meet the Masters, after we came here. Everyone talks about them. They have ceremonies, to give them thanks. But whoever sees the Masters? Kadro thought they were a myth. He thought that was the whole secret . . .'

'But who runs the city?'

'You've already met him.' She stifled another strained laugh. 'Ethmet.'

'What, that . . .?'

'That nice old man? That was what you were going to say, weren't you?' Petri chewed at her lip, which was already ragged from it. 'The First Minister rules Khanaphes. He says he's only a servant of the Masters, and that the Ministers know everything, see everything. There are palaces and halls in which the Ministers are supposed to serve the Masters, but Kadro was sure they were empty. It's Ethmet, telling everyone the lie.'

'I can see why it might be dangerous to find out the truth of that,' Che said slowly. 'Although I can't see how you could really keep that fact secret from a whole city.'

Petri collapsed back on the bed with a groan. 'You won't let them take me?' she pleaded.

'Nothing's going to happen to you, now that we're here,' Che assured her. 'You're not alone any more.' She saw Petri's shoulders shake, realized that the woman was barely stifling an outburst of sobs. *Whatever the truth, something happened here.* On the heels of that came a more selfish thought: *I hope she recovers soon. We need to learn what she knows.* Che was ashamed of it but that made it no less true. She went to the door as quietly as she could, prompted by the sudden, irrational feeling that there was a servant there, silent and listening, just a moment before. *That way madness lies*, she decided.

From the bed Petri began murmuring, just a noise at first, then becoming words. 'But when he had done his researches . . .' she said, though Che could barely catch it. 'When he had gone into the desert, and spoken to the Marsh people, Kadro started doubting it all. At the end, just before he vanished, he was talking as though there was another secret inside the secret . . . as though he had begun to believe in the Masters after all.'

Che stood there waiting for a long time, but there was no more. At long last, sleep had found Petri Coggen.

Beyond the windows the city of Khanaphes bustled,

bright with sunshine, busy with the simple industry of its people, and happily concealed under the mask of its own innocence.

'I hope I get used to them soon,' Berjek grumbled. 'It's all very decadent having them around, but . . .' He shook his head. The grand entrance hall to the makeshift Collegiate embassy was opulently decorated: with wall friezes depicting scenes of hunting and farming; with twin statues of Khanaphir soldiers cast in bronze; with those countless pictograms carved in their eternal lines. Mostly, however, it was decorated with servants. Standing halfway up the broad marble-faced staircase, Berjek could see a good dozen of them going through the never-ending business of keeping the edifice spotless. One was even retouching tiny chips in the friezes.

'I know what you mean,' Praeda Rakespear said. 'I woke up in the middle of the night and thought we were being robbed. They never seem to stop working.'

'I like it.' Manny smirked at them. 'I could live here. It's like being in the Spiderlands without having the Spider-kinden.' From sounds heard last night, Che guessed he had enticed one of the female servants into a different kind of service. She also suspected the woman had simply seen that as part of her duty.

'Remember this is just because we're honoured guests,' she reminded him. 'The common people of Khanaphes don't live like this.'

'I've never been common anywhere I went,' Manny replied airily.

She shook her head, about to make some suitable remark, when a servant stopped on the stairs beside her and straightened Che's robe, tugging the creases and folds expertly into place as though the girl had been born in Collegium. Che was left with her mouth open, the words evaporating. Manny cackled.

'You're happy to stay here on your own?' she eventually asked Berjek. 'Only, I promised—'

'Madam Coggen, yes,' Berjek finished for her. 'I was never one for gatherings, whether formal or informal. In fact I became a scholar of dead ages just to avoid the onerous chore of talking to the living. Go and suffer it, by all means. I would rather stay here and make notes about the wall-hangings.'

'And make sure to look in on Petri, every so often,' Che reminded him. 'And check that the servants don't . . . bother her.'

'And that, yes. Now go. Our hosts will be waiting for you.' There was a hint of a smile on his face and, inwardly, Che thanked him for being reliable.

The messenger the Ministers had sent to them was still waiting patiently by the door, and had done so for an hour as the academics changed into their formal robes. When they descended the stairs, Che, Manny and Praeda, they looked every bit the proper representatives of the Great College of the most enlightened city in the world. Skipping after them, half walking and half gliding down the stairs, came Trallo, whose baggy Solarnese whites provided a close enough match to their finery.

There was abruptly a Vekken at the foot of the steps, waiting for them. Che had assumed they would not be interested in a formal reception and, in truth, had not taken many steps to let them know about it. Still, here was one of them, which one she could not discern. At first she was going to remonstrate, or try to, since he was dressed in full armour, chainmail hauberk hanging to his knees and sword belted to his hip. *But why not? We wear the dress of Collegium. He dresses as an Ant. Let our hosts judge for themselves.*

'Are you ready?' she asked him. In that strangely nervous moment, with the mystery of unknown Khanaphes waiting just beyond the door, she almost felt like offering the grim-faced Ant her arm. He would not have known what to do with it, she thought glumly – would probably mistake it for an attack.

He nodded curtly. No doubt the other one would be lurking about the embassy somewhere, receiving reports or making notes.

The messenger was a woman, although it was difficult to tell with these locals. The females' off-shoulder tunics were cut slightly differently, so as to hide both breasts, and it was the garments, more than the facial features, that distinguished one gender from the other. Che sensed it was not so much a close kinship, as with the Ants, but simply a willingness to be interchangeable.

*But what do I know about it?* Che reproached herself. *I'm just being an ignorant foreigner.*

She led the way, after the messenger, towards the grand arch at the far side of the Place of Foreigners. Behind her she heard the others following her: Manny's slightly laboured breath and the faint clink of Vekken armour. As the messenger darted ahead, through the archway, Che followed, and stopped.

'Oh,' she remembered saying. Just that and no more. The others backed up behind her, but at that moment she didn't care.

The square beyond was twice the size, and the buildings lining it correspondingly grander, great facades rising four, five storeys, ranked with pillars in the shape of horsetails or scaled cycads, or of battle scenes where the faces of square columns continued the scene that unfolded on the wall behind them, so that the figures – as the watcher passed – moved behind one another, locked in their endless combat. Everywhere torches were lit, making a whole constellation out of each majestic facade. Che stepped forward with eyes wide, oblivious to most of the pageantry and seeing only what lay straight before her.

It was a stepped pyramid that took up most of the square's

centre, and rose thirty feet to an oddly squared-off apex. But there were figures up there, great shining figures, and Che rushed forward to stare up at them. For a moment she felt their heavy regard, their cool amusement at this plain foreign girl who dared invade their presence.

She fell to one knee. She had no choice. 'I'm sorry,' she said. 'I'm all I have. I'm sorry.'

'Cheerwell . . . Madam Maker!' It was Praeda's voice, and Trallo's small hand was busy plucking at her robe. She blinked, looked back towards them, then was staring up again.

'What is it?' Trallo was saying, and Praeda added: 'They're statues, Cheerwell, only statues.'

Che stood up slowly, shaking her head. On closer inspection in the dance of the torchlight, they were merely forms carved of white marble, gazing down on her from their lofty vantage point. *But they are not only statues, never that,* an inner voice insisted. Even seeing them as dead stone could not strip them of their majesty. These effigies were cousins to the great watchers that flanked the Estuarine Gate, and they possessed the same callous beauty, the same thoughtless power.

'Who are they? Who were they?' she asked, because they were not Beetle-kinden, nor any kinden she had ever seen. The thought was irresistible: *These were surely the Masters, when they lived, but who were they?*

She allowed Trallo to guide her towards the most imposing of the edifices bordering the square, and there she spotted Ethmet, framed by torches. Her eyes met his, and she found there something quite different from the reserved patience that she had come to expect. His attention focused on her, just for a moment, with such intensity that she almost felt the heat of it.

# Fifteen

Che had been expecting some kind of formal banquet, perhaps, but what she got instead was a kind of menagerie, with herself and the visitors from Collegium the prime exhibits. The building Ethmet stood waiting in front of looked like a tomb designed for a dead giant. Its exterior promised dingy windowless rooms and cramped passageways, but instead they emerged into a massive hall, its lofty ceiling supported by two rows of columns – carved figures of Khanaphir men and women reaching up to support the colossal weight of the roof. They were painted, stylized, and the craft that had gone into them was as nothing compared with those alien faces that topped the truncated pyramid outside. In between these caryatids, frozen in their eternal labour, light issued from a hundred shafts that burrowed upwards through the fabric of the monumental building. The effect tricked the eye into believing that the sun shone from all directions at once, although the day was growing late even before Che and the others had entered.

'There must be mirrors,' Praeda had been murmuring. 'Mirrors and lanterns and lenses perhaps. It's remarkable.'

Che remembered the intricacy of the Moth-kinden architecture at Tharn, and the tricks they could play with stone. Ancient techniques: Inapt craftsmen making up in ingenuity for their lack of artifice.

'Honoured and Beautiful Foreigners,' Ethmet addressed

them, 'be so kind as to let me introduce you to my cousin Nafir, who is Minister for the Estuarine Waters.' Nafir had been pressed from the same mould as Ethmet, albeit more recently. He made the same genuflection, spreading hands out from his stomach, and Che did her best to copy the gesture. The great chamber was scattered with other Khanaphir men and women, two score at least, and it reminded her enough of the Collegium Assembly to suggest this was the combined Ministry of the city, gathered here expressly to scrutinize the foreigners. They did not crowd around: Ethmet would no doubt lead her past them all in turn. Instead, they were gathered in small groups, talking quietly. Only a few sat, although there were several stone benches arranged around the fountain that burbled gently in the hall's centre.

Nafir made some polite comments, and was soon left behind. Next a group of three turned out to be called Hemses, Methret and Pthome, and already Che's mind was swimming with the names. Of the faces she had lost all hope because, although the features varied, their expressions were so unified that she knew it would be impossible to recall them later.

A musician had struck up somewhere, playing something plaintive on delicate strings. At the far end of the room there was food laid out, a complex arrangement of meat, insects and unfamiliar vegetables. The sight of it obviously broke the back of Manny's patience, because he was off in that direction with a mumbled apology. Che looked around and saw that Praeda had already abandoned her, was now sitting studying the fountain. The Vekken, whichever one he was, remained standing sullenly in the shade of a column, the scale of its carving making him look like a sulky child.

'And here . . .' Ethmet went on, and introduced her to yet another Minister, and she smiled and nodded, and reflected that there were certain ubiquitous aspects of the Beetle-kinden character she could happily do without. Stenwold had always tried to avoid attending these kinds of receptions, and she wondered now if it had been to spare the visiting ambassadors from one more bewildering introduction.

'. . . is Amnon, the First Soldier of the Royal Guard,' continued Ethmet blandly, and Che started to repeat her threadbare greetings but, in the end, just said, 'Oh,' instead. To start with she was speaking to his chest, because he was more than a head taller than she was. It was a chest covered in gilt-edged metal scales, she noticed, for Amnon was wearing the most magnificent cuirass she had ever seen. She remembered the splendour of the escort that had welcomed them at the docks, and decided that they must have been wearing their everyday garb, because this, *this* was a dress uniform. Each scale had been enamelled in turquoise, and then minute figures painted on top, images of soldiers parading, throwing spears, giving battle. There was room for plenty of scales, too, because Amnon was broad as well as tall, his bare shoulders and arms bulging with muscle. He was grinning down at her with dazzling white teeth and, despite everything, she felt a flutter within her. She had never met anyone quite so robustly *physical* before, a man who looked as though he could break steel bars with his hands.

'It is of course a pleasure to meet one so distinguished,' he announced, and made an elaborate genuflection, beginning with the stomach and ending with the forehead. 'I shall look forward to when I know you and your fellows better. The First Minister has suggested that I arrange a hunt in your honour.'

'I'm sure that won't be necessary,' stammered Che, but he was already magnanimously overruling her.

'The great land-fish of the Jamail have grown fat and fierce,' he declared grandly, 'and the Marsh folk wait only for my word before they take up their spears and bows. No personage of distinction should be absent, for it shall be the greatest hunt in a tenyear.'

‘Well, that’s very kind,’ she managed. The sheer robust presence of him was overwhelming. She was grateful when Ethmet moved her on to meet someone less energetic.

Eventually, of course, she was left to her own devices, with her head already leaking names and faces and titles. Ethmet had proved the perfect, mild-mannered host throughout, so it had been difficult to countenance all the dire warnings of Petri Coggen. She had bearded him at the end, though, declaring, ‘The work of the First Minister of such a great city must be hard.’

‘It is not so,’ he had assured her modestly. ‘I am only here to give reality to the wishes of my Masters.’

‘And how might a poor foreigner seek an audience with those Masters?’ she had asked carefully.

His smile had not altered. ‘Alas it cannot be so. If they request to see you, then so be it, but you may not petition them. They are beyond such dealings, and you must content yourself with this poor servant.’

She had responded to that with the necessary compliments, and all had been well. There had not been the slightest pause in their conversation to warn her of dangerous ground, but she had felt the pit yawning at her feet, despite it.

She looked round to check up on the rest of her party. Manny was in close conversation with two of the women, who Che thought were young enough to be servants rather than Ministers. She decided it was probably the safest place to leave him. Praeda was still sitting at the fountain, staring silently at the waters as they swelled and leapt from their bed of coloured stones. As Che watched, she beckoned a servant over and put some question to him. Beyond her, Che noted the dark form of the Vekken ambassador, standing near the display of food but obviously unwilling to risk eating any. She felt a sudden misplaced surge of sympathy for a man so obviously out of his depth.

She was already regretting the impulse before she reached him, but she pressed on regardless. His glance towards her was less suspicious than usual, but only because their strange surroundings had already stretched his capacity for suspicion to breaking point.

'Are you . . . Is there anything you need?' she asked him. 'Should I introduce you to anyone here?'

He looked at her as though she was mad, not unreasonably given the interminable round of meeting and greeting she herself had just endured. 'I am waiting,' he replied flatly.

'Waiting? For?'

'You know what I mean.'

She sighed, because she did. He was still waiting for the trap to be sprung. He had been holding his breath for it, no doubt, ever since he had left Vek. *How can anyone live in such a ferment of constant hostility?* She wanted to explain to him that there was no great dark motive for their coming here, but he would never have believed her and, besides, was that actually true? *I have my own motives and they are not those of my uncle, or the scholars accompanying me. Perhaps the Vekken have sensed that.*

'If they wanted to kill us, it would not be by poison,' she said tiredly. 'We are defenceless in their city. We would be dead if they wanted us dead.' Deliberately, she broke off a sliver of meat and swallowed it. It was tender, flavoured with honey, and she discovered that she was hungry enough to take a larger piece. His eyes followed her hands as though she concealed a knife in them.

'We can't win, can we?' she said, still chewing. She felt the sudden need to be candid with him: his mulishness drove her to it. 'If, at the end of the day, we sail back to Collegium with no evidence of plots, no tricks, nothing but an academic study, then you'll just think that you didn't manage to root it out, that we hid it from you successfully. Is that it? Is there no chance of any trust?'

He blinked quickly three times and she saw his hand move to his sword-hilt, not to draw the weapon but for the comfort of it. She could not put an age to him but his naivety made him seem as young as she was. She was about to assure him that he need not answer when he said, 'What is it, to trust? It is to know, beyond doubt, the heart of the other. Yet you are silent to us. Your minds throng with all deceptions and lies, and we can never know you.' He was quivering slightly, still blinking rapidly. 'How can we trust such silence?' Almost defiantly he grabbed for the food and, not even looking at it, forced a piece of fruit into his mouth. Then he was gone again, stalking off into his own personal silence. *I wish I hadn't asked*, she thought, having found out more than she wanted to know about the Vekken. *How can mere diplomacy hope to break through those walls?*

'The First Minister offered to introduce us,' said someone close behind her, 'but I explained that we were already old friends.'

Although she had been half-expecting it, the voice opened a door in her mind, releasing a flood of remembered images: a dusty chain of slaves marching from Helleron; the interrogation rooms in the governor's palace at Myna; the dingy back room of Hokiak's Exchange.

'Thalric,' she replied, and she turned to face him, only with reluctance. He had dressed the part, in a pure white tunic and cloak edged with little geometric patterns picked out in black and gold. She knew enough to look for the delicate chainmail concealed beneath the cloth, and even without a sword his kinden never lacked for weapons. 'What do you want?' she asked.

'Diplomatic relations?' He smiled easily. 'The war's over, hadn't you heard?'

'I thought it was only my side who were supposed to believe that.'

'Oh, good, very good.' His glance about the room told her that their meeting was being observed. 'You look harassed, Che. Surely the locals aren't getting to you? We've both been in worse places than this.'

She felt a sudden rush of frustration and, for a moment,

she nearly hit him, and would not have cared who was watching. 'Why can't you decide just whose side you're on, Thalric?' she hissed between her gritted teeth. 'Why keep crossing the same old road, back and forth? You're Empire now, aren't you? So what do we two have to talk about?'

She had done it again, just as on the first time she had ever met him: ten minutes of conversation inside his tent, and she had chanced on some random barb that had struck home and drawn blood. She saw his face tighten, his stance change as he mentally rolled with the blow.

'We could talk, for a start, about what Collegium is doing here so far from home,' he said.

'We could talk about why the cursed *Empire* is here, for that matter,' Che countered. She had known he was here and had been waiting for this, and yet he had caught her wholly off balance. Just seeing him and hearing his voice, she was instantly ready for a fight, reaching for the sword she had not brought with her. She looked into his face and saw the signs of tension pass. His smile returned, or at least some ghost of it.

'Well, perhaps you can tell me why *I'm* here, and I'll tell you why *you're* here,' he suggested.

That nearly caused her a twitch of the lips. 'Why here, Thalric?' she said. 'You're the lord high grandee of the Empire. Surely that's guarantee enough that I can't just keep running into you.'

'Apparently not.' He paused, and she imagined that he was measuring the distance between them – not the physical space, but the miles that time and allegiance had interposed. 'I apologize, Miss Maker . . . Ambassador Maker, I should say. I now formally present myself as your . . . opposite number here in Khanaphes. I'm sure your staff will see fit to call on my own staff, in due course.' The words were said crisply, with a blithe smile, but she detected the wintry sadness behind them.

He nodded his head, took a few steps back, and then

turned to find someone else to talk to. Che was left knowing there were other things she wanted to say, but still uncertain as to what they were.

She heard Mannerly Gorget's braying laughter from across the room and saw him talking now with the First Soldier of the Royal Guard. Amnon was nodding and grinning, and she hoped Manny was not being undiplomatic. With that thought, she looked around for Praeda, and felt a lurch in her stomach as she realized that the woman was no longer in the hall at all. *Vanished? Like Kadro?* She shook this dark thought off irritably and beckoned a servant over.

'Excuse me, I'm looking for one of my party,' she said. 'The . . . the other woman, taller than me.' *The one with hair, the only other woman with hair in this whole building.* The servant looked around in quick, jerky movements and opened her mouth as if to say that she did not know. But then she pointed to where Praeda was now emerging out of a small doorway to one side of the hall.

Praeda spotted Che and hurried over. Her facade of calm had cracked, revealing a scholarly fire in her eyes. 'Che, you've got to come and see this,' she rushed out, almost falling over the words.

'What? What's happened?'

'Nothing's happened,' said Praeda. 'It's just . . . It's incredible, really remarkable. Come with me . . . No, wait, come here.' She caught Che's hand and tugged her towards the fountain. 'Do you see? Do you?'

'I see a fountain,' replied Che slowly, watching the water bubble up between the stones and subside again. 'Praeda, please just be more clear.'

'*Think*, Che,' Praeda insisted. 'Yes, it's a fountain, but how do fountains work?'

'I . . .' *I no longer know,* and she could not say it.

Praeda shook her head impatiently. 'Did you assume this was just a natural spring or something? Che, think! We're above the level of the river here.'

Che vaguely understood what she meant, but that knowledge was dim and distant. 'Just get to the point,' she demanded, to cover up.

'The point is . . . follow me,' Praeda dragged her across the room to the little servants' door she had recently come in through.

'This is . . . rude,' Che protested. 'We're supposed to be guests here.'

'Manny can keep them occupied. He's loud enough and fat enough for all three,' Praeda sneered. She was pulling Che onwards through a series of small turns. The servants' passages were low-ceilinged and cramped. There were little doorless rooms either side, some filled with boxes and sacks, others with tables for preparing food, or with desks for scribes. Praeda paid them no notice whatsoever, nor the surprised servants they passed on their way.

There was a black-clad figure ahead and for a moment Che thought it was the Vekken, inexplicably involved in Praeda's schemes. Then she saw it was a man in dark armour, with a full-face helm tilted back to reveal sandy Solarnese features.

'Well, now, here you are at last,' he said as the pair of them approached him.

'Who's this?' Che demanded. 'What's going on here?'

'The name's Corcoran, Bella.' As he said it Che noticed his tabard, though the smoky lamplight made it hard to pick out the open gauntlet embroidered there.

'Iron Glove,' she observed automatically. As he grinned in acknowledgement, she thought back, seeing them dealing with Dragonflies at the oasis, or on the streets of Solarno. 'Who are you people?'

'We just happen to be the newest and most successful trading cartel out of Chasme,' Corcoran replied. He was a wiry individual with a pointed face that smiled shallowly and easily. 'Weapons, Bella. We deal in weapons and the accoutrements of war.'

'Here?' Che asked. 'I thought they weren't keen on . . . innovation here.'

'Oh, pits to innovation,' said Corcoran dismissively. 'We can sell them better *swords* than they have. You don't need *innovation*. We provide what they lack. It's purely good business.'

'This man isn't what I brought you here to see,' Praeda explained impatiently. 'It's what he showed me. Come on.'

She pushed past them both, leaving Che to blunder in her wake. The corridors were lit erratically by bowl-shaped oil lamps, or the occasional stone-cut shaft. Corcoran seemed almost to melt into the gloom as he followed, his dark leathers merging easily with the pooling shadows. Only his pale face, the gleam of his teeth, betrayed him.

'Here.' Praeda stopped abruptly then and darted through an even lower doorway. Che followed her, and almost tumbled down a short flight of steps. The room beyond was bigger than she expected, excavated down into the earth. There was a . . .

There was a *something* within it.

Praeda was obviously expecting comment, while Corcoran was lounging about at the top of the stairs, watching. Che did not know what to say.

'What . . . am I looking at?' she asked.

'Oh, Che, honestly,' Praeda chided, losing patience. 'Look here, these stone pipes must lead to the river – or to some pond where they keep their purified water. That's done by those reed beds we saw, by the way, but I'll tell you about it later. Anyway, the water is at a lower level than the fountain, so they have to draw it up somehow. That's where this comes in, you see?'

Che still didn't see, though. There was a vertical pipe, carved as intricately as everything else, with a metal rod jutting from it, and there was some kind of fulcrum there, and a weight . . . *I'm supposed to be able to understand what this is,* she realized. Deep inside herself, she began to feel ill.

'Tell me . . .' she said hoarsely.

'It's a vacuum pump, though, isn't it?' Corcoran said delightedly, from behind her. 'The cursed'st one I ever saw, but that's what it is. They get some poor sods of servants to haul the weight up, and then the weight comes down slow – probably there's some sand emptying out of somewhere else to keep it that way . . .'

'The weight descending draws up the plunger, expanding an airless space that the water then rushes up to fill,' Praeda went on. 'Really, Che, this is apprentice stuff. The water possesses enough momentum to gush through the smaller pipes and into the gravel fountain. It then probably flows right back down to where it originated.'

Che did not trust herself to speak, merely put out an arm to seek the support of the wall.

'Of course,' Corcoran was saying, 'we could sell them a pump the size of your shoe that would do a better job, and not need some bugger hauling a weight up every morning, but they won't have it. Mad, they are, around here.'

'But that's not right . . .' Che began slowly.

'What do you mean?' There was a look of perfect incomprehension on Praeda's face.

'The Khanaphir . . . they're Inapt, surely.' She glanced from the academic to the Iron Glove factor, whose expressions mirrored each other exactly.

'Inapt?' Praeda said slowly. 'Che, they're *us* – they're Beetle-kinden. Of course they aren't Inapt. What were you thinking?'

'Go out of the city,' Corcoran put in. 'Go upriver, they got watermills, cranes, they can do all sorts of clever things with levers and weights. Take a look at the Estuarine Gate some time! It's just, they've no more than that. No imagination is what I think.'

'No . . .' Che sat down on the steps. She could feel something slipping away from her, and she thought it might be her hopes. Beyond Praeda's concerned face the stone pump ground minutely on, obstinately destroying everything she had come here to find.

*Am I alone now? Now that the Khanaphir are just Apt, and merely backward, rather than some great survival from the Age of Lore? Can I admit to myself that I'm a freak and a cripple, and simply get it over with?*

'Che, what's wrong?' Praeda asked. And then Ethmet was there.

'Forgive me, forgive me, Honoured Foreigners,' he said. 'Alas, you are used to better hospitality than our poor city can afford. Forgive me that we have bored you thus, that you have fled us into these unfit places. I shall call for dancers. I shall have Amnon order his men to fight for your pleasure.'

'Please, First Minister,' said Praeda, abruptly stand-in diplomat. 'I think that Che . . . that is, Miss Maker is ill.'

'Alas!' He crouched beside her and, despite Petri's predictions, his lined face showed nothing but concern. 'We shall have a physician sent for at once.'

'No, please.' Somehow Che got herself to her feet. She saw that Corcoran had made himself scarce as soon as the Minister arrived, perhaps not eager to be implicated in robbing this man of his guests. 'Please, I just need to rest. I just need to go to my rooms.'

'Well, it is late,' Ethmet agreed. 'I shall have some servants escort you.'

*They have servants for everything,* she thought muggily. *Even to make their machines work. They have machines that are powered by people, how strange.* She was wailing inside her head. She wanted to go home – away from this place that had so decisively betrayed her – but Collegium was just as strange, and she could not now say in what quarter home lay.

They all headed back to the embassy together in the end. Manny was singing loudly, a girl on each arm, and Che was glad that her room was located at the opposite end of the building from his. *Not that I will sleep, anyway.* The discovery that had so thrilled Praeda had filled her with dread. *I had everything worked out, and what a fool I've been!* At every step, she felt she should plunge into the chasm that had suddenly opened up before her. *Nowhere to go*, she kept thinking. *I have nowhere to go. This has been a fool's errand, and I was the fool for it.* Another hour, another dawn facing that realization seemed unbearable.

'Manny,' she said, and then repeated, 'Manny!' when he wouldn't stop singing.

'What can I possibly do for you, Honoured Ambassador?' he drawled, and the girls giggled. Possibly, in their eyes, he seemed full of exotic allure. Overfull, maybe.

'You have drink, strong drink?' she enquired, though she already knew it to be true.

'I am drunk,' he considered. 'Also, I do have drink. Do you wish to retire with me and my new friends to my room so we can explore just how strong it is?'

She grabbed his robe hard enough that he halted abruptly and almost toppled over. 'If you ever dare say anything like that to me again, Mannerly Gorget, I will cut off your parts.' It was not fair, really, since she was not angry at *him*. He was just a broad and easy target for how very angry she felt with all the world, and with herself. 'I want at least two bottles of strong drink from wherever you've stashed it, but I will not be sharing them, do you understand?'

He goggled at her: her stern expression brooked no argument. She released him and strode off through the arch and into the Place of Foreigners.

*This world has too many sharp edges*, she brooded, *and I have cut myself too often on them. I will blur them and blur them, and perhaps tonight I will not dream, and tomorrow I will not feel like putting a knife to my wrists.*

# Sixteen

The pen scratched as it went dry, and Thalric shook it irritably. He would have preferred a simple quill of rolled chitin, but the Regent must have only the best. These reservoir pens – manufactured in Helleron, or copied in Sonn – carried their own store of ink. No more constant dipping and messy inkwells. He found that they worked unreliably and that his handwriting became unrecognizable. Such was progress.

It was long past dark now, and well into the silent watches that dragged their way towards midnight, and Thalric was still writing his report.

> *Contact made with the Khanaphir First Minister. Relations generally friendly. The precise power structure here is opaque. Mentions have been made of certain 'Masters', but this would seem to be a purely ceremonial position, from my observations.*

He had already written his assessment of the Khanaphir people, their character, their defences. He concurred with Vollen:

> *If the Empire brings force against Khanaphes, then there seems no prospect of a successful resistance. Their ground defences seem antiquated, and the Khanaphir have no visible means of defending their city or its holdings from the air.*

So far so good. Yet he had barely written a new line for over an hour now, the pen poised, then scratching out letters, then crossing them through, pages being copied to disguise his indecision.

It was all academic, of course, since Marger would be preparing his own report. If the purpose of this expedition fell into Rekef territory, then it would be Marger giving the orders. Thalric was only an adviser. Still, here he was playing the Rekef officer because it was all he knew how to do.

> *I have made contact with the Collegium embassy. Their ambassador is Cheerwell Maker, niece of their general, Stenwold Maker.*

He crossed it out and started again. His Rekef past and his more recent past hung on scales in his mind, each balancing the other. He found he did not want to be the man who put her name into the thoughts of General Brugan. The Rekef remembered names and he had no way to describe the two sides of Cheerwell Maker. List her accomplishments – fomenting rebellion in Myna, resistance in Solarno and Tharn – see her that way and she was such a threat that the Rekef death-orders would be signed the moment his report found home.

*And yet I know she is just a foolish girl. She bumbles about the world meaning well, and trying to do the right thing, then gets it wrong as often as not, and must run to catch up with events.* No, he did not want to be the man responsible for putting her on the List – inscribed beside her uncle – of those people the Rekef would remove when the new war broke out.

*I am a poor Rekef man, a poor Imperial soldier.* He had always tried to be loyal to his friends and comrades, but that had almost never worked. *So where is my loyalty now?* It seemed absurd that the sticking point for his much-abused fidelity could be a Beetle-kinden girl working for the opposite side.

*Everyone else recognizes the risks.* Maybe that was it. Che Maker never seemed to realize the danger she constantly put herself in. Watching her progress through life was like witnessing a constant series of near-misses, like seeing someone sleepwalk through a battle.

He shook his head. Once more he had written, *The Collegium ambassador is known to me*, but that begged the obvious question. He put down the pen and rubbed his eyes, smudging ink across his cheek. He was willing to bet that Marger would have completed his own report hours before, despite having the added chore of reporting on Thalric.

There was a scream from outside, so shrill with terror that Thalric leapt up instantly, spilling everything from the desk. He went to the window, found it too narrow to exit through. There was a lot of shouting from downstairs and from across the square. The scream was repeated, like the desperate cry of a man on the rack. *An attack! But on who?* He grabbed up his sword, discarded the scabbard and bolted out of his room.

He ran into a half-dressed Marger on the stairs, and with a common glance the two of them made for the door. As they hit the cool night air they found Gram outside, sword already drawn, the other hand held out with palm open towards the building on the other side of the Place. There were people spilling out of it, too, and Thalric spotted one of the Vekken already armoured, and glimpsed Che's Fly-kinden as well. Both of them held crossbows.

*Oh, this could get messy.* Gram and the Fly began shouting at each other, each demanding to know what the other had done. Without having to look, Thalric knew that Vollen, with his sting ready, would have taken station at one of the windows.

'There!' Marger snapped, and pointed. Thalric saw the body at the same time. Near the larger arch, a man lay on his back, one hand upraised as if to ward something off, the other arm flung over his eyes.

It was Osgan.

Thalric's heart sank as he ran across, dropping to one knee beside the fallen man. There was a lot of shouting going on, the pitch of tension rising and rising. 'Get them to shut up!' he told Marger, who backed away to quieten things down.

Osgan was shaking violently and he clung to the proffered arm as Thalric went to touch his shoulder. His face was a mask of tears and he reeked of alcohol. He kept pointing, though, and was trying to get some words out. Thalric followed the trembling finger, and for a second felt a twitch of what Osgan must be feeling. Then he cursed the man wearily and rounded on the escalating confrontation behind him.

Che had emerged now, bundled up in a grey Moth-kinden cloak and calling for her own side to back down. Thalric could sense that Gram was more than ready for a fight, and even Marger had abandoned his easy manner and had drawn his sword.

'Down! Swords down! Back inside!' Thalric bellowed, and for a moment he was neither Rekef nor traitor, but Captain Thalric of the Imperial army shouting at a bunch of recalcitrant soldiers. 'We are not about to restart the war with the Lowlands here in Khanaphes. There is no problem, there is no attack. Everyone get back inside and go to sleep!' Even as he shouted it he could hear his words echoed by Che Maker ordering her people to do the same.

'Accius, listen to me,' she was yelling. 'Or Malius, whichever. Just . . . I will find out what's going on . . . Trallo, put that cursed crossbow down.' An old Beetle had come out, wearing a nightshirt and carrying a sword, until Che turned and swore at him, telling him to get back inside and leave this to her. 'This isn't a fight,' she insisted. 'Nothing's happened.'

*Not yet,* Thalric thought, *but it very nearly did.*

'That man of yours is a liability,' Marger remarked disgustedly.

'Right now we're all liabilities,' Thalric told him grimly. 'I'll deal with Osgan. You get your men back inside.'

It seemed to last for ever, this moment on the edge of violence. Then Marger turned away, and Gram followed him with such a belligerent backwards stare that Thalric guessed he must have scores to settle with the Lowlands, left over from the war. The Vekken had already stamped back inside and Che was shepherding the rest of her errant people out of sight.

Osgan had crawled over to the pond and was splashing water on his face. In the sudden quiet, Thalric could hear the ragged catch of his breathing.

'You bloody fool,' he said, but quietly. Osgan rolled over onto his back. He looked ill.

'You can't know . . .' he got out, 'what I saw—'

'I know exactly what you saw,' Thalric snapped, 'and be grateful I understand enough not to hand you over to Vollen and Gram,' He glanced over at what had spooked Osgan: just a statue. It was partly overgrown, hidden in greenery until now, and depicted a Mantis-kinden standing with his clawed gauntlet on, the blade folded back along the line of his arm. *And I do understand. Tisamon could have modelled for it.*

The release of tension left him feeling weak, shaking his head. He had no will left to discipline Osgan. The whole business just seemed ridiculous. He sat down heavily on one of the benches as Osgan eyed him cautiously.

'I'm sorry, Thalric. I'm sorry,' he mumbled.

'Oh, shut up,' Thalric said, without rancour. *We could have been killing each other, over this.* He chuckled despite himself, resting his head on one hand and staring into the water.

'Midnight manoeuvres for the Imperial army, is it?'

He jumped up and turned to find Che standing not ten feet away, still clutching that grey cloak about her. He snorted half a laugh before he could stop himself.

'Just an . . . It's not a problem.'

'Is he all right?' She peered round him at the prone figure of Osgan.

'He's fine. He's drunk.'

'Lucky him.' To his surprise one of her hands came up holding a clay jar from which she took a swallow. 'He's more than drunk. What happened?' She asked the question without guile, not a Lowlander agent prying for information – just Cheerwell Maker and Thalric caught up in another awkward situation.

'He ran into that statue over there, the Mantis one, and it gave him a bit of a fright,' Thalric explained. One harsh winter during the Twelve-year War, he had crossed a frozen lake on foot, his armour weighing him down too much for flight. He was reminded of that now: just pressing on carefully while waiting for the ice to give way, for everything to fall apart.

'Well, I can understand that.' She sat down with a whoosh of breath, raising the jar to her lips again.

*Everyone gets a drink tonight except me*, he thought. *Now is that fair?* 'I don't suppose,' he said, still negotiating the ice, 'there's enough there for a swig?'

She gave him a long look, and in his mind he heard the ominous creaking and cracking, but then she passed it over. He knocked back a gulp, tasted harsh spirits, far stronger than he had expected. He choked, forcing it down, then handed the jar back wordlessly.

Che gave a delighted shout. 'You know, I always thought temperance was one of your lot's virtues. I don't think I ever saw a drunk Wasp before.'

Osgan began to protest about being called drunk, but he slurred the words so much he was incomprehensible.

Thalric felt himself smile. 'Oh, bring three bottles of this gutrot to my room some time, and I'll show you one.' He waited for the final crack, the sudden icy cold, but she laughed out loud, the sound ringing around the Place of Foreigners. What Marger and the rest must have thought, he had no idea.

'I'm not . . . not that drunk. I'm not that . . . that drunk,' Osgan muttered, getting one elbow on to a bench and dragging himself into a sitting position. 'That . . . not that drunk . . . but . . . but I saw – *it*, *him* . . .' The words fell off into a choking sob.

Thalric gave Che a look of exasperation but realized she was nodding. 'Oh, the Khanaphir are far too good at statues,' she agreed. 'I had enough of a fright when I saw our door guards.'

Thalric glanced across at the Collegium embassy, not understanding for a moment, then reinterpreting the stone Moth-kinden there. 'Of course,' he added more quietly, 'he is dead.'

'Yes,' Che echoed. 'Yes, he is dead.'

'I'm sorry.'

'Are you really?' And the ice began to give way, just as it had in the Commonweal.

'You forget, I knew him,' Thalric said, in a tone that was quick and clipped. *Why do I care what she thinks I think about her dead Moth?* 'We went through that mad business in Jerez together. For that matter, I did my best to stop him getting stabbed.'

She was nodding, slowly. Another step taken and he hadn't fallen yet. 'I wasn't there. He wouldn't take me with him.'

'You . . . wouldn't have been able to change anything,' he declared.

She glared at him. 'Would I not, then?'

He turned away from her to look into the water again, his own expression looking as distant as those of the statues themselves. 'It's just what one says, in these situations, to spare people. To tell the truth there were things happening that night that I will never understand.'

There was a long pause, and he found her studying him, nodding slowly. 'I believe you,' she said, almost too softly for him to catch. 'I believe you, because I understand it a little, now.' He frowned at that and she shook her head, casting around for another topic of conversation. 'What's your friend got against Mantids?'

Osgan gave a hollow laugh. 'You can't know. You weren't there.'

Che frowned at Thalric. 'Where?'

Osgan struggled further up onto the next bench, and lay back on it, gasping like a dying fish.

'He was . . .' It was not a pleasant tale, would seem even less pleasant to her. Thalric pressed on regardless. 'He was a guest of the Emperor during a celebration to mark the anniversary of the coronation. There was a big blood-fighting match. He had the honour of serving as the Emperor's scribe for the evening. For the Consortium it's a real accolade.'

'Oh, I was doing well, back then. Well, well, well,' Osgan interrupted. 'I was flying high.'

'So what happened?' Che asked. 'Did the Emperor—?'

'Oh, the Emperor nothing,' Thalric said. He waited for Osgan to speak, then filled in the silence. 'It was because of your friend. I wasn't there, but I've heard all about it. Your friend the Mantis.'

'Tisamon.' Che breathed. The very name seemed to make the night more chill, and she shivered under the cloak, leaning closer to him, anxious to hear the rest.

'He was fighting for the Emperor's pleasure, but he got up into the stalls somehow. He went . . . mad,' Thalric said slowly. 'Tisamon went mad, that's what I heard. There were guards that tried to stop him, but . . .'

'You . . . weren't there,' said Osgan clearly. 'You can't know. They tried to stop him. They ran in from in front of the Emperor, and from all sides, and they flew from across the pit. They tried . . . they had stings and spears and swords, and they were trying to get between him and the Emperor, but he just . . . killed them.' His voice sounded raw, like an unhealed wound. 'He killed them and he killed them, and they didn't have a chance. They were throwing themselves on to his blade. They – so many – they were . . . so brave, all of them so brave. They were dying for the Emperor, and the Mantis wouldn't stop killing them. They didn't have a chance.' He choked again, descending back into his misery. 'So brave,' he got out one last time.

Che was looking somewhere beyond Thalric now, while automatically passing the jar back to him. 'She never said,' she murmured. 'Tynisa would never say just how it happened.'

Thalric put a hand to her shoulder, without thinking. *All these dead we have in common.* She covered it with her own, still peering into her own mind. For a moment, lost in memory and in drink, she had forgotten who he was.

'And the Emperor died, of course,' said Thalric. *And from there come all my woes.*

She focused her gaze on him again, and instead of the anger he had expected there was only puzzlement there. 'What are you doing here, Thalric?'

'Keeping an eye on you.' He said it before the Rekef in him could prevent it. 'And you?'

'Me? Oh, I'm mastering the art of self-deception. The others, they're here to study – although I don't expect you to believe a word of it. But I myself came here looking for . . . something else.' She gave a fragile smile. 'Something that isn't here, that never was.' No longer clutched so tight, the cloak had fallen open as she leant closer. Beneath it he saw the thin shift she wore, and under that, the swell of her breast. He felt a stab of arousal, absurdly inappropriate but powerful, and made to remove his hand from the warmth of her shoulder. For a second she held on to it, then let him reclaim it.

'We are such fools, aren't we?' she said. 'Brawling in the streets.'

'To the great amusement of our hosts,' he agreed.

'Well, Thalric, where does this leave us?'

'I don't know,' he said. 'Are we enemies, here and now?'

She met his gaze. 'You made a slave of me.'

'Che—'

'You would have had me raped. You would have tortured me – you *would* – don't think I've forgotten.'

He had gone cold. The ice had finally cracked and he had forgotten to be ready for it. 'I won't deny it.'

'I didn't think you would. You've never been less than honest.' She shrugged. 'And Uncle Sten thinks there's even hope for the Vekken, so why not you? What are you asking for, Thalric?'

'A truce? Until things degenerate between our factions again. A truce between you and me.' He took that final step across the perilous ice. 'For old times' sake.'

She snorted with laughter, but he was now on firm ground. He grasped her hand when she offered it to him, though he saw the faint flinch, her memory of what Wasp hands could do.

'We are both a long way from home,' she conceded, draining the last dregs from the jar. As she stood up it took her a moment to get her balance. 'We . . . we run out of old friends, do we not? They die, or they leave.'

He knew what she was saying: both of them marooned here at the ends of the earth. With whom did they share a past, however bitter, but with each other? He knew she would never have admitted it without the drink, but it was said now, impossible to retract.

'A truce,' she said. 'I know you're no good servant of your Empire, Thalric.' He must have twitched because she said quickly, 'and I'm no better. I came here for my own selfish reasons, however misconceived. A truce until the others start fighting again. Why not?' She squeezed his hand briefly, then released it.

He turned to Osgan and kicked the man's foot, drawing a startled exclamation.

'What—?'

'If you're intending to sleep, at least sleep indoors rather than under the stars like a Roach-kinden,' Thalric reproached him, and half-hauled the man to his feet. He glanced at Che again, and she gave him a fragile smile, a lop-sided shrug.

'Until next time,' she said, and turned for her embassy.

Petri Coggen was wide awake the next day – more awake than Che felt, certainly. Without fatigue to loosen her lips, she was now close-mouthed about the things she had said previously. Instead she eyed her fellow Collegiates cagily. *You all think I'm mad*, was written plain on her face.

'We will talk later,' Che whispered to her. After all, her great confessions had been disclosed only to Che, who was frankly not ready for further details. Between the disappointment and the drink she was feeling the morning keenly.

'You've lived for a while amongst these Khanaphir,' Berjek remarked. They were sitting together at a magnificently carved table, eating a local breakfast of honey and seedcake. The airy wave of his hand took in the city beyond the window, but ignored the servants that glided past him. 'I confess to seeing here a great deal that has mystified me. Their culture is not at all like ours, and yet we are of the same kinden.'

Petri Coggen nodded gloomily. 'Yes, they are not like us,' she said.

'Technologically, in particular,' Praeda put in. 'Which I think we can take as a valid yardstick of any culture—'

'Oh, nonsense.' The objection of Berjek the historian to Praeda the artificer.

She ignored him. 'These Khanaphir have a marvellous architecture, it's true, and I'm told they have some achievements in basic water-powered or weight-and-lever devices, but . . . but when Che first saw this place, she even thought they might be *Inapt*, and I must admit I can see why.'

*Oh you can't*, Che thought, around her headache. *Really, you can't.*

'Do you know much of their history?' Praeda asked.

'They do not talk about their history, for the same reason fish don't talk of water,' Petri told them. 'They are swimming in history. So much of this city is ancient, and so much more simply copied from that.'

Manny seemed to be suffering worse than Che, and had been listlessly chewing the same mouthful of seedcake for twenty minutes. Now he swallowed forcibly, and said, 'Maybe they achieved Aptitude more recently than we did.'

The others looked at him quizzically.

'Yes, yes,' he said irritably, 'I am a Master of the Great College. I may not be as respected as either of you two, but I'm a cartographer. I study maps, and I know that sometimes there are maps that I can't read: maps made by the Inapt, who frankly have no concept of how to draw one. But sometimes there are maps that are . . . trying harder. Those of the Fly-kinden, for instance. Fly-kinden maps dating from a couple of centuries ago are illegible, but modern ones, most of them, are clear as day.'

'It's a possibility,' Berjek allowed. 'The transmigration of Aptitude over time is a . . . contentious issue, academically speaking. I'm not sure that's something I want to get into.'

'Corcoran said something . . .' Che blurted out. What was it the Iron Glove factor had said?

'Corcoran advised us to study the Estuarine Gate,' Praeda recalled. 'I think we should take him up on it. He told me where their consortium has its factora located. I'm sure he'd be happy for us to engage his services for the day.'

The bright sun provided no antidote to a harsh night. Che staggered like a blind woman half the distance to the Estuarine Gate, before her eyes and brain reluctantly reached a détente with the new day. Corcoran seemed in annoyingly jaunty form, more than happy to help his fellow foreigners. He had been in Khanaphes for a while, she gathered, but the locals would not let him forget that he did not belong. He was enjoying the novelty of some company.

'The thing is . . .' Corcoran began, running his hand along the intricately cut stone of the Estuarine Gate's nearside pillar. 'No – tell you what, you take a look at it there, then you tell me.' He beamed around at the academics. Che could not yet make up her mind about him. He had the demeanour of a mercenary, and wore the dark armour of the Iron Glove at all times, but he talked like a merchant, instantly familiar, endearingly irreverent. His Solarnese features looked infinitely honest and Che would not have bought a kitchen knife from him.

Berjek and Praeda both stepped forward to take a look. The great column that formed the eastern Estuarine Gate towered above them, incised at every level with those ubiquitous pictographs that Khanaphes had tattooed itself with. Che forced herself to examine them, aware that behind her Manny Gorget had drifted off to accost a sweetmeat seller, while Petri Coggen stood biting at her nails and flinching away from the many Khanaphir that bustled past.

In frustration, Berjek had dismissed the designs as merely decorative. Che's eyes gave him the lie. They caught on the orderly lines of carving, drawn into following them. On most of the buildings it was like seeing a madman's scrawl, always promising sense, delivering nothing. Here on these ancient stones . . .

She blinked. For a moment just then it had seemed as though she saw words, had heard voices almost. *In that day . . . Honour to . . . So it was . . .* She averted her eyes, her headache stabbing sharply behind the eyes, then forced herself to look again. It was as though the sense they conveyed was hovering like a fish just below the surface – distorted, deceptive, but nevertheless there.

'Corcoran, tell me,' she said, 'what are these cursed carvings they engrave on everything?'

'No idea.' He grinned briefly. 'Just part of the Khanaphir

way, their traditions. When they build something in stone they have special craftsmen come and put these squiggles on them. It's just what they do.' He gave a half-shrug, clearly not so bothered. 'They say the carvers train especially from a great book of the designs that the Ministers have, that shows all the permitted pictures they can use. Good luck in seeing that, though. Our hosts don't make it easy to understand them.'

Che filed the information away. *I will see that book if I have to steal it.*

'I really don't know what I'm looking for,' Berjek admitted, backing away from the towering structure. 'Or do you mean the statues on the estuary side? We saw those coming in.'

*Didn't we just,* Che thought. She had dreamt last night of Achaeos, the drink betraying her. He had been hunting her, the lethal lines of a snapbow in his slender hands, and she had tried and tried to hide, but he had always tracked her down, his white eyes blazing in fury. It had been Khanaphes he was hunting her through, a city empty of people, and with those colossal statues, in their eternal cold beauty, looming at every corner.

'I have it,' Praeda said at last. 'This is not of one piece. There are four sides to it, and it is hollow.'

'Very good,' Corcoran smiled. 'You can hardly tell, I know, but the cracks are there. Now look across at the side of the west gate, facing us. You see the groove there?'

'There is . . . Is that a chain?' Praeda leant out, alarmingly, over the river. 'It can't be.'

'They don't call this a gate for nothing,' Corcoran confirmed. 'Below us, way below the draught of any ship, there is a great big, bronze-shod, wooden gate, and inside those towers there must be the biggest drop-weights you ever saw. When they want to close the river, they close the river, though I've never actually seen it done. They tell me it was last raised about forty years ago, so I reckon it's in good working order still.'

'Still?' Berjek echoed. 'Yes, but "still" from when? Oh, it looks old enough, but then everything here does. When was this mechanism put in?'

'That I can't tell you,' Corcoran admitted, and when the academics turned sour faces on him, he raised a hand. 'Believe it or not, I wanted to know that as well. I'm an artificer, after all, and you get curious. The locals just say it's been here for ever, whatever that means. No help there, then. But I got friendly with a Spider-kinden captain, and she did a bit of digging for me – in exchange for a cheap deal on some crossbows from the Glove. She found some records of once when a Spider Arista was stopped at the gates by the Khanaphir – some diplomatic incident – and the Spider-kinden families don't forget insults. Their description of the gate is perfect, same then as now.'

'And when was this supposed to be?' Berjek asked, annoyed by the man's air of showmanship.

'Hold on to something,' Corcoran said, 'because it was at least – *at least*, mind – five hundred and fifty years back. And it didn't say anything about the gate being *new*, even then.'

Berjek stared at him. 'Well, that's impossible,' he protested, but something tugged at the corner of his mouth and he added, 'Isn't it?'

'Could Collegium have built this, then?' Che asked.

'No,' Praeda said simply. 'That long ago is before the revolution, back when we might really have been Inapt.'

'But the Khanaphir can't have been Apt for fifty – maybe a hundred? – years longer than we have,' said Berjek, scandalized. 'Just look at them! What happened? Are you telling me that all their artificers just gave up, closed their books and locked their workshops?'

'I'm not telling you anything,' Corcoran said mildly. 'They do the most impressive things you ever saw with simple mechanisms, and they'll have nothing to do with anything more, even if you promise to install it free of charge. You're right, it makes no sense, but that's the way it is.'

*It doesn't make sense,* Che agreed inwardly. *And so there must be some reason for it that we have not found. Aptitude? It is all about Aptitude. This city has not truly taken to it, so . . . so . . .*

*So there may be something left, some survival, that the tide of progress has not washed away.*

She fell back from the bickering academics to join Petri Coggen, who looked at her fearfully. Che could not blame her.

'You know this city,' Che began. 'You know it better than any of us.'

'What do you want?' Petri asked her, voice shaking slightly. There was clearly something in Che's expression she did not like, and Che was not surprised.

'There must be something . . . Even in Collegium, if one searches hard enough, one can find a mystic, some old Moth or halfbreed peddling prophecy from a doorway. You can't tell me there is nothing of that here.'

Petri stared at her aghast. 'But . . . why?'

'Never mind why,' Che replied, with more force than she intended. 'I want you to think carefully about what I have asked and then, when we can go without these scholars bothering me, you will show me what I want to see.'

Petri was already shaking her head slowly. 'I'm not sure . . .'

'You have told me your fears,' Che persisted. 'I have not dismissed them. In fact, I agree with you: there is something at the heart of this city that is very wrong indeed. But I must use unusual methods to find it.' It was dishonest, putting it like that, but she was desperate. 'Did Master – did Kadro go to those places?'

There was a very long pause, as shock registered on Petri's face.

'He did,' she whispered. 'I don't know how you know that, but he did.'

'Then so shall I.'

# Seventeen

They had sent Corcoran advance warning of the ship, but the vessel was now three days late and he was not a man to be out sitting on the dock every morning in loyal vigilance. Instead, for a handful of coins he had a boy keep watch for him. He meanwhile did his best to show autonomy and importance, for the position of foreign traders in Khanaphes was an uncertain one. A man had to work hard to get invited to the diplomatic functions that Corcoran enjoyed. Still, when the boy came running to the Iron Glove factora bringing the news, Corcoran got himself to the docks absolutely as quickly as possible.

He spotted the ship straight away, even amongst the perpetual dance of other vessels docking and leaving. Following his advice, they had come in under sail, but he could see the tarpaulin-covered bulk of the engine and paddle wheel at the stern, which had cut across the Sunroad Sea in defiance of wind or weather. The gauntlet badge of the Iron Glove was displayed on the round shields that lined her rails, a practice borrowed from the Mantis-kinden and more decorative than functional here. The sail was blank, but they seldom had to resort to it: only here, where time stood still, was being at the mercy of the elements considered good form.

Corcoran got himself to the quay just as the ship drew in, making himself evident in his dark armour and shifting tabard. Though he liked to consider himself a free spirit, there were certain people whose continued favour was essential to his livelihood, and one such was currently on this ship.

*And why is Himself taking all this so very personally?* A simple message from Corcoran had confirmed when the Lowlanders were expected, and the reply had come back by return: *I am coming*, and projected times and dates. *None of my business*, Corcoran decided. *He's worried about the competition, no doubt.*

Once the dockhands had finished tying the ship off, a section of its metal-plated side fell open to form a gangplank. Corcoran drew himself up straight as the passengers began to disembark.

*Life alive,* he marvelled. *He doesn't do things by halves.*

The man in the lead wore armour of black, fluted steel: an intricate mesh of fine mail and sliding plates, and each section cast in ridges and folds to give it more strength for less weight. Nothing of his face showed between the slotted helm and a high gorget. His Iron Glove tabard was edged in silver, but beyond that it was only the sophistication of the armour itself that marked his rank. Behind him came a full dozen Iron Glove mercenaries armoured in leathers, like Corcoran himself, but under plain breastplates and blackened steel helms. They all carried spears and swords, and Corcoran guessed at the disassembled crossbows or snapbows lying hidden in their packs.

*It's not a delegation, it's an invasion*, he thought. Already there would be word rushing upriver towards the Scriptora, so they would receive their official welcome soon enough.

'Welcome to Khanaphes, Sieur,' he said. The eye-slit of the helm waited, and he hastily corrected himself, 'Sir, rather.' *And why they have to use Imperial, rather than good honest Solarnese words, I don't know.* 'Are you not hot in all that armour, sir?'

The man gave a hollow laugh. 'A little, but giving the

right impression is important. What is the situation here? Where do we stand?'

'Would you not rather retire to the factora first, sir?'

'I'm sure I will be required to speak with the locals shortly, so tell me what I need to know.'

'Well then, nothing much has changed,' Corcoran explained. 'The Collegiates have been here almost a tenday now, and they've been meeting with the Ministers and poking at the statues, all what you'd expect. The only business was some kind of midnight scuffle with some Imperial types a few days back, but nothing further seemed to come of that.'

'How long has the Empire been here?' the helm enquired.

'Oh, about a couple of days longer than the Lowlanders. And yes, I know, obvious conclusions: one of them's here to watch the other. Or both of them are.'

His superior nodded. 'And the Lowlander ambassador is . . . who I suspected?'

'She is, yes.'

'So.' There was a fierce edge to this single word that made Corcoran guess that Che Maker was in for a complicated future. 'Where have they put her?'

'The old embassies. They've reopened them.'

'Make sure you have people watching her constantly. Know where she goes, who she meets.' The gauntleted hands clenched.

'Of course, sir.' *And why's that then?* But it was not Corcoran's place to ask questions of this man.

'And now I think we have our welcoming committee.'

Corcoran turned to see a full score of Khanaphir guardsmen hurriedly pushing their way through the crowds towards the docks. Although not caparisoned in the gilded splendour of the Royal Guard, they had the great form of Amnon striding at their head. They halted and formed up at a respectful distance as the two groups of armed men watched each other cautiously. Corcoran, caught in the middle, began to feel exposed.

'Now then, who have we here?' boomed Amnon as he stepped forward. When he came to stand before Corcoran's master he seemed quite oblivious of the spear-tipped ranks poised ready to close on him. 'Iron Glove, then? *More* of you? We're a little taken aback, my good friends, since we were not expecting such numbers. Our hospitality may not stretch to it.'

'We don't need much,' replied the Iron Glove leader, as he tilted his helm back, revealing a tan-brown face with that slight mismatching of feature that spoke of mixed blood.

'You must think our streets very dangerous, to come in such numbers,' Amnon murmured. His countenance was all good humour, but Corcoran could sense his displeasure, ready to make a fight of this if the Iron Glove's answers did not satisfy him.

*I only hope they read everything I wrote to them about how to deal with the Khanaphir*, he thought. Corcoran wanted to edge away, to slip out of that invisible line of tension strung between the city guard and the mercenary newcomers, but he had an image to maintain. The Iron Glove did not show fear.

'The world's not safe. Without these men I'd not have arrived at all,' the Iron Glove leader replied. 'Indeed, some pirates saw our little trading coaster here and marked it as an easy prize.'

Amnon nodded. 'And did you outrun them . . .?'

'They discovered their mistake.'

'I hate pirates.' Amnon's face split in a grin. 'Those that dare strike near the mouth of the Jamail are the rightful prey of my ships. I am glad to hear you sent them to the bottom.'

'Not at all. I put men on their vessel and had them sail her back to Porta Rabi. We of the Iron Glove are well known as traders, and wealthy ones. We become targets, by land or sea. We show them in exchange that we who sell war can use what we trade in. That way they will soon realize that we always fight, and that any attacks will cost them more than they could ever gain from us.' He glanced back at his followers, still standing at the ready. 'So there you have the reason for this force. As for my men, they can lodge here on the ship, or wherever you wish in the city.'

'I will have rooms prepared at your factora,' Amnon decided. He had been nodding with approval throughout the man's speech, and with these words the tension eased, his guards standing down with a tiny shuffle of feet. 'Well then, allow me to welcome you to our city. I am Amnon, First Soldier among the Royal Guard.'

The Iron Glove commander threw a brief glance at Corcoran for confirmation, before announcing, 'Ah, so we have a gift for you, I believe.'

Amnon nodded. 'That is no surprise to me, after all the measuring and prying that your man here has done.'

'It may surprise you yet,' the Iron Glove man remarked. 'I am glad to be here in your city.' He thrust forward his armoured hand and clasped Amnon's larger one. 'My name is Totho, once of Collegium. I think you have some of my kin here.'

'Apparently there's going to be a hunt of some kind,' Manny reported. The other Collegiates looked up from their breakfast in mild interest. 'Their big fellow, Amnon, came round yesterday while you were all out,' he went on. 'We're all invited. In fact it's in our honour. I, for one, am looking forward to it.'

'Are you sure you're feeling well?' Berjek asked him. 'This hunt, presumably it will involve some manner of exertion – running around or that kind of thing. Not your favourite pastime at all, I would have thought.'

'Very funny.' The fat man gave him a sour look. 'I am a

natural historian and a cartographer, do not forget. Neither of which I can do much about while sitting idly here in this city. I want to go out and make a few sketches, and this hunt sounds like the best chance I'll get – anyway, it's on the river and so all I'll have to do is recline in a boat while some local beauty fans me with a frond or something.'

'Some local *bald* beauty,' Berjek pointed out.

Manny's expression remained supremely unconcerned. 'I happen to find that quite attractive.'

'Are you planning to deflower the entire female population of Khanaphes before we're done here?' Praeda asked testily.

'They don't object.'

'They've probably been warned that their families will be executed if they don't indulge the important foreigners,' she said. 'That's the only way I can account for it.'

'Trallo, what sort of hunt is this likely to be?' Berjek turned to the Fly. 'Dangerous?'

'Could be, if you get too close,' Trallo replied. He had been idle recently, his work in Khanaphes already done, and Che suspected he might soon ask for his pay and take his leave. 'They usually put the spectators out in mid-river where they can watch safely, while the real business goes on in the shallows or on the shore. Of course, they'll respect you all the more if you ask to take part.'

Petri Coggen appeared just then, bleary-eyed. Che studied her with a matching expression. Her own dreams had been bad again, too, but Che remembered only fragments. When she awoke the ghost was boiling in the air beside her bed and, in conjunction with her latest nightmare, she had not been able to suppress a scream. Its seething frustration was palpable: she could feel its thoughts, and they were all contempt and rage at being trapped, and all directed at her, for keeping it so.

'I'm sorry!' she had cried out to it. 'Please, tell me what to do!'

But instantly it had been gone, just as Trallo had burst in, half-dressed and with a crossbow in his hands.

*I can't take much more of this,* she thought. This city that had promised so much had betrayed her, and she was falling apart.

Praeda and Berjek were heading out into the city again. Che was still not quite sure what they were looking for, and she guessed that neither were they. Once they were out of the door, Manny laughed vaguely. 'She might come over all Mistress Detached, but I know something she doesn't. Remember that party at the, what's the place called?'

'The Scriptora,' Che supplied.

'Right. Their man Amnon, he had some interesting questions to ask me.'

At the mention of the name, Petri shuddered, but Manny was too concerned with his story to notice.

'He was asking me, you see, whether our Praeda Rakespear had a man back home.' He smirked. 'I think he thought that she and I might be . . . you know, but when he found out we weren't, he was asking if there was anyone else. I think our big dumb brute has taken a liking to the Cold One.'

'And you wouldn't have encouraged him in that at all?' Trallo tried to sound stern, but could not hide his grin.

'Perish the thought.' Manny winked.

Tiring of this conversation, Che caught Petri's eye and jerked her head towards the next room.

Out of earshot of the others, she said firmly, 'Today, Petri.' It had been several days since she had first made her request, and she knew that Petri was trying to put her off.

'I'm really not—'

'Today,' Che repeated quietly. She sat down on a canvas-covered stool. 'You are not the only one of us this city is destroying.'

'You don't understand.' Petri actually knelt before her. 'This thing, it is banned by the Masters . . . the Ministers,

I mean. It is illegal. What would they think if they found you . . .? They call the very practice "the Profanity".'

In Che's mind the ghost howled again, and Achaeos's blank eyes held only hatred. She could feel her hands shaking, ever so slightly. *I will break*, she decided, *if I cannot claw some release from this city.* 'I don't care,' she told Petri. 'Let that be my worry.' The words tasted foul in her mouth.

'But the people . . . you must see, the people who practise Profanity, they are criminals, outlaws, outcasts. If you venture among them, they might just cut your throat.'

'I am looking for mystics, whatever shabby oracles and seers this place can throw up,' Che said stubbornly, 'not for some den of murderers.'

'They take their mysticism very seriously here. If the guard caught them, they would be executed. It is . . . a vice, an illegal pleasure. *Fir*, they call it.'

'Fear?'

'Fir,' Petri pronounced it more carefully. 'But it is not like taking some Spiderlands drug, or exotic women, or that kind of vice. There is . . . a whole under-society based around it, and they are mad, unpredictable. They might kill you on the spot – you can never tell. Kadro, he was good with such people, but he still didn't like to go looking for the Fir-eaters.'

Che clenched her fists in frustration. She felt as though she was already experiencing withdrawal from some drug, cut off from a normality that she had breathed and eaten and slept with for twenty years. *I cannot be doing what I am now doing. I am Cheerwell Maker, scholar of the Great College, citizen of Collegium, niece of Master Stenwold Maker. I am no criminal. Give me some other way to turn!*

'But they *are* mystics, or at least they talk like mystics do, about the past, and . . . impossible things,' Petri continued hoarsely. 'I do not know who else there is.'

'Then take me to them,' Che demanded, before she could change her mind.

*

The man Petri found was a starved-looking Khanaphir. He was bare-chested and Che could see each of his ribs distinctly beneath that taut skin. It was clear that sustenance came second to some greater love in his life.

They met him at an 'open house' near the docks, meaning a place where the locals offered drink and other services to foreign mariners, so that they would not be tempted to venture any further into the city. The place was crowded, squalid, the outer shell of an older building fitted out with as many benches and tables as possible. Solarnese and Dragonfly and Spider-kinden sat shoulder to shoulder, and argued and drank and brawled.

The lean man hunched forward towards the two Beetle women. His eyes were cavernous, hollowed. 'I hear you seek something this place here cannot provide,' he said. Che had to strain to catch the words.

Petri glanced nervously at Che and then nodded, her hands clutched each other anxiously on the tabletop. 'Something special,' she explained. 'I know . . . someone I know said you could find it for us.'

There was a bleak cynicism in the thin man's eyes. 'Be careful what you seek. The Profanity is not for all palates. It is not for foreigners.'

'Do not presume to know who I am,' Che interrupted. The words came from within her, yet no conscious thought had formed them. As she snapped them out, she found herself pincering the man's bony wrist with her fingers. His recoiling twitch whiplashed down his long arm, but her grip held tight.

'What do you want?' He was afraid now, not of them but of something else, something she could not see.

'You *know* what I want.' Che's heart was racing. She felt as though she was hurtling downhill, and sometimes she was in control and sometimes she was just falling forwards. Something had come over her, some sharp inspiration.

Could that be Achaeos's ghost, speaking through her?

The lean man bit his lip, staring at her. 'This other . . . no, but you . . . Who are you? Where do you come from?'

'I've come a long way.' Che finally released him, saw the shadow of her grasp on his skin, that he rubbed at resentfully. He would no longer look at either of them.

'If you want, then you shall have. But do not complain, afterwards, that it was not what you sought.'

'Just take me there,' Che said. 'Petri, you can go. You don't have to come with me.'

'But . . . you can't just go off alone with him,' Petri protested. She dragged Che away from the table, out of the man's earshot. 'He'll kill you,' she insisted.

'He might.' Che's hand moved to her sword, buckled on now that politeness was no issue. 'What else can I do?'

'No, Che!' Petri hissed, casting the thin man a venomous look – as though she herself had not been the one who had led Che here.

'Will you come with me, then?'

'With him? Into the Marsh Alcaia again?' Petri bared her teeth in desperation. 'Not again . . . don't make me . . .'

Someone right beside them rapped on a table with something hard, a dagger hilt. Both of them turned to see a Fly-kinden man, his face half hidden beneath a broad-brimmed hat. The neat beard gave him away and Che felt her stomach lurch at the thought of discovery.

'Trallo,' she gasped.

He tilted up the brim of the hat and gave her a broad smile. 'I reckoned you were up to something foolish,' he said. 'Thankfully you have people interested in keeping you safe, so I decided to keep an eye on you.'

'Trallo, this isn't your business now.'

He took a long breath, a tiny spot of calm in the rowdy open house. The lean man still watched them, clutching at the edge of his table.

'You're about to do something really unwise, I can tell that. You're about to go somewhere very dangerous.'

'It's my decision.'

Trallo glanced from Che to the shaking Petri, and back. 'Fine, I'll come with you. That's *my* decision.'

Che was caught in mid-protest, suddenly thinking, *Was that not what I wanted?* Trallo would surely be of more use than poor Petri, and Petri just as surely would not come willingly. 'Do you know . . . You know Khanaphes. You should know what we're about before you make such an offer.'

Trallo shrugged. 'Like I said, our friends have asked me to ensure you're safe. They're worried about you.'

Che thought of Berjek and the rest, and would not have believed that of them, but here the Fly was, all the same.

She leant close to him. 'We are going to the Fir-eaters. You've heard of them?'

'Heard of, but never met.' He made a face. 'Tell your hungry friend there to pack his bags, then. Bella Petri, you get yourself back to the embassy – and not a word of this to anyone, you understand?'

Petri nodded gratefully and, before anyone could retract the offer, she was hurrying for the door.

'I'm grateful for this, Trallo,' Che said.

The Fly spread his hands. 'What are friends for?'

And she was happy enough with that answer not to notice the signal he gave, as they left the open house.

# Eighteen

There had been Scorpions keeping pace with them for at least three days, and Hrathen guessed probably a while longer. Since that morning they had let themselves be silhouetted against the barren skyline. On foot, or seated on their beasts, with spears held high, they had stared at the odd caravan but made no move against it.

*Why would they,* Hrathen thought wryly, *when we are so obligingly going where they want us to go?* Imperial mapmakers had not made much inroad into the Nem. It was a wasteland of stones and dust, of coarse ridges of bloody-minded grass that cut the skin like knives, and of ruins. Here and there some fault in the rock beneath opened narrow root-space with access to underground water, nourishing stark, barrel-trunked trees with fleshy leaves shaped like the sort of arrowheads the Empire used to pierce strong mail. The going was uneven, the dusty terrain rising and falling with the stony bones of the land beneath. Sometimes those bones speared through into crags and juts of red-black rock that the coarse wind had rounded and bowed.

The Imperial scouts, mostly staying with the dubious safety of the Slave Corps, had nevertheless ventured far enough to pinpoint a Scorpion-kinden camp, and it was this tenuous landmark that Hrathen had set his compass by. Overall, it was Brugan's plan but Hrathen's details. Hrathen found he liked this mission, as Brugan had known he would, and in liking it, he would remain faithful to it. *Until it suits me otherwise.* Such was the constant clash of his mixed blood: the Wasp crying, *Serve yourself by serving the Empire*, while the Scorpion roared out, *Do what you will.*

The Scorpions of the Nem were not so dependent on outside trading to make their living as the Dryclaw tribes Hrathen had known, but still, a caravan of this size walking obediently towards one of their camps had attracted a lot of interest: three heavily laden automotives grinding their monotonous way over the desert ground, and each of them with two draught beetles plodding meekly in traces before them, not labouring as yet but ready to haul the wagons if they broke down or ran out of fuel. Hrathen had asked for a score of the Slave Corps's most intrepid, and Brugan had not stinted on obliging him. They were like old friends, to him, for he knew them for men who adulterated Imperial writ with their own self-interest, willing to go further and risk more for the sake of their profits and their pleasures. Proceeding alongside them were a dozen who wore the armour of the Light Airborne, but who mostly kept to themselves with a quiet discipline. Hrathen had marked these as Rekef agents, and guessed that they would be keeping a close eye on him.

*Still, twelve of them? He flatters me.* Or perhaps Brugan had some other mission in mind, and that was an unwelcome thought. If these men had received orders to assassinate the Warlord of the Nemian Scorpions, then this expedition would be everyone's last service to the Empire.

After the soldiers came the experts, who got to ride while the others walked. Chief amongst them, and most vocal, was Dannec, the political officer of the Rekef and its most overt representative. He was a thin-faced, ambitious man who did not relish being sent off into the wilderness, not even by the Rekef's supreme commander himself. He wasted no chance to complain, and even now he was suggesting that they drive the Scorpions off the ridge over to their left. Hrathen had ignored him from the start, and by now everyone else did, too. Aside from Dannec, there were eight men from the Engineering Corps, led by a grey veteran named Angved. They formed a mysterious and silent cabal of their own, and Hrathen was looking forward to putting them through their paces.

The sky was darkening but the horizon ahead was heaping up with a range of stark artificial shapes: one of the famous ruins of the Nem desert that the Scorpions had made their own. There were flames to be seen there, burning bluish-white. They were fuelled by a rock-oil, Hrathen understood, that the Scorpions, or their slaves, extracted wherever it bubbled to the surface. Here in the desert it was more readily available than wood, and continued burning for days.

The Scorpions began to close in now, bringing their mounts nearer and nearer until they had turned from scouts to an escort. They rode humpbacked black desert beetles that skittered along on high, long legs, fast over the dusty ground. They also rode low-slung scorpions, whose claws had been capped with sharp iron, sitting on them in strangely made offset side-saddles to keep the riders out of the path of the curved stingers. Others were on foot: tall and burly men and women with waxy-pale skin and snaggle-toothed underbites, wearing brief garments the colour of dust. About half of these had armour too, some merely with primitive carapace scale, but many with mail or plated leather. One even wore an undersized banded cuirass that had once borne the Imperial colours.

'Savages,' Dannec muttered, but Hrathen smiled to see them. He stood up from his seat on the lead wagon, letting all the Scorpions see him and know him as the leader. Enough of them were now riding ahead towards the camp to ensure there would be the right kind of welcoming committee. These were not the Aktaian Scorpions he was familiar with, but there was enough traffic between their two peoples for him to know he could expect similar customs.

*Here is fringe desert, with sporadic contact with the Empire,* he reminded himself. *The Warlord will not be so familiar or predictable. I must not become complacent.*

Sure enough, the whole camp had turned out to see them arrive. The ruins here were no more than three or four stone buildings that looked as though some ancient fire had started what wind and time had subsequently brought close to finishing. The camp itself was no more than awnings propped on sticks, a scattering of canvas all around. Scorpions were a hardy folk and not a private one. Simply getting to sleep up against the stone walls here would be a sufficient mark of rank and favour.

As the caravan approached the camp a flurry of creatures rushed out to investigate. These were more scorpions, three or four feet long not counting the over-arching tail, and they scrabbled forth with their claws held high in threat. Hrathen heard Dannec swear and saw him recoil in fear. He himself jumped down from the wagon and dropped to his knees in the path of the leading beast, summoning up his Art, which had slumbered for so long.

It was an Art little known, these days, though all kinden possessed some facet of it, and he guessed it had once meant sheer survival to people when the world was young. Now few deliberately sought it, fewer still chanced upon it. Hrathen had always been the exception.

He extended his mind and felt the small, aggressive barb that was the beast's.

*Well, now,* he thought to it, *how is it with you, little brother?*

The creature was slowing, but its claws were either side of his head when it finally stopped. He could sense its confusion at the sound of the engines and the smell of the machinery. Confusion made it angry and it wanted to sting something.

*Oh, I know how that feels,* he told it, *believe me.* It did not quite understand the words, but it felt the sense of them, and calmed. When he went to walk beside the lead wagon, it trotted at his heels, its claws now drawn in. The other animals were unsure at first, thrusting spread pincers at the newcomers, darting towards Hrathen and the slavers in mock charges. The lead beast had been the dominant one, and by earning its trust he had thwarted them all.

He saw the chieftain approach, a hefty Scorpion wearing overlapping metal plates across his chest and shoulders. His hands were big and Hrathen could imagine them clenched into fists so as to free those scythe-like claws for fighting. The chief strolled up to the lead wagon as the artificers braked the engine, putting one taloned hand on the machine's flank.

'We were not expecting such wealthy visitors,' Hrathen heard him say. 'Perhaps we should be wearing our fine clothes for you.'

Hrathen faced him, making his stance a challenge. 'My name is Hrathen, of the Empire.'

The Scorpion turned to squint at him through small yellow eyes. 'You do not look "of-the-Empire" to me, but I have met with the slavers before, and I know they are slack in what servants they take on.'

'Is that so?' In fact it was indeed so. Some of the Slave Corps that Hrathen had once led had not been good Wasps: there had been Spider-kinden amongst them, rogue Ants and halfbreeds. Still, it did not do to let insults go unchallenged amongst the Scorpions.

'I am Kovalin,' the chieftain rumbled. 'What is this you have brought me, Of-the-Empire?'

'I bring many gifts for the Warlord of the Nem,' Hrathen said, loud enough for them all to hear. 'Will you show me to his camp?'

'She will be grateful. She loves gifts,' said Kovalin, and Hrathen blinked at that revelation. *Thinking like an Imperial, shame on you.* Scorpion women fought just as fiercely as their menfolk, and indeed there was little to tell them apart. A little slighter at the shoulder, a little fuller at the chest, but otherwise as hairless, fanged and clawed as the males. They were no other race's ideal of beauty.

'However,' Kovalin went on, revealing no more than Hrathen had expected, 'she does not love outlanders, not from your Empire, not from anywhere. It would serve better for your gifts to be given to her by one she knows well and loves well, such as I.'

'No doubt,' Hrathen said, 'but that is not my plan. I will give her these gifts myself, with all my men present, and explain the workings of them.' He saw that his people, even Brugan's shadowy lot, had done exactly as he had forewarned them. They were arranged in a loose double line either side of the first wagon, swords out and pointedly ready to fight. There were perhaps fifty fighting Scorpions before them, once Hrathen discounted the rabble of attendant children. The locals were not obviously about to attack, but there was not one of them that did not have a spear or axe or halberd to hand.

'And if I just take these things?' Kovalin asked. He was taller than Hrathen, his claws far larger. Hrathen's impure blood had given him a broad Art, but neither parent's inheritance showed as strongly as in a true-breed.

'Why need to take gifts that will be freely given?' Hrathen said easily. He shrugged his shoulders, loosening his joints for the coming fight.

'I take what I wish,' Kovalin declared. 'I give you the chance now: gather up your people and return to your Empire. You are not wanted here.'

'Do you fear me so much?' Hrathen asked.

Kovalin went very still, and two different waves of tension passed through the camp. The Wasps were ready for an explosion, and though he had ordered them not to intervene unless the rest of the Scorpions made a move, it seemed to them now that things were poised on the very cusp of violence. But Hrathen knew that the Scorpions were excited, not angry. They were about to be entertained.

'Come on, then,' he said. 'Let us have this out. With nothing more than nature gave us, yes?'

Kovalin eyed his rival's claws, eyes narrowing suspiciously. 'You may know no better than bare hands, Of-the-Empire, but I have this. He unslung a long-hafted axe from his back. The head was solid, dark metal, shaped in a vicious, heavy crescent.

'Well, then.' Hrathen drew his Imperial-issue shortsword. Against the axe it was tiny, and Kovalin roared with laughter.

'A knife!' he cried. 'Of-the-Empire has a knife!' And then the axe was in motion, a great sweeping slash that sent Hrathen diving aside, rolling in the dust. He knew Kovalin would be coming straight for him then, the axe still in motion from that first swing, so he kicked himself back on to his feet. He thrust his free hand out and summoned his Art.

The flash of fire struck Kovalin about the neck and shoulders but did not stop him. Hrathen made a circular parry that took the axe-blow just past him, then loosed his sting again and again. Kovalin was already reeling when the third bolt caught him directly in the face. He fell to one knee, began struggling to rise, whereupon Hrathen backed off and lashed out at him with his Art until at last the Scorpion collapsed.

There was a silence, and Hrathen received a keen sense from his own people that they suspected this would mean foul play, that the Scorpions would descend on them.

*They have no concept of foul play*, he thought. *No codes of honour, no complex laws – no noble savages here. All they have is a fierce respect for strength in all its forms, and that includes cleverness.*

'I have no wish to take his place,' Hrathen announced loudly, 'for who would want to lead such wretches as these?' Again the Wasps behind him braced for the fight, but he was playing by Scorpion rules. He was proclaiming his strength. Flattery was only for the weak.

A woman approached him, her face claw-scarred. 'He was food for the animals before you came. His death is nothing to boast of,' she said. 'Stay here tonight and we will send you on your way tomorrow. I think the Warlord will be curious to meet you.'

She was tall, but not as massive as most Scorpions across the shoulders and back. Her arms and legs were long, and she stood with a poise that few of her kinden possessed. Just from her stance Hrathen could tell that this was an exceptionally dangerous woman. He would not want to try the same tricks that had killed Kovalin against her, and he was thankful that his plan did not call for it. If the Rekef men here with him intended to kill her, then, looking at her, he wished them luck.

She was young, too, although Scorpions never got very old out here. Still he guessed she was younger than thirty, and yet already Warlord of all the Many of Nem. Her face was half-hidden behind a crested helm, eyes glittering from within it. She had capped her tusks with gold, and her white skin, wherever exposed, was decorated with twining patterns of black and red. They meant something, of course, but Hrathen was beyond his range of knowledge now. He would have to hope that these people had not diverged too far from the customs of their Dryclaw brethren.

He saw how she had made the best of the equipment her people scavenged. She wore a mail hauberk of a fineness he had never seen before, the links silvery and flowing like water. Panels of cruder mail riveted at the front and sides showed where they had broadened it to fit her. She had steel greaves on her shins, plated leather guards strapped to her thighs. One arm was completely covered by interlocking metal plates, only the claws jutting forth from a ravaged gauntlet. She held a spear, its slender head comprising almost a third of its length.

They had spent nine days in the desert, just to reach this

place. Although Hrathen had made sure they would have ample supplies, he had traded with the Scorpions along the way. If he had not, they would have decided he had too much, and would have made a move to take it from him. Dannec, of course, had been critical of such expense, such waste. He had let the man simmer. They had attracted many Scorpion-kinden from the desert, come to stare and to question their guides about these intruding foreigners. Twice there had been attacks, but the Wasps' stings, and the resistance put up by what had previously been Kovalin's people, had driven their attackers away easily.

A day ago they had come within sight of these ruins, and had expected to reach them sooner. The sheer scale defeated them: this was no fallen farmhouse or outpost. Here was a city of the old days, the days before the Nem had become a desert. Even Dannec's endless carping had faltered to a halt as they approached, to witness those great cracked walls, the massive plinths whose statues were severed at the ankle or the knee. It seemed a city built by giants, but however mighty the hands that had laid stone upon stone here, time and the desert had finally undone them. As they passed in through a break in the wall, they bore witness to a desolation that only the usurping Scorpions had brought to life again: streets and squares of fallen stones; stretches of wall so shot through with gaps that they looked like the teeth in a battered skull; pillars lying like so many sticks cast at random; the cracked and collapsed eggshells of fallen domes. The Scorpions had descended on this place with a scavenger's eye. They had dug out the ancient ruin's old wells and found the waters still clear. They had made fields out of the dust, now watered and tilled by their slaves. They had dug through the ruins for metal they could melt and reforge. Whoever had built here had been wealthy beyond measure, and what they had left behind, for the Scorpions, seemed riches worth taking. Hrathen had never known Scorpions to settle in one place. In the Dryclaw they moved constantly on and on through their desert, preying on each other, trading with the slave markets, raiding border farms and towns. Looking around the ruins, he could see that they had been here for generations, and any building still owning to three walls had become a permanent dwelling, now completed in cloth and wood. The children were everywhere underfoot, chasing and fighting each other. It had become a Scorpion city, as though the ghosts of its builders had stayed on to teach the newcomers some shadow of their old way of life.

As with the camp previously, a crowd of the locals was fast gathering, but here there were hundreds of them, too numerous to count. Many scrambled atop walls and buildings to overlook the wagons, clasping axes and spears ready to throw. A few even held bows, but to make a good bow required suitable wood, and the desert denied them that.

*That's good,* Hrathen decided. *That fits with the plan.*

He jumped down from the wagon again, observing the woman who was their leader. Her complete mastery of them was evident in the way she stood, and in the way they gathered around her. He had to remind himself: *This is not just any chief, this is the Warlord of the whole Nem desert.* It would be a hard title to win, a harder one to hold. Something about this woman had brought them under her rule, and it must involve more than mere skill with a spear. He would have to be careful with her.

'I am Hrathen of the Empire,' he declared. The other Wasps had again taken up their fighting stance, but if things went badly here it would not matter. 'I seek the Warlord of the Many.'

'You have found her,' the woman replied. She approached, two or three steps at a time, and then stopped again, regarding him. 'I am Jakal of the Many, and my people have brought me word of you. I hear Kovalin lies dead in the sand.'

'Do you mourn him?' Hrathen asked. *Strength, always.* There was no room for sentiment here.

'You have spared me the chore of killing him myself. It would have been dull work,' she said. The words were for the crowd, and the crowd liked them. Behind that helm, though, her eyes were careful, wary. 'What brings you to the Nem, Hrathen of the Empire? What brings you to my citadel of Gemrar?'

Hrathen heard Dannec snort at the mention of 'citadel'. The Rekef officer had a Wasp's eye for other nations, and he had decided from the first that the Scorpions were barbarous savages, and Hrathen little better.

'The Empire brings you gifts,' Hrathen announced. 'There is nothing in these wagons that you may not have.'

'That would be so, whether you willed it or not.' Jakal had moved closer, yet had not so much as glanced at the automotives. 'However, it is always pleasing to hear that we are known and feared by your Empire, who wish to bribe us so. You may join me at my fire tonight, and we shall discuss what you have brought me.' She was standing right before him at last, a few inches taller than he was, so that he had to look up to her. Hrathen was a man of instincts, and they were all telling him now to make a distance between them, to take himself backwards out of the reach of her claws. It was entirely possible she would kill him right there, and he realized he could not discern, from her stance, whether she would do it. She was impossible to decipher.

From the shadow of her helm her eyes challenged his. 'Good,' she said eventually. He had not moved or backed down. 'You are welcome amongst my people, until I change my mind. If any vex you, bring them to me and I shall remind them of their place – and mine.'

'I would rather kill them myself,' Hrathen replied, because that was expected of him. He saw her fanged lower jaw curve in a smile.

'Then perhaps we shall have some sport, later,' she said. 'We are not all as weak as Kovalin was.'

*

'You think I am ignorant,' she said, when they had re-gathered after dark. 'I know of your Empire. My advisers have told me of it.' The bluish light of the burning oil made the Scorpions' pale skin gleam and glow.

'The Empire's fame deserves to travel,' said Hrathen. He had called upon Dannec, of all his people, to sit with him at the Warlord's fire. The ragged circle was made up otherwise of Jakal's people, and he was surprised to see several there who must have been aged forty, fifty even, wrinkled about the eyes, with tusks missing or broken, skins spotted with time. *Her advisers, then?* Age had always been a death sentence in the Dryclaw but, with their more settled life, the Nemian Scorpions had clearly found some use for wisdom. A clay jar of something was being passed around, but it avoided the visitors scrupulously. Hrathen had meanwhile broken the neck on a bottle of Imperial wine, and was taking careless swallows of it, to Dannec's disapproval.

'My advisers tell me the Empire is a great beast lurking to the north, that is always hungry. That each year it moults and splits its skin and grows larger by eating another of its neighbours.'

Hrathen laughed at that, but Dannec drew his breath in sharply.

'The Empire is not as you describe,' the Wasp protested. 'Those brought within our borders only benefit from our rule. So, many of our neighbours beg to join us.'

'Fascinating,' Jakal said, dismissing with a word everything he had said. 'Tell me' – she returned to Hrathen – 'how long before we are your neighbours? We do not beg.'

Hrathen glanced at Dannec, who replied, 'There will be no need for bad blood between us. After all, we are here now to strengthen bonds of friendship, are we not? Why talk of war?'

'One cannot strengthen that which does not exist,' Jakal retorted, amidst a mutter of laughter from the other Scorpions.

'But alliances are always to be wished for, are they not? We have things you lack,' Dannec pointed out. 'I do not believe your advisers realize what the Empire has to offer.'

'Tell me,' Jakal said, pointedly to Hrathen, 'is this your lord, that he talks so much in your place, or is he perhaps your mate?'

The other Scorpions loved that, and Hrathen smiled, too. 'You are right, of course. I shall have words with him.' He turned the smile on Dannec and, as the man opened his mouth to speak, he rammed a thumb-claw as far as the knuckle into the Wasp's throat. Dannec, words abruptly gone, stared at him. With faint interest Hrathen saw his own bloody claw-tip within the man's gaping mouth. He jerked his hand three times, feeling the sharp bone slice flesh and arteries, and then withdrew his thumb with a practised movement. He turned back to Jakal as the Rekef man's body slumped lifeless to the ground, thinking, *Thank you, General Brugan. He was perfect for the purpose.*

The Scorpions were still laughing, but their tone had changed from mockery to appreciation. Strength again, and a strong leader did not tolerate weakness in his followers.

'Very good,' Jakal said quietly. 'I admire your performance.' Her tone told him that she had seen through the device but still appreciated the effort. The next time the jar came round, she passed it over to him, and he took a great swig of the fierce, fiery liquor.

He let the Scorpions talk amongst themselves for a while, let Jakal watch him and wonder, and then excused himself, wandering off into the dark to relieve his bladder. On the way back, he located the artificer, Angved, leaning on a capless pillar and carefully watching the group at the fire.

'Well?' Hrathen asked him.

'Well, I never liked the man, but even so,' the old man replied. He wore his armour still, even the helm. Field engineers seldom had to fly, and represented years of

Imperial training, so they had better mail than anyone else except the sentinel heavy infantry.

'All part of the plan,' Hrathen said. 'Don't tell me you didn't see it coming when I called him to the fire.'

'I know *he* didn't,' Angved remarked. 'Tell me, sir, when do they descend on us with sword and axe and cut us all into pieces?'

'When we're no longer useful to them,' Hrathen informed him. 'Have you guessed at your duties?'

'Doesn't take much to work that out.' Angved spat. 'Can't see them as quick students.'

'Living out here, you learn anything fast, so don't underestimate them,' Hrathen warned. He assessed the artificer as a level-headed man, someone who could be relied on. Considering the man would suffice, he headed back to the fire.

'So why does the Empire seek out the Many of Nem?' Jakal asked him, as he sat down again. 'I am not such a fool as to believe you fear us. You are far away and strong, so if you are giving gifts to us, it is because you want gifts in return.'

'Tell me about Khanaphes,' Hrathen said, and the Scorpions went quiet again. 'Are the people of Khanaphes your friends?' he persisted. 'Do they pay your warriors tribute? Do they send you gifts?'

Jakal tilted her helmet back. The face she revealed was a hard one, even for a Scorpion. Her eyes were red, and the oil-fire made them shine with a mad light. 'We raid the Khanaphir all along the Jamail,' she replied. 'We strike at their farms, their merchants and tax gatherers. When they are strong they hunt us, but we are fast and they are slow. When we are strong, they fall back to their stone walls that we cannot breach.'

'The Empire wishes an end to Khanaphes,' said Hrathen. The Scorpion laughter was derisory, but Jakal held up a clawed hand to quell it.

'Why?' she demanded. 'What offence has it caused, being so far away?'

'Who can say why?' Hrathen had asked himself the same question. *It must be because Brugan wants to see if the Many can be put to work for the Empire,* he had decided. *Khanaphes is simply the most convenient testing ground.* But there was more to it than that, and he guessed that the detachment of Rekef agents he had brought were to be involved in it. 'Perhaps some citizen of Khanaphir has insulted our Empress . . . It only matters that the Empire wishes it done.'

'And the Empire wishes me to do it,' Jakal said.

'Do you not wish to do it?'

'If the riches of Khanaphes could be mine, I would already have taken them. Do you think I would have stayed my hand?'

'You need stay it no longer, then,' Hrathen told her. 'For the gifts I bring you are weapons. I bring two thousand crossbows and more, supplied with bolts, and the men to teach you in their use.'

'We know of crossbows,' said Jakal coolly, but he could see the interest in her eyes.

'Also, we bring a dozen siege engines – leadshotters, they are called,' he continued. 'The walls of Khanaphes shall stand in your way no more than the walls of this old city here.'

They did not cheer at that. Instead they stared at him avidly, whilst word of what he had said was passed back and back, until the whole usurped city knew it.

# Nineteen

'What is this place?' Che asked, feeling as though she had stepped into another world. From the fierce, dry heat of the sun outside they were suddenly plunged into a thick, muggy, sticky humidity. The daylight had dimmed to a coloured gloom as it filtered through tight-stretched canvas, silk and linen. Ahead of them the emaciated Khanaphir had stopped again to wait for them.

'The Marsh Alcaia,' Trallo pronounced. 'Even a city as polite as Khanaphes needs somewhere to break the law. At least when the guard come looking, they know exactly where to go. People will always have vices they need to indulge.'

'But this?' Che took a few steps deeper, beneath the cloth ceiling. It was like walking under water. She felt an almost physical resistance to her intrusion.

'Don't worry about that, worry about why our friend seems so fond of you,' the Fly advised her.

'What do you mean? *I* sought *him* out.'

'I mean that he could have run while we were bickering in the open house, and he could still run now, and we'd never find him in here. Think about it.'

She tried to, but here, in the stale heat, it was hard to match the pieces. Their guide was drawing ahead again, making them hurry to catch up with him. All around them were Khanaphir and foreigners intent on their purposeful errands. Amid the fragile aisles lined with people crying their wares, the sounds and smells were overwhelming.

He always stayed just in sight, always paused by each new turning he took, and always looking back at them – at *her* – with that hollow, hungry gaze. Trallo was right: it was not because she was a foreigner, or anything to do with the money she might carry. Instead, something had sparked inside him, as soon as he had taken a proper look at her.

*Is this really what I am looking for?* The stifling air was making her feel dizzy, while odd thoughts and feelings kept passing through her mind.

'Wastes, but we're going in deep,' Trallo observed. 'Never been this far into the Marsh Alcaia.' He cast a glance backwards, teeth bared, and Che drew back, suddenly feeling trapped. She opened her mouth to suggest turning back, but then something twisted in her mind and she saw it. There, just beside the skeletal, hurrying figure of their guide, she saw the air seethe and darken: something of the night fighting to be seen, to make itself known to her. She imagined she even saw it pointing after him, urging her onwards. After that she had no choice.

Again, the lean man was waiting for them at the turn, leading into yet another alleyway. Roofed with heavier cloth, it was cooler there, and the air was thick with darkness. Che let her Art cut through it, spying a tent at the far end, with four or five figures seated there.

'This must be it,' she told Trallo. He nodded grimly. She saw that he held his hand near his knife-hilt.

The thin man was now kneeling in front of the tent: a low, ragged structure, patched and filthy, its original colour lost beyond recall. The doorway was hung with charms and lockets, little bits of brass and bronze and tin that dangled and jangled on slender chains. Someone inside was speaking slowly in a low voice, as Che paused before the entrance to reach out for one of the swinging fragments of metal. It had been crudely cut with a symbol that reminded her of the stone carvings to be seen everywhere about the city. Again she felt a stab of anticipation.

'Why have you brought these here?' demanded the voice. Only now did Che identify it as a woman's, so deep and rough it sounded.

'She was asking, asking questions, and she found me,' the lean man explained. 'Mother, when she asked . . . I saw . . .'

Che saw a bulky form shift within the tent, half hidden by the hanging drapes. 'I see her. She is foreign Beetle-kinden. I know them and they have nothing. They are lost to the old ways. She is wasting her time. You are wasting mine.'

'Only look at her, Mother!' the lean man almost howled.

'May I speak?' Che intruded, trying to keep her voice steady. She saw the figure shift again, still shapeless behind the drapes.

'Come forward at your own risk,' the half-seen woman replied, and Che could hear the soft whisper of daggers and knifes tasting the air.

'I mean you no harm,' Che persisted and, although Trallo was shaking his head fiercely, she crouched to enter the tent on her knees.

There were three Khanaphir inside, two men and one woman who each held a leaf-bladed dagger and stared at her with mute hostility. Another denizen was a halfbreed, Khanaphir mixed with something else to produce skin of a green-black hue. He was hollow-cheeked and thin-shouldered and yet with a gut that bulged over his belt. Che's eyes were now fixed on the woman beside him, the one whom the thin man had called 'Mother'. She was another halfbreed, and a halfbreed of halfbreeds, until it was impossible to tell just which kindens' blood ran through her veins. She was grotesquely fat, her huge frame shuddering with each breath even as she reclined on silken cushions. Her face was round and sagging, a dozen vices writ large there in pocks and blemishes, a true degenerate except for the eyes. Her eyes were blue and clear and piercing and, looking into them, Che felt an almost physical shock, like sudden recognition.

'Well, now . . .' the woman called Mother rumbled.

Che heard Trallo step in behind her, staying close to the door.

'My name is Cheerwell Maker,' she said. 'I . . . I come seeking . . .'

'Enlightenment.' Mother pronounced the word as though she were eating a sweetmeat. 'Oh, yes, you do, don't you.' She leant forward, her shapeless body bulging. 'What are you, little traveller? Do you truly know what we do here? The thing they call the Profanity?'

'Tell me,' said Che, and the woman smiled slyly.

'O Foreigner,' she said, 'you know nothing of the Masters of Khanaphes, and yet here you are. You have been led here – by what, I wonder?'

'I have heard of these Masters, but nobody will tell me anything about them,' Che replied, and some of her frustration must have leaked out, because Mother chuckled indulgently.

'Then listen, O Foreign child,' she said. 'Once, many, many generations ago, the Masters walked the streets of Khanaphes, and exercised their power over the earth as naturally as we ourselves would breathe and eat. They were lordly and beautiful, and they knew no death, nor did age afflict them, or disease or injury. Their thought was law, and the city of Khanaphes knew a greatness that today is only a shadow.'

'Only a shadow of a shadow,' murmured the halfbreed man, and then the three Khanaphir in chorus. Che felt Trallo shift nervously.

'But that was our Golden Age, and all things fade. So it came about that the Masters were seen no more on the streets of Khanaphes, and the decline of our people began. Oh, the Ministers will claim that they hear the voices of the Masters, that the Masters reside still within their sealed palaces, ready to save the city should they be called upon, but we know that the true glory of our city is long passed, and it is many hundreds of years since this soil knew the tread of the Masters.' Her brilliant eyes were fixed on Che and she licked her lips thoughtfully.

'So what is it that you do here?' Che asked her. *I am almost there. Just a handful of words and surely I will understand.*

'Though the Masters are gone, they have left their legacy. There are those that possess some spark, some trace of their old blood,' Mother said slowly. 'They find the world of today hostile and confusing, perhaps? They are tormented by dreams and visions? They long for something more . . .?' Her lips split in a smile. 'I thought as much. O Foreigner, I see in you something of their touch, their mark. All who are here with me are your kin. We carry within us the bloodline of the Masters, and were the Ministers just, we would be elevated and praised for it, instead of hunted like criminals.'

Che glanced at the others, and she noticed now that even the Khanaphir had a strange cast to their features, uneven, slightly disfigured, perhaps some distant trace of mingled bloods. A cynical part of her said, *It probably does not take too much belief to turn a wart into the blood of the Masters.* Another voice was saying, *Are they talking about Aptitude? Is it the lack of it they discern in me? Is all this a memory going back to when this city was Inapt, before their revolution? And were the Masters their seers, who were cast out after they discovered their new artifice?*

'But . . .' Mother continued, and let the word hang for a moment in the stuffy air, 'there is a way for those of us that still bear the ancient gift to touch those far-off days. There is a substance that can yet wake memories of the golden days of Khanaphes.'

'Fir,' Che suggested, and the woman nodded ponderously.

'It brings true visions, echoes of the past, a sight of the Masters perhaps. There is nothing else in the world. It is our only link with our birthright and heritage.' She had reached out for the halfbreed man to give her a pot in which something glistened. 'O Foreigner,' said Mother, 'having come so far at the call of your blood, will you not eat Fir with us?'

Che glanced back at Trallo, who was staring wide-eyed. For the first time ever her capable Solarnese guide seemed out of his depth.

*Why else have I come so far, if not for this?*

'Let me eat of it,' she agreed. 'I need to understand.'

Mother extended her hand and the halfbreed man drew a small blade delicately over one thick finger so that a drop of her blood fell into the pot. Then he lanced his own hand and did likewise, before passing the pot to the three Khanaphir. His dark eyes were fixed on Che all the while.

The pot came to her, and they watched her patiently until she took out her own knife, pricked at her thumb and shook a drop of blood into it. The halfbreed retrieved the vessel jealously, as though she might run off with it, and with his blade stirred the viscous contents, the red droplets streaking and blurring into the clear jelly.

He finally passed the pot to Mother, whose eyes were now closed in naked anticipation. She stuck two fingers into the thick mess and drew them out, gleaming with a gob of slime. With a hedonistic shiver, she licked it from her hand.

The pot was passed around, each of the dingy celebrants taking a share, and now it was back with Che. She stared into it, fighting down bile, having no idea what the Fir consisted of, even before it was tainted with blood. Mother was already shuddering, eyes firmly closed while the others seemed to be falling one by one into a trance.

Che had scooped some up, without even realizing it, her hand responding to no conscious command. Out of some bizarre consideration she put the pot down, lest she spill some.

She raised the hand to her mouth. The Fir was odourless,

colourless, sticky and dense. She closed her eyes, already gagging. *I came here, so I must do this. I wanted to learn the secrets of Khanaphes.*

With a jerky, convulsive movement she put the smeared fingers into her mouth. The slime was so salt and sweet she almost choked, but she swallowed it down, shuddering and retching.

She looked round for Trallo to tell him something, but whatever she had been going to say was already gone from her mind. He was now too far away to hear, anyway, sliding further and further into the gloom of the tent, as the oppressive heat of the Marsh Alcaia lifted from her, and she fell into time.

For a long while she just sat there, still falling but unable to move, feeling the rushing of the world as it left her on all sides at great speed. Eventually she recovered her balance, as though she had discovered some other Art of flight to arrest that endless descent.

As she stepped out of the dingy tent, she could not have said whether it was herself moving, or whether the world had just been diverted sideways. All around her the Marsh Alcaia was disintegrating, stripping itself down to its struts and poles, as though a great host of invisible locusts had descended on it, tearing the fabric away as she watched. Soon even the poles themselves were gone, and she was turning towards the city itself. The great statues of the Estuarine Gate seemed to glow with a white fire as she passed them by, and she was walking on the river itself, and it seemed natural that she should do so.

Khanaphes had begun fading. In sections and pieces, the clutter of low buildings was losing substance, passing away, leaving only broad avenues and arcaded promenades between the great palaces and temples that had been the original Khanaphes. The city now transformed itself, whilst staying intrinsically the same, merely sweeping away all the accumulated detritus of five hundred years.

She sensed a presence, a collective presence, whose mind filled the city completely. The Masters remained invisible to her, but she was touched by their attention – the entire city was blanketed in it – and she knew that, after she woke, its absence would seem as shocking as a broken tooth.

*Let me see you,* she thought, as the streets and walls of Khanaphes wheeled and darted around her, but they were always around each corner, just out of sight.

The city was hard to focus on, its edges blurred, the light it radiated painfully bright. *Perhaps this is the city's memory of itself, before the march of years eroded it all away.* She moved close to one wall, trying to discern the carvings embellishing it, and in this half-dream they were words, as clear and comprehensible as a book written only yesterday. She read and read, the histories and learning of ages, and yet nothing stayed with her. The understanding flowed into and out of her head like a stream that barely disturbed the pebbles of her mind.

*Is this it? Is this the Profanity?* This sad half-life, this feeling of meaningless wonder. Was this what the Fir-eaters craved? She thought of their tent, their faces. *It is not real, this, but it is more palatable than their reality.*

She found the square before the Scriptora, lying open and bright. The city eddied and turned about her but something kept her here, some nagging feeling, until she realized it was wrong. *Where is the pyramid?* she asked. *Where are the statues?* In the centre of the square there was nothing but an old well. *Is this not even the real city? Is this all some hallucination*? There was now a bitter taste in her mouth.

*Is this no more than a common vice? Have I been fooled again?*

*Yet I am thinking very clearly, for a dream-vision.* She looked around the square once more. *If I were dreaming this, it would be as I had already seen it.* She suddenly had the feeling that this was indeed the reality, that the place she had seen and remembered was the falsehood.

*I do not carry their precious blood, how can I? Is this vice wasted on me?* But she knew, with the absolute certainty of dreams, that what the Fir-eaters saw as a bloodline was something more tenuous. It was to do with Aptitude. It was some old strain of the Inapt that they laid claim to, some persistent reminder of those old, old days.

*Show me!* she called out, and the voices of the city said, *We have shown you.* She drifted towards the Scriptora, and found Khanaphir men and women there, bent over tablets, scribing industriously. She thought she saw Ethmet there, too, or someone that looked very like him. *These are the Ministers, back in the days when they were no more than servants of the Masters, but where are the Masters themselves?*

*Is that really what you are looking for, little one?*

Her mind was full of voices and she felt a spurt of panic when she realized she could not tell which was her own. The thoughts flitted in and out of her, free as flies.

*What am I looking for?* She was catching thoughts with her bare hands, holding them, as they crawled and buzzed. What did the Masters of Khanaphes matter to her, truly? She had become so distracted by the means that she had forgotten the end. She had not come here to meet the Masters, for all that they were just out of sight, forever in the corner of her eye. She had travelled here to come to terms with her own nature – and to reach a détente with her ghost.

*Achaeos!* she cried. *Achaeos, you led me here, so come forth now and speak to me.* She did not know for sure whether she could survive regaining him here in this dream-place, only to lose him again. Perhaps this would be the end of it. She would take his hand once more, embrace him one last time, look into those white eyes of his, and then she would die and be with him, wherever the Inapt went after they shed their bodies.

*Please, Achaeos, I love you, but I cannot continue living like this. Either come forth and show me what you need, or leave me. I cannot stand in twilight for ever, between what I was and what I am.*

But no grey-robed figure came towards her in that flickering, painful light. She shouted out in frustration and anger: *You brought me here! You drove me here! Now come forth, I demand it!*

The city fell very quiet as the echoes of her unspoken words rolled back and forth across the walls of the Scriptora. The scribing Beetles were gone, even the presence of the Masters seemed to have drawn further back.

*Achaeos?* she asked, tentatively, because she was now sure that *something* was approaching.

The earth before her cracked open, the stones of the antique well shifting as something began to claw its way up the shaft. Without transition, Che felt very afraid of what it was that she had awoken. *It is not Khanaphes that I have called up: it is something within me.* She wanted to flee, but the cracking earth about the well-mouth was hypnotic, and she could not tear herself away. The *thing* rushing upwards sounded like distant thunder on the edge of hearing.

*Achaeos . . . help me . . .* she thought, and the thunder grew more and more urgent, getting closer without ever becoming louder, and she knew that whatever it was had now reached the very lip and was about to burst forth in all its force and fury.

There was nothing, only silence, but Che was not fooled. She knew that it was waiting at the very lip of the well.

A single tendril reached up from the darkness, quested briefly in the air, then arced downwards to dig into the sundered earth. She saw it was a briar, studded with thorns, and the sight of it instantly turned her stomach. She managed a single step back . . .

Another followed it, and then another, coiling and twisting as they were liberated into the open air. A darkness clung to them that she well remembered.

*Oh no, oh no no no . . .*

Something else came out, unfolding and then unfolding again – a great hinged arm, hooked and barbed, that clutched at the well's edge and tore the stones loose. The ground bucked and buckled, something vast ripping its way free. She saw long antennae spring upwards, another raptorial arm, then a triangular head with immense eyes burning with a green fire. Pierced and re-pierced by those arching thorns, the mantis lurched its way out of its chrysalis of earth, and Che felt a silent wail of horror in her mind.

*The Darakyon . . . he was touching the Darakyon when he died. Have they* taken *him now? Is that why he needs me?*

The mantis's killing arms wept blood, and its monstrous eyes were fixed on her as the thorns continued to penetrate its flesh, riddling it with wounds. This was the true Darakyon, the very personification of all Mantis-kinden fury and pride and futility.

*Run*, came a voice in her head, and she turned and ran, but the monstrous thing was immediately on her heels, red blood spilling from the myriad wounds the thorns had bored in its carapace, the shadows of its claws raking the ground on either side of her. She had called out first to Achaeos, but in the end she had just called – and she had awoken the ghost of the mad, embittered Darakyon instead.

Che felt something lurch in her stomach, a sudden feeling of disorientation. The bright light was dimming . . . The monster that had been about to seize her in its jagged arms was suddenly very far away, receding and receding. She felt dizzy, nauseous, impossibly weak. The enclosed, baking air surrounded her again, amid the tatty gloom of the tent. She collapsed on its floor, and heard again the husky voice of the halfbreed woman they called Mother.

'She has the touch of the Masters. She has it as pure as I have ever known,' and then, after a moment's smothering of any conscience, the woman ordered, 'Kill her. Kill her and take her blood.'

Che tried to reach for her sword, but her arm was leaden.

She heard a shout and something passed over her, Trallo lunging knife-first and wings a-blur. There was a hoarse cry of pain, and Trallo cried out again, words this time.

'Now!' he was yelling. 'Now! Come on!'

She could barely turn her head, just heard a scuffle and the cursing. Her vision was eclipsed and she saw the halfbreed man loom over her. His teeth were bared into a snarl and his dagger was raised high.

*Achaeos!* she called, and she would not have cared if the Darakyon had answered her again.

For a second the interior of the tent was lit by unbearable brightness, then a wind seemed to hurl the halfbreed away from her. Che heard the woman known as Mother begin to scream in rage and grief. Trallo staggered away past her, bleeding across the scalp. One of the Khanaphir came after him, but again there was that burst of pure light, and the bald man reeled back, his chest just a blackened hole. Mother kept screaming and screaming.

'Che! Che, get up!' Trallo was shouting at her, pulling at her arm. She made all the effort she could, her limbs like jelly. Someone grabbed hold of her, strong hands digging under her arms to haul her to her feet. She was leaning against someone, as her world swam. Her stomach was squirming with the abomination she had swallowed. She tried desperately to focus, to see who had come for her.

'Achaeos?' she asked.

'Not Achaeos,' said a clipped voice in her ear, and then they were out of the tent – out into the confusing underwater colours of the Marsh Alcaia – and the world was swimming, spinning around her, and she could hold on to it no longer.

Thalric almost fell over as Che's full weight dragged against him, but he got an arm behind her knees and hoisted her off the ground. *Cursed Beetle girl could stand to lose some weight,* came the thought, but then he had a firm grip on her and was backing out of that horrible tent. He noticed movement and turned awkwardly, seeing someone running towards them. He twisted a hand free, almost losing hold of Che again, and let his sting flash. The man, an emaciated Khanaphir, fell back in a tangle of limbs.

'Let's *go*,' he grated. 'Come on, Fly-kinden.'

Trallo was already on his way, trying to wind back the string on a pistol crossbow as he went. The denizens of the Marsh Alcaia had begun to show all too much interest in a Wasp lugging a foreign Beetle girl about.

'Stupid, stupid woman,' Thalric was cursing under his breath. 'What did you think you were doing?'

'Lucky you were keeping an eye on her,' said Trallo, having finally got his crossbow cocked. Now that he brandished it so openly, interest from the street people was fast diminishing. The Khanaphir didn't seem to possess such weapons themselves, but everyone here seemed to know what it was capable of. Loosing a crossbow bolt in a confined space bounded entirely by cloth walls would be an interesting exercise, Thalric thought.

Trallo was leading the way confidently, left, left, then right. Merchants and gamblers watched narrowly as they passed, making Thalric keenly aware of just how much Che's unconscious body was hampering his progress. *If they jump me I'm dead*, he thought, and then, *and I bloody well deserve it*. He was conscious that dressing this episode up to satisfy his Rekef colleagues would be nigh impossible. *But I knew – I knew she would get involved in something like this.* Cheerwell Maker, as usual, blundering through a world of sharp edges with her eyes shut.

The uncomfortable truth: *I have a problem, here,* and then Trallo shouted something, and Thalric tried to turn. Something hit him in the jaw hard enough to snap his head back. He staggered, his legs suddenly weak, and someone tried to wrestle Che from his grasp. There was a moment of fumbling that, to a disinterested observer, must have seemed hilarious, and Che was pulled out of

Thalric's hands. The abductor had botched it, though, tripping and falling backwards so that the weight of her drove the breath from his lungs. Abruptly free of her, with palm open and ready, Thalric turned to receive another hammering punch that knocked him flat on his back. A dark-armoured form loomed over him just as he heard the clack of Trallo's crossbow. Impossibly the little bolt just danced off the attacker's mail and those gauntleted hands now came up with something ugly and short-barrelled: *a cut-down snapbow!*

'Flee!' Thalric shouted, as two of his attackers began hauling him to his feet. He struggled furiously, trying to turn the palms of his hands towards them. 'Trallo, flee!' he yelled again. He saw the armoured assailant sight down the wicked little snapbow, then lower it.

*Telling a Fly-kinden to run,* it occurred to Thalric, *is surely unnecessary.*

'Watch his hands!' the man warned, but they were already holding Thalric's arms out straight and back, putting pressure on his elbows to keep them that way. Their dark armour was mostly plated leathers, and only their leader wore steel mail, of a design Thalric had never seen before. It was a moment before he recognized the emblem on their tabards.

'What—?' One of them wrenched his arm and he hissed in pain. 'What do the Iron Glove want with me? I am Imperial ambassador in this city!'

'Are you?' He could see himself reflected dimly in the armoured man's helm. The eye-slit gave no clues. 'And what does the Empire want with abducting Lowlander women?'

'I was . . .' But he was what? *What can I say that will not incriminate me?*

'Your name is Thalric, my people tell me,' said the Iron Glove man, and a chill went through him.

*Assassins?* He had all but forgotten, given the challenge of this new city and its distractions. *Are you so weary of your life that you forget such things?* But he was far from the

Empire, and the attack outside Tyrshaan now seemed like something long ago.

'My name is Thalric,' he admitted.

'It has been a long time,' the armoured man replied slowly. 'I saw you only briefly, on the *Sky Without*. But she told me what you did to her, in Helleron and in Myna.' There were knives in that tone which mocked the terrors of mere assassins.

'Who are you?' Thalric demanded.

'Me?' The faceless helm came closer. 'Why, I'm no Rekef officer, Master Thalric. I'm no lord of the Empire or grand ambassador. I'm just a poor halfbreed boy who's had to make his own way in the world.'

A name hovered at the very edge of Thalric's memory, but he could not bring it to mind.

'But look at me now,' the man continued. 'I've not done so badly. Look at what I can do.'

Thalric saw him draw back his fist for the blow, amateurish and clumsy if only he himself had been able to dodge. Then the metal-clad fist slammed into his stomach and doubled him over, only the layer of copperweave saving his innards. He sagged against his captors, who instantly jerked him upright. The armoured man was examining his mailed fist speculatively.

'Look what I can do,' he repeated, wonderingly. When the gaze of the helm tilted towards Thalric again, it was as though they were collaborators in this new exercise of power.

'You don't understand what's going on here,' said Thalric, and because he was speaking he was not ready for the next blow, which lashed into his cheek, splitting his lip and throwing him out of the grip of his captors. He hit the ground hard, clawing at the dust, trying to extend a hand out to sting. The boot came from nowhere into his ribs and he cried out at last, curling about the pain, bracing for the next blow.

There was no next one, though, and he forced himself to

look up. The snapbow was directed at him, at his face, at his eye. *Well, I always knew the mail wouldn't save me every time.*

'This is personal, between us two,' the armoured man explained. 'The Iron Glove wouldn't thank me for killing an ambassador. Be grateful that your Fly got away to tell tales. It's enough now that you know you're beaten.'

Two of them still supported Che between them, and the two others that had been holding him now had their crossbows out and ready. The company started moving away through the Marsh Alcaia, only the armoured man pausing a moment, staring down at Thalric.

'If I ever see you again,' he said, 'know that I haven't even begun to avenge what you did to her.'

Thalric tried to sit up, unkinking bruise by bruise, his breath ragged in his throat. No broken ribs, just pain all over and a bloodied lip. He had suffered much worse. The halfbreed had no idea just how much Thalric had endured, before.

There was a flurry of movement nearby, and he instinctively jabbed an arm out towards it, reaching for his sword with the other.

'It's me, it's me!' Trallo shrilled, coming to rest beside him, surveying him critically. 'They did a real job on you, didn't they?'

Thalric groaned, pulling himself fully to his feet, light-headed and breathing through waves of pain.

'I hope you can walk,' Trallo added reproachfully. 'There's no way I'm carrying you.'

'I can walk.' *And I can think up some explanation for Marger and the others, as well.* He was still ransacking his memory for the name of the armoured halfbreed.

# Twenty

She awoke, and was in a strange place.

She was still in Khanaphes, because the city signed every brick that composed it, but this was nowhere she recognized. The ceiling was too low, the windows too small: it was certainly not the splendour of the Place of Honoured Foreigners.

Nor was it the coloured cloth of the Marsh Alcaia, and that was something to be grateful for, at least. She gathered up the pieces of her last recollections and tried to put them in order. The Fir dream came back to her with shocking suddenness: the mantis of the Darakyon, reaching out with bloody claws towards her. She sat up with a start.

'Achaeos?' she whispered the name, out of force of habit, but his ghost was not there, not even a tremor in the air to hint of it. She was in some kind of dormitory, lying on a narrow cot that was one of five. It looked like a room allotted for servants.

*They were going to kill me,* she recalled. The woman they called Mother had urged, *Take her blood.* Was that why she was now here? Were they going to farm her blood, syphon it off in cups and quarts? Che realized she was not tied to the bed, but she was willing to bet that the door was locked, and the single window was too small to let a Fly in.

*Trallo?* Perhaps the Fly had escaped. Perhaps there would be a rescue, after all. *By who, though?* She could not imagine

Manny and Berjek charging in with sword and pike, but at least they could always go and seek aid from the Khanaphir. It would be a diplomatic embarrassment, of course, and if the truth of her deeds should become known they might be thrown out of the city – or worse. That might still be better than being bled to death by Fir-eaters over the course of a month.

She recalled Trallo shouting something. Had he been shouting for help? *And hadn't help arrived?* She had an image of a bright figure with its hands on fire. The Fir-eaters had been screaming . . .

There was water and soap laid out for her at the foot of the bed, and the sight of it brought a surge of relief out of all proportion, since the Fir-eaters had not looked as though they cared much for washing. There was even a towel folded over the bed-end, Collegium style. *Someone's trying to make me feel welcome.* After washing, she drank a great deal of water from a pitcher, trying to rid her mouth of the bitter taste of the vices she had dabbled in. *Perhaps this is some kind of Khanaphir hospital?*

They had laid out a robe for her too, and she eyed it suspiciously. She was still wearing what she considered as her working clothes, hardwearing and practical even though they were filthy and malodorous.

Realizing her sword was gone, she cursed quietly. Her new situation seemed subtly balanced between comfort and threat. *Am I a prisoner here, or a guest?*

She decided not to change clothes. Instead, she tried the door, and found it opened out into a corridor. Immediately she was surrounded. There were three of them, men in dark leathers and helms, shortswords at their belts. One closed the door neatly behind her, another was off and away at a run. She swung round, reaching again for the absent sword. 'What is this?'

'If you'll come with us,' one of them said, the tone of his voice strictly neutral.

'You're – wait a moment, you're Iron Glove. What's going on?' she demanded.

'Just come with us, Bella,' the man repeated. The two of them were standing on one side of her, blocking the narrow corridor. She backed off the way that the third man had gone running, and they followed smoothly.

'I'm the Collegiate ambassador,' she told them, trying for authority. 'I insist you tell me where I am and what is going on.'

They gave no reply to her bravado, which was perhaps all it deserved. She was retreating and retreating, seeing only closed doors on all sides, or doorways and stairwells where other Iron Glove men stood and watched, barring any escape.

'Is Corcoran here?' she asked desperately. 'I know him. He's a friend.' *An acquaintance, barely.* 'Please would you go find him. He's in charge here, isn't he?'

'Not any more,' one of the men said flatly, and her heart sank. *What have I got myself into? Some schism amongst them? And how would that involve me?*

She realized that she had unthinkingly backed into a larger room, and turned, groping for her bearings. It was a dining hall, still low-ceilinged but wide, and windowed on one side beyond a row of pillars. This was a little more like the Khanaphes she knew.

The long table that dominated the room was set with fruit and some sort of fish, simple local fare. The sight of it made Che realize how hungry she was, but there were only two chairs set there, and until the other one was claimed she was not going to sit down. The two Iron Glove men had now retreated to the doorway she had entered by.

'Someone,' she insisted, 'had better tell me what is going on.'

Even as she spoke, that someone entered the room from the far door. She saw a broad-shouldered man in intricate dark mail, pulling off his gauntlets even as he approached.

He went to stand by one of the chairs, which was drawn out for him by one of his men. Cautiously, Che approached the other.

He laid the gauntlets on the table, undid the chinstrap of his helm and took it off. Che stared into the solid, closed face of a stranger, a halfbreed, strong-jawed and heavy-browed, touched by that faint discontinuity that so many of mixed blood were tainted with . . .

As she studied him, something shifted inside her, as though the ground beneath her feet had turned suddenly treacherous.

'Hello, Che,' he said, and she was rushing around the table to get to him, throwing her arms around the fluted breastplate, feeling his own arms hesitantly encircle her, almost too gently to feel, as though he was desperate not to break her.

She stood back a pace, looking him up and down. That face, which a moment ago had been as full of mystery as a stranger's, had that familiar half-bewildered expression that brought back long-ago days in the Great College.

'I can't believe it,' she said. 'I can't believe it's you. Look at you!' The sight of him unleashed a whirl of memories. 'I thought they must have killed you,' she continued. 'I was sure they must have found you out. I never heard anything more . . .' A cold thought came to her. 'You're not . . .?'

'With the Empire? I am not,' he said firmly. He was trying to smile at her, but a lifetime of hiding his hurts and joys was making it hard for him. 'And the man who found out what I had done was no normal Imperial officer.' He made an awkward gesture at the table. 'Eat, please. Will you eat with me?'

'Of course.' She sat herself down hurriedly, hands moving rapidly to the food under urgent directions from her stomach. She glanced back towards the two men who had shepherded her into the room. 'How did you go from the Empire to these Iron Glove people anyway? Are you turned merchant now?'

As he sat opposite her, a smile broke through at last. It made his face look unfamiliar: a hard thing born from the years since they had left Collegium, not something of the boy she had known at all. 'Che, I *am* the Iron Glove,' he replied.

She frowned at him, bolted a mouthful of fish and said, 'I don't understand.'

'A year ago I fled the Empire with my . . . business partner. We came to settle in Chasme, and started work. Now we're the biggest artificing house around the Exalsee, and expanding every day. The trading is secondary. It's the research, the manufacture, that's the point.'

'And you sell . . . weapons?' Che recalled.

'We sell war.' From his expression, it was a reflexive answer, and perhaps one he would not have given her if he had thought it through. 'Weapons, armour, machinery, with Exalsee innovation, Lowlander craft and Imperial methods. We've built it up, Che – *I've* built it up – and we've only been in Chasme for a year and a bit.' His face was desperate for some validation from her.

'You always did like your weapons,' she said and, although that was not it, her fond smile seemed to satisfy him. 'And that's why you're in Khanaphes now?'

'There's a market,' he said, and she heard behind the statement things left unsaid. *He could not have come all this way just to meet me*. But her memory snagged on that letter, the one Achaeos had found, in which all of Totho's soul had lain scraped bare.

'I suppose I was lucky that you came along, in the Alcaia.' She said the words lightly, but she watched, and saw the beat, the moment's hesitation in his reaction. *Or you were seeking me out, or you were watching me . . .?* 'Hold on a moment.' She paused, the fork halfway to her lips. 'Where's Trallo?'

'What's Trallo?'

'A Fly-kinden. He was with me in the Alcaia . . .' A sudden chill struck her. *Did they kill him? Had I abandoned him?* She had been so concerned with her own surroundings, with this man from her past, she had not wondered what had happened to Trallo.

'He . . .' She saw Totho frown. 'He was yours?'

The chill increased. 'What did you . . .? Tell me you haven't hurt him, please.'

'No, not hurt . . .' His face remained without expression. 'There was a Fly, but he fled, when we took you from the Empire. I was sure he was on their side.'

She gave that one a long pause, trying it from all angles, and finding that it would not fit, no matter how she turned or forced it. 'The Empire?' she finally said, in a small voice. 'It was natives, Totho.' She could not bring herself to mention her foray into Profanity. 'The people who attacked me were natives.'

'Then they must have been in the Empire's pay,' he insisted. 'I took you from the hands of the Empire. A Wasp – and not just any Wasp . . .' She had held up a hand, but he barrelled on, determined to convince her. 'It was that man who had you captive in Myna. Their Rekef man. I took you from him though. I rescued you.'

He looked for approval, but she sank her face in her hands. She was suddenly feeling ill. 'Totho,' she said quietly, 'what have you done? Have you killed him?'

'The Iron Glove trades with the Empire,' Totho replied slowly, 'and this Thalric is their ambassador here. I merely took you from him . . . by force. I did not kill him.'

She was surprised at the relief she felt. *Thalric had been there, in the tent:* the bright figure with hands of fire. She had been rescued from her rescuer. *And how many people were following me, and keeping track of me, when I went to commit this crime against the Khanaphir?* How could she have missed so many spies and agents following on her heels?

'There's no reason for you to have known, but he worked for Stenwold during the war,' she said. 'It's . . . complicated.'

'He's the same man that enslaved you, tortured you,' Totho argued stubbornly.

'It's complicated,' said Che again. 'That's all. I had better go and see just what sort of a diplomatic mess has happened in my absence – whether they're searching the city for me.' She shook her head, seeing his suddenly aggrieved expression. 'Or could you at least send someone to my embassy to let them know I'm safe, and then I can finish dinner.'

He made a signal, and one of his men went running from the hall. In that same moment she felt uneasy with him. She could reconcile the face, the voice, but not the man. *What has he become, after all this time?* In all his designing and making, he had reinvented himself into this man of authority, dark-armoured, close-faced, hard-edged.

'It's good to see you again,' she told him, but was not sure, looking at Totho, how much she was still seeing of her old friend, or what had been brought in to replace what she had once known.

'So what happened to you?' Marger asked, eyeing Thalric's bruises.

'Diplomatic incident,' Thalric replied shortly. He had stormed back into the embassay only a few minutes ago, knowing that one of the Rekef would be with him as soon as they could decide who best to send.

'With the Lowlanders?'

'No, with the locals. Tell me about the Iron Glove.'

Marger took the two statements in, and made the connection without comment. 'What's to say?' Another in his long series of shrugs. 'Trading cartel from the Exalsee, weapons and armour, operating out of Chasme. They've done well for themselves over the last year.'

Thalric leant back in his chair with a disappointed sigh. 'Come on, Marger, I knew that much myself.' *Talk to other Rekef men, and it feels as though I'm debriefing some enemy agent I've turned.* It was ludicrous, considering his business, but he missed the trust and the certainty of honest spy-work.

Marger's expression offered nothing but wide-eyed sincerity. 'What do you mean?'

Thalric sighed. 'You're thinking of me as a courtier, Captain Marger. You're thinking of the Regent, some fop who's never done a day's work for the service. I didn't get my Major's rank through family or favour. I earned it. I know full well that if a group like the Iron Glove was muscling in on your area of operation, you'd get briefed.'

For a long time Marger kept his usual easy smile, no more than the puzzled junior officer. Then it collapsed, and he gave a single hard-won nod. 'Well then, Major, we didn't know they were here, but it seemed likely enough for me to hear something. Nothing certain, mind, since they're tight with their information. They travel all over the Exalsee and beyond, in those helms and that black armour, and they manufacture arms that are strong, cheap, top quality. For special customers they offer more than that, new designs that have the Imperial artificers in fits. The Exalsee is already ahead of us, in some branches of artifice, and the Iron Glove is keeping ahead of them, too.'

Thalric digested this. 'And we trade with them? We should do.'

'As of recently, we do,' Marger confirmed. 'It's difficult, though. We want their schematics, their plans, but they're only prepared to sell us the finished articles. Reverse-engineering is always time-consuming, especially at the level of complexity that the Iron Glove are working at. And there are . . . other complications.'

'Tell me.'

Marger shrugged again, but it was a shrug from the heart. 'Like I said, they're secretive, and we don't know for sure who's running the cartel. Only . . . there are rumours.'

Thalric made an impatient gesture.

Marger grimaced. 'You must have heard of the Colonel-Auxillian? That mad halfbreed artificer who captured Lans Stowa and Falme Dae and Tark? Official records have him dead, along with the rest of the garrison at Szar, but . . . the rumours keep coming back that it's him . . .'

Thalric was thinking hard now. The armoured man had got the blows in, but he had lowered his guard in order to do it: he had let Thalric know who he was, and his armour alone marked him as a man high in the Iron Glove hierarchy. Where did Stenwold's renegade artificer fit in, though? Where had he gone after Helleron?

*He wasn't* at *Helleron.* The recollection came suddenly, like a splash of cold water. *He was the one that Scyla replaced, because the boy had run off to . . . Tark.* Tark, where the Colonel-Auxillian Dariandrephos had been practising his siegecraft.

'Send to the General,' he told Marger, who looked suspicious at the instruction. 'Get some clerk to dig out names of the artificers who were assisting the Colonel-Auxillian.' *Am I right?* He knew he was right, but he had no evidence. *Drephos had survived or, if he hadn't, someone who worked with him did.*

*Oh, my armoured friend, I shall have you yet – if I have to use the Empire to beat you to death.* The thought brought a rush of satisfaction, soothed both the bruises and his damaged pride.

Marger was still looking at him. 'Actually, Major . . .'

'What?'

'I'll be sending to the General as soon as I can get a messenger, but my report is incomplete. I need your help to complete it.'

'Of course, just ask.' In that moment, Thalric felt confident enough to be unassailable.

'You have been somewhat on your own recognizance,' Marger said. 'I understand that you were sent here because of your familiarity with the Lowlanders in general, and now it would seem that we extend that to certain individual

Lowlanders that are here. I need to know what your plan of action is, so that the General can endorse it, and so that you and I won't trip over each other.'

*And there's a good question, for which I have no answer.* 'I am still gathering information,' Thalric remarked.

'You seem to have established a rapport with the Collegiate ambassador,' Marger noted. 'I can see the benefit of that. Do you intend to seduce her?'

The question stopped Thalric dead, both in thought and action, leaving him looking at Marger with a half-framed expression on his face. At the same time something stirred inside him, that might have been anticipation, and the automatic answer: *Why not?*

'You're direct, Captain,' he said, expecting and receiving a shrug in return.

'She seems young for an ambassador,' Marger said. 'Inexperienced. It is easy enough to keep track of the others, but she seems to appear and disappear almost at random. If you were able to establish some kind of a hold on her, it would serve us well.'

'I'll . . . consider it,' said Thalric, his throat unexpectedly dry. In his mind the face that loomed before him was not Che's but that of the Empress. *What word will wing its way back to Capitas now? When she draws me back there eventually, what other treasons will I have committed?*

Amnon arrived shortly after Che had left, which spared Totho the burden of too much introspection. She had not quite warmed to him yet, but it had been two years, and the circumstances of their last meeting had hardly been conducive to fond memories. She had assumed he was dead, while he himself had done his best, in that time, to discover where she was and what she was doing. The resources of the Iron Glove stretched to a little spying, and Drephos had tolerated his eccentricities.

The Captain of the Royal Guard sauntered in with a broad smile. His sheer robust energy made Totho feel tired.

'So, we are ready for my fitting then,' the big man began, with an enthusiasm that was almost childish. *It doesn't matter how strange these Khanaphir are, everyone loves a new toy,* thought Totho. Corcoran had picked out the First Soldier as the man they should primarily impress, in order to further the Glove's influence in Khanaphes. He was loved by the people, high up in the city hierarchy, and yet he was a hands-on commander always to be found in the front rank. It made him an ideal customer.

'My people are unpacking the armour even now,' Totho told him, once he had led Amnon to a room they set aside for testing. There were weapons on the walls, breastplates and helms displayed on armour trees. He imagined this man would want to try out his new mail as soon as he had put it on.

'I see you're wearing your own, still,' Amnon observed. 'Is it so light?'

Totho could not suppress a slightly shamefaced smile. 'It is new, so I'm wearing it as much as possible to get used to it. It's not the weight, so much, just the way I need to move in it.'

Amnon nodded approvingly. 'Armour and mounts and women, you have to get used to them all,' he said. He started to say something else, but paused to rethink. In a man normally so positive, the hesitation caught Totho's attention.

'You are one of these Lowlanders, are you not?' the big man said eventually.

'From Collegium, although I've travelled since then,' Totho told him. He felt the time since he had left Collegium as a physical distance, a desert that he could never recross.

'Collegium, excellent.' Amnon made a show of examining some of the weapons on the wall. 'Will you advise me, then, on a matter regarding Collegium?' His accent gave the familiar name an exotic sound.

'If I can.'

'How is it with the women there?' Amnon said, still not looking at him directly.

'The . . .?' Totho let the sentence hang. *Do I want to know what he means?*

'It is like this.' Amnon turned to him, and his big, amiable face wore a defensive expression for once. 'One of the Collegium delegation has caught my eye. In fact, I find her quite the most beautiful woman there is.' He said it quickly, without fumbling the words in any way. 'I know she is not wed, or intended, but I have not spoken to her of my feelings yet. I am not sure how things are done where she comes from.'

Totho felt a sinking feeling. 'Is it . . . the ambassador?' he asked. *No more rivals*, he thought. *And certainly not this man, this absurd specimen of physicality.* He tried to imagine competing with Amnon, with all his smiles and prowess and position.

'It is the woman Rakespear,' Amnon announced, and Totho felt a wash of relief. He had only a vague idea of who Amnon meant, but it was not Che and that was all that mattered.

'In Collegium, one normally speaks to her father or her guardian' – *and that worked well for me, didn't it?* – 'but there is no reason not to speak with her direct, or to offer her gifts. I think you'll find that Collegiate women are probably quite forward compared to what you're used to.'

'Good,' said Amnon, and he was about to say something more when Corcoran came in, not with the armour but escorting another guest. Amnon straightened to attention immediately, and Totho recognized the robed figure of the First Minister standing there with his quiet smile.

'My lord,' Totho bowed to him quickly, 'we had not expected you, but you are welcome, of course.'

'Of course,' Ethmet replied, glancing from Totho to Amnon. 'I had heard our First Soldier was to receive some gift today. It is very kind of you, Honoured Foreigner, and I would see it presented, if I may.'

'We would be happy,' said Totho, aware of a feeling of discomfort from Amnon. *Is he breaking some rule of theirs?* But Corcoran had done his groundwork, surely, and presenting gifts to high officials was every bit a part of Khanaphir life. Ethmet's face offered no clues.

They brought the armour out just then, four of his men manhandling the table on which it was laid. The mere empty shell of it, cast to Amnon's proportions, made Totho feel dwarfed.

'This is forged in what we call aviation steel, that the Solarnese developed for their flying machines,' he explained, as the Iron Glove men buckled the arming jacket on Amnon and then began to piece the armour onto him. 'It's very light, and still very strong, but they had never thought of using the material for armour until we came along.' The mail undershirt was already on, and Totho relished Amnon's surprise at how light it was. 'The mail rings are drawn from silver-steel wire, and they'll bunch on impact to block an arrow or a sword.' Totho walked around, observing as his people attached the metal plates, watching Amnon slowly disappear, becoming something huge and metallic. It was a glorious transformation, in Totho's eyes. 'The plates themselves are machined into flutes, which makes them as strong as much thicker metal, and which also helps deflect an enemy's weapon. Every surface a blade might impact on is curved or, where those curves meet, is an angled line. That means that you have the absolute maximum of protection against attacks from any angle. With the mail, and the jack beneath, the only weak points are the groin and armpit, although there is fine mail even there.' When the helm was lowered onto Amnon's head, they had to stand on the table to do it.

For a long moment there was silence. Totho watched Amnon making small movements, feeling the way the metal slid over metal. He looked like some creation of artifice, some colossal war-automaton. They had stripped from him all human frailties.

Then, 'No,' said Ethmet softly.

Amnon's helm turned quickly to face him.

'First Minister?' Totho asked, uncertainly.

'We cannot accept this gift,' the old Khanaphir declared. There was some expression, at last, on his face. He was shaken by what he had seen. 'We had thought it was mere armour. This is not armour as we understand it.'

Amnon wrenched off the helm, looking aggrieved. 'But, First Minister, I like this armour. It is lighter than my battle-mail. I have never worn anything like it.'

'No,' Ethmet said again, 'we regret that Khanaphes cannot accept this.'

'But, First Minister . . .!' Amnon began again, till Ethmet turned on him sharply, his glance alone quelling any argument.

'The Masters would not approve,' he proclaimed, and Amnon's face sagged. The Minister's expression was still stern as he turned to Totho again. 'Trade us your arrows and your swords, your shields and such things as we approve of, but you are henceforth warned, O Foreigner. There are limits, in this city, to what may be done, and the Masters' will may not be crossed.'

'I don't understand,' protested Totho.

'I think you do.' The man facing him now was a stranger, stripped of all the mild patience of the First Minister. There was no compromise at all in that face and Totho saw that Amnon was visibly frightened. *He could snap the old man in half with one hand*, but things didn't work that way, it would seem. *What does this remind me of, that I have seen before?Mantis and Moth, that is what it reminds me of. The strong whipped into submission by the weak.*

As they stripped the armour from Amnon, his expression remained resentful but cowed. Whatever power Ethmet held over him, it was something that the First Soldier would not provoke at any cost. *Who exactly are these Masters of Khanaphir?* Totho wondered. A fiction, Corcoran had assumed – some invention of the Ministers, to ensure their continuing power. Totho himself had not been sure, until now. *Nothing but such a deception could allow this old man to get away with it.*

'I had thought that the Honoured Foreigner might come on my hunt,' Amnon muttered, almost too quiet to be heard.

'It is not appropriate,' Ethmet replied, as though Totho was not there. 'Your hunt is for dignitaries, not for merchants.'

The two of them departed after that, the old man shepherding the huge warrior out of the Iron Glove factora, leaving Totho quizzing Corcoran futilely in an attempt to understand what it had all been about.

# Twenty-One

The boat cut through the water at a surprising pace, its shallow draught moving cleanly and with almost no wake. Che huddled inside her cloak and felt miserable.

'I don't see why I have to join this circus,' she complained. Her last few days had been hectic – the Fir was still giving her occasional stabs of queasiness and she had not come to terms with meeting Totho either – so the last thing she wanted was to be dragged from her bed to go on some hunting expedition.

'It's in your honour,' Manny explained airily. 'Or perhaps our honour.'

'Berjek didn't have to come along.'

'Master Gripshod isn't the ambassador.'

Che shook herself irritably. The locals had come to fetch them two hours before dawn, which had been a surprise to everyone except Mannerly Gorget. Manny himself had been downstairs and ready, drinking hot spiked tea, having neglected to tell anyone else of the arrangements he had made. It had meant a bungled rush for Che and Praeda to get dressed, and then be bustled down to the docks. They had reached the river to see the first bare streaks of dawn kindling in the eastern sky.

The boat that awaited them there was not what Che had expected. For a start it had no mast, and it seemed very small. It was a long, slender craft that rocked alarmingly when Manny transferred his bulk on to it, little more than an oversized canoe. At both prow and stern the curving shape tapered and rose into a stumpy carving of something that Che could not identify.

There were two boat crew, standing fore and aft, and although they must already have been waiting an hour they did not show it. Che, cowled and half-asleep, did not get a proper look at them until they had cast off and were under way, each standing upright to paddle with great strong strokes, alternating left and right. Then, belatedly, she realized that they were not Khanaphir. They were slender, with silver-grey skins, and though they had shaved heads and simple tunics like Khanaphir servants, Che recognized their angular features instantly.

'Mantis-kinden?' she exclaimed, blinking herself wider awake.

'They call them the Marsh People,' Praeda informed her. 'They seem to be attached somehow to the city, under its control, though the relationship between them and our hosts seems complex. We're going out into the delta now, you see. It's their place.' She spoke distractedly, something else clearly on her mind.

They had just passed between the great pillars of the Estuarine Gate, and Che carefully did not look back at the morass of cloth that was the Marsh Alcaia. 'I didn't realize the Khanaphir had subject peoples,' she said. 'The city's not exactly cosmopolitan.'

'And more than just the Marsh-dwellers,' Praeda confirmed, 'but they keep to their places. I've been asking to go upriver, to see some of the other settlements. The Dominion of Khanaphes has at least four disparate kinden within it, I believe.'

'What keeps them in line?' Che said softly, almost to herself. She looked up again at the nearest Marsh-dweller, silhouetted against the lightening sky. The Mantis woman did not glance down, but kept paddling strongly, stroke after stroke. *What do they get out of this servitude? Who can manage to hold Mantis-kinden in thrall?*

*The Moths could – Achaeos's people.* The thought came automatically, and she knew she was touching the secret again, hearing the pulse of Khanaphes's hidden heart. The Moths were a sorcerous, Inapt race, whereas the Khanaphir were not . . . or at least that was the face they showed to the world.

The river beyond the gates was swathed in mist: white curtains of it rose from the waters, cloaking the banks and muffling the deep ratcheting of the crickets and the boom of a distant cicada. Abruptly they were within it, and the world had been left behind, only the pale and ragged sheets of the mist itself coursing over and around them.

'We're not just going out alone are we?' Che whispered. 'Aren't there supposed to be more of us?'

'They'll be waiting for us further out on the river,' said Manny, with slightly hollow confidence.

'Do we have any idea what we're supposed to be hunting?' asked Praeda. Even she sounded slightly nervous.

'Fishing,' Manny said dismissively. 'After all this, it's only fishing. So I intend to get a decent look at the local fauna while everyone is fooling about with nets and things.'

There was a slight sound from the forward Mantis, which might have indicated humour. Che looked up abruptly to see a definite smile being fought off the woman's face. Her stomach sank, knowing that Manny's research had not been as thorough as he thought.

Something loomed ahead in the clearing mist, and Che made out a greater boat, a broad barge that was ten times as long as their little punt, equipped with a bare mast and a canopy to keep off the sun that would soon be burning the mist away. Che saw several robed figures standing at the rail, watching them with polite interest. She recognized Ethmet and a few of the other Ministers, obviously come to watch the sport.

‘Why aren’t I on that boat?’ she asked.

‘Ah, well,’ said Manny, in a tone that admitted guilt even while he was choosing his words. ‘We were given the choice, of course, but I reckoned we’d see nothing from up there.’

‘Manny, are we . . . *participating* in this hunt?’ Praeda asked him.

‘Well, not so much – not unless you wanted to. I just wanted to make sure we were close enough to the water to see what was going on, get a decent look at the wildlife.’

There were other boats now skimming along the side of the barge. Che saw that they were tiny, barely five feet long and with a single Mantis-kinden poling or paddling them, poised with impossible balance as they scudded across the river. Those craft were not of wood, but merely bundled reeds, and where the bunched reeds were lashed together, at front and rear, they formed the original of the wooden carving that her own boat was capped with. She turned to point this out to Praeda, but the woman was already bent over the boards of their own craft, examining its construction.

‘Fascinating,’ she said finally. ‘You realize there are no nails in this boat at all?’

‘Don’t be foolish,’ Manny sneered. ‘What’s holding it together then?’ He shifted his place and the craft rocked alarmingly. The Mantis crew accommodated the movement with a slight shift of balance, as though it had all been rehearsed between them and Manny the previous day.

‘Rope,’ Praeda revealed. ‘Just rope, passed round and through and round again. It must shrink in the water, to hold everything together. But it’s perfect Inapt boatbuilding. The techniques must be centuries old.’

*Just like everything around here*, Che thought.

Another boat came up beside them, the mirror of their own but twice as long, four Mantids back-paddling to bring the craft alongside. Amnon was standing at its carved prow, stripped to the waist and wearing only a kilt. Che heard Praeda murmur, ‘Oh, grace and favour, look at him!’

in civilized horror. She kept looking at him, though, Che noticed, and when she glanced away her eyes were drawn back to him soon enough. A conversation with Manny recurred to her, and Che wondered if similar word had crept round to Praeda.

The big man grinned down at them. 'Welcome!' he said. 'At last you are with us: the hunt can begin. It is my honour that you have agreed to participate as bold hunters along with us. In this way shall the skill and the courage of Collegium be known.'

Che grimaced up at him. 'Captain, I think you should first let us know just what we are hunting, and how to go about it,' she said weakly. 'We are rather new to this.'

'Of course, of course. You should watch me make the first kill, perhaps.' He put a bare foot up on the side of his boat, scanning the riverbank beyond them, then jabbing out a finger. 'There, you see,' he said. 'They come to warm themselves in the sun. Do you see them there?'

'Fish basking in the . . .' Che could see nothing but rocks amongst the foliage, but she heard Manny whistle in astonishment, and then one of the rocks opened a bulbous eye to appraise her. There were half a dozen of them, the least of them the size of a man. Slick-skinned, brown creatures with stubby front fins like arms, and high-set, goggling eyes, they lounged half-in and half-out of the water. One of them yawned, and its mouth was cavernous, the needle-sharp teeth glinting in the dawn light.

'Oh, loose knives and bloody thunder,' Manny said in awe. 'They're fish. Those are the fish they're hunting.'

'Land-fish,' Amnon said proudly, as though he was personally responsible for their existence. 'But we will not hunt these, of course. They are only young. It would not be fair to pit our skills against them until they have fully grown.'

'I want to go on the barge,' said Che, but the Mantids were suddenly thrusting the boat forward, almost toppling her backwards. Amnon's crew did the same, and she saw a few other boats like their own coursing ahead over the water, moving beyond the wallowing barge.

'Catch these!' Amnon called out. 'You must have the tools to hunt them!' He took up a leather-wrapped bundle that was as long as he was and cast it, with no appreciable effort, across the water towards them. Manny took it full in the chest and would have toppled overboard with it had Praeda and Che not grabbed hold of his robes. With a certain avid interest he unwrapped it, spilling arrows into the bottom of the boat. There was a brace of shortbows, too, curled forward ready to be strung, and a spear with a barbed head attached to a neatly coiled line.

'Nets and things,' said Che pointedly to Manny. 'What have you got us into?'

'That Amnon, he claimed it was fishing,' the fat man protested.

'Well, to *him*, this probably *does* count as fishing,' Che snapped. 'We will keep well clear of all this hunting, and Waste take the honour of Collegium.'

'Agreed,' said Manny, slightly shaken by this turn of events. Che sat back and put a hand to her head. Land-fish stared at her with sleepy suspicion from the banks, and so she turned her back on them, looking out at the other boats.

From the far side of Amnon's craft another boat emerged. It had two Mantids poling it forward, but a third man was standing near the bows, spear in hand and cloak billowing. It took Che a moment to recognize him.

*Thalric.* And of course what she should be doing *now*, instead of performing this ridiculous charade, was talking to Thalric and smoothing things over. But it would have done no good to seek him out, she saw, because she was not the only ambassador to have been invited on the hunt.

He glanced over at her, and on his pale face she could see bruising, and her heart sank. *Totho thought he was rescuing me.* Trallo had explained to her how Thalric had taken her from the Fir-eaters, only to lose her to the Iron Glove. *I am changing hands so often, they should put customs duty on me.*

She raised a hand to send a feeble greeting over the water. She saw him nod in response. That small contact, the opening of negotiations, brought her a disproportionate relief. *Has Totho now usurped him as the person I know best in this city? Or do I know Thalric even better, at this remove? Thalric has been drifting nearer, while Totho began close to me but he seems so far away now.*

There was a series of shrill whistles that Che could not locate. As they sounded again she realized they came from beyond the river proper, amid the channels and marshes of the delta which spread its tangled fingers from here all the way to the sea. Amnon's boat went coursing towards the sounds, and her own followed under the swift, sure oar-strokes of the Mantis-kinden. She saw Thalric's craft leap forward also, his wings flickering to keep balance. There was another Wasp sitting in the boat behind him, looking every bit as ill and miserable as Che herself felt. She thought it might be the same man who had reacted so badly to the Mantis statue, and wondered how he was getting on with their boat's crew.

Two of the little reed craft suddenly shot on to the broad waters of the river as though they had been spat out, their occupants poling them with precise grace and astonishing speed. There was a line trailing from one – Che could see it cutting ripples on the water – it was attached to—

It was attached to one of the land-fish, but a creature almost as long as Amnon's boat. Its maw, snagged by a harpoon head and gaping with fury, could have swallowed Che whole. It powered over the mud and ferns, its stumpy front fins granting it a startling pace, and then sloughed into the river with a bellowing grunt. Amnon's boat was cutting close, as the big man stood ready with a bow strung and drawn back. For a second the fish was invisible in the brown wash of the water, but something guided Amnon's hand as he loosed the arrow into the murk, and then the fish leapt to the surface to meet this fresh assault.

*They want it in sight of the barge,* Che realized, *but still in the shallows, where it can't escape.* Amnon and the Mantis-kinden were playing a dangerous game, herding the enraged monster up and down the river bank, not letting it slip into any of the smaller channels, nor vanish into the depths. Time and again it hurled itself at Amnon's boat, but the Mantis crew pirouetted and sliced through the water, always cutting aside from the creature's furious charge. Everyone on the boat, Amnon and his crew alike, remained standing throughout, as the big Beetle sent arrow after arrow into the furious beast. It turned from him towards the other boats, those fleeting little reed constructions, but they nimbly skittered out of its path. Once it was too quick for them, its jaws slamming down on a bundled stern. The Mantis poling the boat was in the air at once, wings glittering, as the monster shredded her craft into scraps with mindless rage.

'What a barbaric spectacle,' Praeda remarked, sounding disdainful, but she was clutching tightly at the boat's side. Manny just stared, silently, fingering one of the bows they had been given.

At last it was done. The cornered fish, jaws agape in threat, reared up out of the water, its hide bristling with arrow shafts. Amnon held a spear now and took precise aim, spinning himself completely around to give the cast more force, yet barely rocking the boat as he did so. The heavy-headed lance plunged into the monster's throat, and Amnon leant forward to take hold of the butt and drive it further in. The great fish recoiled under the shock of it, thrashing down on to the mud, and Amnon took up the bow again. He sighted on the beast's eye, the arrowhead moving in minute twitches to track the creature's death throes. His fingers released the string.

Che grimaced. 'I think I prefer fishing the Collegium way,' she said weakly.

'Nonsense,' Manny declared. 'Can't visit a foreign place and not try a few of the local pastimes. String this for me, would you?'

One of their crew took the bow from him and bent it back effortlessly, seeming to turn the curved wood almost inside out before she hooked the string over the notched end.

'You're not planning to use that, are you?' Che demanded.

'Might as well look the part,' the fat man said jovially. 'After all, I hear that fish-hunting is a proper hero's pastime, and I want it to be said that I did my bit. A reputation for heroism around the city could work wonders'

'You're drunk,' Praeda retorted flatly. 'Or you're mad.'

'I am only slightly drunk,' Manny assured her. 'And, as to the other, neither you nor I am qualified to diagnose. Let us hunt the land-fish!'

'Let us stay close to the bank,' Che advised, 'and watch, if you have to. While we're all on this boat, you're not taking it near one of those creatures.'

The other boats were splitting away now, some hunting down the channels of the delta, swiftly lost to sight amongst its riotous vegetation, others coursing across the clear water of the river, waiting for game to be flushed out. Che huddled in her cloak. The land-fish terrified her, their bloody fate appalled her. It was a very foreign land she now found herself in.

'Remind me why we're doing this again?' Osgan complained. He had his arms wrapped tightly about both himself and a bottle, but he still looked uncomfortably sober.

'They wanted the Imperial ambassador to come hunting with them,' Thalric explained. 'They gave me a chance to sit on the barge and merely watch, but Marger and I agreed it was not politic to choose that option.'

'You're going to kill one of those things, are you? With just a spear?'

'Spear, sting,' Thalric said vaguely. 'Wings, too. We're better equipped for this sport than our hosts imagine.'

'I'm not the strongest flier.'

'So long as you can fly better than a two-ton fish, you'll be fine,' Thalric replied. He was conscious of forcing the humour, but it helped. It gave him an act to maintain, which meant he did not have to think about more awkward matters. He was playing the role of Imperial ambassador, upholding the honour of the Empire by showing these savages just how good the Wasps could be at whatever they turned their hand to. That was easier than brooding over his revenge on Totho of the Iron Glove, or reflecting on his recent conversation with Marger.

Marger was up there on the barge, of course, since there needed to be someone to keep an ear open for what the Ministers were saying. The Fly, Trallo, was there, too, ostensibly as a servant of the Lowlanders, but then he was a servant of Thalric as well. He had many pockets, Trallo, and he could take anyone's gold. Useful, but not a man to trust.

At Thalric's direction, the two Mantids guided their boat into one of the channels. There were several reed punts moving ahead, hunting out a land-fish of suitable dimensions. Smaller beasts flopped and grunted on the mudbanks, staring back at the intruders with their huge eyes, raising bright red fins in warning.

A chorus of whistles from somewhere ahead signalled the scouts finding suitable quarry. With a word, Thalric bid his crew urge the boat forward. 'I think Imperial honour will be satisfied by our driving one of the beasts into the river,' he decided. 'Let Captain Amnon deal with the bloodletting.'

They noticed the commotion ahead, then the little boats were hurrying back towards the river, while the humped back of a fish, fin raised like a banner, came surging through the shallow water after them. The Wasps would be too late,

Thalric guessed, but he would be able to make a show of it, anyway, perhaps burn a few holes into the beast as Amnon dispatched it. His boat reached the fish's wake, abruptly jolting over the disturbed water so that he had to use his spear to push himself off a stand of reeds and keep his balance. He saw others rushing out amidst the green, following the hunt on foot as they dodged between the giant horsetails and rushes.

He had turned to order his crew to chase the beast when the image of the runners struck a chord in his mind. *Where have I seen that?* followed by, *What was I seeing?* Those dashing figures, skipping swiftly between mud and greenery, *walking on the water.*

The first arrow knocked the Mantis at the bows right off the boat. Thalric saw him arch backwards, mouth open in silent surprise, and then vanish into the waters with barely a splash. Thalric's wings flared, and he kicked off from the rocking craft. Another arrow sped across the water, and he heard Osgan cry out.

He saw them clearly then, or some of them. They were skipping over the water, crouching low from cover to cover. He had assumed they were the local Mantids at first, but they had long limbs and short bodies, all angular elbows and knees. They wore cuirasses of darkened metal scales, and they all carried bows. He saw three, in that brief moment, and one was aiming up at him already.

He let his sting speak for him, the old reflexes coming back. The arrow shot off to one side of him as he shifted in the air, but his own aim was true, the impact of his fire striking the man between neck and shoulder. In an instant the assassin was gone, his Art dying with him, the water receiving him at last.

The other two were shooting then and the air offered nowhere to hide. Thalric dropped down to just above the river's surface, hovering near the boat. 'Get moving!' he snapped, but the Mantis woman had snatched up a bow, a little recurved thing, and was kneeling at the stern to sight up on some target invisible to Thalric. His heart lurched when he spotted Osgan lying groaning in the bottom of the boat. There was an arrow all the way through his upper arm, digging an inch into his ribs.

The Mantis let fly with her arrow, and at the same moment a shaft struck Thalric in the side. He was not wearing his army-issue mail, but the copperweave was hidden beneath his tunic. The arrowhead – broad-bladed to cleave flesh – did not pierce through, but the impact knocked him into the water.

His wings were abandoned at once, and for a moment he could do nothing but splash. Then his feet found the bottom and he reached up to drag himself into the boat.

The killers had broken cover, were racing towards them over the water, shooting as they came. One of them sprang backwards, with an arrow punching through his mail. The last assassin leapt up from the surface of the water onto the boat's side, drawing back his bowstring again and aiming straight at the Mantis.

From river-level, Thalric put a hand out and loosed his sting, catching the man at a range of five feet, splintering his bow and melting his mail, hurling him back off the boat into the water. When Thalric cautiously lifted himself up and into the boat, there was no sign of any of them, all their bodies reclaimed by the river.

*Skater-kinden from Jerez,* he named them, acutely aware that there could be more of them nearby, and another team of three would just about settle matters here. *Skater-kinden?* It was a long way from Jerez to Khanaphes, but of course there were Skaters in service to the Empire, with all the skills and the temperament necessary for the assassination game. That someone had sent them this far afield said a lot about how much they wanted Thalric dead. *And if I had stayed in Capitas, what might they not have sent against me?*

He had grown complacent, stopped thinking like a Rekef officer, and it had come close to killing him.

'Get this boat back on the main river,' he snapped. 'If we're to deal with assassins, let's have witnesses too.'

But the Mantis woman did not move, peering still into the tangled ferns. 'There are more,' she said, nocking another arrow. 'Between us and the rest of the hunt.'

*Fly*, thought Thalric, and it would be simple enough – save that even in that short space between here and the barge he would become a target for any halfway competent archer. It would mean leaving Osgan as well. Crouching low in the boat he studied the injured man. Osgan was shaking, skin gone pale, but he was conscious still.

'Now,' the Mantis said, and stood up suddenly to loose her arrow. Thalric raised his head briefly, saw a confusion of movement, heard a cry. Another arrow zipped past, a foot over his head. He saw the Mantis sighting up again.

'Out of the boat,' she urged abruptly. 'Into the trees.'

'What . . .?' Thalric started saying, but she kicked hard at the boat's side and it capsized neatly, dumping its two Wasp passengers into the murky water. Thalric, one hand still clawing at the curved hull, felt it quiver twice, knew that arrows were hammering into it from the far side. The Mantis woman had sprung into the air, her wings flickering. She loosed another shaft at a target he could not see, dodged in the air as a return shot sped past her. The arrow that jutted from her side was as unexpected and unlooked-for as a magic trick. She hissed in pain, fell towards the overturned boat, still reaching for her quiver.

'Go!' she spat, and Thalric waded two steps, then turned to haul up Osgan, who was spluttering and splashing fitfully. The man cried out as Thalric jogged the arrow through his arm, but there was no time to do anything about it. Thalric dragged him through the water, sometimes with Osgan's help and sometimes despite it. The Mantis woman landed beside him, just as he reached the nearest stand of ferns, and she shoved Osgan forward into the green and the mud. She collapsed shuddering beside him, the spine of the arrow in her side jerking in irregular time with her breathing.

Thalric crouched, watching, but he saw nothing more. That the assassins were still out there he had no doubt, but the same leaves now keeping him alive also hid his persecutors. Osgan gasped loudly, and Thalric hissed at him, 'I know, you're shot. Keep quiet.'

'She's dying,' Osgan's voice responded, sounding more controlled than Thalric would have expected. He glanced back to see the other Wasp sitting up with his back against the segmented trunk of a horsetail. Pain was written in sharp lines about his eyes, but it had chased the drink away at least.

The Mantis was still lying on her back, her teeth bared in defiance at something Thalric could not see. The arrow had penetrated deep but it was that final effort of getting her charges to cover that had finished her. Thalric reached over and took her hand, and she gripped it fiercely, the spines on her arm flexing.

'Still between us . . . and the river . . .' she got out. 'Further in . . .'

'I know,' Thalric interrupted. 'Don't speak.'

She coughed violently, and he felt it racking through her, holding on to her hand until the final spasm and the quiet that followed told him she was dead. It was no more than the Rekef man had always tried to do. He had always done his best for those that served him.

'What now?' Osgan asked, with a tremor, but some vestige of the career quartermaster of old had dragged itself to the surface and was holding the man together for now.

*And indeed what now?* The thought had come to Thalric again that he could just trust to his wings. He could flit from green to green until he had the open river before him, and then he could skim for the cover of the boats and hope that the assassins valued secrecy over success. But that would involve leaving Osgan here alone, wounded and fair game for any killer or predator that found him.

What would the Rekef man in him do? And he knew that same Rekef man had possessed one oft-boasted and overriding virtue, which was loyalty. Even though the Rekef itself had been torn out of the heart of that man, the loyalty remained.

'Further in, like she said,' he told Osgan, and draped the man's good arm over his shoulders, sinking calf-deep in mud to lever him to his feet. 'We'll take a curved path, head back for the river somewhere closer to the city.' Looking about him, searching for bearings in this baffling maze of channels and fronds, Thalric kept his voice confident for Osgan's sake. 'And when we get back, I'll give Marger something worthwhile to put in his cursed report.'

# Twenty-Two

They were still trying to roust a second land-fish for the hunt when Che saw it, glimmering amid the foliage on the far side of the river as though it was a ragged cloth caught amongst the leaves.

*No!* she thought, but that part of her, the part inside that was helplessly anchored to him, was already responding. 'Take the boat across,' she heard herself say. She was pointing right towards the shuddering blur that only she could see. 'Take it there.'

She heard Manny say, 'That's more like it,' and knew that they were also heading for where the hunt was. *I'm doing it again. It's the Fir-eaters all over again.* Only this time it was two bewildered academics she was dragging into danger alongside her. *Can I not just turn my back?*

She could not. It was not even love, now. She was cursed. Her life, her understandings, had been taken from her. Chasing this ghost was the only way she might ever get them back. *And what am I willing to pay for that, at the expense of others?*

The ghost was gone but she had seen it, felt it. It would come back to her. Whatever it wanted, it wanted here. The Mantis crew tacked their boat to what passed for a riverbank, barely more than stands of reeds and ferns jutting from the winding water. Manny put an arrow to his bow and tried to look heroic, while Praeda huddled as low as she could manage in the boat, trying to look bored. Che stared into the shadow-maze of the delta and searched for Achaeos.

Something was moving out there, she saw. There were quick flashes of rush-boats speeding, she heard shrill whistles and, across the river, Amnon's boat turned and began heading towards them.

'I think . . .' she started, and then a land-fish burst through the reeds not ten feet ahead of their boat, careering over a mudbank and into the river. Che toppled back into the bottom of the boat, on to Praeda, as she heard the distinct twang of Manny's bowstring releasing the arrow.

'Manny!' she shouted. 'Tell me you didn't shoot it!' She levered herself up, saw the land-fish now rearing and plunging past Amnon's boat, being herded by the smaller punts of the Mantids. Manny stood at the prow of their own vessel with the bow in one hand, mouth open.

'No,' he said. 'I just . . . it startled me. I shot the river, I'm afraid.' He turned a sheepish smile on her, but just then one of the Mantis crew gave a warning shout, pointing.

There had been a line attached to Manny's arrow, and it was pulling taut, unspooling from the bottom of the boat and whipping into the water faster than Che could watch. She met Manny's uncertain gaze.

'You shot something more than the river,' she said, but then the line went suddenly slack. Manny gave a great sigh of relief.

'Well, whatever it is—' he started, before Praeda cut him off.

'Whatever it is, it's stopped moving away. It's coming *back*, you fool.'

The Mantis crew had snatched up short-hafted spears, as Che stared at the murky waters of the Jamail. *What have we woken?*

It struck them from the opposite side of the boat, the narrow wooden hull almost kicked over by the force. One of the Mantids took to the air; the other crouched at the stern, holding the boat with one hand, and spear raised high. For a second there was nothing but churning water, then segmented arms began hooking on to one side of the boat and the creature was doing its best to climb in with them. Che saw a rounded carapace break the water, and below it a small head with fist-sized faceted eyes the colour of fresh blood and a beak like a shortsword. Manny's arrow jutted from the joint between the creature's head and body. The barbed arms scrabbled at the wooden hull, and then made a great effort to climb. Surging out of the water, it was twice the size of a man.

The boat tipped towards it, and then flipped over entirely. Che felt her wings flare automatically, dragging her up to hover inches above the river. The Mantids knelt stabbing at the insect as it continued to try and haul itself onto the boat, mindlessly seeking an enemy it could not understand. Then Amnon's boat was in the water alongside them, and he had brought company.

The second land-fish was not yet dispatched but Amnon had come to their aid even though the maddened creature was tethered to his craft. He reached down and grabbed Praeda's thrashing arm, dragging her, one-handed, up into his boat. His crew had set their spears against the enraged fish that was attacking them from the other side, while the smaller boats speeding past it loosed arrows to distract its attention. Che saw Manny floundering, first pawing at the capsized boat, then clinging to one of the water-insect's legs as it hung from the upturned vessel, more frightened of the water itself than of the things that lived in it. She tried to get closer to him, but Amnon was already there, the land-fish drawn away from him for the moment. Bracing himself, he caught hold of Manny's robe, pulling upwards with all his strength until he had tugged the fat man halfway out of the water. Praeda appeared beside him, grabbing for handfuls of Manny, too, and then a Mantis joined in on the other side. The real help came from the marauding insect, which finally claimed the keel of the capsized boat as its own, and pulled Manny up with it. For a second he hung there, dripping and shivering, still clinging to the creature, and then Amnon's boat closed the last foot of distance and they tipped him into it. The insect turned to stare at them, flexing its beak, then Amnon leant forward and grasped the arrow's shaft. For a second neither moved, and then the creature went for him, driving itself forward from the overturned hull. Amnon jerked back just as the lunging insect struck the side of his boat, shoving it away, then the creature vanished into the depths of the river. Amnon's hand now held the offending arrow, which he brandished aloft like a trophy.

*Cheerwell.*

She turned, still hovering ponderously over the water, and spotted him. He shuddered and stained the air, like paint running, an anguished grey form within the trees.

*Here, Beetle girl, here!*

*No!* she told it, but she knew she could not deny its summons. *Just tell me what you want! What can I do?*

*Power. Strength*, replied that harsh voice, the same commanding tones that had dragged her from her bedroll by the oasis. *There is power here. I need it.*

*Achaeos . . . I cannot live like this.* But she lumbered into the treeline, wings a labouring blur, chasing that fleeting, smearing image. *Achaeos, I would free you if I could.*

*We would be rid of each other*, returned that deathless voice, and it pierced her sharply. She fell from the air, landing thigh-deep in murky water.

'Don't say that,' she demanded of the delta and its myriad denizens. 'Please, Achaeos . . .'

*Come!* was the order it delivered and she felt it tugging at her mind with all its insubstantial fury.

'Is it . . .?' She choked over the words. 'Is it so bad to be with me?'

*Agony. I am pierced and pierced.* For a moment the encroaching green all around her became the twisted corpse of the Darakyon, and she shuddered away from it. The ghost, its hook fastened in her mind, was still dragging at her, just strongly enough for her to feel. He was throwing all his might – all that death had left him – into drawing her somewhere, some place he had sensed.

'I'm coming!' she told him, and she floundered her way forward, heedless of monster fish or insects, determined finally to shed this burden, to set him free – and so to free herself.

'Give me your alcohol,' Thalric ordered. He had snapped the arrowhead off, although with so much wrenching that Osgan had briefly passed out. Now the stricken man was conscious again, pasty-faced and sweating.

'Don't know what you're talking about,' Osgan responded faintly out of the corner of his mouth, past the cloth bit that Thalric had given him to clench his teeth against.

'You've come out here with something to drink. Hand it over,' Thalric demanded. He was acutely aware of the target his back provided but he knew he had to fix this sooner rather than later. He had a feeling that Khanaphir medicine would be as primitive as the rest of their culture.

Osgan's good hand made a feeble gesture towards the pockets of his coat, and Thalric delved into them, ripping them open one after another until he found the bottle. He uncapped it and let the clear liquid drip onto the graze running down Osgan's ribs. Osgan hissed and twitched at the sting of it and, with that distraction, Thalric yanked the arrow from his arm.

Osgan's scream sounded even through the cloth gag. He fought so hard Thalric had to kneel on his chest, dragging the arm out straight to douse both sides of the wound with burning spirits. Strips torn from Osgan's much-abused coat were all the bandaging he could muster.

'Five minutes,' Thalric decided. 'Then we move.' He left Osgan sobbing quietly and went to see what attention their noise had brought. They were deep inside a stand of canes, as defensible a spot as he had come across. Now, dropping low, he crawled cautiously forward. The marshlands of the delta did odd things with sound: the foggy air deadened and distorted it. The assassins would most likely be unsure precisely where the sound had come from, unable to follow it up.

*How many?* He guessed at four dead and reckoned at least a pair of them must be left. Two teams of three felt logical, and he had sent such men out on Rekef errands enough to trust his own judgement. *This is not just some Tyrshaani malcontent.* Somebody with power in the Empire wanted Thalric dead very much indeed. *And then what? Kill the Regent and then what? Is my death the trigger for some uprising? Has a conspiracy eluded General Brugan?* It was information he had to get back to Capitas, along with news of his own continued survival. *Assuming that news is still current by the time I get a chance . . .*

Again the thought came to him: leave Osgan to the mercies of the swamp. If there were only two killers left, there was enough cover between here and the river to evade them. *Assuming I still know which way the river lies.*

There had been no movement visible out there. The assassins were elsewhere, or they were close by and waiting patiently. There was no way to tell.

'Osgan,' he said, as loud as he dared, 'time to move.'

The quartermaster was now sitting up, looking as though he had died and come back to life. Thalric's uncharitable thought was that, without the wound, he'd have just assumed the man was suffering after a night's heavy drinking.

'Move where?' Osgan managed to ask, and he was clearly doing his best. Old military instincts were struggling to make themselves felt.

'Away,' Thalric replied. There was only one clear entrance to the stand of tall canes they were hiding in: one clear exit, too, therefore. Any killers that were watching could not help but appreciate that. 'We're going out the back way,' Thalric decided.

'What back way?'

'Have you the strength to use your sting?'

Osgan closed his eyes. The Wasp Art that had taken the Empire so far was tiring to use: it lived off the body's own strength. He nodded wearily.

Thalric levelled one hand towards the canes behind Osgan, and the quartermaster hauled himself round and did likewise. Worms of light now flickered and crawled across Thalric's open palm.

He unleashed the golden fire, putting a hand up to guard his eyes from splinters as the searing fire of his Art shattered the canes apart. Something inside them was flammable, the pith exploding like a volley of snapbows. He and Osgan turned their faces away as a score of canes combusted together, flinging fragments and splinters across them.

'Move,' Thalric urged, and he was already pressing through the gap that had been scorched between the canes. He lurched forward, across an open patch of water, ducking into the reeds on the other side. Laboured splashing behind him told him that Osgan was trying to keep up. He turned, tugging at the man's good shoulder, just as an arrow cut across the water, clipping the ripples they had left. Thalric loosed his sting instantly, guessing at the archer's hiding place, then they were stumbling and staggering through the mud, the waist-deep water, burrowing ever deeper into the delta as the foliage around them grew taller and thicker, stilt-rooted trees and gigantic horsetails making a half-drowned forest out of the Marsh.

'Thalric . . .' Osgan's voice, hoarse with effort, came from behind him,

'Just keep moving.'

'Thalric – water's getting deeper.'

He did not stop, still plunging on, dragging himself forward in sudden bursts, then letting Osgan catch up. The man was right, though. Surely if they were heading into denser plantlife they must be reaching the river banks, the shallows. Then it came to him just where they were. *This is a delta . . . the tide . . .* Of course the water level would be rising. The tide was coming in, and that was why all the trees around them were on stilts. Soon their spidery roots would be submerged. Worse, the rising levels would not hinder their Skater-kinden pursuers, but it would drag Thalric and Osgan to a standstill. *Can Osgan swim?* Not with only one arm, was the answer to that. Time was running out.

Thalric came to rest, dragging Osgan down beside him. They were in the shadow of some tall ferns, as hidden as he could make them. As they crouched, the water came to their chests. *We cannot just run. We need a plan.* Osgan was breathing heavily, sucking at the air in great gasps. There was little more flight left in him. The wound and the heat and the man's habitual dissipation were killing him.

'I'm sorry I brought you to this,' Thalric said quietly.

Osgan lacked the breath to respond, just shaking his head in a denial that could have meant anything. He grasped at Thalric's arm abruptly, pointing something out.

*Assassins,* was Thalric's first thought. He hunched forward, putting a hand out ready to sting. Osgan continued pointing, jabbing a finger urgently. Thalric tried to follow the direction of it, seeing only more green, more ferns and rushes and canes, and . . .

There was a regularity to some of it, a distinctiveness to the angles. Something leapt inside him. Ahead of them was something that was not grown naturally, but built. *But what? Where in the wastes are we?* The question was swiftly followed by, *It doesn't matter. We have no other compass point.* Thalric lurched up, slinging an arm around Osgan to haul the man to his feet.

'Go,' he urged, and cast himself off into the water, his wings surging instinctively to half-carry him, with Osgan a weight at the end of his arm. It was all too slow, he realized at once. They were too exposed. He gave his wings their full rein, ignoring Osgan's protest as his unwounded arm was almost wrenched out of its socket. Between the trees, Thalric spotted crude huts, barely more than platforms raised above the water and roofed with leaves. He saw movement too, spreading out to either side of them. They had been noticed.

'Khanaphes!' Thalric shouted out. 'Khanaphes!' hoping it would be enough to save them.

An arrow danced past him from behind, a hurried shot surely. He did not turn, continued towing Osgan through the water, knowing only from the man's curses that he was still alive. He had a brief glimpse of a silvery-skinned Mantis woman with bowstring drawn back, the arrow loosed instantly. There was no sound from behind, but from her very expression Thalric knew she had found her target.

He dragged Osgan on to a mud bank. They were sprawled at the edge of the village, no more than a cluster of spindly shacks gathered about a mound of higher ground cleared of vegetation. Knowing that nothing he could do now would matter, Thalric collapsed onto his back, feeling his muscles burn in protest. Osgan was wheezing and choking beside him, shuddering like a dying thing, but somehow still alive. He had sprouted no new arrows since, and Thalric could only hope that the assassins had not survived their clash with the Marsh's own killers.

He sensed movement nearby and pushed himself up on to his elbow. The Mantis-kinden were approaching, arrows nocked to their bows and spears levelled. These Marsh people were smaller than the Lowlander kinden that Thalric was familiar with, but they had the same poise, the same angular grace. Their faces had the same insular hostility, too. He held up a closed fist to them. 'We are friends – we are guests of the city of Khanaphes.'

They had formed a ragged horseshoe around the two Wasps, leaving open the path leading to the village. One of them, a woman looking older than the rest, jabbed her head in that direction, and Thalric let out a great sigh and struggled to his knees.

'Come on,' he told Osgan, but the man would not move.

'Can't . . .' he whined. 'No further . . .'

Two of the Mantids were there instantly, catching him by the arms and lifting him up, ignoring his screams as the sudden movement tore at his wound. Thalric pushed one of them aside, moving to catch Osgan. Then he was very still.

Osgan swayed, still supported by one of the Mantids, almost clinging to him. His injured arm was held tight to his chest, the bindings newly bloody. Thalric felt the tiny pinpoint of sharp pain that had come to rest under his jaw, assuming at first it was a spearhead, then knowing it for an arrow-point. He took a good moment, in lieu of any fatal attempt at action, to study their rescuers.

These were not the shaven-headed servants who had been poling the fishing boats up and down the river to Amnon's tune. They were not clad as Khanaphir menials, merely a little hide and chitin and fish-scale to cover their modesty. Their long hair was pale, bound back with rings of bone and amber.

'We are not your enemies,' Thalric said carefully. In his mind the sands of the archer's strength were running out. She must soon either take the arrow away, or loose it. 'We mean you no harm. Return us to Khanaphes and you shall be rewarded.'

Osgan gave a bark of pain, dragged without warning towards the village. Thalric twitched, poised on the point of the arrow and knowing that there were enough of them to make an end of him whichever way he turned. Without warning the archer took a step away, the point still unwavering. Thalric followed Osgan's halting progress, conscious that every arrowhead and spear was aimed at him. Ahead, Osgan gave out a horrified cry.

The mound of earth that the village was strung around

was not empty, not quite. They had erected something there, that Thalric had not registered before, his first glance letting the crude canework merge into the struts and poles of the surrounding village. He blinked, trying to identify what it was. Osgan was struggling now, shrieking for them to let him go, but three of them continued propelling him towards it effortlessly.

*It's a statue*, Thalric realized, a statue reworked to the locals' resources. Just as they had not a coin's-worth of metal in their possession, even their weapons being made of bone and wood, so there was no stone to their statue, just a lattice of canes lashed together into a shape that seemed abstract at first. Until he stood directly before it, and the shifting angles and planes of it suddenly made a picture.

It was a mantis, an openwork sketch of a mantis rendered in three dimensions, its killing arms raised high above them. The chamber of its body was large enough to fit a man, and Thalric knew this because the bones of the last occupant were still inside, buzzing with flies and dripping with a few lingering maggots. Osgan was still kicking vainly and crying out, and Thalric knew that somehow this *thing*, this idol, had become Tisamon in his mind, that what he was fighting against was more within his own head than outside it.

'What is this?' Thalric demanded, his throat suddenly dry. 'Do you kill the guests of the city so close to its walls?' The Khanaphes card was the only one he had to play, but he had put it on the table three times now without eliciting any interest. Now, at last, an old Mantis woman stepped between him and the idol. Uncomfortably close, she rested one forearm on his shoulder, so he felt her fighting spines dig slightly into his neck.

'You are ignorant,' she said, and it took him a moment to unpick her accent. 'You are from far away and know nothing.'

'I know that they will send people to look for me – that my absence will stir the city up, and my own people as well.'

'Do not threaten us on our sacred ground,' she warned him, voice still soft but the spines jabbing him briefly. 'The city shall not come here, and you were hunted here by other foreign hands. There shall be no search to find your bones. We have made our pact with the Masters: any that cross this far are ours. It is our right.'

*Another bloody thing the locals could have told us: that their tame servants have murderous relatives just a short walk away!*

'I will fight,' Thalric said. His understanding of even the Lowlander Mantis-kinden was limited, so he had little to work with. 'Let me fight for our freedom. Choose your best, if you will.'

The old woman smirked. 'Your death shall not be at our hands, foreigner. Your blood shall be drunk by the earth, and by the avatar. Your comrade first, though. We must shed his blood while he still has it.'

They were opening up the wicker casing of the effigy. Osgan had collapsed, all his limbs drawn in, shuddering and lost to his own terrors. *And perhaps that's a mercy.* Thalric made a sudden lunge back from the woman, feeling the barbs of her arm gash his flesh. He tried to put a hand out towards her, with some wild idea of holding her hostage, but someone struck him with a spear-shaft behind his knees as another glanced from the back of his head. He joined Osgan on the ground, reeling. Around them, the Mantis-kinden had begun a soft humming, barely audible save that they were all doing it, a slow tune, but a gradually building one.

'Osgan,' Thalric said, hunching closer. 'Osgan, snap out of it!'

The former quartermaster gave a great gasp, staring upwards at the latticed idol above them. 'We're going to die,' he said.

'Then die like an Imperial Wasp soldier, not like a Fly-kinden coward!' Thalric spat at him.

'You don't understand,' Osgan said hollowly. 'You didn't see.'

Thalric opened his mouth to make some harsh comment, but the Mantids had stopped humming.

Someone else had entered the clearing.

As she walked into the village, Che barely saw the Mantis-kinden. The guttering, flickering grey fire of Achaeos was all that was worthy of her attention. Then her mind broadened to include the wicker idol and her mind was briefly racked with memories and images, some that she owned and some that were alien to her. *This is the thing that Tynisa would never speak of.* She saw it with Inapt eyes, and she saw it running with death, quivering with a thousand years of adoration and sacrifice. It spoke of skulls to her, it leered blood, so that she flinched back from it even as the ghost surged forward.

Then she saw the Mantids, brought into sharp focus as their leader pointed towards her. It was a Mantis woman standing before the idol, and Che did not notice the two Wasp prisoners before her, only that old woman silhouetted before the empty effigy's power.

'The land has been generous to us today!' the old Mantis cried out. 'Take her and bring her here!'

A dozen of the Mantis-kinden were instantly in motion, falling on Che with expressionless faces, with hungry eyes. She raised her hands to ward them off, and the old woman suddenly screamed.

Inches from laying hands on her, they stopped. She saw their reserve crack, surprise and shock taking hold, expressions not native to Mantis faces. They were looking back to see their leader on her knees, covering her face. Before her was Achaeos's blurred ghost.

The Mantis warriors could not see it, Che realized, but their leader could. Despite everything she had been through, the revelation hit her like a hammer blow. Che dropped to her own knees, staring at the old woman. The Mantis leader – *priestess?* the unfamiliar word came into her mind – was scrabbling at the muddy, bone-littered ground in front of the idol, trying to claw some distance between herself and the shuddering grey stain in the air. Her eyes were wide.

*Give me your power.*

Che heard the imperious command, and she thought of the old saying, *Servants of the Green, Masters of the Grey*, and how the Moth-kinden had always commanded, and the Mantids obeyed.

The old woman was well clear of the idol now, and the ghost flowed into its vacant frame, its trailing edges boiling and dissolving into the surrounding air.

'Che?' said someone, and she blinked down from the supernatural to the mundane to see Thalric and his comrade staring up at her.

*What can he think?* But she was too far removed from any world that Thalric might know. He would only see the Mantis-kinden backing off from her as though she was on fire, as though she was sacred. She held out a hand to him, and somewhere in the gesture it turned from an offer of help to a plea for it. She felt the world swimming, her eyes drawn relentlessly back to the ghost of Achaeos hanging within the idol as though it was caught on the bars.

Thalric and Osgan were crawling towards her, trying to avoid notice. The Mantids had no time for them any more. They watched only their leader and she watched Achaeos.

Within the prison of the idol, the grey smudge waxed and grew, forming shapes – hands, features. Che waited for him, waited to recognize those blank eyes, the sharp features. *I set you free*, she thought. *Please, be free.*

It was not working. The ghost billowed and surged within the prison of the canes, but she could see that this was not enough. She heard that same harsh voice again, this time almost spitting the words. *Is this all? How many years and how many deaths have led to this? Has all your duty and reverence and labour been to give birth only to this nothing?*

The old woman wailed, hiding her head, and if there were words there, Che could not catch them. The other Mantis-kinden were slipping away into the trees and the water, as if unwilling to witness the torment of their leader.

*You wretched wasters of power!* the ghost continued. *You traitors to your past! There is nothing here, nothing! Betrayers of your kinden and your heritage!* There was no trace in that raging voice of the man she had once known, and Che thought, *He is going mad, tied to me, tied to this world. I do not know him any more.*

The tirade continued, showing no sign that it might ever stop, and Che wanted to rush forward, to shout into the face of the idol that he should stop it, that it was doing no good – but she managed one step only. The sheer fury that rippled through the ghost's substance was too much for her. She had not known that he was capable of it. Perhaps it had taken death to bring it out of him.

'Che, we have to go,' said Thalric, sounding distant, and she knew from his tone that this was not the first time he had said it. He was barely audible over the ghost's rantings, but of course he could hear none of that. Only Che herself and the Mantis woman could. *But I am not the only one, and I am not insane, and this is real.* Something in her, some echo of her past, wailed that this was all impossible, but she found in herself an acceptance that the world was made of these things, that the world worked by such means. It was clear to her now, in the way that the workings of a crossbow or a lock would never again be.

'We must go,' she agreed, and turned to find Thalric holding up his friend, who was pale and shaking. He met Che's eyes: two harrowed gazes, each with its load of untranslatable grief. Then she too put an arm around Osgan, keeping clear of the crude bandages, and the two of them helped guide him off into the swamp towards the river. The going was hard enough to limit any further words until the boats found them and they became separated once again.

# Twenty-Three

They sat in silence in their room within the Collegiate embassy, one standing by the window, the other one by the door: Accius and Malius, the Vekken ambassadors.

They had been invited to join the hunt, of course: they had ignored the invitation. Instead this had seemed to them a golden opportunity for a little quiet, some space to think without the Collegiates crowding them with their constant noise.

*We have watched for long enough,* Malius decided. *The King would expect some action from us by now.*

*The King does not know the conditions here,* Accius thought darkly.

*We are merely being distracted. No doubt that is the intent.*

*Agreed.* Accius watched Khanaphir servants outside as they tended the gardens of the Place of Honoured Foreigners. *This city is irrelevant.*

*Primitive,* agreed Malius. *There is no advantage to be secured for Collegium here. Even ten thousand Khanaphir soldiers could not stand for more than a moment against a Vekken army. Bows and spears!* In the voice of the mind, derision was so much purer and more satisfying.

*So why are they here?* Accius posed the riddle they had been slowly pondering for days.

*Their scholars are almost certainly nothing more than that,* Malius admitted reluctantly. *They may have other standing orders that have yet to come into effect, but we have witnessed nothing about them to suggest that their claims hide anything more devious.*

*They are the typical irrelevant chaff with which Collegium always hides its true purpose,* Accius agreed. *Which purpose—*

*Which purpose is therefore embodied in the person of their ambassador. No doubt we were intended to watch the academics, or the city itself – the Collegiate contempt for the abilities of others, once again.* Malius loaded the thought with particular emotion. It was their one pastime, really, this disparagement of their enemies. It enlivened the silence, and it even made the noise more bearable.

*Her movements have been mysterious. She has been evading scrutiny and she has been impossible to track,* Accius thought. *She has an agenda that even her foolish compatriots do not realize. She is the real reason they are here, and they can look at all the stones and rocks they want. That much is clear.*

*That much is clear,* Malius echoed. *And we must now unearth her purpose. It is obviously something more than we had thought.*

*The King was wise to send us on this mission.*

*Indeed. We have seen where she visits most, who she associates with.*

*And that skirmish in the courtyard,* Accius recalled. *How swift she was to disarm it, and then spending so long speaking to the Wasp.*

*It is clear they have come here, so far from the Lowlands, because it is a neutral city where arrangements can be made.*

They both paused then. Their joint conclusion, inexorable, was sufficiently dire for neither to wish it voiced. At last it was Malius who finished the thought.

*Collegium has no stomach for another war, therefore they seek an alliance with the Wasp Empire.*

Neither needed to state the obvious consequence of that. Where else could the combined eyes of such an alliance turn, save to Vek?

*We must prevent this, at all costs,* Accius decided. *We must create disharmony between our enemies.*

*There is only one way,* Malius concluded for him. *Their secrecy shall be their undoing. We must kill both ambassadors. For the glory of Vek.*

Scorpion dens were seldom quiet places at night. The darkness was punctuated by the sounds of drinking, brawling, vendettas abruptly realized, the crash of pottery and the clash of steel, but when the explosion ripped across the night of the city-camp of Gemrar it was of a different order. The entire city was shocked into panicked motion instantly, Scorpions surging out naked or half-dressed, weapons in their hands, shouting at each other or rushing for the gap-toothed outer wall to confront the attack. Even Hrathen himself was momentarily disoriented. He felt the desert chill and in his mind he was back in the Dryclaw during the war, bellowing orders to the Slave Corps officers who had followed him into infamy. *The Empire has found us*, was his first thought, as he shrugged on his banded armour, took up his shortsword and stepped into the night. His eyes scanned the sky, looking for the Light Airborne or the square bulk of an Imperial heliopter.

Then he remembered. This desert was the Nem, not its domesticated cousin. He was far from the Empire's reach.

'Report!' he bellowed, hoping that one of his men was in earshot. Most of the Scorpions were still rushing outwards, roused to a single purpose by the thought of an assault on their capital. There was a counter-current, however, that was calling some of them somewhere within the city's bounds. Hrathen joined the latter, sheathing his sword and tightening the buckles of his armour. Whenever the Scorpions got in his way he elbowed them aside, for all that they were bigger than he was. It was the only way.

He smelled the smoke soon enough, the acrid bite of spent firepowder in his nostrils. *Has some fool fired the magazine?* But the resulting explosion would have been greater than that, and besides, they weren't so easy to light, for the firepowder was packed in small charges, little metal-bound barrels not much bigger than a man's fist. The Imperial engineers had made the stuff as safe as possible, if only because it would be them who would be standing next to it most of the time.

He spotted the dark-and-light of an Imperial uniform up ahead. 'Report!' he shouted again, shouldering forward through the gawping crowd. Once he got clear of the scrum, the story was written plain ahead of him, although it took him a moment to take it in.

Those ravages time had begun in one of the ruined buildings of Gemrar, an instant's work had completed. What had previously been a sound enough shell of a building, a small dome-roofed structure with three intact walls, was now a broken eggshell, punched in upon itself, so flattened that very little of it still stood stone upon stone. Hrathen went close enough to see, in the bluish lamplight, what must have been at least three bodies lying torn apart within. He glanced back along the line of devastation, into the mouth of the leadshotter, still wisping smoke. Lieutenant Angved, the engineer, had arrived by now and, true to his trade, was inspecting the weapon for damage, heedless of the carnage nearby.

There was a Scorpion standing near the device, Hrathen saw, who looked defiant, and pleased with himself. That was all Hrathen needed to see to complete the picture.

'Where is the Warlord?' he asked.

'At your elbow, Of-the-Empire.'

He had not sensed her, though she was standing very close. She wore only a long hide hauberk, but she had her spear to hand and her helm on. He felt those red eyes studying him coolly.

'Do you regret giving us these weapons now, Of-the-Empire?' she asked him. He amused her, Hrathen knew.

He was Scorpion enough to touch on her world, but she found the Empire and its ways tedious, pointless. When in her company, he almost felt he agreed.

'I am only glad that I have given you some enemies to turn them on,' he told her. 'A man has a right to use his strength. If his strength is in the mind, then so be it.' He gestured at the siege weapon and its victims. 'This is no business of mine.'

'That he took your weapon, does that not anger you, O possessive Empire?' Beneath the rim of the helm, she was smiling through her fangs.

'It is yours, given to you and your people. If he took it from you, then the theft is yours to punish,' Hrathen said, trying to match her grin. She put him off balance, and he knew it was because his Scorpion side – his rapacious father's side – wanted her. She was no whore like the Empress, though, who ruled through others' weakness. Jakal was strong and would seek only strength. She would yield herself to his strength, or else he would force her, or she would kill him. *And now she drives me to the second of those, or perhaps the third.*

'So glib,' she berated him. 'You change your colours, Of-the-Empire, but the black-and yellow-stain lies ever underneath.' She turned away suddenly, calling out, 'Genraki!'

The Scorpion that Hrathen had picked as the culprit came forward. He stopped a safe distance from Jakal, obviously not entirely sure of his own daring now.

'You have long warred with the Friends of Hierkan,' Jakal observed.

Genraki merely nodded, keeping a hand close to the hatchet on his belt.

'Are the Friends of Hierkan here to witness? Do they wish to match weapons with Genraki?'

There were enough glances cast at the staved-in house for Hrathen to suspect that the man had done his work well.

Jakal spread her arms, walking over to inspect the ruin of a ruin, stepping up on to cracked and tumbled stones, heedless of the bloody jumble beneath. 'See these stones I stand on now?' she addressed her people. 'The walls of Khanaphes are made only of such stones.'

They went absolutely silent, all of the watching Scorpions, and Hrathen found his heart catching in his chest at the sheer simplicity of it. *How many challengers to her authority has she killed, how many conspiracies has she rooted out, that she leads them so deftly?* He knew it was more than that, more than just the same brute force that prevailed in the Dryclaw. The Many of Nem had begun to recognize the true value of their leaders and their elders. They followed Jakal through respect and belief in her, and not only because she could put a spear through any one of them.

*But she could.* The knowledge excited him, and he forced his thoughts back to business. *I am Captain Hrathen of the Imperial Slave Corps, of the Rekef.* His heritage, his despoiled blood, surged within him, testing the bounds of his duty.

He found Angved still checking out the leadshotter. 'Report,' he said.

'No damage that I can see.'

'I don't mean the machine.'

The engineer looked up at him, and there was a tightness around his eyes. 'I don't know what to say, sir. It's a four-man job to move and load this thing, yet apparently he did it on his own.'

'A good student, then?'

'Not my best, I would have said.' Angved shook his head. 'I can't believe they're going to let him get away with it.'

'Look at what he's accomplished,' Hrathen pointed out. 'He's ended a feud, he's proved himself strong and wily. Why should they punish Genraki when he's exactly what they want?'

Genraki himself was returning to them, with a couple of others following in his wake. 'I shall return the machine,

Lieutenant,' he said to Angved, with a surprising deference. The engineer nodded, faking a smile, and the three Scorpion-kinden made light work of wheeling the leadshotter away.

'They learn fast,' Angved observed. 'You were right on that, sir. They're not disciplined, and it's difficult to get a decent speed up, because they always want to watch the shots, see the damage and have a bit of a talk about it, but they're strong and they're tough. Make good Auxillians, is my report.'

Hrathen nodded, wondering again if that was why they were here – *and if not, what then?* 'But you're not comfortable with them,' he finished.

'Permission to speak freely, sir?'

'Go ahead.'

'Are *you* comfortable with them?' Angved enquired. 'I know it's the fashion to call people like these savages, but with *these* people it's true. It's not that they're stupid, it's just . . . they have no rules. Shedding blood means nothing to them, either their own or anyone else's. I can't even understand how they survive from generation to generation. How do their children even live to full growth?'

'You want to know?'

'I want to understand, sir.'

'When she's close to term, the mother leaves the camp, goes off and fends for herself in the desert,' Hrathen told him, remembering. 'She stays there two, three years – a Scorpion child learns fast, grows fast. By then it can walk, run, fight with the other children. Then she comes back to the camp and gives the child to the tribe, and it has no mother or father from that day. They hold their children in common, and soon enough nobody recalls ancestry. No families, Angved – nothing to stand between the individual and the group.'

'That sounds harsh, sir.'

'Life *is* harsh. Life in the Dryclaw or the Nem is harsh. If a child was linked to its mother, it would become a weapon against her. Their best chance for survival is anonymity: it breeds strength, self-reliance.' Hrathen smiled, and he saw Angved pale at the sight of those underslung tusks in a Wasp-kinden face. 'It breeds a callous disregard for others, but think how much effort the Empire puts into teaching us something the Scorpions learn for free.'

Angved remained carefully silent after that.

Hrathen chuckled. 'Just teach them to destroy,' he said. 'Teach them to break walls with the leadshotters, to break men with the crossbows. Then we will take them to Khanaphes and simplify the maps – one less city in the world.'

'Why, though?' Angved asked. 'What's the point? Why does the Empire want Khanaphes gone?'

'Think like the Scorpions,' Hrathen told him, not unkindly. 'We do it because we can.'

Hrathen sought out Angved the next morning, finding him not at the leadshotters, amidst the noise and the smoke and the curses, but hidden away beneath a lean-to of chitin over wood. The engineer was cooking something, or at least heating something in a small pan.

'Not deserting your post, is it?' Hrathen asked, looming. Angved looked up at him, unalarmed.

'At the moment we're just working on speed, Captain, seeing if these brutes can manage faster than a shot every twenty minutes. They already know what they're doing, but they lose focus so quickly.' The engineer shrugged. 'My lads out there can shout at them without me needing to strain my throat, so I decided to do a little investigating.'

'Really?' Hrathen knelt by him. 'Beyond your brief, isn't it?'

'Engineers and Slave Corps both, we think for ourselves,' Angved replied, meeting Hrathen's small, yellow eyes. 'This rock-oil of theirs, they use it just for lighting, yes?'

'What else is there?' Hrathen asked. The engineer smiled at that.

'It's a slow-burning stable mineral oil, sir. That's useful for engineering, and there are pools of it all over, probably entire lakes of it underground. Would they trade it, do you think? For more weapons?'

'I don't see why not. Like you say, there's no shortage of the stuff.' Hrathen, no artificer, shrugged the idea off. 'Are they going to be ready?'

'It's up to them, now. I'm keeping the artillery under my thumb, but the crossbows are already out there – the warriors we taught are teaching the others, as best they can. It's not difficult, to point a crossbow. That's why we like them.'

Hrathen nodded, standing up straight. It had been like watching a slow-building rockslide, seeing the Scorpions take to the crossbows. The weapons were old Imperial Auxillian standard issue kit, second-hand and almost obsolete, but for the Many of Nem they had been a revolution.

Jakal had ordered her two advisers to examine them first. The old man, with his fetishes and charms of cogs and gears, had climbed all over them, muttering to himself, testing the action on the weapons, thrumming the strings with his thumb-claw. He had reported that they were good, a worthy armament for the Host of the Nem. Next, the young man, wearing a cloak of clattering chitin shards, had walked round the wagons with his eyes closed, trailing one hand near them. He had then announced that the land believed it was well time for the city of Khanaphes to be broken open like an egg.

Scorpion-kinden made bad archers, and Hrathen knew it well. It was their claws, arching over forefinger and thumb, that got in the way, snagging or even severing a bowstring as the arrow was loosed. Those few of the locals who still preferred the bow had cut notches into their claws to hook the string with, but they were poor shots even so. Most reverted to throwing axes, spears and javelins.

The big, pincered hands of the Scorpion-kinden could manage a crossbow, though. They were still slightly clumsy with it, but they were strong enough to re-cock their weapons without the bracing and ratcheting the makers had intended. Once the crossbow was loaded they could pull a trigger as well as anyone. Eyes that had learned to foresee the flight of a spear could adjust to the swift shiver of a crossbow quarrel. There were hundreds of them, now busy eating through the stock of bolts that Hrathen had brought with him. Hundreds more were crafting new quarrels, with more and more confidence, out of chitin and wood and pillaged metal. There were not enough crossbows to go round, but about half the Scorpions were unable to use them anyway, crippled by their Inapt heritage. These would become the shock troops, the warriors of the traditional way, using greatsword and halberd and double-handed axe. There was a new fighting nobility emerging, though, and it brandished a crossbow.

*We have brought a revolution*, Hrathen reflected, and was slightly awed by the thought. The population of Gemrar had doubled in the last tenday, was set to double again. Allied tribes had been summoned out of the mid-desert, eager to have their part in the destruction of their age-old foe.

'Why do your people hate Khanaphes so?' he had asked Jakal once.

'Of-the-Empire, you try so hard to be Of-the-Scorpion, but you will never succeed,' she had replied, with a cruel smile. 'So we are told that our ancestors fought with theirs when this land was yet green, when these broken cities still thrived. So we are told that, of all the peoples in their Dominion, only we did not bow the knee to their Masters. So we are told all of this. What other reason do we need but that we can, and that they are there?'

'Jakal means to leave in a tenday,' he told Angved now. 'Enough time?'

'We can practise on the road, when we camp,' the engineer said. 'They'll be rough but they'll be ready, as we say.'

'Good.' Hrathen passed his eyes over the camp, not quite looking and yet finding. He saw the dark armour of a small knot of men and women. A stab of annoyance pricked him.

*We should do something about them sooner, rather than later,* he thought.

They were traders, he understood – the only traders who had dared to come into the Nem to deal with the Scorpions, men and women in dark leathers or dark metal, and with that defiant open gauntlet emblazoned on their tabards.

'Since when do you tolerate merchants?' he had asked Jakal.

'Since they show us they are strong,' she had replied. 'Is Of-the-Empire jealous?' He knew she was leading him on, and part of him knew that he was letting her. She was drawing a reaction from him, and it would eventually lead to a coupling or a blood-letting. He was uncomfortably aware that the choice would be hers.

'Strong?' he asked, but then she had pointed out to him the Iron Glove's chief factor in the Nem, and he had understood. Scorpion-kinden were powerful, standing half a foot or more over the Wasps, but in the midst of the Iron Glove people stood a Mole Cricket, watching his minions distribute swords and metal ingots. Now Hrathen could see the same giant walking with impunity amongst the Scorpions, overseeing business.

*Yes, we will have to deal with you, slave.* There were three Mole-Cricket enclaves in Imperial hands, their populations decreasing, generation to generation, as the Empire siphoned off their menfolk for work in the mines or for the army. That prodigious strength and stamina, and their way with rock and earth, was too useful to conserve. The Empire spent it all too lavishly.

The huge creature noticed Hrathen's interest and strode over, putting him under its shadow. *A runaway slave,* Hrathen decided, *or an Auxillian deserter.* How else would a Mole Cricket come to be here? The Iron Glove had a lot to answer for.

'You wish to make a purchase, Captain?' it rumbled. It had a name, and its name was Meyr.

Hrathen stared up at the creature. *The bastard must be eleven feet tall,* he reckoned. Meyr wore a vast hauberk of leather with metal plates sewn into it, and an axe the size of an ordinary man was thrust through his broad leather belt. His monstrous hands had great square nails that looked every bit the equal of a Scorpion's claws. Certainly, Meyr was the face of the Iron Glove as far as the Scorpion-kinden were concerned, big enough and strong enough to protect his people from their depredations.

*I'll deal with you, soon,* Hrathen promised himself, but he said nothing, just ignoring the creature and walking away.

Instead he went to find the officer of the Light Airborne that he had brought with him. The man was packed ready to go, along with half a dozen of his men. Their leader was a hollow-cheeked type, his receding hair cropped close. His mouth crooked up on one side into a dry little half-smile, as though enjoying some small joke that only he was privy to. As he was the ranking Rekef officer here, Hrathen thought that might be true. His name was Sulvec and he was obviously Rekef Inlander to the core, for Hrathen knew enough to recognize a man who had given himself over heart and mind to the service.

'Not forgotten anything?' Hrathen asked him, realizing that if his own task was intended to be a suicide mission, then Sulvec would be his executioner. He wanted to show the man he was not afraid. *Scorpion thinking, since Wasp-kinden tread carefully where the Rekef are.* The fact that half of Sulvec's men were staying with Hrathen's party had not escaped him. He was plainly not trusted, but that was hardly news.

'We'll depart presently.' Sulvec's fragment of smile made its inevitable appearance: it signalled disdain for everything Hrathen was or could be. 'Don't be too long in coming, Captain.'

'Scorpion-kinden move fast,' Hrathen told him. 'Make sure we don't outstrip you.'

'Hm.' A slight noise was the response, all the humour the

man would voice. 'We'll liaise with you when you arrive with your thousands, Captain.'

Hrathen just nodded, and in the next moment the seven Rekef men were airborne, streaking across the sky towards distant Khanaphes with a speed born of well-practised Art, and Hrathen had no idea what their orders were, for implementation once they arrived in Khanaphes.

*And if they are to betray me? Do they plan to win the Khanaphir by betraying the Many of Nem?* He considered the possibility coldly. *Then they do not understand what the Scorpion-kinden are capable of*, he decided, and left it at that.

With Hrathen gone, the Mole Cricket-kinden called Meyr took stock. He had a dozen people here: enough, when allied to his strength, to dissuade the Scorpions from precipitate action. The Scorpions would trade whenever there was reason not to steal or take. The Iron Glove turned up with small shipments, always promising more in the next, each visit a tentative link in the mercantile chain. Meyr was a cautious man like most of his kind and, given a free choice, he would not want to be the Iron Glove ambassador to the Nem. He paid his debts, though. Totho had taken him in when he had been fleeing the Empire, and Meyr had been a slave long enough that working for a living, to another man's orders, had become second nature. He might hate it in himself, but he could not deny it.

'We're going to have trouble soon,' he said softly. His second-in-command, a Solarnese woman named Faighl, was nodding. She was a tough, compact woman, a mercenary out of Chasme for more than a decade before signing on with the new-formed Glove. She had already killed two Scorpions who assumed that her size meant weakness rather than a killing speed. Now they gave her space at their fires and drank with her.

'Pull out?' she asked.

Meyr was a big man to be balanced on a knife-edge.

Pulling out was safe, but he would not be thanked for it. It was not the trade that mattered, it was the information. Something was happening here that the Glove had to be informed of. The Empire was in the Nem, and had become everyone's best friend, giving out free presents and holding lectures. The Scorpions had no idea of secrecy, so word of their target had come to Meyr almost as soon as he and his team had arrived with their packs and crates.

*But why? It makes no sense.* Meyr knew the Empire well enough to understand, that, whatever their evils, they did nothing without reason.

'We stay,' he replied heavily. 'But . . . Where's Tirado?'

'Here, chief.' The Fly-kinden man ducked forward under Faighl's arm. 'What, where and who?'

'I'll write it out,' the Mole Cricket decided. One of his people snapped open a folding desk, a square of wood smaller than Meyr's two open hands. He knelt by it awkwardly, taking a fresh slate out from his pack. His Art rose within him, and he put the corner of one fingernail to it. Back home, his people wrote their letters in stone. Pens were lost in his grasp and paper tore under his nails. His people had ways with the earth, though, which was why the Empire enslaved them so enthusiastically.

The tip of his nail scribed, carving blocky, close-packed script into the slate as though it was wet clay. He filled the square of stone from edge to edge, a solid mass of writing, trusting to Totho to decipher it. When he made an error he smoothed the stone over and wrote again.

When he was done he wrapped the slate in cloth and handed it to Tirado in a comedy of scale: the receiving hand would barely match one of Meyr's fingers for size.

'Fly to Totho at Khanaphes, swift as you can,' he instructed. 'This information must be known.'

# Twenty-Four

'The hunt . . .' Amnon wrinkled his nose. 'I thought it had gone well. Perhaps I was wrong.'

Totho watched him empty the dregs of a beer jug. The Iron Glove staff had brought in plenty, though, and then left the room at his command. Totho had assumed that the Khanaphir First Soldier was coming to talk business, but it turned out that Amnon was seeking something simpler, and at the same time more fraught: a sympathetic ear. *And I'm the ear?* There was a whole city of Khanaphir out there, any of whom would have been honoured to receive the First Soldier of the Royal Guard as their guest. But Amnon was out of sorts, Amnon had worries, possibly for the first time in his life, and he wanted to bare his soul. Perhaps that was not something the Khanaphir did with one another: their secretive, mirror-placid nature went deep. Somehow, Amnon had looked on Totho and seen a kindred spirit.

*I'm willing to bet the Ministers don't know he's here either.*

Iron Glove business in Khanaphes had not been good over the last few days, after Ethmet's displeasure had filtered into the city. Totho reckoned it was only a matter of time before they had to write this city off as unprofitable. They would have been leaving soon enough, anyway, denied an outlet to practise their true craft. Totho had no real interest in bulk orders for ordinary swords and arrowheads.

'We took four of the land-fish, one as large as any I have

seen,' Amnon explained, and then sighed massively. 'I do not understand these Collegium women – are they not impressed with such prowess?'

Totho found himself wondering what Che must have made of it. 'They're a perverse lot,' he agreed, feeling a pang of the old bitterness. 'Believe me, I tried to . . .' *And am I revealing this now, and to him, that I have kept to myself for so long?* The beer and Amnon's blithe innocence encouraged him. 'I tried to help the girl I . . . tried to show her how I felt and what I could do. I even went halfway across the world to rescue her. For nothing.'

'So what do they want?' Amnon demanded, taking up another jug. 'Has she enemies I can slay? No, it is all diplomacy with them, and I am not allowed. How am I to *show* this woman?'

'They're very sentimental, Collegium women,' Totho told him. 'Sentimental to a fault. They read too much.' A sweeping statement, but he had just decided that it was true. *Am I drunk?* It seemed likely. The empty jugs littering the table between them were not entirely the fault of Amnon. Mind you, just because he had been drinking, it didn't mean that it wasn't true. 'They prefer a hollow gesture to all manner of sincerity,' he added. *One touch of Moth-kinden mystery and she virtually forgot I was even there.*

'So you think I should woo her gently?' Amnon said. It did not quite match with what Totho thought he had just said, but he let that be.

The big man was thinking. 'I had not wanted to seem too forward.'

'You'll get nothing by hiding your fire. They never notice, if you do that,' Totho replied sagely. 'And they don't care about what success you make of yourself either. You could be general of the world and suddenly it wouldn't matter.' *And, in that case, what am I doing here? What is it I really want?*

'I am observing this, with her,' Amnon agreed heavily. 'I must make a grand gesture – an unmistakable one.'

'Tell me, then,' said Totho. 'Tell me what she did, on your hunt.'

'She seemed not the least interested in anything of it,' Amnon reported gloomily. 'Even when I pulled her from the water with my own hands, she did not seem to see me.'

'No, no, not your Rakespear woman,' Totho interrupted. 'I mean Che – the ambassador.'

'Ah, that I cannot tell you,' Amnon replied ponderously. 'For she vanished for some time, strangely, leaving her companions very concerned. When our search parties finally found her, she was with the Imperial ambassador and his clown.'

*I am not drunk any more.* Indeed he felt abruptly, coldly sober. Totho wrestled a polite expression on to his face, glad that Amnon was being too introspective tonight to notice. 'Is that so?' he asked.

The big man nodded. 'It is not safe, to venture so far as she did,' he said.

*It is not,* Totho silently agreed. *I was asking myself what I want here. What I undoubtedly want is to make sure that Che does not fall into the hands of the Empire. Surely that is what I want,* and on the heels of that, came the wretched thought, *And how many rescues will it take, to make her mine?*

In her dream, Petri Coggen found herself standing at the door of the embassy, looking out at the Place of Foreigners. A breeze brought cool air from the river, but the sky above was almost cloudless.

*This isn't right.*

In the dream there was a strange feeling laid on her, of calm and acceptance. As it enveloped her like a blanket, she took three steps out towards the pond and its benches. Deep inside her something flinched. That part of her trying to wake was thrashing, fighting, but buried very deep. The numbing calm they had laid upon her was smothering it.

*This isn't right.* Still that note of discord. *This is not the*

*Place of Foreigners.* There was enough awareness left to her to force her head around, to look closely at her surroundings. It was a dream, but she *knew* it was a dream, and that behind this dream there lurked something much worse. Somewhere, out beyond her sight, they were waiting. She could feel the leaden weight of their attention.

The statues in the garden of Honoured Foreigners were now watching her. As the moonlight caressed them, it touched not cold stone but cloth and flesh. Deep inside, a shiver of horror went through her – because if these statues could live, then why not others? – but her outer calm was barely cracked, staring at them.

They made no move, just stood in their places, but she saw them shift slightly, and their eyes tracked her as she crossed the garden. The Moth-kinden watched her with inscrutable patience, the Spiders with arch disdain. From his hiding place within the foliage, the eyes of the Mantis warrior gazed with narrow suspicion. Other kinden, some that she had never known in life, stared down on her, as their names were dredged from her memory: long-limbed Grasshoppers, hunchbacked Woodlice, poised and beautiful Dragonfly-kinden.

*No Ants, no Beetles, not even a Khanaphir.* But in the dream she understood that. It was because they were so very lowly: who would waste the fine white stone on a statue of Petri Coggen or any of her relations? They were the servants, the minions, the countless running hordes, whose myriad deaths and births passed unmarked season to season. These, here, were the nobility.

She turned away from their scathing looks and found herself facing the grand arch that led into the Place of Government, towards the Scriptora and the pyramid with its eternal watchers.

*And tonight the statues have come to life.* The struggling part of herself was rising to the surface fast now, howling for her to wake up. Here in her dream there were things that she did not want to see. Her feet were moving her forward, a pace at a time, with a sleepwalker's slow inevitability. She felt the collective gaze of the foreign ambassadors prickling against her back, but none made a move to help her.

*Help me*, and yet there was no help, and her traitor feet kept taking her, pace by pace, towards that arch ahead. She tried to close her eyes against it, but this was a dream and she could not block it out.

*All I wanted to do was leave*, she wailed in protest, and the answer, in crystal-clear tones, came back to her.

*We do not wish you to leave.*

*But what about what* I *want?* Except that was beyond the point. She remembered then that she was a slave, that all her race were slaves, and that this dream came from the far past, when what any Beetle-kinden woman wanted carried no more weight than a grain of sand.

*But we have broken from all that! The revolution …*

But it was a dream from the past, and the revolution had never happened, and besides: this was Khanaphes where her people carried their shackles inside their minds every day, and were joyful about it.

She was now at the arch and stepping into its shadow. The steps of the pyramid rose before her. If she craned her gaze upwards she could see the first hint of white stone.

*No!*

She made a sudden, furious effort to wrest herself away from the dream – and abruptly she was falling, lurching from her bed in a tangle of sheets, and striking the floor with a cry of panic that must have woken half the embassy. She stayed motionless but trembling, waiting for some revenant left from the dream to rise up from within her mind and recapture her. Then she heard footsteps, and people suddenly shocked into wakefulness were shouting at one another.

*I must tell Che,* she thought. *She's the only one who might understand.*

*

Che had not gone outside since the hunt. The rooms of the embassy had become her shell, the blather of the academics her unseen shield.

She had not seen Achaeos's agonized form again since the hunt, either. She imagined it still hanging there inside the wicker cage of the idol, haranguing the Mantis-kinden for their lack of proper faith.

*I am running out of places to turn.* She felt that the world was waiting for her to step outside, yet some sense, previously unknown, kept feeding warnings to her. Seen out of the window, the day gone by had been piercingly bright, cloudless, like all Khanaphir days. But when she turned away and closed her eyes, her mind embroidered the unseen sky with louring grey, a towering thunderhead of storm. *Something is about to happen!* The feeling made her head ache, made everyone seem suspicious in the way they looked at her. In the corners of her eyes, those indecipherable little carvings that marched their endless rounds in every room, along every wall, seemed to jump and gibber. The scholarly pedantry of Berjek and Praeda seemed rife with double meanings, hidden secrets. She clung to their presence, though, for anything was better than being alone. Berjek was intent on his studies and nothing more, therefore no good company, while Praeda had her own worries, remaining quiet and thoughtful, as though something was eating at her mind.

*Where now?* There was one 'where now' left to her, but the thought made her heart tremble. She had skulked in the shadows of this problem all this time, and was not sure that she could take up a lance and strike to the heart of it. To do so would, at the very least, destroy any standing she retained as an ambassador.

Berjek and Praeda reached some kind of impasse in their discussion, and she sensed them turn towards her. She opened her eyes, to see that the sky beyond the windows was already darkening. 'What?' she asked.

'We are in need of your services,' Berjek said. 'As an ambassador, they may listen to you.'

'What do you want from them?' Che asked blankly; their words had passed her by.

She saw Praeda make an exasperated face. 'Che, we need this code-book of theirs, the one for their carvings,' she said. 'There is supposed to be a book containing a translation – a meaning – for these symbols. Berjek and I agree that this is more than idle decoration. There is information encrypted here, but we can't read it, so we need the book.'

'It's one of those things where they clam up as soon as you mention it,' Berjek said glumly. 'They just change the subject, ever so politely.'

'Sacred,' remarked Che, and they stared at her.

'What a peculiar notion,' said Berjek at last.

'It is a very old word,' Che said softly, 'but it's the right word.' She saw him bursting with questions but she held a hand up. 'Don't ask me,' she warned. 'I don't want to talk about it. I don't even want to think about it. I cannot explain it in any way that you would understand.'

Berjek rolled his eyes and was about to say something very sharp, but then a drum began sounding out in the garden, a simple, low beat. The three Collegiates exchanged frowns.

'Some local custom . . .?' Berjek suggested, and then a stringed instrument, high and plaintive and intricate, had added its voice to whatever was going on. As one they passed out onto the balcony to see.

Whatever it was, it was happening right below them, where they would have the best view. Khanaphir servants had staked out torches that blazed with a steady, rosy light, outlining a rough circle on their side of the pond. Che saw some movement in the Imperial embassy across the way, the Wasps emerging to watch in equal puzzlement.

The two musicians, still playing quietly, sat cross-legged outside the circle. Four soldiers had stepped inside it:

slender Mantis-kinden wearing chitin and hide cuirasses and helms, and bearing spears. They knelt at four points, spears pointing upwards and inwards, their razor tips describing a smaller space within the larger.

'Is this a play?' Berjek wondered.

'Or an execution?' Che said darkly.

Another figure came striding up towards the circle, and Praeda said, 'Oh, hammer and tongs, look at him,' hand to her mouth, for it was Amnon. The torchlight picked out the grim expression on his face. He wore only a kilt of white with a golden belt, and the dancing red light picked out the lines of his musculature. In each hand there was a sword, not the broad leaf-bladed things his soldiers carried, but blades like curved razors, thin and wicked-looking and extending longer than his arm. He went to the heart of the circle, within the threat of the four spear-points, and Che saw him take a deep breath. He raised the swords, one held forward, one underhand. Che glanced at Praeda and saw the woman had a look of exasperation on her face, one of clear disapproval at whatever the big man was going to do. The thought came to Che, *And yet she is still watching, to see what it is all about. If her mind had matched that face she would be back inside already.*

The music stopped.

Amnon looked up, and Che knew he was seeking the face of Praeda Rakespear. His expression was so bleak that she thought, *He's going to kill himself. This is some kind of Khanaphir suicide ritual.*

The drum exploded into greater life, the strings rattling alongside it, and Amnon began to dance.

Che had never seen anything like it. Like a man possessed, the First Soldier had gone mad. From that utter stillness he had become a leaping, spinning maniac and, wherever he went, the swords were weaving about his body in a blur of killing steel. He was in and out of the spearpoints, over and under them, whilst the Mantids that held them kept absolutely still, without a tremor. The swords passed everywhere, cut nothing. Amnon looked neither at the swords nor at the spears nor at his feet. His eyes were always fixed upwards, seeking out Praeda Rakespear.

It should have been ridiculous. Without the music it *would* have been ridiculous, but the swift, insistent rhythm was working some magic all of its own. Che felt something catch at her emotions, even though this entire spectacle was for a purpose to which she was purely incidental. *He wants to reach out to her so much . . .* But that great-framed man could not just bare his heart. Behind the armour of his office and the worship of his troops, he was as human as them all. He was dancing to display his vulnerability, even as he danced to show his skill.

Che glanced over at Praeda; the woman's face still showed nothing. *The Cold One, that's what they called her.* It seemed impossible that Amnon would not injure himself, or kill one of his soldiers, but the music forced him on and on. The sweat glowed on him, and Che wondered if there was an end to this, or whether he would go on until he took one wrong step and drew blood.

The music was still building, she realized. *There is more to come.* Amnon's feet moved in a rapid patter, yet every step in perfect place. There was no margin for error in his dance, no chance to recover from placing a foot wrong. The spears glinted ivory in the red light; the swords seemed already stained with blood. Even the musicians seemed gripped by the same frenzy that made Amnon leap and spin.

He gave out a cry that must have come echoing back from the river, then sank down on one knee within the fence of spears. The swords, still unstained, were raised above his head, but the spearheads, all four, lay severed about him on the ground. At last he was looking down. At last he had freed Praeda from the barb of his attention.

Praeda had one hand to her mouth and there was a colour to her cheeks that seemed alien to her. Che's first thought was that she had found the whole thing embarrassing. Praeda would not meet anyone else's eyes, as she hurried inside.

Below them, with Praeda gone, Che saw Amnon finally allow himself to relax. His bare back heaved for breath, and he lowered the swords to the ground.

*What would I feel, if that had been for me?* Che wondered, and felt, at the edge of her mind, just a flicker of that fierce attention. In the face of the brief stab of envy she felt, despite herself, she wondered whether her assessment of Praeda's reaction had been correct. *She's cold, but you'd have to be frozen through not to feel that warmth.*

'Remarkable customs,' Berjek said, returning inside himself, giving every impression of being the muddled academic missing the point of everything he had just witnessed. In his wake, Che was now left with only one person on the balcony beside herself.

'Help me,' Petri Coggen implored her, as she stood there in her nightshirt, hands clutching each other before her. 'Please, Che, before it's too late.'

It had not occurred to her that the First Minister of Khanaphes would be waiting for her. Of course, he made a great show of finishing up business first. When she stepped into the great hall of the Scriptora, with its traitor fountain playing its serenade to the Aptitude of its creators, she found him at the far end, giving quick instructions to a clutch of clerks. Even as Che approached him, though, the menials began to disappear, bowing backwards off into oblivion, leaving Ethmet to turn and beam at her politely. She knew, then, that he had been here for this reason only: to meet with her.

'O Beautiful Foreigner, O Ambassador,' he said to her, 'what favour may the city of Khanaphes enact for you?'

'I need to speak with you,' she said. She had resolved to be blunt, because she needed answers both for herself and for Collegium.

'Of course. Nothing would be of more pleasure,' he assured her. 'Would it displease you if I pass about my duties as we speak?' If he had been a younger man, and of another city, she might have accused him of mockery. *The Khanaphir could revile you to your face, though, and you would never know it for sure.*

'We would need privacy, I think,' she said. He was already turning away, pottering off into the next room, so she was forced to follow.

'Ah, well, there are only servants to hear us, and they know their duty is to keep their ears close about them,' Ethmet said absently. *He plays the part of the avuncular old man so well.*

The room he had passed into gave her a moment's pause. It was a library, she guessed, or perhaps just some grand office of government. The circular floor was picked out in an intricate mosaic design devoid of meaning, and the walls were lined with wooden racks, criss-crossing diagonal beams that reached up to the high windows visible far above Che's head. Steps on either side led to balconies for access to the higher shelves and, when they entered, there were at least two score clerks removing scrolls, filing them, or amending and updating them. Within a minute of Ethmet's entrance, and without any signal that Che could discern, they had all carefully rolled up their work and departed from the room. Each one's manner suggested merely that they had been about to do so in any case, and that Ethmet's entry had not swayed them in the least. A moment later, as the shuffling of sandals receded, Che and Ethmet were left alone in the echoing room.

'You wished, I believe, to have words with me?' the old man enquired. He was standing at the nearest desk, a simple slab of stone with some half-furled scrolls resting upon it.

Che seized her courage in both hands, determined to crack the First Minister's shell. 'What happened to the scholar, Kadro?' she asked.

Ethmet did not even blink. 'We have been unable to locate him, I am sorry to say.'

Che gritted her teeth. 'It has been . . . suggested to me that he may have been asking awkward questions, that the Ministers of Khanaphes may not have approved of his researches.'

Ethmet's smile remained distantly polite. 'I understand only that your compatriot was given to asking his questions, impolitic or not, in unwise places. He was seen much in the Marsh Alcaia, even out in the desert, where the writ of the Khanaphir Dominion runs regrettably thin. In seeking such company it would seem most likely that the manner of his researches, and not the subject of them, proved the cause of his difficulties.' He gathered up some of the scrolls and made his patient way towards a flight of steps.

'You're telling me that you gave no orders . . .' Che trailed off. *In the face of such denial, such a wall of denial, what can I say?*

'None at all. Why should we?' Ethmet replied, taking the stairs one at a time. Even in those few words, Che had the absolute certainty that he was lying. *I can prove nothing, but Petri is right.* She was becoming used to intuitions that arrived without logic, with nothing but an assurance of their own truth.

She followed him up the steps, trying to formulate the words that might trip him up, expose the man behind the mask. Then he remarked, as blandly as ever, 'I understand that you have succumbed to the vice of Profanity.'

She stopped, as thoroughly thrown as she had ever been, ice coursing through her veins. *This trap has sprung the wrong way.* Ethmet was not even looking at her, carefully filing the scrolls, one by one.

'I . . .' she began, her heart hammering. She waited for the guards to suddenly spring out from their hiding places, but guards there were none, just herself and the old man within the big, echoing chamber.

'We make it a crime,' Ethmet continued, still at his deliberate filing, and she thought, *The First Minister does not do a clerk's job. He has brought me up here for some reason.*

'I . . . I know,' she stammered. 'What . . . What will you . . .?'

'Do not fear.' He looked at her directly then. 'It is a law that is enforced only against those who are not . . . worthy.'

'I do not understand.' And she genuinely did not understand. He was waiting for her, testing her.

'Word has reached us, O Foreigner, of you and your unusual heritage.'

'They thought I was of the blood of . . .' She could not bring herself to say it, but he completed the thought for her.

'Of the Masters. But you are not.' He was at the balcony rail now, hands resting on the carved stone. 'But you are *special* nevertheless, or so we have been led to believe. Not for many ages has Khanaphes welcomed one like you. The eating of Fir is a practice not forbidden, but restricted. Through Fir do those of us bearing the blood hear the voice of the Masters.'

She gaped at him. 'But you don't mean . . . you mean that . . . the Ministers? You?'

'The sin of Profanity is profane only when committed by the unrighteous who seek to steal that which is given freely to those who deserve it.'

She clenched her fists, utterly lost now. 'Tell me what you're talking about,' she urged him. 'Just tell me . . . tell me something plainly, please.' She had joined him at the balcony's edge, but his gaze did not even flick towards her.

'You *know*,' he said. 'Am I plain enough in that?'

'But I *don't*—' She stopped and, at last, followed his gaze down to the tiled floor of the chamber. After a moment she said, 'Oh.'

The mosaic, the tiles of sepia and black and grey, swam before her eyes, and she felt Ethmet take her arm to keep her from simply pitching over the rail. What had been an abstract arabesque down below was suddenly recognizable, stylized but familiar. The floor was a map.

Khanaphes lay at the centre, she now saw plainly, but the extent of the map was large, the world stretching away on every side. She found the Sunroad Sea, and from that guessed at north, seeing nothing of the Empire, no Capitas, none of the centres of Imperial Power. *But that city is where Myna stands today, and that other one for Maynes.* Her eyes were drawn westwards: Darakyon was a living Mantis Hold, and west of that lay Tharn, but no Helleron. There were other cities marked, whose names she could not guess at, of kinden that perhaps she had never heard of. The edge of the Commonweal was picked out in a glorious detail beyond her own people's modern knowledge of it. She followed the unfamiliar lines of what should have been a familiar land. There was a coastal city there that she knew must be marked 'Pathis', for the name 'Collegium' was only five hundred years old. This map was from an age that made close cousins of the Wasp Empire and her own home city – and infant cousins at that. A map that had been scuffed by the feet of Khanaphir clerks for . . .

'How long?' she asked.

'I cannot say, save to say that the Scriptora was not young, when the Masters ordained that a map of their world should be placed within.' Ethmet's voice was soft and sad. 'O Honoured Foreigner, you see it plain, do you not?'

'I do,' she said. This was not a map as she had once been used to, drawn from the precise cartography of grids and measurements that the Collegium mapmakers taught. There was no regular scale down there, and the lands around the Jamail river were shown disproportionately large, but it all fell into place before her eyes. It gave up its secrets with barely a struggle.

'I have never seen it,' Ethmet whispered.

She could not drag her eyes from the map. 'What do you mean?'

‘I know it as a map, for our older records speak of it as such, but I am not so blessed as you. I have a touch of the blood of the Masters – in truth, enough to pursue my duties as my fathers have done before me – but you are truly blessed.’

She turned to him at last, tearing her gaze away from the inlaid patterns. ‘But the Masters are gone, aren’t they? That pyramid out there is their tomb, their monument. That’s what I . . .’ Had anyone actually told her that? ‘That’s what I always thought . . .’

‘Oh, it is indeed their tomb,’ he whispered, and suddenly he stood uncomfortably close. ‘But they are not dead. They shall walk their city once more, and in time they shall call for you – and you shall go to meet them.’

# Twenty-Five

'There's post waiting with your lunch, sir.'

Totho nodded absently, brushing past the man. He was in a poor mood. He had spent a restless night thinking towards some way of reclaiming Che, but reaching no conclusions. He only hoped that Amnon was having better luck with his chosen Collegiate woman.

*Of course he is*, the little voice inside Totho – the one he had been born with, that had started speaking to him as soon as he had been old enough to realize what he was – piped up again. Amnon was big, handsome, charismatic. He would not need to do much to get the woman to notice him. Life had been kind to Amnon. Totho doubted the big man had ever had to work too hard at getting anything.

*I have had to work, though.* It felt bitter. Even in Collegium, which prided itself on its industry, the dream was to become rich enough not to have to work. That dream was inherited from the past, when Beetles had worked and Moth-kinden had spent their time in idleness, living off the sweat of their slaves. The dream was further honed by the effortless lives of the Spider-kinden Aristoi, who had nothing better to do in life than intrigue against one another. *Whereas I have had to work for everything.* Delivered to an orphanage by unknown parents, tinkering with mechanisms from the age of five, competing against dozens of others for a College place that would have been his for the asking, if only he had been some rich magnate's son. Yes, he had worked: to get where he was now, he had not only got his hands dirty, he had steeped them in blood to the elbows.

*I rearmed the world, equipped it in my own image. I destroyed an army. I halted the Empire, drove them out of Szar.* But he did not like to think of Szar. He was not yet ready for that. *If I had been some magnate's son, I would have needed to do nothing, to secure my future. To come this far I have had to wade hip-deep in bad choices and bad deeds. And still she turns away from me.*

Lunch was set out for him, but he spared it barely a look. There were some sealed documents beside it, and a roll of cloth tape – and a Fly-kinden man. 'You're post, are you?' He raised an eyebrow.

'Tirado,' the man confirmed. 'Message from Factor Meyr, your eyes only.'

'Well, get out until I've finished eating,' Totho snapped, deciding that cocky Fly-kinden annoyed him. Some of them seemed to think that rules and authority didn't apply to them. The Fly looked put out, but he stepped down from the table and flitted out through the door. Totho sat down, pushing the food away despite his recent words. The papers were all manifests, he could look those over later. He broke each seal, to be sure, then laid them to one side.

The tape was another matter, a little spark of daylight showing through the clouds that were on his mind. He reached into his pouch and took out one of the Iron Glove's newest artifacts. It was hand-sized, and looked mostly like a very small drum with a winding handle, as though someone had decided that even a drum was too complex to learn to play, and had therefore invented an automatic one. Where the handle joined the drum there was a spidery little arrangement of teeth and tiny pins.

Totho took the reel of cloth, a woven strip barely an inch across. It was an ugly piece of work, the threads jumbled together without pattern, looking like some clothier's reject remnant. With the utmost care, he fed the end of it into the teeth of the machine until it caught. He then wound it through a few inches, listening carefully. The sound that echoed from the drum was almost too faint to hear. Patiently, Totho fiddled with it, turning the clamps to increase the space inside the drum itself. In this small exercise of his skill, he had forgotten about Che or Amnon, or all the rest of it. The intricacy of the device itself consumed him.

He wound the cloth back, and then began winding it forwards again, letting the delicate pins brush against the rugged fabric, and their vibrations carry down to the drum itself. Into the room, small and distant-sounding, came a voice.

It was a voice Totho knew well, after two years' association and more. It was the voice of the senior partner of the Iron Glove, and the man after whom the entire enterprise was named.

'Hello, Totho,' said the scratchy tones.

'Hello, Dariandrephos,' Totho replied, even though there was nobody there to hear him. A sense of wonder still came to him, although they had been using these similophone tapes for two months now. It was the secret of the Iron Glove. Only he and Drephos possessed the drum-like similophone ears, and so far Drephos had the one weaver, the machine that took the sound of his voice and wove it into cloth. He was working, however, on a model that was portable.

The winding handle carried the tape further, projecting Drephos's voice, dry and tendays old, into the factora in Khanaphes. Totho was careful to keep his speed steady, so as to pitch the man's voice right. When the first similophone tape had been heard, he had been left in stitches, making Drephos squeak and drawl as he tried to match the pace.

'First,' came the tiny voice, 'you should know that the Empire has made some advances in retroengineering the Solarnese-style aeromotives that we sold them. I understand that they will be in a position to upgrade their Spearflight models within the next two months, at this rate. Our new design of rotary piercer has exceeded expectations to the extent that I am uncomfortable with allowing them onto the market without consideration, and I would value your input when you return, which I trust will be shortly. Matters with the Empire are likely to reach a head soon, one way or another.

'Less importantly, our fourth factory assembled and test-fired the first greatshotter design yesterday. The results were remarkable, but the damage to the prototype was such that it required complete disassembly: the barrel integrity does not stand up to the pressures generated. I am loath to look for new materials right now, but aviation steel, in the thickness required, does not offer the absorbent flexibility . . .'

Totho let the details wash over him, considering each, letting them settle in his mind. *This* was the important thing. In such a wash of technical minutiae he felt happy, as he always had, and such imprecise calculations as the affections of Cheerwell Maker could be temporarily shunted aside. At this late age, in this foreign land, he had found for himself a surrogate father. Oh, Dariandrephos was a monster, for certain: he had no conscience, no humanity, no regard whatsoever for any who could not contribute to the world of artifice. He would destroy Khanaphes without a thought if he needed to, because he considered the city a waste of stone and wood and flesh. Drephos was all these things, but he was a man whose priorities struck a chord in his protégé – and he valued Totho. For the sake of Totho's artificing Drephos indulged him like a spoilt child, even when Totho's preoccupations went beyond the older halfbreed's comprehension.

The tape kept ravelling on, and Totho leant back in his chair and listened to it as though it was music: the pinnacle of artificing used to bring to him the furthest advances in artifice. It was how life should always work, and so seldom did. And if he missed any of it, or wanted to hear it all again, then he could do so. He could recoil the tape and wind it through again and again. Drephos's words, anybody's words, need never be lost. The Iron Glove had found a way to cheat time and death.

*We should take one to Collegium, record some of Stenwold's speeches . . .*

At last the report came to its close, leaving Totho smiling slightly, still, at the ingenuity of it. Belatedly he remembered the Fly-kinden, now kept waiting for an hour or more. With a scowl, Totho called him in. Tirado had obviously been reminded about being a good Iron Glove employee in the interim, because he saluted properly this time.

'What's happened to Meyr?' Totho demanded.

'Nothing when I left, but that's a state of affairs not likely to continue,' Tirado reported. He handed over Meyr's wrapped slate. Totho was still slouching easily as he started to read but, after only a few words, he sat bolt upright and started paying real attention.

It was late in the day when she finally broke away from the Scriptora.

She had expected the guards, after what Ethmet had said. She had expected to be thrown into the cells to await the Masters' pleasure – a pleasure that would surely see her rot before it was made manifest. She had come to believe that the Masters' bloodlines might still echo within Khanaphes, in men like Ethmet or women like the Mother, but not their voices or footsteps. That was the fiction that the city was built on – and that perhaps Ethmet even believed – that the Masters would one day come forth again and take up the reins. It was a foundation that was concrete as long as it was believed, that would be shifting sand the moment it was doubted.

He had shown her the book, which had made all the difference. She was becoming used to sharing her life with the miraculous, but the book made the miraculous commonplace. Ethmet had taken her to a small room in the Scriptora where stonemasons were working. They were carving out the hieroglyphs that infested Khanaphes like indecipherable locusts, and they had for reference a book.

They had not liked her being there, those craftsmen: they were members of a select and occult fraternity. However, Ethmet's word, his mere glance, had been law. They had given the book over to her and she had opened its pages, and her mind had jolted at what she had seen.

She had thought it might be something simple, perhaps with a text in hieroglyphs set out on one leaf, and letters on the opposite, or even like a reading primer for children, the glyphs drawn large and their meaning inscribed beneath them. But no.

The pages of the book had been layered end to end in hieroglyphs, drawn in large, bold strokes, page after page after page. Her eyes had been bombarded by their cryptic images, but after that first page she had ceased to see them as impenetrable symbols, but simply as the words that they represented. There was no apparent meaning to the book, no story, no sense of grammar, nothing but a cascade of images but, as she turned the last page, she had looked from it to the walls and read: '*All praise to the Masters, the lifeblood of the Jamail, the sweet rains and the rich earth,*' and the words had struck her in the heart.

She had looked to Ethmet, and then at the masons, and she had known, beyond the frailest doubt: *They cannot see this. Ah, no, their own history is opaque to them, but I can read it.* The pages of the book had worked a magic in her. Wherever she now looked, the stories of Khanaphes unravelled their meanings for her, on every wall.

But not on every stone – the individual words, yes, the stories no. As she looked upon the greater book that was the city, she saw the cruel theft that time had committed. On the walls of the Scriptora, on the elder buildings, were tracked the countless voices of ancient Khanaphes. Merely in passing from the masons' room back to the library, her eyes snagged on every passageway, at each turning or pillar: '*In this year the great Batheut ventured into the Alim with his nine hundred . . .*'; '*Of grain, fourteen baskets; of oats, nine baskets more, and he shall . . .*'; '*And she sang the songs of her far homeland, and all who listened were . . .*' until she had to almost shut her eyes to keep out the thronging meanings that would not leave her alone. Where new construction had been made, though, the script fell into babble: '*She boat sun leap shoe coral great if . . .*'

And then she understood: *They have lost their ancient language. It died when their Aptitude was born. Generation by generation, those carving hands became more Apt, less arcane, until they were merely going through the rotes. In their secret little brotherhood, they copy and they carve, but it has no meaning any longer.* The informative had long since become the merely decorative.

And Ethmet knew it. She could see it in his face. He looked at her and there was hope in his eyes, a terrible, misplaced hope. It was as though her reading of the book of glyphs had revealed the key to his expressions as well.

She had assumed he would keep her, but he had let her go. He believed, despite his Aptitude, in destiny. He believed she would come back to him voluntarily, to fulfil whatever role he wished of her. As an Inapt Beetle, her very curse had made her his messiah. Her mind was now reeling as she set off for the Place of Foreigners. She did not dare look at the pyramid, with those statues placed irregularly about its top, for fear of the stories it might tell her. She was painfully aware that she had failed Petri and Kadro, and that her own selfishness was to blame, once more.

As she reached the archway leading through to the embassies, something stopped her, snapping her back to the here-and-now. She found her hand on her sword-hilt, yet no danger in sight. *What is it?* Some sense she had not known before was calling to her . . . *No, I have known this. The desert, the Scorpion raid.*

‘Achaeos?’ she asked softly, feeling an edge of tension that was external to her, the result of some other’s keener senses.

Someone moved in the shadow of the archway. Up until then, she had not so much as glimpsed him. When she saw him she started to relax, but whatever had alerted her kept its hook in her twisted tight. It was one of the Vekken, she realized. As usual she could not have said which one.

‘Were you waiting for me?’ she began.

He stared at her blankly and she saw, so very late, that his sword was clear of its sheath, blackened with pitch. Her reactions caught up then, her hand clenching on her own hilt as she looked into his hating eyes.

There was a rapid flutter of wings, and Trallo was standing beside her, all smiles. ‘Ah, there you are, been looking all over. You do wander off some, Bella Cheerwell!’ His hollow cheer washed over them both, but Che guessed at once that he knew where she had spent the day. The Vekken looked from her to the Fly-kinden, then stalked away without a word. He had already told her more than he had intended. *Something has snapped in the Vekken’s ambassadorial calm.*

‘Trallo, what’s going on?’

‘You’re asking *me*?’ The little man shook his head. ‘Nothing’s happened at the embassy. The professors are all off looking at rocks down by the river, for reasons unknown to man or insect. Oh, and Sieur Gorget is being more insufferable than usual, but apart from that . . .’ He was staring after the Vekken ambassador, rubbing at his beard.

‘Manny is . . .?’

‘Oh, it might be that Bella Rakespear received a certain Khanaphir beau this morning, in her own chambers, but more than that I have no knowledge of.’

Che managed to raise a small smile at that. They passed through into the Place of Foreigners, and she took a seat by the pond. *I need to speak with the Vekken, but I first need to know what’s set them off.* She remembered that brief moment of confrontation. *This is more than injured pride.*

'That's twice you've been there for me, Trallo,' she noted. It was a train of thought she had stored away a while ago, now dragged out into the sunlight again. The little man merely shrugged, and did not look surprised when she continued, 'I don't recall you asking me for any pay recently.'

'Well, you know . . .' he replied, but he was waiting for what she said next.

'You're a business-minded sort.' She wanted to pick her words with more care, but it had been such a long day. 'The plan was that you'd be back in Solarno by now. Talk to me, Trallo.'

'You've a complaint about my services?' he enquired, light-heartedly, but with a brittle edge.

'Quite the opposite. Talk to me.'

He smiled. 'You're a popular woman,' he explained. 'You have a lot of friends, and they're anxious that you're well.'

'We're not talking about Berjek and the others. I know that much,' she said flatly. 'Trallo, are you taking orders from the Ministers?'

'From the . . .?' She saw in his expression immediately that she was wrong. He laughed out loud, in fact. 'They already have a thousand Khanaphir watching you, Bella Cheerwell. They don't need me to keep an eye on things as well.'

'Then . . .' *And who was it who pulled me from the tent of the Fir-eaters – for all the good it did him? And I never stopped to ask what he was doing there so deep in the Marsh Alcaia, so close to me.* A terrible bleakness settled on her. 'Are you taking the Empire's coin, Trallo?' she asked.

'Not a bit of it,' he told her. 'Bella Cheerwell, I like you, so I only take coin from those I think have your best interests at heart. That way they're paying me for something I'd want to do anyway, if I could afford to do it on my own.' His grin was so guileless, it cut her like a knife. 'I wouldn't take Imperial coin, Bella Cheerwell, but I might just take the coin of Sieur Thalric.'

She stared at him. 'You've been spying on me for Thalric,' she said.

'I've been watching out for you, for Thalric,' he confirmed, absolutely candid. 'That's what he asked, that's what I've done. He doesn't think you can look after yourself, you see.'

'Oh, doesn't he?' she snapped. 'Does he not?' She heard her raised voice echo back from the embassy walls. Trallo waited, still smiling slightly, but not so close that he could not get out of the way if she went for him.

*Diplomatic incident,* her mind told her. *He's broken the truce by spying on me. Blast the man – just as I was getting somewhere with this city the Empire comes butting in.* Another part of her was saying, *You should not have asked the question if you did not want to hear the answer – especially as you have known all this, if you had only thought about it, long before.*

And, a fragile voice: *And he dragged you out of the Fir den, and what if he had not?*

'I want to be angry,' she complained. 'Why aren't I?'

'Beetle-kinden are a phlegmatic lot,' suggested Trallo, and then skipped back a step as she glared at him.

'And Flies are a pragmatic one,' she shot back. He shrugged at the truth of it.

She glanced back towards the Collegiate embassy, which was where she should now be going. But the Vekken would be there, and she did not feel ready to deal with that problem yet – if it was even capable of being dealt with. Petri Coggen would be there too, another person Che did not want to see just now. She would have accepted the company of Manny Gorget or the others, but they were out doing what they were supposed to be doing. *How simple some people's lives are.*

'Let's go have a word with Thalric,' she decided. Trallo raised his eyebrows, and she had the chance to turn his smile back on him. 'Why not? In this new climate of brutal honesty, I want to ask him why he's suborning my staff.'

She marched off around the pond towards the Imperial

embassy, feeling a mean spark of pride that she had wrong-footed the Fly-kinden for once.

A servant was already opening the door to greet her.

'Cheerwell Maker, the Collegiate ambassador, here to see her opposite number,' she announced smartly. The servant ushered her into the hallway, where another was already padding off to deliver the news. Aside from the ubiquitous Khanaphir she saw no one, certainly nobody serving under the Imperial flag.

'Where are they all?' she asked.

'Off watching your lot, I imagine,' Trallo said. 'You have to remember the way the Empire thinks. They don't believe for a moment you're just here to catch fish and look at stones.'

'And do you?' she asked him, because his tone had seemed doubting.

He spread his hands. 'I don't need to believe anything.'

As they stood in the hallway, Thalric appeared at the stair-rail above them, his expression suggesting that he had not believed the servant's message. Behind him there was a Beetle-kinden, a bulky Imperial of about Stenwold's age and dimensions.

There was a beat, a moment's pause, before Thalric turned and descended the stairs, saying, 'Ambassador? Is there a problem?'

'Possibly.' Che saw Thalric's gaze touch on Trallo and then slide off, noticed the quickly suppressed flicker of understanding.

'Ah, well,' he said, then turned back to his Beetle companion. 'We'll have to break, Corolly. I'll leave the board set.'

The big man nodded. 'I've got paperwork to catch up with.' He gave Che a vague half-salute, like a man unsure about the formalities, before retreating into one of the upstairs rooms.

Thalric had paused near the foot of the stairs, and stood

looking at her with a slight smile on his face. 'I suppose you should come up then, unless you want to keep this formal.' He singled out one of the servants. 'Get us some decent wine or something.' Then he was trekking back up the stairs, leaving Che to follow him. Trallo had already flitted up to the landing and, judging from his expression, Thalric must have given him a foul look as he passed.

The room she followed him into matched her own across the other side of the Place of Foreigners. She had to force her eyes away from the walls, where ancient hands had inscribed a valedictory epic to a kinden she was not even sure she recognized, but that she imagined were depicted in the tall, hunchbacked effigies that flanked the main embassy doors. To one side there was a low table on which some kind of game had been set up, with two couches facing each other for the players. The two ambassadors took their places on either side of it.

'How's . . . your man, the . . . injured one?' She had been about to say 'the drunk one', but that might not have been diplomatic enough.

'Osgan? Fevered,' Thalric said. 'Being tended, expected to recover. Getting yourself cut open in a swamp's a stupid thing to do.' Thalric shrugged. They had not spoken since the hunt, and she had no idea what he thought of what had happened there, in the village of the Mantis-kinden.

'Did he . . . did he say what he saw there?' she asked tentatively.

'What Osgan sees is not regarded as reliable testimony,' he replied shortly. 'Even at the best of times.'

*He did see something then.* Had this man become so caught up in Tisamon's final moments and the death of the Emperor, that he was now able to grasp something of the Inapt world? She knew that she was unlikely ever to find out. 'Thalric . . .' She frowned down at the game board and, in place of chastising him over Trallo, she just said, 'You're a really bad chess player. These pieces are all over the place.'

He had been waiting for something serious, and he snorted at that, caught off guard. 'What it is, is that you Lowlanders have no idea how to play chess,' he replied.

'I came third in the College trials, I'll have you know.' It had meant a lot to her, at the time. Now, facing his amusement, her sense of pride was dwindling.

'You play Ant-chess,' he said. 'Trudge-trudge-trudge. I couldn't believe it when I first came to Helleron – all that lining up and slogging. In real chess—'

'They fly,' Che finished for him. 'Of course, if chess is a war, then . . . war is different for the Wasps.' Such a simple thing, but it seemed to say a lot about the gap between them.

'Blame the Commonwealers. It's their game,' he said, but his smile was slipping fast. 'All right, Che, out with it.' The wine arrived then, a further stay of execution, but he was still braced and waiting when the servants bowed their way out.

'You have been keeping watch over me,' she accused. 'Using Trallo here, who has his kinden's sense of free business, I think.'

'And his kinden's ability to keep his mouth shut, I see,' Thalric added.

The Fly gave an amused snort and Che turned to him sharply. 'You've got something to say, at this point?'

'Only that you're both making a great fuss over nothing,' he said easily. 'He wants you looked after, so what? She knows about it, so what? There's no conflict here, no difference of opinion. Why all the secrecy, eh?'

They were both staring at him in exasperation. Then Che said, 'Don't you understand anything?' and paused, trying to put into words just why the Fly was wrong. 'Perhaps . . . you'd better go wait at the embassy while I sort this out,' she said finally.

Trallo rolled his eyes at that. 'If you insist on complicating matters, Bella Cheerwell.' He bowed to them both, before stepping up on to the window ledge and letting the air catch him beyond it. Che could not keep herself from going to the window to make sure that he was not simply still hovering there, eavesdropping.

'Solarnese Fly-kinden,' she complained. 'What can you do with them?'

'It's all because their Spider mistresses let them get away with murder,' Thalric remarked.

She looked over at him, her expression undecided. 'So you told him it was all for my own good, did you?'

'Wasn't it?' he asked.

Slowly she returned to her seat. 'What right do you have—' but he was smirking at her in that patronizing way he had always done, from the beginning, and she demanded, 'What?'

'I had forgotten,' he said, 'how you Collegiates aways talk of rights – rights of humanity. This is nothing to do with having a *right*, according to some obscure philosophy. Che, I look after my comrades, past or present. It's an Imperial virtue, believe it or not, although one that's seldom practised these days.'

'And I can't look after myself, is that it?'

He looked at her, fighting for a moment to hold in the response, and the laugh that went with it. 'No,' he let out, finally. 'Oh, Che, even when we first met it was after you had gone to great lengths to put yourself straight into the hands of the man most likely to betray you to me. When we were in Myna together you managed so well with the resistance that they were about to execute you as a collaborator. Che, from what should I believe that you will keep yourself safe?'

'You . . .!' As she stood, her indignation was strangling any chance of getting coherent words out. 'How—! Why you—!' He still had a faint smile, which maddened her even more, and she slapped the little table, flipping it over entirely and scattering chess pieces to the four quarters of the room. 'Bah—!' she got out. Thalric was not looking suitably chastened, instead was plainly fighting not to laugh out loud.

*Oh, that does it.* She went for him, then, catching him completely by surprise. She was not entirely sure what she intended, save perhaps to strangle the smile from his face, but she knocked him backwards off the couch and landed on him hard enough that she heard the breath whoosh out of him. Shocked at her own success, she dithered, sitting back on his stomach. His recovery was impeded more by his laughter than her weight.

'Hammer and tongs!' she exclaimed. 'What?'

'You don't change,' he choked out at last. 'You must have been a riot in the debating circles. Do you attack everyone you don't have an answer for?'

The humour of it got through to her at last. The anger burning but a moment ago, now seemed to have died a death, not even an ember left. She met Thalric's eyes, feeling his body twist beneath her, testing himself against her weight, and there was a moment when something passed between them. Che felt suddenly uncomfortable and scrabbled backwards, ending up perched on the couch he had just vacated. Thalric picked himself up and dusted himself down, then plucked a chess piece from the floor, where it had been digging into his back.

'I've escaped another mauling from Corolly, then,' he said vaguely. She knew, from his abruptly subdued tone, that he had felt that fleeting something too.

'Thalric . . .' she began, but did not know where to go next.

'They suggested I should seduce you,' he told her, the words ambushing both of them without warning.

She stared at him, agog. 'What . . .?'

'Good Rekef practice.' Instead of looking at her, he was busy picking up game pieces.

'Why are you telling me this?'

'I'm trying out honesty,' he said. 'I'm just telling you what they suggested.'

'I should go,' she said. He was still hunting chessmen,

though, and she did not want to go until he had at least turned to face her. 'Thalric,' she said, more urgently, and he looked at her at last. The expression he had been hiding from her left some traces still, on his face. He looked a little uncertain, a little shaken. She tried a smile on him, saw the corner of his mouth twitch in return.

Something crashed downstairs and they heard the servants scream.

Che was out of the room in an instant, reaching for her sword. She saw the Beetle, Corolly, surge out onto the landing, dragging at the string of a crossbow. There were soldiers in dark armour rushing up the stairs already, who reached him before he could cock the weapon. One of them smashed Corolly across the face with the butt of a snapbow, knocking him to the ground. Another put a foot on the Beetle's chest, levelling a long-barrelled weapon at his face. The rest were surging towards Che.

She brandished her sword, and only then did she recognize them.

'Totho?' she faltered. The lead figure was wholly concealed in armour, black metal plates cast into elegant flutes and ridges. She was not even sure that she had identified him correctly until he spoke.

'Che.' She could barely recognize the hollow voice from within the helm. 'You're coming with us.'

'*You!*' Thalric spat the word out from behind her, and she felt a sudden plummeting in her stomach at what was about to happen.

Totho raised some kind of weapon, levelling it directly over her shoulder, but Thalric was quicker. The flash and flare of his sting warmed her cheek before it struck Totho across the breastplate and pauldron. He reeled back with the impact, the short weapon in his hands snapping a bolt into the ceiling. The seething fire from the Wasp's Art merely boiled off his armour, leaving it patterned with pale lines but unbroken.

'Everybody stop!' Che cried out at the top of her voice. 'What is going on?'

Totho grabbed her – just reached out, took hold of her tunic and hauled her towards him effortlessly. As her back was pulled hard up against the grooves of his breastplate, she could feel where it was still warm from Thalric's shot.

Thalric stood in the doorway of his chamber, hand again spitting golden fire. A man beside Totho went down, a fist-sized hole charred through his leather armour. The weapon in Totho's hand snapped again, striking stone-dust from the lintel and forcing Thalric to duck back. Che was struggling to escape from Totho, but he held her close with a grip she could not break. 'What are you doing?' she demanded over and over until he roared in her ear, 'Just shut up for once, Che. You're coming with me!' The vehemence shocked her into silence, mouth left open in mid-complaint. The Iron Glove contingent, some dozen men in all, began retreating back down the stairs. She heard Thalric call her name as he ran out onto the balcony, and his hand blazed again. Then a snapbow bolt tore across his arm and another skimmed his ribs, and he fell back.

'Where in the wastes are the rest of them?' someone was asking, and she recognized Corcoran's voice. 'Setting an ambush?'

Totho paused, and Che could almost feel the workings of his mind, transmitted through the armour that was digging into her back. If the rest of the Imperials were elsewhere, then Totho could accomplish more than simply dragging Che away.

Deliberately she began fighting him again, and she heard his curse echo from inside his helm. Corolly had appeared at the balcony rail again, crossbow loaded now. A snapbow bolt made him duck back. Totho came to his decision.

'Let's go. We have what we came for.'

Under the gaze of the aghast servants, the Iron Glove men retreated from the Imperial embassy. They left a dead man on the balcony, irrevocable proof of how they had broken the peace of Khanaphes.

*What can he mean to do?* Che asked herself helplessly. *They will hunt him down for this. The Ministers will set Amnon and the Mantids and everything they have on him.* She envisaged being manhandled to the docks, a swift flight through the Estuarine Gate before the alarm was raised. Totho was not taking her towards the river, though. As she was marched briskly on, she understood where: the Iron Glove factora. *He must be mad. What will he do, holed up in there?* 'Totho, tell me what's going on,' she pleaded, but he said nothing, just hustled her on through the streets of Khanaphes, under the increasingly concerned attention of the locals.

She stumbled, as a memory revived within her like a cold knife in her, leaving her suddenly sick with the thought. *It is just like before.* She pictured a mountainside outside Helleron, and a sudden abduction by a familiar face. It had been her lost Achaeos that had stood before her then, rather than Thalric of the Empire, but the face of her kidnapper had still been Totho's.

*But it was not truly him,* not then. That first time, it had been the Spider-kinden shape-changer, Scyla. *And now we are come full circle, and this time he really has done it.*

# Twenty-Six

She had expected Totho to at least sit down and talk to her, after they bustled her into the Iron Glove factora. He seemed to have no time for her, though. She had assumed at first that this was some mad impulse of his, and that he could not know what a nest of hornets he would be stirring. Now she saw that he had planned everything.

They had moved her from room to room within the factora, ahead of a wave of fortification. Allotted such primitive facilities, the Iron Glove were not content to let them lie: the solid stone framework of the factora building was being re-edified even as she watched. She caught brief moments of the process as they moved her deeper inside. They were fixing metal grills over the windows, with apertures large enough to admit a snapbow's barrel. They had replaced the main door with something iron-bound and reinforced. Iron Glove people were running everywhere, now, strapping on breastplates and buckling on helms, checking the workings of crossbows and snapbows.

*He's making ready for a siege.* She could understand the logic. The Khanaphir could not stand by and allow these foreign merchants the run of their city. *But they are not merchants.* The staff of the factora had transformed their headquarters into a fort, and themselves into soldiers. She had no doubt that they practised regularly with all the different weapons that they sold.

At last she caught a brief glimpse of Totho again, helmet pushed back, his face appearing almost transformed. It was a look she remembered from when she had found him engaged in some artificing project or other, where everything was coming together just at the last moment.

She called out his name, even as two Iron Glove men began manhandling her up some stairs. She saw his head turn, then he strode over, leaving half a dozen metal-clad men waiting on him. He still wore his own elegantly fashioned mail, that made the serviceable equipment of the others look like something that should be hanging in a museum.

'Later,' was all he said, from the foot of the stairs, and then turned to go.

'Totho, tell me what's going on!' she cried, struggling furiously with the men that held her. 'This is *me*, Totho!'

'Yes, it is.' He turned sharply back to her, and he was actually grinning. It was an expression of desperation and elation all muddled together. 'Oh, I'll tell you all right what's going on, but not now. Soon enough I'll tell *everybody* what's going on.' Then he was off once more, marching back to his troops, and Che continued being hauled backwards up the stairs.

'Curse you!' she shouted after him. 'You can't *do* this!' She was about to add that he had no right, but Thalric's words came back to her, about what her 'rights' were worth.

'Bring her in here now.' She recognized the voice as Corcoran's, though his helm left him as anonymous as all the rest.

'You are all going to regret this so much,' she warned him, because she had nothing else to say.

'I imagine you're bang on the money there,' Corcoran concurred. 'Mind you, it's too late to be having second thoughts now, but I'm sure Himself will find a way out of this.'

'He's gone mad,' she hissed. Poised in the doorway to her

latest prison, Che wrestled around to confront him, seeing his leather-clad shoulders rise and fall.

'And what manner of man hasn't said the same about his employer, once or twice?' was all Corcoran could offer before they propelled her inside. She heard a click – and saw that even the lock was new, bolted on to the solid Khanaphir door. She had to concede that she had clearly not done herself proud as a diplomat.

*Are ambassadors kidnapped on a regular basis? And what is the diplomatic response? Are you supposed to remain calmly polite and thank everyone for the personal service?*

The room they had put her in was located two storeys up, and they had not yet barred up the window. The opening was barely big enough for a Fly-kinden, though, which meant there would be no escape there. Scuff marks on the floor suggested that the Iron Glove had been using this as a storeroom, but now it was practically empty.

Someone else moved inside the room, and she froze, reaching automatically for the sword they had taken away from her. He had been standing by a desk in the corner of the room, small and still enough for her not to have noticed him.

'Trallo . . .' She heard the uncertainty in her own voice, on realizing he was no prisoner. A Fly-kinden could go in and out of that window as often as he pleased.

'Hello, Che,' he said, with an awkward look on his face, suggesting they had at last punctured his cheer. She gave herself a moment to rein in a temper that had been increasingly on its own recognizance of late.

'Just how many people,' she asked sharply, 'are paying you to "look after" me?'

He grimaced. 'Well, the thing is, you see . . . after that scuffle in the Marsh Alcaia, your Iron Glove fellow sent me a message, wanted to do business. Now, you know, in my line of work, you don't want a bad name with any of the big traders.' Seeing her darkening expression, he hurried on.

'And it was just . . . I was watching out for you anyway, and at the time it didn't seem that there'd be a problem about it.'

'I'm sure the shiny money blinded you to the obvious. And now?'

'And now I have what's known as a conflict of interests,' Trallo admitted. 'How was I to know that this Totho fellow would lose his mind so completely?'

Che stared out of the window. There was no crowd gathered yet, but it would only be a matter of time. It was not that she herself was so very important, but the sovereignty of their hosts had now been challenged. She knew how seriously they would take that. 'He's not mad,' she decided. 'I don't really know what he is, any more, but he's not mad.'

'Old friend of yours, he claimed.'

'He was, yes.' She thought about the man she had met after the Battle of the Rails, where it had still been possible to see her friend somewhere behind the scars that his recent history had scored across him. But the man she had met in Khanaphes had been all scars, and barely a hint left of the shy, awkward boy who had once helped her in her studies. *Have I done this to him, somehow? Or is it Stenwold's doing? We cannot leave the Empire with all the blame.*

She heard a rattle at the lock, and then they were around her again, bolting a grid across the window. This time she went with them without a struggle, accepting defeat. Trallo pattered along beside her, the Fly finally caught in the trap of his own diverse loyalties. She found she could muster scant sympathy, especially as he had taken her down with him.

They led her down one floor and into a long hall, where Totho was waiting with a dozen of his men.

'Now,' he addressed her, 'no more secrets.'

'Then tell me,' she said.

'I will, right now and, more than that, I'll make it a public proclamation.' He seemed on a knife-edge, as if waiting to see whether his carefully crafted project would succeed or fail. Out of everything about him, only that was painfully familiar. 'Come out onto the balcony with me,' he said.

'Totho . . .'

'No, no, let's . . .' He put on a smile. 'Let's – what do they say? – take the air? They're all out there now. The Empire, your people, lots of the locals.'

'I'm not surprised.'

'Neither am I, because it's what I wanted,' he told her. 'I've armoured this place up so that it's even given Amnon pause for thought, and now they're going to hear me out. And so are you. Come on, Che. You say you want to know what's going on? Now's your chance.'

*Who would have imagined any of this?* Looking over the gathering crowd, Thalric confessed to himself that he was surprised that some paltry Exalsee traders could achieve so much. Diplomatic history was being made. It was a tactic he might recommend to the Rekef: manufacture a common enemy and the world falls into your lap.

They were all here, that was his initial conclusion. Probably there were some people somewhere in Khanaphes who knew of Cheerwell Maker but had not turned out, but he could not think of any names. Her fellow Collegiates were here, of course. The three academics – old man, fat man and distant woman – were standing in a close-knit clump and looking worried. Separated from them by a pointed distance were the two Vekken ambassadors, who had arrived with their crossbows and their closed expressions. Near them was gathered the formal delegation from the Scriptora.

Ethmet himself had put in a personal appearance, together with at least a dozen of his fellow Ministers. They stood in their simple, one-shouldered robes like a gaggle of clerks, save for the respectful space that everyone else gave them. Behind them was the army, or that was how it looked to Thalric. Amnon had turned out the Royal Guard in their gilded scale mail, with their pointed shields, spears and bows. The big man was looking angry. What had happened here was a personal affront to his authority and, with perhaps a hundred men at his back, his authority was looking more and more sensitive to insult.

*Did the halfbreed know what he was asking for when he opened the door on this?* Thalric wondered. Looking at the way the Iron Glove had turned their factora into a fortress, he had to conclude that, yes, he had. *But why? Is the man so mad for Cheerwell Maker that he will see his entire delegation slaughtered?* Beyond the guardsmen were a mass of the ordinary Khanaphir, many holding staves or sickles or slings. Word of the outrage had gone quickly through the streets, no doubt tacitly encouraged by the Ministers.

*Any welcome for the Iron Glove has finally expired,* Thalric thought with satisfaction.

There was a silence falling on them now, a quiet focused on Ethmet, although he had made no sign. More soldiers were just arriving, who carried, slung between them, a bronze-shod tree-trunk. Appreciating the hush, they lowered it gratefully to the ground. Thalric eyed the reinforced door and decided the ram would burst it open after a dozen or twenty blows. He could see movement behind the metal-latticed windows, and knew the Iron Glove would be ready to defend themselves. There would be two prodigious bloodlettings, in Thalric's professional opinion: one to get the door open, and another inside once the horde of the Khanaphir began tearing every single Iron Glove man apart.

Up on the balcony that extended above the door, a handful of the Iron Glove emerged, bearing snapbows but keeping them low. The archers amongst the Khanaphir already had arrows to the string, just waiting for the command to draw.

Totho came forth next. Although most of those come to cause his ruin would not have recognized him, the sight of his armour, and the way his men deferred to him, singled him out. One of his men passed him a speaking horn, and Thalric felt a wrinkle of contempt for a man without a parade-ground voice.

Cheerwell was pushed out to stand next to him, looking angry and stubborn, and Thalric felt a twitch of relief to see her still alive. He had not expected otherwise, but still . . .

Totho coughed into the cone, the noise emerging garbled and tinny. 'Is everyone here?' he asked. His voice boomed back across the crowd, echoing from the walls across the street.

'Explain this!' Ethmet demanded, needing nothing but his own lungs. Thalric would not have thought the old man had it in him, but he would have made a fine drill sergeant. 'What is this insurrection? Have you declared war on the Masters of Khanaphes, O merchant? What is this barbarism?'

*And not just on Khanaphes,* Thalric thought, *but the Lowlands and the Empire, all in one. I would not have thought it possible to make so many enemies so swiftly.*

'You're owed an explanation,' Totho replied, and his voice, even amplified, was that of an awkward artificer trying to sound forceful. 'I will give it, but I wanted everyone to hear it. What I have to say is important.'

'Release the Collegiate ambassador,' Ethmet snapped back at him. 'We will listen to nothing until she is free.'

'She will be released,' Totho said. 'I won't hold her. I wanted her out of the hands of the Empire, that's all.'

'Do you make your merchant venture a sovereign state now?' Ethmet called. 'How do you dare meddle in the affairs of your betters? Release her!'

'Oh yes, we are ambitious, we in the Iron Glove,' said Totho, and his confidence was already building. 'You may not know, but Che here can fly. She can leave us right now.' He turned from the speaking horn to say something to Che, and Thalric saw her glance at the Iron Glove snapbowmen. Her wings flickered, putting her up on the very rail of the balcony.

‘Say what you have to say,’ she told Totho, loud enough for many of the crowd below to hear. Thalric saw another figure nip out to join her on the railing, and it took him a moment to recognize the Fly, Trallo. The sight gave him a slight edge of unease. *And what has that villain been doing with the Iron Glove? Had they captured him, for information about me?*

‘Thank you.’ Totho had returned to the horn. ‘As I say, I owe you an explanation. I beg you to hear me.’

‘Explain, and then gather yourselves to leave,’ Ethmet told him.

‘You have been deceived,’ Totho’s voice boomed out. ‘You are victims of your own generosity, O Ministers. You are betrayed by your very guests.’ There was a moment’s murmuring before Totho caught up with the crowd’s response. ‘I don’t mean *myself.* I don’t mean *this,*’ he said. ‘This is nothing, a moment’s misunderstanding, to be soon forgotten.’ He waited, letting the murmur die down. His eyes sought out Thalric.

‘There is an army marching on Khanaphes even as we speak,’ Totho declared. ‘An army of the Scorpion-kinden called the Many of Nem. Your enemies.’

There was a ripple of alarm through the crowd, but Amnon was having none of it. ‘So they come again?’ he roared out. ‘So let them come, and we shall beat them back, as we have before. Totho, we made you welcome here, and what are the Scorpion-kinden compared to the thing you have done?’

‘This is no army such as you have ever faced before,’ Totho said, forcing sincerity into his words, overstressing them. Thalric realized he must have rehearsed all this, must have written his own script for this confrontation. ‘These Scorpion-kinden possess new weapons, terrible weapons the like of which Khanaphes has never seen before. And why? Because they work for new masters. The Many of Nem now march under Imperial officers, and they wield

Imperial arms. The Empire has set them upon your city, while their own ambassadors lurk within your walls and speak of peace!'

It was unexpected enough that Thalric ran the words back through his mind before fully grasping them. By that time he realized that everyone was now staring at him, the lone Imperial representative in all that crowd. Che was looking at him, too, and he returned her gaze and shook his head.

'What nonsense!' he said, pitching his voice to carry across the whole crowd. 'There is no Imperial attack on Khanaphes. Why would we? We have no ambitions here.' He heard that old empty promise of the Empire on his lips, betrayed a hundred times. *But we have none, for what would we do with Khanaphes anyway? Give us ten years, and perhaps* . . . 'There is no attack or, if there is, then these Scorpions come of their own accord.' He felt slightly unsteady in his stomach, though. *And has there not been some piece missing, of all of this, ever since we arrived?* Still, it made no sense. There was no attack. He would know if there were. *They would tell me* . . .

'Send your scouts west!' Totho demanded. 'Or just wait a day, perhaps two, and you will not need my warnings. Perhaps your hunters and farmers can already see a dustcloud on the horizon. The Empire is nearing with its Scorpion tools, I swear to you – and knowing that, what plans might they have had for the Collegiate ambassador? What could I do but rescue her from their grasp?'

The crowd was in uproar. Some were already hurrying off, perhaps to seek out family or friends. Totho's words would be across all Khanaphes before morning. Ethmet's call for silence might have stilled them, but he did not give it. Instead, he was conferring with his fellow Ministers and then with Amnon. The Royal Guard stood uneasy, looking sidelong at each other, still under their rigid discipline.

Che stepped out from the balcony, letting her wings carry her to the ground. She landed in front of Thalric, in the suddenly widening space that had appeared about him.

'I swear,' he protested, 'I know nothing of any attack. There is no attack.' He found his heart racing. *They have me believing it now.*

Che studied him for a long time, enough to tell him about the distance that had re-opened between them. 'Those are two different things,' she said.

'Yes, yes, they are,' he admitted. 'I must speak with Marger and the others. There has been some mistake.'

'Why would Totho make such a claim, if it were not true?'

'To buy himself time, no doubt. Or perhaps the Scorpions are raiding, for truth, and he wishes to paint them in black and yellow?' Thalric shook his head. 'There is no attack. I will speak with my people—'

'Ambassador Thalric.' Amnon appeared, abruptly looming at his side.

Thalric looked up at him. 'I need to return to my embassy—'

'You must first speak with the Ministers. They require assurances.' There was no hint of a request in Amnon's tone. Thalric cast a desperate look at Che: *Trust me.* There was no sign of trust in her face, though. *And I have given her enough cause to doubt me, over the years.*

He let his shoulders sag. 'Lead me,' he told Amnon, and fought down the urge to look back at her, as he went.

Che watched him go, biting at her lip. She felt strangely wretched for Thalric, and on the back of that came the thought: *I believe him. For once in his lying life, I actually believe him. He has been out-danced by his own people.*

She had to go to the embassy. She had to talk to Berjek and the others, who were even now being ushered back to safety there. This was, of all things, a diplomatic situation, but she had no idea what she, as ambassador, was supposed to do.

*Come to us.*

She stopped in mid-step. She was aware that, on the

balcony above, Totho's people were talking to him, fast and all at once. He was trying to look her way, but he had kicked the wasps' nest, and now he had to deal with the consequences.

*Cheerwell Maker, hear us.*

It was not words. It was a feeling, an intense feeling washing over her like an unexpected tide. It came from all about her, from beneath her, from the very stones of Khanaphes.

*Come to us.*

She could not, of course. She had her duties now, whatever they might be. There were the scholars to take care of. There was Totho. There was Thalric.

*Come to us, Cheerwell Maker.*

She felt herself fading, drifting . . . the city around her losing focus. *Like the Fir.* But she had consumed no drug and still she felt the ghosts of ancient Khanaphes all around her. The walls swam, their idiot hieroglyphs abruptly thrusting their meanings at her, shouting at her from every wall, some of them couched in sense, some in gibberish.

*Come!*

She turned and walked away, but not towards the embassies. She turned and walked away, and was soon lost in the city.

His men had been picked for their ability to fly long and far. They had stopped for a few scant hours since leaving the Scorpion horde, making such time across the desert that the towering column of dust, the great battle-standard of the Many of Nem, had long been lost behind them. Now Sulvec of the Rekef had found Khanaphes.

*And what a wretched place I've found.* Sulvec was a major in the Rekef Inlander, by definition an ambitious man who fed his ambition any which way. This assignment would be the making of him: he would become Colonel Sulvec on his return, or not return at all. Like so many who climbed the Rekef ladder, his loyalty to the ideals of the Empire at large had been burned away by the duties he had been given. Now his loyalty was to his own advancement, in the sure knowledge that only the Rekef could reward him as he desired, and no other would punish him so hard if he failed.

*And General Brugan met with me in person to give me this mission.* Sulvec had been startled, at first, but he had long since ceased to question his assignments. It was not his place to act as moral arbiter. He was the hand of the Rekef, and that was all the sense of righteousness he needed.

He spared a thought for bumbling Hrathen, playing barbarian warlord with the Scorpion-kinden. He would do his work well enough, for he had been given the tools and he had just enough rough charisma to keep the savages pointed in the right direction. *So much effort for such a little thing*, Sulvec considered. *There must have been simpler ways.* He supposed that the Scorpion assault would serve other purposes, too, that perhaps the Empire might even genuinely want to assess the Many as shock troops, useful Auxillians for the future. *We will probably have to kill Hrathen, though: he grows too fond of his role.*

His third Rekef assignment had been to spy on a friend, to bring the man in and interrogate him about the Broken Sword cult. He had drunk himself into a stupor for a week, after that. Thenceforth, when the Rekef had sent him out for any task, he had been ready. Thenceforth, the lives of others had been just pieces to be moved or removed, as policy demanded.

He circled over the city, looking for the mark. His men had been ensconced in a farmhouse beyond the walls, sufficiently distant to avoid notice. The sky over Khanaphes was so clear, and he was the only human being in it. Nobody below would be looking up except his compatriots.

He saw the black and yellow flag singling out the roof of a large building. He made his swift descent, coming down on the roof's edge, between two statues of Woodlouse-kinden. Seeing no watchers, he dropped down to the balcony below and slipped inside.

It was a mere two minutes later that he had them assembled: three Wasps and a Beetle-kinden, representing the Rekef Outlander's presence in Khanaphes. A lean Wasp-kinden stepped forward, eyeing him with suspicion. 'I'm Captain Marger. I'm in charge here.'

'Are you indeed?' Sulvec replied, handing over his sealed orders, which Marger accepted reluctantly. There was a moment's pause before the man broke the seal, as though he was feeling out the future through the parchment. His shoulders rose and fell, and then he cracked the paper open. His eyes flicked over the few words there, checked the brief identifying sketch of Sulvec's face, noted the signatory.

'Says here we're at your command, Major,' Marger observed without inflection, handing back the paper. 'You've got commands?'

'I'm calling you out of cover, first,' Sulvec told them. 'From now you are no longer a diplomatic mission. You are soldiers of the Rekef. Now, who should I be giving orders to?'

Marger looked at the others, shrugged again, took a backwards step. The Beetle-kinden pushed forward and saluted. 'Corolly Vastern, Captain-Auxillian,' he rumbled. 'This is Vollen, this is Gram. I'm ranking Rekef Inlander here. What's going on?'

'Where's Major Thalric, first of all?' Sulvec asked.

'Diplomatic duties,' Corolly said. 'There was an attack on this embassy.' One thick thumb indicated the broad bruise across his face. 'He's been in with the natives for hours now, but he got a message out to us, and it made interesting reading.' The Beetle's eyes were suspicious. 'It's being claimed that we're attacking Khanaphes, sir. Using the local Scorpion-kinden.'

*And how did that news outreach me?* Sulvec already had his suspicions. 'Consider it fact, Captain,' he said. 'We have one official duty left to perform in this building, and after that we resort to stealth procedures. We will soon not be welcome in this city.'

They exchanged glances, none of them happy about it, but none of them about to say so.

'So what's the one duty, sir?' Corolly asked, expressionless.

Sulvec smiled like a knife. 'Tell me, when's Thalric expected back?'

# Twenty-Seven

'We've left it too late,' Faighl observed, watching the idle movements of the camp around them. 'We should have moved yesterday.'

Meyr said nothing for a long time. The Scorpions of the Many of Nem were just going about their normal evening business after another swift day's travel. By Meyr's guess they would be on Khanaphir territory before midday next morning. Farms would burn. The city would be readying its forces. *And I have bought them a few days, if the message was passed on, and if they listened.* It was a matter of supreme indifference to him, for he owed the Khanaphir nothing. He knew only that there was an Iron Glove presence within the city, and therefore the Glove should know of this development.

They had stayed on, accompanying the Scorpion horde, for that sole reason. He had wanted to gather as much information as he could, before they pulled out and made their exit. Now he was forced to agree with Faighl. They had left it too late.

It was not the Scorpions themselves, for nothing had changed in their restless, aggressive manner. They were quick, abrupt in their preparations, as they unfolded tents and unloaded their pack beasts or sharpened weapons. Some were training with crossbows, shooting at old shields propped on stones. The leadshotters that had sounded like practised thunder last night were still hitched in trains to the Imperial automotives. It was within the Imperial camp that the change was visible.

Meyr had seen the looks their halfbreed commander had been directing towards the Iron Glove. At first it had just been because the Glove was competition for whatever scheme the Empire had in mind. Then it had been because Meyr himself was a deserter, a runaway slave. Now it had boiled down, under the sun of the march, into something more concrete. The Empire would brook no interference here. Any outside influence would have to be excised from within the Many of Nem. Meyr understood that, yet he and the others had lingered. Lingered too long.

'Gather everyone,' Meyr instructed at last. 'Armour and weapons.'

'Will it do any good?' Faighl asked him, as one of the others ran off to spread the word. 'We're only eight, so even if the Scorpions don't get involved . . .'

Meyr shrugged massively, letting his pack slide off his shoulders with a scrape of metal. 'What else is there?' he asked. The thought of it was hard, that Faighl and the others would all die. He, Meyr, might also die, it seemed possible. The others would be dead for certain.

*If we had only left yesterday?* But he was not sure they would have been allowed to go. They had survived this long by moving as the Scorpions moved, by not raising a ripple against the current. To leave, or to be discovered in clandestine flight, would be seen only as an invitation to these violent people. It would be the excuse they were always waiting for, with outsiders, or even with their own.

He began to unpack his armour. It was a splendid suit. They had cast it for him specially to see if it could be done, to see if the principles underlying the Glove's new mail could be scaled up in size to armour-plate a giant. His spade-nailed fingers began securing buckles as big as a normal man's hand. Around him, with surreptitious professionalism, the other Iron Glove were putting on their own steel, breastplates and helms over reinforced leather. They were assembling snapbows and checking the weapons' action. Meyr himself had a shield large enough to serve the Imperial leader as a coffin lid, and an axe that put the Scorpion halberds to shame.

'Coming now,' Faighl hissed the warning.

Meyr patiently buckled his greaves, sensing his people form a rough semicircle before him, weapons at the ready. He could feel, through the parched ground, the approach of the Imperial contingent, and he reckoned on about a dozen of them. The numbers would count only at the beginning, though, as they were about to light a spark in a firepowder keg.

He stood up, rising from amongst his followers, and saw the Imperials falter for a moment, just a moment, at the sight of this great dark-armoured monster. He had become a colossus of dark steel, a machine of destruction. He now saw that there were closer to fifteen Wasps, mostly dressed in Slave Corps uniforms, of bitter memory. They were lightly armoured, with the short Imperial stabbing swords and a few crossbows, and almost all of them had one hand free: Wasps never lacked for weapons. In their centre was the halfbreed, that bastard mix of Scorpion and Empire, who now gazed up at Meyr and put a smile onto his malformed jaw.

The forces were not so very uneven, after all. The Wasps had the advantage of numbers, whereas the Iron Glove equipped its adherents with more care. Scorpions all around them had stopped to watch, eager to see some blood shed before nightfall.

The Wasps were professional soldiers, veterans of battles and skirmishes and brawls. The Iron Glove handful was a mix of mercenaries and merchants, trained but not nearly so well blooded.

Meyr took a deep breath. 'Ready bows,' he instructed.

'Behind and above!' Faighl cried out, and even as she got the words out, Meyr felt something punch into the small of his back.

He felt a brief moment of warmth as the Wasp sting boiled away off the ridges of his armour. 'Eyes front!' he bellowed, for the fight was upon them.

Two of his people went down instantly, distracted by the Wasp stings from behind and then shot from the front. There were at least three Wasps on the ground in return, lanced through with snapbow bolts that cared nothing for armour. The halfbreed leader shouted out a command and then they were moving in close with their swords.

Faighl placed her back to Meyr's, sniping up at one of the airborne Wasps and bringing him down with a single shot, trusting to the giant to guard her from the main assault. The Mole Cricket leant out over the heads of his followers, snapping his great axe forward with all the length and strength of his arm. The heavy head of it caught a Wasp slaver in the chest before the man even realized he was within Meyr's reach. Ribs snapped like sticks and his suddenly limp body was swept sideways into the next man, living and dead tumbling over in a tangle of limbs.

A couple of the Iron Glove had got their shields in place before the Wasps hit them. One was a Solarnese artificer, a hammer in his other hand making a slaver's helm ring before a sword jabbed up over the shield's rim and caught the artificer in the throat. The other shieldman was a renegade Maynesh Ant, who held firm. His shortsword never ventured forth but he danced left and right with his shield, successfully holding off three Wasps as they tried to overrun him. When they pushed him back, Meyr's thundering axe hacked into them, lopping the head clean off one man and forcing the other two to stumble back.

*This will not last another minute*: the unhappy knowledge came to Meyr with certainty. He had lost near half his people already. The Wasps were spreading out around them, while more were taking to the air. Flexibility and mobility had always been the Imperial way, in battle and in skirmish.

He felt Faighl die, the woman slamming against him, head rebounding from the small of his back. A moment was all he could spare to mourn her. He felt he had barely known her, although they had worked together for months. A sword-blow was turned by his legplates, a sting coursed across his shield.

The Ant-kinden before him reeled away. The halfbreed Imperial had hold of him, one clawed arm hooked over his shield. The other hand, empty, rose as if to stab down at the man's exposed face, but then fire bloomed from it, snapping the Ant's head back. Meyr roared and hacked at the enemy with his axe, but the halfbreed dived and rolled out of the way, and abruptly it was all over. They had now pulled away to form a circle out of his reach, and at his feet, Meyr saw his fellows.

The Wasps had killed them all in less than a minute. Faighl and the others, loyal servants of the Iron Glove, they had not stood a chance. Meyr glowered now at the Wasps, at their halfbreed leader. He saw more than that. He looked beyond them at the Scorpions, all lovingly fingering their spears and knives. The blood and the violence had been like food and drink to them.

With the bodies of his followers strewn at his feet, he met the gaze of the halfbreed. The man was smiling slightly, and Meyr tensed for a gesture, the smallest sign that would signal the attack.

Instead, the man grinned openly as he stepped back three paces, letting a Scorpion pass him to his left, and another to his right. All his men kept widening their half-circle, until it was the Many of Nem that Meyr faced, and not the Empire. The Scorpions all wore the same hateful smile as their half-caste cousin. Step by step they closed in on the giant, pausing just out of the reach of his axe.

*So, we are weak, in their eyes.* Meyr found, belatedly, that he despised them. They had signed themselves over to the Empire, and they did not even know it.

One of them hurled a spear, almost without warning. Meyr got his shield up, felt the strength of the missile rattle against the aviation steel. Something else, perhaps a hand-axe, rebounded from his pauldron, striking from behind.

They came for him then. Without a war cry, with nothing but a glitter of raised weapons, they descended like ravenous beasts.

'I spit on you all,' Meyr roared at them, and then let himself fall into the earth.

That night, around the fires, Jakal came to find Hrathen. She crouched beside him, one sharp elbow knocking a Wasp slaver away and clearing a space. She did not spare the unseated man a glance.

'You are very clever, Of-the-Empire,' she began.

'Am I?' he said, carefully neutral. Her presence, suddenly so close, had fired his pulse a little. *Is it that I genuinely admire her, or simply because I cannot have her?* he asked himself.

'Walk with me, great conqueror,' she said, standing again. 'We will talk of your deeds.'

*It is because she challenges me,* he thought. *She cares nothing for rank, nothing for the Empire. She is the pure savage, and she would cut my throat in a moment – will do so, when I am no longer of use.*

And the thought came back, *And she would do the same with any other here, and so I am one of them.* It was bittersweet, that thought. The Rekef in him jeered at it, but that part of him whose actions had seen him brought in for treason, that man understood. He launched himself to his feet and followed her off into the dark.

'What would you hear of my deeds, O Warlord?' he asked her, trying to match her tone. Away from the fires, he could not see her face clearly but he knew she was smiling.

'I shall tell you of them. You are a cunning creature,

Of-the-Empire. You knew that the giant would escape my people.'

He shrugged. 'I was a slaver for the Empire. You learn about the Art of the lesser races. I knew that some of his kinden could walk within the earth.'

'How do you ever keep them enslaved?' she asked.

'Many don't have the Art. Most have kin that don't. For every runaway, every act of rebellion, we punish those we still have.' He spread his clawed hands. 'That man bought his freedom with the blood of his people. He's unusual. They're clannish, the Mole Crickets, and most of them just offer their backs to the lash and get on with their work.'

She gave a brief laugh. 'So your generosity gave the giant to my people.'

'And if they had killed him, they'd have thanked me,' Hrathen said. 'And if we'd gone for him and he'd escaped, we'd look weak. Do you disapprove?'

'No. I love cleverness. There are chieftains stronger than I, more skilled, more savage, but none is more clever, Of-the-Empire, remember that.'

'Must you call me that?' He surprised himself with the complaint. It was a weakness, to seek to avoid the name, but it jabbed him like a stone in his boot every time she used it. Perhaps it had surprised her, too, for she paused, appearing nothing but a darkness within the night. He sensed her staring back at him.

'What else am I to call you? That is all you are, to me: you are the Empire's halfbreed hand.' She sat down, looking back at the fires, at the hasty tents of her people. 'So tell me, Of-the-Empire, tell me of yourself – if there is more than that.'

He joined her carefully, within arm's reach of her. Now that his eyes were growing used to the dark, he saw how the distant wash of the oil flames gave her pale skin the faintest touch of blue fire.

'I was a slaver for a long time, working the Silk Road

mostly,' he said. 'Then I was a Rekef man, keeping an eye on the slavers. It looked like that was all I'd ever be, travelling up and down the Dryclaw with the Scorpion-kinden—'

'I know of them,' she interrupted dismissively. 'The tame ones, we call them.'

He digested that, nodding. 'Then the war came,' he continued. 'War with the Lowlands. First strike was against an Ant city-state off the Silk Road, an army moving through the desert to get there. Throwing money at the Scorpions to act as guides. Suddenly I was important: the Rekef were leaning on me, wanting the Scorpions this place or that.'

'And who did you betray?' she asked, keen as a razor, enough to make him pause for one second, thinking: *Is she Rekef? Is this the reckoning for me, here and now?*

'To run with your kinden, even the "tame ones", one must live like you, share your values,' he explained. 'When the time came that they seized on the hand that fed them, I did not restrain them. Perhaps they could not have been restrained, anyway. Imperial supplies began disappearing. It was only a matter of time. If they hadn't gone on to hatch this plan, I'd be on crossed pikes by now.'

'Yes, this plan.' After that she was silent for a long time and, although he opened his mouth to speak several times, he could not find the words.

Eventually she sighed. 'Your Empire thinks us stupid,' she said, and then, 'I had the omens read, today, from the blood spilt on the sand.'

He had nothing to say to that, so he waited for her to elaborate.

'The haruspex told me that we would advance like the desert wind, that we would break the walls of Khanaphes and scourge them from the city's streets.'

'That sounds a good omen.'

'Does it?'

He gave her time to explain but she said nothing, and her melancholy was now infecting him. Eventually he said,

'I don't . . . we don't have omens and such in the Empire. Even amongst the Dryclaw tribes. I don't know what you mean.'

She laughed softly. 'Oh, the desert storm is a terrible thing, but where does it go to, when the wind is blown out? When the sand has settled again, where shall we be? The world is changing, Of-the-Empire. The Khanaphir do not realize it, and so they will be destroyed, but the world is changing. As for us, what do we build? What do we craft, save weapons? What do we create? And now we have your Empire to our north, and we look upon the tame ones and we can see our future. How long will it be before the Nem is no longer ours to rule? Perhaps I am the very last who can truly call herself the Warlord of the Many.'

He said nothing to this, because he could deny none of it.

'But in these last days we are strong,' she said, and with that she had banished her mood back to where it could not be heard or seen. 'And if the grave-marker of my people shall be the ruin of Khanaphes, so be it. Let them look upon those broken walls and know that once the Nem was free.' He saw the faintest movement of her face turning to him with its distant phosphorescence. 'You will never be one of us, Of-the-Empire, but I think you will never be of the Empire either. Men like you are cast simply for moments when the desert storm strikes. And then they are cast away. And then cast away, remember that.'

Next morning found Hrathen out of sorts, Jakal's words still echoing faintly inside his head. All around him the war-host of the Many was mobilizing, buckling on their armour and forming into their mobs. Their cavalry was already harnessed and ready. Riders with long lances sat in offset saddles strapped on to great scorpions that had been plated with armour, clattering forth with claws agape and stings raised high. Lesser beasts were put in pairs or fours to draw the Nemian chariots with their jagged-hubbed wheels, each beast with its outer claw sheathed in metal, like a shield. The chariots were traditional, light, chitin-built things for shock assaults, but now, behind the charioteer, they carried two crossbowmen apiece.

The great mass of the host went on foot, and it surged and quarrelled and milled as it formed up into marching order. There was a discord to them that he had not witnessed before: someone had drawn lines and boundaries about their naturally chaotic exuberance. That someone was Hrathen himself. While once they had all been warriors, now he had sieved them, divided them. Some of them were checking over the leadshotters, now drawn by animal carts and the Imperial automotives. Some carried their crossbows, standing distinctly apart from the rest. Others were simple soldiers with greatsword and halberd and axe. There was barely a shield amongst them, these hard, close-quarters traditionalists. Their place would be to bleed for the Nem when the battle was joined.

These were a people who possessed little, and put it all into their wars. Metal was not so scarce in the desert, for they melted down the wealth of past ages, from the Nem's ruined cities, to make their sword blades and axe heads. They scavenged armour of a dozen different styles then stretched and mauled it to fit their larger frames. Wood was harder to find, but they hunted the desert locusts, in their season, for the strong chitin shafts of their legs. A thousand insects had been trapped and killed to make hafts for the forest of halberds that Hrathen saw waving and weaving amid the host's advance guard.

'It makes you laugh, really, doesn't it?'

Hrathen turned to see the engineer, Angved, who had been busy these last few days, working with his picked artillerists. He might not like his students, but Hrathen could not fault him on his duty.

'Why laugh?' Hrathen asked him.

'The old and the new,' Angved said. 'You know, among these people, two in three aren't even Apt.' His lip curled in derision. 'They'd make the worst of slaves, back in the Empire, strong backs and nothing else. It didn't matter to them before, though – they didn't know any better. Then we turn up with a job lot of crossbows, and we make a warrior elite out of the best of them.'

'You've yet to say anything amusing.' The engineer's words were close enough to Hrathen's own thoughts to make him surly.

Angved cocked an eyebrow. 'Well, think about it. Who are the Inapt kinden that we're familiar with? Spiders, Moth-kinden, Grasshoppers. Not one of them that could go a day in full armour without collapsing from it. Thin and delicate, the lot of them. And yet with these lads, it's the Apt that get the decent jobs. Your host of bolt-fodder out there, with their swords and pikes, they're your Inapt. And they'll die, battle after battle, until it's only the Apt left of them. You reckon that's how it was with us, way back?'

Hrathen stared at him. 'You're quite the philosopher, suddenly.'

Angved shrugged. 'We're making a new nation here, sir. We've taken a rabble of monsters that was no use to anyone, and we've put a mirror to it, and made a kind of mockery of the Imperial army. All we need to do is paint them black and yellow, and they're ours.'

'And is that your brief?'

'Mine?' The grey-haired engineer laughed at that. 'I'm just an engineer, sir. I just have an inquiring mind, and I see the future, here. We've discovered the great natural resource of this desolate waste. We've struck the richest lode of Auxillian soldiers you could ever want to find. We just need to break their pride enough so that the Empire can put a foot on their necks. And it'll happen – not today, maybe not in this generation, but it will.'

Angved seemed to find all this reflection a cause for

humour, but his words felt like lead to Hrathen. 'Go look to the siege engines,' he snapped. 'I want them ready for a field battle, not just to assault the walls.'

Implacable, Angved saluted and strolled off.

*Is he Rekef?* was the instant thought, and it was not the first time Hrathen had considered it. The artillerist would make a good watcher, someone Hrathen could not dispense with. Sulvec need not be the only sneak on this mission.

The Many of Nem were all ready now, proving Angved right as they made formations that looked like a child's sketches of Imperial battle order. Hrathen strode towards the automotives, aware of all eyes resting upon him. The Scorpions saw him as an outcast, as a foreigner, but also as a warrior, as a provider of this golden opportunity. They would follow him for now, and they would tear him to pieces if he failed them.

*Then let their claws rend me now.* But he stopped by the lead automotive and looked back towards them. *If this is to be the last flowering of the Many of Nem, then let them go to it gloriously.* They were not his people, but then he had never had a people, so they would do.

Without warning, Jakal was there beside him. She vaulted up on to the automotive's footplate and directed her spear ahead. 'Ruin!' Her voice sang clear out over the throng. 'Ruin and dust on the Khanaphir!' Hrathen saw her tusks bared in a mad grin, visible beneath the lip of her helm, her lithe body held straight and proud as she clung to the automotive's rungs, the spear thrust forward like destiny. 'Let the Jamail run red! Let us dam it with their corpses! Onward to Khanaphes!'

Watching her, as the automotives growled and rumbled, and were drowned out by the roaring of the war host, Hrathen felt his heart leap, wanting her as he had never wanted a woman before. He hauled himself up beside her as the machine began to surge forward, and she turned to look at him with flashing eyes.

He looked behind, to see the barren landscape crawling dark with the great mass of Scorpion-kinden and their beasts. *Ruin and dust*, he echoed, *and curse the future.*

The dust was bitter in his mouth as he trudged on through the wasteland, heading eastward, ever eastward. Meyr's people possessed a solid endurance, such as had endeared them to the Empire's slavemasters, but by now he was ready to drop. Sheer stubbornness alone kept him stomping on towards the river Jamail and the city of Khanaphes.

The journey through the earth had been taxing enough. It was an Art hard-learned, and draining to use. He had clawed blindly through the sand and grit, the compacted strata of the dust of centuries, and through the bones of rock beneath, as if swimming through the earth's very body. In grindingly slow sweeps of his massive limbs, he had dragged his way out from under the Scorpion camp. Then, feeling his strength failing, he had struggled for the surface, hauling himself hand over hand from the solid darkness into the light.

He had still been within sight of the Scorpion fires, so he had made pitifully little progress, for all his exertions. He could not rest, either. There was a long way to travel.

His shield and axe had been abandoned within the earth, deep within the rock where they would never be found again. He considered abandoning his armour, too, but they had made it for him especially. It had been the armoursmiths' greatest challenge, to adapt their designs to his mighty frame. It barely slowed him, anyway, and, more to the point, he did not feel that he had the reserves of mental strength to undo all the buckles.

So he had set forth, away from the Scorpions, with a slow and deliberate tread. Some uncounted hours later, he had observed the sun rising, and adjusted his aim to where the landscape first lit up red. It had been a cool night, the breezes from the distant sea treacherous with their promises. The sun, even while still low in the sky, had banished all that, beginning to roast him with its infinite patience.

*We are not a people made for this.* The Mole Cricket-kinden could toil in the earth for hours without complaint, but they had never been built to travel. He had long since stopped listening to the muscles of his legs. Their complaints had nothing new to tell him. He had retreated into some small part of his mind, focused on nothing save the horizon.

And it was all futile, he knew. He did not look behind him any more. He had already seen the great wall of dust that the Many of Nem were stirring up ahead of them. They were fresh, fierce and anxious to taste the blood of their enemies. They would easily overhaul a poor Mole Cricket lost in the desert. If he was lucky then their natural bloodlust would see them kill him in the moment of finding him: he knew them well enough to expect worse if he fell into their taloned hands alive.

*I have regrets.* His people were close-mouthed and inward-looking: even among their own kind, they said little. Perhaps there was little needing to be said. *I should have let the Wasps kill me there in the camp.* But the will to survive was deep-entrenched. Even another hour of life, even another hour of crawling through this barren, loveless land, was life enough. *We are so tenacious, and for what?*

His people were philosophers of a sort, but their philosophy was a fragmented thing. Few in number, slow to act, seldom roused to passion, they had been slaves in the Days of Lore, and they had been slaves ever since. Mere strength, sufficient to shatter stone and bend steel, was powerless against the imprisoning chains of history.

Something passed overhead, only a shadow on the earth to indicate it. He felt almost relieved: *They have me, then.* He had wondered if the Imperials would send scouts out after him. Perhaps they were not even looking for him at all, but simply flying ahead to see what defences Khanaphes had prepared. It mattered not, either way, for word would return to the host and then they would send out some cavalry, perhaps, to run him down.

He trudged on. He would not make their task easier, even if such resistance accounted for only a hundred yards more of effort for them.

There was something ahead. He heard the movement: the creak of harness and chitin. *Already, then?* There must have been other scouts earlier, whose shadows he had missed. Abruptly something went out of him, that guttering spark that had driven him so far, and he stopped. For a moment he swayed, his body thrown out of its plodding rhythm. Then his legs gave way, and he fell to his knees.

*Make it quick*, was all Meyr could think.

'Hey, big man, no time for that,' he heard a voice say – neither the clipped Imperial accents nor the mangled, mumbled Scorpion speech. He forced his head up against the brightness of the sun, and started at what he saw.

There were three great beetles on the ridge ahead of him: black-bodied things with their bulbous abdomens held high, their long legs as awkward and stilt-like as scaffolding. They twitched their mouthparts and antennae, lifting their feet off the hot ground in careful sequence. Each was saddled and harnessed, and each with a Khanaphir rider: two men and a woman in scale armour, bow and lance scabbarded beside their saddles.

'Come on, Meyr, have you looked behind you?'

That voice again. Meyr tilted his head and this time saw the tiny figure of Tirado, his messenger. The Fly nodded urgently and flitted off towards the beetles. With a supreme effort, Meyr got to his feet and craned his head back in the direction he had come.

The western horizon was a single wall of dust. He even thought he could make out the dots of the Scorpion vanguard.

'Meyr, we haven't got all day!' Tirado shouted and, with

infinite weariness, the Mole Cricket stumbled towards the waiting animals.

There was no complaint from the beast as he hauled his huge body on to its back, just a patient redistribution of its feet to take the additional weight. Then the three riders were urging their animals round, heading back east towards the city with a rapid, skittering gait, bringing news that the war host of the Many of Nem was in sight.

# Twenty-Eight

There had been no easy answers forthcoming. The Ministers of Khanaphes had put question after question to him until, at the last, he had realized that they just would not *believe* him.

Thalric paused on the steps of the Scriptora, looking at the stepped pyramid that dominated the square ahead of him. At its top was poised that maddeningly asymmetrical ring of statues, frozen in their dance. It seemed that they smiled mockingly at him, from their barren, perfect faces. He had a strong urge to just sit down, right there, and put his head in his hands. He had a stronger urge, however, to seek out Che and try to make her, at least, believe him. He needed someone's belief, and his own was a washed-out, faded colour, after all the questioning. *Could it be that they told me, and that I somehow didn't notice? Could a planned invasion have passed me by somewhere in the minutiae of my briefing?*

They had not asked him whether Totho's claims were actually true. They had not even bothered with that preamble. Instead they had gone straight to probing him for details of the attacking force. They had wondered by what means the Empire had spurred the Many of Nem on to this act. They had enquired how long the Empire had been in contact with the Scorpions, what degree of control the Empress had over them. At no time had they left enough space for his denials.

Most of the time, he had just shaken his head. 'I have no knowledge of this,' he had stated, over and over. They had nodded sagely, those bald-headed men and women in severe robes, and their scribes had written all of it down.

They had conferred together: he remembered acutely the sound of their quiet, polite voices. Then they had come back to sit before him again, some score of Ministers, with Ethmet at their head, and they had asked him, in so many words, the exact same questions again. Their patience was infinite, their manner told him. Again he had made his disclaimers. The Empire had no such plans, he assured them. He, as the Empire's ambassador, would surely know of any such intention. If the Scorpions were coming, it was without any mandate from the Empress.

They had made no threats, had not even raised their voices. He had been free to leave at any time, save for the bonds of his ambassadorial duty, which kept him there as if bound by steel chains. He had begun to experience the despair of the man who knows nothing, faced with the questioner who does not believe him.

It had been hours before they had finally, and for no obvious reason, lost interest in him. Even then they had suggested that he remain available for any other further questions they might think of.

He had no idea where Che might have gone, meanwhile. She might be holed up with the Iron Glove, for all he knew. The entire Collegium delegation might have left the city. Worst of all, he had no idea, here on the steps of the Scriptora, if there really was a Scorpion army at the gates.

*I must find Che.* That was a traitorous thought because what he *must* do, without question, was make his report. This was Imperial business: the name of the Empire had been sullied. *Or else the Empire's designs have been exposed.* He no longer knew which. The relentless questioning had stripped him of any certainty he might have possessed.

*I must find Che.*

It was only a small detour, surely. To step through into the Place of Foreigners and turn left to the Moth-fronted embassy, and not right towards the building guarded by stone Woodlouse-kinden. It would require only a moment's disloyalty.

*And if she doesn't believe me, either?* It seemed more than likely. He had not exactly given her any reason to trust his unevidenced word.

*And why do I care?* His instinctive response had grown rather stale now. *I care because she is a clumsy, naive, foolish Beetle-kinden girl, yet her regard matters to me. Because I find her company easier than that of my own kind. At least with her, I do not feel the knife at my back every moment.* He doubted that she felt the same way.

His shoulders slumped, as he set off down the steps for the archway leading to the embassies. *I have only ever had one virtue, and that one so often pawned as to have become near-worthless. Still, I used to pride myself on my loyalty. Therefore I shall make my report.*

Something made him pause, as he passed through the arch: his Rekef senses had not quite left him yet. Some part of him, though overlaid now with uncertainty, was still living behind enemy lines. The quiet of the garden – the stillness of the pool – was an illusion. He found his fingers twitching, baring his palms by purest instinct.

He saw them then, two shadows of the evening standing near the Collegiate embassy. They were like statues, or the shadows of statues, dark instead of pale marble. They watched him, and he watched them back, ready to use the archway as cover if they were assassins come after him. Some small and detached part of him thought, as he hesitated, *Is this the way of things now, for me? Will it be assassins for breakfast? Will I wake to them each morning? Is that what it means to be Regent? I would rather live the life of a spy. At least spies sleep well sometimes.*

He was no Fly-kinden or Spider, possessed of good

night-eyes, but the light of the sunset still greyed the west sufficiently, and it told him enough about their build and stance to identify them as Ant-kinden. *The Vekken, of course.*

He had no wish to have any dealings with the Vekken, for a number of reasons. Their customary stare of absolute antipathy was born of their city's isolation, and its recent history with the Empire. It was not usually *personal.* On the other hand, if they knew that it had been his word that had prompted them into their disastrous assault on Collegium, then he had no doubt that they would kill him.

The sight of them brought back a great deal that he could have done without, just then. He remembered the neatly soulless city of Vek. Perhaps to a native it had seemed bustling with cheer. He did not believe it. The sole impression he had received was one of cold pride exemplifying all that was Ant-kinden and honed to a brittle edge.

He remembered their general boasting of her army, as it had marched past in its perfect ranks. What came to him, across the bloody stretch of intervening time, was a colossal arrogance. Such fierce and overweening confidence they had then possessed, such joy in their anticipated victory: a city of soldiers making war on a city of scholars. *And they had lost.* He had been, at that point, in no position to appreciate Collegium's victory, but the details had come to him later, as they would come to any competent spymaster. Collegium had won because of its own unique virtues: ingenuity and allies. Vek had lost because of its bankruptcy on either front.

Thalric's lips were pursed tight He had been in no position to cheer the victors, because he had left the Vekken camp by then. His mind recalled with perfect clarity the severing of the ties that had bound him to the Empire. They had not been cleanly cut, either, but crudely hacked until they parted, the blade running red. Even the thought made his side twinge, a relic of the old wound that Daklan had given him, the scar that bore mute testimony to when he should have died.

*Would the world be a better or worse place, I wonder.* His bleak thoughts would not leave him. A lot of the man he had once been had died on the point of Daklan's knife. He had been so loyal, and every atrocity that his hands had worked had been justified by the cause he served. He found that he was frightened by the man he had once been. *If I met him, that burning idealist, I would kill him if I could. Far too dangerous to let him live.*

He thought too much, these days.

The Vekken had clearly come to some decision, under his silent scrutiny. They made a quick exit by the passage alongside the embassy, vanishing from his sight, if not his thoughts. He made no attempt at pinning a motive on them. Ant-kinden were all mad, he decided: living constantly in each other's heads could not be healthy. He had never met any Ant-kinden, of any city, that he had actually liked.

He turned aside for the Imperial embassy. *And why the Woodlouse-kinden at the door? Do they mock us with our own slaves?* The statues reminded him of Gjegevey, one of the Empress's favourite tools. That brought a whole new fleet of grim thoughts into port. He realized, standing before the heavy-lidded stone stare of the Woodlice, that he had no idea where his life was going now. He had lost hold of it. He had rejoined the Empire, but it had not let him back in. He did not understand it any more.

'Thalric!' A hoarse whisper.

He recoiled from the Woodlice statues, took three long steps away from the embassy, eyes raking the gloom.

'Thalric! Here!'

The stand of trees, with its burden that had so appalled Osgan, was hissing at him. He was frozen, old instincts rusty, trying to pierce the shadows between them with his gaze.

He discerned the paleness of the Mantis statue, but there was something dark lurking at its base. He had his hands palm-outwards as he approached, but they dropped back to his sides once he saw what it was. He walked over to the very trees, and leant in further, peering down.

He could not imagine what it must have cost the man, to come here. It was not just the wound – Osgan's face was pale and sweaty with it – but the fear. He had forced himself to crawl in among these trees until he sat at the very feet of the Mantis statue. He was resolutely facing away from it, and yet every part of him aware of it.

'What are you doing?' Thalric demanded, despairingly. 'You shouldn't even be up yet. Is it so important to get to a taverna that you'd kill yourself for it?'

Osgan stared up at him, teeth bared. 'Thalric, you mustn't go inside,' he managed to get out. His breathing was ragged, and there was still fever in him from the arm wound. It must have been all he could do to haul himself this far, and it was not drink that had drawn this effort out of him. Thalric felt something sharp-edged turn in his stomach.

'Report,' he said, as if he was still the Rekef officer, living in a straightforward world.

Osgan held his eyes. 'A new officer's flown in,' he croaked. 'Rekef . . . He's taken charge. Given orders . . .'

'Orders?'

'To have you killed.' Osgan clung to the Mantis effigy, grappling with its stone legs to haul himself half-upright. 'They're waiting inside, right now . . . I overheard it all. They'd forgotten about me, or they didn't think I could move . . .' Hooking an arm about the stone waist, he sagged, just some drunkard making a fool of himself.

Thalric felt something building up inside him, a great rushing wave that cried out: *It's happening again. It's happening again.* He felt Daklan's dagger go in, the keen cleanness of the man's strike.

He could not keep himself from laughing. After all his recent brooding, the worst had already happened. However hard he had tried to reattach himself to the Empire, his knots had slipped, his bindings frayed. He laughed because he had suddenly been cut free.

*I am a dead man.* But it was still funny.

Osgan stared at him, shivering. 'Thalric, we've got to get out of here,' he pleaded.

Thalric's grin was keen as a razor. 'Of course we do,' he replied. 'You'll know some low dive where a couple of foreigners can hide up. I doubt there's a drinking den in this city you haven't tasted.'

'I know . . . places.' Osgan struggled to stand, and Thalric helped him up, slinging the man's good arm over his own shoulder.

'Then let's go,' Thalric said. 'Suddenly I have no appointments.'

All the leaden chains of doubt had just clattered to the ground with Osgan's halting words. From the bewildered ambassador he had become the hunted agent in a hostile city. It was a role he felt infinitely more comfortable with.

For as long as she could stave off sleeping, she had not slept. She knew that, in her dreams, the other Khanaphes was waiting for her: Petri Coggen, passable scholar, graduate of the Great College, Beetle-kinden student of the past, and fugitive.

She did not run, this fugitive. She hid in the Collegiate embassy – no, in the embassy they had painted over as Collegiate, although it had the marks of the old Moth tyranny underneath. Being a historian was becoming a curse, now that the accumulated centuries of Khanaphes, the city where time had died, were rising up to choke her with the dust of ages.

She needed help, so she had gone to Che – but Che had her own worries. The other academics regarded Petri with disdain. She could not speak to them more than five words without stammering and shaking. *They did not understand.* They looked at the carvings and the statues and the colonnades, and they thought it was simply the past. They did not understand that it was all still *alive*, the truth of it lurking beneath the surface, glimpsed only from the corner of the eye.

She was seeing a lot from the corner of her eye these days, after nights of resistance to sleep. The world was alive with motion as the ghosts of old Khanaphes whirled about her. Even when the servants came to her with food, she shied away. She could not be sure if they were real or not. The servants of five centuries ago would have looked no different, she knew.

She needed help, but there was nobody here who could, and if she ventured out on to the streets . . .

She had not left her room in two days. The encroaching taint of history arisen had crept even into the other parts of the embassy. The net of Khanaphes was closing on her.

*Sleep* was closing on her . . . She pricked herself with a knife. She stripped the rugs away and sat on the cold floor. She twisted her fingers in turn, searching for pain enough to keep her awake. She considered driving the blunt blade through her foot. She held it poised, quivering, ready to ram it down. She heard her own sobbing breath loud in her ears.

She could not do it. She lacked the courage or the resolve or whatever mad quality it was that enabled people to mutilate their own bodies. She let the knife fall clattering to the stone floor.

The claws of sleep rose again for her, eager to hook into her mind, and she had no defences left. None.

In her dream, Petri Coggen was outside, alone in the midnight streets of Khanaphes. It was the same dream, or another segment of the same dream, as it thrust itself slowly upwards from the depths of her unconscious. Each dream was another lurching progression further forward. Each dream took her deeper into the city.

Now she had arrived.

The Scriptora rose behind her, a wall of darkness. She reached back to feel the stone-carved scales on the columns that fronted it. The night was chilly, the moon veiled in ragged cloud. The air was damp with the breath of the river.

In her dream she could feel her awakening fear like the pounding on a distant door. This was the hub of her nightmares. This was what kept her behind the safe walls of the embassy. *Khanaphes was out to get her.*

In the end, Che had not believed her. Che had not even given much thought to the absent Master Kadro. The ambassador had other matters on her mind. Petri had not even tried confiding in the other academics. She had just been clinging on, day to day, waiting for when they would pack up and set sail for Collegium once again, because surely they could not deny her passage then.

And each night the dreams returned, and each night they grew worse, until now.

She turned away from the hulking presence of the Scriptora to face the steps of the pyramid. The pale statues at its summit regarded her with an impartial coldness. She felt her feet begin to climb, taking her with them. It was *her* dream, but she had no control of herself. *I don't want to see what lies within.* She knew with a passion that whatever secret Kadro had unearthed would prove fatal, that a mere glance would seal her doom, would cut her off for ever from the comforting world of Collegium and the Lowlands. Still, her feet kept climbing, step by step by step. She could hear her waking fears wailing, feel them battering at the inside of her mind. In the dream, in her dream-mind, she remained placid, even content, to be taking this journey. In the dream the never-ending carvings almost made sense, and the city around her was rich and vibrant with a life that the waking mind could not see. So it was in the dream, but at the same time she knew it was a lie.

And she stood atop the pyramid, but fought the impulse

that would have her look down. The shaft was at her very toes, while either side of her those majestic and inhuman statues kept their eternal watch.

Her head was being drawn down: the dream wanted her to see. She teetered on the edge of waking, the facade of her dream cracking. *Don't want to . . . I don't want to . . .* Because there was something down there, and it was rising up.

She woke with a sharp start, as though she had been slapped. For a moment the dream still clung to her, its sights, sounds, the very texture of the air confusing her. *Where am I?*

She froze. The air around her was chill and damp, kissed by the Jamail. She was high up, and the cloud-strung moon's light settled on little, but it settled on the pale stone of the statues looming across from her. They had always looked outwards before, but now one was turned towards her – and it was smiling slightly as if in amusement at her folly.

She screamed, a short and ugly sound, as she felt the sudden rush of air from the pit at her very feet – *as if something was rising from the depths.*

She stumbled backwards, abruptly without sure footing, tripping back towards the descending steps of the pyramid. She reached out for a support, grasped the arm of one of the statues, expecting cold stone. What she touched was slick and slippery, not stone but flesh.

She screamed again and let go.

*Part Four*

# The Voice of the Masters

# Twenty-Nine

*On this day, the one hundred and seventy-fifth day of the seven hundred and forty-second year from the founding of the Bounteous City, were the tallies made of all peoples who dwell under the hand of the Masters, happy are we to stand in their shadow . . .*

*Also in this year the harvest was of unexpected richness, so that the stores of the city were increased by three parts in one hundred for the coming years. The word of the Masters has cautioned that our storehouses must remain full, for there are lean years foreseen in the east . . .*

*Also in this year . . .*

'Bella Cheerwell?'

The words – her own name – startled her from her reverie. Che blinked, stared at the wall she was crouching before. For a moment the hieroglyphs only marched their incomprehensible procession before her eyes. Then they swam and twisted, as though suddenly viewed through tears. Comprehension came as naturally as breathing, and she saw: *Also in this year did the First Soldier of Khanaphes take to the West River Plains so as to turn aside the advances of the Many of Nem . . .*

But what did that remind her of . . .?

'Che! What's wrong with you?'

It was an irritation that would not go away. She shook her head and looked up to see a figure standing beside her.

Beside her, not over her, though she knelt, for it was Fly-kinden: a man in a traveller's garb and cloak, with a little snarl of beard at his chin, in the Spider manner. His face seemed familiar to her . . .

A tenday of personal history slipped, like a great rock mass long hanging, and descended on her without mercy, leaving no survivors. Che gasped, flinched back from Trallo so hard that she bounced her head against the wall she had just been studying. *Khanaphes – the Fir eaters – the hunt – Thalric – Totho – the Empire – war!* It was all so much to fit in place that she nearly choked on it.

'Trallo—?' She stared at the Fly wildly, trying to work out precisely where they were. Khanaphes, yes, but she did not recognize this district. Beyond the worried-looking Fly, the shaven-headed people were going about their business in a narrow street, without even a glance for the mad foreign woman. They continued herding their goats and sheep and aphids, carrying jars of water or oil, or baskets of grain.

'Che,' said Trallo patiently, trying to capture her attention. 'I have been looking for you for two days.' He let that sink in before adding, out of sheer exasperation, 'And do you know how difficult it is to stay out of *my* sight for two days? People have been worried sick. All sorts of things have been going wrong. You're supposed to be an ambassador and—'

'And whose money paid for all this searching? Which of all your masters?' she snapped back at him, before she could stop herself. She grimaced instantly. 'Trallo, I'm sorry . . .'

'No, that was a fair shot,' he said, not seeming at all hurt or even repentant. 'My own house got a little untidy towards the end, but then I wasn't expecting open war between the Iron Glove and your Wasp fellow.' His expression soured. 'I wasn't expecting open war, full stop. Che, I won't pretend that your halfbreed friend hasn't wanted me to track you down, but it's your own people who are going mad right now. After all that's happened, they want to get straight out of town – and, to be frank, so do I.'

'All that's happened?' *Ah yes.* 'So . . . the rumour . . .'

'The Scorpions are coming, and they're going to be here, well, really soon. Really, *really* soon. Whether they've had all the Imperial help that the Glove have been claiming, that's unproven for now, but they're coming sure as death and taxes. The Khanaphir are putting their army together as though the point of the whole exercise was just to give them the chance to hold parades. You can't move through most of the streets of this city for soldiers marching about and crowds waving at them.'

Che stood up, realizing as she did so that her robe was filthy, ingrained with dirt and dust. *How long have I . . .?* 'I have been researching,' she explained uncertainly.

'Surely you have,' Trallo replied. 'Now let's just . . .'

'You don't understand. I have been reading the histories of Khanaphes – the true histories.' She waved towards the wall with all its bewildering array of sigils. 'These old walls, they're the ones that matter. It's all there in plain view if you can only read it.'

Trallo was staring at her as one stares at the suddenly mad. 'Surely,' he said again. 'You're a credit to the College. Now, how about you come on back to the embassy?'

'Who were the Masters of Khanaphes, Trallo?' she asked him abruptly.

'You want my call? There never were any,' he replied in a harsh whisper, with a suspicious look at the natives passing behind him. 'Now let's—'

'But there were,' she said simply. What knowledge she had deciphered, during those missing, dream-lost days, was filtering back. 'They write about them all the time, their commands, their wishes, their guidance.'

'Sure, sure – and all of it through the Ministers, I'll bet. Now—'

'They speak of them walking through the city, Trallo.'

The Fly took a deep breath. 'Now listen, Bella Cheerwell, things have gone all to the pits since you disappeared, and we've a good way to drop yet. Can we *not* just stand here talking about something that's so long ago it matters less to me than a midge's fart, and perhaps just come back to the embassy where you're supposed to be, perhaps, maybe?'

'It matters, Trallo,' she told him firmly. 'It's more important than anything.' *How did I manage to lose two days?* she was asking herself, horrified, but something of that calm, that supernatural, overwhelming obsession, still clung to her. *It tastes like Fir,* she thought. *But I do not actually need the drug.* She had not even needed to memorize the alphabet in that book that the Khanaphir stonemasons now copied from in mindless rote. Simply being exposed to it had operated some change within her. *The magic of ancient Khanaphes,* and then the inevitable thought: *The voice of the Masters calling to me from five hundred years ago.* She still did not know who they had been, those lost Masters, but it was as though, across all the intervening years, they wanted her to find out.

*It was their voice that led me away, to come here . . .*

'Trallo, I can't come with you—' she started, but his face took on an ugly cast.

'Petri's dead, Che.'

She stared at him, wordless.

'Is that immediate enough for you, Bella Cheerwell? Has that got through to you?'

'Dead?'

'They found her on the steps of that pyramid in front of the Scriptora – I saw her body, before the locals took possession of it. Broken neck. She'd fallen backwards off it. But I saw her face.' He shook his head, unable to properly describe it.

*Petri's dead?* Petri Coggen's babbling tirades about this city being out to get her, her delusions, her fears, her pleas to be taken out of Khanaphes. *And she confided in me, and I did nothing.* It was like cold water washing the dust away from her. The last ebbing of the trance was falling from her.

'Poor woman,' she said, hollowly. 'Poor, poor woman.' When she met Trallo's gaze again, her eyes were steady. 'Let's head for the embassy. We can talk on the way.'

As they approached the side arch leading through to the Place of Foreigners, her thoughts turned inevitably to the maze of diplomacy she saw awaiting her. *And what am I going to do with Thalric now?* 'What's the Imperial reaction been, Trallo?'

'Blatant guilt,' he said, from her elbow. She halted, frowning down at him,

'Explain.'

'They've gone, Bella Cheerwell. They've upped and left. If they're still even in the city, they're keeping their heads down.'

'All of them?'

'Every single stripy one of them.'

The news seemed oddly leaden. Trallo was right: it indicated guilt, surely, to leave so suddenly and secretly, once the news was announced. *Have they gone to join their fellows amongst the Scorpions?* And then: *So I will not talk this over with Thalric, then. I suppose he has made his decision, once again.* It seemed incredible that one man had been given so many choices in life, and made them all so differently.

'What's the feeling among the others?' she asked.

'Manny wants out of Khanaphes yesterday. Our great warrior has decided that war isn't for him, after all,' Trallo said drily. 'They raised the chain on the river, though – that big old gate your lot were so interested in? Worked like it was made only last tenday in Solarno. Old Ethmet has said they'll let you out, when you're ready to go. He's very apologetic. And distracted, too, what with suddenly having a war to run.'

'What about Berjek and Praeda?'

'Berjek is being patient, but I get the impression he's about ready to pack his bags as well. As for Bella Rakespear . . .' Trallo grimaced. 'Well, that there's gotten complicated.'

They were at the door of the embassy, as Che gave Trallo a sidelong look. 'Meaning *him?*'

'He does appear to have got to her somehow,' Trallo murmured. 'It was all that dancing he did, I reckon.'

Che tried to envisage them: cool, detached Praeda Rakespear with the giant, vital Amnon. They seemed utterly opposite. *Then again, at least they're of the same kinden. I'm no one to judge.*

'So what does she want to do?' she asked the Fly.

'Bella Che, I don't think she knows herself. We were all hoping you could talk her into making a decision.'

The city of Khanaphes resounded to the tread of marching feet.

From atop the wall it was a spectacle, but Totho found that he could no longer appreciate mere spectacle. The regiments of Khanaphir soldiers were still leaving the city, each parading in mighty armed pomp through the streets before assembling in front of the west gates. Totho was no novice when it came to armies, and his mind afforded plenty of comparisons. *In fact I am probably the best-qualified person in the city to say to Amnon what must be said.* Except for some of the fugitive Imperials, perhaps, and they were unlikely to be handing out strategic advice.

It was not a Lowlander army, that much was clear. *Correction: it is not a Lowlander army such as has been seen these last three centuries.* The troops were still arriving by barge from the tributary towns further upriver, but the city itself had mustered a surprising number of soldiers. They were not Ant-kinden here, where every citizen would take up a sword at a moment's unspoken notice, but the Ministers had been able to mobilize a lot of the city's population in the short time they had been given. That would be Amnon's first boast: *We are used to fighting off these savages.*

*The sands have finally begun to move in the glass, though,* Totho thought. *What you are used to, friend Amnon, is what was, not what is.* Time, that long-denied guest, was finally marching on Khanaphes.

Amnon leant on the parapet, looking down with a broad smile as his soldiers assembled. He was dressed in his full armour, the scaled hauberk and the crested helm. *He would be better served by what we tried to give him,* Totho knew, but the Ministers had forbidden it, of course. Totho watched another unit of neighbourhood militia leave the gates. The Khanaphir army looked a strange amalgam to his eyes, unwieldy and awkward and lacking in vital parts. The core was Amnon's Royal Guard and some other heavy infantry: scale-armoured shield-and-spearmen backed by armoured archers. They were greatly outnumbered by the light militia, vast expanses of men and women without armour, with only shields and spears or leaf-bladed swords, or archers who could back up their bows with nothing but a dagger. Although they could stand in neat enough rows, Totho doubted they had seen much of a battle before. *It is not an army, rather it is a levy. A levy of citizens that the Khanaphir can ill afford to lose.*

There was cavalry on either side of the main force, and Totho was unused to seeing that. The swift, long-legged sand-beetles were ranged in their skittish, twitching ranks, each bearing a lancer and an archer. Smaller beasts were yoked to little two-wheeled carts which carried a pair of archers apiece to keep the driver company. Totho had never seen the like of them.

'The Marsh people have answered our call at last,' Amnon rumbled, pointing them out. A straggling column was heading upriver from the delta, and Totho turned a glass on them to see them better. They were the silvery-skinned Mantis-kinden from the swamps, perhaps a couple of hundred men and women wearing no armour, but armed with spears and recurved bows and the Art-given barbs of their arms. *Mantis-kinden, still,* thought Totho, but he had seen how the Mantids fell at the Battle of the Rails, and he knew he would be seeing it again, if he was fool enough to march alongside Amnon.

*And if the Emperor had not died, then this would be a full Imperial army coming.* He had not considered that before, but the timing felt right. The expansion of the Empire would have reached this far south by now, had it not been for all the internal squabbling. Perhaps the Khanaphir stood a chance against their age-old Scorpion-kinden enemies, even re-equipped and retrained as they now were, but if it had been the Imperial Eighth Army . . .? Twenty or thirty thousand Wasp-kinden and Auxillian soldiers descending on this lumbering mass of Beetle-kinden and their allies? Even if the Khanaphir and the Many of Nem could have put their differences aside, the Empire would still sweep across them and leave not a man. There would be no room for a battle in amongst all the slaughter.

He looked upon the army of Khanaphes and his artificer's mind cried: *Where is their air-power? Where is their mechanized support? Where the engines of war? Where the crossbows and nailbows and snapbows and all the other accoutrements of modern battle? Drephos's heart would break if he saw this.* Even the new toys of the Scorpions were merely old war-surplus, by Meyr's reckoning, outdated and obsolete weapons and engines that the Empire was well rid of. It seemed the unmaking of all of the great artificer's work in advancing the science of war. Small consolation that all this, this very way of life, now stood to be unmade in turn.

'Amnon,' he said.

'Speak, at last,' the big man turned to him. 'I have sensed your words unsaid all this time.'

'You have heard the reports of my people,' Totho said.

'The Ministers have heard them,' Amnon replied vaguely.

'I don't care about the Ministers,' Totho snapped, grabbing for the man's attention. 'You yourself have heard. You, the First Soldier of Khanaphes. The man who will lead.'

Amnon regarded him silently.

'You are now going to go and have the same fight you always have with the Scorpions,' Totho continued. 'Or that is what you think. That is what the Ministers have told you. You are going to go and put your shields up, and expect them to charge, and charge again. You see, I've done my research. I'm not just an ignorant foreigner. That's how it's done, yes? The wild Scorpion-kinden descend on you with axes and beasts, and you shoot them with arrows and brace your shields, and eventually they run out of manpower or will-power, and then they go away. They're just the mad desert savages, while you're the solid soldiers of Khanaphes. That's what you're all thinking?'

Still Amnon said nothing. His expression discouraged further pressing, but Totho looked up into his dark gaze without a flinch.

'You haven't understood a word that any of us have said. My people have spent time with the Many, long enough to see that the wind's changed. The Empire has been busy sharpening the sword, and the Scorpions, at least, aren't so attached to their cursed past that they're too proud to change. They have crossbowmen now, Amnon. Hundreds of crossbowmen. At medium range, a heavy crossbow bolt will go through a wooden shield without slowing much, and those Scorpions have the muscle to recock a heavy crossbow without breaking sweat. And you know what I see out there? Half your militia are carrying shields of shell or wicker.'

'I listened to you,' Amnon said, turning back to view the assembling army. 'I heard.'

'Then *what?*' Totho demanded. *Why am I even getting involved?* It was not just that he liked Amnon, although he found that was true, but this situation was an offence to his profession, and a criminal waste of raw material.

'The Masters have spoken,' Amnon said patiently. 'We will meet the Scorpions and defeat them, as we have always done. What can I say against that?'

'But—'

'No!' Amnon clenched his fists, knuckles swollen by his Art until his hands were like maces. 'Do not think I did not listen, when you spoke. Do not think I have not heard all this before, from one dearer to me than you are. She told me . . . She said such things . . . But she did not understand. I am commanded. The will of the Masters has been made clear to me, Totho. Therefore we will fight them as we have always fought them.' His breathing sounded ragged with repressed emotion. 'I have given some orders, that go beyond my own. I have ordered . . . a rearguard, if need be. In case we need to find our walls in haste. That is all. Even in that, I betray the Masters with my lack of faith.'

*But there are no Masters!* But Totho knew that to say this would be to go too far.

'I must go find my own mount, and then join my soldiers,' Amnon said. 'May we meet again.'

Totho clasped hands with him. 'Technically all my people and I have been banished from the city. It's just that so far they've not had the spare hands to make us go. I will try to stay for your return, at least. So, yes, may we meet again.' Totho tried to smile, but he saw doom reflected in Amnon's solemn nod.

Amnon's tread was heavy as he descended to the stables. Totho's words were like a weight on him – and not the only weight.

Amnon was not a stupid man, by any means, for the First Soldier's role could not sustain a fool in office. He oversaw the city watch and the militia's training, received reports from every settlement along the Jamail river, liaised with the Marsh people. It was more than just shiny armour and parades.

He believed Totho's story. It was not simply the Many of Nem on their way, who the Khanaphir had repulsed a hundred times before. The Empire, too, was coming by proxy. The Empire was coming in the shape of the new weapons they had gifted to the Scorpion-kinden. *And why does this Empire hate us so?* The answer was clear and uncomfortable. *They barely know we exist. They woo the Scorpions with gifts, and bid them make use of them. It is simply because we are here, waiting for their attentions.*

But Totho did not know the might and the will of the army of Khanaphes. The halfbreed's own people were strange, aloof and passionless. They spoke too much and too loud, these foreigners. They strutted and bragged, and had many marvellous inventions, but they lacked true spirit. This was what the Masters had preserved their city from, this shallowing of the soul.

His mind tugged itself towards that marvellous suit of armour, strong as stone, light as leather, that Totho's people had made for him. It had been forbidden him. The Ministers had spoken and, through them, the Masters.

In the stables, amidst the muted smell of the insects, he instructed grooms, 'Saddle up Penthet. I will ride him into battle.' To command his army truly, he would need to be mobile when the battle came. He flexed his broad shoulders, hearing the slight scrape of metal scales. The Many of Nem had not raided so near the city for eight years now, and never had they come in such numbers. That alone lent Totho's warnings more truth than Amnon needed to hear.

*Why is he still here? Does he seek to profit somehow from the fight?* It was an uncharitable thought and Amnon regretted it instantly. The unhappy halfbreed was still here because he was bound by chains that all his artifice could not break. Amnon understood, because he felt the tug of those chains himself.

He had gone to Praeda last night, seeking distraction, finding only argument. *She thinks she is so clever, with all her learning. She does not understand.* She had not understood when he had told her he must go to war on the morrow. Her objections had been Totho's objections, taken from that patronizing position of superior culture that all these foreigners seemed to hold, and not know they held. Amnon had weathered it – he was good at that – and in the end she had broken down, swearing that she would never speak to him again, that he could go hang himself if they could make a rope thick enough to hold him. The expressions on the faces of the other foreigners, the old man and the fat man, had been horribly embarrassed, as he made his exit. It was clear they had heard every word.

And, of course, he had thought that she might come here, before the army marched, with some last words to clear the bad air between them. She had not come.

One of his grooms brought him his favourite bow, short for cavalry work but curved back and back on itself, coiled with tautly strung power, of Mantis craftsmanship. He slung a broad quiver over his back, the arrow-tips spreading out like a chitin-fletched fan across his shoulders, ready for his fingers to pluck. When he turned round, it was to find a Beetle woman standing there.

It was not *her*, though. It was the other one, the ambassador who was shorter and rounder than Praeda. She was looking awkward, yet she had talked her way into the stables of the Royal Guard, and for no other reason than to see him.

'Yes, O Foreigner,' Amnon addressed her, 'how may I assist you?'

'Just Cheerwell, please,' she said. 'Or even Che.' She looked ragged, as if she had been short of food and sleep for a good while. 'Amnon . . .' she started, and stopped.

'Speak,' he told her.

'I've been talking to Praeda.' And she paused again, scowling at her own inability to push the matter forward. Then the grooms brought out Penthet, and she exclaimed, 'Hammer and tongs, what's that?'

The question brought a slight smile to his face. 'He is Penthet. He is a desert locust. My grooms raised him for me, from the very egg. We two have been companions in the fray for many years.' He ran a hand down the long, segmented flank of the creature, and it resettled its legs, one glittering eye watching him from above the constantly-working mouthparts. 'From his back I shall command the battle.' His hand moved to the high-ended saddle that sat so naturally over the locust's thorax, just in front of the wings. His face darkened momentarily. 'I am glad to see there is one part of war that you wise foreigners do not understand. Perhaps your predictions are not so all-knowing as you think.'

'Amnon, she could not make herself come and see you,' Che told him.

He nodded grimly. 'I had assumed as much.'

'She fears for you. It is true that we do not understand your ways here – of all people, I know that! – but you do not understand what is coming, with the Scorpions. They are bringing a part of our world against you – the worst part. Praeda . . . she fears that she will lose you.'

'All men must die. Warriors die in battle. Your world is not so different, I am sure,' he said. 'What would she ask of me? That the First Soldier of Khanaphes hides away, while his army fights?'

'She would have asked, I think, that you changed your battle plan – that you changed your ways as the Scorpion have changed theirs,' Che said. 'She would have asked that you took all the weapons and armour that Totho could sell you, and thus sent the Scorpions back to the Empire asking for more and better in return. She is a logical woman, but she does not see where her logic would lead. Besides, I myself have seen battles, and she has not. You cannot change an army in a day. Order and discipline are built from practice. The Scorpions cannot have had so very long to become used to their new toys.'

He regarded her for a long time before responding, 'Speak the rest, O Foreigner. I see it in your face. These crossbows . . . Totho tells me they are a simpleton's weapon, that any fool can take them up and shoot. And the Scorpions have had many tendays to practise. Who knows how long the Empire has been dwelling amongst them? And the Many of Nem are truly *many*, in their war host. Never have we known the like, this swarming of them.'

'You see it all, don't you?' Che said.

'I see that we must fight. That is the true word of the Masters. What can we do but defend our homes? The Scorpions will accept no peace, give no quarter. They seek only to loot and kill. The Empire may have armed them, but it will not have changed them.'

'And we cannot change you.'

As he met her eyes, the force of his gaze was almost like a blow. 'The Ministers declare that the Masters will save us, at the end.'

'Do you believe that?'

'I will believe it at the end. I will have nothing to lose then.'

# Thirty

It was a bright, cloudless morning, as they always seemed to be here. The dust of an army on the move had not yet started to choke the air. The war-host of the Many of Nem was just stirring.

In the distance, within a day's hard strike, the green that was the river Jamail was in sight, with all its treasures. Through a spyglass, focusing the little device awkwardly with his clawed hands, Hrathen could see the walls of Khanaphes in some detail. He passed the glass to Angved the engineer. 'Your professional opinion?'

Angved spent a long time passing the telescope back and forth, in minute increments. 'Big walls,' he said at last. 'Big old walls. Carved real pretty too, it looks like.'

'That doesn't count as a professional opinion,' Hrathen growled. 'How will the leadshotters fare?'

'Sir,' replied the engineer, 'given that it never rains round here, they might as well have made those walls of paper and spared themselves the effort.'

Hrathen frowned down at him. 'So confident?'

Angved shrugged. 'I've seen Beetle-kinden walls, and those aren't them. Those are great big blocks of stone set one on another, all beautifully cut and dressed, but there are walls and walls. We could bring those walls down with trebuchet and rock-throwers, maybe a tenday's investment, maybe less. With leadshotters? We'll have a breach in two days at the most. This is old, sir. It's all *old* work. When they built these walls, my trade wasn't exactly foremost in their minds.'

Hrathen nodded thoughtfully. 'So now we just have to get there.'

'They've moved their army out, then?'

'Just started to come for us, it looks like.'

'It's what I'd do, too. With walls like that, they must know they can't withstand a siege. A victory on the field is their best chance.'

Hrathen shook his head. 'Not like that, apparently. It sounds like this is what they always do whenever the Scorpions come for them. They tend to win, too, so you can see why they've not changed the recipe. The Scorpions have all sorts of excuses, but it comes down to basics. The Khanaphir are better disciplined, and the Many were never *this* many, before. Also, the Khanaphir had a superiority at range – with bows and the like.'

'Well, I can't say we've entirely solved the discipline problem,' Angved observed. 'Still, your woman there, Jakal, she seems to have them well in line.'

'We work within our limits,' said Hrathen. He had spent last night with Jakal, talking over what tactics they could reliably impose on the Scorpion warbands. Talking them over, and nothing further, despite what he had hoped for. *The bitch is stringing me along, and she's enjoying every minute of it.* He could challenge her, he knew. He could try to take her by force, but that would not achieve the Empire's goals here. *And let me be honest with myself: I don't think I would succeed.* She had not become the Warlord of the Many by anything less than ruthlessness and skill.

'The crossbowmen are looking good,' Angved remarked idly. 'They've picked up the idea of shooting all together, at least. When we started they were all for just popping off a shot and then up with the axe and go charging in. We were lucky to find that caravan. Live targets make all the difference for practice.'

The caravan had been a little convoy of foreigners, tomb robbers and relic hunters set on pillaging the ruins of the outer desert. They had been heavily armed, forming up around their wagons and hoping to stand the Scorpion outriders off, but instead of simply descending on them with knives and hatchets, Hrathen had sent for the crossbowmen.

It had been bloody work, and not swift. The thieves and their hangers-on had tried to stay together, to find cover, as the crossbows had loosed and loosed. The Scorpions had begun to learn the joys of killing at a distance: now the same crossbowmen would not trade a kill at thirty yards for all the savage delight of getting their claws bloody. It had been a useful object lesson, as they had begun to understand the archer's pride and joy in seeing the enemy wither and fall, without ever having a chance to fight back. For a Scorpion it was no great mental leap.

'Your woman's coming,' Angved reported, and prudently absented himself, heading off to check the siege engines. Hrathen turned to greet Jakal, finding her in her full armour, spear in hand.

'I have spoken to the chiefs,' she said. 'We have our battle order, as you call it.'

'Is it as we discussed?'

Her strange eyes regarded him. 'I have taken those I like least, or those who will not stand the fight, and made them our centre. I have gone among the others, telling them not to worry if these break, since they are marked as weak. The crossbows will make the claws on either side, with the better warriors, and you yourself have the sting.'

'Lieutenant Angved has the sting, yes,' Hrathen agreed. 'The weapons are designed for siege, not open field work, but it has been known. It will test the crews.'

Jakal shrugged, one clawed hand spread wide. 'Let them be tested, then. Have you found a place for yourself in all this planning, Of-the-Empire?'

'Of course. I shall drive your chariot.'

He had amused her at last. 'Will you, indeed? And you are so used to chariots in your Empire that even the word was strange to you, at first.'

'But your beasts will know their work,' he said. 'And I shall speak with them, and let them instruct me.'

'And you will follow my orders, without question?'

'I have brought you weapons, and the knowledge of how to use them,' he reminded her. 'Now you must use them – use them as you will. I shall bow my head to you, for as long as the battle lasts.'

Beneath the rim of her helm she was smiling. 'Have I conquered the Empire now?' she teased, one thumb claw coming up to rest along the line of his chin. 'Well then, you shall indeed have that honour.' Her eyes met his directly now, bold and fierce and utterly unlike the eyes of any Imperial woman. 'Perhaps you shall have other honours, when we have driven them from the field. Perhaps we shall celebrate, you and I, if I am pleased with you.'

The plume of dust that the Khanaphir army was raising was more clearly visible. They wanted to fight the Scorpions far enough from the city that the river would not become a barrier at their back. Hrathen was fretting at a lack of scouts, but he did not want to risk any Wasps to the bows of the enemy, and the Scorpions had no fliers, and slower cavalry than the defenders. He was obliged to rely on his telescope and the reports he had heard of older conflicts. At least the Khanaphir did not seem to be the type to innovate.

The difficulty, as he had discussed with Jakal, was to make best use of the Many's new-found advantages. The crossbows were slower than the shortbows the Khanaphir favoured, but they outranged them. *And perhaps not really so much slower, for that matter.* They were the old Imperial heavy crossbows for which the archers were supposed to draw the string back by winch, but most of the Scorpions had notched their thumb-claws and were tensioning the weapons by hand in half the usual time. The Empire had not considered just how *strong* they were. There would be more than a few broken claws by the battle's end, more than a few broken crossbows for that matter, but they had quickly made the weapons their own. It only remained to give them the best chance to use them.

The normal Khanaphir tactics were reliable and unimaginative, from what he had been told. They fielded an infantry-strong army with good cavalry wings and archer support. It was not something out of the Imperial tactics textbooks, but he could see the strengths and weaknesses. The Scorpions were more mobile, so that meant that, for a decisive victory, the Khanaphir would at some point have to come to them and follow them up. Otherwise the fight would go on all day, with the Scorpions picking and choosing the targets of their strikes.

The Khanaphir would understand the same thing, Hrathen was counting on it. The plans had been made, so no point worrying about them now. They would deform and change as soon as they met the enemy, just as plans always did. The Scorpions were not a disciplined force, but the Khanaphir knew that too, and it became just one more factor that a clever general could use.

He stretched and went off to see about Jakal's chariot, to have a talk with her beasts and set them straight.

The army of Khanaphir marched tirelessly, as Beetles could. To Hrathen it was a great row of white squares, reinforced with steel in the centre where their heavy infantry was posted. On the flanks there was an odd mixture of the Mantis-kinden skirmishers, Khanaphir archers and chariots. The beetle cavalry, seated on its long-legged black animals, was taking a wide path in order to flank the Scorpions when the forces were engaged.

'How do their riders stack up to ours?' he asked. Their chariot jolted and bounced, finding its place on the Many's left flank. He could feel the minds of the animals, keen and hungry. Each had an armoured shield fixed to its outside pincer and barding of chitin over its back.

'They are faster, but scorpions will kill beetles if they catch them. They will hold off until they can catch us unawares, perhaps come all the way round behind us,' Jakal told him. The chariots are different . . .' She stopped, gave a particularly vicious laugh. 'Or they were until we got your crossbows. I've told them to aim for the beasts first.'

'And your soldiers will stay with the plan?' The chariot was in place now, amongst a slew of other vehicles arrayed about the Scorpions' left flank.

'Probably.' Jakal shrugged. 'Mostly.' The Khanaphir had stopped now, waiting. Hrathen saw their front rank bristling with spears. Behind them were archers, identifiable at this range because they had no shields. The Beetles would wait for as long as it took, Hrathen knew. They were a naturally more patient people, but it was all taken care of in the plan.

Jakal took up a bulbous horn made from a hollowed-out stinger, took a great breath and sounded it. The strange, wailing note sounded out across the restless, uneven lines of the Many's war host. Instantly it was eclipsed by a great roar, a thousand Scorpion throats cheering on the initial charge. The centre of the lines surged forward, a great mass of halberdiers and axemen rushing for the Khanaphir centre. Hrathen steadied the chariot beasts, feeling in his mind their instinctive urge to follow, looking to his right to assure himself that not *too* much of the host had just committed itself. He felt a wash of relief when he saw that at least two-thirds of the infantry was still waiting, although milling angrily, obviously exercising every drop of restraint they possessed. On either side of that belligerent centre were the crossbowmen, looking already more ordered and disciplined, as though he had sewn Wasp brains into their heads. He and Jakal had gone over the plan with their chiefs in great detail, so they knew their glory would come.

The sky above the charging Scorpions turned abruptly dark. The Khanaphir archers had loosed their first volley, arrows arching over their own spearmen to impact among the onrushing warriors. If the Scorpions, unevenly armoured as they were, had come charging in a block, then they would have been slaughtered. Their own lack of discipline helped them in this one thing, for their running mass was so loosely knit that, although the sleeting shafts killed many, there were just as many missed shots as the arrows fell into the gaps between them.

That was the first volley, and the shortbows of the Khanaphir did not have the range of a proper battlefield weapon, but the second volley caused havoc amongst the Scorpions' rear ranks as they pressed closer in anticipation of making impact – the Khanaphir arcing their arrows high to fall on them, making exquisite use of the limited tools they possessed.

Hrathen grinned, his hands tightening on the reins in anticipation.

The Scorpion vanguard struck, and he saw the enemy line bow under the force of them – under the great cleaving blows of axe and halberd. Scorpions were not soldiers at heart, but they were warriors: they knew how to fight. They were taller, stronger, longer-armed and vastly more bloodthirsty by nature than their foes. The Beetle lines bent before them, even as dozens of Scorpions died on the enemy's levelled spears.

The charge had struck at the point where the Khanaphir light infantry met the Royal Guard. The unarmoured militia buckled helplessly, shields cracking and splitting under the Scorpions' ferocious blows, the men behind trying to give ground in order to stay out of the reach of the hacking polearms. The Guard pressed forward even as the Scorpions advanced and Hrathen saw swords rising and falling behind their solid line of shields. They were now butchering the men confronting them, turning their front line into a flank, rolling up the Scorpion advance. Behind them, more shields were stepping forward to keep the line intact. It was an impressive display of military order.

Now the Scorpions were falling back. The Khanaphir pursued them a dozen yards before re-forming seamlessly, as though they had not lost a man. The Scorpions outpaced them in their retreat, then turned around ready for another charge. By now their numbers were greatly reduced, but they did not seem to care. *Fighting spirit,* Jakal had called it, and their blood was up. She seemed to think it made them more dangerous as a people, though Hrathen had kept silent and reflected on how an Imperial army would exploit such a weakness.

The Scorpion vanguard tried another assault under the raining arrows of the Khanaphir archers. Hrathen could feel the restlessness of the main army reaching a fever pitch. Even as he had the thought, he heard Jakal say, 'We can't keep them back much longer. Nature shall take its course.'

The second advance was a shambles. The Scorpions faltered before the strike, losing even more men to the archers and denying themselves the impetus of their charge. When they struck the Khanaphir line, they broke and ran almost at once, an utter rout. The Khanaphir followed them up, further this time, no doubt heartened by the predictability of their foes.

There was a shrill whistle from Hrathen's right, blown by one of Angved's engineers. It told him that the Khanaphir host was now within crossbow range.

'Over to you,' he said to Jakal. He then looked out for the Khanaphir cavalry, seeing the nearest detachment still far to his flank, waiting on a rise for their chance.

*And if it never comes?* He ducked his head as Jakal sounded her horn again, the note cutting stridently through the shouts and yells and screams. The main host should now be separating into three blocks, opening up two avenues that led down towards the advancing Khanaphir. Most of that did not happen: it had proved too much to try and teach the Scorpions in the short time they had. Thankfully, Angved would be aiming high.

*A count of twenty,* Hrathen thought. It was all the pause Angved would leave. Obligingly the Khanaphir forces had halted again, waiting for the next charge of the Many. This was how they had won their previous battles: short, unstoppable advances whilst the enemy wore themselves down against their interlocked shields.

He put himself into the minds of the beasts, warning them, steadying them. *There will be a great noise,* he told them. *It is not for you to worry about.*

The whole chariot quivered with their fear, even so, when a dozen leadshotters spoke in rapid succession. He looked back to see the great plumes of smoke from behind the Scorpion army, marking where the firepowder-charged engines had discharged their shot. For a moment both armies seemed in disarray, and then the missiles began to land. Angved had not used the solid balls that would soon crack the walls of Khanaphes: instead he had something purpose-made for this moment. Each shot would smash and shatter as it impacted, scything metal fragments into the tight-packed ranks of the surrounding enemy.

Well over half the shots missed the Khanaphir army altogether, impacting behind or beside them in colossal clouds of dust, but two or three landed directly on their mark, crashing down amidst those shoulder-to-shoulder squares of armed men.

This was part of any modern war, Hrathen knew: acceptable, unavoidable losses. Soldiers too spread out were inefficient, hard to command, ineffective against any solid enemy force. Only Ant-kinden possessed the almost supernatural discipline to change from close to open formation at will. It was part of any modern war, but the Khanaphir had never fought a modern war until now.

Angved had made history: he was the first man to bombard the people of Khanaphes.

Hrathen had half thought they would break then and there, but they were made of sterner stuff. They held together, reeling and milling, and all the time the leadshotters were reloading. Command was slow in coming: no mindlinks here for instant readiness. They stayed still, and Hrathen admired the restraint of his own crossbowmen in not playing their hand too early. The army of Khanaphes reordered its ranks, and then the leadshotters spoke again.

His artillerists had been given a chance to correct their aim, and some had over-corrected. One shot struck within the Scorpions' own front line, and another, worse still, ploughed through thirty loose ranks of Nem warriors, exhausting itself before it ever reached the enemy. Hrathen felt the shock whip through his forces, knew that he must find a use for them soon or they would attack their own artillery.

Two shells had missed the entire army again, proof of the practice the Scorpions still needed, but the rest were on their targets, eight separate explosions rocking the Khanaphir lines.

*And there's more where that came from*, Hrathen thought. *Work it out.*

He cast another look to his left and saw the Khanaphir cavalry mustering, falling into a phalanx.

'Messenger!' he bellowed, and one of his Wasps dropped down beside him.

'Send to Angved, have him ready his crossbowmen. The cavalry are readying for a charge.'

It was the right thing to do, of course, assuming there were no more surprises. Just as the main army was about to do the 'right thing', on the same assumption.

Whoever was commanding the Khanaphir centre had now realized that staying still was a death sentence. The bombardment, a mere friendly greeting by Imperial standards, had killed more of them than both of the Scorpion charges, and it did not take any great mind to see that such tricks would be of limited use once the armies converged.

The Khanaphir army sounded the charge, and their ranks of locked shields thundered towards the disordered Scorpions with a great battle-cry. Their chariots began to rattle forward on either flank.

Hrathen took a deep breath, waiting for the whistle. Angved took his own time over it, but then it sounded high and clear over the sounds of battle. *Second whistle: crossbows loose.*

He was expecting a rabble of individual shots, but the crossbowmen had inherited a kind of pride from their teachers, and that paved the way for something more military. When they loosed, each unit was mostly together. The staggered crossbow discharge caught the Khanaphir in mid-charge. Their right flank managed to take the brunt on their shields, stumbling to a crawl but keeping their lines intact. The Khanaphir left, on the far side from Hrathen, fell apart instantly, men lanced through or speared in the leg, men falling over fallen comrades. That entire flank of the Khanaphir army was crashing into itself, utterly still, the uniform advance ruined.

The crossbowmen would be drawing back their strings with all of their strength. The Khanaphir centre had slowed to keep pace with its comrades, the charge faltering. The crossbowmen had made, by their discipline, their own chance for a second shot.

It struck, without the previous savage cohesion, now that they were getting excited, but it was enough. The Khanaphir right began pulling inwards, retreating. On the broken left it was the unshielded archers that took the worst of it, dropping in their scores. The left-flank chariots had mostly stopped, some wheeling in disarray, others stilled, their beasts brought down.

Hrathen looked back at Jakal and was about to signal to

her, but she had the horn to her lips already, sounding it loud and long.

*Third horn blast: charge.* It was the end of tactics, for the most part, but tactics had played their part. Now the great host of the Many of Nem descended upon the halted Khanaphir line with all of its ferocious might, and the real killing began.

From his station amongst the cavalry, Amnon felt abruptly hollow inside, on hearing that earth-shaking roar from behind the Scorpion lines. Something in him had cracked. His former certainty was leaking out.

It was not immediately obvious to him what had happened, but something had struck within the infantry lines. He saw the dust, heard the distant cries. It was some device of the Empire, but he could not link cause and effect. It seemed like magic to him, that the enemy could simply punch ragged holes into his army.

He hesitated, four score of riders about him trying to calm their high-strung mounts, which were baring their mandibles in terrified threat at the very sky, as though to challenge the echo.

Then the sound came again, and he managed to connect it with the smoke of a moment before, the line of brief flares visible behind the Scorpion host.

'Form me a wedge!' he shouted out, but he had to give the order three more times before his troop got their animals under control. The beetles were pattering about madly, gaping their jaws and flaring their wingcases in threat, trying to scare off the future. Their riders, lightly armoured men and women, with shields slung over their backs, struck the beasts with the butts of their lances or the reins of their Art until they were back under control. By that time, Amnon's officers had set the main army to moving forward. It was the right thing to do.

'Charge with me!' he cried out. He could not remember

what name Totho had given to the weapons but he recognized the description. 'They are exposed at the enemy's rear, these noisemakers. We will kill the men who operate them.'

They were mostly behind him now. Penthet the locust bucked uncomfortably beneath him, folding and refolding his wings. He and Amnon had been through a lot, and the insect's simple mind trusted him.

He put his spurs in and the locust leapt twenty feet forward, the banner of Khanaphes streaming out behind him. The beetle cavalry would come scuttling after at their top speed, long-legged over the uneven ground, catching him at the end of each jump and then being left behind again. He readied his first lance, letting it rest between Penthet's antennae as the world wheeled and plunged about him.

Enemy cavalry was already moving to intercept him, but the armoured scorpions were sluggish compared to his own fleet warriors. Only the swiftest outriders of the Scorpion-kinden were in time to cause him any inconvenience. Amnon couched his lance and let Penthet choose his own path down, wings steering so as to bring the steel point thrusting through the chitin of a scorpion before the creature or its rider even realized he was upon them. He unslung his bow as a rabble of the Many's fleetest riders bore down on him. His own fastest follower caught the closest of them with a lance, skittering in from the side and hooking the Scorpion cavalryman off his mount, while the Beetle archer seated behind the lancer was busy loosing his shafts at more distant enemies. There was a chariot rattling down towards Amnon, two beasts yoked to a two-wheeled cart. The soldiers within were training some weapon upon him, but Penthet sprang obediently into the air and Amnon sliced an arrow back down at them, killing one of their animals and dragging the chariot to a stop. A moment later, he and the bulk of his riders were past the enemy cavalry. The last few of his wedge would meet them, he knew, peeling off to throw themselves at the enemy's stings in order to buy time.

He spared a glance for the main army and saw that something was wrong. They were now locked in with the Scorpions, but were being forced back, the host of Scorpions surging to both sides of their formation.

Before him he spotted the strung-out line of weapons, long black tubes that the Scorpions were swarming around in some arcane ritual. He goaded Penthet onward, knowing that the riders behind him would take up the pace.

There were other Scorpions rushing to get between him and the weapons, but he knew a cavalry charge would break them. The Scorpions had no decent spear-wall to fend off riders, and their own cavalry was hopelessly outmanoeuvred.

Penthet came down before them, and he realized his next leap would clear the mob of Scorpions entirely. He felt the locust's hind legs bunch with all the power of their colossal muscles, knowing that his charging followers would scatter and smash the Scorpions and join him on the other side of them.

Even as he jumped, he saw the enemy crossbows let fly into the charging riders.

He came down right behind them, within three yards of the hindmost Scorpions, and turned to see his cavalry. By that time, more than half of them were dead.

Something tightened inside him. The ground the Scorpions faced was strewn with fallen men, with dying animals. Riding beetles, whose shells could shrug off javelins and axe-blades, had been pierced through with holes, the short, heavy bolts barely slowing for chitin or barding. They lay on their sides or on their backs, legs twitching and kicking in uncomprehending agony.

By now, the survivors had struck the Scorpion line, which fragmented before them, the enemy simply running left and right. Though many of the crossbowmen fell to the lances of the riders, or under the feet of their mounts, there were still plenty left.

'Onwards!' Amnon cried, although he heard his own voice sounding raw with grief. Penthet took him another great stride towards the enemy weapons, and his men followed without question. The crossbow shot began to fall on them from behind now, and from the left where the main Scorpion army was. The bolts zipped through the air like wasps. One bounded from Amnon's shield. Another skipped across Penthet's thorax right in front of him, leaving a shallow gouge, barely slowed.

The Scorpions were fleeing from the nearest weapon but he was too quick for them. He came down in their midst, his lance impaling one, and then his sword lashing out to kill two more. A scattering of riders reached him, slaying the rest before they could escape. He felt Penthet prepare for the next leap.

They had shifted the next weapon round, he saw. Some of the crew there were not Scorpions but Wasp-kinden, such as had so recently been the guests of Khanaphes. The gaping maw of the leadshotter was now facing him.

Amnon gave out a wordless cry, feeling two crossbow bolts impact into Penthet's side. The locust kicked off from the ground, unevenly but high.

The thunder spoke.

It was not just that one, but many, the others dropping shot on to the rear edge of the Khanaphir forces. That one weapon filled Amnon's view, though: the flash of fire followed by the plume of smoke. The lead-shot ball struck into his cavalry just as it was forming, smashing three riders and their beasts smashed into bloody shards.

The crossbows loosed again, and now there were just two riders behind him. The crew of the weapon ahead of him had scattered, and he did not have the numbers to hunt them down, or the strength to break the iron of the weapon itself.

He came down again, his two survivors still with him. 'Rejoin the army!' he bellowed. 'Fly!'

Penthet could fly, not strongly but enough. The beetles could manage a brief hop: a frantic, buzzing barrelling through the air. It would have to suffice.

The locust launched itself into the air, wings spreading into furious motion right behind him, battering Amnon with their force. The beetles lifted more slowly, clawing for height. One faltered, the bolts finding it an easy target, piercing its underbelly in a dozen places and bringing it down. The other one took three bolts but stayed in the air, in a single strained burst of effort that took it down behind the Khanaphir lines. Amnon felt the shuddering impact as another quarrel took Penthet in the abdomen.

Amnon's officers had already begun the retreat. With what discipline was left to them, the Khanaphir forces were falling back. In places it was already a rout, but the centre – the Royal Guard itself – was holding the Scorpions at bay, selling their own lives at a ruinous cost to the attackers.

Behind them, on the approach to the river Jamail, there lay farms and tributary villages, herders' hovels, dozens of little homes that had trusted to Khanaphes's protection. The army retreated through them at the best pace it could, and the Scorpions, who might have harried them right up to the very walls of the city, fell away to seize on this immediate chance to loot.

So it was that the remnants of the army of Khanaphes regained its city. Half of the men and women who had marched out that morning never came home.

Jakal came to him at last, that same night, after the host of Nem had made its camp amongst the burned-out farmhouses, the ruined fields. When the last prisoners had finally been tired of and slain or packed off for slaves, when the bloodlust of the battle had simmered into an anticipation of the morrow, she came to him, at last, naked save for a belt where a long dagger was sheathed.

In the gloom of his tent, by two guttering oil lamps, he

could see her well enough. The bluish light tinted her pale skin with an undersea glow. She was lean and muscled, her breasts small, little of the feminine about her. Hrathen was more used to slave women, Wasps or other kinden of the Empire. Jakal's jaw jutted with narrow fangs, her hands bore claws curving over thumb and forefinger.

Gazing on her, he felt such a surge of arousal as he had never known. She was the Warlord of the Many of Nem, on whose word the horde of Scorpion-kinden fought and died. She had marked him out from the start: a constant teasing, backed with steel, that had found all the gaps in his Rekef facade. Her eyes still glinted with amusement at the victories she had won in her own personal campaign.

'Do you not trust me, yet?' he asked, looking at the dagger. She knelt beside him, pressed one hand to his broad and hairless chest, pushing him back on to his bedroll.

'I will never trust you, Of-the-Empire,' she replied, 'but this is our way. We are a fierce people, after all, and couplings turn into killings sometimes. Claws, daggers . . . perhaps I should take one of your crossbows into bed with me, to mark today's conquest.'

He had reached for his own sword-belt, but she pounced on his arm, pinning his wrist with her claws, gripping hard enough to draw blood.

'What need have you of steel?' she demanded. 'I know you are never unarmed, Of-the-Empire, for your Art lives in your hands – the Art of both your kin.' She drew his hand to her mouth, biting at it gently, the rank of her fangs barely denting the skin. He felt her tongue lick his palm, as though exploring where his Art came from. He could feel his palms warm with the sheer excitement of it. She released his hand and laughed at him delightedly.

*She is ready to kill me*, he thought, but that was no revelation. She was equally ready to kill him at any time, for any reason. It was how they lived, the Scorpion-kinden, and it meant he belonged.

She was upon him in an instant and they wrestled briefly. He might have been the stronger by some small margin, but she fought with more fire – the Warlord of the Nem demanding nothing less than a complete surrender, pinning him down beneath her and clasping him between her claws.

Her eyes held his, and he thought: *Claws first, and then sting. Always the way of it.* His death was now in the forefront of her mind, being contemplated, and that did nothing but inflame him more.

She thrust herself down on to him, and he was more than ready to enter her. Locked together, still grappling, his hands warm against her cool skin, in that moment he abandoned the Empire, all the games and rules and weaknesses.

Later, separated, they lay watching each other, as the watches of the night turned towards morning. Scorpion-kinden did not slumber in one another's arms. Jakal had fallen back out of arm's reach, perhaps close enough still that the claws of her hands could scrape against those of his.

'Let me in,' he said, barely more than a whisper. 'What is it that I cannot understand of your people? I want to be part of your world.'

'Have I not let you in, this very night?' she asked him, amused.

'I have worked with your kinden for years, in the Dryclaw,' he told her, feeling an urgency about it. 'You are not like them: they have been corrupted by the Spiders, by the Empire. How is it you have not?'

'They forget their true enemies. They forget their past,' she explained, with a one-shouldered shrug. 'They tell no histories, they keep no lore. We hold firm to our histories here. Perhaps you had not thought of us as scholars?' He saw her fangs bared in a grin. 'Our histories are our grudges, told by each generation to the next. We hold to those grudges, and we would never let them go. Let our cousins of the Dryclaw be seduced away from their past. We remember.'

'But remember what?'

She eyed him, still smiling. 'And why would you know?'

'Because I would be a part of it. Your grudges are mine.'

'So besotted, Of-the-Empire?'

'I will kill you if you name me that again.' The words came out flatly, but sharp-edged. She paused a long moment, regarding him, turning his death over in her mind once again, but the smile stayed put.

'At last you speak as we do,' she said. 'A warrior needs no more reason to shed blood tomorrow than because the sun shines, but perhaps you should know our story, at last. We *remember*. We remember to the time when the desert was green. Long and long ago, when the desert was green and the cities of the Beetle-kinden were strung across it like dew on a spiderweb. Long ago when we lived in the dry fringes. When the whole world was ruled by the Masters of Khanaphes, and we alone would not bow the knee.'

Hrathen felt an odd feeling stir inside him, as though he was at the edge of a chasm, looking down. *How many generations?* he wondered. *How much was 'the whole world' when that was true?*

'Year on year, mother to daughter, and the slaves of the Masters tried to tame us. They forced us to the very edge of the world, but we would not be their slaves. We alone, of all the kinden of the world, would not surrender, nor would we flee to seek other lands and other masters.'

*Other lands and other masters?* Hrathen had never been a student of history, but he guessed this must mean what they called the Bad Old Days, those times in which the world had belonged to very different kinden: Moths, Spiders. *Were these 'Masters' in fact Spider-kinden? It sounds like their way.*

'Then the dry times came,' Jakal went on, 'and the green lands faded and the Beetle-kinden departed. Year on year, mother to daughter, the land dried, and the Beetle-kinden returned to their river, where it was always green. It was not that they could not have survived in the drier lands, but that their Masters could not, and where their Masters' power failed, so they failed also, for they were slaves always to their Masters.' Jakal's telling had started to sound almost ritualized, recalled words told over and over, told to him now in this tent in sight of Khanaphes's walls. He sensed history all around them: the clawed and brutal story of the Scorpion-kinden.

'So we came unto the lands that had once been green, and we came unto the cities of the outer desert and the mid-desert, and all the things that the Beetles had left behind. We took their metal and made swords from it. We took their wood and made spears of it. Such was the wealth they had discarded that we yet mine their cities for the commonplace treasures they have left behind. Only the cities of the inner desert are barred to us, for there the Masters posted their guardians, and those we may not disturb.'

*The inner desert?* Hrathen shivered again. Nothing lived in the inner desert, of course. Even the Scorpions could not survive there. That had been the Imperial understanding, at least. It had not been considered that fear of something *worse* might keep them away.

*Once Khanaphes is dust*, he thought, *I shall go there and view these cities*, But it was a hollow boast because, in absorbing the Many's history, he was adopting their strictures too.

'Yet still,' Jakal watched him carefully, 'still our enemies kept to the river, and held all the land that was still green, and penned us up in the dry lands, year on year, mother to daughter. Until the strangers came from the north and brought us many weapons, and showed us how to take those green lands from the Masters' servants. And we smote the servants of the Masters and tore down their walls, and slew them, women, men and children, each and every one,' and she said it sweetly, very sweetly indeed, and he loved her for it.

# Thirty-One

*We have lost control.*

Malius's gloomy response came back. *We never had it.*

*We cannot remain long in this city,* Accius told him. *This war of theirs has no relevance to us.* The Vekken were sitting side by side on one of the beds in their room, in their customary silence. The movements of the Collegiates, their babble and clumsiness, intruded on them through the closed door.

*It has been claimed that the Empire is behind the attackers,* Malius reminded him.

*I am not convinced. I can see no gain for the Empire.*

*We are not best placed to know what the Empire seeks.*

Accius sighed inwardly. *They talk and talk of leaving.* He referred to the Collegium delegation, who had been packing their belongings frantically, but yet never seemed to make any definite plans. The implication was clear.

*A poor deception then: they intend to stay.*

*Denying us our chance to return home.*

*Home,* Malius echoed, and his inner voice was wretched. *But we cannot give up all hope.*

*Could we even find home, if we left this city on our own?* They compared maps, mind to mind, trying to stitch the borders of where-they-were to those of where-they-knew. But Vek had lived in isolation for such a long time, it barely acknowledged Helleron and Tark, let alone the Exalsee. *We are lost. Only by staying with the Collegiates can we ever hope to reach home. We could put a blade to their throats and force them to guide us, if need be.* Accius was warming to the idea. *Or we could take their Fly-kinden slave and force him, instead. Fly-kinden are pliable.*

*A plan,* Malius admitted. *But what would we tell the Court, after we found our home again? What have we accomplished? What have we discovered?*

*That Collegium seeks common cause with the Empire!* was Accius's prompt response. *That our enemies gather against us.* Another thought followed swiftly on: *They pretend to leave, but they must wait here to betray the local Beetles to the Empire. Perhaps that is what they have promised, in return for Imperial help against Vek.*

*Plausible,* agreed Malius. Feeling the other man's alarm at the thought, he fed him caution in return. *We must accomplish what we have set out to do. We cannot return empty-handed. We must attempt to spoil their plot.*

*We care nothing for this city,* Accius argued. *In fact, we hate it. This is a crude, loud, chaotic place.*

*Still, it is being attacked by our enemies. In following our course of action, we deprive our enemies of their advantage. We must kill the ambassador, as we planned.*

Accius's mind signalled frustration. *She seems to be able to appear and disappear like a Moth-kinden. Whenever she is present, others watch her. That Fly slave has his eyes on her often, yet at times even he cannot find her, or that is what he claims.*

*That is what he claims,* Malius echoed. *We no longer have the time to do this properly, like soldiers. We must resort to other facets of our training. They fight their battles even now. We must be expedient.*

*I understand you.* Accius signalled his preference for a simple killing, out of sight and without subtlety, but he felt Malius holding firm and ultimately knew the other man was right. They were not, after all, diplomats by profession, nor were they wholly soldiers. They could fall back on other resources, if need be, and that need had made itself amply apparent.

*She is here, in this building, right now*, Malius told him, building his confidence. *She has returned to her fellows. Tonight she shall sleep in her own bed. I shall watch out for the others and, when she is settled, you must make your move. It must be swift.*

*The swifter she is dead, the sooner we can make the others leave this place and return us to the Lowlands. To our own city.* Accius felt a tremor of the old homesickness rack him momentarily, leaning on his comrade for support. *This is a vile place, and we will be well rid of it.*

Malius stood up, stepping out of the room and on to the landing, to look down at the bickering Beetles in the main hallway below. He was out of the room but not out of Accius's presence, and so he could feel his friend begin to prepare, removing his armour, blacking his sword. The assassin's knife would now be whetted for Ambassador Cheerwell Maker. She would be found dead by one of the others. Then they would leave.

*Or, if they do not leave, we will cut them until they agree to*, Malius thought with a spike of anger. He could feel Accius's approval radiating to him through the wall.

Below him, the Beetles were still arguing. Their Fly-kinden slave had just flown in with news that the Khanaphir army was returning.

'And in cursed poor shape,' the little man was saying. 'They got a bloody nose, and then some. They're all kinds of beaten up.'

They were all of them down there: the old man, the fat man, the ambassador woman, but their attention was focused on the other woman, the one who normally seemed so admirably detached. Malius saw, with disapproval, that her creditable reserve had broken down. She had her hands to her mouth, eyes locked on the Fly in some kind of emotion that Malius found uncomfortably overstated.

'I'm not going,' she insisted. 'I'm not going.'

'Praeda . . .' the ambassador started, but the other woman shook her head.

'No, I couldn't . . . How could he *do* this to me? Men!' She rounded on the fat man, for want of another target. 'This is *unfair!* How often I've been wooed by some fool – she prodded him in the chest – 'by some ignorant oaf, and I've not cared. It's never touched me, before.'

'Now, look . . .' the fat one started, but she would not be diverted. Leaning on the stone rail of the landing, Malius found himself perversely fascinated. All this bared emotion, it was almost as if he could actually look into their minds. It was as eye-catching as someone throwing a screaming fit in the street.

'And now he comes along,' the woman complained, 'and he . . . he was different. I thought: there's something special here. Because he wasn't just some magnate's son, flashing his wealth, some scholar all full of himself, or a merchant adventurer. He was *real.* He was genuine. He was honest. And then, the moment he's got my attention, he goes off to war and gets himself killed.'

'You don't know that,' the ambassador protested.

'Trallo, did you see him there?' the grieving woman asked.

The pause the Fly allowed made the answer obvious. 'Not as such, but there were a lot of people about.'

'If he's still alive, he would come here,' the woman insisted.

'He might be thinking exactly the same about you,' the fat man pointed out. 'Bloody women, honestly.'

'He *would* come here,' she said again, sitting down. 'And I will wait for him here. I'll wait all night, if I must.'

*Mad, all of them*, was Accius's silent comment. He was ready now for when the house went to bed. The ambassador would get her throat cut, and thus the last tie holding the expedition to Khanaphes would be severed. *It's just as well the other woman's lover is dead. We might have had to kill him, then. Or her.*

*Luck has been scarce recently*, Malius thought. *We were owed some.*

She felt the straps taut about her wrists and ankles, falling into that familiar nightmare once again. Che did not need to open her eyes to know where she was: the interrogation room in the Myna palace. It was the room that she had personally witnessed being gutted by the resistance, every implement there destroyed, but in her mind it remained whole and unassailable.

*And he did not even use the machines on me*, she reflected, half in and half out of the dream. *Yet still it haunts me. How quickly would I have broken under torture, had he ordered it? And would they ever have been able to put the pieces of me back together?*

And she opened her eyes, seeing above her the poised arms, the drills and saws and files of an artificer's trade now horribly suborned. The sound of the steam engine was turned up, the noise that Thalric had used to hide his conspiracies. She looked around for him now, for this was not the first time her dreams had dragged her back here.

But it was not Thalric, at the levers. It was a slighter man, in grey robes, and she did not need him to turn around to recognize him. Turn he did, though, regarding her coolly with those white eyes, and she cried out, 'Achaeos!'

'Why do you make me do this?' he asked, his hands hovering over the controls. She was fully in the dream, now, and no escaping. It had all become terribly real in such a short space of time.

'Let me go!' she begged him, wrenching at the straps. 'Achaeos, let me go!'

'Not this time,' he said. His voice was quiet but she could hear it clearly over the whine of all the drills and the rumble of the steam. 'Che, look at us.'

'Achaeos – what is it? Why are you doing this?'

'Because you force me, Che,' he explained.

'Just tell me what you want me to do,' she said quickly, tripping over the words. 'I've tried! I've tried to follow you when you appear to me. I've gone everywhere you led me.'

'You do not understand,' he said. 'You do not understand at all. What do I want, you ask me? What do you think I want?'

'*I don't know! Tell me!*' she shrilled, for the drill arms were descending jerkily now, under his ministrations

'What do *you* want, Che? Freedom? To be let go? Do you think I would do this if you were not forcing me?'

The wrongness, the discontinuity of the situation, tried to speak to her, but the drill was very close, glittering within her vision, and it took all of her attention. She squirmed and twisted, trying to shift herself from underneath it.

It dropped, and she screamed—

And she woke.

The darkness of Khanaphes at night. The cool air from the river. There was no sound of distant battle, or of nocturnal assault by the Scorpions. The city was not yet under siege. She took a deep breath, still shaking.

*I cannot survive many more of those nightmares.* And, following from that: *What if I do not wake next time, as the drill comes down?*

The slightest sound then, and she went cold all over because there was someone in the room with her. She was instantly and absolutely sure of it. *Achaeos?* she wondered, but the ghost had never announced itself by sounds – just a smudge in the air, or the harsh, authoritative voice in her head.

Her Art penetrated the darkness, leaving her with that muted grey clarity that must have been how *he* always saw the world. Her heart caught, on seeing the cloaked figure crouching by the window.

'Oh, you have gone too far now,' she berated him, sitting

up. 'Thalric, what . . .?' And then her horrified pause as he stared through the darkness, towards her voice – because, of course, she had not seen him since matters had fallen foul with the Empire. *Which of your flags are you flying tonight, Thalric? Is it the black and the gold once more?*

'If you're here to kill me, you've missed your best chance,' she told him, sounding remarkably calm even to herself. She had a sword within easy reach of the bed, a habit learned from her uncle. He could sting her before her hand reached it, of course. She heard a ragged release of breath.

'I need your help, Che.'

He was not quite looking at her, just vaguely in the direction of the bed. She kept forgetting how the Wasps possessed no Art against the darkness. Seeing him more clearly, he looked as though the intervening days had not been kind to him. His clothes were creased and torn, and he was unshaven, hollow-eyed. He stayed close to the window, one hand reaching out towards the sill, as if ready to jump.

She swung her legs off the bed. In her flimsy nightshirt she would be just a shape in the dark to him, but he still made her feel self-conscious. She pulled on a tunic, telling herself it was against the chill.

'Help?' she asked him. 'Help against what?'

'The Empire,' he said, and she laughed at him. She had not meant to, and she saw his hurt expression, unguarded because he thought she could not see it.

'I'm sorry, Thalric, but—'

'I know,' he said flatly. 'I lose track myself, of whether they want me dead or alive. I certainly lost track this time, but now I know they want me dead. I don't know for what reason, but the orders must come from high up. I need your help, Che, because there's nobody else I can turn to.'

She had her sword in her hands now, not to wield but for the comfort it brought her. She padded towards him, seeing his eyes track her approach with difficulty. Little enough of the moonlight got in at her window.

*How strange to see him so helpless.* He sat himself back on the windowsill, within arm's reach of her – a man at the end of his resources but not defeated, never that. He had a wild look to him, the patient Rekef officer cast off for the moment, and she thought, *This is how he looked in Myna* – a man with nowhere else to go, and all the more dangerous for it. *He will make some other Wasps pay for putting him here again*, she thought, and it was oddly comforting. *So he is on my side again. At least I know.*

'What do you need?' she asked. 'If I can help you, I will.'

The sudden smile surprised her. *He thought I would cut him loose. And why not? Do I need these complications, when everything else is falling apart?* Despite the thought, she knew she would not turn him away.

'Osgan's on the run with me, and he needs medical help. We're holed up in a drinking den. I need . . . What I need is just someone who has the freedom of the city, to come and go. Someone to fetch for me and tell me what's going on. Above all, someone I can trust.'

'Major Thalric, are you trying to recruit me?' she asked with a slight smile, then collected her satchel, which held some basic medicines in it. When she turned to him again, his expression surprised her in its thoughtfulness.

'I have just described an agent's work, haven't I?' he said. 'No matter how hard I try, the old instincts just won't leave me alone.' He shrugged. 'Just as well, for I'll need them. Ready?'

She felt an odd leap of excitement at the thought, something she had been missing since the war. *But I hated all of that, surely.* She had served as her uncle's agent, therefore plunging into the invisible otherworld of the spymasters. Since the war's end, her life had been better in so many ways, and yet . . .

'So long as it doesn't interfere with my duties or endanger other people,' she told him, 'you have my services, Master Thalric.' It seemed a small enough promise to make.

‘We should leave now,’ he said, ‘so I’ll show you where Osgan and I are lying low. We can talk there, securely. Shall I meet you downstairs, outside?’

‘No need,’ she told him. She had her cloak on, now, and sandals, so she was ready to go. ‘Lead on.’

He let himself fall backwards out of the window, his wings quickly catching him. She followed, pausing, with a knee on the sill, to look out over the silent city.

She let her wings carry her through the window and into the air, clumsy beside Thalric yet able to follow where he led.

Behind her, in her room, the door was pushed open once the sound of voices had faded. A figure crept in, and found the empty bed. A brief dialogue of puzzlement passed between the intruder and his kinsman, before the Vekken stalked over to the window and stared out, baffled and frustrated, at the night.

There was a sudden commotion behind him, somewhere within the building, and Malius’s immediate command: *Hide!*

It should have been a simple job.

Vollen had gone over the details both with the newcomer Sulvec and with his Rekef commander, the Beetle-kinden Corolly Vastern. This covered the second stage of the Rekef operation in Khanaphes. Although Thalric, maddeningly absent, was still the primary target, they had some Imperial obligations to the force that would appear outside the city’s walls soon enough.

Vollen himself had gone off to creep around some of the unoccupied embassies, enough to satisfy himself that each was built to a similar plan. *Mustn’t show favouritism to any of the ambassadors,* he supposed. What it meant, in fact, was that his job was that much easier. He had never seen inside the Collegiate embassy, but now he knew for sure he did not need to.

They had gone over the complement of the Collegiate delegation, so in his mind there was a concise list.

'It's very simple,' Sulvec had explained. 'It is better for the Empire if word does not reach Collegium of what has happened until much later. Certainly not word brought by their own people. Therefore . . .' He had made a dismissive gesture with one hand, which had abruptly ended up with it raised and open, facing Vollen. *Therefore kill them.*

Sulvec had spared him seven soldiers. The Rekef force inside Khanaphes was not large, but that should be enough.

They burst in through three windows at the front of the building, two of which had not even been shuttered. The sound of the third window's wooden frame giving way was the first warning the Collegiates had of an attack.

'Into all the rooms. Drag everyone out to the main hall,' Vollen snapped at his men, setting himself down beside the front door. He could hear various sounds of confusion from the house, but no outright panic yet. 'Tell them that they'll live so long as they cooperate,' he added. It was not true but it might be effective. He wanted them all rounded up, as peaceably as possible, and the entrance hall was the quickest place for it. His men were already spreading out, some to the downstairs rooms, others heading up the stone steps to the landing and the bedrooms. Once the residents were gathered in one place he could put them up against a wall and make an end of them all together. Vollen was a neat-minded man.

He waited, looking at the blandly ceremonial decorations with which the Khanaphir had adorned the hall. They were different to those in the Imperial embassy, and yet they might as well have been the same. Their hosts clearly had a taste for the meaninglessly ornate – like all those little carvings they put everywhere.

His men were returning now, and he began his count.

The fat man came first, ballooning out his nightshirt and

complaining vociferously. He had a half-full bottle in his hands and nearly tumbled down the full length of the stairs, saving himself only by clutching at the soldier who escorted him.

'What in the wastes is going on?' he demanded of Vollen. 'I'm a Master of the College of Collegium, curse you!'

'Shut up,' growled Vollen, and backhanded him into silence. In the ringing echo of the blow the fat man reached up to touch his reddening cheek and there were actual tears in his eyes. His flabby lips phrased words of protest, but no sound emerged. Vollen smiled approvingly.

The others were appearing now. A half-dozen servants had been rounded up by two of his soldiers, young Khanaphir men and women, wide-eyed but docile, being herded like beasts out into the hall. *Best to kill them as well,* Vollen decided. *No witnesses, then. Not that this will be any great mystery, but let them wonder about it nonetheless.*

The older man and the proud-looking woman were being hustled after them. He wore a loosely belted robe that bared his dark chest, wiry with grey hair, and thin enough for Vollen to have counted his ribs. The woman had obviously succumbed to the Khanaphir heat, for she was wrapped in a bedsheet and he guessed she was naked beneath. She was a good-looking piece of flesh as well, for one of inferior kinden. For a moment he wished he had more liberty and time to spare on this mission. She would have proved a welcome reward for staunch Imperial service. The Rekef came before personal pleasure, though, and besides, his men would all want a piece. That was bad for discipline, and this was not the Slave Corps, after all.

'Hurry it up,' he hissed, mostly to himself. There was another coming now from upstairs, a black-skinned Ant-kinden who was fully dressed, even to the now-empty scabbard at his hip. The soldier with him kept a few steps behind, well out of striking distance. Of the lot of them, he was the only one who looked dangerous.

There was a flurry of activity further along the landing. A small figure flitted out and over the rail, landing so close to Vollen that his forehead and Vollen's palm were just an inch from touching.

'Vollen, isn't it?' Trallo began, with a cheerful nod. He was fully dressed, and Vollen guessed he had been flying in and out this night already. They had not expected him to be here.

The Fly was now smiling up at him. 'What's going on?' he asked, looking around the academics and the soldiers.

'Just stand with the others, Fly-kinden,' Vollen told him sharply.

'Now, wait, you know me and Ambassador Thalric . . .' The sentence died as Trallo registered Vollen's expression. Vollen saw something click into place in the little man's head, an understanding quicker and deeper than any to be found amongst the Beetles.

*He goes first*, Vollen decided. *If anyone has a chance of escaping, it's him.* 'Keep a stern watch on that one,' he instructed his men.

The last of his force was leaning over the landing rail now, waiting for orders.

'Where are the others?' Vollen demanded of them.

'That's all there are, sir,' one of them reported. 'We've gone through every room.'

*That's not right.* There was that woman who had met them when they arrived, and most of all there was the ambassador. Something else was niggling at him too, but he could not immediately place it.

'Where's your ambassador?' he demanded of the old man.

'Abed,' was the dignified reply. 'My name is Berjek Gripshod and if you have diplomatic business, at this late hour, I shall assist you.'

'There's nobody else here, sir,' the soldier left on the landing insisted.

Vollen put a hand out to pincer the old man's chin with thumb and forefinger, the heat of his sting already warming his palm. 'Where,' he said again, 'is the ambassador?'

'She was here.' It was the Beetle woman. 'She's been here all day, and I saw her going to bed.'

*How did she know?* was Vollen's immediate thought, because he understood instantly that the woman Cheerwell had somehow fled the embassy already, abandoning her companions to their fate.

He had a sudden and unwelcome conviction that she would be somewhere with Thalric. The two of them had seemed too close for Imperial propriety.

'Where is the other woman? The . . .' What was the name now? 'Coggen.'

'Dead,' Gripshod explained. 'Some days back.'

Vollen released him, stepping back and levelling his hand. It seemed to him that he had heard something of that, now it was mentioned.

'What is going on?' the old man asked, rubbing at his jaw. 'You must be mad.'

'Vollen, listen to me,' Trallo spoke quickly. 'Vollen, there are other ways than this. There's no war between Collegium and the Empire – not yet. Do you really think that this will go unnoticed? Vollen, nobody wants these kind of complications, really, when you think about it clearly, come on—'

Vollen turned his open palm on the little man, choking off the words. *Fly-kinden – loathsome, treacherous vermin, and this one most of all.*

'Deal with them,' he snarled.

The crossbow bolt took him by surprise, lancing into the back of the man standing nearest to the Vekken prisoner. Vollen's own stingshot went wild as the Fly-kinden ducked desperately away. There was another Vekken on the balcony. *There were two of them? Of course there were two of them!* So little had been seen of either of the Ants that somehow the two had become one in his mind. The ambassador's had been the absence that Vollen had fixated on.

The soldier on the balcony turned his sting towards the newcomer, but the Vekken had closed already, and they were sword to sword instantly.

'Kill them!' Vollen shouted. 'All of them!' The first Vekken was now wrestling with another of his men, holding both wrists away, trying to bend the Wasp backwards. Vollen turned back to the Beetles.

The fat man moved. It was a ponderous lunge at the man next to him, but unexpected. The bottle smashed over the Wasp's head, and one thick hand closed about the man's sword-hilt and wrenched the blade from its sheath, hard enough to spin the Wasp half around. With a grunt of effort he drove it into the disarmed soldier as hard as he could. It punched into the man's armour, leaving a savage dent and knocking the man off his feet. The Wasp's sting flashed, more by instinct than intent, knocking the fat Beetle backwards.

The old man made a try for Vollen, but the Wasp punched him in the face as hard as he could, laying him out on the floor. The Khanaphir slaves were cowering away, keeping as low as they could. Vollen snarled and looked around for the woman with his hand already extended.

Something struck him hard, almost throwing him from his feet. He felt a blade scrape across his armour, and then the Fly-kinden, Trallo, was fighting with him, trying to wrench his arm aside. Vollen made a grab for him, but the little man was agile, tugging and pulling at him and escaping his clutching hands – a nuisance with a small knife, but a nuisance that was taking all of Vollen's attention.

The Beetle woman lunged at him and broke a chair across his back, smashing the priceless Khanaphir craftsmanship to splinters. Vollen hit the ground hard, feeling his shoulder take the brunt of the attack. He turned onto his back, palms up. The woman grabbed one of his arms, trying to twist it flat. Trallo raised his dagger, his face a white mask of fear.

The flash of the soldier's sting warmed Vollen's face, and the little man was thrown halfway across the entrance hall by the impact of it. The woman screamed and leapt away, staring at the Fly's charred body.

Vollen whisked himself to his feet with a flick of his wings. 'Right,' he said, fully aware that he would receive no commendations for this. Then the front door burst open.

He turned to see a huge Beetle-kinden in Khanaphir armour, a sword in his hand and bloody murder on his face.

*Emperor save us!* he thought. *It's the First Soldier.*

Amnon made a wordless sound and charged. Vollen's sting spat its fire, melting a hand-sized section of scale mail but not slowing the giant in the least. Then Amnon's leaf-bladed sword was thrust, effortlessly to the hilt, into his chest.

Vollen fell to his knees, everything around him suddenly more than he could cope with. Amnon had his sword raised again, and the two Vekken were still spoiling for a fight. Two of his men fled out of the windows, the rest were already dead save for one man, who made a feint at Amnon and then plainly decided the big Khanaphir was too much to deal with. He tried to fly away, too, but the Vekken crossbowman picked him off even as he lifted into the space of the entrance hall.

Feeling the world fall from him, Vollen toppled face-first onto the tiles of the Collegiate embassy.

Praeda crouched beside Berjek Gripshod, calling his name and shaking him roughly. At last his lips moved and his eyelids fluttered. Peering up at her from floor level, his gaze was unsteady. 'Uncalled for,' he murmured. 'Quite uncalled for.'

'They killed Trallo,' she got out. 'Oh Berjek, they killed Trallo.'

She looked up, and saw another fallen body. Her hands went to her mouth again, she was feeling ill. 'Oh, Berjek . . .'

The old man levered himself up, and then saw what she had seen. He struggled to his feet, a hand to his head, and staggered over.

'Gorget! Get up! Manny . . .'

Praeda saw him stop as he reached the great sprawling form, then drop painfully to his knees. She joined him there tentatively. There was no doubt at all from the outraged expression in those open eyes, or from the char-edged burn-hole in his chest. Mannerly Gorget was dead.

Praeda stared about her, as though, somehow, someone would be able to help. *Do magic. Bring back the dead.* She saw the two Vekken standing close beside each other, like some trick with mirrors. *And we would all be dead, if not for them.* Then her eyes found Amnon. His face, though expressionless, was watching her.

Trembling, she put out a hand towards him. Without a moment's thought he swept her up in his arms, clasping her to his broad chest where the armour was still warm from the Wasp's stingshot. There she let herself go, sobbing into his embrace, shuddering over and over until at last she could manage the words.

'You came,' she said. 'You came for me.'

'It should have been sooner,' he said gently. 'But I had a dying friend I could not leave. This has been a night for death. First my Penthet, and now your companions. I am sorry, I should have come sooner.'

'You came,' she said.

Berjek gave a long, sad sigh. 'This is too much,' the old man's voice came to her. 'Too much to bear. War . . . murder . . . the time has come to cut our losses, Praeda. We should have left long before, while we all could.'

She felt Amnon's arms tighten slightly and she said to her colleague, 'Go. You must leave. The Khanaphir will find a ship for you, and lower the Estuarine Gate.' Around Amnon's shoulder she met his gaze. 'But I will stay.'

'I suppose I should not be so surprised at that,' he said

sadly. 'And, as for Cheerwell, she will not leave, I am sure. Something in this city has its hooks in her.' He glanced up at the Ants. 'And you two?'

'We have a task unfinished here,' replied one of them. Berjek could not guess at the conversation that they were holding, in the space between their heads. 'We may decide to leave with you, but it depends on other factors. Perhaps, if the ambassador leaves with you, she could assist us on the journey back.'

# Thirty-Two

'I've done what I can for your arm,' Che said. It had involved more of her night's work than her earlier talk with Thalric. The wound was infected, and she had cleaned it out and applied whatever salves she had handy to keep it pure and deaden the pain. Osgan was conscious but pale, his forehead shiny with sweat even in the cool of the night.

'Thank you,' he croaked.

'If we were in Collegium . . .' Che shrugged. 'I can't guarantee that you'll keep the arm, though. I'm sorry. It's not gone rotten yet, but . . .' Her gesture took in the shabby little room that Thalric had found them, a cellar dug out beneath a drinking house and with one of the walls cluttered with barrels. The first dawn light glimmered through the two wide shafts cut into one wall, where the river-borne goods came in. They were also the way Thalric would escape, if the worst came to the worst.

Osgan nodded weakly.

'There isn't a proper doctor in this whole wretched city,' Thalric complained. 'They don't know the first thing about medicine.'

Che thought about that. 'I think you're right, actually.'

He barked a brief laugh. 'The legendary cosmopolitanism of Collegium is rubbing away, is it?'

'Apt medicine and Inapt medicine are very different,'

Che reproached him. 'You and I have good cause to remember that.'

It took Thalric a moment to catch the reference, but she saw the understanding dawn in his face. *Achaeos, in Collegium, asking to be taken back to his own people – for all the good it did him.*

'These Khanaphir are Apt,' Che went on, 'but they're . . . they're trying to live like the Inapt, for some reason.'

Thalric made a derisive face. 'They're just backward, holed up at the east end of nowhere.'

'It's more than that,' Che argued, the pieces falling into place one by one. 'They trade with the Exalsee ports, and they're close enough to some of your Imperial cities, for that matter. So it's not geography, it's . . .'

'Wilful ignorance,' Thalric suggested.

'It's something like that, yes. They are fighting tooth and nail to ignore the last five hundred years. It's like with the Moth-kinden, except . . . except these people are Apt.'

'Imperial doctrine would say that this is why the Empire's intervention is so necessary,' Thalric said drily. 'In this case, I'm not sure I disagree.'

'They're Apt,' Che repeated, trying to catch the fugitive train of thought, 'but they once had masters who were Inapt . . . whoever they were. And they still remember those masters so keenly, with such reverence, that they refrain from anything that might have offended them back in the Days of Lore. They hold themselves back simply out of respect.'

Thalric regarded her doubtfully. 'Well, now it's come back to sting them blind, frankly. The Scorpions will be all over this city in a tenday, at the most. Half the Khanaphir army's dead in just the first engagement. If it wasn't *us* out there, I'd be advising the Ministers to seek Imperial protection right now. We'd make better masters than the Many of Nem.'

'Is that the plan?' Che asked him. 'Avenging Empire sweeps in and puts the invaders to flight? Imperial governor gratefully received by the city? I don't think that would work so well, not here.'

'I lose track of the plan,' said Thalric. She saw his face sag, for just a moment showing her how tired he was. 'The plan seems to be to kill me first, the city second. I do not understand why they so badly want me dead.' Seeing her expression, he pressed on before she could speak. 'Oh, I have done things sufficient to warrant my death, but this makes no sense. This is the high Rekef's work, that much seems sure. This is . . . this stems from someone standing beside the throne, if not the throne itself. It's *personal*.' He shook himself impatiently. 'Che, you have to go now. You know what you must do.'

'As your agent, yes.' She smiled sourly. 'After I've spoken with the others, I'll find Ethmet or some other senior Minister. I'll warn them that the Imperial force within the city will be looking to sabotage the defence, assassinate their leaders and the like.'

'It's what I'd do,' Thalric confirmed. And then: 'It's what I've done.'

Che went over to the shafts, paused there and looked back. 'Be safe, Thalric. I'll come back for you.'

'Send Trallo with messages, if you can,' Thalric said. 'Che . . .'

His urgent tone turned her back, as she was about to call upon her wings. He stood regarding her with a calculating expression, as if making his tallies and finding that they did not add up. This was Thalric the spymaster, she realized, the old Thalric – and somehow she was about his business.

'Why are you not just leaving, Che? I don't believe you think your intervention can save Khanaphes from the Scorpions, even if you cared to. What is this place, to you?'

The spectre of Achaeos rose in her mind, and all the frustrations of her Inaptitude. 'Do you need to know?' she asked him. 'Really?'

After a thoughtful pause he shook his head, and she

scrambled out of the hatch, heading above and into sight of the river.

She found the embassy unoccupied save for servants. In the moment she entered, the desolate scene fell on her in pieces: the feeling of abandonment, the eerie silence, the men and women industriously cleaning the floor of an unmistakable stain.

'What has happened here?' she demanded hoarsely.

They pointed her towards the Scriptora, and there she found Berjek and Praeda, who had been hurriedly ensconced in guarded rooms. She found them sitting together, looking tense and fearful, whilst one of the Khanaphir ministers hovered nearby.

'Bloody ink and seals!' Berjek swore, as he saw her. 'You're here! We weren't sure you were even alive.'

'What's going on?' Che asked, because the Khanaphir, in their private way, had not told her.

After Berjek had done with his halting narrative, when the borrowed room had been loaded with two absences, one large, one small, Che remained very quiet.

*Too slow, Thalric, with your warnings. You must be losing your touch.* 'Manny, Trallo and Petri. Was Petri their victim as well?'

'Unlikely.' Berjek shook his head. 'They mentioned her by name, as if expecting to find her at the embassy. Che, if it hadn't been for Amnon and the Vekken—'

'Where are the Vekken?' Che demanded, feeling an uncomfortable twitch at the thought. She was not so blind to the way they had been looking at her. She did not know what conclusions they had come to in their hermetic little asylum of a shared mind, but none of it boded well for her.

'They . . . would not accept our hosts' hospitality,' Berjek said, with an embarrassed glance at the Khanaphir Minister. 'Certainly not after what happened this morning on the river.' Seeing Che's frown, he hastened to explain. 'The

Scorpions are here, Che. They arrived with the dawn, and they're setting up outside the walls.' The old Beetle sighed. 'I was determined to leave today. I came here looking for a ship out of here. That's how I met Tathbir, here. He's the Minister of the Oceans.'

The short, podgy Beetle genuflected briefly, bobbing his shaven head.

'But when the Khanaphir lowered the river gate this morning, the Scorpions were already waiting for them,' Berjek explained. 'They put a leadshot into a fishing boat, sank it with all hands. They see that the river could be used to land a flanking force, is my guess. It doesn't take a tactical genius to see the opening. They've got a pair of leadshotters waiting out there to hole any vessel that comes out. Meanwhile, nobody's going anywhere until that can be dealt with.'

'We have sent messengers to the Marsh people,' Tathbir added. 'They will take this matter into their own hands. Until it is done, though, we cannot lower the Estuarine Gate. We are sorry.'

'The assault on the city has yet to start,' Berjek put in. 'The Scorpions are displaying unusual patience for their kind, I understand. Some small groups have come within bowshot of the walls, to their regret, but the rest are setting their engines to loose upon the city's defences. I know my field enough to know that the walls of Khanaphes were not designed to resist leadshotters.'

It was the suddenly stiffened pose of Tathbir that heralded the new arrival, the frisson of indignation radiating from the man. A shadow fell through the door: a man in dark armour, one whose face Che used to know.

'Are you yet in the city?' the Minister demanded. 'I am sure the First Minister banished you.'

Totho's stare remained intense enough for the stout man to take a step back. With his snapbow slung under his arm, within easy reach, there was something of the pirate about

Totho now, a man outside rules. 'I was called here,' he said flatly. 'The First Soldier wishes to consult with me, so how could I say no?' His eyes dismissed the Minister utterly. 'Che, I need to talk with you.'

'I suppose you do.' This was not a conversation she had been looking forward to but, at the same time, she had been expecting it. 'Elsewhere,' she decided. This was not for Berjek and Praeda, or for the Ministers.

She chose the pump room, eventually, out of some perverse need for the appropriate – the secluded room with its primitive vacuum pump that she no longer understood.

'Are you going to start with pointing out how right you were?' she began. He had paused in the doorway as though there might be an ambush waiting. Now he stepped in and found himself a seat on the horizontal shaft of the pump.

'Would that help? Probably not,' he replied, his shoulder-plates scraping as he shrugged. 'The Empire never changes, as I should know well.'

'You were wrong about Thalric,' she told him, before she could stop herself.

'Was I?' There was no admission of it in his face. 'You think he hasn't betrayed you, just because you haven't found out about it yet.'

'The Empire wants him dead,' she said.

'The Empire has wanted him dead before. And then it calls, and he comes like a trained cricket. He's spent the last four months sleeping with the Empress.'

The thought cut her more deeply than she expected. She had known it, of course, but had steered her mind deftly away from it, every time. 'You've done your research.'

'He hurt you,' Totho said simply, 'so I found out what I could. We in the Glove have sources in the Empire. You'd have to walk a long mile before you found a man as untrustworthy as Thalric.'

She could feel a wave of anger rising in her, hearing the man attacked behind his back. Nothing but the truth, surely, and yet because it was a truth Thalric himself owned to, with his chequered past so openly admitted, she felt that she should be defending him.

'New topic, Totho?' she said. 'Unless all you wanted to do is come here and complain about Thalric.'

She saw his lips purse, but then he said, 'I can get you out of Khanaphes. You and your friends.'

She stared at him, waiting for the catch. He, however just waited for her response, looking down at his hands as they rested on his knees.

*He got that from Uncle Sten*, she thought, and asked, 'How? They say the Scorpions have engines watching the river.'

'My ship is the *Fourth Iteration*, and she's fast enough to dodge leadshots, tough enough to shrug a few off before suffering. She's a Solarnese corsair with a reinforced hull. She even has some smallshotters for the rails. She can leave as soon as the Khanaphir lower the gates, and for us they'll lower the gates because they want rid of us. Even with the Scorpions outside their walls.'

She stood up, with desperate hope. 'Take Berjek and Praeda,' she said. 'Please, take them away from here.'

'No,' he said.

'Totho . . .'

'I will take you,' he said. 'I will take you, and with you, anyone you wish – save for Thalric. I will not leave here without you.'

'Totho, the city's under siege now. What will you do here, if you don't leave? Don't be a fool.'

'I'll just have to make sure the Scorpions lose, then, won't I,' he said.

'You *are* a fool,' she decided. 'You'd risk your life, your followers . . .'

'Yes, I'm a fool. One among many.'

'But why?'

'You *know* why.' He was on his feet suddenly and she shrank back from him. 'Che, you don't need to ask that question. I will stay, if you stay. I will also leave if you will leave with me. That's because I love you. You know that I love you. That I always have, since we were students and you were copying down my answers in class.'

'You're right. I didn't need to ask,' she replied, and then: 'I wish I hadn't.'

He took the blow, rolled with it. 'I never knew what you saw in the Moth,' he said, 'but I knew what you missed in me. I've tried, Che, to make something more of myself. I've tried to patch the defects that nature gave me. I'm still a halfbreed, but I'm a magnate now. I've money, prospects. They'd kiss my feet in Helleron, if I walked in under Iron Glove colours. My hand is on the tiller of artifice.' He looked into her face, forcing her to avoid his gaze lest it scorch her. 'And I can see, though – I can see it's not enough. So tell me what you want me to be, Che. Tell me what it is I'm still missing. Or is it the blood? It didn't seem to matter to you, of all people, that I was a half-caste.'

'It's not your heritage,' she said. 'Do you really think I care about that?'

'No,' he said, fiercely. 'No, I don't. I really don't. So tell me what it is that's wrong with me.'

'Oh, Totho,' she sighed, 'all this time you've been trying to make yourself into what you think I might want . . . but I can barely see the friend I once knew, let alone anything beyond. You've built yourself a suit of armour for the inside as well as the out. Just listen to you now!' She felt suddenly frustrated with him. 'You're bargaining for my affection with the lives of my friends, yet you spent most of the war working for the Empire.'

'To save Salma!' he put in hotly, but she came back just as hard.

'Was it?' she demanded. 'Was that what it was? And did they never give you a chance to leave them, after that? Totho, you rail at Thalric for all the things he has done, and, yes, he has done terrible things, but at least he tried to divert his course *away* from them. You have just moved *towards* and *towards*. Totho, tell me you could not have escaped from the army, if you had wanted.'

'And what would have happened then?' he demanded. They were almost nose to nose now, an inch from drawing swords. 'I beat them in the end, Che. I beat the Empire, in Szar. What would have happened there, if I had just snuck off and left?'

The moment teetered in the balance, the weights of recollection dropping. Che had been in Myna, of course, and she had heard the news from Szar, in more detail than she needed. It had been a great victory against the Empire, but nobody had felt much like celebrating it, not even the Szaren.

'Szar?' she began. She had not seen the twisted bodies of the Wasp garrison, but there had been no shortage of description. An entire force of thousands, with their slaves and servants and Auxillians, dead in a single night, and in agony. The last she had heard, there was still a whole district of their city that the local Bee-kinden did not enter, for fear of the coughing sickness that might still come to cull them. They said that the air still smelled of sour death, there, when the wind was in the wrong quarter.

'Che . . .'

'Szar. That was *you*?'

His face was that of a man who would do anything just to retract a few words. 'Che, you weren't there. There was nothing else . . .'

She was retreating from him, back to the doorway, staring at the creature that wore her friend's face. He called her name again, but at the mere sound of it she fled from him, leaving him in the darkness of the pump room, her skin crawling at the thought of what he had done.

Amnon summoned him soon after. The defeat on the field had not managed to stifle his fierce energy. Totho felt tired just looking at him.

'You called for me, First Soldier,' the artificer said, feeling in no mood for this now. No mood at all.

'You are still in the city,' Amnon observed.

'Is that it? Is that why you sent for me?' Totho demanded. 'Yes, I am still in the city. My people are still in the city. So what are you going to do about it? Shed a little blood early, before the Scorpions come for the rest?'

'I will make use of you, if you will let me,' Amnon suggested. 'Totho, will you walk the walls with me?'

'Walk the . . .? Why?'

'Because I need to understand,' the big Khanaphir said. 'I need to know what to do, Totho, and I need your wisdom to guide me.'

'Wisdom?' Totho managed to say, strangled by the need to laugh at the word. 'I've precious little wisdom, Amnon.'

'I'll take anything I can get,' Amnon said, quite seriously. 'Will you do this one thing for me before you go?'

'Of course,' Totho replied, finding that he meant it. He liked Amnon: there was some trace of commonality between them, despite their disparate cultures and histories. Both of them, at this moment, were where the metal met.

Khanaphes was gripped by panic. Totho saw people cowering inside their homes, saw groups of soldiers rushing here and there, seemingly with no aim at all. Passing over the great span of bridge that linked the two halves of the city, they heard a hollow knocking sound, distant and harmless save for the plume of dust that rose beyond the walls. Amnon started, but Totho put a hand out.

'That wasn't an attack. There's been no attack yet.'

'They are raiding all the farms, burning the fields,' Amnon spat. 'Also they know that by making us wait, they also make us fear.'

'And by launching a few rocks over the city they'll make you fear even more,' Totho agreed. 'They want you shaken up by the time they meet you hand to hand.'

'No,' Amnon said firmly, 'they simply want us to fear.

That is their sport, to know that the good people of my city live in terror of them for this interval of time, before the end comes.'

From the lofty arch of the bridge they could see the city's soldiers atop the walls. Totho took his telescope out automatically, panning its lens across the battlements. The Khanaphir sentries were rushing back and forth, and then he noticed a sudden haze of dust rising from between the great stones of the wall. The sound of the leadshotter's discharge came a moment later.

The walls of Khanaphes had stood a long time. They were tall and thick, built of massive slabs of rock, curving slightly as they rose. There was a walkway along the top to allow two men to walk abreast, with stone steps leading up to the parapet every two hundred yards. Those walls would have seemed a remarkable piece of engineering even two centuries ago, let alone whenever they had actually been built. Totho knelt as he reached the top, pressing a hand to the stone to feel the grain of it. In his mind were the fortress designs that Drephos had sketched out on scrap paper, in order to resist a siege by modern weapons. They were all planes and edges, thrusting out into the besieging force to give the widest arc of shot, and slanted to let the enemy's weapons glance off them.

'Tell me,' Amnon asked him, 'will we hold? They tell me that the Masters would never let the walls of Khanaphes fall. What do you tell me?'

Totho went to the ramparts and the sight beyond struck him hard, although it must strike any Khanaphir observing it that much harder. The Many of Nem were encamped outside, a squalid mess of tents and lean-tos against a horizon thick with smoke. They had laid waste everything that lay within a day's ride, pillaged everything worth taking. *They must expect a quick siege, otherwise they will starve.*

The artillery positions were well ensconced within the front ranks of the Scorpion horde. Clearly the Scorpions, or their Imperial masters, knew how vulnerable unattended engines could be. There was a bank of ten leadshotters, positioned quite tightly. Through his glass Totho could recognize the model as an old Imperial make that had first seen service before the Twelve-year War. It would still do the trick though.

*Three rounds?* No, the Khanaphir walls were too thick and solid. *Twelve rounds?* Perhaps, yes. The stones were not properly mortared, not as a Lowlander Beetle would have built them. They were not hard, either. With a dagger's blade he could scratch deeply into them, turning stone to sand by his own tiny industry. How accurate were the Scorpion artillerists? *Twenty rounds then, at most.*

'Your walls will not hold,' he declared, and the shudder of fear that ran through the men around him made him feel like some doomsaying prophet. 'Unless they lose the use of their engines, or are very short on ammunition, your walls will crack and then fall.'

Another single leadshotter boomed out its plume of smoke, and Totho felt the faint vibration as the shot hammered into stone. It was obviously a day of idle practice for the Scorpions, since the war host was still reassembling after a day's hard looting. *If we had the full army of the city with us now, perhaps we could have broken them,* Totho thought. They had already left too many dead on the field, though, and hope and morale now lay out there amongst the broken weapons and the corpses. The Khanaphir did not have it in them to sally out and attack their besiegers.

'What can we do?' Amnon asked softly.

'I don't know,' Totho said. 'I'd suggest surrender but, given the enemy, I don't think that's an option.'

Later, Totho sat in the Iron Glove factora, listening to the sounds of his men packing up everything for their departure. Soon they would come for the crate he was sitting on, down here in the cellar. For now it provided a quiet place to think:

about Amnon and about Che, and about what Che had said.

*What if . . .?* It was a poisonous game. It was a game for weak people who would rather not live with the decisions they had made, or who had made no decisions at all and had found a bad end by following the river's flow.

*I have always made my own decisions.* It seemed a fragile thing to be proud of but he clung to it. His past was like a string of beads, each representing a point where he could have chosen otherwise. *Should I have stayed with Stenwold and Che rather than running away?* That begged the question of 'What if Salma had gone to Tark alone, without Totho's help?' and it was unanswerable at this remove. *But if I had stayed, I would have done something I would regret. I would have killed Achaeos, or else got myself killed. I could not have borne the two of them together.*

The next bead was, 'What if I had not saved Salma, by selling myself to the Empire?' *Salma would be dead, no what-ifs about it.* But then Salma had died anyway, on some bloody battlefield. So it became just another choice he had made and that he would have to take responsibility for. Which led to Che's question of whether he could simply have taken off the shackles and fled.

*It has always been so easy for Che, so clear-cut.* He did not have the words to explain to her how he had found a place for himself under the black and gold flag, at the side of the maverick Colonel-Auxillian. *There was nowhere in the world that was home to me, until I met Drephos.* He could not pretend ignorance of her likely reaction to all he had done. He had done it, in fact, to try to exorcize himself from her influence. Che, his nagging conscience, his residual sense of right and wrong, just a gnat in the face of Drephos's comforting philosophy of technological advance.

*But, even then, I helped.* Another straw to cling to. He had saved Che from the interrogators once more, and alone this time, without any killer Mantis or Mynan resistance to help him. He had passed the snapbow plans to the Lowlands, arming Stenwold and his allies with the fruits of Totho's own invention. He had liberated Szar.

He had liberated Szar. In doing so, he had saved the Mynan resistance, created the Three-city Alliance. He had remade the map. He, Totho, the halfbreed.

Yet she hated him for it. Even this great Right had become a wrong. *And if I had killed them all with a blade, like Tisamon? Would that be right, then?* It was the means, the coldly efficient means, that so horrified the woman. He could eviscerate as many Wasps as he wanted on the battlefield, but woe betide him if he preferred to use his brain.

*We use whatever tools are given to us. I am no great warrior, but is that what she'd prefer? To have me dead alongside Salma, sword in hand?*

Perhaps that was indeed what she would prefer. A dead Totho of unstained character would be easier for her to file away and forget.

He heard boots on the steps leading to the cellar, and Corcoran peered down at him. 'Sir,' the Solarnese man enquired, 'how's it going down here?'

'How's the ship?' Totho asked him from his seat on the remaining crate.

'Every bolt tightened, ready to go, sir,' Corcoran reported, taking the last few steps down. 'The lads are wondering when we're moving out. Those Scorpions won't wait for ever before kicking this place in like an egg.'

'We should leave here,' Totho said.

Corcoran regarded him dubiously. 'Well yes, sir, that was the idea.'

'What will happen to the city, after we're gone?' asked Totho.

Corcoran stared at him. 'Same thing as if we were still here. It's not as though it was ever going to be much of a market for us. Come on, chief, give us the word. We'll leadshot their gate down, if they won't open up for us.'

Totho rested his head in his heads. 'Corcoran . . .'

'Sir?'

'Are we doing the right thing, do you think?'

'By leaving? Absolutely. Staying about would be a bloody stupid thing to do, sir.' The Solarnese was beginning to sound unnerved.

'But it would be the right thing,' Totho murmured, almost to himself. 'That's how *she'd* see it.'

They heard a heavy, slow tread above them. Meyr the Mole Cricket was negotiating the steps.

'Here you both are,' the big man said, the gloom of the cellar no barrier to his sight. 'What's this?'

'Meyr,' Totho said, standing, 'do you think we should leave?'

The Mole Cricket was now halfway down the stairs, hunching forward, yet with his back and shoulders still brushing the cellar ceiling. 'I think we should,' he said carefully, but in a tone that invited further comment.

'And what do you yourself want to do?' Totho asked him.

'My people are slow to anger,' Meyr said ponderously. 'We lack the fire to make us proper fighters. Still.' He let the word sit there for a moment. 'Still, I would very much like to kill some Scorpions and Wasps. Very much so.'

*And is that right? Is it right that Meyr blames himself for the death of Faighl and the others, and now wants vengeance? How good the Wasps are at teaching us their own motivations.*

'Come on, now,' said Corcoran nervously, looking from one to the other.

'Send a message to the *Iteration*,' Totho decided, 'and tell them to stand ready. Corcoran, go yourself, have them load the smallshotters and warm the engines over.'

'Because we're going?' the Solarnese said, without much hope.

'Have every fighting man armed and armoured by dawn tomorrow. Meyr, you're in charge of that.'

'Right,' the Mole Cricket rumbled.

'I have a conversation with Amnon to finish – and one he's not going to like,' Totho explained. 'When I get back, I want to see every Iron Glove man ready for war.'

He found Amnon up on the walls, of course. The Scorpion leadshotters had been idly throwing shot at the stones, or over them and into the city. Totho took a moment, on gaining the battlement, to spy out a leadshotter crew with his glass and assess their technique. The Scorpions themselves were the very essence of brutality, but he could pick out Wasp-kinden overseeing them and the savages were swifter and more practised than he would have thought.

The First Soldier was leaning on the ramparts, staring out at the enemy that he could not defeat. He glanced at Totho, then looked back at the great ramshackle chaos of the Scorpion camp.

'Come to say your farewells?' he asked. 'I shall have the Estuarine Gate lowered for you.'

'Not just yet,' Totho told him.

'Oh?' Amnon turned, barely flinching as another solitary leadshotter spoke thunder, the shot whistling high over the city.

'I have an answer,' Totho said. 'The only answer that I can give you on how to defend your city from the Many of Nem. It's not an answer that the Ministers would approve of, and I doubt you'll like it much either, but it's an answer.'

'Speak,' Amnon said, bracing himself for it.

'The Scorpions out there are not an army; they are a huge mob of thugs. A proper army has supply lines, logistics. This lot are living directly off the land, and that cannot support them long. They need a quick victory, so it follows that if you delay them long enough, perhaps two tendays at the utmost, they will not be able to sustain their attack.'

'I had thought as much.'

'Exactly. You don't need to be a tactician to see it,' Totho agreed. 'But they'll burst through these walls tomorrow or the day after. No doubt of it. You've probably already noticed a few cracks, where they've struck home.' Totho could see the truth of that in Amnon's eyes. 'So the wall will not hold, and they can keep knocking holes in it. If you put men in the breach, they can knock holes in them too. And their infantry is well suited to taking advantage of a breach, I think: fast-moving, hard-hitting. They're not men for standing in line and taking a charge, but men for breaking through shield-walls and pushing forward. So, the wall ceases to be a defensive asset very quickly. In fact, once they've taken the wall, it becomes a disadvantage. Their crossbowmen will soon make full use of the elevation.'

Amnon nodded, taking it all in. 'So,' he asked, 'what is your answer? How do we save our city, even for a short while?'

'Abandon the western half of it,' Totho said, expecting a strong reaction. In truth, he half expected Amnon to throw him off the wall. Instead the big Beetle just twitched, as he had when the leadshotter had loosed a moment before.

'Have your soldiers go house to house, instructing everyone to evacuate the western city. Have them take every single boat to ferry people across the river, and then paddle back for more. Have them cross the bridge in their hundreds. Have them carry only what is easily to hand, and primarily whatever footstuffs they can cart. *Everyone.* Everyone moves east, across the river. Because the river becomes your defensive wall, Amnon, and the leadshotters cannot tear it down. There is only one bridge, and we take every single boat to the eastern bank. Barricade the bridge where I shall show you, and put your best men there to hold it, with archers on the east bank, ready to pick off any makeshift thing they do try and send over. That's the answer: let the river hold them off.'

'You know what you are asking me to do, how many people must be moved,' Amnon said. And then: 'The Masters would not approve.'

'I have no other answer for you,' Totho told him.

Amnon gazed out again at the sprawling host. 'I will give the orders,' he confirmed quietly.

Totho only realized then that he had not expected this man to take his suggestion. *Am I become a tactician now? Am I a warleader?* And in the shadow of those thoughts followed another one: *Would that find favour with her?*

'For the men holding the bridge, it will be hard,' Amnon said slowly.

'Put up as much of a barricade as you can. Funnel them in until a small number of your best men can stand them off,' Totho said. 'Those men will face repeated charges, crossbows, Wasp stings. They must be your best. If the Scorpions manage to force the bridge we will never hold them.'

Amnon nodded. 'I myself shall stand on the bridge,' he said simply. 'I shall ask for volunteers from my Guard to stand with me.'

Totho felt the ground lurch beneath him: no leadshot, not Amnon hurling him down, but the vertigo of his own next words getting to him. 'I shall stand beside you.'

Amnon clapped a hand to his shoulder, sending him staggering. Totho saw the degree of emotion in the man's eyes. *Ah, but it is the right thing to do. She would say so, too, were she here.*

'I shall give orders for the evacuation,' Amnon said. 'We shall start right away. By the morning we shall not be finished, but we shall at least have what time the walls shall buy us.'

'There are other ways of buying a little time,' Totho said. The thought was heavy on him, loaded as it was with memories of the last time, but he persevered. 'A night attack on the engines may disrupt them, buy us a few hours. If you have those available who can make the attempt.'

Amnon nodded fiercely and beckoned one of his men over.

'Get me Teuthete,' he ordered. 'Then bring me all my officers.'

# Thirty-Three

Her name was Teuthete. The word she used to define herself was 'Chosen'. The title was woven through with history: the long and complex interactions and accords between her people and the Masters of Khanaphes.

She was slender, five feet and a half tall at most, far shorter than any of her distant western kin. Her skin was silvery grey, like light shining on silty water. She wore the armour of her people: a breastplate, shoulder and leg-guards of wicker and wood woven together tightly, interlaced with sinews and tightly plaited cords of hair: enough to turn a sword-stroke or snarl an arrow. Her own hair would have been white, except that she had ceremonially re-shaved her scalp before this mission. That was the mark of her servitude, her calling.

Being Chosen was not just about being in service to the city, for she was something more than the levies of their army or the followers of their hunts. She was hostage for the freedom of her people, for the continuance of their ancient ways. Her personal loyalty bound her people to the city, and protected them from the wrath of the Masters. Such wrath had not been felt since time out of mind, but it was remembered nevertheless. They had warred with the Khanaphir, in that very distant past. The Marsh people had fought with all their skill and stealth, and their diminishing numbers, until the Masters had offered them a truce. A truce of servitude but not slavery, for Mantis-kinden could never abide slavery. With their backs to the wall they found other names for it and called it loyalty.

And now Khanaphes itself looked to be facing its last days. Teuthete was no fool: she had read Amnon's face even as he delivered to her the word of the Masters, or what was left of that word once it had passed through him. Amnon did not seem frightened. She reckoned the man did not quite know what fear was. He had been severed from hope, though. This was not a man who looked forward to the next dawn.

It would be easy enough for the Marsh people to withdraw now, to step into the mists and shadows of their murky realm and wait until it was over. The Many of Nem were not equipped to hunt Mantids through the waterways, and if they tried it, they would regret it and then die of it, in short order. Teuthete's people were not directly threatened, and the descending rod would strike only the backs of their age-old taskmasters. The mission they had given her, given her people, was a death waiting to happen. It seemed to her that they would none of them see their villages again.

She had thought – and the thought shocked her – of turning away from the Khanaphir in their time of need. It was only a thought, though. To act upon it would be to break an oath her people had sworn generation after generation, and that she herself had sworn as their proxy, as their Chosen. The sense of honour that bound her would have been entirely understood by her kin in the distant Lowlands, whose existence she did not even guess at.

She had a score of her people with her, as many as she dared take. They were all Marsh hunters, skilled in the ways of silence, blessed by their Art to strike fast, to step unseen. They padded wordless out of the Marsh on the west side of the river, with the walls of the city standing bravely to their right, the festering camp of the enemy directly ahead of them. It was three hours before dawn, those longest hours when sentries slumbered and it seemed the night would never end.

They carried their bows made from layers of different woods and sinews bound together with fish glue, curved and recurved so that, when unstrung, they coiled forward like worms. The Mantids would hold one end down with a foot, bracing their entire bodies, wrestling the rebellious strength of those composite materials until they had turned them inside-out, then secured them with ten-times interwoven hair and imprisoned all that straining power within a bow that looked small enough to be a child's toy. Their arrows normally had heads of stone or bone; the best of them were tipped with the hard, sharp chelicera of a certain water spider, and were lethal with venom. They had spears, too: long, flexible weapons headed like their arrows. They had the flexing spines that sprang from their forearms. There was not a piece of metal on any of them, and they were barefoot. The Scorpion thousands, equipped with their halberds and armour, their greatswords and axes and usurped Imperial weapons, awaited them.

The sentries were sporadic, loose, inattentive. There were even gaps where several had deserted their posts. Teuthete found one, though, staring directly out towards the Marsh. She crept close enough to see clearly the man's narrow eyes, trusting to her Art to hide her. She nocked an arrow tipped with a spider's fang. The first blood must always be shed properly. To stint on that now would be to curse their mission.

She drew the bow back slowly, with incremental motions of her arm, her shoulder, her entire frame taking the strain of it. Another Scorpion was passing by, weaving slightly, already drunk on looted beer. She waited, untiring, until he was gone.

Then she loosed. The arrow was gone from her bow, had lanced through the man's eye, without seeming to cover the brief distance between. Instantly she and her fellows were on the body, and had hauled his heavy corpse off into the night.

She took out her best knife, its blade a serrated razor of stone. The others of her party gathered around reverently. Before a hunt of this importance, these things must be done. There were rites that must be observed.

She cut the dead man's armour free and opened him up, spilling as much of his blood as she could on to the earth. Dabbling her hands in the gore, she anointed her fellows one by one, placing a handprint in steaming red on each forehead, the fingers of it curling over each shaved skull.

'Now let us hunt,' she said, and they surged into the Scorpion camp, at a fast rush that was not running, but a silent, ghostly charge.

Amnon had explained to her what they must do, and she had not completely understood, other than that at the camp's heart there were some great iron weapons that the Khanaphir feared. Amnon's foreign creature had tried to tell her how best to disable them, but his words had shattered on the shield of Teuthete's Inaptitude, and she had not grasped them. In his frustration the foreigner had offered to come with them, but Amnon had dissuaded him in time. No outsider could hunt alongside her people and live to tell of it.

The Scorpions remained oblivious as Teuthete's hunters passed between their tents. Most of them slept but there were plenty still wandering about in the dark, laughing, fighting, drinking. However stealthy they were, the Mantids were not invisible, not quite, so it was inevitable that they would be spotted eventually. Meanwhile, they continued soundlessly, deeper into the camp, relying on their speed to take them close to where they needed to be.

She could see ahead of her the tarpaulined shapes that matched Amnon's words. There were many Scorpions nearby, some sleeping, some not. One of the weapons had its cover stripped back, and a foreigner was doing something to it, prodding and poking.

*We have come far enough.*

Teuthete drew back her bowstring once more, and around her the others followed suit, save for the few that trusted their spears more and were getting ready to leap.

The arrow sped from the string, plunging through the foreigner so far that its stone head shattered on the iron of the weapon he was busy working on. Simultaneously, a dozen other arrows rammed home into the Scorpions standing around him, killing them instantly. Teuthete was already moving forward, bow now slung over her shoulder. There was no time to admire her handiwork.

The Mantids screamed as they came in, each one of them giving a high, whooping yell that froze the Scorpions briefly in their tracks. The spears then lunged in, flickering fast. Many of the enemy wore armour that could have broken the bone spearheads or snapped the stone points, but the Mantis were precise. They lanced eyes, throats, skewering under arms or into groins. When they had left no target standing, they began killing those on the ground, those just now waking up, with brutal efficiency. Half of them continued loosing arrows into the bulk of the camp at every new figure that presented itself.

Teuthete vaulted on to the uncovered weapon with a brief shimmer of her wings. It was mostly composed of a solid iron body. There were various holes and pieces to it, but it seemed invulnerable to her. The foreigner's instructions had been just words and they had made no sense to her.

One of her hunters fell, a stubby arrow protruding from the man's lean body, having punched through his woven armour as though it were not there. Her own archers kept loosing over and over. She noticed a bright flash from somewhere, a bolt of golden flame that she danced aside from.

There was a bowl of blue-burning oil nearby, by which light the foreigner had been working. She snatched it up and poured the contents into the orifices of the weapon.

She could not tell if it did any harm, but the burning oil was flooding across the surface of the machine now, and perhaps its innards would be more vulnerable to flame.

The Scorpions were now rallying, alerted to the killers in the heart of their camp. Teuthete saw a shambles of a charge, a score of half-dressed men and women with axes and swords, but it was cut down by her archers before they got within a spear's reach. Another three of her people were now dead to the Scorpions' own bowmen.

She found more burning oil to splash over the covers of the remaining weapons. The heavy canvas smouldered fitfully.

Her people called a warning to her. There was a much greater Scorpion force forming: at least half a hundred of them dressed in piecemeal armour, with a scattering of their guard-beasts as well. Arrows lanced into them, each shot exacting a death, but they gained in numbers all the time, and then rushed forward in a single body.

*Now we come to it.* Teuthete and her spears confronted the onslaught. They did not even wait to receive the charge but launched themselves into the Scorpions' midst, half-leaping and half-flying. The spears were lost instantly, each through the body of a foe, and they resorted to their spines, dancing and cutting. driving the bony spikes of their forearms into faces and throats. The Mantis archers were still loosing into the throng, impossible to miss at this range.

Teuthete killed: it was what her kinden did. It was the red heart of all their rituals and mysteries, their oaths and honour. It was what they put up all their masquerade of customs to hide. She killed because that was what she was made for. It was not glorious or noble, merely efficient.

Scorpions were not slack in that regard, either. They, too, had mostly cast aside their axes and blades. They had an understanding, their two kinden: *unarmed is best.* There was a pleasing simplicity in it, unmatched by the later layers of civilized war. Claws against spines, they slashed each other,

Teuthete's handful a blur of blood and motion within the Scorpion host. The archers were not shooting now, but engaged in their own close combat.

It was over, and she knew it. She could feel it in the surge and swell of the melee, as each of her followers died. Not one of them departed before their path had been smoothed by the death of many enemies. Her own time was coming, and she accepted that without question. If she was Chosen, this was what she had been chosen for.

There was sudden thunder out of a clear sky, and she felt a mighty hand take hold of her, take those around her. Most were thrown flat, but she, with her wings momentarily outstretched, was hurled into the sky.

One of the weapons had died. Its death-agonies, instantaneous but colossal, had wrecked a space of the Scorpion camp and broken open the weapon next to it. It had been the same one she had poured burning oil into, she realized.

*So that is how you kill them.* It was too late now to exploit this knowledge.

The air was abruptly busy with stubby machine-shot arrows sleeting up at her. The moment had gone. She saw three others of her kinden also airborne, although one was picked off as soon as she noted him.

She darted higher, labouring her way into the air. Her kinden were not strong fliers but the darkness cloaked them. The three survivors swooped over the camp, heading towards the city walls. Something tried to follow them, some flying foreigner in banded armour, but she turned in the air with her bow ready in her hands and spiked an arrow through him.

*I live.*

It was unexpected and she was not sure how she felt about it. The shackles of Khanaphes were still fastened upon her, but that would not last long. Amnon would find other ways for her to die. It was what being Chosen meant.

*

In the dawn's first light, Hrathen surveyed the damage. Angved and his engineers were picking over the damaged artillery. The bodies were being looted and then hauled off into the ravaged farmlands to rot. Scorpion-kinden were not sentimental.

'Give me a report,' the halfbreed growled. Angved clapped one of his men on the shoulder, telling him to carry on, and stood up.

'I counted around a hundred Scorpion dead,' he said. 'Half of those fell in the initial ambush.'

'Ambush?' Hrathen spat. 'How can we have an ambush occur in our own camp?'

'Well, whatever the word is.'

'What loss to your artillerists?' Hrathen pressed.

'Of the Scorpions? Three or four. They'd expected our crews to stay with their machines, I suppose. In that case, they don't know how much of a shambles this camp is. No great loss there. However, one of my better engineers got himself killed. One of the shotters had a jammed cartridge and he was working double-time trying to sort it out. Shows what you get for being too keen. Oh, and one of your Slave Corps lads got killed because he was stupid enough to chase their survivors into the dark.'

'Enemy dead?'

'Seventeen bodies recovered. Some kind of local Mantis-kinden, like we saw in the battle. I fought Mantis-kinden in the Twelve-year War: this could be a nightly occurrence.'

'Camp security is very much on my mind,' Hrathen assured him. 'What about the engines?'

'We've lost two, neither repairable. Our guests cleared the jammed cartridge by setting fire to it, and of course it was chock full of the good stuff,' Angved confirmed. 'Thankfully we'd managed to drill it into the Scorpions not to leave the shotters loaded overnight. Otherwise we might just have lost the lot.'

'Well done,' Hrathen told him. 'I want those walls down by evening.'

Angved looked away from him over to the city, that yesterday's festivities had confirmed to be within easy bombardment range. 'Quite possible,' he said. 'Normally you don't have the luxury of setting up this close, what with enemy engines on the walls and the like. Because we can, we have all the benefit of our ranging practice of yesterday, without having to spend two hours finding our mark again. I reckon we can organize a concerted barrage on the walls and gate, and punch through in good time. Or I can give you three breaches by the end of tomorrow. Just one breach might become a big choke-point.'

Hrathen nodded, conceding the thought. A moment later a man dropped to earth next to him, making his claws twitch with the suddenness of it.

'Captain.'

'Report.'

'The streets are full of people, sir. Absolutely packed full,' the scout told him. 'They're all on the move.'

'They're going to fight? What are they doing?'

'On the move away, sir. Looks like everyone who can is shifting across the river. I saw what must be a hundred boats, of all sizes, ferrying people over.'

Hrathen stared at the scout for a moment, with Angved waiting at his elbow, and then he laughed. 'I see it,' he said. 'I see it plain. Jakal'll love it. We've scared them to death already. They're giving over half the city before the walls are even down.' His face darkened. 'And it isn't necessarily a bad move for them. They'd never keep us out, and they know what will happen to every man, woman and child once we get inside. We've been guilty of thinking like an Imperial army.'

'The river,' Angved agreed.

'Quite. It wouldn't stop an Imperial advance for a moment. We'd just send the airborne over to take the far bank, worry about the rest of it later. But of course, we have no airborne, and I don't think our friends here are good swimmers.' Hrathen chuckled, the sound of a man whose day has become more interesting. 'Get me a single breach as quick as you can,' he ordered Angved. 'Clearing half a city of people takes time. Even if they started yesterday, there'll still be some sport left for us if you can have the walls down by dusk.'

'And what about tomorrow night?' Angved asked him. 'More attacks?'

'There was a tribe responsible for keeping watch, last night,' Hrathen told him. 'By midday they will be extinct. The Warlord has taken their failure as a personal insult. That will give the army something to enjoy while they wait for you to do your job. Tonight our watch will take their jobs more seriously.'

At dawn, Amnon sought out the Iron Glove factora, eluding his officers and advisers. The Ministers had been making demands to see him, and he had a pressing invitation to the Scriptora to explain his decisions. In the meantime the evacuation of western Khanaphes had been going on all night, the discipline of his troops managing to control the panic and fear of the people. Every boat that could take to the water had been transporting the people of Khanaphes to the east bank of the Jamail, the sailors and fishermen and traders shuttling back and forth across the river. They stopped only if their boats were in danger of sinking or falling apart.

The Ministers had not countermanded his orders, and in its own small way that brought home to Amnon just how bad things had become. Their fearful forbearance would not last, he knew, so he was determined to achieve as much as possible before they confronted him.

And he had promised this one indulgence to himself. It meant a lot to him.

Totho met him within minutes of his arrival, already wearing half of his mail. All around them was the sound of a company of mercenaries preparing for war. Corcoran was already on the river with the *Fourth Iteration*, helping with the general evacuation.

'How's it going?' Totho asked him.

'Well enough, but there is a great deal left to do. When they start attacking the walls, we will have to make a choice.'

'Priorities, you mean,' Totho appreciated. 'People or foodstuffs.'

'If we strip the western city of food, we could starve the enemy, as you say . . .'

'But you won't do that,' Totho finished for him.

'I have a duty to the people, first of all. I am their First Soldier,' Amnon said. 'I cannot leave them to the Many of Nem.'

'I understand,' said Totho, and Amnon could tell that it was that particular civilized brand of understanding that these foreigners seemed so adept at. Totho could understand Amnon's logic with his mind, but not feel it with his heart. If it had been Totho in command, then the choice would have been different.

*And I am lucky to have a man on my side who can think like that*, Amnon decided. *Or we might have simply sat here behind our walls until they fell on us.*

There was a distant concussion and he thought he felt the ground tremble slightly. Totho had lifted his head, like a hunter listening for his quarry, and said, 'That was all of them at once. It's started.'

'Then make me ready,' Amnon urged him.

'Come with me.' Totho led him into the factora, seeking out that same room he remembered. 'How is the work at the bridge?'

'Going well. We will be ready,' Amnon replied. It had been a nightmare, in truth. A true nightmare for masons and labourers to carry out such precarious work in the dark. They had set up a pair of hoists on the bridge, and thus lifted stone blocks up on to its arching span, and then wooden boards and planks had turned the stonework into battlements, narrowing the path across the bridge to only a few feet across. Now the leadshotters had begun, that narrow gap could be closed entirely, and the makeshift wall of stone and wood would block off the bridge. A handful of good men and a scatter of archers could hold it. They would have to, since it was the only chance of stalling the Scorpion advance.

*How long?* Amnon tried to picture himself standing atop that barricade, that had been put up so hastily. *They will come in all the numbers the bridge will allow them. They will sink their claws into the wood and tear it away. They will swarm up the stone.* In the back of his mind was the thought that, even if they stood off the Many for a tenday, it would not be enough. Two tendays or three, it was all delaying the inevitable.

*Then we will delay them until we have no blood left to spill.*

'Of course you can destroy the bridge,' Totho said, 'or try to. I'm not sure if we have enough explosives on the *Iteration* to manage it.'

Amnon did not need to think of the outrage such a suggestion would cause amongst the Ministers. He felt an echo of it himself, rising unbidden. 'The stones of that bridge are amongst the oldest of the city, Totho. The Masters themselves decreed its construction. It is like the Scriptora, the Place of Foreigners. It is the genuine old city that the new city has grown within. It would be . . . unthinkable to turn against it.'

'The Scorpions are going to tear down as much of your old city as they can get their hands on,' Totho pointed out harshly.

'That is why they are our enemies,' Amnon said flatly.

They had arrived at the arming room, where the black plates of aviation steel were laid out ready for him. He remembered how they had felt: smooth, weightless, a second skin of impenetrable steel.

'Put it on me,' Amnon directed.

Totho, with no further comment, set about the task like an artificer, taking up the pieces in their precise order, and remaking Amnon piece by piece. He buckled together the breastplate and backplate, drawing the straps tight, and feeling a strange sense of triumph. *Logic and reason can grow even in this soil.*

He heard lightly running feet and did not need to glance up. The messenger was expected, and the Fly-kinden, Tirado, burst in.

'How are they looking?' Totho asked him.

'They're all over the place,' the Fly reported. 'It's going to take them three volleys at least to all focus on the same mark. And they're two engines down by my count.'

'That tallies with what your Mantis said,' Totho noted.

'I am glad her people died for something,' Amnon remarked. 'She will join us on the bridge.'

'Will she indeed?' An odd shiver passed through Totho. 'It's been a while since I fought alongside Mantis-kinden.'

'Oh, and I spotted the grand old man on his way here,' Tirado added. 'Meaning the top Domino.' It was a word the Solarnese had coined for the male Khanaphir leaders. In Solarno the heads of the leading houses were Spider-kinden, therefore women, and referred to as Domina. The new-minted slang had obviously failed to reach Amnon, however. Totho tugged the pauldrons tight and explained, 'He means First Minister Ethmet.'

He felt the stance of the man stiffen, a warrior readying for an attack.

'I can keep him out,' Totho suggested. 'Right now I don't think they have the spare men to make an issue of it.'

'I will see him,' Amnon declared.

'Your choice.' Totho nodded briefly to the Fly-kinden. 'See he's well received, then bring him through.' Once

Tirado had gone, he put in, 'We could keep him waiting. Drinks, food. It doesn't have to be now.'

'I want him to see this,' the big Beetle said forcefully. Just then there was the sound of hasty footsteps, the voices of Totho's staff being cut off in mid-civility. Ethmet burst into the room, mouth open to rebuke.

He stopped dead, the abruptness and his expression both suggesting he had been stabbed. His mouth opened and closed a few times as he watched Totho industriously lacing Amnon into the black plate.

'How dare you?' he managed at last, and it was almost a whisper. 'This has been forbidden. How do you dare this? Do you think the title of First Soldier puts you above reproach? Do you put my authority aside so lightly?'

'The role of First Soldier,' said Amnon, not even looking at the old man, 'is heavy enough on my shoulders that I require support.'

'Amnon . . .' The First Minister was scandalized, barely able to get the words out. 'You know the Masters have spoken on this matter!'

'Have they?' Amnon had abruptly moved a step away from Totho, and was now looming over the old man. 'They spoke to you, did they? And perhaps they also spoke to you about the battle we fought, how it would go, and what I could have done to save half our army from the sword? Because they didn't say a thing to me.' He was shaking with rage, all that anger, so carefully husbanded, now out in the world. 'I have listened to you all my life. I have been your dutiful servant and done whatever you said, whether it made sense to me or not. I have always done the Masters' bidding, imparted through you, and taken it for granted that you heard that voice that I never could. But if the Masters are so wise, how could they leave so many of my soldiers dead on the field? If the Masters are so great, why are they intent on keeping from me every advantage that might save our city?'

'What you would do – what this *foreigner* would do – would destroy us as surely as the Scorpions would,' Ethmet snapped back. 'When he had finished, with his ideas and his machines, what would be left here would not be Khanaphes. He would take the city away from those who have cared for and ruled it all these years!'

'From you!' Amnon shouted down at him. 'From you, you mean! You and the other Ministers, who tell us every word you spout is repeating the voice of the Masters!' His hands were clenched, as if itching to pick the Minister up and rattle him. 'I will fight to save this city. I will die fighting to save this city. But not for you. Not for the Masters. For my people. For the memory of those I have already led to their deaths, on your command. I will do this, and I will do it with Totho's advice, because I can hear *his* voice and it speaks sense to me.'

'The Masters will not brook such disobedience!' Ethmet almost wailed.

'There are no Masters!' Amnon bellowed at him, a full furious roar of rage. 'There are no Masters! It's *you*! It's you who would sacrifice this city rather than loosen your cursed grip on it an inch!'

After he had said it, he looked shocked, horrified by his own daring. Totho lifted the helm, the last piece of his mail, and held it out. Mutely, Amnon accepted it.

'You will be exiled,' Ethmet said, aghast. 'You will be stripped of your rank.'

'If the Scorpions leave enough of me to suffer your punishments, then exile me to the ends of the world. I care not,' Amnon growled. 'Now leave. Leave and do not show yourself to me again, you or any of your siblings, or I swear by all that I have sworn to protect that I shall march into the Scriptora and kill every last one of you.'

Whether by a renewed concentration of effort amongst the Scorpion artillery crews or some weakness within the

Khanaphir stonework, the walls of Khanaphes were breached at three hours past noon that day, and the Scorpion war-horde rushed for the yawning gap. Beetle-kinden archers hurried to either side of the tumbled stones to rain arrows on them, even as the leadshotters picked a new space of wall near the breach, and began to pound it.

Atop the tumbled rubble and stones, two companies of the Khanaphir neighbourhood militia took station, directing their spears down at the onrushing Scorpions. They had been picked by Amnon and tasked specially for this last service to their city. They were men and women whose homes stood at their backs, who knew that their families were even now being rushed towards the river.

Roaring, raging, surging up the rubble, the first Scorpion charge broke against their shields, axemen and halberdiers of the Nem impaled on the spears, run through and wrenching the weapons from their wielders' hands even as they died. The leaf-bladed Khanaphir swords came out. The militia held fast, and the Scorpions fell back amid a hail of arrow-shot. The archers leant out further to loose at them, feeling the walls rock and totter with each leadshot that struck home. The impacts were coming fast now: the crews had got into their stride.

The Scorpion host struck out again, their long legs taking them up the rubble swiftly and sure-footedly. Axe heads split shields, javelins sank into them and dragged them from their owner's grip. The brutal halberds descended over them, hacking down men in the first and second rank.

More defenders pushed in from behind to stand over the fallen, using the slope to deny the Scorpions any progress. The bitter struggle swayed back and forth, but the Beetle-kinden dug in for all they were worth, with the legendary endurance of their kind, and they held firm. Amnon had chosen them well. They held.

After they had repulsed four charges, with grievous losses on both sides, Hrathen sent the crossbows in. They loosed volley after volley, the bolts powerful enough to punch through shields.

The Beetles held their ground. The archers above killed enough of the Scorpion crossbowmen that they fell back, aware of their value, their place as a military aristocracy that did not have to suffer casualties. The Beetles held, standing bloodied and ragged behind a barricade of the dead.

Hrathen found Angved and gave his orders. They had no time to play this out for honour's sake, and the Scorpions cared nothing for it in any case.

The first three thunderous shots were delivered to establish the range, impacting on either side of the breach and showering the militia with shards of stone and dust. The fourth shot was on the mark, right in the centre of their close-packed bravado.

Even then they tried to hold. Even then they brought up what few reserves they had left to fill the gap. They had a courage drawn from ignorance. *The enemy have done their worst,* they assumed, *and we stand.* They stood between the lips of broken stone and braced their shields, spears held high in challenge.

The next two leadshotters spoke in unison and wiped them out. Angved had made calculations for the lighter load and used scrap-shot, a bag of nails and stones and jagged metal that burst halfway from the engines' mouths. No shield could protect them, nor their desperate bravery. The leadshotters' load scythed them like corn, tearing men and women in half, ripping off limbs, breaking their bones like dry twigs.

Some few had survived, those standing closest to the shattered stone walls. A handful, only, they could not so much as slow the Scorpion advance as it howled its way into the breach, but they fought anyway. They had been stripped of choices.

Scorpions ravened up the walls and killed the defending archers. The bowmen fought to the last man, using fists and daggers against all the weapons of the enemy.

The war-host of the Many of Nem entered Khanaphes in a bloody-handed rush. Their army had instructions to run straight for the river, but the open city was too tempting. The Scorpions diluted themselves in looting and burning, even as the evacuation was drawing to a desperate close. Amnon's words to the boatmen had been clear: on no account, at any cost, must the Scorpions be allowed to take any vessel. Even as the Scorpions sacked the westerly neighbourhoods the boats were still taking on fraught and weeping passengers, just one more load, just one more handful of the dispossessed and homeless, even as the smoke began to rise and the victory cries of the Many drifted through the air.

When the vanguard of the Scorpions came to the river at last, it was near dusk, and still the boatmen's work was not done. At the sight of that rapacious horde, though, they cast off with their last cargoes. They wept, many of those oarsmen and sailors, on hearing the cries of those they had left behind. Hundreds, hundreds were still left on the west bank for the Scorpions to find. Hundreds, but not thousands. Not the tens of thousands who had made western Khanaphes their home.

At dusk, the Scorpion host was a dark mass along the riverbank staring across the water at their enemies. They bunched at the bridge's mighty foot, seeing the barricades above, guessing at the archers and soldiers beyond the peak of the arch, and they made their camp, and planned for the morrow.

# Thirty-Four

It was hard work running Thalric's errands, but that was because the city was falling apart.

Even moving through the streets was getting difficult. The eastern city was packed out with refugees, and with soldiers trying to find a place for them all. In the last hour before dark it seemed to Che like the end of the world. The uprooted citizens of Khanaphes, clutching their children and their scant possessions, were herded sobbing and whimpering through the streets, to be bivouacked in markets, along pavements, in homes and storehouses, anywhere there was space. Che forged her way through it all with a foreigner's awkwardness. The distraught crowds were all part of the same world, despite their distress, while she was from elsewhere. There were currents and signs that allowed them to shoal like fish through even the narrowest parts of the city, where Che was left battered and bewildered. From all sides she heard them calling on their lost Masters, their city's ancient heritage. They were praying, beseeching invisible and absent entities for aid against the invader. She saw fervent belief on so many faces.

She had done her best to keep track of her remaining compatriots. Berjek and Praeda had been arguing earlier, now neither was speaking to the other. Berjek wanted to leave at once, given that the Scorpions had reclaimed their leadshotters from river duty to make up for the engines the

Khanaphir had destroyed. Praeda would not go.

Che could still not quite believe it. Praeda herself bore an expression of puzzlement, whenever caught unawares, at the colossal entity that had come thundering into her life. It was not that she had not been wooed before, Che knew, for plenty of scholars and magnates had set their sights at her, demonstrating their erudition, their wealth, their good taste and sensibilities. She had been pursued in all the civilized ways known to Collegium, and had stood them all off with her icy reserve. It had been claimed that her heart would not be won until some artificer devised a clockwork husband for her.

But, of course, Collegium did not hold wooers like Amnon. He was something from the violent, brutal past. He was fierce, burning with energy, strong and swift. He had never sat on a committee, drafted a paper, given a lecture or brokered a bulk purchase. He would not know what to make of any part of Praeda's world, and that, for her, was the attraction. More, he had an aura about him, of youth and strength and infinite capability and, despite his status and his allegiance, and the hundreds of Khanaphir women who surely coveted him, he had looked just once at Praeda Rakespear and thought, *Yes.*

Che had to admit, that would be a hard offer to resist. The simple, pure adoration of Amnon the First Soldier was nothing to be cast aside lightly. Perhaps Praeda had been waiting, all this long cold time, for the warmth of a man such as he.

*And he will let her be what she wants to be,* she thought, battling still through the packed streets. *No scholar he, nor merchant, he will not compete with her, or try to be her better.* In Collegium it was always maintained that men and women were equals. Artisans, militia, artificers, scholars, all could boast women within their ranks. Still, Che had seen the Assembly, and seen that at least three of every four were men, and the ratio was worse amongst the merchant magnates. Helleron's Council consisted of twelve men and one hard-nosed woman. *We are not the Wasps, with their strict patriarchy, but we should take a long look at what we actually are.*

She ducked in at a convenient corner to get her bearings. She had received plenty of news from the battle front, which was even now advancing on the river. None of it seemed good. She had seen Totho and Amnon in conference several times, and it seemed that the Iron Glove was taking some personal interest in the outcome. Despite her harsh words for the man, she could not help but think, *I hope Totho knows what he's doing.* Certainly a great deal of the city had been surrendered already. In the sky to the west, the sunset was darkened with smoke.

She had been keeping her eyes out for the Wasp-kinden. They were out there still, and it seemed clear that both she and Thalric were on the menu as far as the Rekef were concerned. They would be holed up somewhere here in the east city, but they would be working at a disadvantage, because Khanaphes was not the sort of city they were used to. The word had gone out now that they were enemies of the Ministers and Masters, so a Wasp-kinden face would find few friends here. They would be forced to seek their agents and spies amongst the lowest of the low: halfbreeds, criminals and those few foreigners who had not fled when word of the Scorpions came. Even there they risked exposure and betrayal to the city's authorities. They would have to tread carefully.

Of course, Thalric had the same problem himself, hence his need for Che. She had done her best to explain to the Ministers that Thalric himself was no part of the Empire's plan. They had nodded and smiled with their usual politic blankness, leaving her unsure whether they had believed her or not. She also half expected to get back to find that the drinking den's owner had sold him out.

She spotted a foreign face within the crowd, just for a

moment. She had been looking backwards, along the way she had come. It was the brief discontinuity that had caught her, another person not quite in tune with the crowd. But it was not the pale flash of a Wasp face. It was a face darker than her own, than any local: coal-black Vekken features.

She cursed, moving out into the crowd again, knowing that the other one of them would be somewhere about. *What do they want?* But that was an old question. They wanted to kill her, of course, and she had to assume they were following some distant Vekken directive, because she had surely given them no recent cause. They must have received their instructions before any of them even set out from Collegium, and on that list, triggered by who knew what, was the directive: *Kill the ambassador.*

*Uncle Sten and his stupid ideas.* Peace with the Vekken, indeed! She had already gathered enough understanding of them to know that it was simply not an option. *They hate us. They fear us. There is no common ground.*

She picked up her pace, jostling and pushing, sensing in the back of her mind the two Ant-kinden trying to reach her through the crowd. One was likely ahead of her, trying to find an ambush point, silently guided by his comrade. She changed direction several times, trying to be unpredictable. She was meanwhile looking for any kind of public building.

She saw a large house that had obviously been opened up for refugees. As swiftly as she could, she ducked inside. The place was lined wall-to-wall with people: each had inherited a space of stone floor in place of the home they had abandoned across the river. She pushed through them, making for the stairs, ignoring their complaints. She imagined the doorway now darkening as the hooded Vekken came inside after her.

Upstairs, still stepping and stumbling over destitute Khanaphir, but she had seen a window large enough to admit her. She rushed for it, squeezed through it, let her wings catch her as she dropped. She was a clumsy and awkward flier, but it was an Art the Vekken could not attain. She let her wings carry her across a flight of buildings, across two alleys, dropping down into a roof garden and then making her way across to the street, past more surprised locals. *Let that put them off the trail.*

She was uncomfortably aware that they would not give up hunting her, though. They had a kind of blind, idiot patience in that regard, an Ant trait. She would have to confront them eventually.

*Then let me choose the time and place, and let me choose my allies too.* She had no doubt that Thalric would back her, should she ask him. The thought gave her an odd surge of confidence: to have a friend, no matter who, one who would not ask the wrong questions. Just to have a friend.

She was getting close to his retreat now. It had taken her long enough. His hideout was across an open-air market from her, although the stalls had now all been turned into surrogate housing. Rows and rows of Khanaphir were huddled together beneath the awnings, hundreds of them sitting there with bland acceptance, simply waiting to be told they could go home.

It was an instinct that came with flying, an instinct that precious few of the locals could possess. Entering the market, Che had glanced up at the rooftops.

They were there. She saw two of them clearly, one to her left, one to her right, crouching on high and watching: Wasp-kinden. They were cloaked, but their simple presence said it all.

*They've tracked him down.* For a moment she thought they might have killed him already, but then why would they still be watching? Surely not for her? *It's still daylight, just, and they won't risk anything until after dark.* She could not be sure of that, but it seemed to make sense. If she went into that drinking den now, she could be walking into a trap, but if she did not she could be leaving him to his fate.

*Was this part of the bargain we made?* But that was not a

question worth asking. Her difficulty now would be getting in without being spotted by the Wasp sentries.

She put a shawl up over her hair, so that she now looked as much a Beetle-kinden as the locals. Once that tell-tale was covered, there was nothing in her appearance that should scream *foreigner* at them. Nothing except the way she moved.

The crowd was settling, the streets were emptying as dusk drew on. She must go now if she was to take cover amongst these, her distant kin.

*But what a gulf separates us. We are of different worlds.* The thought was irresistible, sweeping over her with the feverish insistence of a Fir dream. *O Masters of Khanaphir, aid me,* she mouthed. *Hide me from the eyes of my enemies.*

She stepped into the crowd and moved through it, and it opened up before her. It was not that people parted for her; that would hardly have served her purpose. Instead, they were always just out of her step, not in her way, not snagging her elbows or stepping on her feet. She coursed through the settling crowd like a true part of it. Her mind reeled at the continuing strangeness, waited each moment for everything to come crashing down, but somewhere deeper it felt natural to her, as though she had finally started to listen to a voice she had been trying to ignore.

She reached the den's entrance, knowing better than to glance back and thus show her face.

A thought struck her just before she entered the building, and she let her smooth course carry her past and then down a side alley, seeming nothing more than one Beetle amongst hundreds. She was keenly aware of time, the hour latening, the Wasps surely readying themselves to swoop. Still, she continued on to the riverside, towards the building's rear, the hatch that was Thalric's fall-back. With eyes that were not hindered by the gathering dusk, she managed several quick glances at the rooftops, seeing no one.

*But why would the Wasps not be watching here?* It felt wrong. They were Rekef, therefore neither fools nor amateurs. Still, aside from a few ambling Beetles going homeward, their eyes fixed on the far bank and its bristling newcomers, she saw nobody.

She walked right around the building and slipped back to the front, ducking inside. It was increasingly difficult to keep her pace nonchalant. She could almost hear the sands dwindling in the glass.

The place was nearly empty: the Ministers had yet to commandeer it to house fugitives and, with the city sundered in two, it was not a night for drinking. Khanaphes was frightened. Of the three people there, one was audibly murmuring some invocation to the Masters, and she wondered if this was something they had always done when faced with life's trials, or whether the emergency had brought them back to it.

She slipped into the cellar after a single look at the proprietor. His eyes regarded her bleakly and he made no move to stop her.

'Thalric.'

He picked up on her urgent tone and was on his feet at once. 'They're here?'

'Right outside the front,' she said.

Osgan was sitting up, looking pale, but stronger than he had been. It was just as well.

'They followed you?' Thalric asked her.

'No, they did *not* follow me,' she snapped, put out by the suggestion. 'They tracked you down. They were here long before I returned. They're waiting for nightfall, is my guess. So we have to move right away.'

'What about the back?'

'I didn't see anyone.' She nodded at his expression. 'I know, I know, but I looked and there were no Wasps there that I could see. That doesn't mean they weren't there.'

'We move now,' Thalric decided. 'We try to lose them. There are a few other places that we could hole up in, but they're none of them far enough from here to shake off a chase. That means we'll have to go wide, then double back to one of them. Osgan, on your feet, now.'

'Can he—?' Che started, but Osgan groaned and shook himself, and clawed his way up the wall until he was standing.

'Let's go,' he croaked. He was red-eyed, unshaven, but Che wondered if a lack of drink had not taken over from his fever as the main antagonist.

'Can you fly?' Thalric asked him.

'Enough to get up the chute,' Osgan confirmed weakly. 'No roof-hopping.'

'We'll be staying on the ground,' Thalric decided. 'You two are both dead if we go above roof level. You might as well hover there waving flags.'

'Oh, really?' Che glared. 'And you'd just vanish into the night like a Moth-kinden, I suppose.'

'That's exactly what I'd do,' he told her. 'Now, when we hit the street above, make a left, and then run along the river until the third alley – then left again, into it. I'll bring up the rear. I want to see who follows us.' He had bundled himself in a cloak, but Che could not see him passing for a local any time soon. He was too tall, too pale; there was a violence evident in him that Beetle-kinden did not own.

He paused under the barrel chute and then kicked off, wings throwing him upwards. A moment later he said, 'Clear, come on.'

Che made Osgan go next. The man shook his head wearily. His arm was still bound up and she knew she should change the dressing, but they did not have the time. She heard him swear under his breath and then his wings flared, barely a sputter of them but getting him high enough to hook his good arm over the sill. Thalric hauled him up from there, and Che followed right behind, pulling herself through the hatchway. For a second they crouched there, just three more refugees among so many. She heard Thalric's breath emerge in a long hiss.

'Nothing on the roofs here, just like you said.' He grimaced. 'They could have someone with a glass positioned across the river, but that's not a recipe for a quick response. Let's move.'

They scattered down the narrow muddy track running beside the river, Che helping the wheezing Osgan along, whilst Thalric followed near-soundless behind them. The west bank was lit up by fires, and she found it hard not to brood on that. *I should have duties at a time like this, as an ambassador.* Save that those duties had dried up. *Diplomacy has failed.* Indeed, through the instruments of the Empire, she was now as much a target as was the city of Khanaphes.

*You do pick my errands well, Uncle Sten. Just keeping me safe again, were you?* Behind it all lurked a kind of specifically selfish despair. *What if it should all come down, the city falling in ruins before I ever understand it?*

'Move!' Thalric's voice hissed, and she picked up her pace, slinging herself and Osgan into the chosen alley. There was a thin rabble of locals still on the street and she just battered past them, with Thalric, running now, behind.

'Stay where there's people,' she got out. 'Won't risk drawing so much attention.'

'Don't bet on it,' he shot back. 'Go right, now.'

When he said 'now', he meant it. She and Osgan almost fell over each other's feet making the sharp turn into an even narrower alley. She saw that this one was roofed off with canvas, struts and spars, reminding her of the Marsh Alcaia with all the emotional baggage that carried. The Wasps, who had surely been tracking them from the skies, were momentarily confounded. Thalric paused for a second, whilst Osgan leant heavily on Che and coughed. The ex-Rekef man looked back at her: that was how she saw him, just then. He was smiling, a man on the edge and loving it.

He kicked in a door, without warning, at random. There was a scream from within. Then he was inside, leaving Che and Osgan to trail in his wake.

'Can't keep this up much longer,' the ailing Wasp grated in her ear. She had no words to spare him, just hustled him along as best she could.

Thalric had found another door to kick down, and Che guessed they were into the next building now, or just part of some extended family home. He was finding windows in turn, glancing out of them at the dark sky.

'Here!' he said and, instantly throwing the shutters back, had hooked his way out. She bundled Osgan through, more and more without any help from him, and followed after to find herself in the middle of an alleyway choked with people. The authorities had nested a host of refugees here, almost shoulder to shoulder, under the cover of a few wretched awnings. Thalric had already elbowed himself some space, and then he made some more, pushing dispirited people aside mercilessly, until the other two could join him.

'Now we wait,' he said.

'Until?' Che asked him.

'Until I say go.' He had hunched himself as low as he could in his cloak, slumped and abandoned-looking as any local. Osgan was lying on his side, breathing heavily, coughing again.

'Have we lost them?' Che whispered.

Thalric kept his eyes on the sky, surreptitiously. 'I don't see any fliers. They'll broaden their net in a while, thinking they've missed us, that we're still running. They know they can move faster than us, so they'll try to make the best of that advantage. So we use it against them instead. We just let them fly away.' He was still grinning slightly, not at his own cleverness but at the game. It was the only game, once you had tasted it: the spy game, the intelligencer's game – the Dance, as the Spiders called it. He was in the thick of it again, and it seemed to have taken years off him.

'You look like Tisamon,' she told him.

'The Mantis? What do you mean?'

'He was like that, too. When he was up against it, he'd be smiling always. He loved being challenged.'

'Tell me you don't feel it,' he said, fixing her eyes with his.

And she did, that was the terrible thing. There was Osgan to protect, and there were Trallo and Manny and Petri dead, and there was a city out there that would be put to the torch tomorrow, but through all that she felt a leaping spark of excitement inside her. She was an agent again, not an ambassador, and it was just like old times. She let herself smile, just enough for him to see.

'Stenwold was always lucky, having you as his left hand,' Thalric said softly, surprising her.

'You've taken every cursed chance you've been offered to point out my inadequacies in that field,' she reproached him. 'How can you say that now?'

'You must have something going for you, Che, some trick of the trade that I've never grasped. Think of all you've survived, all you've come through intact.'

*Not intact,* she thought. *Not when you tally the friends I've lost.* Thalric bent over Osgan and she heard him say, 'We'll have to move soon enough. Unless they find us again, we'll take it slowly. If we're lucky, we can get to another hiding place without them picking up the trail.'

'We should head for the Scriptora,' Che suggested. 'We'll be safe there.'

'You might be,' Thalric told her, 'but those old men and women will have us two executed as Imperial agents. The funny thing is I'm not sure whether that's true or not.'

'I'll speak for you. Ethmet will listen to me.'

'Not unless we have no other hope,' Thalric argued. 'I don't trust the Ministers an inch. If they come to believe that the Empire does want me dead, they'll probably hand me over to the enemy to try and buy their city back.'

'You're not a trusting person, are you?'

'A very good judge of character is what I am. Now, let's make a move slowly. Try your best to look local.'

They had picked their way halfway down the narrow street, stepping over legs and bodies, moving as steadily and wearily as any evicted local, when Thalric's hiss alerted them: 'They're on us already. Run!'

*Here?* Che thought, already automatically picking up her pace. There were people all around them, a hundred witnesses to each move they made. It seemed impossible that the Wasps would make such a public move against them.

*But they will be gone*, she thought. *They will be over the rooftops and away.*

She heard the first crackle of a stingshot, and the people all about her were suddenly jumping up, panic on their faces. Most of them must have thought it was some Scorpion advance guard, over the river already along with their Imperial allies. Instantly the alley ahead of them was choked with alarmed people, a wall that Che crashed into, fighting her way through them with Osgan stumbling in her wake.

'Push on! Push through!' she heard Thalric shout, with two or three more stings backing up his words. Che tried, but her ability to forge a way through the Khanaphir crowds had deserted her. She was just one more awkward foreigner, and the Wasps were closing fast.

Thalric cursed, catching up with her. She saw his hand jut forward, but until he loosed his own sting she had not realized what he intended.

'No!' she yelled, but people were already recoiling from them, seeing his pale skin and features, falling before the golden fire his Art unleashed on them. He was aiming deliberately high, enough to scare and disperse them. She hoped he had hit nobody.

'Go!' he snapped and muscled forward, virtually throwing aside any local who had not already retreated. His sting spat again, and then another bolt seared past on Che's other side. *The Rekef!* she thought, but it was Osgan, his one good arm extended, following Thalric's lead. Injured and weak as he was, she had almost forgotten that he too was a Wasp.

She had no choice but to keep up with Thalric. There were people screaming and sobbing on all sides, and she made sure she did not look at them too closely. She did not want to see charred wounds, to become an accomplice to murder.

Thalric suddenly shoved her, knocking her sideways into Osgan. A figure had landed ahead of them, hand already extending to sting. Thalric's hand flashed first, punching the other Wasp off his feet. Then they were running again, virtually trampling over his body, taking an abrupt left on to a broader street, straight across into another narrow one. There were no cluttered refugees here, only a couple of late-returning citizens who got out of their way in a hurry.

'Where now? Where's the safe house?' Che asked, trying to keep pace with Thalric. Osgan was still with them, for the moment, driving himself hard. His face was shiny with sweat.

'Behind us,' Thalric got out. He turned in mid-run, loosed a couple of shots backwards, and then was catching them back up again. 'They've done their research,' he said.

'Scriptora!' Che said. 'Only chance.'

He bared his teeth. 'No, we'll tire them out. Flying and stinging's like all Art, it drains the strength. We'll just wear them out.' He had done this before, she realized. He was reliving some other chase, perhaps being hunted by Mercers in the Twelve-year War. He dragged them down another street, changing direction without warning, seeking out covered places where the airborne might lose sight of them.

'Thalric!' Che yelled at him. 'Osgan won't last! Look at him. The Scriptora's our only chance. It isn't far.'

He led them without answer into the courtyard of some wealthy man's residence. There were steps up to a roof garden, and Thalric took them three at a time. At the top he turned, dropped to one knee, hand flashing. Che and Osgan hurled themselves past him, into the greenery beyond.

There was little enough cover in the roof garden but, between the low parapet, the urns and the plants, there was just enough to conceal the three of them. She heard Thalric's sting crack three more times. Then he said, 'That put their heads down. They'll be working their way round. I've been a fool.'

'How?'

'In forgetting they have a Beetle-kinden with them too. That bastard Vastern, I saw him as we were running. Shaved bald as a native and keeping track of me. No wonder they found us so fast. He was right there all along.'

Che had no answer to that. Some old memory within her hands itched for a crossbow, but of course she would not have been able to shoot one even if she could somehow find one here. The locals had bows, but she had never used a bow. It was not a weapon her homeland placed any stock in. *Perhaps I'll have to learn.*

'The Scriptora.' Thalric did not sound happy about it. 'You're right, it's our best chance. But you'd better be able to talk the Ministers round.'

'I will,' she promised, hoping it was true.

'We're going over the wall to our left, then we fly down into the street and run for it. We're almost at the embassy now. It's only three streets from here to the Scriptora proper. Osgan, reckon you can make that?'

'Only one way to find out,' the other Wasp gasped.

Thalric nodded. 'Then *now*,' he hissed, and was up and running for the edge, vaulting over it. Che let Osgan follow first, the Wasp simply toppling off and out of sight. She heard the sizzle of stings even as she herself followed suit. Her wings bore her raggedly and she stumbled as she landed. Thalric was already running across the street, lancing bolts of fire. She saw two or three figures at roof level, drawing back to avoid his aim. Osgan pitched a sting at them, too, before lurching after Thalric. *If only Beetle Art provided some facility like that!* Che ran after them, an enemy bolt scarring the ground close behind her.

They were close to the Scriptora now and she experienced an odd sense of anticipation, beside and beyond her own feelings. *Achaeos?* It was the same sense as before, that feeling of invisible company. *Oh, if I ever had need of you, Achaeos, it's now.*

In the air, the Rekef hunters easily outpaced them, but Thalric used the city to his advantage. The walls of Khanaphes's buildings, its uneven skyline of huge old buildings surrounded by the cluttered new ones, became their allies. Thalric changed direction over and over, each time bringing them back towards the Scriptora. Sometimes he was way ahead, sometimes he lagged, letting Che and Osgan build a lead. Often she heard his sting as he used it to warn off their enemies, forcing them out of his sight, buying a little extra time.

*He is a hard man to hunt,* Che thought. Thalric backed into a corner was a dangerous beast, was at his best, his most alive. It made her heart jump to see him so fervently defiant of all the odds. He was a proper bastard, she knew, but he would make them fight for his blood. None of it was for giving away easily.

'Here! *Run!*' he snapped, as though they had not been running already. Abruptly there were no walls about them. They had hit the Place of Government from an unexpected angle, directly across from the arch to the Place of Foreigners. Ahead of them was the stepped pyramid with its crown of pale statues; to their left rose the Scriptora, huge and dark. There was not a single light in its windows. It looked like a tomb.

*But the Ministers . . .* Che wondered, but there were a hundred possible reasons. They might be sleeping, readying themselves for tomorrow's battle. They might also fear Wasp assassins, and with good reason. They might still be working somewhere out in the city, housing refugees. There was not a sign that anyone remained behind those closed doors. Still, they had nowhere else to run to.

Figures were dropping down ahead of them, swiftly cutting them off. She saw at least four Wasps falling into place. Thalric's sting spoke, but they answered in kind. The range was long, but Che flinched back, changed direction. The Wasps were already barring them from the Scriptora doors.

*And so it ends.*

Thalric had thrown himself backwards, a winged jump of ten feet that put him seven steps up the side of the pyramid, returning golden fire from his open palm. Osgan collapsed beside him, shaking, gasping, one hand held fitfully out towards the enemy.

*Cheerwell Maker!*

That voice, all within her head, was enough. It caught her by the chin and dragged her face round until she was looking *back* and *up* – up the stone slope, up past the poised stone giants.

He hung there, clearly visible even at night, a grey ghost in a foreign city. *Here, girl!* The voice snapped in her head, admitting no patience with her.

The Wasps were advancing: another two had dropped down, one to each side. The square was broad, so the range still defeated their stings, but they were moving in. Thalric was retreating up the pyramid side.

'Up!' Che shouted at him. 'To the top now.' *And why?* 'Take cover among the statues!'

Thalric glanced at her and nodded grimly. *He has no illusions about how this will go.* He reached the flattened top in a sudden rush, darting behind a stone thigh as broad as his own torso. A moment later he was calling out, 'Osgan! For the Emperor's love, come on!'

Osgan picked himself up, stingshot bursting close by him, and looked up.

He screamed, falling back, rolling down the steps and landing on his side at the pyramid's foot. Thalric cried out his name, but Osgan was pointing – pointing at something past and through Thalric. Che, halfway up, stopped in horror and realization.

*He does see it. He sees Achaeos.* She recalled Osgan's history, his fears. *He saw Achaeos at the Mantis village: he thinks he's a Mantis.*

'Come on, you drunken bloody fool!' Thalric roared at him. Che got most of the way to the top before turning. Osgan was clenched up into a ball, but she could still hear him cry out, '*It's him! He's come back!*'

'It's not him, Osgan!' Che called. A stingblast cracked against the stones near her and she fell back, clawed her way over to where the statues could be her shield. 'Osgan, please—!'

The Rekef were now reaching the pyramid's foot. still spread out. Thalric's occasional shots made them start back, leap briefly into the air with a flurry of wings, before settling down again. Despite Thalric's promises, it did not seem that either flight or shot had tired them. They seemed all patience, closing carefully, while they kept a wary eye on Osgan. They could have killed him easily, but it was clear they would take him alive when they reached him. He would provide the leverage to force their other quarry into reach.

It was surreal, Che thought: they were standing in sight of the very fount of governance for Khanaphes, an armed insurrection in the heart of the city, with Rekef assassins running riot, and nobody else seemed to care.

'Osgan!' Thalric bellowed, just as a stingshot blazed from the Wasp on the leftmost flank and seared Che's shoulder. She cried out in pain and fell back. And fell further.

There was no solid ground behind her. What the grey stain of the ghost had been hovering over was the pit: the shaft sunk into the middle of the pyramid. She plummeted, too startled to call upon her wings. One outstretched hand scraped the pit edge, dragging its way through a layer of slime inches thick. Then she was gone, dropping into the darkness.

She heard Thalric call out her name and then he was diving after her. Still falling, in shock from the pain of her wound, she watched him outpace her with his wings flaring, sparking against the sides of the shaft.

Then he had her, arms tight about her, unimaginably painful where he grasped at her injured shoulder. His wings backed, trying to fight against their descent, their combined weight. She had a split-second glimpse of his face, his expression gone taut with the effort.

They struck bottom. She spilled from his arms, landing on her good side, scrabbling for purchase. It was dark, which did not matter to her, but it mattered to Thalric. He went stumbling away from her, arms out blindly. She tried for her feet and got there, swaying. 'Thalric,' she said, and he swung towards her.

There was a light, a lamp. It was getting brighter: from the shaft.

'They're coming!' he spat, backing away from it. She tried to make sense of their surroundings. The shaft gave on to a narrow room – *Just how far below the ground are we?* – and she saw a single passage beyond, branching three ways almost instantly. Thalric was making for it, hoping for cover, and she stumbled into him, clutching at him to hold herself upright. It hurt to move her right arm, but she could still move it. The sting must have just clipped her, for all the pain.

There was something about the tunnels ahead. She could not reconcile it, but there was something wrong there, hanging in the air like a ghost.

A pair of Wasps dropped down the shaft behind them, their stings blazing blind even as they did so, bolts of fire scattering within the confined space, their lantern glaring beyond. Che saw Thalric back away into the passageway, and a stab of panic overcame her, without any reason.

'Run!' she cried, then her wings hurled her at him fast, spoiling his aim as he tried to shoot back. The two Wasps were almost on her heels, charging forward to close with swords drawn.

She felt the stone around them shift, even as she collided with Thalric, striking him full in the chest, propelling him down the centre corridor. There was no mechanism, no click and grind of machinery. The stone moved as if it was alive.

She landed on Thalric hard enough to expel the breath from his lungs with a whoosh.

What landed on the two Wasps, only feet behind her, was the ceiling itself. A colossal block, the same height and width as the passage, thundered down on them. It cut off their scream, which was mercifully brief.

Thalric's eyes were wide, staring, unseeing in the pitch darkness.

She rolled off him with a groan, and lay flat on her back. *Traps*, she thought, *traps for the intruder, the unwary*. Traps laid by the Inapt, though. There had been no pressure point, no tripwire, that had brought that fatal load down. There had been a watching magic, and she had sensed it somehow, where Thalric and the dead Wasps had not.

She peered about herself at last, saw that the room was not large. There was Khanaphir picture-writing on the walls, but in bolder and larger characters than she had seen before.

There were no doors.

Sulvec perched on the lip of the pit, as the resounding crash died away below him. He had heard the momentary cries of the two men he had sent after Thalric.

'Gram!' he called down. 'Gram, report!'

Only silence replied.

Marger and the soldiers joined him there, crouching among the statues. They would have to go in, he realized.

No matter what had happened to Gram, they would still have to go in. He opened his mouth to give the order.

At that moment he felt fear. It came steaming up like cold breath from the slime-edged mouth of the pit. It caught him in mid-word, freezing him, wrenching at his stomach. He felt himself gripped by an unreasoning terror.

*We should not be here.* The placid faces of the statues had become nightmarish without ever changing expression. They looked down upon the intruding Wasps with condemnation. Sulvec heard his own breath sounding ragged in his throat. *We should not be here. This is a terrible place. Something terrible has happened to Gram.* Those screams, so brutally stopped, had unnerved him, but now fear had taken hold and was shaking him in its jaws.

*I am a Rekef officer!* But in this faraway city the Rekef seemed just a pale dream. He looked over to Marger, saw the man's eyes wide, his hands shaking. The other soldiers were retreating down the pyramid, away from the statues and the dreadful pit.

'Back.' The word was dragged from him. 'Go back. We . . .' He could give no reason for it, could not justify the order. He only knew that to stay where they were, in this forbidden place, meant death.

None of them needed to be told again. They fled down the side of the pyramid gratefully, gathering near the archway to the Place of Foreigners.

'They must be dead,' Marger was saying. 'Thalric and the Beetle girl. Surely they must be dead, all of them.'

Sulvec wanted badly to agree with him, but he had been given his orders most specifically. 'He's survived a lot,' he got out. 'We have to see the body. Absolutely sure.' Two of his men had a prisoner, he noticed. The wretched Osgan was hanging limply in their grip. The man looked half dead.

'What now, sir?' Marger asked him, a man with the luxury of not having to make decisions. At that point, Corolly Vastern caught them up, looking like a local with his shaved head.

'Why did you come down, sir?' he asked. He had obviously seen something of what went on. Sulvec opened his mouth, reaching for answers. *I can't just say 'because I feared.'* His mind progressed to: *So that cannot be the reason, but I must have had a reason. I do nothing without a logical reason.*

'Sir, Guards coming,' said one of his men, and his mind leapt. There was a squad of Khanaphir soldiers arriving at the far side of the square, no doubt drawn by all the noise. *I must have known that,* Sulvec told himself. *I heard them coming. I knew that they would catch us, if we were still up there.*

'Marger, keep a watch on this place. If Thalric comes out again, I want to know about it,' he snapped out. 'The rest of you, fall back with me. We'll return tonight if they leave it unguarded, or we'll be back tomorrow night, whatever. We have a job to do here. Come on.'

He could not entirely keep the trembling from his voice, still feeling that dread gnawing at his innards. *A perfectly rational feeling: fear of discovery. Good trade-craft. A Rekef agent's instincts.* The words rattled about inside his skull looking for acceptance.

# Thirty-Five

Dawn stole in from the east to find the city of Khanaphes at war with itself, split by the no-man's-land of the river Jamail.

On the eastern bank was arrayed the remainder of the Khanaphir army, ready to repel all comers. Some Scorpions had spent the night desultorily nailing together pieces of wood to make rafts – ugly, awkward things worked from first principles. In the harsh dawn they quietly abandoned their labours, for there were archers out there, whole detachments of them, both city folk and Marsh folk. Anyone paddling a raft towards them would be riddled with quills as soon as they came in range. The Scorpions lacked the craft to make vessels of any greater complexity. Unless they could somehow lure boats from the far shore, then a crossing would prove fatal.

They had kept some prisoners over, following their triumphant surge into the city. Jakal now ordered each one brought forth before the eyes of the defenders. The Scorpions were inventive and gleeful in their treatment of such prisoners, and they spared nothing, hoping to provoke some futile attempt at rescue. They spent two hours of the first day in burnings and cuttings and rape.

The Khanaphir would not be drawn, however. They watched, each one of them, from their Ministers down to the lowest peasant militiaman, and they saved their resentment for when they could pay it back twice over. They were too disciplined to take the bait.

*Which leaves the bridge*, Hrathen decided. It was a painful conclusion, if only because the enemy had reached it too. They had fortified the bridge even while they were evacuating their people from the west city. Past the crest of the span they had put up a great barricade, of stone and of wood, while beyond the raised sides of the bridge his glass could make out constant movement there. He saw spear-tips waving, indicating a small, compact force ready to repel the invaders. They would not need many to hold there, at that choke point.

'They are fools,' Jakal said. 'They should have brought their stones to the bridge's top. They waste their archers.' They had found a vantage on one of the roofs, the better to spy out the enemy.

'If only they had.' Hrathen let out a long breath. 'Angved, explain.'

The old engineer glanced nervously at Jakal. 'Well,' he said, 'if they'd built on the actual zenith of the bridge, we'd be able to shoot them off cleanly with our leadshotters. Simple as that: they'd give us a direct line of sight on them, and we'd knock them straight into the river. Which shows they're finally thinking like a proper army. They're using the arch of the bridge itself as cover.'

'So your weapons are useless now,' Jakal said.

'Oh, I could take them down, sure,' Angved told her calmly. 'Problem is, that bridge is built like their city walls, same stone, same style, save that the bridge isn't even *meant* to stand off an attack. I hit that bridge with a few shots and, odds on, I might just knock a great big hole in it, and then how do we get across? In fact, if they've any explosives to hand, we'd better be careful of them doing the same.'

'Where would the Khanaphir get explosives?' Jakal demanded, but Hrathen made an unhappy noise in response.

'They're no longer fighting this alone,' he told her. His spyglass raked across the barricade, seeing blocks of stone built to four feet high, wooden boards added above. It looked solid but not indestructible. 'I've noticed people in dark armour out there. Not locals, for sure. Not many of them, but it looks like they're giving the orders. I think it's our friends from the Iron Glove wanting a little blood.'

'So where does that leave us? I shall ready men for the assault,' Jakal decided.

'Send in some dross first, a couple of waves of chaff you won't mind losing,' Hrathen advised. 'After that we'll try for a surprise. Angved, get me a petard readied.'

'They're massing!' Tirado's high-pitched voice came clearly to them from his hovering point twenty feet up. Totho felt the stir amongst the Khanaphir, the gathering of nerves and determination. The archers were stringing their bows with the ease of long practice, bending the simple slats against their calves to hook the string over. Some were already positioned aloft, standing on the stone barrier with four foot of wooden barricade to cover them. They had been complaining, Amnon said, that they would not get a good enough shot at the Scorpions once they charged, but they had no idea what he had saved them from by having the barrier put up this far back from the apex.

Caltrops were another invention that had never reached Khanaphes. Totho's people had not been allowed the chance to make many, but the ground before the barriers was liberally strewn with the jagged little four-spined iron things, looking like spiders in the dawn light.

The danger he had foreseen was that the Scorpions would come around the sides, clambering and grappling about the edges of the barricade and using the walls of the bridge itself as purchase. They had built the sides out as far as he dared without creating a safe target for the leadshotters, but he had indulged in a little psychology as well. He had sacrificed some of the centre, made a low point where the spearmen would be standing, to give the Scorpions a target. It would seem easier to them to force their way through that choke-point. It would be the task of Amnon and his people to stop them.

*Time.* Totho had no idea how long they could hold, but the first few waves of attack would provide useful data. *How long until the Scorpion host breaks up, hungry and frustrated? How long before masses of them start raiding further upriver?*

*There are so many of them.* He was beginning to see the enemy as the locals did. Compared with the size of the Imperial armies he had travelled with, both sides here were betting with pocket change only. Here and now, though, there really were a lot of Scorpions ranged on the other side of the river.

*If they just come at us, if they just charge and charge and charge, climbing over their own dead like mad things, we'll be swept off here within hours.*

He shifted his shoulders, letting the plates of his pauldrons settle. This new armour had seen no battles yet. This one would be its first. The hush falling on the Khanaphir, as the three of them had arrived, had been shocking. Totho, big Amnon, giant Meyr: three war-automata, things of faceless black metal, lords of war. *We are making legends here,* he thought, and then: *but only if we win.*

He had hoped Che would be here. She wasn't, and there was no help for that, but he had hoped she might hear of what he was doing, and come to see him off.

He saw the Mantis woman, Teuthete, leap up on to the barricades, with her recurved bow in one hand. There was a scattering of her people here, all archers. *It really has been a long time since I fought alongside the Mantis-kinden.* That felt like another world, another epoch, a story of once upon a time.

Amnon vaulted up to take the centre, of course, his shield on his arm and his spear drawn back. To either side of him were the pick of his Royal Guard, men and women in scaled hauberks, with their elliptical shields and long spears. They were braced, and Totho could hear the thunder of the Scorpions, the roar of their battle cries, as they rushed up the facing slope of the bridge.

*Rush on,* he thought, *and welcome to the modern age.*

He did not even have to look. The first screams each denoted a caltrop for him, and he imagined the charge stumbling over itself, warriors trying desperately to stop, feet run through with agony, while being shoved from behind by their heedless fellows. The archers were busy, methodical and unchallenged, as they emptied their quivers into the enemy. There were always more arrows.

Totho clambered up, not too proud to take the offer of a helping hand. The Scorpions were already in retreat, leaving a great bank of their dead that was still yards short – spike-studded yards short – of the barricade. The archers continued to let fly, sending their arrows over the arch of the bridge on to the fleeing host, heedless of individual targets.

The second and third Scorpion advances were desultory. They came without enthusiasm, barely got within the sight of the archers before they were falling back in a scattered and dispirited rabble. The Khanaphir cheered as their opponents disappeared back beyond the curve of the bridge.

'We can't have broken them,' Amnon stated, stepping down from the breach. He had not yet bloodied his spear. 'They are stronger than that.'

'They're preparing something,' Totho said. He leant back against the stones, feeling their reassuring solidity against his backplate. 'They've got a plan. This is just to keep them busy while they work it up.' He glanced at Amnon, but the man's open, honest face was now a metal carapace, just a dark slot for the eyes.

*We look evil in these helms.* It was a child's gleeful thought. He imagined the Scorpions seeing Amnon the deathbringer, the black-armoured warlord at the centre of the line. It must give them pause, he thought. It must shake them. The sight was worth a fistful of caltrops, at the very least.

There was a call from the barricades and Amnon stepped back up. A moment later he shouted, 'This is it!'

Totho scrabbled at the stones hurriedly, using his Art to clamber up to the archery platform. What he saw from there wrenched his stomach.

*Oh Che*, he thought, with a fervent hope that she never learned about this small stratagem.

The Scorpions again crested the bridge's arc, and this time they had brought company. Ahead of their line, herded forward by spears and halberd-points, were perhaps two score Khanaphir, prisoners who had so far escaped torture or butchery. Some were children. Totho glanced at the archers around him, with their strings drawn back, and saw faces abruptly torn with shock.

*Shoot them*, Totho thought. *Shoot them and save the caltrops for the enemy.* He opened his mouth, looking to see if Amnon would give the command. *Shoot them! Do not even think to break ranks and let them through.* The lines of spears, Amnon and his Royal Guard, all held fast but no orders came.

Bowstrings twanged. It was the Mantis-kinden, drawing and loosing with casual speed, between the prisoners and over them. Totho did not know whether they were confident of their aim or heedless of the consequences. Still, the Scorpions were slowed by their own trick. Each arrow brought a death, winging from over the wooden parapet to plunge through Scorpion mail, through flesh. There were only a dozen Mantids at the wall, though, and the Khanaphir archers still held back, arms trembling and teeth bared.

'Loose!' bellowed Amnon, and Totho wondered whether he had simply not seen the problem, with his vision limited to that unfamiliar slot. Even with his orders, most of the archers did not shoot. Those that did pitched their arrows high, trying to curve down on the Scorpion rear ranks. The advance was now at the bank of bodies that the first wave of attack had left behind.

A great roar went up from the Many of Nem, not just the warriors on the bridge but the whole host on the west bank, and they pushed forward. The rearmost of the prisoners went down at once, lanced through by spears, hacked by axes. The rest fled.

Totho braced himself for it, but it was brutal. As tactics went, it had a clever simplicity that Drephos would have approved of. The prisoners fled towards their fellow citizens, heedless of the spears, but it was not the spears that took them. They plunged on to that unplumbed no-man's-land, and screamed and fell and clambered over each other, and fell again, lanced through by the caltrops. Totho felt the defenders shudder, saw the spearpoints ripple as the soldiers fought against their own instincts. They were an inch away from breaking forward to recover the fallen.

'Hold!' he shouted, and who cared that he was in no position to give orders. 'Hold and ready!' he commanded, just like a real battlefield officer, like a Wasp captain who had only his voice to keep his unruly soldiers in line.

*Oh, if only artifice could give us the Ants' mindlink.*

But they held. It was their discipline or Amnon's steady presence, or even Totho's exhortation, but they held. There were tears in some eyes, and hands shook. The Scorpions were coming.

They enacted a savage mercy upon the fallen as they came, stamping and hacking at them, working themselves into a greater frenzy. Arrows, long restrained, punched into them, but they were at the barricades now, and the dead Khanaphir were a few extra inches of height to assault the spears.

Still, it was fully four feet of stone and a wooden lip, and a fence of spears beyond. The Scorpion assault broke against those defences. Lean, tall men and women, like fanged and clawed monsters, were run through a dozen times as they leapt up like madmen. They fell back, pulling the spears along with them, as they died faster than new lances could be passed from the back. Halberd blades cracked shields, even split the wood of the barricades. The shock of that first impact whiplashed back through the Scorpion lines, but it did not stop them. This time they kept coming.

Totho fitted a magazine to his snapbow, the model he had made with his own hands, and set to work. As the archers either side of him fitted their arrows, drew back and let fly, he directed the weapon into the enemy and depressed the trigger, feeling the minute kick, the explosive snap-snap-snap-snap-snap as it discharged. Five bolts, and he had remembered to swing his arm to rake this volley across the host. Otherwise he would have put them all virtually in the same target, killing one wretched Scorpion so unnecessarily dead that anatomists would have refused the body as a teaching specimen.

Totho ducked back behind the parapet and charged the battery, not lever-pumped as with the originals, but wheel-pumped for smoothness and speed. His gauntleted hands spun the little winch-handle with the ease of long familiarity, and then he was ready to empty the other half of the magazine into them.

*No bloodlust required*, he thought. *No howling hordes, no particular strength, not even any real skill, at this close range. I have made war a province of the intellectual.* Snap-snap-snap-snap-snap, the finger-sized bolts punching through armoured men, sometimes two or even three at a time, unstoppable. They had no idea what was killing them, and most of them were dead on impact, a narrow hole drilled through chest or skull becoming a fist-sized gob of gore by the time it made its exit. He took another magazine and clicked it into place with his thumb, forcing the old one out into his waiting hand.

*I did well, when I made these.*

Something struck him in the chest, and he was abruptly

airborne, flying for a moment before he struck the side of the bridge hard enough to hammer the breath from him. The armour saved him from broken bones, but for a moment he just lay there, unable to understand what had happened. He levered his helmet back, craning to look down. There was a dent and a long scar across his mail, and his professional understanding supplied: *crossbow bolt*.

He looked up just as one of Amnon's people was punched backwards, the short end of another bolt lodged in his throat. Shields were being raised along the line, and he saw how the archers had pitched their aim higher, shooting further. Totho levered himself to his feet, feeling the pain of a body-length bruise. Despite it, he levered himself onto the barricade again, to get a look over the parapet.

There was a line of crossbowmen up on the very apex of the bridge, not shooting all together but each man intent on dragging the string back and loosing as swiftly as he could. Before them stood a rank of Scorpion-kinden with shields, trying to keep them under cover from the Khanaphir archers. The shields were all of city make, Totho noticed, so the Scorpions had not been idle in their pillaging.

*Shields, is it?* There were plenty of arrow spines bristling on those captured shields, for the Khanaphir shortbows did not have the strength to penetrate them. Totho grinned to himself, within the privacy of his helm, and charged his snapbow again.

Teuthete loosed a shaft that split one of the enemy shields, lancing on through to kill its bearer outright. The Mantis recurves had a prodigious power to them, but Totho carried something better.

He sighted up on the Scorpion line, using the notches and the little annotated scale he had meticulously cut into the weapon's sight, thus adjusting for his best guess at distance and elevation. It was like employing a little siege engine.

He loosed, more careful this time, pausing after each shot to find his next target. When he was done, there was a gap five shields wide in the Scorpion defence. He dropped back to recharge his weapon. *Let the archers get busy now.*

'Totho!' Amnon bellowed, and he was on his feet in an instant.

'What is it?' Totho's eyes scanned the surging Scorpion host, trying to spot what the other man had seen. He wasted precious time trying to fit a view of the entire battle into the slot of his helm, before he dragged it off to see. 'Oh . . .' And what? For a second he was frozen, not a military man at all but an artificer feeling abruptly out of place. Then: 'Shoot them down! The bearers! Shoot them!' It was too close, though. Too close already. The Scorpion lines were falling back raggedly, many of their men staying on alone to hack at the defenders. *They must not realize what it is.* Totho knew what it was, though. A petard. An explosive. A wall-breaker.

Too close. He ran along the width of the barricade and hooked one hand under Amnon's pauldron, before hurling himself back, shouting, 'Get off the wall!'

For a moment he thought Amnon would simply not budge and he would be left hanging from the man's armour like a trophy. Then his own weight told, and Amnon was falling back as, for the second time, Totho dropped from the barricade.

*If Amnon falls on top of me he'll kill me.* It was an odd candidate for potential last thoughts.

He struck the stone of the bridge and skidded, actually seeing a few sparks from the ridges of his breastplate, then he heard an almighty clatter as Amnon fell by his feet.

Totho braced himself as best he could.

There was a pause in which he wondered, *Has it failed to go off?*

It went off.

The force of the blast shook every stone of the bridge, even though it had been such a small petard. The shock lifted Totho up and put him down half a foot further back.

He got to his feet, head ringing with the sound of it, turning to see what extent of ruin had been wreaked on them.

The barricade was still there, incredibly. The stones of the centre had been shoved back six feet so that the entire construction was a funnel now, and the upper stones had been toppled from the lower, stripping two feet off the centre's height. At least ten of Amnon's spearmen were dead, torn apart by the blast. Three times as many Scorpions must have stayed in the fight and been ripped into pieces. For those who had remembered to fall back, there was now a great hole yawning in the centre of the Khanaphir defence.

He could not hear them charge but he felt it, even as he frantically charged his snapbow, hoping its mechanism had survived the fall. Amnon lurched to his feet, too far and too late now to hold the breach. Totho saw the Scorpion vanguard surge forward, the surviving Royal Guard trying to form up against them.

His sight of them was suddenly half blocked by a wall of black metal. Something impossibly huge surged forth to meet the Scorpions, armoured head to foot in black, with a shield the size of a door, and propelled by an irresistible momentum. Meyr was entering the battle, wielding in one hand a spiked bludgeon that had been made for a strong man to hold in both. Totho actually saw one Scorpion warrior switch abruptly from slavering charge to a frantic halt, as the colossal metal warrior rose in front of him and the weighted mace came sweeping down.

The Empire had long known that Mole Cricket-kinden were superb labourers, craftsmen, miners and porters, but also that they were poor warriors. Their huge strength was a slow strength. An insect of their size could have moved like water and lightning in the fray, but they themselves were weighted with clumsy flesh and bone. Their first strike would shatter armour and bodies, but skilled soldiers would slip within their reach and be bathing in their blood before they could strike again.

The Iron Glove had cured that deficiency. The Scorpions struck at Meyr with their greatswords and their axes. They were strong, fierce warriors but Meyr was armoured in aviation-grade steel layered three times over. As the Khanaphir spears jabbed past him from either side, the Mole Cricket simply stood in the front line and smashed every Scorpion he could reach – and his reach was long. They were still coming from behind their fellows, crushing together, so he could not miss. The warriors in the fore were soon fighting against their comrades, trying to get out of his way. After Meyr smashed his mace apart he snatched a Scorpion halberd, and then one of their five-foot swords, striking so hard with it that he bent the blade.

They surged and pushed at him, trying with sheer numbers to drag him down. Something was dancing about his shoulders now, and Totho experienced a moment of confusion before he could work out what it was.

It was Teuthete the Mantis. As though she weighed nothing, she was crouching on the shifting pauldrons of Meyr's armour, shooting down into the Scorpion throng. She danced in time with him, used him as her personal platform, swaying contemptuously aside from the crossbow bolts that sought her.

Amnon was beside them next, hacking with his sword at any Scorpion who managed to escape Meyr's onslaught. Totho knew that he should join them up there and put his snapbow to use, but he just watched and watched in awe as that impossible trio and the Khanaphir soldiers turned back the tide, killing with skill and fervour and monstrous brute strength, until even the Scorpions lost their taste for bloodshed and fell back under the constant rain of arrows.

Totho felt exhausted, beaten black and blue, and he had not so much as struck anyone with his fist. Another squad of the diminishing Royal Guard had come forward to seize the breach. Meyr, when he turned round, was painted red, coated with what he had made of the Many of Nem. The giant sat down on a fallen stone, knees up at chest level. He pushed back his helm and inhaled breath in vast lungfuls.

'Well done,' Totho commended him.

'We're . . . not done yet,' Meyr panted, between breaths. 'Have you seen how *many* of them there are?'

'I know.' Totho laid a hand on his shoulder, such a tiny gesture in comparison. Some of the Khanaphir had come forward with water, and they began to clean the Mole Cricket's armour as though it was a sacred honour for them.

It was noon, or so the sun said. They had held the Scorpions at bay for half a day.

'Tirado!' he shouted out, realizing that he had not seen the Fly-kinden for much of the fight. His call was immediately followed by the small figure landing beside him. 'Where in the wastes have you been?' he snapped.

'Keeping myself out of trouble, chief,' the Fly said. 'You wanted?'

'Go to the Scriptora. Find . . . find Maker, the Collegiate ambassador, and tell her . . . Tell her I want to see her. Ask nicely—' He stopped, on seeing figures approaching from the east shore. 'Never mind. Wait on.'

They were Khanaphir civilians, carrying baskets of food for the soldiers, but among them strode a tall woman with a full head of hair. Even as Totho recognized her, Amnon strode past him with arms outstretched. It was Rakespear, the Collegiate scholar, who threw herself against his breastplate, and then stepped back to stare.

'My life, look at you,' she said. 'You look like a sentinel.'

'If you say so.' Amnon managed a tired grin. 'Thank Totho for it. It's saved my life already.'

'Then I do thank him.' Praeda Rakespear nodded to Totho briefly. 'How is the defence?'

'Too early to say. They'll come back,' said Amnon. The

food was being distributed among the defenders, and Totho found a cloth-wrapped parcel pushed into his hands. Being used to Solarnese cuisine, which was spicy and hot, he had found Khanaphir food too bland or subtle for his taste. Just then he was hungry enough to eat anything.

'Mistress Rakespear,' he said, 'is Che . . . is Mistress Maker . . .? I was wondering if she would come here, to speak with me.'

'Che?' Praeda frowned at him. 'Do you know where she is?'

Totho stared. 'Is she not with you? With you and the old man?'

'Nobody seems to have seen her since yesterday,' Praeda told him. 'I've asked the Ministers, but they don't seem to understand. She's gone missing before. She . . . she's not been acting rationally.'

'Tirado,' Totho ordered. 'Go and find her.'

'Right you are.' The Fly bolted whatever he was eating, and lifted off into the sky, wings glittering, heading across the river towards the east. Totho grimaced. *That bloody woman can't keep out of trouble to save her life*, and then, *But am I really in a position to judge her?*

He found a flat space of stone away from the locals and set to eating as quickly and efficiently as possible, so as not to be interrupted.

Someone sat down beside him. He started in surprise and looked up to see one of Amnon's Guard, a woman ten years his senior, her scaled armour streaked with blood. A younger man sat on the far side of her, his helm removed, his bald head gleaming. Totho regarded them both cautiously.

'I am Dariset,' the woman announced, before biting into the hunk of bread they had given her.

'Ptasmon,' said the man.

'Halmir, me,' said another man appearing on the far side of him. There were soon quite a few gathered, sitting on stones or the ground, in a loose circle that now included him.

'Totho,' he said awkwardly, 'of Collegium.'

'You have done much for us, Totho,' Dariset said. 'Much that you did not need to.'

*And to please a woman who won't even turn up and witness it*, he thought, but he just nodded noncommittally.

'We are honoured that you and your giant and your people fight alongside us, Totho,' said one of the others, and something clicked inside Totho, as he thought, *This is the first time that any of them, save Amnon, has called me something other than 'Foreigner'*. He looked into their faces, the faces of simple, hardworking people who were prepared to die for their city. *This is something that Drephos never did. He never knew the names of his soldiers. He would never have cared.*

It was a terrible trap, though. They would die, he knew. Perhaps even today. Perhaps in an hour's time or less, Ptasmon would be writhing in agony with his gut ripped open by a Scorpion halberd, or Dariset would lie still with a crossbow bolt through her eye. In knowing their names, in making them real people and not components of a machine, he was baring his flesh for the lash. *They are meat for the war machine*, he tried to remind himself but, sitting there with them, it came hard.

He was going to say something dismissive, cast them off, become the Foreigner again in their eyes. They were now going about their midday meal industriously, talking amongst themselves, in between mouthfuls. *But these people are so solemn and silent, almost like Ant-kinden*, he thought, but the notion was easily corrected: *They are like that only in front of strangers. Like Ant-kinden, amongst their own they behave like all people.*

He said nothing further, just let them talk. He learned about the widow that Halmir was hoping to woo, and that Ptasmon did not yet know whether his family had got safely over the river. He learned that the scarred man called Kham was Amnon's cousin, yet was openly critical of much that the First Soldier did. He learned that Dariset had once gone on an expedition to scout the ruins in the heart of the Nem, but they had turned back on seeing the shapes that moved there, and the signs that those shapes left behind: crucified Scorpions poisoned and desiccating in the sun and sand, and yet some of them still alive.

*I should not have shared in this.* He felt their lives loading him with emotional baggage that Drephos would have scoffed at. He remembered when he had let so much similar baggage slough off him, during the siege of Tark. He had been granted a kind of icy rationality at that point, a clarity of vision he would be loath to lose. But, he now considered, had he ever truly been free of sentiment?

*Remind me again why I am still here, and not gone from this doomed city?* Che's face, in his mind, never failed to twist something inside him, some organ that seemed designed purely to wreck his life and ruin his every dream. *Cursed woman! Wretched wasting woman! Can you not let me be, after all this time?* He had tried – oh how he had tried – to excise the callow, clumsy youth who had been so besotted with her, but no matter how deep his reason cut, up to its elbows in blood and tissue, his younger self always grew back.

*And so we are brought to this pass. I will fight to defend a city I should care nothing about, and then I will most likely die, and so will those who follow me. Drephos would laugh himself to death if he knew. Or would he weep for me? If Drephos could weep for anything, it would be at such a futile waste.*

He looked over to Meyr, saw the huge man still sitting, Teuthete standing by him, their heads almost on the same level. The Mantis was speaking, but Totho could not hear her quiet words. The Mole Cricket shook his head slowly, and she put a hand to his chest, her arm-spines flexing.

A shout went up from nearby and suddenly they were all in motion again, rushing for the barricades, cramming a last mouthful before taking up weapons. Meyr pulled his helm forward over his face. Totho saw Amnon embrace Praeda one more time and then take up his shield.

The next wave of the Many were coming.

Corcoran felt the engines of the *Fourth Iteration* turn over, first slowly and then with a building urgency. The crew were casting off, letting the rudders and the current of the river pull them away from the quays.

There was already a movement among the Scorpion-kinden in anticipation. A great mass of them was gathering by the west pillar of the Estuarine Gate, anticipating that the ship would have to come close enough for them to rake it with crossbow shot before it quit the city. *And we should, we really should*, Corcoran thought. *What we should be doing right now is leaving. Khanaphes was never going to be a market for us, and soon it won't even be a city any more.*

He did not understand his leader: Totho seemed to have gone mad, caught some local fever. Gone native, perhaps. Where was the profit in this, to defend one pack of primitives against another? What could they possibly gain? Especially as the beast they had backed was going to lose. It didn't take any tactical mind to see that.

Corcoran was not a soldier, despite the armour. He was a merchant, from a family of small traders. When the Iron Glove had hoisted its banner over Chasme he had seen the opportunity. He had been in near the start, and done well out of it. It had been worth exchanging the cluttered security of Solarno to make that bid for profit. He was a merchant and profit was his business. That was what he understood. Profit allowed him to live well and be a pleasant and amiable person, because to be pleasant and amiable in this world you needed a buffer between you and its woes.

The world's woes were coming right back at him today. *Sure and I'm very sorry for them all*, he thought, but it wasn't as if they were family. The Khanaphir were having their last days on the map before the Scorpions consigned them to the past they had dwelled in for so long.

But the halfbreed had decided that the Iron Glove should be making some kind of idiot *stand* now. It was beyond comprehension. Corcoran wanted so very badly to sail the *Iteration* towards the river mouth and demand that they raise the gate. Surely he would then be doing what was best for the consortium. Totho had plainly gone mad.

If it had been any other man, perhaps, but Totho was a favourite of the Grand Old Man himself. It was well known that he and the big chief had built the Iron Glove with their own hands. Whatever Totho did would be given the nod, no matter how insane. Which left Corcoran out on the river, turning the bows of the *Fourth Iteration* towards the bridge.

They were fighting up there. Totho was fighting up there. *And maybe there'll be some justice and he'll get killed before I do.* There would be a signal, but the *Iteration* had to be in place by then.

'Take us in closer!' Corcoran called, and the order was relayed down to the engine rooms. 'And get the smallshotters loaded and on the rail,' he added, trying to sound adequately military. His hands were clenched on that rail themselves because otherwise they would be shaking.

The *Iteration* was a good ship, made to stand the perils of hostile seas and hostile seafarers. In the river current it handled choppily, the engines constantly adjusting to the water's flow. Corcoran had the bulk of the Iron Glove people aboard with him, both to handle the craft and to man its armaments. They were short-handed even so. They had left a fair slice of their crew on the Spider-kinden pirate that had tried to overhaul them on the way to Khanaphes.

The Scorpions on the bank were watching, fascinated, as the ship completed its cumbersome turn and chugged towards the bridge. With its mast down and sails stowed the *Iteration* might just have scraped under its arches, in another breach of Khanaphir tradition. *That lot can rot*, Corcoran thought. *If they'd had any sense they'd have bought a job lot of snapbows off us, and they'd already be chasing the Scorpions back into the desert about now.*

'Keep us steady!' he called, as they neared the bridge. 'Steady here.'

'You want the anchor out?'

'No, just keep us steady.' He was not a sailor, either. Let his crew wrestle with engines and rudders to fulfil his orders. If Totho didn't have to make sense, neither did he. He did not want to be anchored down, though, since the Scorpions were not exactly powerless to retaliate.

They had not seen the ship as a threat, he realized. There were masses of them gathered, set on funnelling on to the bridge. The *Iteration* had turned to put its broadside towards them and the crew were clipping the smallshotters to the rail. Tiny compared to the Scorpions' own siege weapons, they could shoot balls three inches across that would make a mess of a wooden hull, but were even more useful against human targets.

'Grapeshot,' Corcoran ordered. His people industriously dropped bulging little paper sacks into the weapons' muzzles, each one a careful measure of firepowder and shot.

*Might as well make the first one count,* Corcoran thought. 'We'll give it them all together,' he shouted out. Then he started as a small figure dropped on to the deck beside him.

'Himself says now would be a good time,' Tirado told him.

Corcoran nodded. 'Let them have it on my mark!' he cried, and then, 'Three, two, one – loose!'

The combined shock of a dozen smallshotters detonating at once rolled the *Iteration* back in the water amid a bellowing of smoke and fire. The fistfuls of lead shot tore through the massed Scorpion warriors, ripping dozens of them apart. Corcoran was glad enough he didn't have to witness it. The aftermath, as the ship righted itself, was bad enough.

'Load and loose in your own time,' he instructed his crew,

seeing the Scorpion host boiling and reeling from this new assault. *That will have taken pressure off the barricades*. 'You go back now and find out how long he wants us here,' he told the Fly, and Tirado kicked off from the deck, darting upwards towards the bridge itself.

The smallshotters were discharging independently, each at the speed of its own crew, lashing at the Scorpions wherever they were thickest. There was some return of crossbow bolts, but the distance defeated them, only a few coasting far enough to bounce back from the ship's armoured hull.

'They're bringing up the big engines!' someone called. Corcoran glanced up at the bridge. Surely they were done by now? Surely Totho didn't need them to stay out here. Perhaps Tirado had been killed or hurt, or simply forgotten to deliver the message.

'Try to keep them busy,' he shouted. He located one of the big leadshotters, and saw that it was some way inland, taking advantage of its own better range. The *Iteration* was armoured, but it was designed to be proof against the sort of pieces that another ship would carry. No ship had ever put to sea with something as heavy as the Scorpion ordnance. A few hits near the waterline would soon take care of the *Iteration*.

'It'll take them a while to find the range,' he said, hearing his own voice tremble. Over the sporadic boom of the smallshotters he could barely be heard anyway. The bulk of the Scorpion advance had scattered, seeking shelter from the *Iteration*'s salvos. The fighting above must falter, surely, the grinding wheels of death no longer fed by a flow of fresh bodies. Corcoran gritted his teeth, watching the Scorpion crews load their massive weapons.

They were quicker than he had assumed. He saw the gust of smoke from one leadshotter and instinctively dropped to his knees.

A tremendous column of spray spouted from the river,

a full twenty yards past them and astern. *They hurried their aim*, he thought, and it was oddly reassuring to know that he had done enough damage to secure the enemy's attention. A second leadshotter roared even as he thought this, and the water erupted a few yards off the bows, between the *Iteration* and the piles of the bridge. Corcoran clung to the rail as the swell rocked them. Meanwhile, some of the smallshotters were loosing solid shot, trying for enough range to trouble the Scorpion artillerists.

Tirado dropped almost on to his shoulders, swerving in the air to make himself a harder target. 'Time to go,' he announced. 'Pull back to the docks, and be thankful this river's so wide.'

'Stop shooting and let's get out of here!' Corcoran shouted to the crew at the top of his lungs. He had to repeat it twice, running down the length of the ship, before everyone had pulled the smallshotters back and the ship's engines started to turn them. Another plume of water exploded nearby, but they had become a moving target now, spoiling the enemy's calculations.

*But they'll be ready for us the next time, won't they just . . .*

Above, on the bridge, the latest Scorpion assault was falling back, unsupported, shot through with arrows. Yet the host of the Many of Nem seemed barely diminished.

# Thirty-Six

She woke up because he had stepped on her arm. The sudden pain, and waking into utter dark, left her wholly bewildered. Che had no idea where she was. Someone was apologizing to her but all reference escaped her. For a brief moment she was nowhere, and had no idea even who she was.

Then she remembered her Art: it was still not second nature to her. She let her eyes gradually find their way, and saw Thalric a few paces away, looking frustrated.

'Clumsy bastard,' she told him, and enquired, 'I've been asleep?'

'Unless you've been snoring just to annoy me.' He was not quite looking at her and it took a moment to realize that it was because he could not, of course, see her. Her voice, in the confined space, must be hard to pin down.

'You swallowed some of that herbal muck you were giving to Osgan,' Thalric went on. His eyes were very wide, futilely trying to stare the darkness down. 'Because of your shoulder. Then, after a while, you were sleeping. It's been a long night.'

'And then you trod on me,' she pointed out. 'How long has it been?'

'I have no idea.' He was moving about the room again, feeling for the walls. 'I used to think I had a good sense of time, but there are no clues down here: no light, no sounds. It's been hours, anyway. It must be daylight outside.'

'Thalric,' she said, 'what are you doing, exactly?'

'Trying to get a proper idea of this place – which has turned out to be surprisingly difficult, and somewhat disgusting.'

'Do you want me to help you?'

'I'll be fine.'

'Only, I can see in the dark.'

He stopped abruptly, turning towards where she was. His expression was completely unguarded. 'Since when?'

*Since you locked me in your heliopter after Asta* – but she wasn't going to say that. 'It's a Beetle Art, Thalric. Granted, it's not common, but it's there.'

His lips moved, but whatever he was going to say died there. Abruptly he sat down and put his head in his hands. *How long has he been feeling his way around this place? How many hours of going round and round?* She was treated to a brief moment of Thalric in absolute despair. Then he lifted his head, and he was already adjusting. 'So tell me then,' he said, 'what do we have?'

She clambered to her feet, feeling her shoulder twinge, peering about. Her Art-sight leached the colours, turning Thalric's skin pallid and his clothes drab. She suspected there were few enough colours in their surroundings to begin with.

'It's a room maybe twelve paces to a side,' she decided. 'The ceiling's about the same extent high. A cube, then, but the walls slope slightly inwards as they go up. There's an archway in each wall. Trapezium-shaped.' She stopped.

'And no doors,' Thalric finished for her.

'And no doors,' she echoed. 'There are just . . . the archways just have stone behind them. And one . . . one of them's been blocked off by the trap.'

'I felt carving on the walls,' he said weakly.

'It's the usual old Khanaphir script,' she said. Even with her Art-enhanced eyes it was hard to discern it. She moved to one wall, using a sleeve to wipe at it. At the first touch she made a horrified noise and flinched back. 'There's something on the walls.'

'Yes, there is,' said Thalric, with some satisfaction. 'Every cursed surface here is coated with it. It's made my explorations a real joy.'

*I can't see it*, she realized, but then logic reasserted itself. There was a thin layer of transparent slime coating the walls, coating the floor too – at least from the state of her clothes and the sounds her sandals made. As there was no light to gleam off it, it was completely invisible, even to her. It showed only in a blurring of the carvings beneath.

*And why go to the trouble of writing all of this here, in this little room of death?* Of course, the Khanaphir engraved these things everywhere, but she could tell just by looking that this script was the real old hieroglyphs, not the meaningless babble that was all the modern masons could manage. Someone had deliberately put a message here, for those with eyes to see and minds to understand it.

'This wasn't really how I thought we'd end up,' said Thalric quietly.

'We haven't ended up yet,' she told him.

'Only a matter of time. The air can't last for ever.'

'What happened to the old resourceful Thalric then?' she asked him, feeling suddenly annoyed that he was just sitting there. 'Don't the Rekef teach you to be ready for anything?'

'The old resourceful Thalric is currently blind, slimy and trapped in a cell underground with no possible way out,' he said, 'and very, very tired. Some of us here haven't been getting our beauty sleep.'

'Not that it would do much good, in your case.' She wiped away slime from more of the carvings, feeling the thick gunge caking her sleeves. It had a feel to it that was familiar, but unpleasantly so. She hunted the memory down, associating it with guilt, panic, danger . . . 'Hammer and tongs!' she spat. 'Thalric, this is Fir.'

'What now?'

'This slime, it's Fir. This is the forbidden elixir of Khanaphes, that the Ministers will kill you for sampling.' *And that the Ministers themselves eat gallons of.* 'This is their link with the Masters, they claim. There must be enough down here for everyone in the city to go out of their minds on.'

'Are you suggesting we spend our last few hours drugged into a stupor?' Thalric asked her acidly.

'No, but don't you see . . .' *But he doesn't see. He doesn't understand what Fir is. So, do I?* Fir, the drug that somehow opened one's mind to the past, that the Khanaphir underclasses swore let them look on the faces of the Masters, that the Ministers thought opened a direct link by which they could hear their Masters' voices. Did she still believe that there were Masters yet, or that there ever had been? Yet the Khanaphir believed. Ethmet believed. Was their entire culture built on hallucinations derived from this slime? *No, there has to be something more to it than that.*

'I've been knocking on the walls,' he said. 'No echo anywhere. I've even tried my sting against them. That slimy stuff smells vile when you burn it. The stone underneath barely warmed.'

'I think I need to read these inscriptions,' she decided. 'Give me your cloak.'

He frowned at the dark, but shrugged the garment off without question, holding it out blindly until she took it from him. She began scrubbing at the walls, clearing away the Fir that had turned those crisp carvings into illegible smears.

'Since when,' Thalric said after a moment, 'can you read that gibberish? Since when can it even be read?'

'It's a long story.'

'Well, I didn't have any other plans.'

She stopped, gazing back at him. He was still sitting in the middle of the floor, head turned vaguely in her direction. Something of his normal expression was gone, that hard mockery that was usually there when he spoke to her. *Has he really given up hope?* She realized it was far simpler than that. Just as her face was invisible to him in the dark, so he had not considered that his was not invisible to her. This was Thalric caught unawares, without his customary armour. She took the chance to study him: the years of hard deeds, of bitter loyalty, all the betrayals that could be traced on his face. Each had put its grip on him, twisting and turning to fit him to the mould, yet finally he had not fitted. At the end, after the scars and the fingerprints, there was still a core that was only Thalric. *Only a man who truly knows himself could have come out of all that still recognizing himself in the mirror.*

'What?' he asked suspiciously, into the silence. She felt suddenly ashamed, as though she had been spying on the spymaster.

'Just looking at the carvings,' she claimed, although her voice held no conviction. 'Look, if you want a conversation, why don't you talk? I've had enough of you interrogating me.'

He gave an amused snort and she was surprised at how familiar it sounded. *How well do I know him? Sometimes it seems that I know him even better than my own family. My life has been riddled by the holes left by his passing, like some kind of grub.*

'You could tell me, for a start, why the Regent-general of the whole Empire is currently buried alive in a nowhere city out here on the Sunroad Sea,' she said. 'Because I myself don't understand it. Life just keeps giving you chances, and you waste every one of them. You were the big man of the Empire, after the war, so how did this happen?'

For a long time he remained quiet, while she kept on industriously cleaning up the carvings. Fragments of their meaning drifted loose into her head, but nothing that she could string together.

'The Empress,' he said at last, slowly. 'The Empress Seda the First. And if you ask me how that happened, well, I wasn't there at the time. An Empress? Nobody had ever heard of such a thing: a woman in charge of the Wasp Empire.'

'Well, we know about your people's attitudes towards women,' Che said primly. 'Although you've had your share of women agents, haven't you? The Rekef, at least, isn't so blinkered.'

'Mistakes, all of them,' he said darkly. 'Arianna tried to kill me, and I actually did kill Scyla, or at least I'm as sure of that as I can be. No, I've not been the luckiest man with women.'

'You were married, though, weren't you? I thought you told me that once? What happened to her?'

'She was only too glad to yield place to the Empress,' Thalric replied, with a brief laugh. 'Not that she'd have had much choice, but we hadn't seen each other in years. I had a son, too. I still have, I suppose. The union was all for the Empire, and part of my duty. I was never that interested. It was just something you're supposed to do before you go off and die in the wars. I'm sure the woman was compensated.'

'I'll never understand your people – or like them, frankly,' Che remarked.

'Well, maybe I'll join you in that, seeing as they seem to want me dead yet again. Maybe it's *her*. Maybe she's decided I'm now surplus to requirements.' Thalric grimaced sightlessly. 'While the provinces were in rebellion she needed a man as a figurehead that her people could be reassured by. That was me, at the time, but now the Empire's pretty much together again. Maybe it's as simple as that.' He paused in thought. 'But in that case she could simply have had me executed, or assassinated, when I was last in the capital. It wouldn't be hard for her to do away with me. There'd be no reason to go about it like this, snuffing me out in some distant corner of the world.'

'What's she like?' Che asked. When he did not reply, she urged, 'Come on, tell me. The woman who rules an Empire, what's she like – your new match?'

Still he did not answer, and she turned from her work to

look at him. His expression was far away, somewhere that he did not want to be.

'Thalric?' she prompted, and his eyes flicked towards her.

'You really want to know?' he asked. 'The best-kept secret in the Empire? You want to know about Seda?'

'It doesn't look likely that I'll get a chance to gossip about it much,' she pointed out. *Do I really want to know?* she asked herself: something in his face had disturbed her.

'The Empress . . . Seda the First,' he said, and she had now lost her chance to avoid the knowledge, whatever it would be. 'She is not quite eighteen yet, younger than you by a year or two. She was eight when her father died, Alvdan the First, and she told me how she'd lived in fear of death ever since. She was the only sibling of the new Emperor to survive his coronation. He kept her around because making her afraid was one of his pastimes. That's how she tells it.'

Another pause. Che kept scrubbing away diligently.

'I wasn't there when the Emperor died,' Thalric said. 'In fact I was imprisoned in the cells beneath the arena, where they keep the fighters and the animals. When I found out about what she had become, the Empress, I searched out someone who could tell me exactly how it had happened, because it seemed clear to me that *something* had gone very badly wrong indeed.'

'Osgan,' Che filled in.

'Osgan,' Thalric confirmed. 'The same man who was stupid enough to follow me here, and who's surely paid for it now. But Osgan sat beside the Emperor, and saw it all. And then I heard what he had to say, and it made no sense.'

'Tisamon killed the Emperor,' Che said. 'That's what Tynisa said.'

Thalric was silent again.

'Or what? Did he just die? Did he have a weak heart?' Che prompted. 'Tisamon and that Dragonfly woman came charging out of the fighting pit and killed just about everyone they could get hold of. Did the Emperor just die coincidentally?'

'I don't know,' Thalric said. 'All I know is that something happened, something . . . very *wrong*. The Emperor was there, and Seda, and General Maxin, and some slave of the Emperor's. This is not just from Osgan. I've spoken to a few others who were there, too. It's amazing how people remember . . . or don't remember. Everyone remembers the mad Mantis killing the Emperor: it's just that none of their versions quite match.'

'And what does your new wife have to say?'

Another pause, terminating in a laugh that was surprisingly free from bitterness. 'You bloody Beetle woman,' he said, but fondly, 'why can't I ever have a conversation with you, just once, where you don't manage to trip me up? This . . . being here, in the dark, it's the whole situation with us, from the start. You've always seen things in me I've wanted to hide, while you . . . I can't make you out at all.'

'That's because what you see is *all* of me, Thalric,' she told him. 'And you're not used to people who aren't hiding things from you.' But even as she said it, she realized that it was no longer true, that it had not been true for some time. *Even I have secrets now.* 'So what did she say?' she pressed on, to turn his attention away from the subject.

'She said that Tisamon didn't really kill the Emperor. That the Emperor's old slave – nobody seems to have known who he was – was in the middle of the conspiracy to put her on the throne, only she's glad he's now dead. He's dead, Maxin's dead, the Emperor's dead. It's only Seda left from the royal box. Seda and Osgan, of all bloody people.'

'So who killed the Emperor?' Che asked. 'According to her story.'

'She says I wouldn't believe her,' he replied. 'And she says she won't tell me. And, knowing what I do about her, I don't think I want to know.'

'You're going to soon run out of ways not to tell me,'

Che said, moving on to the next wall. 'So why not just say? What's so wrong? What's the problem? I don't think there are many Wasp excesses that could surprise me.'

'Oh, is that so?' he said quietly. She heard him move closer to her. 'You want me to tell you?'

She put out a hand that brushed his shoulder. He flinched back from its touch, then took it briefly, confirming what it was. With that frame of reference, he got himself facing her directly, and his expression told her that he had been keeping this to himself for a long time. *And wanting to tell someone for a long time, and not been able to . . .*

'She's mad,' he said. 'She's completely insane. She thinks she . . . She thinks she has powers. Not Art, but magic powers.' His expression was almost embarrassed on behalf of the Empress, but Che was abruptly paying full attention, the carvings forgotten.

'Her powers, these powers she thinks she has, they derive from blood, you see,' Thalric explained. 'It's something to do with this old slave, some nonsense he told her, but she must have blood. And when an Empress sets her heart on something . . .' The corner of his mouth twitched. 'The thing is . . . there's someone inside there, just a Wasp-kinden girl who's had a hard life, and who's terrified of what's happening to her, but the madness, it takes possession of her. Then she gives the orders, and another two or three slaves are bled. For her bath. To fill her cup. She says it makes her powerful.' A shudder went through him. 'I have drunk from that cup, too, when she has asked me to.'

Deep inside, Che felt an unease that was nothing to do with the overt horror in Thalric's story. Something else had connected with her, and she did not know what. Something was trying to tell her that this was important, and at first she thought, *Achaeos?* She heard no harsh voice in her mind, but there was some link there, something close to her.

'The thing is, though,' Thalric continued, the words sounding as if they were dragged from him, '*something* happened to her. When the Emperor died . . . I don't know how to explain it, but something went terribly wrong. She was changed. It drove her mad. She was . . . wounded.'

'What do you mean?' Che whispered.

'She has . . . lost something,' Thalric said raggedly. 'Something in her mind has broken and driven her mad. She has lost her Aptitude. She is like some other kinden now, not a Wasp at all. That connection, that understanding . . . her mind is changed utterly. She does not think like we do any more. The worst thing is that she is not just mad, but she is Inapt and ruling an Apt Empire.'

Che slumped back against the slick wall, feeling something within her plummet. 'Oh that . . . that is the worst thing, is it?' she got out, but she was finding it difficult even to draw breath.

He got her reaction wrong, of course. 'I'm not talking about your Moth lover,' he protested. 'You can't imagine it. It's as though she's not human any more. Some part of her mind has just been cut away, and it's the part that would let anyone else understand her. It's turned her into a monster.'

She felt her heart lanced through with horror, with anger, even with that old revulsion at what she was, that she thought she had put behind her. 'And me,' she said. 'Would you say that of me, Thalric? Am I a monster?'

'What are you talking about?'

'Answer me? Am I a monster, too?' The anger was triumphing. Her fists were clenched. He would never see the blow coming.

'Che, I don't understand you.'

'No, you don't. Because some part of me has been cut away, Thalric. I'm Inapt. I lost it at the end of the war, when Achaeos died. I'm the same as her, so I suppose that makes me a monster too.'

She watched him, secure in the knowledge that he could not see her. She had felt like hitting him, but it was fast dissolving in a morass of despair at what she had lost. *Who's to say he's wrong? Perhaps I am a monster. Something's wrong with me. I've been crippled where nobody can see.*

It was his hands that drew her attention. His fingers twitched, in and out, closing for safety, opening for danger. *Hammer and tongs, is he going to kill me for it?* She always forgot who he was when she spoke to him, forgot *what* he was. It was a small room. He would not need many blind sting-shots to find her.

'No,' he said, and he sounded surprised at his own conclusion. 'No, it doesn't. It makes her a monster, but not you under any circumstances. Perhaps she was more monstrous to begin with. Something to do with her kinden, probably.'

When Che said nothing, he began to look around, imagining that she had moved elsewhere. 'When I found out about her, about her loss, it made a kind of sense of her, of all her other habits – of the blood. But you . . . I find I don't honestly care. I *know* you. I know you're not what she is.'

*Am I not? Perhaps not, but I think I could understand why she does what she does.* 'I've only ever told Uncle Sten,' Che admitted. She had just realized that her secret, her terrible secret, was now known by two others, and one of them was a Wasp.

He reached out and, more by luck than judgement, brushed her hair, then found her uninjured shoulder. She held his hand there with her own. *He does not flinch or struggle, at having to touch the monster.*

'You don't believe in magic,' she said. 'How could you?' It reminded her of a conversation she'd had once with Salma, long ago. 'But you must have seen some things, during your life . . .'

'Some,' he acknowledged grudgingly. 'I saw the spy, Scyla, doing her tricks with my own face. It was no Art, and yet she did it – and I cannot say how.'

'The world is full of the inexplicable,' she said. 'I find it easier to see that now.' She felt his hand tense for a moment, then relax. 'Or at least, I cannot explain such things for you, but I can navigate them. Would you believe that?'

'Just because I cannot explain something does not mean that there is no rational explanation,' he replied. There was a faint edge to his voice that told her, *He's frightened. He knows just enough to be frightened.*

'If I told you that I sensed the trap, where you saw nothing, you would say it was because my eyes and my Art let me see better. If I told you that I can read these carvings *because* of what I have lost, you would say it was merely because I had studied.' It made her feel lonely, saying it out loud, the way that she had been cut off from so much of the world. 'If I told you that I did believe in magic, you would think me mad.'

Through each revelation, she could feel him on the point of pulling away from her, but he never quite did. 'Che . . .' he began. His hand tightened. 'Actions are more important than beliefs. You believe what you want, so long as you don't start bathing in the blood of slaves.' His lips twitched, the long-absent mocking smile coming back. 'An Inapt Beetle? You've finally found a way to make yourself completely useless to everyone.'

'What?' she snapped, and pushed him in the chest, hard enough to make him stagger. She tried to follow up, but now he had the measure of where she was. In a moment he was holding her against his chest, her forehead on his shoulder. She did not dare look up and see what unguarded expression he wore.

She had expected him to let go, while he made some other barbed comment, but instead he stood quite still, his breath rising and falling against her.

'Thalric . . .' It felt strange, comfortable and horribly guilty all at once. She kept expecting the spectre of Achaeos to loom large in order to castigate her, but it seemed to have absented itself since enticing her to this place. 'What if I told you now that I could open the doors to this room, from what I have learned in the carvings here? Would you say it was just artifice?'

His breath quickened. 'You can open this room up?'

'I don't know, for sure,' she said. 'But the carvings say I can, if I try.'

'Then I'd say it was magic and not care who heard me,' he said quickly, but she knew that was not true. *Achaeos was right: belief is easy in the dark, but soon banished by sunlight. If we ever get out of this he will invent some explanation to settle his mind.*

She pulled away, was held tight for a moment and then released. *Oh this is wrong.* Stenwold would be mortified. In fact the list of people who would recoil from her was long: Tynisa, Achaeos, Totho . . . How many was she betraying by feeling this way about a Wasp, a Rekef Wasp? About *Thalric.*

It had been growing on her since she spotted him in this city, a face if not friendly then familiar, amid an ocean of strangers. It had been growing since she found such common territory with him, her opposite number, her old adversary. Now, looking at his face, she did not any longer automatically think of the cells in Asta and Myna, of the interrogation and what he would have done to her, for the Empire's sake. The past had reclaimed its own. She had acknowledged the account was settled, through what he had done later.

'I remember Myna,' she said, and saw him stiffen, expecting rebuke. 'The second time, I mean. I remember that you gave yourself up for the resistance – and for me.'

'These things never quite work out how you plan them,' he said.

*I remember Collegium, too, and the signing of the Treaty of Gold. That moment we were able to speak freely, before the diplomacy claimed him.*

She felt a wellspring of emotion about to burst, and fought it down. *Not now. Not here. But how strange that it should come to this.* 'You try and rest,' she advised. 'You look as though you need it. I'll work on getting us out of here.'

# Thirty-Seven

*We have reached a turning point, I think*, was Accius's conclusion. The two Vekken were crouching in the shadows of the archway that linked the Place of Foreigners to the square fronting the Scriptora. They had, from one vantage or another, been watching the pyramid since last night, taking turns to sleep for short periods, knowing that the sleeper would wake the instant the sentry called on him.

Last night they had tracked the fugitive Beetle ambassador, street by street, silently and with grim determination. The Wasps had helped. The Vekken had followed Cheerwell Maker's trail by watching the sky and hunting the hunters. Their chase had been tireless, careful, and the Wasps had never guessed that they were acting as beacons in a greater pursuit.

They had been in time to see the Maker woman and her co-conspirators bearded at the pyramid. They witnessed the Wasp advance, one fugitive captured, the other, along with Maker, disappearing into the edifice itself. Two Wasps had followed them. There had been a sound.

Cheerwell Maker had not returned from inside that pyramid. Nor had any of the Wasps, either her companion or their pursuers. The Imperials above had fled the structure, seemingly without cause or warning.

*The Wasps still keep watch*, Malius noted. *They believe as we do, then, that they are still within.*

There was a moment of silence between them, an understanding close enough that even unspoken words were not needed. Neither one said, *We could let this rest here,* but each knew the other was thinking just that.

*I do not like that place,* Accius decided. *It is an irrational reaction, but something I cannot define disturbs me about it.* He compared his perceptions with those of Malius, and was comforted to find the same disquiet in his colleague. *The behaviour of the Wasps cannot be fully accounted for. They fled very swiftly, from nothing that was apparent to us. I cannot say what, but some other force is at work here – some force as yet invisible to us. We can see only its effects.*

*Agreed.* Malius hunkered down lower, while checking the action of his crossbow. Again there was a pause in their thought-conversation, each steeling himself.

*Our suppositions to date are challenged.* It was Malius who voiced this silently. *The Collegium ambassador's game is not so simple as one of loyalty or betrayal. There is division in the Imperial camp also. We came here to determine the Collegiate plans, and how they might affect our city. We know less now than we thought we did yesterday. We cannot return without gaining more concrete information. Otherwise we would have failed our city.*

*It is clear, then, that whatever the Collegiate ambassador is up to, it is substantially more complicated than we thought,* Accius agreed with a sigh. *Only a proper interrogation will reveal it, and for that we must catch her alive. And for that . . .*

*We must follow her,* Malius finished. They both felt the strange dread exercised by the pyramid, but each took strength from the other.

*I feel that this journey shall only be one-way.* Accius was saying what they had both been thinking. *There is something down there, something that I cannot give a name or shape to. There is only one way to do this. We must separate.*

*I shall—* Malius started, but Accius overrode him. *No,* I *shall. I shall venture within. You must stay hidden up here and I shall report to you all I encounter down below. If I meet the ambassador, I shall relay her explanations to you. If matters come to their worst . . .*

*I shall find my way home,* Malius stated firmly. *No matter what, I shall take what you learn there back to our city. Your sacrifice shall be known. I only wish there was some other way.*

*None suggests itself, none to be achieved with honour.* Accius took a deep breath. *I fear.*

*Take strength from me.*

*I do.*

*They shall know, back in Vek, that you did your duty.* Malius shifted position, eyes still on the pyramid. The sky above was darkening towards dusk, the square empty of life. *What words for your comrades?*

*None but the usual: that through me the city shall prosper, and our enemies fail.* Accius stood up slowly, seeking for inner calm. The alien, hostile city all around them seemed to encroach, to loom and threaten.

*I shall speak personally to your mate and children,* Malius assured him. *I know you are fond of them. Is there any specific message?*

*What more could I want for my children, since they enjoy the greatest gift already? They will be brought up as soldiers of Vek.* Accius slung his crossbow. *The Wasps will see me as I approach the pyramid.*

*If they move to attack you, I shall draw their attention,* Malius assured him. *A death or two should serve. I shall be with you, brother.*

Accius nodded, the bond of Art between them more potent than any clasping of hands, and then he was moving at a swift, low run out towards the pyramid and up the steps. Within moments, he was lost amongst the statues.

They had tied Osgan professionally. At least they had tied him in a chair, their rope-work rough about the elegant Khanaphir carvings, his hands bound together behind its back, palm pressed to palm, to stifle his Art.

They had even given him some wine, feeding two bowls of it to him messily, perhaps simply to keep him quiet. It had cleared his head a little, but he still had no real image of what had happened at the moment they caught him.

There had been a sound, a thunderous sound like a leadshotter going off . . . and screams. Not Thalric's scream, though, for they were not done hunting him. Thalric was one of life's survivors. Even brought to Capitas in chains as a traitor, he had got out of it – though he'd had to marry the Empress to do so.

Osgan shuddered, on recalling the hints Thalric had dropped about *that* situation, when his tongue had been loosened by drink down in the palace cellars. Terrible things, terrible secrets. Osgan's life contained enough terrible things on its own, without Thalric loading him with any more. Was that the price he must pay for Thalric's unreliable patronage – to be steadily eroded by ghastly secrets that he had no place knowing? He had survived his own moment of horror, while crouching there by the Emperor's side as *He*, as the avenging monster, had come for them both.

Osgan felt the terrors building in him again, his muscles twitching with them, making the chair creak. He was in some half-stripped room, some abandoned upper storey where the Rekef were hiding out. If he cried out, only the guards would hear, and then they would strike him again. His face was already overwritten with their despite of him.

But *He* had been there. They did not understand. Even Thalric had not understood. *He* had followed Osgan to Khanaphes. He had been hovering over the summit of that pyramid. Osgan had not actually seen that cruel face, nor any material form, but he had known it as sure as if the Mantis had stood there in plain view.

It did not matter that he had already seen the man dead, his blood mingling with the Emperor's. It only mattered that he was *here,* and that he had found Osgan at last.

Osgan whimpered, feeling the shakes build up inside him,

and this time he could not control them. He fought against his bonds, wrenching the joints of the chair, while he cried out in fear and frustration. He cried out for help, though in all the world there was not one with the ability and the inclination to help him.

Perhaps it was his mother that he cried for, in the end.

The door kicked open and he flinched, but it was not one of the guards this time. It was Marger, supposedly Thalric's second at the embassy, now revealed as a Rekef double-agent all this time. Not even the senior man, he was a puppet, a mere mouthpiece. Sulvec and the Beetle were both his masters, and Marger was a man dethroned.

'Shut up,' Marger told him, 'or we'll gag you. Don't think you won't get your brain boiled if anyone hears you and comes looking.'

There were tears in Osgan's eyes, amongst the puffiness of the bruising. Marger came over and examined him more closely.

'Waste it, just look at you. What's the point of you? You were a fool to come.'

*Oh how true,* but Osgan could say nothing. His lips were pressed tight to keep himself from sobbing.

There was an uncomfortable expression on Marger's face, which might have been pity or disgust. 'Call yourself an Imperial soldier?' he asked, shaking his head. 'Curse you, but they did a proper job on you, no mistake – not that it'll make much difference in the long run.' Marger was talking too much, hiding some nervousness.

'And . . . and you?' Osgan got out. 'How are they treating you? What's it like as a professional betrayer?'

'In the Rekef? Ask your friend Thalric, should you get the chance.' Marger shrugged easily, but it was clear that there was something else on his mind. 'We're going back tonight, you know.'

Osgan felt a moment of freezing horror. 'Back to the . . . to the . . .'

'To the ziggurat. We've had it watched all day, and nobody's come out. That means Thalric's still in there, skulking somewhere about. Maybe he's waiting for darkness too. If so, we'll be ready for him, because we're going in and we're taking you with us.'

'No!' Osgan choked. 'No, you mustn't! You don't understand what's in there!'

'So tell me.'

'It's . . . It's *Him*.'

Marger rolled his eyes. 'Don't make me slap you. Just tell me who's *him* now?'

'It's . . . I saw him . . . the man who . . . who killed the Emperor.' There, it was said, but Marger just shook his head.

'How long have they left that arm without tending it?' He scowled. 'You better not get so feverish that you stop making sense. Give me a plain answer and I'll get you some more wine. You'd like that, right?'

'I'm serious . . .' Osgan started, but saw the man's face turn sour. 'What do you want? What do you want from me?'

'Thalric, ideally. Then we can all get out of this backwater. We'll take you into the pit because Sulvec reckons if we start cutting pieces off you then Thalric might – *might* – come running. No guarantees, though, because he might not be such a sentimental bastard as all that. Unless you've got any better ideas?'

'Please,' Osgan whispered. 'Kill me here. Kill me now. Kill me slowly. Just don't take me back there. Not with *Him*.'

Marger frowned at him, clearly a little shaken. 'Nothing about this damn job makes sense,' he complained. 'Nothing about this damn city makes any sense. And *that* place.' He shuddered – not his customary shrug but a shiver that Osgan could well relate to. 'There's something not right about all of this, so give me answers. Right now, while it's just you and me. Don't make me call the others in here to cut it out of your hide a strip at a time.'

'What do you want to know?' Osgan asked him fearfully.

Marger took a moment to formulate the question, with a glance at the door that suggested he was not supposed to be conducting this solo interrogation. When he spoke again it took them in a new direction.

'What in the wastes has Thalric done?' he demanded.

'When? What?' Osgan replied weakly. His head was beginning to ache, and the entire room seemed to shift around him as the fever rolled back over him.

'Tell me what the pits is so important,' Marger insisted, his voice now a hushed whisper. He crouched beside Osgan's chair like a conspirator. 'Why do they want him dead so badly?'

'Ask your big Rekef man out there,' Osgan suggested. 'Surely he's told you.'

'Oh, they haven't even told *him*,' Marger said. 'But they've told him just how far they intend going just to have him dead. Do you think the Empire really cares two spits about Khanaphes or those Scorpion savages? Oh, maybe the Scorpions would make good Auxillians, but that's not the *point*. They're here just for Thalric, all of them. All the thousands of them currently attacking the bridge out there – they're here because the Empire wants Thalric dead.'

'I . . . don't understand,' stammered Osgan.

'No, *I* don't understand,' Marger told him, 'because it makes no cursed sense at all. Someone wants Major Thalric the Regent-General so very dead that they've sent Skater assassins and a Rekef team and engineers and leadshotters and a whole desert full of Scorpion-kinden, and they'll see forty thousand Beetles dead so long as his corpse lies somewhere amongst them. I swear they'll kill every living thing within miles of here just to make sure he's dead. That's what it's all for, because the Empire doesn't care a toss about this city. Someone very highly placed within the Empire wants Thalric dead, as dead as he can possibly be and – and this is apparently the important thing – every trace of *how* it happened buried under the rubble of a dead city so that nobody can ever pick up the pieces of what went on or work out who to blame. Now what in the wastes is going on?'

Osgan goggled at him. 'Why are you asking *me*?' was all he could say. 'It's nothing to do with *me*.'

'Because I hoped you would know,' said Marger, abruptly exhausted by the whole business. 'I really did. Because nobody is talking about it but we all know it's mad. Something's gone wrong back home, to have all this happening out here in the sticks. I mean, I don't dislike Thalric as a man. I really don't. But when orders come down from the bloody *palace* to see him dead by any means, including exterminating an entire people, then you jump to obey.'

Someone called out Marger's name from the next room, and the man started guiltily, putting some paces between himself and the prisoner. 'In here,' he said loudly.

One of Sulvec's men put his head around the door. 'Word from the sentries,' he announced. 'There's been some movement at the pyramid. It's dusk anyway, so time to move.'

The Scorpions had not stopped hurling themselves continually at the barricade until the sky began to darken in the east. In the thick of it, loosing snapbow bolts as fast as he could charge the weapon, Totho had wondered whether they might not eventually whittle the horde down to nothing, slaying so many of them that their corpses mounded up against the barricade and fell off the bridge into the river on either side.

There were only five left now of the original thirty Royal Guard who had held the breach, and many of their replacements had fallen also. The Khanaphir losses were far less than the Many's, but the Nem had far more warriors to lose. The Scorpions did not even have to kill them, only to force their way through the breach just the once. They had come close to it several times, but Meyr and Amnon had held the line, in their mail that was proof against axe and crossbow bolt, fighting like murderous automata until the force of the latest Scorpion charge ebbed.

Halmir, he who wooed the widow, had lost half his face to a Nemian halberd and Totho did not know if he lived or not. Dariset had her shoulder laid open by a greatsword, but her armour had saved her, leaving the wound messy but shallow. She still fought on. Old Kham had broken two shields defending Amnon's back at the moment when the Scorpions were closest to breaking through, and he would not let his cousin forget it. Totho had already shot several hundred bolts, and sent to the *Iteration* for more.

He had sent new orders for Corcoran too. Having looked out at the west bank and seen the monstrous mass of fires out there, he had realized that, despite all its losses, the war-host of the Nem had so far been spending only the small change from its pockets. Tomorrow would be worse: Amnon could only trust the Royal Guard to hold the breach, but so many of them had already perished out on the field. Their numbers grew slender, and the archers had taken their losses too, under crossbow bolts, axes, javelins. They could all be replaced, but only by weakening the force that waited, up and down the shore, for any rafts or boats the Scorpions could scrounge together.

There were some fires burning now behind the barricades, a force of soldiers waiting in case of an assault. Marsh folk were stationed on the wall itself, their eyes better in the darkness. Any creeping force of Scorpions would be rudely surprised by their arrows.

Totho found Amnon fiddling with the straps of his armour, his gauntleted hands clumsy with the buckles.

'Hold still,' Totho said. 'I'll take you out of it.'

'Tighten it,' Amnon told him. 'If they attack tonight, I will be needed.'

'If they attack tomorrow, you will be needed too, and

then you will be in need of sleep,' Totho said. 'Meyr and I will quarter the night between us.'

'The three of us will take a third each,' Amnon argued stubbornly.

'As you will, but you sleep now. I'll take first watch, Meyr will take the middle, you the last. Meyr can see in the dark, anyway.'

Amnon sighed. 'Get me out of this, then, but I will sleep here alongside my people.'

Totho stripped off his own gauntlets and stood close to him, finding the buckles from long experience. 'Tomorrow will be ugly. They have enough fresh troops to force the breach,' he observed, his tone neutral.

'I know.'

Totho glanced up, but the firelight revealed no expression on Amnon's face. 'You have a plan?'

'I have some thoughts for delay. It will be only delay. A second barricade at the bridge's foot, supported by every archer who can still draw a bow, deployed from the bank and the rooftops.'

'That will last only until the Scorpions think of bringing a leadshotter to the bridge's peak,' Totho said sadly. 'Then . . . no more barricade. We are now at the only point where we can hold without their shot smashing us to scrap as soon as they find the range.'

'I'm glad I listened to you regarding that, at least,' Amnon said. 'One less failure that could have been mine.'

'You? You've fought like a hero!' Totho assured him.

'Yet still I have failed my people. I am First Soldier. Who else should take the blame?' A tremor ran through him, and he tore himself from Totho's ministrations. 'Except you, old man!' he exclaimed.

Totho looked up, taking a moment to see the robed figure of the First Minister. Faced with the weary soldiers, the fires, the vast host of the enemy lit up red along the western bank, Ethmet was looking twenty years older.

'I came to see . . .' he began, and his voice trailed off.

'Well, you have seen,' Amnon replied. 'No doubt the Masters have already told you how this will all end. In truth it needs no prophecy, but I would spare my soldiers your words of doom. What do you want here?'

'The Masters . . . are considering,' Ethmet almost mumbled. He looked confused, an old man out too late, who has forgotten the way home. 'They . . . I wait for them to instruct me.'

'Oh, really?' Amnon said, but there was a catch in his voice, and Totho thought, *Still he believes, despite all he says. If these Masters were to rise up now and smite him for his failures, he would not care so long as they saved the city.*

'Amnon,' Ethmet came close, 'you must tell me.'

'Tell you what?'

'Tell me what will happen. The Masters . . . are silent.'

Totho saw different expressions at war in Amnon's face: compassion and anger in bitter feud.

'We stand firm. We will stand until there is none left to stand, and only then we will fall,' he said. 'I am no seer to tell the future. The Masters have never spoken to *me*. All I can do is set an example for my soldiers, as the first into the breach, the last to walk away. And these foreigners are contributing as well, despite the welcome they have received from you. We would be lost already had it not been for Totho and his followers.'

Ethmet blinked rapidly, and Totho realized with horrible embarrassment that the old man was crying, the tears running freely down his lined face. 'I am sorry,' he said, and it was not clear whether he referred to his treatment of Totho or of Amnon. 'I am so sorry.'

There was a whoop from the barricades and Totho heard the creak and twang of the Mantis bows, the shouts of surprise from the Scorpions beyond. He was reaching for his snapbow but, by the time he had a magazine in place, the attack was over, the Scorpions startled into retreat.

Ethmet had clenched his hands together over his chest. 'What can I do?' he whispered. 'What can I do?'

'If this bridge falls then you must lead all you can out of the city,' Amnon told him. 'It does not matter where to. Have them sail out to the sea. Have them flee towards the eastern plains. Anything but stay here within these walls.'

'Leave . . . Khanaphes?' Ethmet gaped. 'Leave our city?'

'It will not be our city at that point.'

'But this is the Masters' city,' Ethmet protested. 'They would never let it fall. They would never abandon their people . . .'

'If they ever lived at all then they have left us now,' Amnon replied harshly, a man trying to convince himself.

'No, I have heard them . . .' And Ethmet's tone was the same.

Amnon shook his head tiredly. 'Go home, First Minister. I have told you what you must do, if the worst comes to the worst, but I cannot make you do it. Go home, and we shall bleed here for as long as we can, and hope that the Scorpions run out of food or bloodlust before we ourselves run out of blood.'

Ethmet nodded, still trembling. He nodded and turned and tottered off down the bridge, and even Totho felt a fragment of sympathy for him.

'You go home too,' he told Amnon.

'I'll sleep here—' he began.

'And Praeda? Don't you think she wants to see you tonight?' Totho felt a catch in his throat, but he forced the words out anyway. 'If . . . if . . . if I could go to Che tonight, and if she would have me, I would. I wouldn't care what happened here. I would go and . . . kiss her, and lie with her, if she'd let me.' He was shaking, without warning or precedent, as he unlatched the last of Amnon's buckles. As the greave fell free, he did not rise, but pressed his hands against the stonework of the bridge for strength. 'If . . . if I could, that is what I would do.' *In that other dream world where things worked out for us, for me . . . where some cursed thing in this whole wasted world actually went right for me.*

As he stood up, Amnon clapped a hand to his armoured shoulder. The big warrior was Ethmet's reverse, looking suddenly as young as Totho, even younger.

'You are right. I will go to Praeda,' he said. 'I don't know why I need a foreigner about to tell me the obvious things, but you are right.'

Totho arranged Amnon's armour carefully so that it would be easy to don quickly in the morning, and because he was badly in need of something to do just then. Amongst other concerns, Tirado had not been able to find the first sign of Che anywhere in the free half of the city.

# Thirty-Eight

When Che nudged him with her foot, he contracted into a ball and then sat bolt upright, eyes wide and staring in the darkness.

'I wasn't asleep,' he said, automatically. She could see him looking wildly about, fingers clawing at the slick floor. 'Oh,' he said at last, 'here.'

'That's right.' Che stood back. 'For a man who wasn't asleep, you do a good impression.'

'We're still in the trap,' he said bitterly and then frowned. 'Are we?'

'Only because you were sleeping so soundly that I didn't want to wake you.'

'I can hear . . . what can I hear? The echo's changed.'

She was impressed by that. 'The echo's changed because one of the doors is open.' It had been a long haul for her to get that far, a seemingly timeless eternity down here beneath the earth. Those carvings were not intended to be read by some Beetle-kinden freak who just happened to be Inapt. Achaeos would have been able to make easy sense of them, but when she most needed his ghostly presence he was gone, lost somewhere far away from her, or hiding deep in her mind. The carvings had been a test, she was sure, and one that she did not deserve to have passed. The task had called on something inside her that she had not even realized she possessed – something that she surely had not possessed before Achaeos's death, and the catastrophic backlash that had maimed her mind. *Or perhaps he was guiding me after all, in ways too subtle for me to tell.* It had been like practising Art-enhancing meditation, which she had never been able to manage. Her concentration had not been up to that, but then it had never meant life or death before.

She had sat there in the dark, sealed room and pressed her mind into the places that the builders had left, like picking a lock with a crude, improvised tool. Whilst Thalric slept, she had laboured at it for hours, constantly slipping and faltering, losing her train of thought, succumbing to distraction, until she had taken hold of her mind with a grip of iron and just *done it.*

Thalric had stood and was now walking forward, hands extended. 'What's out there? What do you see?' he asked. 'Can we get out?'

'It doesn't seem to link up with anywhere we've already been, or not within sight at least,' she told him. 'It . . . goes on for a long way. There's a great hall, high-ceilinged and vaulted, with alcoves all along it. I haven't left this room yet, to investigate, so maybe some of them are actually other passages. The carvings are everywhere but I haven't gone to look at them.' *In case the door closed again and I could not reopen it.* She did not say that, but she saw him understand her.

'I suppose we start walking then,' he suggested. 'I shall put a hand on your shoulder, like a blind man, shall I?'

He managed it only after a little clutching at thin air, then touching her injured shoulder first and making her wince. She set out slowly, trying to open her mind to whatever other signs it could apparently now register. There might be more traps, after all.

Their soft footfalls echoed cavernously in the open space, even muffled by the slime: it all seemed vastly too large for them. Che's vision could just reach to the far end of the hall, where there was a dais with something on it. *A throne? Down here?*

'What is this place anyway?' Thalric murmured. 'It seems too grand for sewers. Cool enough to be a storeroom, but . . . the air's damp. I can smell mould, a little.'

'I think . . .' Her courage failed her for a moment and then she pressed on. 'I think it's a tomb.'

A pause while he digested that, and then said, 'Well, that's a cheery thought.'

'They never spoke of this place, or of the pyramid,' Che remarked. 'It was always right there, in front of the Scriptora, at the very heart of the city, and they just overlooked mentioning it as though it was invisible. Which means that it's important. I think the word the Khanaphir would use is "sacred". They avoid the subject out of respect.'

'Respect for what?' Even hushed, their voices resonated down the length of the hall.

'For the only thing that they reserve such a degree of respect for,' Che said. 'The Masters. Their lost Masters who still dominate everything they ever do. The Masters, who haven't been seen since before the revolution. Not that the revolution ever reached here.' *And when I myself dreamt of the city's past, when I took the Fir, I saw the square before the Scriptora and the pyramid was not there. That was the city of the Masters, when they still lived.* 'The Masters of Khanaphes are dead,' she said. 'They've been dead a very long time indeed, for all that the Ministers have kept their name alive. And this is the last testimony to their rule. This is their tomb.'

'Guarded with traps,' Thalric reflected. 'I have heard of such things. There are people who make a living out of cracking open tombs like this. The yolk inside is often golden, I understand. Do you think we'll find a king's treasury?'

'Would you like that?'

'I wouldn't object to filling my pockets, now it seems I'm freelancing again.'

A shiver went through Che, an innate reaction of innate revulsion. 'That's disrespectful,' she chided, unsure precisely where this thought came from.

'What have these Masters done to earn my respect?' he argued. 'Aside from cripple their own people until a rabble of Scorpions with a few siege engines can barge in and level their city.' Che had halted suddenly, so that he nearly ran into her. 'What is it? Don't tell me now you've become a convert?'

'I . . .' She had wanted to say 'look', but that would have been meaningless. Instead she said, 'I see . . .' For a moment she could find no further words for it. 'Garmoth Atennar,' she said. 'Lord of the Fourth House, whose Bounty Exceeds all Expectations, Greatest of Warriors.'

'Che?' Thalric demanded, but she pulled forward out of his grip and knelt down, smoothing slime away from the inscription.

'That's what it says here,' she whispered, 'on his tomb.'

'Che, tell me what you see.'

'There is a great stone slab here, a giant block cut into . . . a coffin, it must be. And on the side they have written those words. And on the top . . .'

It was an effigy of a man, carved as if sleeping: ten feet from head to toe and heavy-framed, cut in white stone with a skill and delicacy that Che marvelled at – and had seen before. Those statues atop the pyramid, the giants who fronted the Estuarine Gate, they were all of a kind with this man. His stone features were proud, handsome and heartless, and Che was glad they had been cut with closed eyes. Even a semblance of waking life might have seemed too much in that perfect, imperious face.

'Garmoth Atennar,' she repeated softly.

Thalric felt his way forward, touched the statue and recoiled, his fingers trailing strings of slime.

'You were right enough, then,' he said. 'So much for the Masters of Khanaphes. I suppose all those people above are probably now waiting for the dead bastards to come back and save them.'

'Yes. Yes, they are,' Che replied, standing up and stepping

back. There was a feeling of loss, of tragedy, about this place, much more than could be lent to it by the simple word 'tomb'. It signified the death, unrealized and unacknowledged, of an entire era of history, leaving only an unnaturally extended shadow of itself, a mummer's show enacted by increasingly uncomprehending slaves. There was a chasm of time and place between herself and those aristocratic stone features, one that she could never bridge.

'Of no kinden I have ever known,' Che stated. 'If his body was laid here within the stone then the carving must be greater than life-size, but even so . . . Thalric, if this is a tomb . . . people don't usually build tombs with exits. We might still be in trouble.'

'The air moves,' he observed, and she was surprised she herself had not noticed it. His blindness had obviously made him aware of things that she overlooked. 'The air moves, and is cool and moist. There is a way out of here, and it is to the river – though why build a tomb with river access I do not know. Can you swim?'

'I don't know.'

She saw him smile at that reply. 'I can swim. I can swim with you, if I have to. Lead us to the river, and I will get us both out.'

She turned towards the far end of the hall, towards the throne that she had dimly noticed before.

Her heart froze.

The throne was occupied.

Sulvec landed on the roof beside the Beetle Vastern, dropping immediately into a crouch. Around them the other Wasps – Marger and the handful of soldiers he still had left – were also setting down. Three of them were guiding a foundering Osgan through the air, twisting his injured arm whenever he faltered.

'It is a joy to be in a city where nobody ever looks up,' Marger remarked, and Sulvec shot him a venomous look.

'Well, if you feel that way, then perhaps I can arrange for you to be posted here permanently.' Since Sulvec had taken over the operation, he had felt a certain sense of friction with Marger. The Beetle, ranking Rekef among the agents who had accompanied Thalric here, was cooperative enough, but Marger had plainly grown too used to his fake authority. Also, Sulvec suspected that he was finding the business of turning on his former companion slightly straining. He was Rekef Outlander, after all: he had not been properly hardened in the Inlander fires.

Marger just shrugged, in that irritating way of his, and went off to secure the gasping Osgan. The prisoner was a liability to them, Sulvec knew, but there was a chance that his suffering would cause Thalric sufficient concern to draw him in. The Rekef never disposed of a potential tool until it was well and truly broken. Indeed, sometimes the breaking of it was the point.

'Report,' Sulvec instructed.

'All quiet until maybe fifteen minutes ago,' Corolly Vastern told him. 'Then someone comes pelting up the steps from the direction of the embassies, and just drops straight inside, quick as you like. I marked him as Ant-kinden, which suggests one of the Vekken, although he went so fast that I couldn't be absolutely sure.'

'There's always the chance that he broke both his legs and is still lying at the bottom,' the Beetle suggested. 'Not known for their airborne, the Ant-kinden.'

'That shaft is easily scalable, if you have the Art,' Sulvec said, dismissing him. 'So the Vekken are allied with the Collegiates?'

'That's the way it looked, from the job on the embassy,' Corolly confirmed with a grimace. There had been few enough survivors to tell the tale.

Sulvec took a long breath, staring up at the pyramid in the gathering dusk. 'We will have to make our entrance, and ensure that Thalric is dead. Or make him dead, if he has the poor grace to be still alive.' He became aware that his hands were flexing nervously, so he clenched them into easy fists, trying to appear calm to his men. He still recalled the way he had felt the previous night, however he might try to explain it away. 'We have to go in,' he repeated, looking at them each in turn. The other Wasps shuffled unhappily. Only Vastern, who had not been there the night before, nodded readily.

'We've all seen the orders,' the Beetle agreed. 'Thalric must be dead at all costs. So let's kill him and get out of here while there's still a city to get out of.'

Sulvec fought down his feelings of dread. 'Follow me over to the top of the pyramid.' Before he could have second thoughts, he had called up his wings and coasted over to the jumble of statues that ringed the pit. The irregularity of their placing bothered him, random enough that he could not have sworn that there were the same number and arrangement as before. *They must have given up before they finished constructing this monument, whatever it is.* But there was no real sense of absence, only an instinct that whatever pattern the statues had been laid out in was one that his own mind could not grasp.

They had all followed him, the other Wasps, even Osgan and his forcible escorts. The prisoner dropped to his knees as soon as he was released, almost toppling forward into the narrow abyss. He was whimpering, but not from pain. *He knows something about this place,* Sulvec thought.

'What's down there?' he growled, crouching by their wretched prisoner. Osgan ignored him, trembling and sobbing quietly to himself, till Sulvec clutched his collar, hauling the man up to face him. 'You tell me what you know,' he warned. 'What's down there?'

Osgan stared at him wildly, eyes red in a grey face. 'The death that comes for Emperors,' he replied, quite clearly, and something stabbed deep inside Sulvec, an echo of last night's fear. He dropped Osgan, turning the gesture into an angry one, his eyes challenging any of his men to make an issue of it.

Corolly Vastern had caught them up, slogging his way on foot up the steps. 'There's not a light on in the Scriptora again,' he remarked. 'It's like they know we're here, and they're trying to ignore us.'

'You think it's a trap?' Sulvec asked him.

'I don't know what to think, but a trap could be the least of it,' the Beetle replied. 'Something got Gram and Dreker last night. If I could make a suggestion, sir?'

'Make it.'

'I'll go first.'

'Why?' Sulvec was instantly suspicious. He felt absolutely on edge here, amongst the statues overlooking the coolly breathing pit. Everything seemed like a threat, a challenge. He tried to calm himself.

'I can see in the dark, with my Art, and I can climb down the walls,' Vastern explained. 'If there's an ambush below, from Thalric and the Vekken, say, then either I'll see their lights, or they won't be able to see me. When I get down, I'll signal if it's safe.'

It was absurd that a man in Sulvec's position should be putting more faith and trust in an inferior kinden than in his own kind, but the other Wasps were clearly not at their best. Marger's expression was openly rebellious, and the rest weren't far off.

*I didn't join the Rekef Inlander to make friends*, Sulvec reminded himself harshly. 'Do it,' he snapped, and Corolly approached the pit, feeling round the edge and examining the glistening slime left on his gloved fingers.

'Lovely,' the Beetle muttered. He had strung his crossbow in a moment, and now slung it over his shoulder. Then he perched on the pit's edge for a second, hunched forward and, hands clamping to the side, descended head-first down the shaft.

They waited for a long time, hearing barely a scuffle or

a clink from him, all crouching in the statues' shadows. The sheer scale of the stone figures was beginning to oppress Sulvec. Standing straight, his head would barely come past their waists, and their faces above him were obscurely intimidating. They made him feel *small.*

'There, sir!' one of his men called out, and he peered over the edge into the darkness. A tiny spark was dancing there, as the flame of Vastern's steel lighter flickered on and off at intervals. He counted the pattern.

'That's it. We go down.' Sulvec expected to feel once more the clutching grasp of fear, but his decision passed unmarked. His men were all staring at him expectantly, and he knew that, if he did not go next, neither would they.

He stood at the edge and stepped off, letting his wings catch him as he fell down the stone-walled shaft until he felt the sides widen out. The darkness below was almost total, save for what waning light still came from above. One by one the others joined him. Osgan and Marger descended together, landing awkwardly in a tangle of limbs.

'Report, Vastern,' Sulvec said.

'Three passageways running parallel, the centre one blocked off by a stone block the size of a house. There's . . . a boot sticking out from under the block. Army issue.'

Sulvec heard the uneasy shuffling of his men. 'Any sign of Thalric or the others?'

'No sign of anyone, but the clear passages head off as far as I can see. This place is big.'

'Light a lantern. Keep it low and shuttered.'

He did not have to ask twice. One of his men carried a little gas lamp, and even the faintest glow from it was welcome.

'If Thalric's under that stone, he's gone,' Vastern observed.

'If,' Sulvec replied. *Trust the bastard to go and die in a way that we can't check.* 'We'll move deeper in. If he survived at all, we should find some trace of him.' None of them liked the suggestion but that wasn't the point. 'Vastern, walk ahead of the lamp, quiet as you can. We'll take the left-hand way first.'

'Right, sir.' Moving surprisingly softly for a bulky Beetle, Corolly Vastern padded off into the darkness with his crossbow levelled. *Dark-sight*, Sulvec understood. *A useful Art, but rare. Perhaps we should try to breed Beetle-kinden for it.* The Wasps were creatures of the day, and night attacks had caused havoc among them several times during their war with the Lowlanders.

He gave Vastern a long enough count to get well ahead, then gestured for his men to follow him, using the faint gleam of the lantern to navigate by. It was tempting to turn the flame up, but Thalric and the others could be waiting there in the pitch dark, watching for the faintest glimmer. *In which case Vastern will see them before they see him.* In the back of his mind ran the litany: *Be dead, Thalric. Be dead and let us find your corpse.*

Then he spotted the Beetle ahead, waiting for them. 'What is it?' he hissed. 'You've noticed movement?'

'Not movement, but signs.' Vastern gestured at the floor, which showed Sulvec precisely nothing. 'It's hard to see but there's been a disturbance here. That slime, that's everywhere here, it's been disturbed. Looked odd to my sight, and now the lamp really shows it up. Tracks, more than one.'

'Thalric and the Beetle girl?'

'Best guess,' Vastern confirmed.

'Then follow him and find him and kill him,' Sulvec managed to get out. The dark and the weight of stone above were oppressive. 'Or perhaps we'll start cutting his friend up, until he comes to investigate. Either way I want him dead before dawn, and then I want us out of this city.'

'No argument there, sir,' concurred Vastern wholeheartedly.

Che had recoiled with a strangled cry, tumbling into Thalric and nearly knocking him backwards onto the effigy-crowned tomb.

‘What, what is it?’ he demanded, hand outstretched and directed futilely at nothing he could see.

‘I . . .’ Che took a deep breath, a better look. Her heart was still hammering from the shock. For just a moment . . . ‘It’s nothing. It’s – I just got a bit of a fright, that’s all. The throne . . .’

‘The what?’

‘At the far end of this hall there’s a throne. Only – it’s not empty.’

Thalric said nothing, waiting for more. Che took his sleeve and they both took a few steps closer until she was absolutely sure. ‘Armour,’ she explained. ‘There’s a suit of armour sitting there. Hammer and tongs, but it gave me a start.’

She edged closer, then closer still, because the scale and the repeating ribs of the hall’s buttresses played tricks. ‘Look at that,’ she breathed.

‘I can’t,’ Thalric pointed out. Che continued to stare, trying to take it in.

‘It must be the oldest suit of sentinel plate in the world,’ she decided. It was true plate armour, an intricate suit of interlocking pieces that had been posed as if its missing occupant was deep in thought, elbow on knee, with the raised gauntlet supporting the edge of the open-faced helm. *It must be wired together*, she thought, staring into the cavernous emptiness of the helmet, and then realized: *The slime is holding it together, like glue*. ‘It’s absolutely huge,’ she said, shaken. ‘It would fit a Mole Cricket-kinden, I’d guess.’ *It was made to fit one of those statues,* came the next irresistible thought, but she shook it off. Perhaps that stone coffin held only ashes, or perhaps they had folded up Garmoth Atennar before putting him inside. Perhaps the box was actually the mouth of a pit and they had buried him standing up, or even standing on his head. She didn’t *know*, so there was no reason to get jumpy about it. *Garmoth Atennar, Greatest of Warriors, sitting silently upright on his plinth, those dead stone eyes opening at last.*

*I have to get out of this place. It is not healthy for the mind.* 'I have seen workmanship like this before,' she said, 'in drawings in very old books mostly, but once or twice in life, and never a complete suit. It's Mantis work. It's beautiful. I wish I could see it in the light, to look at the colours of the metal.'

'The Masters of Khanaphes were Mantids?' Thalric frowned.

'Not if their statues are anything to go by, but they would have possessed the best of everything. A complete suit of Mantis-kinden sentinel plate like this . . . You could buy half the Assembly for the price of it.'

'Che,' Thalric interrupted, and the tone of his voice had changed. She felt her hand stray instinctively for her sword-hilt, ready for trouble.

'What is it?'

'I can see light.'

'Daylight?' she asked him instantly.

'No, not daylight.' His inflection said there was no doubt about it.

'You'll have to guide me, then. I just *see*, here, and I see greys and shadows. If there's light coming from anywhere, I can't make it out.'

'Somewhere to our left. It's very faint, but it looks . . . bluish. I think I can make out something . . . a further hallway there?'

'There's another hall each side,' Che confirmed, 'but I suppose we go left then.'

'It must be daylight,' Thalric said, without conviction. 'What else could it be?' His stance changed suddenly. 'Or it could be lamplight. The Rekef?'

'It could,' Che confirmed. 'So let's creep up on them very carefully and find out whether it is or not. They won't see us, after all.'

'If it is Rekef, we'll have to kill them all,' Thalric said flatly. 'If we catch them by surprise, my sting can take two or three down before they have a chance to react. We should be grateful for what happened in your embassy. That cut the numbers down a great deal.'

Che paused a moment before saying, 'Thalric, two of my friends died in that fight.'

He stared back towards her, caught out, torn between spymaster and human being. 'Of course they did. Forgive me.'

'But you're right,' she said. 'If there's a chance we can surprise them, then we have to do it. I have my sword.' Her voice trembled just a little.

'Pray you don't have to use it,' he said.

They crept forward, and this time Thalric took the lead. It was a long time before Che's sight began to tint and waver, the light bleeding in to curdle her Art. It was not daylight, certainly: a strange unhealthy pale blue that picked out the alcove walls in stark contrast. More, it was not still, but dancing and guttering, playing up and down the floor and ceiling and making the slime gleam and glitter. It was clear that it was no kind of lamp that the Rekef could be expected to carry. They approached with trepidation.

Before an open archway they found them: two metal bowls, each a foot across, on elegantly worked, coiling legs. Some oil within them burned almost smokelessly, its scent rusty to the nostrils. Che and Thalric stopped and stared, half ducking into an alcove. It was not fear of the Rekef that made then seek cover, but a feeling of trespass, like two children lost in a giant's castle.

'The oil burns,' Thalric observed. 'So it has been lit – but by who?'

*If I said by magic, would he believe me?* she asked herself. *Perhaps now he would.* 'I think that we have . . . caused them to be lit. I think that our presence here has made this happen.' *Ancient enchantments – but why give tomb robbers light to work by? Why this long-dead hospitality?*

'Some device . . .' Thalric mused. 'It's possible.' Yet he

did not seem eager to examine the braziers for artifice. Che looked past them into the next hall. There were other braziers there, glowing and flickering with pale light. *Did I notice those before?* She could not be wholly certain that she had.

*What are we nearing? How large is this place?* She felt they had been exploring, admittedly at a cripplingly cautious pace, for hours.

They stepped through the archway and stopped. For a long time they simply looked.

The ceiling was at least another six feet higher, and it was supported by great columns that had been fantastically worked into the shape of abominations. It was an old motif. She had seen carvings like it in Tharn, but never as grandly detailed as these. Human features were merged with those of beasts so that each column became a monster with its arms or claws raised high to support the earth. There were spiders with the faces of women, and scorpion-tailed men with pincered hands, beetle-headed, wing-backed, joint-legged. One depicted a woman who was partly consumed within the shell of a great mantis, and this image in particular Che turned away from, finding it obscurely, disturbingly familiar.

Between the columns were the tombs, arrayed in earnest now. Where Garmoth Atennar, whoever he had been, had kept a lonely vigil, here were an even score of great stone sarcophagi interspersed with the grotesque carved pillars.

The eerie light leapt and dwindled on them, these sleeping statues, the ranks of the forgotten, the Masters of Khanaphes. She saw their names: *Hieram Tisellian, who Raised the Temple and brought Life to the Parched Land, Lord Architect of all Time . . . Killeris Jaenathil, the Beautiful, the all-Knowing, Lady of the Utmost Sorcery . . . Iellith Quellennas, Bringer of Death, the Harvester of the Old Lands, the Chariot of War . . .*

'How many hundreds of years,' Che wondered, 'since anyone last saw this?'

'Always assuming you don't count the lamp-lighters.' The sense of awe and reverence had passed Thalric by, and he was becoming increasingly unnerved, looking up at the hybrid visages of the carved abominations and shuddering. For impossible monsters, they had been rendered extremely lifelike.

They were crude, however, compared to the likenesses that the Masters had decreed for themselves. Each one of these was an individual, as recognizable and distinct as they must have appeared in life. The white stone flowed smoothly over their musculature, each curve of gut and jowl and breast. Theirs was an alien aesthetic, but one that seemed to overrule all others. They were not delicately beautiful as Spiders were, or Dragonflies or Beetles or Moths, or any other kinden. They were simply beautiful *de facto*, commanding and magnetic. Even their stone facsimiles confirmed it.

'No wonder they are still revered as they are,' Che said in wonder.

'Oh, true,' Thalric snapped. 'They'd be able to give our Slave Corps a few lessons: how to keep an entire population under your thumb for a thousand years after you've died! How about that? The greatest slavemasters in the history of the world lie here, and I'm glad that, beyond this stinking piece of sand and stone, nobody even knows about them.'

'How can you say that?' Che demanded. 'Thalric, what we're seeing here . . . it's an age of history that Collegium has never guessed at. In all the Lowlands, there are probably only a few records of this mouldering in the Moth-kinden strongholds. I could go home right now and claim my seat as a College Master just for being here. This is *history*, this is the past right here for us to look upon. Can't you see that?'

'Do you know what I see?' he asked her. 'I see those pillars in the main hall of the Scriptora – the hall with the little fountain, where they held that reception for us both.'

'I don't—'

'They were just like these monsters: pillars carved into

figures that were holding up the ceiling. Very artistic. Only those ones were carved to look like Beetle-kinden. *Your* people, the Khanaphir. What did these dead Masters think? That it was your lot above ground, and monsters for servants once they were dead? They were mad, Che. They're better forgotten, believe me . . .' He trailed off just then, and she heard his breath suddenly become ragged. She turned to see what had caught his eye.

One of the stone coffins was bare.

The sight – the absence – chilled her. For a moment neither of them moved. Then Thalric said, 'So, we're both thinking the same ridiculous thing just now, and we should stop it. After all, they wouldn't be the first people not to finish crafting a tomb. It's something you tend to have built late in life.'

Che walked closer and wiped slime away from the inscription to read it clearly.

'Elysiath Neptellian, Lady of the Bright Water, She whose Word Breaks all Bonds, Princess of the Thousand,' she translated.

'Maybe she didn't care for the likeness,' said Thalric harshly. 'Now, can we get out of this festering place and . . .' His voice choked off and Che looked around wildly.

'What? What now?'

'I . . . thought I saw something . . .' he said, voice openly shaking. 'Ahead there. Something pale . . .'

'The lamps. The shadows of the lamps,' Che said hurriedly. 'The lamplight on the stone.' She was tense as a drawn bow, waiting for whatever terrible thing was about to descend on them. The air was thick with it.

When it came, it came from behind them: a long, drawn-out scream of human agony. Thalric whirled around, his sword in his hand instantly.

'Wait—' Che started but he snarled, 'Osgan,' and was away from her at once, plunging back the way they had come, and leaving her to scurry in his wake.

# Thirty-Nine

Totho was awoken by the sound of stone, great loads of it being hauled up the span of the bridge by sled, and by the noisy efforts of a labouring draught beetle.

*Are we building the barricade now?* he wondered vaguely, but had they not already built it? Had they not defended it for a day already? *I refuse to go through that again.*

He sat up, seeing the great bow-backed animal settle, antennae twitching, as the sled was unloaded. By the barricade itself, the centre had been reinforced, going some way towards repairing the petard's damage, and some complex woodwork was being lashed together, a slope on either side of the central point, with what seemed like a vast quantity of rope lying about. He could make nothing of it.

He jumped up, looking for authority, and spotted Amnon. The big man was supervising the unloading. Meyr, whose watch it was, leant against the barricade well out of the way.

'What's going on?' Totho asked him. 'When did this start?'

'Hour ago,' Meyr said. 'That Amnon, he's got an idea or something. Look down at our end of the bridge.'

Totho did so, seeing a great many torches down below, and what seemed like two hundred Khanaphir busy hauling stone about. *A second barricade*. 'Amnon!' he called out. 'I told you, once they get a leadshotter up here, they'll sweep away anything you put down at the shore. They'll just smash it to pieces.'

'That is indeed what you told me,' Amnon confirmed.

'Then what?'

'I have been speaking with Praeda about the engines of the enemy, and what they are capable of,' Amnon revealed.

'Yes, that's exactly what I meant when I said you should go home to her,' Totho remarked drily. 'So what did she have to say about it?'

'Firstly, she said she is an artificer, and a professor of artifice at their College, so she knows about these things,' Amnon told him.

Totho shrugged. 'That covers quite a range of competences.'

'She then also says that our stones cannot resist their shot, because our stones are rigid. She says that Collegium walls have a soft core to them, where the mortar is, that makes them move when struck, which is why these engines would not beat them down so easily. True?'

'True,' Totho admitted, 'all true. So what's going on?'

'Down there they are preparing a very great deal of stone, all of it we have dressed and ready to place. As of now there is a narrow pass to one side, to let the defenders here escape, but that will be filled at need,' Amnon said. 'We are building bands of wall: stone backed with wood and wicker, then stone again, and so forth, the whole of it a score of feet deep at least, and high as we can build it. The spaces of softer stuff, Praeda says, will give the stones somewhere to go when they are struck. The enemy will take twice as long to batter through. And she says, when the leadshotters shoot at it, they will only be turning standing stones into rubble that they will have to climb across. We will have archers on every roof. What do you think, about my Praeda?'

'I think she's thought it through,' Totho conceded. 'As last lines of defence go, I can't think of a better one. I should have thought of that myself.'

'Good to be appreciated,' he heard a female voice interrupt. Praeda herself came walking towards them up the slope. She had traded her Collegium robes for hard-wearing artificer's canvas, and there was a crossbow of Iron Glove make slung over her shoulder. 'Amnon, you're sure the barricade can hold them off here while they complete the barrier down there, after you fall back?'

'Of course.' Amnon was looking at Totho as he said it, and the wince was evident, that told of the lie.

*Every plan has its flaw.* 'So what's this up here?' Totho asked hastily, to ward off more questions from Praeda.

'When this barricade is due to fall, my soldiers will still need time to flee down to the eastern shore,' Amnon explained. The labourers were loading great blocks of stone on to the ramps that flanked the barricade's mid-point, building them high and securing them against the slope with ropes. Totho extrapolated, seeing two big columns of stone, poised and straining, waiting to thunder together in the centre, an instant breach-blocker.

'That's mad,' he said. 'What if the ropes go? Anyone fighting in the centre will be squashed flat.'

'We make good ropes, and we know our stone,' Amnon replied. 'We have been building like this for a thousand years. The ropes will hold until we cut them. I will be in the centre of our line. It is my own life that I stake on this.'

Totho shook his head at it. *Oh you say that here and now, with that confidence, because your lady is with you. It would not do to point out the cracks in this plan.* It would not take the Scorpions long to break through the barricade, as soon as its defenders had retreated. Another petard would suffice and they would surely have one ready. If there were sufficient bodies on the far side, or if they possessed the Art, then they might even just swarm straight over. At the foot of the bridge the fleeing soldiers would either be trapped by the barrier's completion, or the barrier would not be finished in time, letting the Scorpions through.

*Unless.* But he did not need to voice that 'unless' here. *You are a fool, Amnon. You have more to live for than you know.* Amnon's sense of duty was crippling to be near, and Totho could barely imagine it. If he himself had been born with all the advantages that Amnon owned, with his strength and energy and easy manner, and if he had a Beetle girl who loved him, then there was nothing in the world that would make him turn away from it. Not duty, not honour, nothing.

*But, then, perhaps that duty is what makes Amnon what he is.*

'You should sleep again,' Amnon told him. 'It is your turn.'

'Small chance of that,' Totho grumbled.

'They will be done here soon enough.' It was true, the piles of stone, immaculately placed, were now almost as high as the barricades. The webwork of ropes that held them in place had been run to pulleys fixed on the bridge's sides, and then back to a single ring set in the stonework behind. It would take a sword's blow to those taut ropes to drop four tons of stone together like clapping hands.

'I don't think I'm going to get much sleep tonight,' Totho admitted. 'Tomorrow is oppressing me already.'

Amnon settled down with his back to the bridge's right flank. His glance, away from Praeda towards the western bank, caught him wearing a strangely irresolute expression. 'Praeda,' he said suddenly, 'would you leave us? Return to the city?'

The Collegiate woman frowned at him. 'Actually I . . .'

'You were going to stay to face the dawn,' Amnon finished for her, nodding. 'You bought a crossbow from one of the Iron Glove people. You want to fight alongside me, tomorrow.'

'Yes.' Her expression was determined, set. Totho glanced from her to Amnon, who would not look at her at all.

'You must not,' was all he said.

'I have a right to defend you,' Praeda told him. 'How can you keep me away? I know you're First Soldier of Khanaphes, and all that, but that doesn't mean you're immortal.'

'No, it does not,' Amnon said heavily. 'But you have never fought before, and many will die here who have lived their whole lives carrying spear and shield. And I will not be able to fight to my best, knowing that you are in danger. I will not.'

'Amnon, that's not fair . . . I was up on the walls during the Vekken siege of Collegium. I loosed a crossbow then.'

'Praeda.' He said her name very softly, and that silenced her. In the pause that followed, Totho felt unbearably awkward, a voyeur to something intensely private.

'Praeda,' Amnon repeated. 'Do not make me choose between you and my city. If I knew that you were fighting here, and might be hurt at any moment, I would give commands that would compromise our position so that you might remain safe, or at least safer. If you forced me to it, I would give over my people just to save your life – but I would never forgive myself, after, for doing so. Do not tear me apart.'

Totho saw tears come to her eyes, glinting red in the torchlight. 'Amnon,' she whispered, then she knelt down beside him, throwing her arms around him, kissing him. She was shaking slightly, after she stood up again.

'Come back to me,' she urged him. 'You must.' Then she was running back towards the construction works at the bridge's foot, heading towards the eastern shore.

Totho had been about to pass some comment about how much Amnon loved his city, but one look at the big man's face warned him off it. Instead he sat down beside him, feeling all his bruises from yesterday complain. *And soon I shall have to put the armour on again. Joy.*

The broad shadow that was Meyr joined them, setting a cask down in front of him, and a stack of clay bowls. 'In the Delve, when a great construction is completed, we drink to it,' the Mole Cricket murmured. 'I had called for this, so that we might drink before tomorrow sees the colour of our blood, but shall we not drink to these stones behind us instead? How well they are laid, one on another. Nothing compared to my own people's work, of course, but pretty enough. They will do their job.'

His huge hands laid out the bowls – one, two, three – and then he craned his head to look back. 'Mantis-girl, come and join us in a drink.'

Teuthete stepped down from the barricade, head cocked to one side. 'The Khanaphir do not know how to brew,' she said. 'I will not drink their beer. It is sour.'

'Then drink some Imperial brandy,' Meyr told her, 'which is not.'

'We were keeping that as a gift,' Totho pointed out, 'to cement our trading links with Khanaphes.' He considered it. 'So let's crack it open, why not?'

'Where is Tirado?' Meyr asked, the fifth and final bowl cupped in his hand.

'Your Fly-kinden sleeps like a dead man,' Teuthete said. 'You could launch him from one of the Scorpion war-engines and he still would not wake.'

'We'll save him some,' Totho decided, gesturing for Meyr to start decanting. The little barrel looked just like a cup in the Mole Cricket's broad hands. Teuthete slipped down to kneel beside him, looking childlike in comparison. Meyr passed the first bowl to her.

'My people are pragmatists: we do not acknowledge freedom,' Meyr said, pouring a bowl in turn for each. 'We were slaves of the Moth-kinden before we were ever slaves to the Wasps. There is no one alive who is not a slave, we say: slave to city, slave to past, slave to feelings. Even the wild beast in the wastes is a slave to hunger.' He put the barrel down carefully, replacing the bung that he had dug out with one thick, square fingernail. His own bowl sat neatly in his palm. 'In all my life,' said Meyr, 'I have been no happier than in my servitude to the Iron Glove. Of all my slaveries it is the least onerous.'

'We do not admit to slavery. Where our respect has been earned we serve with honour,' Teuthete stated flatly. 'My people cannot be slaves.'

*Except to that honour*, Totho completed for her, but he left the words unsaid.

They drank. The Empire's purloined finest was smooth on the tongue, fiery in the throat, with an aftertaste of apricots.

'We have no illusions here about the morrow,' said Amnon. 'That is why I sent Praeda away. Not all battles can be won.'

Totho cast a look back at the monumental barrier that was slowly taking shape at the foot of the bridge. 'Amnon, about your plan . . .'

'You have a comment?' Amnon's smile was edged.

'Just to say . . . when the call comes for everyone to run for the east shore, well, I'll be right behind you.'

'Will you now?'

Totho shrugged. 'Well, it's true I've not got a woman or a city's love to live for, and it's true that the woman that *I* love has vanished, and is probably dead by Imperial hands. And that she'll never know what I've done here to try and make her approve of me. But even though you have so much to live for and I so little, yes, I shall be right at your back when the moment comes. You know what I mean.'

'I do,' said Amnon solemnly, 'and I am grateful.'

'And I shall be at your back,' Meyr told Totho.

'There's no need—'

'What? You can be an idiot, and not I?'

Amnon laughed quietly. 'We are four fools. No, three fools and one too honourable woman. What would anyone think of us, sitting and drinking like this?'

'Who cares what anyone thinks?' Meyr asked.

Totho smiled weakly. 'A man of Collegium once said that

the only parts of us to dodge the grave are the memories we leave behind with others.' *So if you live, Che, remember me this way: the man who tried to save a city, not the killer of thousands.*

There was a high, tooth-jarring buzz coming from one of the abandoned buildings that had been swamped by the Scorpion camp. It had begun around midnight and two hours before dawn it showed no signs of letting up. Most of the Scorpions nearby had been evicted by its constant irritation, shambling off to find somewhere else to sleep. Others had wanted to go and silence the noise. The problem was that, in the single lit window, they could see one of the foreigners crossing backwards and forwards. This noise was their doing, perhaps preparing some weapon to inflict on the Khanaphir. To interfere with them might bring down Jakal's wrath. Threat of superior force was one of the few strictures they held sacred.

Eventually they elected a spokesman, by democratic application of superior force. The man chosen was Genraki, most promising of the new-minted artillerists. His use of artillery to settle personal feuds had already been noted and approved of. It was therefore reckoned less likely that Jakal would have him killed if he did something wrong.

Genraki entered, stooping, through the building's kicked-in door. It was a decent-size two-storey, this one, where some Beetle family of means had lived, enjoying their view of the river. The thought amused him, for it was about time the Khanaphir knew fear and hardship. They had lived behind the safety of their walls for long enough. Genraki loved the Empire, for everything it had given his people. They had always possessed claws to cut flesh; now they had a fist to break stone.

The noise, that skull-boring sound, came from above, and he padded up quietly, taking a moment to peer around the corner, from the head of the stairs. There were two Wasps there, and one of them was Angved. They were hunched over some small mechanism, looking duly impressed.

Genraki cleared his throat and Angved glanced up.

'What is it?' he asked, speaking above the sound. 'Hrathen wants me?'

'What is this sound, chief?' Genraki asked him. 'Nobody else can sleep.'

Angved smirked at that. 'A little experiment of mine.'

This close, Genraki thought he could feel his ears shake under it, not particularly loud but terribly insistent. 'Must it go on so long, chief?' The title was based on the authority that the Warlord and the Wasp leader gave the old man, for he was clearly a chieftain of his own tribe of artificers.

'Well, that's the whole point. How long have we had so far?'

The other Wasp, also an artificer, checked some small device. 'Three hours fifty-seven minutes.'

'Shut it off at four hours,' Angved decided, to Genraki's relief. If he had retreated from this place without some result the others would not have been pleased with him. Angved was ushering him into the next room.

'Tell me, Genraki,' he said, 'this rock oil your people use, how common is it?'

'Not so common that it is everywhere, but we know all the places to find it. Where it is found, there is much of it. More than all the tribes need.'

Angved digested this. 'It burns for a long time, doesn't it?' he said.

'That is why we use it,' Genraki confirmed.

'It's been running that little makeshift engine for hours,' the artificer mused. 'Your people trade, don't they?'

Genraki shrugged. 'When we have the patience. We would trade oil for more leadshotters and weapons,' he added, with a fanged grin.

'You may just have got yourself a deal.'

Above their conversation, the whining buzz stopped, at

long last. Genraki could almost feel the whole camp relax with it. Angved's expression was complex: one he could not entirely read but dominated mainly by greed.

There were swift footsteps on the stairs and one of the other Wasps came up, half running, half flying. 'Captain wants you, Lieutenant,' he told Angved. 'Khanaphir have been busy overnight. Time for us to match them.'

Angved did not rush to attend on Hrathen. As soon as he presented himself, the tide of mundane war would descend on him, and he would have his hands full with jobs more befitting an apprentice than an experienced battle-artificer. *Can't we just let the Scorpions get on with it? We've given them half the city, so surely they can take it from here.* But Hrathen was in charge, and it was clear which of his bloodlines the halfbreed had chosen to support. *I hear he's sleeping with that hideous Jakal creature.* Angved shuddered. He himself had never been one to take advantage of the women of lesser peoples. Even if he had, he wouldn't have started with Scorpion-kinden. *Only among Thorn-bugs are there any uglier people in the world,* he decided, *or more dangerous to sleep with. And the Captain definitely gets his looks from the wrong side of the family.* Better, maybe, that the man forced himself on the fanged horrors here rather than good Wasp women back home.

*Am I fooling myself about this rock-oil?* The Nem was largely unexplored, unexploited. The Empire's internal squabbles had set back its timetable for subjugating the world, or there would have been black and gold all the way to Khanaphes by now, and Jakal's people would have become either Auxillians or history. *And maybe I should be grateful that, with all the fuss back home, I'm the first serious artificer to come here and make this discovery.* He was a man growing old for the army, yet still only a lieutenant. If he kept this all to himself, and if it was what he believed it to be, then 'Major Angved' had a nice ring to it. A comfortable retirement position running some research workshop in Sonn, perhaps? He could afford to be pushy, provided his new currency was as pure as he thought.

He had only told one of his crew about his discovery, and already he was considering whether he might have to kill him. Here, among the Scorpions, it would be easy to hide such an act. *This is much bigger than I had thought.* An idle curiosity was giving way to a real fire of ambition.

He found Hrathen at last. 'Reporting for duty,' he said, banishing such thoughts for the moment. The Scorpion woman was nearby, watching them with arms folded. Her expression was sceptical and Angved guessed that she had been expecting more progress. *Half the city in just two days, and still she's hungry.*

The halfbreed nodded to him. 'We take the bridge today,' he stated. 'I've decided. Enough of this attrition.'

Angved waited. *Empty posing,* he thought, *to impress his woman. Well, let him.*

'I want you to get a leadshotter on to the roof of one of these three-storeys,' Hrathen told him, straight-faced.

Angved raised an eyebrow. 'I'm not even sure that's possible.'

'*Make* it possible. Have some locals haul it up the stairs. Build a hoist, anything. When you've got the right elevation, start making calculations to hit the barricade without damaging the bridge.'

'That will call for a great deal of accuracy,' Angved said.

'Then that's what you'll give me,' Hrathen snapped.

Angved kept his expression carefully neutral, wondering whether it was yesterday's or last night's performance that had shown the man up in front of Jakal.

'We could try using the scrap-shot,' the artificer suggested, 'if we can get the range. That way, no danger of weakening the bridge.'

'Whatever you have to do,' Hrathen replied. 'Have the rest of your artificers make grenades. You know the type:

clay pots, wax stoppers, fuses. Fill them with oil, or with firepowder and nails.'

'I'm not sure our troops here will be able to use them effectively. Not on the enemy at least.'

'They're not for Scorpions. I'm committing the Slave Corps soldiers as grenadiers. Any fool can drop a pot.'

*And usually when you least want them to.* 'I'll put my people on it,' Angved agreed. 'We should have a decent stock by mid-morning, after you've warmed people up.'

'Between that and the crossbows, we'll be on the far side before dusk,' Hrathen declared. He was saying it to Jakal, and Agved saw the Scorpion Warlord shrug and turn away. Hrathen's expression, momentarily exposed, was comical. *She has him on a leash,* Angved realized. *This is why you can never really trust halfbreeds.* He supposed he felt sorry for the man, torn between Imperial orders and trying to be a Scorpion savage at the same time. *What will they do with him when we're done here? Will he want to stay on and live with the barbarians? Will the Rekef get rid of him? Will the Scorpions, for that matter?*

*Not my problem,* the artificer reminded himself. *I just need to get out of Khanaphes with my hide intact, and then I can give the Empire a prize that will make all the loot of Khanaphes look like dross.*

# Forty

Sulvec's hand clenched on the knife hilt and the blade twitched in Osgan's shoulder, making his victim shriek again. The sound echoed cavernously in the underground hall, turning into something truly nightmarish as it baffled its way about the distant vaulted walls.

'Come on, Thalric!' Sulvec shouted, his voice blurring amongst the returning echoes of the scream. 'You went to some lengths to keep this man alive. Don't waste all that effort now!' He was shouting just to keep himself steady: inflicting pain on another provided a reliable mantra for the avoidance of doubt and fear. There were plenty in the Rekef who did not get their own hands dirty, who always had others to do the cutting and slicing for them. Sulvec was made of sterner stuff, or at least that was his self-assessment. All around him, his men were gathered, Marger and the survivors of the Rekef force that had come into Khanaphes with him, seven agents whose pale faces and strained expressions belied their Rekef training.

*Weaklings.* Sulvec sneered inwardly, although he could feel what they could feel. It had begun with that wave of fear atop the pyramid, and the hooks of it had never left them. These slimy, hollow halls beneath the earth were no place for honest Wasp-kinden. They were built too huge, vacant yet full of a devouring dark that waited just beyond the reach of the guttering lanterns. When the final cackling echo of

Osgan's cry came back, Sulvec could not definitively label it as such. It could just as easily be something vast and mad gibbering to itself somewhere far off within these endless chambers.

And so he inflicted pain, because it made him feel better. *I hold the knife, therefore I am in control.* It was not a deep cut he inflicted, but he was an old hand at this. The knife's tip was carefully inserted between the bones of Osgan's shoulder joint, so that the slightest tremor would be unendurable agony. Osgan was sobbing, shuddering, fighting to keep desperately still. If he tried to bolt for freedom the pain would have shocked him out of consciousness.

'Thalric! I know you're out there!' Sulvec bellowed. Marger and the others were waiting in a circle round him, with lanterns some distance beyond them both ways. They had turned the wicks up high, so that for Thalric to get within sting range, he would be in their light. Still, he could come from anywhere, at any time. Sulvec was putting on the pressure but Thalric was no fool. If he wanted to make a fight of it, then he would undoubtedly take a few of them with him. *Which is why I'm here in the middle*, Sulvec decided.

He opened his mouth to shout again, but the echoes were getting to him. They made something unpleasant of his voice, as though someone were lampooning him from the darkness. *I'm glad the Khanaphir are going to get theirs. Nobody who builds a monstrosity like this deserves to live.* Yet at the back of his mind hovered a persistent worry telling him that this did not look much like the rest of Khanaphes above. There was no guarantee precisely *what* hands had created this lightless abyss. That started the imagination going, and it did not take much to start him wondering what else might be roused by his calls and Osgan's cries. *What if things live down here?*

'Maybe he doesn't care about the man,' said Marger, deliberately quiet to avoid the echo.

'You said that he seemed to,' Sulvec accused.

'He did seem to, but maybe I was wrong.' Marger was uncomfortable with the knife-work, Sulvec could see. *Another weakling: to be Rekef is to know no limits.* For good measure Sulvec twisted the blade again, holding Osgan down for easier purchase. The prisoner had been a useless babbler ever since they had dragged him down here, going on about some phantom terror that he seemed to connect with the old Emperor's death. Putting the knife in had only vocalized what had been going on in Osgan's head ever since then. *It'll do him good to let it out.*

'He's out there, and he's hearing this, and he'll come,' Sulvec snarled. 'And don't think your reluctance hasn't been noted. When Thalric does make an appearance, you'd better impress me with your dedication, Marger. You don't want to fall foul of one of my reports.'

'No, sir,' Marger replied with a sour look.

For the first hundred strides, Thalric had been running, heading out of the hall of tombs and back the way they had come. Even as Che bolted after him, she heard his footsteps stop as he took wing, skimming along into the pitch dark, finding his way by the roiling confusion of sounds ahead of them.

She had never been a runner but she did her best. Her wings flicked and flared, casting her forward in awkward jumps, and when she touched the ground each time she kept pelting along at top speed, still falling behind him but keeping him in sight. Then he had passed the last of the blue-flamed fires and was into the utter pitch, slowing to keep his course straight. She kept up her mad dash after him, still moving with all the speed she could muster. She was just about keeping level even as the next shrill scream coursed past them.

*Too loud*, the thought was irresistible. Too loud in this dead place. It was not a matter of respect but prudence.

Too loud in the silence, and Thalric was coursing too fast over all the trampled ages that had lain here for so long. The thought that came to her in the midst of her hopping, awkward flight was, *We will wake them.*

There was light ahead, bright lamplight a hundred times more wholesome than the pallid blue of the braziers. She saw that a ring of Wasps were waiting for them, with two men in the centre, one of them crouching over the other. Thalric had gone high, wings carrying him near to the ceiling. *They will spot him at any moment.*

Motion caught her eye. She saw another man there, standing beyond the lamplight. He was a stocky Beetle-kinden with a shaved head, but the crossbow in his hands belied any claim to being Khanaphir.

*In the dark*, she thought, *he sees as I do, and Thalric cannot see him.*

'Thalric, drop!' she yelled at him, with all the breath she had left. She would remember, later, only that he did not hesitate, banishing his wings and falling from the air on to his feet just as the crossbow bolt ripped above him in the dark, to be lost amongst the buttresses.

Then: 'Go! Go get Osgan!' she called, even as he hesitated, and she herself was charging the Beetle man, her sword already out of its scabbard. He saw her coming, but had time only to cast the crossbow away.

Thalric lunged into the air and his hands were already wreathed in golden fire as he hit the lamplight. His sting was his strong Art, burning further and fiercer than most. Even though they were waiting for him he still surprised them. In his mind was the one simple thought: *They need Osgan alive, to trap me. They will keep him alive, so I have a free hand.*

The closest man loosed his bolt too early, the fire skittering beneath Thalric as he launched his own. He saw the Wasp thrown from his feet by the force of the impact, his armour melted through and holed, a fist-sized burning mark in his chest. Thalric did not slow, turning quickly and diving in the air just as the others loosed at him. He let fly another two bolts, missing both times, then was past them, diving fast into the darkness again. *And how good is their leader now?* He heard the words even as he landed again, feet skidding on the slick stonework as he turned himself around. 'After him, you two!' came the order, and Thalric was waiting for them, fingers spread and eyes hunting out their silhouettes.

In the darkness, Che drove in with her blade, with no time to think: *I am killing another of my people.* He was Rekef in her eyes, and that removed any trace of kindred. She ran him through without mercy.

Or that was the plan. The Beetle threw himself backwards but one arm was already sweeping for her swordblade. She felt the flat of her sword taken aside by his armoured forearm, and then he punched her with his other hand.

Even though he was moving backwards at the time, the blow hit far harder than it should have done, stopping her short with her head ringing. He followed up, grappling for her sword hand and driving a solid shoulder into her chest, knocking her backwards. She swung at him again but he was too close. The guard of her sword struck him in the face and gashed his cheek, and then he backhanded her hard enough to rattle her teeth. His fists were weighted with gnarls of bone about the knuckles, a Beetle's Art-given weapons.

She tried for distance, hoping to get him at the end of her sword again while ducking aside from his next blow. He did not give her a moment's peace, already grabbing for her wrist to get the sword off her. She cut his fingers once as he misjudged the distance, but even that did not slow him. His expression was implacable, a man performing a difficult but routine job.

*I am really not a fighter. I forget that.* She broke away sideways, hacking at his head, but he got an arm in the way. The blade bit into the leathers he wore under his Khanaphir clothes, but did not draw blood.

In the darkness of the far side, Thalric's hand flashed fire twice, three times. One of the men barrelling towards him abruptly tumbled out of the air. The other twitched aside at the first flash, and then was on him, faster than either of them was ready for. He had his sword out but Thalric skipped aside from it, and shoved an elbow painfully into the man's jaw. For a moment they were grappling, each trying to find a clear moment for either stab or sting. Then Thalric dragged his opponent down and drove a knee as hard as he could high into the man's ribs, at the point where the armour of the light airborne left off. He heard at least one crack, as the soldier hissed in pain and fell away. Thalric sent a stingbolt after him but it flew wide, the man's wings taking him back into the dark.

*Running out of time.* Thalric let his own wings lift him, and was scudding back towards the lamplight and towards the diminished enemy. The leader in the centre had a sword out now, Osgan kneeling at his feet. Thalric extended a hand towards him, and swooped in with all the speed he had.

In her own fight, Che stumbled back three paces where she had intended one, catching the man by surprise. For a moment she thought she had him. The Beetle was at her sword's end and she drove forward triumphantly. It had been a feint, though, to draw her out. He was already moving aside, after reading her perfectly. One solid hand smashed down on her wrist, the blade spinning clear of her numbed fingers. The other slammed for her jaw, but hit her shoulder instead, hard enough to take her off her feet.

She landed flat on her back, momentarily unable to suck in breath, one hand scrabbling uselessly across the slimy floor for a sword that was well out of reach. The Beetle dropped on her, planting a knee solidly between her breasts. He had his own sword out now, held point down. In a swift, businesslike motion, he raised it to stab her in the throat.

A metal ball bounced and rolled nearby. The Beetle man hurled himself away from it with instinctive fear, whilst

Che just stared. Only later did she realize that he must have thought it was a grenade.

The sphere suddenly clicked open, its top half sliding into the underside to reveal the dancing flame of an oil lamp. *A quisitor's lamp for exploring caves and ruins*, Che recognized it. It was a common enough toy in the markets of Collegium. *But who?*

The Beetle man had come to the same realization, as Che thought, *Well, we're both lit up like a bonfire now.*

She heard the solid crunch of the crossbow bolt, as it took the man in the small of the back and split two inches out of his chest. His face at last wore an expression, although it was hard to categorize. He dropped.

She cast a moment's glance towards the Wasps, and saw Thalric swoop into the lamplit circle and kill one of the soldiers there with a single blast of his hands. The other Rekef spread out, as if trying to get clear of their leader, but Thalric's palm was now right in line with Sulvec's forehead. They froze, waiting for orders, while Sulvec locked eyes with Thalric. He had one hand on Osgan's collar. The other held the sword directed at his prisoner's neck.

'Let him go.'

'Give it up, Thalric,' Sulvec said. 'Marger, take his sword.'

'Not a move,' Thalric warned, and Marger stopped, his own hands ready to sting.

Sulvec smiled.

Che had stared at them for far too long before going for her own sword. Even as her fingers touched it a boot kicked it down the hall. She found herself looking up into the face of Accius the Vekken.

'What . . .?' she said, utterly thrown. There was nothing readable in his expression. With a deft motion he scooped up the quisitor's lamp and flicked it shut.

He grabbed her, finding her in the darkness by simple memory. Even as she recoiled instinctively, he had grasped her sleeve and yanked her towards him, off balance. His arm was about her throat, tight enough to hurt. She pried at it, but it was like iron. *Ant-kinden strength.* Even putting all of her weight on it there was not an inch of give.

'Thalric!' she got out, a strangled squeak. 'Help!'

But as the cry rang out, it was Osgan that moved. He abruptly lunged upwards, his head striking directly under Sulvec's chin. For a moment he was free. A stingbolt lanced over his shoulder, and Thalric returned the favour with both hands, making the Wasp soldiers scatter and scorching Marger's arm.

Sulvec snarled furiously. His shot at Thalric was close enough to singe his hair. His other hand drove towards his prisoner.

The blade sank into Osgan's gut, all the way to the hilt.

Thalric felt it as though it was plunged in him too, the sudden severing of his hopes. *Not after all this! Not after the swamps, after dragging him across the city,* all that thought in a fractured second. Osgan gasped, eyes wide, dropping to his knees with blood welling about the sword-hilt. Thalric had seen wounds like that, had inflicted a few. They were agony, and they meant death in almost every case, and never a quick one.

He bared his teeth, torn. He heard Che cry out again, more distant now. *Don't make me choose*—The stingshots began to burst around him. He made an abortive move towards Osgan, felt one shot sear a line of fire across his leg. His own hands were blazing, aimed he did not care where.

*Che.*

He let his wings spring to life and hurl him backwards into the dark, after her. *I'm sorry. I'm so sorry.* He was Thalric, loyal to those who served him and obeyed his orders. He did not abandon them. *But Che, I can't leave Che.*

Into the utter dark he went, and heard Sulvec bellow for his men to give chase. The crackle of stingshot was all around him. He risked a look back and saw two men coming for him. *To hell with the darkness.* He gave his wings their rein, keeping to where he imagined the centre of the hall was, hands outstretched for the walls. *The blue fires are ahead, yet not so far ahead, and Che will see me coming. She will see me and warn me.*

Marger had darted off after Thalric, as had one of the others. The second soldier crouched by the writhing Osgan, ludicrously looking as though he was checking that the man was all right.

'What are you doing?' Sulvec spat at him, already at the lamplight's edge to follow Marger.

'Putting him out of his misery, sir,' the soldier said.

'Don't,' Sulvec hissed. 'Get after them.' There was sudden movement from behind and he whirled round. It was only one of the soldiers who had followed Thalric, after the man's first lunatic swoop across their torchlit space. He had an arm about his ribs and was grimacing in pain.

Something moved, everywhere around them. They all felt it save for Osgan, whose world had now contracted to the gash opening his stomach.

Sulvec froze. It was hard to say what had just happened. It was impossible, in fact. He did not have the words or the concepts. There had been a shudder, through the stone and in the air and in his mind, like an earthquake that had not moved a physical thing, but had shaken a sense of threat into their very bones.

'Go . . .' Sulvec started, and then he watched blue flames suddenly flash into existence down the hall, way beyond their own lamps. They illuminated no lamp-lighter. He turned round, seeing that the same ghostly braziers had sprung up the other way down the hall, too, leaving only a span of darkness immediately around the Wasps. 'Stay . . .' he got out. 'Marger will do it.' His throat was so dry that his voice was just a croak.

'I saw something, sir,' one of his men whispered, pulling

closer. At his feet Osgan was whimpering with each new breath he took. The sound gave Sulvec courage.

'That will be Marger, no doubt,' he said, forcing the quaver out of his voice. *It had better be Marger.* The three Wasps had now drawn together. Their lamps guttered unnaturally low.

Sulvec crouched low over Osgan's body, noticing their lanterns dip, one by one, and fail. Something was moving in the darkness but he looked away from it, looked to the floor. He dearly did not want to see what it might be.

Thalric's sudden dash had caught up with them just as Accius had hauled his prey into the room of tombs, lit up by the braziers that cast the Vekken's skin in cobalt.

Thalric dropped down just six feet from the Ant, sword in hand and left palm extended. Che stared at him, her own hands still uselessly clutching at the Vekken's arm. She noticed a glitter in the corner of her eye and realized that Accius had drawn his own blade.

'What . . .?' Thalric's eyes narrowed as he tried to understand. 'What do you want with her? Where did you even come from?'

'Vek,' Accius said, his arm tightening so that Che almost choked. She stamped hard on his foot, but his boots were steel-toed and it got her nowhere. 'Vek requires answers.'

'Then seek them from me—' Thalric started, but just then the Ant hurled Che aside, hard enough to bounce her off the wall. A stingshot danced through the air where Thalric had been.

Thalric had ended up on the floor, reacting to some instinct he could not name. He turned on his back, hands out. One of the Wasps went straight overhead, the other dropped straight on him.

*Marger?* He was fighting Marger. The man tried to pin him down with one hand and a knee, his sword drawn back. Thalric was stronger, though, and better at this kind of back-alley fighting. He twisted round, put an elbow into the side of Marger's head, and threw him off. They both loosed stingshots at the same time, and both missed.

'Run, Che!' Thalric snapped. He saw the Beetle girl rise shakily. The other Wasp was coming back fast. Accius was loading his crossbow unhurriedly, with a soldier's calm professionalism.

'Run!' Thalric shouted again, and jumped on Marger, feeling the heat-flash of the man's sting warm his own side. He put a fist into the man's face, feeling Marger's nose shift, and then he had his own sword drawn back. Marger snarled in desperation and slung both of them aside, colliding with Accius as he loosed his crossbow. The bolt vanished into the darkness and the second Wasp had now landed, arm outstretched for a target as Marger and Thalric wrestled.

Accius hit Thalric. He had probably not been aiming at either Wasp in particular, but Thalric had the bad luck to get in the way and the Ant's fist hit him in the stomach like a battering ram. Through three layers of silk, he felt every link of his copperweave armour dent into his skin, and he sat down heavily.

Marger turned his hand on to the Ant, but Accius grabbed his belt and one arm and threw him a full ten feet with a bone-jarring crash. Art-given strength was virtually boiling in waves off the Ant-kinden.

The Vekken turned to find the other Wasp with his hand outstretched, but out of reach. That was when Che appeared out of the dark behind the threatening figure, armed with Accius's own discarded sword, and stabbed him in the back.

The stingbolt was loosed, but flew far over Accius's head. As the Wasp dropped Che stabbed him again for good measure, leaving the sword buried between his shoulders. Thalric saw that her hands were shaking.

He backed off from the Ant, ducking to collect his own sword again, prying it from the oozing ground. 'Che, come here,' he ordered quietly, then looked around for Marger, saw him upright. The Wasp cast a half-glance behind him, and his expression of betrayal revealed, more than any words could, the fact that he had thought there were reinforcements behind him.

'Thalric,' he said wearily. 'Thalric, you've got to die. Let the Beetle go, let the Ant go, I don't care. But they'll just keep coming for you. At any cost. You've got to die.'

'I disagree,' Thalric told him. 'To the pits with Imperial politics.'

'Thalric, this isn't *politics*,' Marger stressed. 'I saw the orders, they were sealed by General Brugan himself. Thalric, if you don't die, none of us goes home alive.' He took a deep breath, steadying himself against one of the tombs.

'Brugan?' Thalric felt a strange chill. He remembered his own briefing with the general, that had sent him here. 'Why?'

'Brugan's currently having this whole *city* destroyed just to cover your death,' Marger snapped. He bared his teeth in utter frustration, crooking his fingers into claws. 'What did you *do?* What did you *do* to piss him off that much? Why won't you just *die*?'

Che glanced sideways, and saw that Accius had retrieved his crossbow, and had recocked it even as the Wasp spoke. He was aiming it at no one, not yet. His eyes flicked between the two Wasps, his face expressionless.

Marger was now approaching, step by dragging step, limping slightly from whatever hurts he had taken when Accius had thrown him. Thalric hefted his sword, levelled his hand. 'Marger . . .'

'Then *do it!*' the other Wasp shouted. 'Because they're going to kill me anyway, if I fail, and probably even if I succeed. Why did you have to go and mess with the General of the Rekef?'

It was obvious, in retrospect, that he had been going to charge just then, whatever the consequences, but instead he stopped, jaw dropping, staring past Thalric and the others. A small, strangled noise emerged from him.

Accius followed his glance, and Thalric heard the Ant hiss, turning and raising his crossbow. With that Thalric could do nothing but glance behind him, despite all his training. Once he had glimpsed what was there, he had to turn to face it too. Although it brought him closer to Marger, he started backing away. They were all of them backing away, the four intruders seeking what dubious retreat they could in the face of what they saw.

'Oh,' Che breathed, watching the apparition walk ponderously into view. It was a woman ten feet tall, and massively proportioned, her frame a cascade of curves running down shoulders, breasts, stomach and hips, voluptuous with fat and yet unencumbered by it. She walked with the assurance of kings, and her hair was long and black, lustrous with the gleaming slime that coated her. She wore only a few folds of cloth about her loins, but she would have been fit for the court of the Empress. Her face – with a majesty no Beetle or Ant or Wasp could ever muster – was that of the effigies on the tombs, the dancers atop the pyramid, the forbidding giants of the Estuarine Gate.

It occurred to Che now that probably more than one tomb was missing its effigy, but she felt with certainty that she could put a name to the imperious woman that stood before her. The words welled up in her mind, and she mouthed them: 'Elysiath Neptellian, Lady of the Bright Water, She whose Word Breaks all Bonds, Princess of the Thousand.'

Accius made an animal sound in his throat and raised his crossbow. The woman extended a commanding hand, with a faint smile on her lips.

The world flew apart.

# Forty-One

The Scorpions had been massing since before dawn, forming up into great clattering, complaining companies along the western bank. The eastern sky barely showed the first grey signs of light as they made their first sortie. It was a rabble. Totho had already seen enough to know that there was a hierarchy of usefulness within the enemy ranks. These were the losers, first to be cast away and first to die. They came in a great screaming horde, and if they possessed any appreciation of their place in the world, Totho could not perceive it.

*If we could bottle that mad fervour,* he thought, *then we could sell it for a fortune to any general or tyrant you'd care to name.*

The archers took their places and drew back their bowstrings. The poor light would work against their aim, and the Scorpion charge was uneven, the faster outstripping the slower and leaving gaps for arrows to fall into. Sometimes poor discipline offered its own tactical value.

Four dozen strings sang almost as one. The militia, denied any use for its spear detachments, had packed the barricade with bowmen, shoulder to shoulder. So far they had been the blade that had killed score upon score of the invaders, whilst the Royal Guard, with their armour and spears, had been the shield to fend off the enemy strike. The Guard had died steadily throughout yesterday's fight, their numbers already savagely depleted from the disastrous field battle. From the way they stood firm, Totho guessed they would do so until the last of them fell.

He spared his snapbow for now, letting the Khanaphir archers do their work. A solid volley hammered into the howling advance just before it engaged, and what reached the Royal Guard was pitiful, thrown back into the arrowstorm without a single loss to the defenders. The very sight of Amnon seemed to turn the Scorpions away.

'More coming!' Tirado shouted down. 'Shields!'

The archers had become old hands at arcing their shots over the curve of the bridge to fall blindly amongst the packed enemy advance. This time there were fewer cries of pain, more sounds of arrows thudding in wood. The Many of Nem were being taught battle tactics the painful way, but they were learning.

The advance was slower now, warriors not used to bearing shields were getting in each other's way. The arrows still found the odd mark, and an injured or dying man with a three-foot shield became a hazard to all around him. Teuthete and her people began loosing their own shafts, the bone and stone heads cracking stolen shields wherever they landed, or clipping the rims to punch home into faces or legs behind them. Totho sighed and worked the snapbow handle, charging pressure. He loosed all five shots at once in a narrow arc, forming a fist that smashed the shield-wall in as his bolts holed shields and flesh and barely slowed. He ducked to recharge, the archers all around letting fly so that each shield soon grew heavy and unwieldy with arrows. Men were running from the construction works on the east bank with fresh quivers. Khanaphes seemed to have an endless supply of arrows.

*If we had a snapbow that could fire a bolt every few seconds, and it had a magazine of hundreds,* Totho thought, *I could hold this bridge alone . . . or with one man to feed in the bolts. I should mention it to Drephos.*

'Crossbows!' Tirado called out, his high-pitched voice clear over the sounds of battle. The Scorpions in the second rank had brought up bows and levelled them over the shoulders of their comrades. The men behind them had shields up over their heads to protect them, a crude imitation of Ant-kinden tactics. 'Crossbows!' Tirado yelled again.

The Royal Guard had braced themselves behind their shields, but the heavy crossbows the Scorpions had been given were powerful enough to penetrate straight through half the time. They could not give up the breach. Tirado could shout at them all he liked.

Totho remained down until he heard the massed clack of two score crossbows. He saw men and women hurled back from the breach, shot through. Others stumbled, taken through the leg, or simply because of the massive impact on their shields. Amnon was crying for them to hold, and the archers kept aiming down for that elusive gap between shield-lines that the crossbowmen were shooting through.

Totho popped up and struck down another handful of shieldmen, giving the archers a clear shot at the men behind. The Scorpions were already surging forward, armoured warriors pressing from behind, the crossbowmen separating to let them through. Amnon cried to hold again, and then the lines clashed together. Greatsword and halberd battered against Khanaphir shields, as the Scorpion finest strove to smash their way through the weakened line with main force. Amnon himself was unmovable. Their strokes slid off his sculpted armour, deflected from his shield. He fought with his spear until the shaft splintered, and then he hacked at them with his sword.

To the right of him the line wavered. A huge Scorpion had leapt up to the barricade, hurling back two of the Guard, laying about him with a double-handed axe. Teuthete put an arrow between his neck and shoulder, shooting almost vertically down into him, but there were another three

Scorpions taking his place, eager to force that one breach that would undo the defenders.

They met a wall of aviation-grade steel as Meyr rammed them with his shield. With all the thunderous momentum he could muster, he flung all three Scorpions back onto the blades of their fellows. The force of his charge took him beyond the barricade, momentarily in the midst of his enemies. He swung at them with a great bronze-reinforced club that had been a scaffolding bar only two hours before. As the enemy hacked at his mail, he hurled them left and right with monstrous blows, making even the burly Scorpions look like children. Amnon was shouting for him to get back in line and the Scorpions were all about him, halberd-blades seeking his throat, his armpits, any gap in his mail. Meyr finally stepped back, finding the barricade's edge by concentration and memory, and then retreating behind the reformed line of Royal Guard.

There was no shortage of the Scorpions, however. They were still packed solid all the way to the western shore, with no sign that they would ever break off.

'Tirado!' Totho ordered. 'Send for the *Iteration*!'

The Fly-kinden saluted, and darted off down the river. The archers were drawing and loosing as fast as they could, sending their shafts towards every unprotected piece of Scorpion skin they could see. Still Amnon held firm in the midst of the Royal Guard's overlapping shields as the Scorpions hurled themselves onto the bloody points of the Khanaphir spears. Now Meyr was fighting from behind the line, using his height and reach to swat any Scorpion that gained a foothold on the barricade. At any moment it seemed that the Scorpions must lose their fervour, that the attack would ebb away in a flurry of final arrows, but still they pressed and pressed. The corpses were mounting up and they used them as stepping stones up to the Khanaphir shields. A score of the Guard had fallen and been replaced, and the numbers of waiting reinforcements were now getting sparse. Totho saw old Kham, Amnon's cousin, jerk backwards with a huge gash splitting halfway into his chest, dragging the Scorpion sword from its wielder's clawed hands as he fell.

On board the *Iteration* they had kept the engines turning over, waiting for the call. In truth Corcoran had hoped that it would be noon before the ship's intervention was needed, but Tirado dropped down on him before the sun was clear of the horizon.

'Already?' the Solarnese demanded.

'Oh, yes,' Tirado confirmed. 'Absolutely yes.' He was in the air a moment later, zigzagging back towards the embattled bridge.

Corcoran cursed, thinking, *It isn't our city*, for the thousandth time. He shouted the orders, though. They had learned a lot from the Empire, those in the Iron Glove. If you wanted to do well, you did what you were told. *Totho's got a plan. Totho's got a plan.* He repeated it to himself over and over, ignoring the way it sounded hollower each time.

They cast off, and the *Fourth Iteration*'s engines rumbled them towards the bridge. Its approach would not have gone unmarked by the enemy, and even now they would be wheeling out the leadshotters, not to be caught by surprise as they had been the last time.

'Get the smallshotters to the rail!' Corcoran called. 'Once we're in range I want every damn one to go off. Cut them a new road back to the Nem: grapeshot and scrapshot all weapons.'

He took out his glass and unfolded it to its full length, raking the western shore for the enemy's disposition. Sure enough, there was a roil of activity there, but the mass of Scorpions pushing to take their place on the bridge was so dense that the crew of the *Iteration* could slaughter them blindfold. *They've stepped it up today*, Corcoran realized. It was barely dawn, and yet the Scorpions were already throwing everything into the fray.

He spied the smoke from the first leadshotter before he heard the sound, clutching at the rail in sudden fear. The shot went short and wide, though, so far off that it was useless even for ranging. *That's it lads, you go and waste your powder.* His own people knew the limits of their weapons. They had their steel lighters ready, carefully withholding their fire until their weapons were well into range.

That first shot from the shore triggered a scatter of copycats, each of them falling short and astern as they failed to take the *Iteration*'s cruising into account. It came to Corcoran that the Scorpions would have no real experience of shooting at a moving target and that leadshotters, even at their best, were not designed for it.

He looked upriver, where there was one obvious impediment to making a strafing pass against the Scorpions. He ran astern to his helmsman, a Chasme halfbreed called Hakkon, mentally trying to size up the *Iteration* with the bridge's arches.

'Can we get past the bridge, if we wanted to?' he asked. There was another scatter of leadshot, and he heard the whoosh of water as the misplaced barrage broke up nothing but the river.

Hakkon tugged at his chin. 'Probably,' was all he would say. 'Let me get closer to see.' The bridge had plainly been built to stop large vessels passing upriver, but for the Khanaphir a large ship had a mast and a sail. The *Iteration* made a sleek, low profile in the water.

'Close to range!' one of his men called, just as another leadshot raised a great spire of water astern, near enough to rock them.

'Keep moving!' Corcoran shouted. 'Just keep moving!' He ran forward again. There was a constant sporadic pounding from the Scorpion engines now, one or other of them hurling metal every few minutes. A scatter of optimistic crossbowmen were loosing at them, standing knee-deep in the shallows. One of the bolts got as near as to rattle off the hull.

Corcoran watched the Scorpion masses still pushing for the bridge. There was a light rain of bodies dropping from where the fighting was, Scorpions hurled back by the Khanaphir or pushed off by their own side.

'Now!'

This time he remembered to hold on, as every smallshotter detonated at once. The fistfuls of stone and metal shot scythed into the nearest Scorpions, killing dozens where they stood.

'Don't slow down!' Corcoran shouted. 'Under the bridge! Under the bridge!' The arches looked smaller than he had gauged. *If I'm wrong about this, we'll look like fools . . . and then we'll die.* A lucky shot from the Scorpion artillery clipped across the deck, smashing the rail to both port and starboard in a hail of splinters. The smallshotters were being reloaded with an artificer's care, upended to receive the shot and wadding, and then turned down again for the little pot that was the firepowder charge. A few crossbow bolts clattered from the hull, and one of Corcoran's men swore as one dug into his arm, shallow enough to sag straight out again.

The swiftest of them managed a second messy shot, loosing back at the Scorpions, and then the shadow of the bridge covered them, ancient stones closing in around them and gliding by on both sides, close enough to touch.

'Keep reloading!' Corcoran told them, his voice echoing back down the length of the massive archway. 'They'll be there on the other side.'

*But their leadshotters won't,* he realized. Almost all the Scorpion artillery had been brought to the south of the bridge, to catch the *Iteration*. Until the Scorpions moved their cumbersome weapons back, the ship could sit still in the water and pulverize Scorpions. Corcoran grinned at the simplicity of it.

The boat's sides scraped against stone, but the crew were fending off the bridge with poles and Hakkon had a steady hand. Now they emerged into the dawning daylight, levelling their smallshotters at a surprised Scorpion army.

Totho crouched behind the barricade again, sliding another magazine into his snapbow. *Field-testing, they call this.* He would need to give the weapon some decent care tonight, as it had seen more action this last day than any other score of snapbows anywhere in the world. *Yes, tonight. Hold on to that thought.*

He had heard the thunder of the *Iteration*'s rail-engines, but the Scorpions were still not slackening off. Their crossbowmen were killing archers from behind their fence of shields, while their warriors were still locked man to man with Amnon's Guard. When Totho had last looked at them, the defenders of Khanaphes had been awash with blood, not one of them without some wound, except Amnon himself, and yet not one giving ground.

He levered himself up cautiously. With a snapbow, he could crouch low, as the Khanaphir archers could not. He had already felt one crossbow bolt bound painfully from his helm, leaving a dent that pressed against his head every time he moved it.

'Fliers!' Tirado shouted. 'Look to the sky! Fliers!'

*Fliers? Scorpions don't fly.* For a moment Totho was too surprised to do the obvious thing and look up. Then he saw the Wasps coming in, only a handful of them, but he caught sight of what their lead man was holding.

'Shoot them down!' he called out, at the top of his voice. 'Kill the Wasps! Kill the airborne!'

He loosed his own shot, but against a swift-flying target it flew hopelessly wide. The other Khanaphir simply had not responded. Their world scarcely admitted an 'airborne' aspect to war. They were busy killing Scorpions on the ground.

Totho shot a second bolt, missed again, and then threw himself off the barricade, dragging the nearest archer with him.

The first Wasp grenade was off target, shattering on the bridge's edge in a sudden flash of fire that startled many but harmed nobody. The second dropped neatly into the massed archers close to where Totho had just been.

It was a simple clay pot with a cloth fuse, but someone had patiently packed it with nails and stones and a solid charge of firepowder stolen from the leadshotters. The simplicity of the device was an affront to artifice: clumsy, inaccurate and unreliable.

On this occasion, simplicity won out. Totho saw the explosion erupt amid the archers, shredding men and women to pieces so that their flesh rained down on friend and foe alike, hurling others off their feet to tumble down on the stones or plummet into the water. A section of the wooden battlement the size of two men was blown off into the Scorpion crossbows, leaving a broad space of the archers' platform unprotected. Totho covered his eye-slit as a rain of splinters and metal and pieces of bone rattled against his armour.

Another grenade went past, exploding on the bridge behind him as the thrower miscalculated his own momentum. A firepot of oil landed amongst the archers on the other side, in a shocking gout of flame. Totho raised his snapbow, remembering the brutal chaos of the siege of Tark, where Wasp airborne had been thick in the sky. He caught one of the men turning, missed twice and hit with his last shot, the bolt tearing through the man's thigh. The Wasp spun out of the air and dropped down past the bridge's side.

Then he heard the *Iteration*'s smallshotters again, but this time to the north of the bridge. A shudder rippled through the Scorpion ranks, and the crack and boom of the ship's weapons sounded again and again, shot overlapping shot in their eagerness. Despite the damage done by the grenades, the Scorpion tide began to ebb. The archers that remained were not letting up, loosing arrow after arrow even as parts of their barricade burned.

At last, their rear ranks continually raked by the *Iteration*'s insistent fusillade, the Scorpions drew back.

They had a pack of carpenters on the barricades trying to repair the damage that the grenades had done, hammering new wood into place frantically, as the Scorpion horde reordered itself for its second charge.

'We can't last another one of those assaults,' Amnon said, finally down from the breach after hours of holding the line. He had his helm off and his face was streaked with sweat, darkly bruised about one eye where an axe had glanced from his helmet.

'Meyr, how many Wasps did you see amongst the Scorpions, back in the Nem?' Totho asked.

The Mole Cricket hunched close. 'Two dozen, three, somewhere around that number.'

'We were lucky,' Totho decided. Amnon just raised an eyebrow, thinking no doubt of all the archers who had burned or been blown apart by just a few hurled missiles. Totho shook his head. 'Believe me, we could have lost it all, right then, except the men who came over were Slave Corps. The Empire's Engineering Corps has trained grenadier squads and they'd have made more of a mess than we could hope to clean up. The Scorpion commander's making use of what they've got, but it's makeshift. Most of what they threw at us went wide, even into the river.'

'They'll come again,' Amnon said. 'It won't take many of them.'

'Leave them to the archers,' Totho told him. 'They're ready now, and I get the impression they take it personally.' The archers had not lost many to the Scorpion main force, only receiving a few casualties from crossbow bolts. It had taken the grenades to seriously bloody them, and Totho knew that when the Wasps came back, they would fly into a sky filled with arrows.

Amnon sighed. He looked impossibly tired. 'It was only

your ship's weapons that drew them off.'

'True. And yes, we can't rely on that. The *Iteration* won't manage such a good round of broadsides again. They'll distribute their 'shotters either side of the bridge, force her to keep moving.'

'The next charge, do you think?' Amnon's eyes held his gaze.

*I should say something reassuring at this point, but I cannot lie to him.* 'The next charge,' Totho agreed. 'It seems likely. After that we abandon the defence to Praeda Rakespear's theory, and I hope it's sound.' He looked back to the east shore where construction still went on.

Dariset approached them. 'There's a stir amongst the Scorpions,' she said. 'They're getting ready, we think.'

Amnon nodded to her and pulled his helm back on, his fingers lacing the buckle without the need for thought. *If only Drephos could see how we field-test this armour,* Totho thought bleakly. *I should put a report in a bottle and drop it off the bridge: Armour performance sufficiently above tolerance to outlast that of the flesh.*

'They're moving!' Tirado cried out. 'Shield-carapace to the front again.' The Fly was crouching atop the wooden battlements, resting there until he absolutely had to take flight again. Totho hopped up to join the archers, but the curve of the bridge hid the initial Scorpion movements. Everyone knew the distances by now. The archers were nocking arrows; they would loose them before the first enemy appeared over the crest of the arch. The Scorpions themselves would take their time in their early advance, and would start breaking into a charge as the first arrows landed on them. The carpenters, their work less than half done, dropped down to the bridge again and fled back to the east bank.

*How many have we killed?* Totho wondered. The Khanaphir cleared the bodies away each time, otherwise there would surely be a ramp of the dead to overcome the barricade. There was still a mighty host arrayed on the western shore, undaunted and more thirsty than ever for blood. Were they hungry yet? How were the sands of time falling on the other side of the river? How long would they have to hold off the Many of Nem before their war-host began to disintegrate?

*I think it is now clear that it will be longer than we have the capability to withstand them.*

The Scorpions came into sight amid a hail of arrows. The first four ranks held stolen shields fore and above, shrugging off the worst of the storm until the painted wood bristled. There would be crossbowmen concealed inside that carapace to either side, and in the centre a core of furious armoured warriors with two-handed swords and great-axes, the hammer that would leap up to strike the Khanaphir guard.

It was as well learned as parade-ground drilling now, by both sides. The shields were raised, the crossbows jutted, the vanguard of the Scorpion host leapt up the buckled stones towards their foes, impaling themselves on spears, splitting shields, trying to break the Royal Guard by sheer strength. The archers loosed and loosed, riddling either side of the charge with arrows, trying for the pale gaps between the dark armour. Crossbows raked them, plunging into the wooden barricades, flying overhead, hurling the unlucky backwards with the impact of their short heavy bolts. Totho trusted to his mail and shot into the fray, knowing that no shield or armour would save his enemies from him.

Amnon was crying again for them to hold firm. Totho saw him in his place at the fore, lending the others his strength. Meyr fought, looming over him, a Nemian halberd held in one hand like a wood-axe. Abruptly there were a lot of Scorpions up on the stones, hammering at the Khanaphir. They were dying, the attackers. They were pierced through with spears, hacked with swords, but they had a courage, an insane and reckless courage, that Totho could not understand. They were dying, but were replaced as quickly, and now the ragged defenders were giving ground. Amnon's voice boomed high above the fray, exhorting them in the name of their city to stand, but it was not their will but their sheer strength that was giving way.

'Fliers!' came Tirado's own shout. 'Wasp airborne!'

The archers, save for those closest the breach, immediately turned towards the sky. There was a scattering of Wasp-kinden coming in fast over the heads of the Scorpions and the defenders' arrows began to reach out for them. They dodged and darted about in the air, two of them dropping as the shafts found them. Totho turned his attention to the breach again.

Meyr was fighting unarmed in the front line now, simply grabbing Scorpions and hurling them off the bridge, or slapping them back into their fellows with bone-crushing force. Their swords and axes rang off his armour, lacing it with scratches and dents. He barely seemed to notice them. Totho saw a halberd slam down on the giant's wrist and just leap back from the double-linked chainmail that covered it. *Stone me, but we built well when we built that.*

There was a wash of heat from a fire grenade, but it had landed amidst the Scorpion flank after its bearer was shot down. The other impromptu grenadiers were veering away, the arrows coming at them too thickly to dodge. Another spun head over heels down into the water.

'They're circling left!' Tirado shrieked, his voice increasingly hoarse. 'Coming in over the water—' A moment later he screamed, 'I'm shot!' Totho searched the sky for him frantically, but the Fly had already been thrown from it, transfixed by a crossbow bolt, a tiny figure writhing amongst the Khanaphir wounded.

'Hold fast!' Amnon cried out, in a voice fit to be heard by the spectators at either end of the bridge. Totho heard the boom of the leadshotters from the shore and knew that the *Iteration* was coming in to try and relieve them. A moment later began the rapid rattling of its smallshotters. The Khanaphir were still holding the breach but there were none of the Royal Guard left in reserve; every man and woman was now committed to the fray. Totho saw Ptasmon and Dariset fighting to Amnon's left. Dariset's face was awash with blood from a gash to her brow, her helm knocked clean from her head. Ptasmon's shield was shattered and he laid about himself with both spear and sword. Totho emptied his snapbow into the attackers and reached for the next magazine, slotting it fumblingly into place. With frantic speed he charged his piece, already knowing he would be too late.

A Scorpion lance rammed into Ptasmon, piercing his scaled hauberk. Totho saw his mouth gape wide, and then Ptasmon had thrown himself forward into the enemy, hacking blindly at them, bringing half a dozen down in a tangle of limbs. Dariset was screaming something Totho could not hear.

Totho drew his own sword. It was a shortsword, as he had trained with in Collegium. There was nothing special about it. He unslung his shield.

*Che . . .*

He leapt down from the archery platform and found Ptasmon's footprints, shouldering his way into the shield-wall. He was no great warrior, but a man adequate through dull practice with the blade. *I trust to my artifice. I trust to the armour that the Iron Glove's intellect has brought into being.* He put his sword into the face of a looming Scorpion, the reciprocal axe-blow bounding from his shield with a force that ran all the way up to his shoulder.

Shards of broken water scattered over the deck after the leadshotters' latest miss, too close for comfort. The *Iteration* was heading for the bridge arch again, keeping itself a moving target, but the Scorpions were gradually learning. The art of the artillerist was not something that should come naturally to a savage pack of barbarians, but field practice was the best practice. Corcoran had the uncomfortable feeling that he was standing in as some kind of training instructor for the entire Nemian nation.

The smallshotters cracked and boomed from the port rail, their crews reloading as swiftly as they could, also now considerably more practised than they had been. It was the sort of thing that Totho or the Old Man went on about, the way that war honed invention and its uses. Corcoran was a pragmatist, though: the philosophy of artifice interested him only in so far as he could make money by selling it.

The next booming impact on the river was right at their stern, rocking the whole metal-reinforced ship as though a giant had taken it up and shaken it. They were in long crossbow range, too and, although the bolts that rebounded from the hull or clattered on the deck were a nuisance, a lucky shot could still be fatal.

He could see nothing of the fighting on the bridge itself, but the Scorpions were crowding the shore again, each pushing for his turn in the meat-grinder. *They're all mad,* Corcoran decided. *They must be. The wise man would step back and wait. No sense throwing yourself into the teeth of the mill.* Plainly the Scorpions felt differently.

A crossbow bolt skipped across the rail and hit his backplate with the force of a light slap, making him stagger into the next swell. His armour was not the aviation-grade stuff that Totho wore, just blackened steel breast-and-back and an open-faced helm, but at this distance it was more than adequate.

'Get those archers off us, someone!' he snapped.

'Get them yourself,' one of his artillerists replied. 'Look at them.' It was true. Since the *Iteration*'s last pass the Scorpions had brought a load of wood and stone rubble to the bank and the shallows. The Scorpion crossbowmen were using this to shoot from, and the scattershot the smallshotters were loaded with could do little about it. It would be wasting time and ammunition to try and winkle them out. Already many of the smallshotters were being loaded with fistfuls of glass, stone and nails. The Iron Glove's quartermasters had not anticipated the Khanaphir delegation getting into a war.

*I never wanted to be in a war,* Corcoran reminded himself. *I just wanted to sell the means to other people. Is that so wrong?* It had been a pleasant time, initially, living it up as a foreign dignitary in Khanaphes, but then it had all gone to the pits.

They were passing into the bridge's shadow now, Hakkon keeping a steady hand on the tiller. One of the leadshotters on the far side touched off too eagerly, and they saw a shower of glimmering water through the archway.

'Speed up! Engines full!' Corcoran decided.

'Not in this space—' Hakkon started.

'Do it! They'll be ready for us else!'

He heard the roar of the *Iteration*'s engines mount until the air beneath the arch shook with it. There was a spray of sparks and a shriek of tortured metal as the starboard side ground into the stone before the helmsman could correct the course. The weapons crews had all unhooked their smallshotters from the rail, for fear of losing them to the sides.

'Brace yourselves, this isn't going to be fun!' Corcoran shouted at them. He had no idea whether they had heard him, but they all looked sufficiently braced.

The *Fourth Iteration* leapt out from the archway on to the open river, above the bridge. The crews were already replacing their weapons when the Scorpion ordnance burst around them.

For a moment it seemed that the entire river had erupted. They could see nothing through the spray drenching them from all sides. Something struck them hard about the bows, heeling the *Iteration* well over to starboard, and pointing her away from the Scorpion shore. Another solid shot came down from its arc and smashed the starboard rail near the helm. Hakkon was wrestling with the wheel, trying to turn them back.

The ship rocked back, engines still churning at full speed. At least one man had been lost over the side, and more than one of the smallshotters had dropped straight past the rail. Corcoran half clawed, half rolled over to the port rail, holding hard to it, trying to take stock.

The first of the smallshotters cracked, sending its fistful of debris into the gathered Scorpions.

*It could have been worse.* There was either a dent or a hole in the bows, but above the waterline. *It could have been worse.*

'Watch out!'

He had no idea who called, in that spare second, no guess in what direction to be watching. He just clung to the rail and closed his eyes.

The impact, when it came, was shattering. The deck jumped beneath him, almost hard enough to throw him overboard. The ship lurched, a movement so unnatural it was as though the water had been changed, for one moment, into something solid and jagged.

Corcoran reeled, staring about. He saw the fresh plume of firepowder smoke, but not from where the main Scorpion artillery was positioned. This was on the flat roof of one of the riverfront houses. *They got a leadshotter onto the roof?* Whoever had been aiming it had been good enough to drop a shot straight on them . . .

He became aware that the clamour of battle was missing one important sound.

'The engines! What's wrong with the . . .' The words died even as he turned. The stern of the *Iteration* was a splintered mess. Whether by chance or skill, the rooftop artillerist had struck true. There was a hole broken clear through the deck. The wheel was gone, and if there was anything much left of Hakkon, then Corcoran did not want to go and look at it. A vast white cloud was vomiting up from the hole. *And that would be steam*, Corcoran decided. *The bastards have cracked a boiler.*

The *Iteration*, turned halfway from the enemy, was cruising to a slow halt, though the smallshotter men were still loosing shot with grim determination.

Corcoran's hands slipped to the buckles of his armour and released them, the mail clattering to the deck. He thumbed off his helmet even as the first of the enemy leadshotters took its next shot at them, clipping the bows by a gnat's wing.

'Time to go!' he called. 'Leave any way you can. Swim, fly, grab a plank and paddle! I mean it, lads!' All around him there were men already taking his advice. They shed what little armour they were wearing with frantic speed. Those who could get airborne, Bee-kinden and a few halfbreeds, flashed open their wings and took off for the far shore. Others were still carrying on the fight, reloading and emptying the smallshotters as fast as they could.

Another enemy shot raised a tower of water astern, and then one struck them full amidships. Corcoran was thrown off his feet, clean across the deck, stopping only when he tangled with the broken rail. He heard the snapping of timbers and the shriek of abused metal. 'Abandon ship!' he screamed to anyone that would listen. His people were jumping into the water in ones and twos. It was a long way to safety across the river, but they were not short of wooden ballast to help them along. The locals did not swim, and surely the Scorpions did not, but most of the *Iteration*'s crew had been born and brought up around the clear waters of the Exalsee.

Corcoran kicked his boots off. The ship was listing at a sick angle, the port rail almost under water. The men who threw themselves into the river from there were providing targets for the crossbowmen, whose bolts skipped across the waves towards them. Corcoran scrabbled and slipped, trying to reach the higher starboard rail to throw himself clear there with the ship's bulk to shield him. There was an escalating shriek from the engines, and he knew that whatever damage they had sustained had not prevented the boiler pressure rising: they would blow at any moment.

With a supreme effort he grasped a strut of the starboard railing. A crossbow bolt struck the slanting deck nearby and fell back into the river.

*Sorry, my love,* he mentally addressed the dying ship, *but it's time we were parting.* He bunched himself for the effort of hauling himself over the rail, but then the engine went with an enormous crack, shaking him loose, and the stern half of the *Iteration* tore itself to pieces in a hail of splinters and shrapnel that scattered even the Scorpions on the bank.

# Forty-Two

The interrogation room was filled with the sound of engines, the hiss of the steam boiler below and the whine and rumble of the tools above her. She could barely hear one word in three of the careful conversation that Thalric was holding with the engineer, Aagen. It was some convoluted piece of Wasp politics involving the governor and the Butterfly-kinden Grief in Chains. She strained her ears to catch it, since any information would be useful.

Thalric had now finished, telling Aagen, 'Now, dispatch it straight,' and the engineer left them swiftly. She felt the straps taut about her wrists and ankles. The mechanical drills and blades vibrated on their extending arms, spread above her like the limbs of a spider. Thalric had gone to the levers and was regarding them cautiously. She realized that he was not artificer enough to know how to turn the device off.

'The one at the end!' she shouted out to him. 'The red band!'

He turned to regard her, with a slight smile on his face. His hand found another lever and pulled it, in a brutal, brief motion, and the tool assembly dropped three feet, until it hovered right above her.

'Thalric!' she yelled, and he headed over, still smiling. One of his hands brushed against the surgical tools laid out beside her, and as it came away he was holding a narrow blade.

'Thalric, listen to me!' she said quickly. 'I'll talk. I'll tell you. Please . . .'

'The time for that has passed,' he said. 'I thought you understood as much. You cannot claim that I have not given you sufficient opportunity to speak voluntarily.' The light glinted on the scalpel blade as he dipped it to caress her cheek. 'Fortunate, really, that your kinden are not such a comely people. I had cause to interrogate a Spider once, and they have so much more to lose.' There was a dreadful reasonableness in his voice and expression that was more terrifying than outright anger could ever be. She felt her breath catch and shudder as sheer terror started building inside her. *Don't cut me. Please, don't cut me.*

'Thalric, listen to me. You don't want to do this. Not when you can just . . . just ask. Just ask and I'll say. You might . . . you might have a use for me later. For me whole. Please . . .'

'There is an economy of information, in the intelligencer's trade,' he told her, reaching up and bringing down a mechanical separator on its jointed arm. 'Information freely given is debased coinage. How can it be trusted, after all? However, when I have excruciated you until you beg and scream and plead, until you would betray everything and anything you have ever loved for a moment's cessation of pain, then you shall give me information of purest gold. There is a point when everyone, be they ever so strong or wilful or honour-bound, crosses over into the realm of pure honesty. We shall find where your point lies. Similarly with your future service, when I have put my mark upon you in sufficient detail, the very memory of it shall keep you loyal, for you will know in full what shall await you if you betray me. You are right-handed, are you not? I shall start with your left hand.'

She stared at him in horrified fascination. 'Please . . .'

His smile only broadened, becoming sharp as the blade he held. He touched the point to the back of her hand, holding her fingers flat.

He cut. The pain was short, sharp, almost lost in her bucking, twitching reaction to it. A shallow incision, but now he lowered the separator towards it, inserting the cold spars of the device between the lips of the wound, and then jabbing down. She screamed for real this time, though it was nothing more than preparation, sliding the machine's fingers between the bones of her hand. There was a delicate clockwork motor contained in the fist of it, and he wound it carefully so that she could hear its contented ticking.

She felt the slightest pressure affecting the bones of her hand. Amid the welter of pain, it meant little to her, but the prongs of the separator would slowly grind their way apart whilst Thalric worked on other parts of her – or even left the room entirely. It would torture her by infinitesimal degrees, all by its mindless self.

She was babbling by then, trying to tell him all sorts of things, about Stenwold, about Collegium, about anything she could imagine the Empire might be interested in. There was a sickness welling inside her, above and beyond the pain. She had not realized, before this moment, just how weak she had always been.

'Now,' said Thalric, ignoring her rush of words entirely, 'nature has gifted you with two eyes. One might almost think this was so that the loss of one would serve as an irresistible inducement to cooperate, lest you face the loss of the other.'

He brought the scalpel up and cleaned it meticulously, as though the intrusion of her own blood might cause her some infection. The pressure against the bones of her hand was noticeably intensifying. She clenched her teeth vainly against it.

His smile as he brought the razor-edge of the blade towards her face was fond, almost doting. She jerked her head back, shrieking at him, twisting as he pulled a strap tight across her forehead to hold her still.

'Now,' he said.

★

The interrogation room was filled with the sound of engines, the hiss of the the steam boiler below and the whine and rumble of the tools above her. She could barely hear one word in three of the careful conversation that Thalric was holding with the engineer, Aagen. It was some convoluted piece of Wasp politics involving the governor and the Butterfly-kinden Grief in Chains. She strained her ears to catch it. Any information would be useful.

*Hold on—*

Thalric had finished, telling Aagen, 'Now dispatch it straight,' and the engineer left them swiftly. She felt the straps taut about her wrists and ankles. *No, wait a moment* . . . The mechanical drills and blades vibrated on their arms, spread above her like the limbs of a spider. Thalric had gone over to the levers and was regarding them cautiously. She realized that he was not artificer enough to know how to turn the device off.

'The one at the end!' she shouted out to him. 'The red band!'

He turned to regard her – *Haven't I been here before?* – and there was a slight smile on his face. His hand found another lever and pulled it, in a brutal, brief motion, and the tool assembly dropped three feet until it hovered right above her.

'Thalric!' she yelled. His tongue touched his lips, wetting them, as he regarded her, eyes flicking to the tool assembly, spoiled for choice. When they rested on her again they were blank white, like milk.

'The interrogator is in an admirable position amongst all trades,' he said to her, one hand coming to touch her cheek lightly. 'There are so very many tools he may employ, and no restraints on him whatsoever. So long as he can turn out his goods, meaning information, he is very much left to his own devices.' His hands found the collar of her tunic and, in a single savage motion, he ripped it down the front all the way to the waist.

*This is wrong* – Wrong, of course it's wrong – *I've been here before. This is the room in Myna . . .*

She was feeling a bizarre doubling in her mind, of image over image. Thalric, with his blank Moth eyes, was trailing his hand across her breasts, whilst the other reached up for some tool of torture. Part of her was reacting with fear and revulsion, terrified of the pain and shame, but on another level she was watching everything as though from behind a pane of glass – or some clever Spider mirror that served as a window from one side. *But this isn't the way it happened the first time. This isn't the way it happened last time.*

*First time? Last time?*

*How* many *times?*

'Now,' said Thalric . . .

The interrogation room was filled with the sound of engines, the hiss of the steam boiler below and the whine and rumble of the tools above her. *Wasn't I just here . . .?* She could barely hear one word in three of the careful conversation that Thalric was having with the engineer, Aagen. *But Aagen just left . . .* It was some convoluted piece of Wasp politics involving the governor and the Butterfly-kinden Grief in Chains. She strained her ears to catch it. Any information would be useful.

Thalric had finished, telling Aagen, 'Now, dispatch it straight,' and the engineer left them swiftly. There was something wrong with Thalric's face. It was pallid, greying, changing. He was slighter than she remembered.

She felt the straps taut about her wrists and ankles. The mechanical drills and blades vibrated on their arms, spread above her like the limbs of a spider. Thalric had gone to the levers and was regarding them cautiously. She realized that he was not artificer enough to know how to turn the device off. *And neither am I for that matter. So why do I say:*

'The one at the end!' she shouted out to him. 'The red band!'

He turned to regard her, and his face rent her more than the knives could ever do: the pointed, grey-skinned visage of a Moth she had once known. His hand found another lever and pulled it, in a brutal, brief motion, and the tool assembly dropped three feet until it hovered right above her.

'The true interrogator,' he informed her, 'can extend a moment into a lifetime. He can stretch time as easily as flesh, denying the subject any chance of escape . . .'

'Achaeos?' *Wrong, all wrong. I know it's wrong. I've been here before, and before that, and before that, and . . .*

He reached up for the tools and she felt cracks all around her, her mind fragmenting into lens after distorting lens, one beyond the other, reaching further and further out. She stared up at the machinery above her. *I don't know how this works. I don't remember how it works. I only remember that I once remembered.*

*And Achaeos could never know.*

*I dreamt this. This is my dream, one of many. What did he say?*

*What did he say in my dream?*

*That I was doing this to myself . . .*

*That I was . . .*

*That I was using him to torture myself.*

That I was . . .

She opened her eyes.

From the steady lamps of that remembered cell in Myna to the dancing bluish flames of the tombs beneath Khanaphes: Che blinked, aware that she was lying awkwardly on one arm, and for a moment unsure where she was. She registered some cool, damp place where the stone beneath her was gluey with slime.

Now she remembered, the pieces falling into her head out of order: the Wasps, the halls, the carvings, the sarcophagi.

The Masters of Khanaphes.

She sat up suddenly, becoming aware of her surroundings.

The vaulted halls seemed to lean in on her, each alcove hosting its own stone memorial.

*Thalric . . .?* But he was there. They all were. Strewn around her were three bodies, not dead but not sleeping either. Their eyes were open but unseeing, and they twitched and kicked in the grip of whatever memory or thought was tormenting them. Thalric kept pulling his hands in as though avoiding something, his expression racked and unrecognizable. The other Wasp's fingers flexed over and over as though he was in the midst of loosing his sting. Accius of Vek had an expression only of concentration, moving not at all save for the shivers that pulsed through his muscles. *And what is he here for? What is his part in all this?*

She reached a hand out to Thalric, hoping he might wake, but his skin crawled under her touch. *I must have been like this but a moment ago, with my mind sent back to the rack in Myna.* What horrors would a Rekef spymaster's memory hold? *Felice's children? Surely he relives his murder of her children.*

She belatedly became aware that she was being watched, that the three twitching bodies were not her only company. Then she remembered, and her heart skipped and lurched as she looked round.

*She* was there, looking as though she had been standing there for hours, waiting for Che to wake – and as though she could stand there for a hundred years if need be. There was a patience about her that would wear down stone. Elysiath Neptellian, Lady of the Bright Water, She whose Word Breaks all Bonds, Princess of the Thousand, the risen denizen of her own tomb. Her gravity and presence made Che feel as though she should kneel, that the mere existence of this woman was sufficient to make a slave of her. She fought off the feeling angrily, and noticed the faintest movement of the woman's mouth. It was not a smile, for a smile on that face would have been fearsome, but perhaps an iota of approval.

Che hauled herself to her feet, still barely reaching above the woman's waist, then realized that Elysiath Neptellian was not alone. Another gigantic figure had emerged from the gloom, and now walked ponderously to stand at her shoulder. He was a thick-waisted man with a fleshy face that spoke of all manner of terrible deeds, and no guilt at all. A second woman now sat on her own plinth, combing her hair in slow, careful strokes, while ignoring Che utterly. Their hair was magnificent, waves of blue-black that gleamed in the undersea light. Both the women wore it down to the waist, cascading in slow ripples down their backs and, like the men, they were clad in little more than a few folds of cloth. Had they been Beetle-kinden, they would have been fat, had they been any other kinden they would have been grotesque, but they carried their bodies with an absolute assurance, without admitting the possibility of ugliness or awkwardness or shame. They were beautiful, all three, and it was something that partook of their bodies and those cruel faces, but that went far beyond. They were royalty, by their very nature, and Che was the lowest of commoners.

She heard steps behind her, quiet but slow, and the apparition she saw, when she turned, sent her two stumbling steps away from it, almost falling over Thalric. His name surfaced in her mind irresistibly: Garmoth Atennar, Lord of the Fourth House, whose Bounty Exceeds all Expectations, Greatest of Warriors, had woken. He had donned the mail that had sat waiting on his throne through the ages. Armour plates of gleaming green-black and gold slid one over the other, boasting the meticulous craftsmanship of decades. The dark clasp of the open helm framed the pale features of a dead king. He stared down at her with a distant amusement, as she herself might have looked at some small animal meandering lost through the rooms of her home.

She tried to speak, but her voice betrayed her, cracking to a mere whisper in the face of them. She finally forced it out, hearing her words tremble. 'You are the Masters of Khanaphes.'

'We are some,' said Elysiath. 'Those that have awoken.' The man's hand rested on her shoulder, while the other woman continued to comb her hair, oblivious. 'You are not one of our slaves, though.' Her eyes regarded Che with arch humour. 'Some few are summoned to us, through some trace of old blood that they carry, or else through their own misplaced curiosity, but you have been called from far places.'

'I . . . did not come because I was called,' Che got out.

'That is what many believe.'

There was a sudden gasp from Thalric, lying at her feet, in reaction to some particular stab of torment in his mind. 'What is happening to them?' Che asked. 'What are you doing to them?'

'Testing them.' Garmoth Atennar's voice rang deep and hollow as the halls they stood in. 'A test which they shall doubtless fail, as so many do. A test which you have passed, for which you may give thanks and rejoice.'

Che glanced back towards him. In his colossal mail, he was even more frightening and less approachable than the others. There was a sword girded at his belt that must have stood eight feet from point to pommel. 'Please,' she said, crouching by Thalric, 'he will go mad.'

'It is likely,' said Elysiath indifferently. 'Soon it will be certain. That is what awaits those who fail.'

'Will you not . . .?' Che's voice trailed off. *Of course they will not. Why should they? We are as the smallest insects to them.*

'We will not stir ourselves to release them from their bonds,' Elysiath told her. 'We will not prevent you from doing so, if you can.'

'Me?' Che demanded, astonishment lending her courage. 'What can I do?'

The huge woman made a face. 'Well, then, perhaps you can do nothing.'

'This is . . . magic.' Despite everything it was still hard to say it. 'This is something I know nothing about. There's nothing I can do for them!'

Elysiath glanced at the man by her shoulder, who was looking bored. 'No doubt it is as you say,' she said dismissively.

'But . . .' Che looked down at Thalric, locked into his own bespoke nightmare. 'I can't . . .' Something inside her was telling her to look, though. *Achaeos, help me now*, she thought, reaching out. And then: *You've ridden me all the way here from Khanaphes. I went up the pyramid because you were there. I've taken you everywhere you wanted, until I looked like a madwoman. Come on, now!*

She felt the presence then, the ghostly half-sense of another being that had plagued her since the war. *What do you want?* she asked it. *Just to torment me? Did I escape the nightmare only because I carry my own around with me?*

*You torture yourself with me.* Not her words, but his, remembered from her dream. She twisted uncomfortably.

*Help me now,* she told him. *If you could ever help me, help me now.*

She sensed his reaction, his violent disagreement. *This man is an enemy!*

*He is a Wasp, not an enemy*, she insisted, but she knew he must surely resent Thalric for the feelings she had discovered towards the man. All at once, and spurred by that thought, her patience vanished.

*To the pits with you, then.* In her mind she did not now see the grey-skinned man that she had loved, just the brooding, bitter, shouting stain on the air that seemed to be all that was left of him. The better parts, the parts that had held her affection, were clearly gone to his grave.

There was a net about Thalric, and she caught hold of it and tore it asunder. Afterwards she could find no words, no language, to account for what she had done. She had simply done it, taken the magic and tugged until it snapped.

*It must have been very weak*, she thought, *But then these victims are Apt, and the weakest of magics can bind the mind that does not credit it. It was weak enough that I could claw my way out from the inside.*

Thalric gasped, kicked out, hands flailing at the sticky ground.

'Calm,' she told him. 'It's Che, Thalric. I'm with you.'

He recoiled from her a moment, and she thought that he had gone mad indeed. Then he clutched at her arm and something of his own character returned to his face.

'Che . . .' he began, seeking out her face.

'Thalric!' a voice cried out in utter fury. Che looked to see the other Wasp, Marger, up on his knees, his face twisted in fear and rage. 'Thalric!' he screamed again, throwing one arm towards the two of them, palm outwards. He was too far to restrain, and Thalric just stared at him, still half-numb.

There was a flash of metal, swift enough for Che to think it must be some new form of magic, and Marger's hand was gone, the wrist a moment late in spraying them with his blood. Marger let out a hoarse, horrified yell, eyes bulging as he brought the stump close to them, unable to accept what he was seeing. Then Accius struck a second time, running him cleanly through the throat and then whipping the blade free.

*All three of them*, Che thought hollowly. *I woke up all three.*

She reached for her sword, forgetting that the last blade she had held had been the Vekken's own, which he must have reclaimed by long habit the moment he awoke. The Ant-kinden was not focused on either her or Thalric, but staring past them, at the Masters – the towering shapes of Elysiath and her two companions. Following his gaze, Thalric looked back also, and Che found it incredible that neither man had even noticed the metal bulk of Garmoth Atennar, who had been right before their eyes, the body of Marger almost at his feet. *They stand so still, like statues indeed*, she thought. *And I see better in these dark places and . . .*

*And I am Inapt now, and so I am of their world.*

Thalric swore softly, so she knew that he could see them, the risen Masters. 'What . . .?' he got out hoarsely.

'Words spoken in these halls leave long echoes,' said Elysiath. 'You do not believe in us, O savage. We are long dead, so you say, if we ever existed.'

'You can't be the Masters,' Thalric sounded dazed.

'Who else are they going to be?' Che demanded.

'But it's impossible, not without half the city knowing that you have – what? – some underground colony here, where you eat what? And drink what? And keep your numbers up over – how long has it been since the Masters were supposed to have ruled Khanaphes?' He was shaking his head wildly in disbelief.

'We still rule,' boomed Garmoth Atennar, and Thalric and the Ant whirled round, separating him from the gloom for the first time as more than just statuary.

'Dead,' stammered Thalric. 'The Masters are dead.' Che put her arms around him, but he continued, 'How long since the Masters were supposed to have walked the streets above?'

'This shall be nine years,' said the man beside Elysiath, 'and forty years. And nine hundred years.'

Che felt Thalric twist in her arms, struggling to his knees. 'Then it cannot be. To have a colony, unseen, unknown, for generation after generation beneath their feet, not even if just the Ministers knew.'

They were smiling now, all of them. Elysiath Neptellian even laughed. It was a resonant, inhuman sound that reminded Che of the stone bells the Moth-kinden sometimes used in their rituals.

'Speak not to us, O savage, of your generations. We are the Masters of Khanaphes, and we have always been so. When we turned away from the sun to seek our rest down here, it was these eyes that looked back one last time, and no other's.'

Thalric stared at her dumbly, plainly not prepared to take up the argument against such invincible assurance, but Che spoke up, as politely as a young student petitioning some great College scholar. 'You can't be nine hundred years old?'

'I am older, and I am not so old, by my kinden's reckoning.' The perfect mouth curved more sharply. 'There is none left living now who raised the first stones of Khanaphes and taught the Beetle-kinden to think, but those were active times, so we could not sleep then so long as we have since. Still, I remember when I walked our dominion as a queen, and they cast flowers before my feet and turned their faces from me, lest their gaze sully my beauty.'

'Madness,' whispered Thalric, but tears had sprung into Che's eyes at the mere tone of the woman's voice, the ancient longings and memories it contained.

'Still he does not believe. Like all savages, they have minds able to clutch only small pieces of the world held close, blind to the greater whole,' said the man at Elysiath's shoulder. 'But she believes. She has comprehended our glorious city, and seen how there is a missing piece at its heart. She knows now that the missing piece is before her.'

'Yes,' Che breathed. Despite the magnitude of what had been said, she found no doubt remaining within herself at all. Khanaphes had been a city that did not make sense. Only by the addition of some such presence as this could it be made whole. 'But how?' she asked. 'How has it come to this end?'

'This is no end,' Garmoth Atennar rumbled from behind her. 'We merely wait and sleep. We shall arise once more, when our city is ready.'

The absolute certainty in his voice struck a false chord in Che. For the first time she doubted them: not their belief in themselves, but the extent of what they knew. 'I don't understand,' she said. 'Help me understand.'

She thought they would not respond, but the woman who

had been combing her hair stood up, stretching luxuriously. 'We shall tell her.'

'Must we?' queried the man. 'I tire of it all.'

'We shall tell her,' said the woman with the comb, firmly. 'Child, I am Lirielle Denethetra, Lady of the Amber Moon, Speaker of Peace, Whose Word Brings Low the Great.' She intoned the litany of her titles with profound meaning, shrouding each with the shadows of a history that Che could never know of. 'Open your mind, little one.'

'I . . . don't know how.' Che said awkwardly. 'I am no magician.' She was aware of Thalric close by her, Accius further away, sword still in hand. When she thought of them, she felt embarrassed by their disbelief, but in the presence of the Masters she found she thought of them less and less.

'It is open as a window,' said the man.

'Then we shall tell you of the cataclysm and doom that came to Khanaphes, and that lies over her still,' said Lirielle Denethetra. 'The tale begins before even we ourselves remember, many thousands of years before the founding of our city, or any city.'

Colours began to rise in Che's mind, swirling and dancing, accumulating into hazy images, viewed as through warped glass. She saw a landscape unrecognizable, green and forested. She saw great plains where beetles grazed between the spires of soaring anthills. She saw no walls, no evidence of the hand of man. She saw other beasts, monstrous things with hair, horrible to behold, that she had never seen the like of in all her waking life.

The voice of Elysiath continued in her mind, saying: 'Such was the world before even we had arisen to walk in it. So stood the world when the Pact was made and the Art was born, but the world was new formed, and not set in its ways.'

'There was a great catastrophe, in the spring of time,' Lirielle's voice now took over. 'We have peered back, and divined as best we could, yet know not the cause. Perhaps there was no other cause, save for the mysterious slow workings of the earth, which moved and fell, and made the lands we know today.' The images in Che's mind blurred and shifted. She had a sense of a great sliding and slumping, a shuddering that seemed to rend apart the entire world. She saw whole lands fall into the sea, then the sea roll back to steal even more of the earth. She saw plains riven in two, the higher broken from the lower by a great sheer cliff. *Is that the Lowlands I see? The Commonweal and the Barrier Ridge?*

'And the people were sore afraid,' Elysiath told her. 'Small wonder that only those tribes who might truly influence the world must step forth to take mastery of it. Mere crafting and making would not suffice, in order to live through those terrible times. So we would come into our estate, and so, later, would come the others in their distant lands. Still, none were so great as we.'

'All long ago and before even our time, and it was long before we came to understand it,' added the unnamed man. 'But it was to dominate our world nonetheless. This is later, though, much later.' There was a city now being built, Che saw in her mind. The people were stocky and brown, like her. At first there was merely a small town on the banks of a river, the dense forest surrounding it being cut back for farmland. Then she saw stone walls raised. There were suggestions of battles with the denizens of the forest, and those of the plains beyond. She saw her kinfolk victorious, and saw great figures standing at their head, pale and slow but mighty in their sorcery. 'These come from my great-grandfather, these scenes – before my own time. Your people had not yet gone east to serve the Moths. There is no Pathis, no Solarno. The Spider-kinden live in caves and fight each other for scraps.'

*Too much, too much,* thought Che, but they were merciless in imparting their knowledge, and she was sure that, for every word said, ten thousand remained silent. She was being given only the gloss, a thin veneer of a deep history that she sensed yawning like an abyss at her feet.

'We raised the first walls,' Elysiath said proudly. 'We first placed stone upon stone. We were the *first* of all the kinden of the world to know civilization.' Even as she spoke, so the city of Khanaphes took shape. *But on what river?* The marshes of the estuary segued into lush forest. The fields were green and bountiful beyond the dreams of the farmers Che had seen along the Jamail. Beyond the forests extended vast plains of grassland where the Khanaphir drove back the nomad tribes, to install their own horses and goats and aphids, to build their further towns. *Did they move the city because of some horror? How could this be?* They did not hear her questions, seeming absorbed in their own histories. 'So we grew great and greater,' Elysiath Neptellian affirmed. 'So the centuries passed by, of majesty and expansion. So our teachers walked the paths of the world, and we brought many kinden the benefits of our just rule. So we made colonies elsewhere, even as far east as the Land of the Lake. In that way we met others who had assumed the mantle of rulers, and we received their tribute and taught them much, for they had much to learn. We were attaining our full grandeur, the very heights of our power.'

'And yet all was not well,' said Lirielle sadly, and Che felt a cold wind of grief and loss wash over her. 'For, even as our power grew, the land itself was betraying us. That ancient sundering was still at work. Decade to decade, century to century, the land gave back less. The forests succumbed not to the axe but to time, the grasslands withered, rivers dried. The patterns of wind and weather had been broken all those ages before, and the land was still changing to catch up. Our greatest sorcerers looked into the past and the future and saw that, despite all we had built, our land would grow only drier and drier, until the plains became a barren desert littered with the skulls of our cities, until the forests had retreated back to the sheltered Alim, until only the loyal river Jamail traced a trail of green through the barren land.' Che saw it all evolve in her mind, the encroaching desolation. She saw the desert rise from the heart of the plains like a devouring monster. *And what did the Lowlands look like, once? Was it once green, as well? And will it, too, become a desert?*

'We spent many decades in debate over what might be done,' came the man's voice again. 'We put off the inevitable. Our dominion declined, became less and less, the borders shrinking until only our sacred city remained of it. We would not believe that all we had built must come to an end. It was bitter for us.' And Che felt the bitterness: his words resounded with it. 'We, who had been masters of the earth, were yet become victims of time. As the land became drier, we could not bear to remain. Our skins cracked under the sun, so we became things of the night, and then of the earth's depths. We knew we could no longer remain amongst our subjects.'

'Yet we would not abandon them.' Elysiath said. 'So we had them build this place, where we would sleep, and from which we could still work our magics: our great ritual that has been nine hundred years in the making and may last a thousand more for all we know. And we selected those that bore a trace of our blood, or those that were most open to us, and made them our chief servants, and their children, and their children's children, so that they would be able to preserve our ways, and not fall into evil. Even then, our servants were gradually drifting from away us, falling into the error that has now claimed almost all of their kind. Which is why we have some interest, little child, in you.'

'Me?' Che started. She felt Thalric move beside her, and realized that, for him, her voice was the only one to have spoken out loud. The rest – that incredible history – had been played out in her head alone. *It is best that way.* 'But I'm not of your blood, or the Ministers' blood, whatever you mean.'

Elysiath eyed her pityingly. 'Of course you are not. Do

not make the mistake of our servants, who believe it is merely a bloodline that we value. No, it is the ability to hear our call, to hear the old ways. You are of more use to us than all the Ministers this last century has seen. You alone have been purified of the taint of recent years.'

She saw understanding of a sort in Thalric's face. *I'm Inapt, yes. So what?* But she did know what. It did not just mean she could no longer use a crossbow or turn a key in a lock. It meant that she saw the world differently. Her mind could stretch to different shapes.

'We called to you – as we call to all those with ears to hear. Some of them come to us as we lie dreaming. Few indeed pass our tests.'

A dark thought occurred to Che. 'Kadro,' she murmured, 'the Fly-kinden from Collegium, he went missing.'

'He was curious.' The man at Elysiath's shoulder nodded. 'He had begun to understand. So we called to him. We even met him at the pyramid's summit. Sometimes, when we awake, we miss the sky, even though it is only the stars of a cool night that we can endure.'

'He failed the tests,' stated Garmoth Atennar flatly, 'and his companion took her own life rather than attempt them.'

A shock of anger went through Che, and she took an involuntary step towards the armoured giant, though minuscule in the face of him. 'You killed them!'

'We?' He looked down on her with faint derision. 'We who have the power of life and death, and whose inescapable rule stretches from horizon to horizon?' She met his eyes then, but his stern face beat her down. There was no admission, in that expression, of any kinship or shared humanity. He was the Master, she a servant, the divisions of the world from before the revolution. She wanted to shout and rage at him, but that reaction would have been as incomprehensible to Garmoth Atennar as the Masters' history would be to Thalric. A Fly and a Beetle were dead, two scholars of the College and, to the immortal Masters, it was as though they had been no more than a beetle, a fly, crushed unknowingly underfoot.

'And me?' she asked.

'You have passed our tests,' Elysiath said. 'You have heard our call. From your distant home you sought us out, and now that challenge is behind you, and you stand before us as a supplicant. Now reveal what you would have of us.'

Che stared at them, and she was distantly aware of Thalric's murmur, 'Be very, very careful what you ask.' It was a needless warning. 'I was sent here by my uncle,' she said. 'As an ambassador.'

Elysiath laughed again. It was a beautiful sound, but cold as winter. 'You may have believed that once,' she said. 'Do you still?'

'I . . .' Che stopped, feeling the world around her totter. *Do I? No, Stenwold sent me. There was . . . I had reasons to investigate an Inapt Beetle city . . . There is a perfectly rational explanation for my being here*. But she found that she did not believe it, not standing before them now. *And you, Achaeos, you lured me here, to this place. You have pulled my strings all the way, as well as tormenting my nights.*

*Achaeos, since you died you've not been the man I knew.*

'I had a guide, to lead me here,' she confessed slowly. 'I . . . am haunted.'

'We see him,' Lirielle said. 'He stands at your shoulder. Have you come this far to be rid of him?'

*To be rid of him?* Her breath caught in her throat. This final confirmation that what afflicted her was more than just a madness crawling inside her brain sent a shock through her. More than that was her instinctive recoil from the offer. *But it's Achaeos* . . . She saw his lost, loved face again in her mind. *My poor Achaeos. I can't just discard him like a cape.* But then she thought of the ghost, not the man: that lurking, looming grey stain with its continuous demands.

'How?' she asked.

'We need only lend it a little strength,' Lirielle explained.

'It is too weak to exist apart from you now, therefore it leans on you like a sick man. We shall help it to stand alone, then it will be about its business and you shall be rid of it.'

'But what if I *am* its business?' Che demanded.

Lirielle's expression suggested that this entire conversation was now boring her. She went back to combing her hair.

Che could feel the ghost hovering close, invisible to her but still present. She recalled the Marsh, suddenly: its dragging her towards the Mantis icon, and its shrieking denunciation of the Marsh people, how they had let the old ways lapse so far. *Power: it was looking for magic, and why else if not to free itself?* She should have considered more that he might want to be free from her, as much as she wanted to be free from him.

She did want to be free from him.

'Please,' she said, 'do it.'

'Che . . .' Thalric was reaching out, but she shook him off.

'Do it,' she said again, grasping her courage with both hands.

Elysiath sighed. 'You are so impatient, with your mayfly lives,' she said. 'See, it is being accomplished even while you demand it.'

She waved one languid hand, and all eyes followed the gesture.

There was something boiling and building in the air, grey and formless, writhing and knotting. Motes of substance seemed to be drawn to it, flocking through the dim air. It turned and twisted like a worm, as flecks of dusty powder fell into its substance. Slowly it was growing a form, evolving from a blur into something that had limbs, a head, the shape of a man.

'Is there . . .?' Thalric was squinting, as if trying to make out something he could not quite see. In another place, Che was sure, any number of ghosts would pass him by, but here, where the darkness was layered with centuries, one on top of another in an unbroken chain, the magic was getting even to him.

She thought she saw bones and organs as the apparition formed. It was still colourless, washed-out, still a shadow, a mere reflection in a dark glass. She found that she now feared to set eyes on him. What would he look like after a year in the void? Would it be Achaeos living she saw, or Achaeos dead?

Thalric made a choking sound, and she knew he must now see it, or see something. His lips drew back in a grimace, his hands spreading open to fight. Behind him the Vekken stood expressionless and she could not know what he saw.

'Is that . . .?' Thalric said. 'What am I seeing? Isn't that . . .?'

'Yes,' she confirmed, and looked back at the ghost, which was near complete, now – and discovered that it was not.

They had lent it enough of their strength, like a thimble filled from the ocean, for it to become recognizable, and more of it was being filled out even as she watched. She now recognized the tall, lean frame, and those sharp features that were, in their cold arrogance, a match for the Masters themselves. He did not wear the slave's garb they had dressed him in to die, but instead his arming jacket, its green and gold bleached grey. The sleeves were slit up to his elbows to give play to the spines of his arms. Even the sword-and-circle brooch that he had cast aside now glinted from his breast again.

'Tisamon,' Che gasped. 'But . . . no! This is the wrong one. This isn't him!'

'Little child, what you see is all the ghost there is. No other clings to you,' the man beside Elysiath declared, plainly amused. 'Are you so particular?'

'But . . .' she protested, and the Mantis's haughty features turned to regard her. 'I don't understand.'

'We see in your past a great convergence of ritual,' the man continued, sounding bored again. 'A magical nexus to which you and he were linked. When he died, you were touching him in some way.'

'But where is Achaeos?' she asked, but she already knew the answer. Gone. Gone beyond, and utterly. Whilst this vicious, martial creature had clung on within her mind, her lover had been like a candle flame suddenly snuffed. The dream-Achaeos had told her, *You do this to yourself.* She had used his memory as a rod and imagined that it was his hand that beat her with it.

'Oh.' She sat down suddenly. The spectral Mantis was staring at them, each one in turn. His eyes lingered long enough on Thalric to make the man tense.

'What do you seek, spirit?' Elysiath asked him. 'What holds you here still?'

Tisamon's pale lips moved, the words seeming to come from a great distance. *Where is my daughter?*

'Go seek her,' Elysiath said without interest. 'She is no concern of ours.'

*Where is she?* demanded the Mantis's bleak, far-off voice.

'You are parted from the Beetle-kinden,' the man told him. 'If you cannot scent your child, free as you are now, then you shall never find her.'

Tisamon's greyed eyes flashed briefly. Che thought it was resentment, but then she read it as triumph.

*She is among the Dragonflies*, the Mantis stated. *Far north and west of here.*

'Go seek her,' Elysiath said again. 'We give you leave.'

Che thought of Tynisa, her near-sister, and daughter of this dead man. She thought of what directions Tynisa's life might turn under this ghost's influence, how it had already turned when he was alive. 'Tisamon,' she protested. 'No . . .'

The angular features stared down at her. *Stenwold's niece,* he identified her, as though he had not been riding inside her mind these many months. *She needs me*. With that, he was stalking away, growing less distinct with distance. She thought she detected half-glimpsed shapes about him, the shadows of a shadow, that were those of briars and thorns.

She looked up at the Masters, whose kinden she realized she must know, from fragmentary legends, folk tales, ancient fictions. She had assumed she would feel hollow with the ghost's departure, whosoever's it had been. She also thought she would feel relieved. In truth she felt neither.

'What now?' she asked them. 'What will you do with us?' She stood up again, and this time Thalric stood alongside her, with fingers spread, and the Vekken too. Sword clutched tight in his hand, the Ant was staring at the armoured slopes of Garmoth Atennar.

'They are less than chaff to us,' said Elysiath, 'but you are the grain. In our dreams we have called and, when you came, we awoke for you. For you alone we have broken our long sojourn. We have much to offer you. We give you a chance to share in the rule of the Masters of Khanaphes.'

Che swallowed, feeling very keenly the ancient weight of the dark halls about her and, even more so, the ageless power of the Masters themselves, who were older even than the stones of their living tomb. *There are things here I would never learn in all my days spent at the Great College*, she thought. *There are things that even Moths could not teach me . . .*

'Your rule?' Thalric interrupted sharply, though his voice shook. 'What rule is that? What do you rule, save this hole in the ground?'

'Though our dominion has diminished, do not think we no longer rule our beloved city,' Elysiath reproached him. 'Though we no longer walk its streets, do not think our dreams no longer guide our Ministers. Do not assume we have taken no pains to keep our people on the true path.'

'Oh, I've seen the path they're on,' Thalric said bitterly, and Che saw the great woman roll her eyes, that this savage would not be silent in front of his betters. Thalric was driven by fear and aggression, though, and would not be stilled. 'I've seen them try to struggle on with the simplest of machines, knowing nothing of mechanics, metallurgy, modern farming. We've all seen where that has left them, for even Khanaphes can't hold back the march of time.'

She stared at him and he blanched, baring his teeth, but no more words emerged.

'Now—' Elysiath began, but Che took a deep breath and interrupted her.

'Do you . . . Do you know there's a war out there?'

There was a moment's pause when it seemed that Che might be struck down just for such an interruption, then Lirielle replied dismissively, 'Wars come and go. We, who have seen so many, cannot mark them all.'

'No, there is a war right now. The Scorpions have come against your city.' Che saw their derision and pressed forward. 'They have broken through your walls! When we came down here, they were at the river. By now they may even have driven your people out into the wastes.'

The Masters exchanged amused glances. 'Our city is proof against what the rabble of the desert can bring against it,' sneered the man. 'Our people shall become stronger for the testing.'

Che stared at them in disbelief. 'Your people are praying to you,' she said. 'It's like nothing I've ever seen anywhere else. The homeless crowd the streets and call to you to save them. You have slept too deeply.'

There was enough passion in her voice, just enough evidence of pain and truth, that their mockery dried up slowly, like the landscape of their memories.

'Such nonsense,' said Elysiath finally, 'but let us witness this prodigy. Watch with us if you will, and you shall see your fears dispelled.'

# Forty-Three

When the *Iteration* blew, it sprayed debris as high as the bridge and beyond, showering it with shards of twisted metal and fragments of wood. They pattered down across the stones, on attacker and defender alike. The thunderous explosion forced the two combating sides apart, halted even the frenzied activity of the archers. Totho broke from the line and rushed over to the bridge's north parapet, peering down at the ship's ruin below. His heart lurched. *Oh, I've done it now.* The pride of the Iron Glove's tiny fleet had been destroyed in some backwater, in a war it had no business taking part in. Drephos would be . . .

Drephos would be interested, if Totho ever got to pass the news back to him. Drephos would see the whole expensive business as a field test, and order someone to work on an improved design. In fact, Drephos would not be remotely upset. The thought of that reaction, shorn of all emotion, washed clean of the blood of Corcoran and his crew, made Totho feel even worse.

Then the Scorpions let out a great roar of triumph and came for them again, made newly bold and fierce by their artillerists' victory. Amnon began shouting for solidarity, and then the charge caught them, denting their line so deeply that Amnon almost skidded off the low rampart and fell back onto the bridge. The Scorpions almost had them then and there, by sheer weight of numbers, for, in the packed crush at the centre, there was precious little room for axe or spear. The Khanaphir resorted to their short swords to hack at their enemies, while the Scorpions used the savage claws their Art had given them.

Meyr loomed behind the lines, reaching past the Khanaphir with his mailed hands, heedless of the blows any Scorpions aimed at him. He caught them up at random, plucked them from their places and hurled them back into the mass of their fellows. It was blind, brutal work. Amnon's backplate was against Meyr's breastplate, and that was the only thing stopping him being forced to give ground.

There was a high, keening cry and Mantis-kinden began dropping among the Scorpion throng. Having discarded their bows, some now wielded knives of stone or chitin, while others relied only on their barbed forearms. It was enough for them, as they plunged into the enemy like strong swimmers and began to kill. Moving with a dazzling economy of effort, they sought out the edge of every piece of armour, aiming for throats and eyes. They were swift, almost dancing across the face of the enemy host where, slender and deadly, they spent themselves on behalf of the city that had conquered them long ago, buying time and room with their blood.

The Scorpions could not match them for speed, but their numbers were inescapable, and their strength enough to kill with a single blow. Totho could track the whirlpools of the Mantids' passing amid the surging sea of enemy, and could track each Marsh-kinden death by their sudden stilling. Soon only a few of them remained, cutting a path of death through the tight-packed Scorpions, then only one. Teuthete herself lived still, and slew, the two inextricably linked in her Mantis mind. By then the Khanaphir line was solid again, though perilously thin, and Amnon was calling her. With a sudden leap she joined him back in the lines, her arms drenched in blood to the shoulders. She was smiling, ablaze with madness.

Totho joined them, climbing to a higher position at one end of the line where he could take a clearer shot. The Scorpions had fallen back a few paces, shields linked again to ward off the archers, but this time they were not going away. There would be no retreating for them now, not until the breach was won. They could smell victory as close as their next breath.

*Moments. We have just moments.*

'Be ready with the ropes!' Amnon shouted.

It took Totho a moment to recall what he meant, that the stacks of loose stone on either side of the bridge were to serve as a defence and a trap.

The Scorpions struck the Khanaphir shield-wall with a single metal sound. They were fighting mad now, heedless of the archers' arrows striking down at them. They howled and foamed and battered against shields, splitting and cracking them with axe-blows or the solid strikes of halberds. They ran on to the Khanaphir spears and yet kept running, dragging the weapons from their wielders' hands. It was down to close-in sword work again in moments.

Totho loosed and loosed his snapbow, reloading and recharging as fast as his shaking hands could manage. *I could do this in the dark, now. I could do it in my sleep. My hands know the drill off by heart.* His mind just watched numbly, seeing the Khanaphir line edge slowly back, anchored at either end by the higher stone of the barricade, in the centre by Amnon, his dark armour awash with the blood of his enemies, backed by the whirling, murderous Teuthete and Meyr's bludgeoning reach and strength. Each time the Mole Cricket lashed out it seemed he held some new weapon. He took up whatever the enemy had left him, laying about him with halberds and axes whose shafts splintered and broke after a few swings, with swords whose blades he bent and shattered under the force of his striking. The centre was holding now, but the line bowing to either side. It would only take one breach for them to lose everything.

A crossbow bolt suddenly ricocheted off Totho's helm, snapping his head back, and he clutched at the stonework, while letting his vision clear. Another struck his pauldron, and flew off behind the lines. He turned his snapbow on the enemy archers, killing them through the shields that were supposed to protect them. *They will remember this*, he thought. *If they are writing the last chapter of Khanaphir history, yet we are writing a chapter of theirs. They will remember all of this.*

'Archers back!' Amnon yelled, and he shouted it again and a third time before they would obey him. They dropped back from the barricades, and fled straight for Praeda's second line of defence: that huge maze of stone and wood that blocked the far end of the bridge.

'Totho, ready with the ropes!' came Amnon's next order, his voice loud enough to be heard clear over the Scorpions' howling. Totho found himself obeying automatically, slinging his snapbow over his shoulder and dropping back to the taut cables with his sword drawn. Between the surfaces of stone the line of defenders still held tenuously, straining and bulging. *If I cut now I'll crush them.* He waited, sword raised, looking back towards them as their line fell apart.

'Back!' Amnon shouted, and they tried, but the Scorpions would not let them go without further blood. A half-dozen of the Royal Guard were able to hurl themselves clear. Most of the rest either stayed and died, or died trying to withdraw. Totho noticed Dariset, half a shattered shield still held high, try to jump away, but a Scorpion moved with her, lunging with claws outstretched. He drove one spiked hand into her chest, and she rammed her sword into the huge man's belly, so that the point jutted from his back.

Scorpions were falling through the gaps in the line. There were moments, moments only to spare.

'Now!' It was not Amnon's voice but Meyr's. The huge man staggered back, slapping a half-dozen Scorpions back into their comrades' halberds with one arm, while he hauled at Amnon with the other. For a moment the Scorpions occupied the breach, but they could not come through it. Teuthete was there, and she was killing them as they came. She had a Khanaphir sword in each hand, and the spikes of her arms were flexed wide, and every edge and point she had was busy taking blood. She was never still, a swift storm of needling death that could not hold them more than a few seconds longer, and yet was holding them nonetheless.

'Now!' roared Meyr – and Totho hacked twice, and three times, then a leaping Scorpion slammed an axe into his back. The force of the blow drove him to his knees, though it twisted from his mail. He fell on the mauled rope and it snapped.

The tons of stone were abruptly in motion for a thunderous second. Totho turned and caught the axeman across the face and the gut, even as the Scorpion turned to look at his fellows. The sound of the stones clashing together was like the end of the world. For many Scorpions it was just that.

Meyr shouted something incoherent, then he and Amnon were killing the few Scorpions who had got through, as gripped by battle-rage as their enemies had ever been. Totho only had eyes for the slender figure now standing atop the tumbled wall of stones. Teuthete had leapt up there with Art-sped reflexes, even as the stone descended on her, and she stood there for a moment, proud and defiant, bloody with the demise of her enemies. The crossbow bolt found her as she stood, took her under the ribs with force enough to throw her from her perch. The fall robbed her of grace, and she was dead as she struck the bridge.

After the pictures had faded, there was a great silence amongst the Masters of Khanaphes. Che put her hands to her head, feeling the world tilt about her. It had seemed so real. She had been there, right there on the bridge. She had been all over the city. Her mind's eye had been dragged wherever the Masters had wished, to the sacked western city, to the refugee-clogged streets of the east. The colours had been over-bright, burning like fever, running like paint, and yet it had all been so real.

*That was Totho*, she thought numbly. *Totho fighting, but why?*

'Che?' Thalric had his hands on her shoulders. 'Che, what happened?'

'They're fighting,' she said, shaking. 'On the bridge. Couldn't you see?'

'Che, there was nothing to see,' Thalric insisted. 'You just . . . you were just staring into the dark.' She saw blank incomprehension on his face, and a measure of the same on the normally expressionless Vekken behind him.

'The city hangs in the balance,' she whispered. 'The Scorpions assault the bridge, and only a tiny few hold them off. It is the end for Khanaphes, it must be.'

'This is a grave disappointment,' said Elysiath. 'Have our servants fallen so low that they will allow our enemies into the city?'

'It does not seem possible,' agreed the man beside her, his tone unhurried, conversational. 'The vagabonds of the Nem should not have been able to pass the walls. That suggests treachery within.'

'Our people have turned away from us while we slept,' Lirielle agreed. 'They flee rather than fight. They are no longer what they once were.'

'How can you say that?' Che glared at them. 'They are dying for you right now!' *Totho is dying. He could be dying even now.*

They looked at her patronizingly. 'They have indeed grown weak. How dare they abandon half the city,' Elysiath said sternly. 'They deserve all they get. They should have trusted in our walls.'

Thalric laughed at them. The sound of his derision broke across their pontificating like a dash of water, shocking them with its irreverence.

'Your walls?' he sneered. 'Your walls fell in a few brief hours to Imperial leadshotters.' The faces of the Masters remained quite composed, but Che could still detect the slight uncertainty in their eyes that showed they did not recognize the word.

'Leadshotters,' Thalric repeated slowly. He had seen it in them too. 'Siege engines. Machines. Old relics of my own people, but great big magic to your poor citizens, because they've been living in the Bad Old Days for the last few centuries.' He took a deep breath and she felt his hands tighten on her shoulders. 'And, from what you've been saying, that's your fault. You've kept them back. You've kept them ignorant. You've kept them *yours*.'

'How *dare* you speak to us thus, O Savage,' Elysiath demanded. Her voice was not angry but cold enough to cut to the bone. 'Utter another word and we will send your mind into a darkness so deep that you will never be found.'

Che expected Thalric to say more but, looking back at him, she saw him grimace, baring his teeth. Whatever he might normally believe, in this dark tomb beyond anything he knew, he believed in that threat.

'And what will you do to me?' Che asked them. 'Tell me, O Masters of Khanaphes? When I speak the same truths?'

'What is this insurrection?' the man said, almost good-naturedly. 'Savages may babble their nonsense, but we discerned merit in you. Our people have grown weak. There is no more than that.'

'A leadshotter . . .' She stopped because she now realized she could no longer explain it as she once had, '. . . is a great engine that throws stones hard enough to shatter a wall. The Wasp Empire in the north possesses hundreds of them. My city has many stationed on its walls. The Ant city-states of Accius and his cousins, they field dozens each. Helleron must make more than a thousand crossbows a year in its factories. There are automotives for freight and for war. On the seas there are armourclads, metal ships that float. In the air they have heliopters and orthopters and ships of the air.' The image of these ravening hordes of progress was making her dizzy, slightly ill just to think of it. 'Look in my mind. I can no longer understand what I remember, but look there. See it all. I gift you with five hundred years of artifice.'

They had gone very still. She could feel them taking up the lifeless stones of her memory with their cool, slimy fingers, turning them over and over. Thalric put his arms around her, hugged her to his chest. She wondered if it was a gesture for her reassurance or his own.

'The world has moved on,' she said. 'Everywhere but here.'

'The Moths have fallen,' observed Lirielle. 'What is this?' Despite it all, there was such mourning in her voice that Che felt sorry for them.

'But the rabble of the Nem . . .' the man began, and trailed off, any confidence ebbing from his voice.

'They will not stand still for ever,' Che said. 'Clinging to whatever life the desert could give, fighting each other for a few scraps, they have been slow to change, but all it took was a prod from the Empire, and they are now inside your city.'

For a long moment the Masters stared at one another, trying to cling on ponderously to what they had believed, in the face of all they had now seen. *They don't know what to do*, Che realized. *They slept too long.*

'You will help, surely,' she pressed them.

Elysiath turned a haughty look on her. 'So much is lost, it hardly seems worthwhile to salvage what is left.'

'But they're your people,' Che insisted.

'They have bitterly disappointed us,' the man stated. 'They have squandered all we left them.'

'They have forgotten all I taught them of war,' rumbled dark Garmoth Atennar from behind them.

'But they're now calling out for you!' Che told them. 'They pray to you. They invoke your aid.'

'Do they?' Elysiath actually cocked her head to one side, listening in some way that Che could not imagine. She smiled faintly. 'Ah, yes, they do. How faint they sound. Ah, well.'

'"Ah, well"?' Che protested. 'Don't you see what that means? It means that they believe in you still. To them, after all these centuries, you are still the Masters of Khanaphes. You are what they have lived for, and now you are the reason why they are all going to die. You still have a responsibility to them. They are your servants.'

'Responsibility? To the slaves?' Elysiath echoed, as though the concept was remarkable.

'You said they'd failed you,' Che told her. 'They haven't. They're fighting for you even now, as we speak. They're bleeding and dying for you, for your city. The first city, remember? The city you built so long ago. They're giving their lives to preserve it from the Scorpions, who will soon turn it into one more desert ruin, and put an end even to the memory of you. And perhaps they'll come down here. If there are enough of them, or if the Empire tightens its hold, then maybe even you won't remain safe. Your tests and traps cannot hide you for ever.'

The man was frowning, as though he had eaten something distasteful. Lirielle toyed with her comb. 'But what can we do?' she said.

'It would be such a waste of our power to intervene,' the man mused. 'The cost would be terrible. It would set us back so much.'

'What were you saving it for?' Che asked him.

'The revivification of the land, of course,' he replied. 'The reversal of the change that the great cataclysm brought about. To bring green back to the desert, that is our great purpose.'

Che blinked at that, at the sheer hubris of it, for she could not imagine that even the Masters could even start to accomplish such a thing. *Are they just living empty dreams then, despite all their power*? 'And who will then profit from this,' she pressed them, even so, 'if your own people are gone?'

The man gave a petulant frown. 'It will demand a great effort, hardly worth it, surely, to preserve so little.'

'So much effort,' Lirielle agreed, as though just combing her hair for so long had exhausted her.

'They're *dying*,' Che said, reaching the end of her ability to explain herself to them. 'As we speak, they're dying.' *Totho is dying. Oh, I am so sorry, Totho.*

'I would rather have slept,' said Elysiath, surly. 'Jeherian, will you lead us?'

The man beside her nodded wearily. 'So much lost,' he said sadly. 'Ah, well.'

Che started, as someone moved past her. Without a sound, another of the Masters stepped forward to join Elysiath and the others, a great bulky man whose lustrous hair fell down past his shoulders. Looks were exchanged between them all. Even as Che noted him, she saw another woman come padding from the darkness beyond them, as tall and voluptuous as the rest, the necklace about her throat bearing a kingdom's ransom in precious stones. Next, another two came, hand in hand, to stand nearby. Then, at last, Che saw what she had long imagined. On the nearest sarcophagus, the crowning statue stirred, stretching languorously, without visible transition from cold stone to live flesh. *Thus do the Masters of Khanaphes sleep out the centuries.*

There were almost a score of them soon, male and female, looming from the dark to join their kin, their grave and beautiful faces all marked with expressions of concern. Che expected chanting. She was waiting for them to enact some ritual, as Achaeos had said the Moths did. It took her a long moment of frustrated silence until she realized that they were already at work.

Each of them was looking up, towards the vaulted ceiling, up towards the embattled city of Khanaphes and the sky beyond. Each and every one of them was sharing in the same act of concentration, staring at some great focal point she could not imagine. She knew she should hate them for their callous detachment, but there was such grief and loss evident on those noble faces that it nearly broke her heart.

*What have I driven them to?* she wondered. *What is this, that they sacrifice here?*

Pictures blurred and stretched in her mind again, taking her back to the city above.

'Would you look at what they've done,' Hrathen said. 'How much effort went into that?'

'So they've brought some more stone to fill the breach,' Jakal replied dismissively. 'It will not stop us. An act of desperation.' She jabbed a thumb-claw towards a nearby Scorpion. 'Call my guard together.'

'We knew they were working on something, and now it looks like they've built the world's biggest single-use nutcracker.' They were standing on a rooftop overlooking the bridge and the river, Hrathen with his telescope to his eye. 'The archers, all the rest, are running for the second barricade.'

'Bring it down,' Jakal told him. 'Use one of your petards. Or move one of the engines up on to the bridge.'

'No need for the sweat,' Hrathen said. 'All that effort, and we'll still crack it in less than a minute.' He signalled to one of his own, one of the few Slave Corps soldiers left. Of late, the Khanaphir archers had become very good at shooting them down. 'Fly to Lieutenant Angved,' he instructed. 'Tell him to sight on that blockage and bring it down.'

'Yes, sir.' The man kicked off and made a short dart over the rooftops to where Angved and his leadshotter were waiting.

Jakal regarded Hrathen with a slight smile. It was not a fond look, for Scorpion faces did not lend themselves to fondness. There was fire in it, though: anticipation of victory had set light to her.

'You'll go in yourself now?' Hrathen asked her.

'Their archers have fled. I shall destroy what warriors they have left. You should bring your engines up to the bridge's crest, so that we can destroy their second wall.' Her understanding of artillery and its uses was increasing by leaps and bounds. 'My warriors must see me fight. They must remember why I am Warlord.'

'Then they will see me fight alongside you,' Hrathen said. 'The engineers can manage without me.'

She looked at him for a long moment, then shook her head. 'Your Empire breeds fools,' she said. 'If my warriors obeyed my words as swiftly as yours obey you, I would not need to shed my blood for them. Still, you shall have the chance to prove yourself, if you so wish.'

'Why do you go, then?' he asked her. 'It's not as though your host is short one more warrior.'

Her smile was scornful. 'I am Warlord because I am the best. I slew many to take the crown, and there are many who would slay me for it in turn. If I did not fight they would all take up arms against me. I too must shed the blood of the Khanaphir, but I shall choose when I shed it. I am not destined to become mere prey for arrows. My people shall see me take the bridge itself, and they shall remember.'

'They shall see *us* take the bridge.'

'Are you strong enough?' she asked him. 'Does your blood run so pure? You may just as well remain behind. My people would not care.'

It stung like a slaver's lash. 'I have the strength of my father's kinden and the guile of my mother's,' he told her, 'as you will soon see. Perhaps it will be I who will challenge you.'

That made her smile. 'I would welcome it.' Below, in the ravaged street, a company of Scorpions had assembled, huge men and women loaded with scavenged armour. A dozen of them stamped and rattled, waiting impatiently. Jakal had chosen them carefully, Hrathen knew, from among the most vicious and bloodthirsty of all her people, thus keeping her potential enemies close to her.

She descended to join them and they greeted her with a roar of approval. Today was their day. The day their Warlord had delivered their ancient enemy to them. Hrathen followed as they struck out for the bridge, after sending back an order to have one of the leadshotters brought up after them.

*Not a great day for the Empire*, he thought. *Probably not even a footnote in the Imperial histories, but I shall know. I shall know that I was true to my father's bloody-handed kinden, at the end. The desolation of Khanaphes shall be my legacy to my people.*

The archers, and a scattering of Royal Guard, were still in sight, fleeing towards the end barricade. Amnon faced the new-formed wall of loose stones and squared his shoulders. Meyr crouched close to him, a hulking, brooding shadow, and in his hands he had a rough-ended beam from the construction works, ten feet long. Totho checked that his snapbow was charged. *I had feared I might run out of ammunition today*, he considered. *That seems unlikely now.*

Another thought struck him, that Drephos would be proud now: not of Totho but of the armour. *Field-testing complete: the aviation plate can be considered worth its considerable cost. We three are the proof of that.* He was amazed how quickly Amnon had adapted to it, but then the man was a warrior born, and Beetles took easily to wearing a second shell.

*If we had come with twenty men in full mail, we would have held against anything the Scorpions or the Empire could throw at us*, he thought. *We could have held off the world.*

'They'll bring a petard up to blow the barricade down,' he warned the others. 'We won't have long before we must fight again.'

'We won't need long,' Amnon told him. 'Just enough time so they can complete the works, close up the breach at the far end. That is all the time we need to buy them.' Totho wondered what Praeda Rakespear was doing right now, whether she had realized that Amnon was not coming back to her. He wondered whether Amnon had left people ready to restrain her, to stop her running up here. Probably he had: it was the sort of thing the big man thought of.

He spotted the plume of grey smoke, and knew immediately what it meant. *Leadshotter on a rooftop.* There were words in his mind to warn the others, but he had no time to give actual voice to them before the missile struck the barricade.

The noise passed by him, the physical force overriding it. A piece of broken rock hit his chest like a sledgehammer, his feet skating from under him, so that he slammed down on his back. The air was all dust, with stone fragments pattering all about them. Gasping for breath, he could not get to his feet yet, but he tried to peer through the drifting white veil, to see what had been done.

The new stones had fallen, forming a broken pavement between him and the barricade, and the Scorpions were coming through the breach. He realized even then that their artillerists would have preferred a second shot, to widen the gap, but the warriors already on the bridge had been so long denied this chance that nothing could have held them back. They surged in along with the stone-dust, as Meyr and Amnon met them at full charge.

It would have been suicide but for the mail. It could have been suicide anyway. There were enough weak points – throat, armpit, groin – that one spear or blade could have ended either of them. They thrust themselves into the thick of the Scorpion weapons, and Totho saw Amnon take a dozen blows, and Meyr twice that number. Each rebounded from the dented plate, frustrated by its fluted curves that turned the strongest blow aside. Amnon's sword descended repeatedly, chopping indiscriminately at the enemy. Meyr laid about himself like a mad thing, crushing the Scorpions, flinging them from the bridge with great swipes of his club.

They tried to drag him down, to get under his reach, but Amnon killed them as they came, shield high and sword never still.

Totho struggled to his feet, feeling sharp pains from his ribs. His breastplate had a prodigious dent to one side, where the stone had struck him. He staggered a little, and then ran up to stand to Amnon's left. With a desperate concentration, he resumed the business of running out of ammunition, emptying each magazine in turn into the host of Scorpions, punching holes in their mail and through their mail, even through one man and into the next. Beyond those that Meyr crushed and Amnon slew, the bridge was heaving with them. He could see bigger, better-armoured warriors forcing their way through the breach, eager to get to the fight. There was no subtlety now, no pretence at tactics. Only three men stood on the bridge between the Scorpions and their prey. Faced with that, it was down to blade and claw. Crossbows, leadshotters, all were forgotten, as the Many of Nem returned to what they knew best.

Amnon was down on one knee, his pauldron bent almost in two by a halberd blow. Totho shot the wielder through the head as he raised the weapon for a second strike.

Meyr's breastplate was buckled, the catches at his side split apart by the stroke of a greatsword. It was impossible to tell how much of the blood on him was his own. There was a broken spear jutting from beside his neck that must surely have pierced his mail. The Scorpions were leaping on him, climbing up him, trying to unshell him with daggers and their clawed hands.

Totho loosed and loosed, reloaded and recharged and loosed again, picking them off every time Meyr remained still enough to shoot at. The giant grabbed them and tore them away from him, roaring in rage. If he got both hands on the same man, he ripped the wretch apart. Totho wondered whether anyone had ever *seen* an enraged Mole Cricket before.

Abruptly the Scorpions facing them were more heavily armoured, larger. They thundered into the shields of the two defenders hard enough to drive them back a step, hacking with sword and axe. Meyr backhanded one into the river. Another slammed an axe at his throat which was deflected by the plates of his shoulders. The strap on Amnon's shield broke under a sword blow and he discarded it, taking his sword in both hands.

Totho slung his snapbow and rushed in beside him, with his own shield on his arm. He received three strikes immediately, two on the shield's curved face and one to his helm that made his head swim. He tried to lunge back with his sword, but it was all he could do to just stand upright, shield held up and being struck at repeatedly by the Scorpions – all he could do not to fall back immediately and yield the breach to them. *I am not a warrior.* All he had was his armour, the one thing standing between life and death for him.

Another blow struck his shield so hard that he was knocked into Amnon. The Khanaphir did not even pause in his sword work, merely pushing Totho back with his free hand.

A stingshot struck Amnon clean in the chest, flaring gold, and he staggered. The Scorpions surged forward, but Totho was there to meet them. He raised his shield and sword against the blows, putting his shoulder to the enemy as though he was trying to hold a door closed. Meyr was being swarmed, Scorpions hacking at his legs, leaping up to drive their claws at his throat, hanging off his armour. Totho felt four solid blows land on his shield, numbing his arm. His sword was battered out of his hand.

A Scorpion woman was abruptly in front of Meyr, stepping aside from his descending fist with a deft grace and then driving her spear up with all her might past the edge of his breastplate, under his arm. Totho saw the shaft sink deep through the sundered mail with an explosion of blood. Meyr struck at her furiously with both hands but she ducked inside his reach and ripped at his throat with her claws. Another man, a Scorpion halfbreed, was beside her, one hand outstretched. Totho saw the bolt of golden light strike Meyr's helm around the eye-slit and the huge man staggered back, rearing to his full height.

The Scorpion woman tore her spear free, turning as she did so and coming back to hurl it into Meyr's throat, where it stuck, shaft quivering. Totho could hear himself shouting something wordless.

Amnon was there. Amnon was there now, but it was too late. Meyr collapsed on to one knee, a hand on the spear-shaft that was running with his blood. Amnon lunged forward at the woman, for a moment not caring if the Scorpions were through the breach or not. The halfbreed got in the way, fending the sword off and reaching out with the open palm of his off-hand. The stingshot struck Amnon's damaged pauldron hard enough to rip it off, then the halfbreed's sword jammed into the Beetle's side, scraping against mail and severing straps.

Amnon rammed his own blade into the man's chest, driving it in two-handed up to the hilt. He was ducking immediately to scoop up a new sword, a sharp, slender piece originating from the Iron Glove factories. *My sword,* Totho recognized it. *My sword.*

The Scorpions had paused a moment with the halfbreed's death, and Totho realized it was to give the woman room. She grinned fangs at Amnon and took hold of her spear with one hand, wrenching it from Meyr's neck. The giant gave out a sound, a monstrous sigh, and toppled backwards.

Totho knew he should find another sword or unsling his snapbow, but he found he could only watch Amnon and the Scorpion woman. Amnon stood unevenly, his weight on one leg. His once-pristine armour was a maze of dents and scratches, missing plates and broken buckles. He had been fighting for too long. It was not the mail that weighed on him, but a deadly weariness. The Scorpion woman looked fresh, fleet, long-limbed and strong. Worse, she looked skilled.

'You killed him,' she said, with a nod at the dead halfbreed. 'You saved me the trouble. I shall kill you now.'

'Do it,' Amnon urged her. 'I'm tired.' He braced himself for it, left hand extended before him to reach for her spear, sword held wide to cut.

A stir of unease rippled back through the Scorpions, and at first Totho imagined it was because of the two combatants, perhaps because they had realized who Amnon was. They were looking upwards, though, more and more of them following suit. He tried to do the same, but the lobster-tail plates that guarded the back of his neck had locked in place. Now Amnon himself was tilting his head back, falling from his fighting stance, and the Scorpion woman too. Totho cursed and wrenched at his helm, finally tearing it from his head entirely.

Something struck him in the face as he did, and then another: tiny impacts like insistent little insects. A third followed soon after. He touched his face, which was grimy with dirt and sweat, and found it wet.

There was a look on the faces of the Scorpions that he could not identify. Amnon had tilted his helm back, the better to see what was happening. His expression looked shaken, wide-eyed with fear.

'What?' Totho demanded of him. 'It's only rain.'

Amnon stared at him. All around them the drops of moisture were slanting down, thicker now, the air grown misty with them, the sound a constant hiss off the bridge's stonework, off the river below.

'Rain,' Totho repeated. Amnon shook his head.

'I know of rain, for I saw it once in the Forest Alim. It rains on the sea, sailors say, but it never rains here.'

'It must,' Totho argued. The Scorpions were actually cowering back. Only the woman still stood straight, clutching her spear as though it was a talisman.

'It has never rained in Khanaphes,' Amnon said firmly, barely audible now over the rain which fell faster and faster, battering at them. 'Not ever, in written record, has it rained here.' He could not have looked more horrified and frightened if the Scorpions had been about to skin him alive. 'It is the wrath of the Masters, their judgement on us.'

'It's just rain!' But Totho had to shout, and even then he was not sure his words were heard. He looked into the sky and saw it boiling and thunderous, full of pregnant clouds that surely could not have been there a moment ago. The sun had gone dark with them.

He felt his stomach turn as he looked upriver, and the sight struck a blow that his armour could not protect him from. There were clouds rolling and seething in the sky all the way north. They were following the course of the river, a great train of deluging clouds as far north as the eye could see, curving with the meanders of the Jamail.

*Impossible*, he thought, but his eyes saw what they saw, although, as the rain became more and more furious, he could see less and less.

Amnon was now crouching, in terror or reverence, and many of the Scorpions were fleeing the bridge or milling madly. They could have captured the eastern half of Khanaphes right then, but the storm had struck them with the same fear as had infected Amnon.

*And what about the other Khanaphir?* Totho turned and peered at the east city. He could see little enough of it, but it seemed to him that the roofs of the houses were dark with people. He went to the bridge's parapet and gazed north again. Abruptly he could not breathe. He wanted to shout a warning, wanted to tell Amnon to brace himself. He wanted even more to deny what he was seeing. Instead he could only cling to the bridge's rail and stare, unable even to close his eyes.

There was a wall of water rolling down from the north. It seemed impossible that it would not dissipate itself along either bank, but it did not. It descended purposefully on the city of Khanaphes with the inexorable speed of a rail automotive. The bridge, of course, stood in its path. Totho had cause to remember the bridge's many pillars, narrowed and lowered to impede shipping. At last he dropped to his knees, still holding on to the parapet.

He counted down the seconds in his mind. He was slightly late for, just as he counted *two*, the entire bridge jumped beneath him. Those still standing, meaning most of the Scorpions, fell down. Some were thrown from the bridge altogether.

*It will destroy the whole city*, he thought, and clawed his way up to look. The river Jamail had burst its banks, the water breaking against the bridge, which still stood despite all laws of architecture. The Jamail had exploded from its course in a ruinous wave of destruction, but heading only to the west.

Totho simply stood there, watching the murderous wall of water roll over the Scorpion war-host, sweeping them without mercy through the pillaged streets of the western city. He saw smaller buildings collapse even as Scorpions sought sanctuary atop them, the detritus of the last few centuries' expansion obliterated in seconds, leaving only the greatest and the oldest of buildings untouched. A few Scorpions managed to claw their way to safety on top of those but, of the Many of Nem, the vast majority were already gone, swept away and drowned by the rushing waters.

The eastern bank still held firm, and that was another thing that Totho knew was impossible. Later he would construct all manner of explanations to account for what he had seen, but right then, faced with the enormity of it, he simply knew that it could not be done, and yet it had been. He had no words for it.

The rain was still coming fast, and hard enough to sting the skin. The Scorpion woman was looking back, watching her people try to flee, fighting amongst themselves to escape, pushing each other from the bridge or being carried away by the roiling waters. When she turned back his way, her face was death.

'Amnon!' Totho shouted, and the Beetle just managed to regain his feet before she was on him. She struck him across the helm with the shaft of her spear, hard enough to stagger him, and then rammed the point into his unarmoured shoulder, drawing a thick welt of blood. Amnon drove for her with his sword out, but she spun aside and struck him across the back of the head, whirling her spear one-handed about her. The claws of her off-hand lunged for him, but scraped off his armour. Amnon cut back at her, making her jump away. He was moving too slowly, though, and she was as swift as a Mantis. When safely at a distance, she stabbed at him with her spear, when within his sword's reach her claws raked for him. She danced about him, never still, forcing him always to stumble after her.

She lashed her spear across the side of his head, snapping him round and sending him to one knee. Her claws pincered around his neck, digging into the mail there. She twisted his helm back and poised her spear above the eye-slit.

Totho shot her through the centre of the chest. The bolt passed straight through her, and she shuddered once, but remained standing for some time before the spear fell from her hand and she collapsed. He turned to face the other Scorpions. He had surely broken some law of single combat, and no doubt they would come for him now.

They were backing off. Although there was only water beyond their end of the bridge, they were backing off. Totho could not understand it until the Khanaphir soldiers passed him.

They were just the neighbourhood militia, untrained civilians with their spears and shields, but they were enough. They swept the demoralized Scorpions ahead of them like the river itself, furious and fierce, and when they had done their work, the Jamail took over. So ended the Scorpion siege of the city of Khanaphes, and the enduring memory Totho had of its conclusion was Praeda Rakespear kneeling beside Amnon, trying to pull his helm free as she wept.

# Forty-Four

For a long time, Angved was too shaken to make any rational decision. The words, *Well, now I've seen everything*, just kept rolling round his head like a mindless mantra. At his back was the leadshotter, half covered by a tarpaulin. By the time they had got that far, it and they had been so thoroughly soaked that the effort had grown pointless. *The only problem with firepowder artillery is that you can't shoot in the rain, even if you would want to.* He knew that damp powder would not have mattered if they had a row of trebuchets, but even then it would be impossible to spot targets in this downpour. Loading would become a nightmare of slips and errors. *I've never known rain like this, never.* In the Empire, the serious rainfall tended to come late in the year, but Angved had visited the Commonweal during the war, where up north in the highlands it rained more, and even snowed. There had been nothing to touch this, though. *An entire army swept away. Well, now I've seen everything.*

His Scorpion crew were crouching beside him, all bravado stripped away. Another half-dozen Scorpions had been lucky enough to climb up on to the roof there, which was now an island in the rising flood. He was accumulating Wasps, too. The other engineers were abandoning their placements to find Angved, because they were soldiers, and in times of chaos they looked for authority.

One of the Slave Corps landed nearby at a skid, shaking

himself. It must be a nightmare to fly through this, but they had been trying to find Hrathen, seeking orders.

'Any sign of the Captain?' Angved asked.

The man shook his head. 'He was in that, last I saw.' He was pointing somewhere, but the rain veiled anything he might be pointing at. Angved knew he meant the bridge. 'The Khanaphir are driving what's left of the Scorpion army into the river. I saw no fliers. He must be dead.'

'Right.' Angved shuddered. 'How's the water level now?'

'Steady,' another of his engineers reported. 'Not risen for a little while, so it must have peaked. What in the pits are we going to do?'

'I'm assuming command as ranking officer,' Angved said, loud enough to be heard. It did seem to him that the rain was now lessening. 'Listen to me and do what you're told, and we'll get out of this yet.'

'And for what?' one of the Wasps asked. 'They'll have us staked up on crossed pikes. This is a total disaster.'

'Maybe not,' Angved said. *There's one thing left that could turn this from a footnote in the histories into an Imperial triumph. After all, who gives a spit about a few dead Scorpions or whether some backwater city gets sacked or not? You just have to step back from things to see what's really important.* 'Genraki,' he beckoned.

'Chief.' The sodden Scorpion looked more oppressed by the rain than by the death of so many of his fellows. They were not a sentimental breed.

'You took to the artillery business fine, didn't you? You enjoyed it?'

The Scorpion nodded cautiously.

'Now things have gone sour for your lot here, but the Empire can always use an Auxillian engineer or two. We need to get back to the Empire, quick as you can. Get us there and you and your men will get paid, rewarded. Which is more than I can say about anything that might happen to you around here.'

Genraki nodded again. 'Away from this city,' he agreed. 'Away from the Masters' anger.'

'Whatever.' Angved felt for the satchel containing his precious samples, his notes and calculations. 'And don't think the Empire will forget about this place. I've a feeling the black and gold might be back in sight of here sooner than you think.' He looked around at the doubting faces of the other Wasps. 'Just you follow my lead,' he told them. 'I'll pull us from the fire yet.' *They'll make me a major for this, at the least, which will give me a nice packet to retire on.*

'Get us to the Empire,' he told Genraki. 'Guide us through the desert. You'll be well paid for it, and if you want to stay on there, we can find work for you – engineers or Slave Corps, your choice.'

He grinned. Life was looking up. Even the rain was stopping.

'It's another dead end.'

Sulvec flinched at the words. 'Look again.' His voice came out as a croak. 'You must be wrong.'

'I checked, sir. I looked everywhere. It's not the way out.'

'Then find the way!' Sulvec shouted at him. They listened to the echoes of his voice pass back and forth down the hall. In their waning lamplight, the Wasps' faces looked pale and drawn. Sulvec's eyes were very wide, as though trying to scoop up as much of the failing light as they could. A muscle tugged at the corner of his mouth. 'How can we be lost?' he whispered. 'Where have all these tunnels come from?'

'We'll have to go back, sir. We must have taken a wrong turn.'

'So many tunnels, all dark and covered with slime . . . so many of them.' Sulvec swallowed convulsively. 'We'll go back. We must have missed a turn, that's all. We're probably just a hundred yards from the entrance.' He ignored the expressions of his men which said, *A hundred yards of solid rock*. 'Get moving!' he snapped at them. 'And bring *him* along too.'

He kicked out at Osgan's collapsed form, which had been keeping up a steady, ragged whimpering. The two soldiers looked at their leader with revulsion that was only half-concealed.

'Sir,' one of them said, after a moment, 'he's going to die anyway. He's stabbed through the gut. I'm amazed he's not gone already.'

'He's not gone yet because I still have a use for him,' Sulvec spat out. 'Now just bring him.'

'Sir,' the soldier said again, 'can't we leave him? What's the point of dragging him around this place? I mean, can't we finish him off?' They were Rekef men, but there were limits.

Sulvec snarled at them. 'What's this? Bleeding hearts in the Rekef? Think this is Collegium, do you? You're taking my orders, and my orders are to bring him.' Sulvec felt as though the world was falling away from him, here in this horrible darkness. Marger had not come back. Thalric had not come back. They had seen no living thing since the fight, and yet the darkness beyond their lamps had seemed to throng with monstrous, massive shapes. He needed Osgan. He needed Osgan because as long as he had Osgan in his power, Osgan who would scream and writhe at Sulvec's whim, he was not helpless. Osgan was his hold on the world.

'Sir—'

'One more word,' Sulvec shrieked at him. 'One more word and I'll make you envy him!' There were tears in his eyes, for his men were on the point of mutiny. He felt his fingers flex and curl with the need to hurt something. He settled for kicking Osgan again, drawing a choked cry. 'Now bring him.' He watched as they levered the mortally wounded man up between them, the strain causing Osgan to gasp and retch. The stricken man's face was nothing but a haggard mask of pain, and Sulvec smiled to see it. *While*

*I have you, I have control.* Osgan sobbed wretchedly, wailing each time they shifted his weight.

Sulvec took up the lantern and led the way back down the hall, peering ahead and yet not really looking, not wanting to see what the lantern might reveal. That was another use for Osgan. The prisoner was an anchor to slow their progress, so that the things in the dark had time to get themselves out of sight.

*When I see daylight again*, Sulvec thought grimly, *I will rip him open. I will pull his organs out of him. I will gouge out his eyes. That's only fair, after he and that bastard Thalric dragged me down here.*

Osgan was suddenly quiet, and a tremor of fear ran through Sulvec. *He's dead? He can't be dead. Not yet. I'm not done with him yet.* He whirled around to face the two soldiers, half expecting to see that they'd cut the suffering man's throat. Instead, he found himself looking into Osgan's face. It had been transformed. The expression written there had gone beyond fear of anything that Sulvec might do to him. It was almost blissful in its terror, the look of the man who sees the thing he most dreads come to pass, and knows he need not dread it any more.

'He's coming,' Osgan whispered.

Sulvec flinched away from him, and the soldiers let go, dropping Osgan to his knees. He knelt there, arms wrapped about his bloody stomach, dragging in halting breaths, and just staring.

The soldiers were already spread out, palms aimed at the darkness. 'Something's coming,' one of them said.

'Nothing's coming!' Sulvec insisted, although he did not believe it. 'Nothing! You're letting a dead man get to you. Pick him up!'

'Sir,' said the soldier, and then he died.

Sulvec saw it happen, as a sudden line of red across his throat, the flash of a blade outlined in blood, and the man dropped. The other soldier loosed a stingshot into the dark, then again and again, backing away from something Sulvec could not see. Sulvec opened his mouth to yell at him, but then the second soldier was dead too, twin sprays of blood from head and body and he had fallen away into the darkness.

Osgan was laughing, the sound twisted into a hideous cackle by the pain he was suffering.

Sulvec backed off, but he was backing off from nothing he could see. 'Show yourself!' he ordered. 'Let me see you.'

And then there was someone there, standing between the two corpses. Sulvec did not understand how he could have missed him. A tall, slender man with pointed features, a Mantis-kinden of the Lowlands with a claw on his hand. Sulvec could see him clearly although the lamps were almost out. Whatever illuminated the Mantis shone on nothing else.

He advanced in a delicate stalking movement that made no sound. The light on him fell from one side, and Sulvec could see only whatever that ghost-light touched. The rest of him was made of darkness that even the lamplight could not dispel.

Sulvec loosed a stingbolt at him, but the Mantis seemed untroubled. The Rekef man tried to draw his sword, but his hands were shaking too much. He backed off, further and further away from the discarded lamps of the dead soldiers. His own flickered and died, its fuel spent.

The Mantis reached Osgan and stared silently down at him until the wretched Wasp was able to lift his head.

A voice came cold and clear to Sulvec. The Mantis's lips moved. *I remember you.*

Osgan made a great shuddering sound that was part sob, part laugh. 'I knew . . .' he got out, with the greatest of efforts, 'you'd come. They said . . . you were dead . . . but I knew . . .'

*You sat beside the Emperor,* came the Mantis's distant voice. *You had your knife, little scribe. Would you have fought to defend your master?* Osgan's strangled response was wordless, incoherent, but the Mantis said, *Yes, I think you would.*

His off hand, the arm jagged with barbs, rested on Osgan's shoulder. *I shall give you more, at least, than these your kin.* There was a moment of understanding, dying man to dead one, and the spectral blade speared down just once, precise and final.

Sulvec saw something seep out of Osgan's tortured frame, saw the racked and twisted man relax at last, muscle by muscle. The long release of breath he heard was without pain, was at peace. It was Osgan's last. He swayed and pitched on to his side, and Sulvec knew for sure he was dead.

The Mantis looked up and his eyes, one lit and one shrouded in shadow, found Sulvec.

'Now,' he said, as the lamps went out.

Che sagged back into Thalric's arms, mind still full of the swollen river, even though the images had now left her. Looking up at the assembled Masters, she saw not one of them was looking at her. *They did not even mean to show me,* she thought numbly. *I just got carried along, when they looked. What have I seen? I cannot take it in.*

'What?' Thalric was demanding. 'They haven't done anything. What's happening, Che? What's wrong?'

She stepped away from him, feeling a tug of resistance and then release. 'Do not ask me,' she said. 'I cannot say. I don't have words for what I've seen. Oh, Thalric, I can't hope to make you understand.'

There was a great sigh from the Masters, and she knew that they had finished. A great burden of sorrow was upon them, their faces disfigured by the dregs of effort. Some simply walked away. Many lingered as though, having awoken, they were unsure what it had been for. Only one was missing: armoured Garmoth Atennar had absented himself, perhaps to take his huge sword to the Scorpions in person.

'Such waste of our resources,' said Jeherian bitterly. 'We

should be angry with our servants for putting us to this, but I cannot find the will to care.'

'But what happened?' Che asked them. 'How did you do it? Such a ritual, brought to bear so swiftly!' Words of Achaeos recurred to her. 'I *know* the Moths would never have attempted it.'

'No,' replied Elysiath, 'but they, like most kinden, are brief and impatient. What you saw was not the making of a ritual, but the breaking of one. It is very simple.'

'Not to me, it's not,' Che insisted. 'Please, you must tell me what you did.'

Elysiath sighed, her shoulders slumping as though the very act of having to explain herself to Che required more effort than she could countenance. 'Little child,' she said, 'we have told you.'

'Yet it is important she understands,' Jeherian put in, surprising Che. 'We have told you how, when we foresaw the changes these lands would suffer, we came to the decision to absent ourselves from the harsh surface above, and to work our great ritual from these our halls. Our ritual is for the restoration of the land, the balance that was broken by that great earthquake and cataclysm so long ago. For nine hundred years we have maintained it, and so we shall for millennia to come, if need be, however long our work may take. For we foresaw that the only way to break the drought was to hurry it to its ultimate ends, spur it on to its worst excesses. Of a dry land we have made a desert, watered only by the deep wells, and by the faithful Jamail.'

'You *made* the desert?' Che asked, astonished.

'By our will it has not rained in these lands for centuries past. It rains over the Forest Alim, where the clouds break on the mountains, and thus the Jamail does not run dry, but from over our city and dominion, we take the rain and hide it from the world, for year after year.'

'That's monstrous,' Che protested in a small voice. She could not conceive of it.

'Who may presume to judge our actions? We who live longer, see further. Without us, the land would dry and dry, over the ages. Instead we have brought that drought before its time, and hold it while the rain gathers, forcing it to burn too bright, to consume itself in its own heat. We have broken our ritual just to save our idiot servants. We have set ourselves back two hundred and seventy-five years of rain.'

Che could not speak. The man smiled, arrogant beyond the dreams of emperors.

'When we shall unleash that hoarded rain, when we have finally gathered sufficient of it, we shall transform the entire world. We shall strike a blow whereby we shall reverse the cataclysm. The land shall be green again, and we shall rule it directly once more.'

His words washed over her, and she swayed under their impact. They were madness and yet, revealed to her by the Masters of Khanaphes, she knew that they must be the truth. Here was a magic a thousand years in the making, and accumulating still, and of such power that the Moth-kinden themselves could not have dreamt of it.

'The *rain* has washed the Scorpions away?' Thalric's voice broke in on them, an outsider intruding. 'I understand nothing of this.' The Masters' expressions clearly told him: *Of course you don't.* 'Tell me one thing,' he went on, and they looked at him without interest as he asked, 'What will you and your people do when the Empire gets here?'

'Your Empire does not interest us,' said Lirielle. 'Mere children and their toys.'

'But you seem to have realized now what those toys can do,' Thalric insisted. 'A pack of barbarians with a little artillery has nearly destroyed your city. The Empire—'

'We can see your Empire in your mind,' Elysiath silenced him at once, 'like a child's chalk drawing of power. They will come, you assume, and seek to command Khanaphes, to make it part of your dominion.' She stretched expansively.

'It would be tiresome to have to destroy your Empire, and distracting. I imagine, therefore, that we will allow you to bring your governors and your soldiers, and thus pretend that Khanaphes is yours.' She smiled at that, at last a real expression, sharp-edged and aimed directly at him. 'But how long do you believe your Empire will last?'

He stared at her blankly and she continued, 'I am nine times older than your Empire, O savage, and I shall still be young when your kinden have become the playthings of some other children. Your Empire will decay and die in due course. Only we are eternal.'

Thalric opened his mouth, but no words came out.

'But enough of such trifles,' Elysiath said. 'Let us instead talk of you.' She was looking at Che. In fact they were all looking at her.

'Me?' Che stared.

'You who have answered our summons,' the woman said. 'You who have been gifted, by chance, with such an open power. You have been separated from the tawdry heritage of your own people. You have been made special.'

'I . . .'

'Why did you come here, really?' Elysiath asked her.

'I was sent . . .' She stuttered into silence, feeling the lie burn on her tongue. 'I was not happy in Collegium. I wanted to discover what has happened to me.'

'And so you heard our call,' the Master told her. 'And you followed your destiny all the way to Khanaphes.'

'But what do you want? Why would you call me?'

'You can see how remiss our servants have been here, and yet you ask that?' Elysiath smiled. 'The old blood that rules our city has grown thin and weak. We should have anticipated that. They hear our commands but faintly. They are only a shadow of their ancestors. We would appoint you as our priestess, instruct you in the ways of our power. We would set you above our other servants, as one who can hear us clearly, and is therefore most dear to us.' The expression she turned on Che was almost maternal. 'You shall become First Minister of our city.'

'Che . . .' she heard Thalric's warning tone, but she shrugged him off.

'Why?' she asked. 'Why would I?' She expected them to recoil from the insolence of the question, to inform her that serving them was reward enough in itself. She was ready for that.

'Because you are a true scholar,' said Elysiath, 'one who seeks knowledge always. And nowhere will you find such understanding as we have, we who have lived out, in person, the ages that are your kind's ancient history. We can give you knowledge that even the Moths have forgotten, and that, even if they possessed it, they would not share. We can tell you the names of all the kinden in the world. We can reveal to you why it is that the Mantids of the Lowlands hate the Spiders so, though even they have let themselves forget it. We can teach you where the Art came from, and how to truly master it.' Her fond look deepened. 'But more than that, little child, where else have you to go? You are in a world that has no place for you, save here. You are no longer one of your people, no longer a creature of your home. You are adrift in a land that cannot understand you. You cannot even understand yourself. We shall explain everything. We shall give you a place here. You shall be honoured, become the messenger of the Masters to their servants.'

Che tried to refuse them, but the words came reluctantly to her mind and she could not force them out. It was their sympathy that struck her to the heart, the understanding that they had promised. They knew what she had gone through, and she felt tears in her eyes. Where else but here would she ever find real acceptance? Better a servant of the Masters than a lonely outcast forever moving on.

'Yes,' she said, her voice choking.

Elysiath's approval warmed her. 'You know what you must do,' she said, 'to be ours, and to enter into our grace.'

At her side Jeherian held out something small, and Che stepped forward, reached up and took it. In her hand rested a curved blade of sharpened copper: a razor.

Kneeling down, she took a fistful of her hair, bringing the razor up to it. Of course she knew what she must do, what the Khanaphir had done since time immemorial in order to demonstrate their servitude.

'Che!' Thalric spoke urgently. 'Don't do this.' She could sense the attention of the Masters focused on her like a pressure guiding her hand. The blade, keener than copper should rightly be, severed the first few strands.

'Che, you heard them,' Thalric persisted. 'They don't care about you. They don't care about anyone in Khanaphes, or anyone in the world. Listen to me, Che, this is insane. You can't want to stay down here in the slime and the dark.'

She just gazed at him, and already felt him as a memory, receding into her past. 'I'm sorry,' she said, not sure who she was sorry for, or why.

'They killed your man Kadro, and that woman his assistant,' Thalric went on. He was fighting to get out the words as though the air itself was smothering him. 'And they don't care. People like us, the Apt kinden, we're just beasts to them, nothing but insects.'

'I know,' she replied sadly, 'but what are we, if not that?' She moved the razor more decisively, severing a handful of her locks, took hold of some more.

'Che, I like your hair. Don't cut it off,' Thalric implored her.

She looked for him again, finding that he was hard to focus on. Even his name seemed strange in her mind.

'Che, please,' he went on, 'listen to me. You know that I care for you. Ever since we first met, there was something about you.' He laughed desperately. 'I'll admit we got off to a poor start, but you can't say I don't have some claim on you. Please, Che, stay with me.'

She shook her head, astonished by his temerity. 'With

you?' she said incredulously, the memories drawn back to the surface of her mind whether she wanted them or not. 'Thalric, when the Masters tested me, do you know what they made me live through? What they chose as the most terrible memory I must relive? It was the interrogation room in Myna. That was the worst moment in my life, and they made me watch you torturing me, over and over.'

'What do you think,' he replied through gritted teeth, 'they made *me* see?'

'. . . What?' She felt as though something deep within her had exploded, yet so far away that she had only heard the hollow knock of it, that the main force of it was still travelling towards her.

'What do you think was the moment in my life they took me back to, if not that? The one moment of them all that I would take back if I could. Not your bastard sister and her father destroying me in Helleron. Not killing my own mentor for some Rekef General's whim. Not my own kind turning on me outside Collegium. Not that bitch Felise Mienn with her blade held at my throat, or being strung up in Armour Square, ready for execution. Not my pain at all, but *yours*. They used their Art, or whatever, to make me hurt you, in my head, and I could not endure it. It would have destroyed me if you had not broken their hold.'

The breath whooshed out of her, and she felt the razor slip from her hand. It left a shallow cut on her thigh as it bounced from her leg, and then clacked onto the oily floor.

'Help me,' she whispered, and Thalric took her hand, pulled her up towards him and held her tightly. She sensed Accius moving forward, until he stood beside Thalric, and belatedly she realized that this was because the Masters were now frowning at them.

She hugged Thalric briefly and then turned to them, and their glowering expressions. The awesome disappointment and disapproval she saw there nearly dried up the words in her mouth. She finally got out, 'I thank you for your offer, your generous offer, but I am not the person you take me for. I am not fit to serve you, surely. We must return to the city. I have friends there.'

Elysiath regarded her sourly, almost petulantly, and Che wondered whether she was the first person to ever refuse the Masters something they wanted. 'Return?' the woman said drily. 'Return to Khanaphes Above?'

'We must, all three of us,' Che said, with more strength. 'I'm sorry.'

The Masters exchanged looks from the corners of their eyes. 'Perhaps you are right,' Elysiath said. 'You are not fit to serve us, if that is what you believe.'

'You have heard entirely too much of our secret histories,' added Lirielle, but Elysiath actually interrupted and spoke over her: 'These two with you, the savages, were doomed from the moment they stepped into our resting place, but you, you had a chance to become something greater than you are. Yet you have turned your back on that chance. You were born amongst the slave races, and now you shall die amongst them. Think only how you could have been more.'

Thalric tensed, hand poised to sting, and she saw Accius bring his sword up. Elysiath laughed, as the Jamail might have laughed when it destroyed the Scorpions. 'Your weapons are nothing here,' she told them patiently. 'Though our dominion may have shrunk from the height of its greatness, you are within it now, for we still rule these halls.' The great pressure of their collective minds hung over the three intruders. Che saw Thalric's hand shake, his Art trapped within it. Accius's face was shiny with sweat, his sword motionless.

'You are not the first to come and steal our secrets,' Elysiath said, raising a hand. 'Nor shall you be the last to pay the price for it.'

'Secrets?'

Che started at the voice, for it belonged to the Vekken beside them.

'Our knowledge is our treasure, and no thieves shall take it outside these halls.' Jeherian told him.

'You have kept no secrets here.' Accius's expression suggested that the worst had befallen him, and he was meeting it joyously. 'Slay me and you set your seal on nothing. You cannot keep us from knowing.'

'What nonsense,' Elysiath said scornfully, but Accius grinned, teeth gleaming brightly in his dark face.

'My brother is at large in the city already. Not you nor all your servants shall catch him. And what I know, he knows.'

A dead silence fell between them, the great Masters regarding the defiant Ant-kinden with what Che realized was dawning puzzlement. At last it was Jeherian's expression that changed, sagging with bitter weariness.

'The old Art,' he acknowledged. 'The old Art of the savages. It has been far too long and we have forgotten too much, how they were in each other's minds, the folk of the Alim and the Aleth.' Che saw realization ripple through them all, stripping away their majesty and leaving a sad bewilderment behind. She found that, despite their malevolence and their vast power, she still felt sorry for them in some strange way – atavisms that remembered only ruling a world that had long passed them by.

'What could we say?' she said. 'Who would believe us anyway? We will return to the sun, and say nothing. There would be no profit for us in being dubbed liars or madmen. We leave you to your rest. Do not think ill of us.'

The Masters of Khanaphes regarded them stonily for a long moment, until Jeherian nodded minutely and said, 'Go.'

Che would remember for ever the sight of them as she glanced back one last time: beautiful by an alien aesthetic, huge and commanding and gleaming in that bluish light. The immortal Slug-kinden, the Masters of Khanaphes.

She led the way back. Thalric tried to at first, but he went off course over and over, leading them in circles through the maze of halls by the light of Accius's quisitor's lamp. The true path to the light was clear only to Che and, once they had finally accepted that, she led them confidently until they found the corpses.

There were four of them there, three close by and one at a distance. Che had not quite identified them when Thalric knelt down beside the middle one of the three. She heard him take a long breath, and only then recognized the corpse as Osgan's.

'Oh,' she said. 'I'm sorry, Thalric. Really I am.'

'I left him behind,' Thalric said. 'He was in pain, but I left him behind.'

'We should go,' Accius said shortly, still very anxious. Thalric looked up at him balefully and Che recalled how it was only because Accius had been abducting her that Thalric had abandoned Osgan to his fate.

'No fighting, no disagreement,' she ordered them flatly. 'We leave here at once, or the Masters may change their minds. Thalric, I'm sorry, but we should spend no more time here than necessary.'

'You're right, of course,' he said, standing up. She took his hand and led them on, past the final corpse, that was twisted, both face and body, into an attitude of unbearable horror.

The thought she had, crossing into the next hall, was, *We must be close now. There is his armour on the throne.* She thought that until she saw the head lift, and the dead eyes of Garmoth Atennar stared out at her. Even then the others did not see, not until she flinched back against them, dragging them round to watch the colossal metal-clad form stand up, sword in hand.

'Garmoth Atennar,' she declared. 'Lord of the Fourth House, whose Bounty Exceeds all Expectations, Greatest of Warriors.' She could remember every word of it. 'We are leaving your realm.'

'I know of your words with my peers,' he boomed. 'Even as our slaves have diminished, so has the foolishness of the Masters grown. Not mine, though, and I care not if you have a hundred listeners. They shall know first-hand the fate that awaits trespassers into these halls.'

The might of his mind oppressed them, but Che found it weaker now that he was alone. She could shrug it off with ease, ward it off from the others, thinking: *Is this magic? Am I a magician now?*

Garmoth Atennar took one great stride forward. His sword dropped towards her ponderously and Thalric pushed her out of its path. His stingshot struck shards from the Master's Mantis-crafted armour. Garmoth changed his grip on the sword and swung it in a scything blow towards him, but Thalric took flight briefly and avoided it, leading the sword point upwards. Accius darted in and rammed his sword into the huge man's knee.

Che expected Garmoth's armour to fend off the blow easily, but the Mantis plate crumpled at once, cracking like fire-warmed paper. With a grating roar, Garmoth collapsed to his knees, and Accius slit his throat, stepping back to avoid the huge body as it toppled to the floor in a cacophony of metal.

In the echoes of that crash, that seemed to go on and on, Che waited for repercussions, but the other Masters made no further appearance. Perhaps they slept already. Perhaps they were as heedless of their fellow as they had been of their servants.

'Rusted through,' Thalric observed. She blinked at him, realized he meant the armour. 'Look,' he pointed, 'the backplate is cracked without a blow being struck. This was no good place to store armour.' He laid a hand on one of the massive pauldrons, and half of it came away without effort.

'Greatest of warriors,' she whispered. *Was he genuinely so, in his day? Or did he rely merely on the awe he was held in to win his battles for him? What have we slain here today?* She felt they should move the body to the pedestal where he had lain for so long, but the three of them could not have managed it, even with Accius's strength.

# Forty-Five

He had awoken several times, but retained only a sketchy memory of each occasion: aware that he was in the infirmary of the Scriptora, and that she was beside him. When he moved, he felt as if every bone and joint had been under the hammer. Amnon, the First Soldier of Khanaphes, opened his eyes.

They had not given up on him, he saw, for this was one of the little rooms reserved for Ministers or people of importance. His soldiers, most of whom had suffered worse than he, would be tended in the communal infirmaries of their barracks, or in converted storerooms. There would be more than enough work today to keep all Khanaphes's cutters and salvers busy.

He remembered, in fits and starts, that the city still stood, that the Scorpions had been washed away, that he had held the bridge just long enough. He squeezed the hand that he found in his, startling his companion from her doze as she sat beside the bed.

'Hello, Praeda.'

She looked haggard and he guessed she had not slept much these last few days. She bit her lip, watching him, and he levered himself up to a sitting position, determinedly ignoring all the complaints of his body. 'Don't tell me I look as bad as that,' he chided.

'I am so angry with you,' she said tightly. Her grip on his

hand became painful. 'I can't believe just how angry I am.'

'You have every right to be.'

'Don't be *reasonable* about it now!' she snapped. 'You have no right to be reasonable now, after what you did. You were going to die, you and those other idiots. You were going to stay behind and die. What . . . What sort of a way is that for anyone to behave?'

'It is what the First Soldier of Khanaphes does, if it is needed,' said Amnon calmly. 'It is what the Chosen of the Marsh people does. For Totho and Meyr, I cannot say why they did it, and perhaps they cannot either. How long have I slept?'

'It's now evening of the day after the battle.'

'And what do the healers say about me?'

'Damn the healers. I stitched your wounds myself,' she informed him. 'We know our medicine in Collegium.'

'So what do *you* say about me?'

'That you're a cursed fool. And you got off lightly. I saw your armour after they'd cut it off you. It looked like someone had thrown it off a cliff and then put it into an industrial grinder. They should have taken you out of it in pieces.'

'You sound disappointed,' he noted.

'Because you won't *learn*,' she said bitterly. 'I know you soldiers, you'll remember that you won and that you survived, and you'll call it glory, and you'll do it again.'

He put both hands on hers, and his mind was abruptly full of all those who had not survived or won: Dariset and Kham and all his Royal Guard, the elite of the Khanaphir fighting forces now pared down to a fragile handful. And of course, Totho's foreigners, the Fly, the sailors, the loyal giant Meyr. 'No,' he said hollowly, 'never glory. That I lived was due to chance – chance and Totho's armour and his help. That we won was . . . I cannot explain it. The glory belongs to the dead.'

Tears shone in her eyes. 'Amnon, I love you. You made

me love you. You just gnawed and gnawed away at me until I caved in. So promise me you'll never do anything so stupid again.'

He took a deep breath. 'I am guilty, as you say, but it is a promise I cannot make. Would you think the same of me if I were merely to stand by while those I loved – or those you loved – were harmed? Surely you would not.'

She gazed at him sadly for a long time. 'I suppose not,' she said at last. 'Although it's hard to live with it, you'd not be the same man if you did. You selfish bastard.'

He managed a smile at that, but then he glanced past her, and she turned to see a shadow hovering in the doorway: it was a stooped old Khanaphir who looked as sleepless as any of them.

'First Minister,' she named him, and Amnon said, 'Ethmet.'

'They told me,' said the old man, 'that you were well, Amnon.'

'I live,' Amnon confirmed.

Ethmet looked very old, standing there. The burden of the city's reconstruction would weigh on his shoulders. 'Your banishment . . .' he began quietly.

Amnon nodded. 'I had not forgotten.'

'Amnon, if it were my decision . . . but the Masters have spoken. You went against their tenets when you adopted the foreigners' ways.'

'And so I lived, when so many others died. And so I held the bridge, with the foreigners, who shed their blood for us. But that doesn't matter, does it?'

'Amnon, I am sorry—'

'Dress it up as the Masters' will if you want,' Amnon interrupted. 'I care not. I am banished, so be it.'

'There is a chance,' said Ethmet, holding a hand up. 'If you were to ask forgiveness of the Masters, if you were to repudiate the foreigners, I think that you might yet be taken back. The Masters are just.'

'Are they?' Amnon said heavily. 'Consider this: if I were a man to beg forgiveness, then I would not have held the bridge until the waters came, and the only thing the river would then have achieved would be to wash all our corpses into the Marshland. So no, I ask no forgiveness. I apologize for none of my actions. I held the bridge and, if I am banished for that, then I shall go like a man. I shall go with Praeda Rakespear to her far country, where perhaps they understand things better than you or your Masters.' He saw the leap of joy on Praeda's face, and knew it was something she had wanted to ask him, and never dared.

'Please, Amnon,' Ethmet whispered, 'your city needs you . . .'

'My city needed me and, needed, I came. Now I have done what was required of me. Now it seems what my city needs is a man who will bow the knee, and I will not. You have set the price for my actions, and I shall pay it, as I have always paid my debts. Now we must both part on our own quests: I for a new city, you for a new First Soldier.'

Ethmet hovered in the doorway a short while longer, wringing his hands but without words, and then he skulked away.

*This has been a disaster*: it was Totho's personal assessment. Drephos would find something positive in it, of course. Drephos would see the whole Khanaphir expedition as an extended field-test to destruction: the ship, the armour, the people . . . He would be pleased, overall, with the performance. Drephos did not care about money, so long as he had enough, and the Iron Glove would not be bankrupted by this petty conflict.

*Still, no market in Khanaphes, and the* Iteration *sunk with most of her crew, Tirado dead, Meyr dead, and also Meyr's people from the Nemian expedition.* Still, Totho knew that he was merely dressing the books now, that the true disaster was a personal one. *And Che gone, too.* Lost to a Rekef knife, no doubt. They had hunted her down one night, and he had not been there to save her. That being so, the final disaster was: *I survived.* He had not meant to. His armour had been too proof, his instincts too cowardly. He had lived when all his fellows had died, save only Amnon himself. He wondered if Amnon felt as wretched as this.

*But Amnon has his woman beside him, while I myself have . . . nothing. And what did I ever have?*

The tide of self-pity was rising like the turbulent waters of the Jamail, and that was something he was adamantly not thinking about. There would be an explanation for the water's intervention, but just now he could not be moved to find it. The sight of those rushing floods encompassing only *one half* of the city had profoundly disturbed him. Time would smooth over the queasy feelings it had left within him, and give him a chance to piece together a rationale. Until then the memories were to stay under lock and key inside his mind.

*And, of course, I am exiled from this place, never to return.* It was a strange thing, to be walking alone through a city that was supposed to have thrown him and all his kind out, with only his snapbow over his shoulder, and his battered breastplate. The truth was that his casting out was still very much in force and, equally, would not be enforced. Not a soldier of Khanaphes would lift a finger against him, nor any of its citizens. The Ministers were too wise to issue the direct orders and risk an uproar. Totho was a hero of the city, they all knew. He had stood with Amnon on the bridge.

*And I should be proud of that, shouldn't I? That I played the hero?* He didn't feel like a hero. He had known heroes in his day, people who would fight for what they believed in, without hesitation. People who did not need time and thought to cajole themselves towards doing the right thing. Salma had been a hero, so Totho had always thought that he must have felt like a hero: knowing no doubt, no fear, worry or uncertainty. *Did Salma feel empty instead, like me?*

*Did Salma do all those things because* not *doing them would only make him feel worse?*

No. Salma had been a hero. Amnon was a hero. Totho was not fit for their company save that chance had thrown him that way. *I did the best I could with bad materials. I botched it together, when the moment came. That's all. I'm not a hero, but we were short of one, so I stepped into the gap.*

He was going to find Amnon, to bid him farewell. There were a half-dozen Iron Glove men left, survivors of the *Iteration*. Totho had found them a ship out of Khanaphes, and it could not happen too soon.

He walked out into the square in front of the Scriptora, and saw her stepping down the pyramid as though she had simply been frozen among the statues on the summit all this time.

*Che.*

It had been a fight to be quit of that place. After Garmoth's death, the tunnels and halls had turned against them, but Che had proved their equal in the end. She had pushed and pushed. They were immeasurably stronger, of course, but they were tired: the Masters most of all wanted to sleep again, and she possessed a Beetle's persistence. In the end she had outlasted them, and forged her way through to the open air, guiding the two clueless Apt with her.

Climbing out into the sunlight was the sweetest thing in the world. She stood still, a statue on either side, as though she was part of their irregular order. Irregular, she realized, and purposefully confusing so that when the Masters came up here to view their shrunken dominion, no eye would note them there, even if the moon was bright.

She pushed out of her mind all she had been told and all she had seen, down below. There would be sleepless nights later for her to digest it. For now, she was free, and the war was over, and . . .

She took one step down the pyramid and saw Thalric

emerge from the shaft and alight, wings blurring and fading. He had the temerity to lean on a statue, looking up at the cloudless sky as though he had not seen it in a hundred years, drinking in the blue.

'I thought I'd never . . .' he said.

'I know.' She turned to see Accius now climbing out, wiping the slime off his hands with an expression of revulsion even on his normally blank face.

He nodded to her. 'Malius and I are discussing what should be done, regarding our two cities: what report we will give,' he said. 'It is true, there are events that cannot be understood.' There was an awkward look about him. 'Events that, if reported, will cast doubt on our competence as reporters.'

'I understand,' Che told him.

'We have stood together, in this place.' The admission seemed somehow prompted, and she wondered if it was Malius or Accius who was making it. 'You released me from . . . some torment that even my brother could not unlock, and we are unsure what this means. We shall confer, and then we will come to you.' He settled his sword in its scabbard, a nervous, reassuring gesture, and stepped off quickly towards the Place of Foreigners.

'Hope yet?' Thalric enquired.

'I don't know. Perhaps. It would please Uncle Sten.'

Thalric smirked at that answer, and she demanded, 'What?'

'War Master Stenwold Maker, spymaster of Collegium and defier of the Empire, now reduced to "Uncle Sten". The Rekef would be mortified to hear it.' His grin faded at the memory of Marger's revelations. 'And that's another problem.'

'Which we'll solve, somehow,' Che assured him. 'For now, though, we're out, Thalric. We're free of the Masters. We're free.'

His smile returned and he caught her around the waist

and kissed her. She heard somebody shout.

Turning, she saw Totho running towards them, and her heart sank. *Oh, timing, Totho, always timing. Your eternal gift.* 'Totho, wait . . .' she started, unsure what she could honestly say. Thalric's wings had taken him two steps up the pyramid, hand held out, but Che was between them.

The Wasp did not loose. Totho did.

He was shooting whilst running. She heard at least one bolt ping from the stones very close to her. Another tore her sleeve. A single shot punched into Thalric's shoulder, knocking him back against the steps. She fell across his body, hoping to shield him, seeing him clutch at the point of impact. Thalric's expression was not pain so much as fury, and it was contagious, leaping to her like wildfire. Totho had stopped shooting by then, was just running forward, shouting her name.

*No, no . . .* But it was too late. Something fierce and mad had arisen inside her at the sight of Thalric's blood, and she wrenched the Wasp's sword from its scabbard and was already turning to meet Totho. She felt empty hands guiding her, and an unfamiliar insanity gripping her mind. A whirl of alien thoughts – honour and vengeance and bitter pride – rose in her like bile. After so many months in residence, Tisamon had left some echo behind, the ghost of a ghost.

She lashed out even as Totho arrived, striking sparks from his breastplate. He called out her name, and she hit him thrice more, denting his pauldron, smashing the snapbow from his hand, and then slamming the sword so hard across his body that he stumbled backwards down three steps.

'Che! It's me!' he yelled at the stranger he saw behind her eyes, and she stabbed him as hard as she physically could, so that the blade of Thalric's sword snapped off close to the hilt, as Totho was punched off his feet. He landed with a hard clash of metal on stone and slid to the base of the pyramid. She was on to him as soon as he started to get up, drawing back the jagged, broken edge of the blade, about to jam it into his upturned face. The urge to kill him keened inside her, not through the Mantis's influence but just the bloody handprint his presence had left.

'You never learn!' she screamed at him. 'You never . . .'

He was crouching at her feet, making no effort to defend himself. The sword at his belt was still sheathed, the snapbow out of reach.

'. . . learn . . .' she finished, staring stupidly at the stump of blade in her hand. She let it drop, hearing it clang and clatter distantly. 'Totho?'

He made some muffled reply.

She looked from him back at Thalric, who was groaning, plucking at his wound. 'Oh Totho, why do you always get it so wrong? I'm sorry, Totho, I'm sorry,' she said, horrified, frightened by herself. 'I'm so sorry.'

He was saying something, the words blurred with tears, and eventually she heard it as, 'I held the bridge. I held the bridge for you. I wanted to do right.'

Horror and pity swept over her, in equal measures, and she thought, *And I never learn either, and I always get it wrong. In that we two are soulmates, if in nothing else.* 'I know you did, Totho. I saw you on the bridge, believe it or not. You did well. You saved the city. I'm proud of you, but you have to let me go, please. Totho, look at all you've built. Don't throw it away for me.'

'I would,' he got out. 'All of it, if you asked.'

'But I won't ask,' she replied. The sudden dispersal of all that rage had left her feeling weak and sick. 'Please, Totho, how often must we go through this? Who else will we hurt?' She stood up, stepped away, feeling sicker than ever. He got to his feet, flinching away when she offered her hand, then taking it like a drowning man. She took Totho in her arms and held him close just for a moment.

'I am not the girl you knew at the College,' she said softly, after releasing him. 'You are not that boy, nor is Thalric the same Rekef man who came hunting us. None of us are those people any more.' A sudden realization struck her that made her feel unsteady on her feet. 'Totho, I understand you.'

He was frowning, desperate for help from any quarter.

'Totho,' she told him, 'you still carry a picture of me in your mind, a memory from all those years ago. You let it torment you, but it's not me, Totho. It's not me that hurts you. I would never want to hurt you. You do it to yourself. Let go of me, please. I'm not who you think I am any more, and you deserve more than that.'

She heard movement behind her and turned to see Thalric. He had a shallow gash across his temple and one hand clutching to his shoulder, but she knew the strength of his armour of old. His old tricks had always preserved him before and, as the bolt had struck him, she had guessed that not even Totho's snapbows were his equal. In the instant she glanced at him, she noticed his expression was pure murder, his hand extended ready to sting. Che quickly interposed herself between them, to protect Totho from the Wasp's rage.

Thalric grimaced, made two efforts to speak, to order her out of the way, his eyes fierce with incomprehension. On the scales, his personal and cultural pride swung up and down against how she would see him if he killed her former friend.

He finally closed his hand and took a long breath, but it still was a long time before he could lower his hand.

'Che . . .?' Totho began quietly, as though releasing her name into a great silent room and waiting for the echo.

'I've used you badly,' she told him quietly. 'I'm sorry. And for what you did during the war, I have no right to judge, because I wasn't there.' She put a hand on his arm, feeling the battered mail. 'Be safe, Totho.'

He closed his eyes, keeping his expression very still, and then he nodded, and she half expected to see a filmy grey shape leave him, the ghost of all of their failed futures exorcized at last.

At last, he smiled, something weak and faint but still recognizable as a smile, and then he turned and left.

Thalric was working patiently with one hand to free the bolt in his shoulder. She reached to help, finding that the missile had punched through the fine rings of his copperweave but was snagged hopelessly in layers of cloth beneath. *Spider silk*, she realized.

'If you're wondering,' he said, 'it still hurts like the rack.' His voice was taut, with pain and the stale dregs of his own emotions. She opened her mouth to reply and he said, 'That was very elegantly handled. You're a born ambassador.'

'What, breaking a sword over him and then mouthing platitudes?' she replied.

'Everyone walked away from it.' Thalric finally held up the bolt and she saw a pinprick of blood at its tip.

'Closer than you'd like to admit?' she suggested.

'Being the pleasant-natured creature you are, and beloved of so many, you cannot imagine how many have tried to kill me over the years,' he told her, and she could not decide whether he was mocking her, and to what extent. 'That halfway artificer hasn't come the closest, and he's more reason than many to attempt it.' His smile was flat. 'I happen to agree with him. I think you're worth killing for too.'

She instantly felt deeply uncomfortable, remembering that he was a killer from a race of killers. At the same time, something responded in her that someone should say such a thing about *her* and not her sister . . . her sister . . . *Tynisa.*

'Where now, Thalric? Where do we take this now?'

'I have some temporary plans, regarding some matters I need to put right. All the more so if you'll be travelling with me.'

'I have plans as well,' she told him. 'There is something I must do.' The feeling of that moment's wrath, that Mantis-fury pure and deadly as forged steel, still terrified her. *Not Tynisa*, she thought. *You shall not have her.*

*

There was a ship that had already departed, and a ship that was preparing to leave. Two voyages to mark the end of this blighted moment in Khanaphir history.

Already on the seas were the Iron Glove men, finally enacting their long-promised banishment. Che had not spoken to Totho before he left, by unspoken consent. The fragile détente they had achieved would not bear too much inspection.

Now there was a second vessel, a Spider trader called *Flighty Drachmis*, and it would be heading to Porta Rabi, and from there one could find a way to Solarno, and from Solarno, home.

They were fewer than they had been, the Collegiate scholars. Trallo of the dubious loyalties had been loyal enough to die for them, and poor Mannerly Gorget too. They were also reinforced though, for as well as Praeda and old Berjek Gripshod, and the brace of Vekken, there was now the looming figure of Amnon, former First Soldier of Khanaphes. Even in his simple white tunic he still looked like a warrior.

'Are you sure you're not coming with us, Miss Maker?' Berjek asked. 'What precisely am I to tell your uncle?'

'I've thought of that,' Che said, producing a folded and sealed letter. 'This will satisfy him. I'll send messengers when I can – if I can. Tell him not to worry about me.'

He huffed, and asked balefully, 'Any other impossible tasks?' After a moment he added, sadly, 'It's not worked out well here, has it?'

'Not so well, no,' she admitted. 'I have had my hand in that, I think. I'm sure I could have done more.' She thought of Petri Coggen, and knew that, of all of their losses, she could have prevented that death, had she not been so wrapped up in her own problems. *I am sorry.* There were so many people that she owed apologies to, and most would never hear them.

'Che, come back to us,' Praeda told her. 'If not now, then soon.'

Che shrugged, unwilling to commit herself. 'I will try. I can make no promises. I have a long road.'

Praeda glared at Thalric, over Che's shoulder. 'And you'd travel with this Wasp, rather than us?'

'Yes, I would.'

The other woman made a wry expression. 'Well, be safe.'

'And you.' After which, Che turned to the last two waiting to embark. They looked back at her from near-identical faces, dark and expressionless.

'What will you say?' she asked them.

Accius and Malius shared a moment of silent conference before Malius finally answered. 'That we cannot understand why you came here, but it involved no plot against Vek. That our cities are both enemies of the Empire. That . . .' She had the impression that Accius was prompting him before he went on. 'That there may be some cause for common ground between us. Perhaps.'

She took a deep breath. *So little conceded, and yet see how far we've come!* 'My uncle is a genuine man, and he does not wish another Vekken war. I know he will treat fairly with you. I know that you cannot take my word on that, but all I ask is that you keep an open mind.'

'That was humour?' Accius interposed unexpectedly. Caught unawares, Che stared at him in surprise.

'Open mind?' she realized at last. 'The Ant mindlink.' A smile forced its way unbidden to her lips. 'Humour, fair enough. Travel safely, both of you.'

'Do not fear for us,' Malius said, halfway between affront and reassurance. It was hard for Che to keep in mind how both of them had been present there beneath the earth, one in body, the other just in mind.

She watched them take ship, as the Spider-kinden crew cast off moorings and let the current take them out towards the Marsh channels without raising sail. Her own route would take them upriver as far as the Forest Alim, and further still.

‘Have you actually any idea where we’re going?’ Thalric said.

‘Oh, yes,’ Che replied, ‘every idea, but you’re not going to like it. You won’t be made very welcome.’

‘That hardly narrows down the list of places I know,’ he said drily.

‘The Commonweal,’ she said, remembering Tisamon’s shade saying, *She is amongst the Dragonflies*. ‘Tynisa is in the Commonweal. Feeling any reservations now?’

‘No, that’s good,’ he said, surprising her. ‘It’s out of the way, and I feel the need to be invisible for a while. News travels more slowly in the Commonweal – although there is a single message that I must send first. Just a little unfinished business.’

General Brugan retired to the desk in his study after a long day. The Khanaphir expedition had returned at last, or what was left of it. Detailed interrogations could wait, but the ranking officer had some plea for mitigation he wanted to make, sounding tiresomely technical. Other than that, Captain-Auxillian Hrathen was dead, which was no loss. The Scorpions of the Nem had been decimated, likewise, and half of Khanaphes had been sacked. How one sacked half a city was a mystery to General Brugan, but it suggested poor planning.

There had been no definite word, however, regarding his chief concern, and that irked him. Sulvec and the entire Rekef team seemed to have died as well, which was a shame. Brugan was left only with the uneasy hope that they had at least accomplished their mission before vanishing so utterly.

It was late now, but the Rekef paperwork would only accumulate if he postponed it. Unlike his predecessor, he kept as many layers of clerks between himself and the sources of information as possible: good, trained men who knew how to judge what was important.

He sorted through the summaries and reports, gleaning the essential information from a quick glance, reading in more detail when it was merited. His mental picture of Rekef operations within the Empire, and without, was advanced by one day.

He came to one sealed scroll and broke it open, and paused. The seal on the outside was top priority from the governor of Shalk, his eyes only. The handwriting within was no clerk's, though, too solid and blocky and uneconomical. It was a soldier's hand, and Brugan knew it already. He felt his stomach twist just to see it, even before he read the words:

*General Brugan,*

*I hope this missive finds you in good health and secure in the heart of your power.*

*You will be pleased to hear that I have solved the matter of the assassinations. It took a few more attempts and a confession for the pattern to become clear, but now I understand. I have been painfully slow in this task, not befitting a Rekef agent, and I apologize for this.*

*I understand that, when I was chosen to stand beside our Queen, it was because I was a man entirely at her mercy, who would have nothing without her support. I was her husband to satisfy the conservatives, while she was my preservation against the crossed pikes.*

*I had not thought at that time what other plans I might be intruding on, but I was given no choice, after all. It is not quite true to say that I would rather the pikes than share Her bed, but there is yet some truth in that.*

*And I know now that it is not enemies of the Empress that seek my death, nor any of that multitude whose lives I have personally ruined at the call of my professional career. It is simply because a man loves a woman, and would remove the only barrier between them.*

*Let me tell you, General: I give her to you with all my heart. She is yours. Keep her if you can. You deserve each other.*

*Tell her I died in Khanaphes. I do not intend to expose the lie. I do not intend that any word of me will reach the Empire for a very long time. If you send more killers after me, though, I will get word to her of your actions, and I do not believe she will see them in a favourable light.*

*Tell her I died. I don't imagine she will mourn for long.*

*But if this does not move you to forget about me, General, then know that, just as this letter has found you in good health at the heart of your own Empire, then so can I. I have one Rekef general's blood on my hands, and I would not scruple at there being two. Keep sending killers, and what would I have to lose?*

*I hope you and the Empress are as happy together as she'll let you be.*

*Yours*
*Thalric, formerly Major.*

General Brugan stood for a long time with the scroll still in his hands, and then he cursed and consigned it to the fire.

# Glossary

## *People*

**Accius** – Vekken Ant-kinden ambassador
**Achaeos** – Moth-kinden, lover of Cheerwell, deceased
**Akneth** – Khanaphir Beetle-kinden tax gatherer
**Amnon** – Khanaphir Beetle-kinden, First Soldier of Khanaphes
**Angved** – Wasp-kinden engineer
**Arianna** – Spider-kinden former agent, Stenwold's lover
**Berjek Gripshod** – Beetle-kinden scholar
**Brugan** – Wasp-kinden Lord General of the Rekef
**Cheerwell Maker ("Che")** – Beetle-kinden scholar, niece of Stenwold
**Corolly Vastern** – Beetle-kinden Rekef agent
**Corcoran** – Solarnese Beetle-kinden factor for the Iron Glove
**Dannec** – Wasp-kinden Rekef officer
**Dariandrephos ("Drephos")** – halfbreed artificer, former Imperial officer
**Dariset** – Khanaphir Beetle-kinden soldier
**Ethmet** – Khanaphir Beetle-kinden, First Minister of Khanaphes
**Faighl** – Solarnese Beetle-kinden Iron Glove guard
**The Fisher** – Khanaphir halfbreed information broker
**Genraki** – Scorpion-kinden warrior

**Gjegevey** – Woodlouse-kinden advisor to the Empress
**Gram** – Wasp-kinden Rekef agent
**Hakkon** – halfbreed helmsman with the Iron Glove
**Halmir** – Khanaphir Beetle-kinden soldier
**Harbir the Arranger** – Khanaphir Beetle-kinden assassin
**Helmess Broiler** – Beetle-kinden statesman, enemy of Stenwold
**Hrathen** – halfbreed Rekef agent
**Jakal** – Scorpion-kinden, Warlord of the Many of Nem
**Jodry Drillen** – Beetle-kinden statesman, ally of Stenwold
**Jons Allanbridge** – Beetle-kinden aviator
**Kham** – Khanaphir Beetle-kinden soldier
**Kadro** – Fly-kinden scholar
**Kovalin** – Scorpion-kinden chieftain
**Malius** – Vekken Ant-kinden ambassador
**Marger** – Wasp-kinden Rekef officer
**Mannerly Gorget ("Manny")** – Beetle-kinden scholar
**Meyr** – Mole Cricket-kinden Iron Glove factor
**Mother** – halfbreed Fir eater
**Osgan** – Wasp-kinden supply officer
**Parrols** – Beetle-kinden aviator
**Petri Coggen** – Beetle-kinden scholar, Kadro's assistant
**Praeda Rakespear** – Beetle-kinden scholar
**Pravoc** – Wasp-kinden colonel
**Ptasmon** – Khanaphir Beetle-kinden soldier
**Seda** – Wasp-kinden Empress
**Stenwold Maker** – Beetle-kinden statesman
**Sulvec** – Wasp-kinden Rekef officer
**Tathbir** – Khanaphir Beetle-kinden Minister
**Te Berro** – Fly-kinden spy, former Rekef agent
**Te Rallo Alla-Maani ("Trallo")** – Fly-kinden caravan master
**Te Schola Taki-Amre ("Taki")** – Fly-kinden aviatrix
**Tegrec** – Wasp-kinden ambassador from Tharn to the Empire
**Teuthete** – Mantis-kinden Chosen

**Thalric** – Wasp-kinden Regent of the Empire, former Rekef officer
**Tirado** – Fly-kinden Iron Glove messenger
**Tisamon** – Mantis-kinden Weaponsmaster, deceased
**Totho** – halfbreed artificer, leader of the Iron Glove
**Tynisa** – halfbreed Weaponsmaster, daughter of Tisamon
**Vargen** – Wasp-kinden governor of Tyrshaan
**Vollen** – Wasp-kinden Rekef agent

## *Places*

**Alim** – forest, source of the river Jamail
**Capitas** – chief city of the Wasp Empire
**Chasme** – city on the Exalsee, noted for its mercenary artificers
**Collegium** – Beetle-kinden city in the Lowlands, noted for its academics
**Commonweal** – Dragonfly state north of the Lowlands, part-occupied by the Empire
**Darakyon** – forest, formerly Mantis-kinden hold and, until recently, haunted
**Exalsee** – inland sea east of the Lowlands
**Helleron** – Beetle-kinden city in the Lowlands, noted for its merchants
**Jamail** – river running from the Forest Alim to Khanaphes
**Khanaphes** – Beetle-kinden city far to the east of the Exalsee
**Maynes** – Ant-kinden city, formerly occupied by the Empire
**Myna** – Beetle-kinden city, formerly occupied by the Empire
**Ostrander** – Ant-kinden outpost on the Exalsee
**Porta Rabi** – Solarnese outpost on the Sunroad Sea
**Sarn** – Ant-kinden city allied with Collegium
**Shalk** – Fly-kinden city in the Empire

**Solarno** – Spider-ruled city on the Exalsee
**Sonn** – Beetle-kinden city in the Empire
**Spiderlands** – wide expanse south of the Lowlands, ruled by the Spider-kinden
**Szar** – Bee-kinden city, formerly occupied by the Empire
**Tark** – Ant-kinden city, formerly occupied by the Empire
**Three City Alliance** – coalition of Myna, Szar and Maynes
**Tyrshaan** – Bee-kinden city in the Empire
**Vek** – Ant-kinden city, traditional enemies of Collegium
**Zafir** – Khanaphir city on the Jamail

## *Organizations and things*

**Assembly** – governing body of Collegium, elected
**Consortium of the Honest** – the mercantile arm of the Empire
**Great College** – academic establishment at the heart of Collegium
**Iron Glove** – a merchant house trading out of Chasme
**Mercers** – agents of the Commonweal's Monarch
**Rekef Inlander** – the Imperial secret service arm devoted to internal security
**Rekef Outlander** – the Imperial secret service arm devoted to external security
**Scriptora** – the seat of Khanaphir government
**Skryres** – the magi-rulers of the Moth-kinden
**Speaker** – the leader of the Assembly
**Twelve-year War** – the campaign waged against the Commonweal by the Wasp Empire.

CPSIA information can be obtained
at www.ICGtesting.com
Printed in the USA
LVHW100042130123
737040LV00001B/3